EX LIBRIS

VINTAGE CLASSICS

CAPTAIN CORELLI'S MANDOLIN

Louis de Bernières is the author of nine books. His first three novels are *The War of Don Emmanuel's Nether Parts* (Commonwealth Writers Prize, Best First Book Eurasia Region, 1991), *Señor Vivo and the Coca Lord* (Commonwealth Writers Prize, Best Book Eurasia Region, 1992), and *The Troublesome Offspring of Cardinal Guzman*. He was selected by *Granta* magazine as one of the twenty Best of Young British Novelists in 1993. *Captain Corelli's Mandolin* won the Commonwealth Writers' Prize for Best Novel in 1995. *A Partisan's Daughter* was shortlisted for the Costa Novel Award 2008 and his most recent book, *Notwithstanding: English Village Stories* was published in 2009. He lives in Norfolk.

ALSO BY LOUIS DE BERNIÈRES

The War of Don Emmanuel's Nether Parts
Señor Vivo and the Coca Lord
The Troublesome Offspring of Cardinal Guzman
Sunday Morning at the Centre of the World
Red Dog
Birds Without Wings
A Partisan's Daughter
Notwithstanding: English Village Stories

LOUIS DE BERNIÈRES

Captain Corelli's Mandolin

VINTAGE BOOKS
London

Published by Vintage 2010

1 3 5 7 9 10 8 6 4 2

Copyright © Louis de Bernières 1994

The right of Louis de Bernières to be identified as the author of this
work has been asserted by him in accordance with the Copyright,
Designs and Patents Act, 1988

The poem *The Soldier* from the collection *Requiem* is reprinted
by kind permission of Miss E.A. Wolfe

First published in Great Britain in 1994 by Martin Secker &
Warburg

Vintage
Random House, 20 Vauxhall Bridge Road,
London SW1V 2SA

www.vintage-classics.info

Addresses for companies within The Random House Group Limited
can be found at: www.randomhouse.co.uk/offices.htm

The Random House Group Limited Reg. No. 954009

A CIP catalogue record for this book
is available from the British Library

ISBN 9780099540861

The Random House Group Limited supports The Forest
Stewardship Council (FSC), the leading international forest
certification organisation. All our titles that are printed on
Greenpeace approved FSC certified paper carry the FSC logo.
Our paper procurement policy can be found at:
www.rbooks.co.uk/environment

Printed and bound in Great Britain by
CPI Bookmarque, Croydon, CR0 4TD

To my mother and father, who in different places and
in different ways fought against
the Fascists and the Nazis,
lost many of their closest friends,
and were never thanked.

CONTENTS

1 Dr Iannis Commences his History and is Frustrated 1
2 The Duce 10
3 The Strongman 19
4 L'Omosessuale (1) 26
5 The Man who Said 'No' 30
6 L'Omosessuale (2) 37
7 Extreme Remedies 44
8 A Funny Kind of Cat 53
9 August 15th, 1940 60
10 L'Omosessuale (3) 68
11 Pelagia and Mandras 75
12 All the Saint's Miracles 84
13 Delirium 98
14 Grazzi 108
15 L'Omosessuale (4) 116
16 Letters to Mandras at the Front 125
17 L'Omosessuale (5) 134
18 The Continuing Literary Travails of Dr Iannis 141
19 L'Omosessuale (6) 148
20 The Wild Man of the Ice 153
21 Pelagia's First Patient 159
22 Mandras Behind the Veil 168
23 April 30th, 1941 175
24 A Most Ungracious Surrender 190
25 Resistance 197
26 Sharp Edges 209
27 A Discourse on Mandolins and a Concert 218
28 Liberating the Masses (1) 228
29 Etiquette 235
30 The Good Nazi (1) 238
31 A Problem with Eyes 246
32 Liberating the Masses (2) 254

33	A Problem with Hands	257
34	Liberating the Masses (3)	263
35	A Pamphlet Distributed on the Island, Entitled with the Fascist Slogan 'Believe, Fight, and Obey'	269
36	Education	279
37	An Episode Confirming Pelagia's Belief that Men do not Know the Difference Between Bravery and a Lack of Common Sense	284
38	The Origin of Pelagia's March	288
39	Arsenios	292
40	A Problem with Lips	296
41	Snails	298
42	How like a Woman is a Mandolin	303
43	The Great Big Spiky Rustball	308
44	Theft	322
45	A Time of Innocence	327
46	Bunnios	332
47	Dr Iannis Counsels his Daughter	340
48	La Scala	349
49	The Doctor Advises the Captain	354
50	A Time of Hiatus	359
51	Paralysis	364
52	Developments	371
53	First Blood	379
54	Carlo's Farewell	383
55	Victory	386
56	The Good Nazi (2)	394
57	Fire	401
58	Surgery and Obsequy	407
59	The Historical Cachette	417
60	The Beginning of her Sorrows	421
61	Every Parting is a Foretaste of Death	428
62	Of the German Occupation	438
63	Liberation	442
64	Antonia	454
65	1953	462
66	Rescue	471
67	Pelagia's Lament	478
68	The Resurrection of the History	481
69	Bean by Bean the Sack Fills	489
70	Excavation	497
71	Antonia Sings Again	509
72	An Unexpected Lesson	514
73	Restitution	518
	Acknowledgements	534

The Soldier

Down some cold field in a world unspoken
the young men are walking together, slim and tall,
and though they laugh to one another, silence is not broken;
there is no sound however clear they call.

They are speaking together of what they loved in vain here,
but the air is too thin to carry the thing they say.
They were young and golden, but they came on pain here,
and their youth is age now, their gold is grey.

Yet their hearts are not changed, and they cry to one another,
'What have they done with the lives we laid aside?
Are they young with our youth, gold with our gold, my brother?
Do they smile in the face of death, because we died?'

Down some cold field in a world uncharted
the young seek each other with questioning eyes.
They question each other, the young, the golden-hearted,
of the world that they were robbed of in their quiet paradise.

HUMBERT WOLFE

I

DR IANNIS COMMENCES HIS
HISTORY AND IS FRUSTRATED

DR IANNIS HAD enjoyed a satisfactory day in which none of his patients had died or got any worse. He had attended a surprisingly easy calving, lanced one abscess, extracted a molar, dosed one lady of easy virtue with Salvarsan, performed an unpleasant but spectacularly fruitful enema, and had produced a miracle by a feat of medical prestidigitation.

He chuckled to himself, for no doubt this miracle was already being touted as worthy of St Gerasimos himself. He had gone to old man Stamatis' house, having been summoned to deal with an earache, and had found himself gazing down into an aural orifice more dank, be-lichened, and stalagmitic even than the Drogarati cave. He had set about cleaning the lichen away with the aid of a little cotton, soaked in alcohol, and wrapped about the end of a long matchstick. He was aware that old man Stamatis had been deaf in that ear since childhood, and that it had been a constant source of pain, but was nonetheless surprised when, deep in that hairy recess, the tip of his matchstick seemed to encounter something hard and unyielding; something, that is to say, which had no physiological or anatomical excuse for its presence. He took the old man over to the window, threw open the shutters, and an explosion of midday heat and light instantaneously threw the room into an effulgent dazzle, as though some importunate and unduly luminous angel had misguidedly picked that place for an epiphany. Old Stamatis' wife tutted; it was simply bad housekeeping

1

to allow that much light into the house at such an hour. She was sure that it stirred up the dust; she could clearly see the motes rising up from the surfaces.

Dr Iannis tilted the old man's head and peered into the ear. With his long matchstick he pressed aside the undergrowth of stiff grey hairs embellished with flakes of exfoliated scurf. There was something spherical within. He scraped its surface to remove the hard brown cankerous coating of wax, and beheld a pea. It was undoubtedly a pea; it was light green, its surface was slightly wrinkled, and there could not be any doubt in the matter. 'Have you ever stuck anything down your ear?' he demanded.

'Only my finger,' replied Stamatis.

'And how long have you been deaf in this ear?'

'Since as long as I can remember.'

Dr Iannis found an absurd picture rising up before his imagination. It was Stamatis as a toddler, with the same gnarled face, the same stoop, the same overmeasure of aural hair, reaching up to the kitchen table and taking a dried pea from a wooden bowl. He stuck it into his mouth, found it too hard to bite, and crammed it into his ear. The doctor chuckled, 'You must have been a very annoying little boy.'

'He was a devil.'

'Be quiet, woman, you didn't even know me in those days.'

'I have your mother's word, God rest her soul,' replied the old woman, pursing her lips and folding her arms, 'and I have the word of your sisters.'

Dr Iannis considered the problem. It was undoubtedly an obdurate and recalcitrant pea, and it was too tightly packed to lever it out. 'Do you have a fishhook, about the right size for a mullet, with a long shank? And do you have a light hammer?'

The couple looked at each other with the single thought that their doctor must have lost his mind. 'What does this have to do with my earache?' asked Stamatis suspiciously.

'You have an exorbitant auditory impediment,' replied the doctor, ever conscious of the necessity for maintaining a certain iatric mystique, and fully aware that 'a pea in the

2

ear' was unlikely to earn him any kudos. 'I can remove it with a fishhook and a small hammer; it's the ideal way of overcoming un embarras de petit pois.' He spoke the French words in a mincingly Parisian accent, even though his irony was apparent only to himself.

A hook and a hammer were duly fetched, and the doctor carefully straightened the hook on the stone flags of the floor. He then summoned the old man and told him to lay his head on the sill in the light. Stamatis lay there rolling his eyes, and the old lady put her hands over hers, watching through her fingers. 'Hurry up, Doctor,' exclaimed Stamatis, 'this sill is hotter than hell.'

The doctor carefully inserted the straightened hook into the hirsute orifice and raised the hammer, only to be deflected from his course by a hoarse shriek very reminiscent of that of a raven. Perplexed and horrified, the old wife was wringing her hands and keening, 'O, o, o, you are going to drive a fishhook into his brain. Christ have mercy, all the saints and Mary protect us.'

This interjection gave the doctor pause; he reflected that if the pea was very hard, there was a good chance that the barb would not penetrate, but would drive the pea deeper into its recess. The drum might even be broken. He straightened up and twirled his white moustache reflectively with one forefinger. 'Change of plan,' he announced. 'I have decided upon further thought that it would be better to fill his ear up with water and mollify the supererogatory occlusion. Kyria, you must keep this ear filled with warm water until I return this evening. Do not allow the patient to move, keep him lying on his side with his ear full. Is that understood?'

Dr Iannis returned at six o'clock and hooked the softened pea successfully without the aid of a hammer, small or otherwise. He worked it out deftly enough, and presented it to the couple for their inspection. Encrusted with thick dark wax, rank and malodorous, it was recognisable to neither of them as anything leguminous. 'It's very papilionaceous, is it not?' enquired the doctor.

The old woman nodded with every semblance of having

understood, which she had not, but with an expression of wonder alight in her eyes. Stamatis clapped his hand to the side of his head and exclaimed, 'It's cold in there. My God, it's loud. I mean everything is loud. My own voice is loud.'

'Your deafness is cured,' announced Dr Iannis. 'A very satisfactory operation, I think.'

'I've had an operation,' said Stamatis complacently. 'I'm the only person I know who's had an operation. And now I can hear. It's a miracle, that's what it is. My head feels empty, it feels hollow, it feels as though my whole head has filled up with spring water, all cold and clear.'

'Well, is it empty, or is it full?' demanded the old lady. 'Talk some sense when the doctor has been kind enough to cure you.' She took Iannis' hand in both of her own and kissed it, and shortly afterwards he found himself walking home with a fat pullet under each arm, a shiny dark aubergine stuffed into each pocket of his jacket, and an ancient pea wrapped up in his handkerchief, to be added to his private medical museum.

It had been a good day for payments; he had also earned two very large and fine crayfish, a pot of whitebait, a basil plant, and an offer of sexual intercourse (to be redeemed at his convenience). He had resolved that he would not be taking up that particular offer, even if the Salvarsan were effective. He was left with a whole evening in which to write his history of Cephallonia, as long as Pelagia had remembered to purchase some more oil for the lamps.

'The New History of Cephallonia' was proving to be a problem; it seemed to be impossible to write it without the intrusion of his own feelings and prejudices. Objectivity seemed to be quite unattainable, and he felt that his false starts must have wasted more paper than was normally used on the island in the space of a year. The voice that emerged in his account was intractably his own; it was never historical. It lacked grandeur and impartiality. It was not Olympian.

He sat down and wrote: 'Cephallonia is a factory that breeds babies for export. There are more Cephallonians abroad or at sea than there are at home. There is no indigenous industry that keeps families together, there is not enough arable land, there is an insufficiency of fish in the ocean. Our men go abroad and return here to die, and so we are an island of children, spinsters, priests, and the very old. The only good thing about it is that only the beautiful women find husbands amongst those men that are left, and so the pressure of natural selection has ensured that we have the most beautiful women in all of Greece, and perhaps in the whole region of the Mediterranean. The unhappy thing about this is that we have beautiful and spirited women married to the most grotesque and inappropriate husbands, who are good for nothing and never could be, and we have some sad and ugly women that nobody wants, who are born to be widows without ever having had a husband.'

The doctor refilled his pipe and read this through. He listened to Pelagia clattering outdoors in the yard, preparing to boil the crayfish. He read what he had written about beautiful women, and remembered his wife, as lovely as her daughter had become, and dead from tuberculosis despite everything he had been able to do. 'This island betrays its own people in the mere act of existing,' he wrote, and then he crumpled the sheet of paper and flung it into the corner of the room. This would never do; why could he not write like a writer of histories? Why could he not write without passion? Without anger? Without the sense of betrayal and oppression? He picked up the sheet, already bent at the corners, that he had written first. It was the title page: 'The New History of Cephallonia'. He crossed out the first two words and substituted 'A Personal'. Now he could forget about leaving out the loaded adjectives and the ancient historical grudges, now he could be vitriolic about the Romans, the Normans, the Venetians, the Turks, the British, and even the islanders themselves. He wrote:

'The half-forgotten island of Cephallonia rises improvidently and inadvisedly from the Ionian Sea; it is an island so immense in antiquity that the very rocks themselves exhale nostalgia and the red earth lies stupefied not only by the sun, but by the impossible weight of memory. The ships of Odysseus were built of Cephallonian pine, his bodyguards were Cephallonian giants, and some maintain that his palace was not in Ithaca but in Cephallonia.

'But even before that wily and itinerant king was favoured by Athene or set adrift through the implacable malice of Poseidon, Mesolithic and Neolithic peoples were chipping knives from obsidian and casting nets for fish. The Mycenean Hellenes arrived, leaving behind the shards of their amphorae and their breast-shaped tombs, bequeathing progeny who, long after the departure of Odysseus, would fight for Athens, be tyrannised by Sparta, and then defeat even the megalomaniac Philip of Macedon, father of Alexander, curiously known as "the Great" and a more preposterous megalomaniac still.

'It was an island filled with gods. On the summit of Mt Aenos there was a shrine to Zeus, and another upon the tiny islet of Thios. Demeter was worshipped for making the island the breadbasket of Ionia, as was Poseidon, the god who had raped her whilst disguised as a stallion, leaving her to give birth to a black horse and a mystical daughter whose name was lost when the Eleusinian mysteries were suppressed by the Christians. Here was Apollo, slayer of the Python, guardian of the navel of the earth, beautiful, youthful, wise, just, strong, hyperbolically bisexual, and the only god to have had a temple made for him by bees out of wax and feathers. Here Dionysus was worshipped also, the god of wine, pleasure, civilisation, and vegetation, father by Aphrodite of a little boy attached to the most gargantuan penis that ever encumbered man or god. Artemis had her worshippers here, too, the many-breasted virgin huntress, a goddess of such radically feminist convictions that she had Actaeon torn to pieces by dogs for accidentally seeing her naked, and had her paramour Orion stung to death by scorpions for touching her fortuitously. She was such a fastidious stickler for etiquette and summary chastisement that entire dynasties could be disposed of for one word out of place or an oblation five minutes late. There were temples to Athene, too, the perpetual virgin who (with great forbearance, compared to Artemis) blinded Tiresias for seeing her naked, was formidably gifted in those crafts which are

6

indispensable to economic and domestic life, and who was the patron of oxen, horses, and olives.

'In their choice of gods the people of the island displayed the immense and intransigent common sense that has been the secret of their survival throughout the centuries; it is obvious that the king of the deities should be worshipped, obvious that a seafaring people should placate the god of the sea, obvious that vintners should honour Dionisios (it is still the most common name on the island), obvious that Demeter should be honoured for keeping the island self-sufficient, obvious that Athene should be worshipped for her gifts of wisdom and skill in the tasks of daily life, just as it also fell to her to oversee innumerable military emergencies. Nor should it be wondered at that Artemis should have had her cult, for this was the equivalent of an infallible insurance policy; she was a troublesome gadfly whose mischief should in preference have been made to occur elsewhere.

'The choice of Apollo as a Cephallonian cult is both the most and the least mysterious. It is the most inexplicable to those who have never been to the island, and the most inevitable to those who know it, for Apollo is a god associated with the power of light. Strangers who land here are blinded for two days.

'It is a light that seems unmediated either by the air or by the stratosphere. It is completely virgin, it produces overwhelming clarity of focus, it has heroic strength and brilliance. It exposes colours in their original prelapsarian state, as though straight from the imagination of God in His youngest days, when He still believed that all was good. The dark green of the pines is unfathomably and retreatingly deep, the ocean viewed from the top of a cliff is platonic in its presentation of azure and turquoise, emerald, viridian, and lapis lazuli. The eye of a goat is a living semi-precious stone half way between amber and arylide, and the crickets are the fluorescent green of the youngest shoots of grass in the original Eden. Once the eyes have adjusted to the extreme vestal chastity of this light, the light of any other place is miserable and dank by comparison; it is nothing more than something to see by, a disappointment, a blemish.

7

Even the seawater of Cephallonia is easier to see through than the air of any other place; a man may float in the water watching the distant sea bed, and clearly see lugubrious rays that for some reason are always accompanied by diminutive flatfish.'

The learned doctor leaned back and read through what he had just written. It seemed really very poetic to him. He read it through again and relished some of the phrases. In the margin he wrote, 'Remember; all Cephallonians are poets. Where can I mention this?'

He went out into the yard and relieved himself into the patch of mint. He nitrogenated the herbs in strict rotation, and tomorrow it would be the turn of the oregano. He returned indoors just in time to catch Pelagia's little goat eating his writings with evident satisfaction. He tore the paper from the animal's mouth and chased it back outside. It skittered out of the door to bleat indignantly behind the massive trunk of the olive tree.

'Pelagia,' remonstrated the doctor, 'your accursed ruminant has eaten everything I've written tonight. How many times do I have to tell you not to let it indoors? Any more incidents like this, and it'll end up on a spit. That's my final word. It's hard enough to stick to the point without that animal sabotaging everything I've done.'

Pelagia looked up at her father and smiled: 'We'll be eating at about ten o'clock.'

'Did you hear what I said? I said no more goats inside the house, is that understood?'

She left off slicing a pepper, brushed a stray hair from her face, and replied, 'You're as fond of him as I am.'

'In the first place, I am not fond of the ruminant, and in the second place you will not argue with me. In my day no daughter argued with her father. I will not permit it.'

Pelagia put one hand on her hip and pulled a wry face. 'Papas,' she said, 'it still is your day. You aren't dead yet, are you? Anyway, the goat is fond of you.'

Dr Iannis turned away, disarmed and defeated. It was a most damnable thing when a daughter pulled feminine wiles upon her own father and reminded him of her mother at the same time. He returned to his table and took a new sheet of paper. He recalled that in his last effort he had somehow managed to stray from the subject of gods to the subject of fish. From a literary point of view it was probably just as well that it had been eaten. He wrote: 'Only an island as impudent as Cephallonia would have the insouciance to situate itself upon a faultline that exposes it to the recurrent danger of cataclysmic earthquakes. Only an island as lacka-daisical as this would allow itself to be infested by such troupes of casual and impertinent goats.'

2

THE DUCE

COME HERE. YES, you. Come here. Now tell me something; which is my best profile, right or left? Really, do you think so? I am not so sure. I think that perhaps the lower lip has a better set on the other side. O, you agree do you? I suppose you agree with everything I say? O, you do. Then how am I supposed to rely on your judgement? What if I say that France is made of bakelite, is that true? Are you going to agree with me? What do you mean, yes sir, no sir, I don't know sir; what kind of answer is that? Are you a cretin or something? Go and fetch me some mirrors so that I can arrange to see for myself.

Yes, it is very important and also very natural that the people should perceive in me an apotheosis of the Italian ideal. You won't catch me being filmed in my underwear. You won't see me in a suit and tie anymore, for that matter. I am not going to be thought of as a businessman, a mere bureaucrat, and in any case this uniform becomes me. I am the embodiment of Italy, possibly even more than the King himself. This is Italy, smart and martial, where everything runs like clockwork. Italy as inflexible as steel. One of the Great Powers, now that I have made it so.

Ah, here are the mirrors. Put it down there. No, there, idiota. Yes, there. Now put the other one there. In the name of God, do I have to do everything myself? What's the matter with you, man? Hm, I think I like the left profile. Tilt that mirror down a bit. More, more. Stop there. That's it. Wonderful. We must arrange it so that the people always see me from a lower position. I must always be higher than them. Send somebody round the city to find the best balconies. Make a note of it. Make a note of this, too, whilst I remember it. By order of the Duce, there is to be maximum afforestation of all the mountains in Italy. What do you mean, what for? It's obvious isn't it? The more trees, the more snow, everyone knows that. Italy should be colder so that the men it breeds are tougher, more resourceful, more resilient. It's a sad truth, but it's true nonetheless, our youngsters don't make the soldiers that their fathers did. They need to be colder, like the Germans. Ice in the soul, that's what we need. I swear the country's got warmer since the Great War. It makes men lazy, it makes them incompetent. It unsuits them to empire. It turns life into a siesta. They don't call me the Unsleeping Dictator for nothing, you don't catch me asleep all afternoon. Make a note. This will be a new slogan for us: 'Libro e Moschetto – Fascisto Perfetto'. I want people to understand that Fascism is not merely a social and political revolution, it's cultural as well. Every Fascist must have a book in their knapsack, do you understand? We are not going to be philistines. I want Fascist book-clubs even in the smallest towns, and I don't want the damned squadristi turning up and setting them on fire, is that clear?

And what's this I hear about a regiment of Alpini marching through Verona singing 'Vogliamo la pace e non vogliamo la guerra'? I want it investigated. I won't have élite troops marching around singing pacifist-defeatist songs when we aren't even properly at war yet. And talking of Alpini, what's this about them getting in fistfights with the Fascist legionnaires? What else have I got to do to make the military accept the militia? How about this for another slogan; 'War is to Man what Motherhood is to Woman'? Very good, I think you'll agree. A fine slogan with a lot of virility to it, much better than 'Church, Kitchen and Children' any day of the week. Call Clara and tell her I'll be coming tonight if I can get away from my wife. How's this for another slogan: 'With Daring Prudence'? Are you sure? I don't remember Benni using it in a speech. Must have been years ago. Perhaps it's not so good.

11

Make a note of this. I want it made absolutely clear to our people in Africa that the practice of so-called 'madamismo' has to end. I really cannot countenance the idea of men of Italy setting up house with native women and diluting the purity of the blood. No, I don't care about native prostitutes. The sciarmute are indispensable to the morale of our men over there. I just won't have love affairs, that's all. What do you mean, Rome was assimilationist? I know that, and I know we're reconstructing the empire, but these are different times. These are Fascist times.

And talking of wogs, have you seen my copy of that pamphlet 'Partito e Impero'? I like that bit where it says 'In short, we must try to give the Italian people an imperialist and racist mentality.' Ah yes, the Jews. Well I think it's been made perfectly clear that Jewish Italians have to decide whether they are Italians first or Jews. It's as simple as that. It hasn't escaped my notice that international Jewry is anti-Fascist. I'm not stupid. I know perfectly well that the Zionists are the tools of British foreign policy. As far as I am concerned we must enforce these employment quotas on Jews in public office; I will not tolerate any disproportion and I don't care if it means that some towns end up with no mayor. We must keep in step with our German comrades. Yes, I know the Pope doesn't like it, but he has too much to lose to stick his neck out. He knows I can repeal the Lateran pacts. I've got a trident up his backside and he knows I can twist it. I gave up atheist materialism for the sake of peace with the Church, and I'm not going any further.

Make a note; I want a salary freeze to keep inflation under control. Increase family subsidies by fifty percent. No I don't think the latter will cancel out the effects of the former. Do you think I don't understand economics? How many times do I have to explain, you dolt, that Fascist economics are immune from the cyclic disturbances of capitalism? How dare you contradict me and say it appears that the opposite is true? Why do you think we've been going for autarky all these years? We've had some teething problems, that's all, you zuccone, you sciocco, you balordo. Send Farinacci a telegram saying that I'm sorry he's lost a hand, but what else

12

do you expect when you go fishing with hand-grenades? Tell the press it was because of something heroic. We'll have an article about it in *Il Regime Fascista* on Monday. Something like 'Party Boss Injured in Valiant Action Against Ethiopians'. Which reminds me, how are the experiments with poison gas going? The ones against the wog guerrillas? I hope the rifiuto die slowly that's all. Maximum agony. Pour encourager les autres. Shall we invade France? How about 'Fascism Transcends Class Antagonisms'? Is Ciano here yet? I've been getting reports from all over the country that the mood is overwhelmingly anti-war. I can't understand it. Industrialists, bourgeoisie, working classes, even the Army, for God's sake. Yes, I know there's a deputation of artists and intellectuals waiting. What? They're going to present me with an award? Send them straight in.

Good evening, gentlemen. I must say that it is a great pleasure to receive this from some of our, ah, greatest minds. I shall wear it with pride. How is your new novel going? Ah, I'm sorry, I quite forgot. Of course you are a sculptor. A slip of the tongue. A new statue of me? Splendid. Milan needs some monuments, does it not? Let me remind you, although I am sure you have no need of it, that Fascism is fundamentally and at bottom an aesthetic conception, and that it is your function as creators of beautiful things to portray with the greatest efficacy the sublime beauty and inevitable reality of the Fascist ideal. Never forget; if the Armed Forces are the balls of Fascism, and I am its brains, you are its imagination. You have a heavy responsibility. Now if you'll excuse me, gentlemen, affairs of state, you know how it is. I have an audience with His Majesty the King. Yes, indeed, I shall convey your profoundest sentiments of loyalty. He would expect no less. Good evening.

That's got rid of them. Isn't this pretty? I might give it to Clara. She is bound to find it amusing. Ah, Ciano is coming is he? About time too. Been hacking his way round a golf-course, no doubt. Damn stupid game, in my opinion. I could understand it if one was trying to hit rabbits or intercept the odd partridge. You can't eat a hole-in-one, can you? You can't draw the entrails of a good putt.

13

Ah, Galeazzo, how good to see you. Do come in. Bene, bene. And how is my dear daughter? How wonderful it is to keep government in the family, so to speak. So good to have someone one can trust. Been playing golf? I thought so. Wonderful game, so fascinating, such a challenge, as much intellectual as physical, I understand. I wish I had time for it myself. One feels so much at sea when talk turns to mashie-niblicks, cleeks, and mid-irons. Quite an Eleusinian mystery. I said 'Eleusinian'. O never mind. What a splendid suit. Such a good cut. And such distinguished shoes too. They're called 'George boots'? I wonder why. Not English are they? Give me an honest military jackboot, Galeazzo; I can't compete with you in elegance, I'll be the first to admit. I'm just a man of the soil, and that's the best thing to be when the soil happens to be Italian, don't you agree?

Now look, we've got to sort out this Greek business once and for all. I think we're agreed that after all our accomplishments we need a new direction. Think of it, Galeazzo; when I was a journalist Italy had no empire to speak of. Now that I am the Duce we do have one. It's a great and lasting legacy, of that there can be no doubt. There is more acclaim for a symphony than for a quartet. But can we stop at Africa and a few islands that no one's ever heard of? Can we rest on our laurels when all about us we see divisions within the party and find that we seem to have no central thrust to our policy? We need dynamite up the arsehole of the nation, do we not? We need a great and unifying enterprise. We need an enemy, and we need to maintain the imperial momentum. This is why I return to the subject of the Greeks.

I've been looking through the records. In the first place we have an historic blot to expunge, an outstanding account. I'm referring to the Tellini incident of 1923, as you no doubt realise. Incidentally, my dear Count, I have been becoming increasingly aware that you have been making foreign policy independently of me, and that consequently we have often found ourselves pulling in different directions at once. No, do not protest, I merely mention this as an unfortunate fact. Our ambassador in Athens is very confused, and perhaps it has been in our interest that he should remain so. I don't want Grazzi dropping hints to Metaxas, and it suits us that they should remain friends. No damage has been done; we've taken Albania and I have written to Metaxas to reassure him and to commend his treatment of King Zog, and everything is going very well. Yes, I am aware that the British have contacted Metaxas to say that they will help defend Greece in the event of an invasion. Yes I know Hitler wants Greece in the Axis, but let's face it, what kind of debt do we owe to Hitler? He stirs up all of Europe, there seems no limit to his greed and irresponsibility, and to cap it all he takes the Romanian oilfields without allowing us any slice of the cake at all. The cheek of it. Who does he think he is? I fear, Galeazzo, that we must base our actions upon a calculation as to which way the dice are falling, and I have to say that it is obvious that Hitler is getting all the sixes. Either we join with him and divide the spoils or else we risk an invasion from Austria as soon as the little man sees fit. It is a question of grasping opportunities and evading perils. It is also a question of expanding the empire. We must continue to stir up liberation movements in Kosovo and irredentism in Tsamouria. We get Yugoslavia and Greece. Imagine it, Galeazzo, the whole Mediterranean littoral rebuilt into a new Roman Empire. We've got Libya, and it's just a question of joining the dots. We've got to do this without telling Hitler; I happen to know that the Greeks have been seeking his assurances. Imagine the impression on the Führer when he sees us sweep through Greece in a matter of days. It'll make him think twice, that's for sure. Imagine yourself at the head of a Fascist legion as you enter Athens on the turret of a tank. Imagine our colours fluttering on the Parthenon.

Do you remember the Guzzoni plan? Eighteen divisions and a year to prepare? And then I said, 'Greece does not lie on our path, and we want nothing from her,' and then I said to Guzzoni, 'The war with Greece is off. Greece is a bare bone, and is not worth the life of a single Sardinian grenadier'? Well, circumstances have changed, Galeazzo. I said that because I wanted Yugoslavia. But why not take both? Who says that we'll need a year to prepare? Some stupid old general with old-fashioned ways, that's who. We could do it in a week with one cohort of legionnaires. There are no soldiers in the world as resolute and valiant as ours.

And the British are provoking us. I'm not talking about De Vecchi's ravings. That reminds me. De Vecchi told you that the British attacked a submarine at Levkas, two more at Zante, and established a base at Milos. I've had a report from Captain Moris that none of this ever happened. You really must remember that De Vecchi is a lunatic and a megalomaniac, and one day when I remember to do so, I will string him up by his copious moustache and remove his testicles without anaesthetic. Thank God he's in the Aegean and not here or I would be up to my neck in bullshit. The man turns the Aegean brown.

But the British have sunk the *Colleoni*, and the Greeks flagrantly allow British ships to take port. What do you mean, we accidentally bombed a Greek supply ship and a destroyer? Accidentally? Never mind, it'll be fewer ships to sink later. Grazzi says there are no British bases at all in Greece, but we'll let that pass, shall we? There's no harm in saying that there are. The important thing is that we've got Metaxas shitting himself. I hope I can place credence in this report of yours that the Greek generals are with us; if that's true, how come they've arrested Platis? And where has all the money gone that was supposed to bribe the officials? It amounts to millions, precious millions that would have been better spent on rifles. And are you sure that the population of Epirus really wants to be Albanian? How do you know? Ah, I see, Intelligence. I have decided, by the way, not to ask the Bulgarians if they want to invade at the same time. Of course it would make it easier for us, but it's going to be a walkover anyway, and if the Bulgarians get their corridor to the sea it's only going to sever our own lines of supply and communication, don't you think? We don't in any case want them basking in glory that is properly our own.

Now, I want you to arrange some attacks against ourselves. Our campaign requires legitimacy for reasons of international polity. No, it's not the Americans I'm worried about; America has no military importance. But remember, we want to invade when we want to invade; I don't want any single colossal casus belli that commits us before we are ready. Avanti piano, quasi indietro. I think we should select an Albanian patriot for assassination, so that we can blame it on the Greeks, and I think we should sink a Greek battleship in such a way that it's obvious that we did it, but not so obvious that we can't blame it on the British. It's a question of judicious intimidation that will weaken the Greek will.

By the way, Galeazzo, I've decided that just before the invasion we'll demobilise the Army. What do you mean, it sounds perverse? It's a question of causing the Greeks to lower their guard, getting the harvest in, and maintaining the appearance of normalisation. Think about it, Galeazzo; think what an acute move it would be. The Greeks heave a sigh of relief, and we flatten them promptly with a hammerblow.

I've been speaking to the Chiefs-of-Staff, my dear Count, and I've asked for plans to be drawn up for the invasion of Corsica, France, and the Ionian islands, and for new campaigns in Tunisia. I'm sure we can manage it. They keep moaning about the lack of transport, and so I've given orders that the infantry should be trained to march fifty miles a day. There is a small problem with the Air Force. It's all in Belgium, so I suppose I must do something about that one of these days. Keep reminding me. I must talk to Pricolo about it; I can't have the chief of the Air Force being the only one who doesn't know what's happening. There are limits even to military secrecy. The Chiefs-of-Staff oppose me, Galeazzo. Badoglio keeps looking at me as though I were mad. One day he's going to look Nemesis in the face and find that the face is mine. I won't have it. I think we should take Crete too, and deny it to the British.

Jacomoni has telegraphed me to the effect that we can expect extensive treachery within the Greek ranks, that the Greeks hate Metaxas and the King, are very depressed, and that they are contemplating the abandonment of Tsamouria.

17

God is with us, it seems. Something's got to be done about the fact that both His Majesty and myself are the First Marshal of the kingdom; one really cannot exist amid such anomalies. Prasca, incidentally, has telegraphed me to say that he requires no reinforcements for the invasion, so how come everybody has been telling me that we can't possibly do it without them? It's gutlessness, that's what. There's no expert so deluded as a military expert, in my experience. I have to do their job for them, it seems. I get nothing but complaints about the shortage of everything. Why have all the contingency funds gone missing? I want it investigated.

Let me remind you, Galeazzo, that Hitler is opposed to this war because Greece is a totalitarian state that should naturally be on our side. So don't tell him. We're going to show him an example of Blitzkrieg that'll make him green with envy. And I don't care if it brings the British in against us. We'll thrash them too.

WHO LET THAT CAT IN HERE? SINCE WHEN HAVE WE HAD A PALACE CAT? IS THAT THE CAT THAT SHAT IN MY HELMET? YOU KNOW I CAN'T STAND CATS. WHAT DO YOU MEAN, IT SAVES ON MOUSETRAPS? DON'T TELL ME WHEN I CAN OR CANNOT USE MY REVOLVER INDOORS. STAND BACK OR YOU'LL CATCH A BULLET TOO. O God, I feel sick. I'm a sensitive man, Galeazzo, I have an artistic temperament, I shouldn't have to look at all this blood and mess. Get someone to clear it up, I don't feel well. What do you mean it's not dead yet? Take it out and wring its neck. NO I DON'T WANT TO DO IT MYSELF. Do you think I'm a barbarian or something? O God. Give me my helmet, quick, I need something to be sick in.

Get rid of this and get me a new helmet. I'm going to go and lie down, it must be way past siesta-time.

3

THE STRONGMAN

THE INSCRUTABLE GOATS of Mt Aenos turned windward, imbibing the damp exhalation of the sea at dawn that served the place of water in that arid, truculent, and indomitable land. Their herder, Alekos, so unaccustomed to human company that he was short of words even in his inner speech, stirred beneath his covering of hides, reached a hand for the reassuring stock of his rifle, and sank once more to sleep. There would be time enough to wake, to eat bread sprinkled with oregano, count his flock, and chivvy them to a place of pasture. His life was timeless, he might have been one of his own forebears, and his goats too would do as Cephallonian goats had always done; they would sleep at noon, concealed from the sun on the vertiginous northern slopes of cliffs, and in the evening their plangent bells might be heard even in Ithaca, carrying across the silent air and causing distant villagers to look up, wondering which herd was passing close. Alekos was a man who at sixty would be the same as he had been at twenty, thin and strong, a prodigy of slow endurance, as incapable of mercurial flight as any of his goats.

Far below him a feather of smoke rose straight into the air as a valley burned. It was uninhabited, and the maquis flamed unchecked, watched with concern only by those who feared that a wind might spring up and carry the sparks to places valuable for their dwellings, their herbs, or their tiny stony fields ringed with the piles of rocks that had been cleared for centuries and opportunely assembled into

19

walls that rocked at the touch of a hand but fell only in times of earthquake. A Greek love of the colour of virginity had caused many of them to be painted white, as though it were not enough to be blinded by the sun alone. An itinerant patriot had daubed ENOSIS on most of them in turquoise paint, and no Cephallonian had seen fit to restore the walls to purity. Every wall, it seemed, reminded them of their membership of a family broken by the aberrant borders of senile rival empires, dispersed by an unruly sea, and victimised by a history that had placed them at the crossroads of the world.

New empires were now lapping against the shores of the old. In a short time it would no longer be a question of the conflagration of a valley and the death by fire of lizards, hedgehogs, and locusts; it would be a question of the incineration of Jews and homosexuals, gypsies and the mentally afflicted. It would be a case of Guernica and Abyssinia writ large across the skies of Europe and North Africa, Singapore and Korea. The self-anointed superior races, drunk on Darwin and nationalist hyperbole, besotted with eugenics and beguiled by myth, were winding up machines of genocide that soon would be unleashed upon a world already weary to the heart of such infinite foolery and contemptible vainglory.

But everyone admires strength and is seduced by it, including Pelagia. When she heard from a neighbour that there was a strongman in the square performing wonders and prodigies worthy of Atlas himself, she put up the broom with which she had been sweeping the yard and hurried out to join the gaggle of the inquisitive and impressionable that had gathered near the well.

Megalo Velisarios, famous all over the islands of Ionia, garbed as a pantomime Turk in pantaloons and curlicued slippers, self-proclaimed as the strongest man who had ever lived, his hair as prodigiously long as that of a Nazarene or Samson himself, was hopping on one leg in time to the clapping of hands. His arms outstretched, he bore, seated upon each stupendous bicep, a full-grown man. One of them clung tightly to his body, and the other, more studied in the virile arts, smoked a cigarette with every semblance of calm. On Velisarios' head, for good measure, sat an anxious little girl of about six years who was complicating his manoeuvres by clamping her hands firmly across his eyes. 'Lemoni!' he roared. 'Take your hands from my eyes and hold onto my hair, or I'll have to stop.'

Lemoni was too overwhelmed to move her hands, and Megalo Velisarios stopped. With one graceful movement like that of a swan when it comes in to land, he tossed both men to their feet, and then he lifted Lemoni from his head, flung her high into the air, caught her under her arms, kissed her dramatically upon the tip of the nose, and set her down. Lemoni rolled her eyes with relief and determinedly held out her hand; it was customary that Velisarios should reward his little victims with sweets. Lemoni ate her prize in front of the whole crowd, intelligently prescient of the fact that her brother would take it from her if she tried to save it. The huge man patted her fondly upon the head, stroked her shining black hair, kissed her again, and then raised himself to his full height. 'I will lift anything that it takes three men to lift,' he cried, and the villagers joined in with those words that they had heard so many times before, a chorus well-rehearsed. Velisarios may have been strong, but he never varied his patter.

'Lift the trough.'

Velisarios inspected the trough; it was carved out of one solid mass of rock and was at least two and a half metres long. 'It's too long,' he said, 'I won't be able to get a grip on it.'

Some in the crowd made sceptical noises and the strongman advanced upon them glowering, shaking his fists and posturing, mocking himself by this caricature of a giant's rage. People laughed, knowing that Velisarios was a gentle man who had never even become involved in a fight. With one sudden movement he thrust his arms beneath the belly of a mule, spread his legs, and lifted it up to his chest. The startled animal, its eyes popping with consternation, submitted to this unwonted treatment, but upon being set lightly down threw back its head, brayed with indignation, and cantered away down the street with its owner in close pursuit.

Father Arsenios chose just this moment to emerge from his little house and waddle portentously towards the crowd on his way to the church. He had the intention of counting the money in the wooden box where folk put coins for candles.

Father Arsenios lacked respect not because he was a walking human globe, perpetually perspiring and grunting with the effort of movement, but because he was venial; a glutton, a would-be lecher, a relentless seeker of alms and offerings, an anthropomorphised promissory note. It was said that he had violated the rule that a priest never remarries, and had come all the way from Epirus so that he could get away with it. It was said that he abused his wife. But this was said of most husbands, and often it was the truth.

'Lift Father Arsenios,' someone called.

'Impossible,' called another.

Father Arsenios quite suddenly found himself grasped beneath the armpits and lifted bodily up onto the wall. He sat there blinking, too astonished to protest, his mouth working like a fish, the sun sparkling off the droplets of sweat upon his forehead.

A few giggled, but then a guilty hush descended. There was a minute of embarrassed silence. The priest flushed crimson, Velisarios began to wish that he could crawl away and hide, and Pelagia felt her heart overflow with indignation and pity. It was a terrible crime to humiliate God's own mouthpiece in public, however contemptible he might be as a man and as a priest. She stepped forward and extended a hand to help him down. Velisarios proffered another, but neither of them was able to prevent the unfortunate cleric from landing heavily and sprawling in the dust. He picked himself up, brushed himself off, and with a most acute sense of theatre walked away without a word. Inside the darkness of the church, behind the iconostasis, he dropped his face into his hands. It was the worst thing in the world to be a complete failure who had no prospect of any other job.

Outside in the square Pelagia was living up to her reputation as a scold. She was only seventeen years old, but she was proud and wilful, and the fact that her father was the doctor gave her the kind of status that even the men were forced to respect. 'You shouldn't have done that, Velisario',' she was saying. 'It was cruel and horrible. Think how the poor man must be feeling. You must go straight into the church and apologise.'

He looked down at her from his great height. This was without doubt a difficult situation. He thought of lifting her above his head. Perhaps he should put her up a tree; it would certainly get some laughs from the crowd. He knew that assuredly he should go and mend his fences with the priest. He could tell from the sudden antipathy of the people that at this rate he would never be able to collect much money from them for his act. What should he do?

'The act's over,' he said, waving his hands in the gesture that signified a finish, 'I'll come back this evening.'

The atmosphere of hostility changed immediately into one of disappointment. After all, the priest deserved it, didn't he? And how often does a good act like this come to the village?

'We want to see the cannon,' called an old lady, and this was confirmed by another, and then another: 'We want the cannon, we want the cannon.'

Velisarios was immensely proud of his cannon. It was an old Turkish culverin, just too heavy for anyone else to lift. It was made of solid brass, with a Damascus barrel bound with riveted iron hoops, and it was engraved with the date 1739 and some swirling characters that no one could decipher. It was a most mysterious, untranslatable cannon that generated copious verdigris no matter how often it was polished. Part of the secret of Velisarios' titanic strength was that he had been carrying it around with him for so long.

He looked down at Pelagia, who was still awaiting a response to her demand that he apologise to the priest, said to her, 'I'll go later, pretty one,' and then raised his arms to announce, 'Good people of the village, to see the cannon, all you must do is give me your old rusty nails, your broken bolts, your shards of pots, and the stones of your streets.

Find me these things whilst I pack the gun with powder. Oh, and somebody bring me a rag, a nice big one.'

Little boys scuffed the dust of the streets for stones, old men searched their sheds, the women ran for the one shirt of their husband that they had been trying to make him discard, and shortly all were reassembled for the great explosion. Velisarios poured a generous dole of powder down into the magazine, tamped it ceremoniously in the full consciousness of the need to prolong the drama, tamped down one of the rags, and then allowed the little boys to scoop handfuls of the accumulated ammunition into the barrel. He followed this with another tattered rag, and then demanded, 'What do you want me to shoot?'

'Prime Minister Metaxas,' cried Kokolios, who was unashamed of his Communist convictions and devoted much time in the kapheneion to criticising the dictator and the King. Some people laughed, others scowled, and some thought 'There goes Kokolios again.'

'Shoot Pelagia, before she bites somebody's balls off,' suggested Nicos, a young man whose advances she had successfully deterred by means of acerbic remarks about his intelligence and general honesty.

'I'll shoot you,' said Velisarios. 'You should mind your tongue when there are respectable people present.'

'I have an old donkey with the spavins. I hate to part with an old friend, but really she's useless. She just eats, and she falls over when I load her up. She'd make a good target, it would take her off my hands, and it would make a terrific mess.' It was Stamatis.

'May you have female children and male sheep for even thinking of such a terrible thing,' exclaimed Velisarios. 'Do you think I am a Turk? No, I will simply fire the gun down the road, for lack of a better target. Everybody out of the way now. Stand back, all the children put their hands over their ears.'

With theatrical aplomb the enormous man lit the fuse of the gun where it stood propped against the wall, picked it up as though it were as light as a carbine, and braced himself with one foot forward and the cannon cradled above the hip. Silence fell. The fuse sputtered brightly. Breaths were held. Children clamped their hands over their ears, grimaced, closed one eye, and hopped from one foot to another. There was a moment of excruciating suspense as the flame of the fuse reached the touch-hole and sputtered out. Perhaps the powder hadn't caught. But then there was a colossal roar, a spout of orange and lilac flame, a formidable cloud of acrid-tasting smoke, a wonderful spitting of dust as the projectiles tore into the surface of the road, and a long moan of pain.

There was a moment of confusion and hesitation. People looked around at each other to see who might have caught a ricochet. A renewed moan, and Velisarios dropped his cannon and ran forward. He had spotted a huddled form amid the settling dust.

Mandras was later to thank Velisarios for shooting him with a Turkish culverin as he came round the bend at the entrance of the village. But at the time he had resented being carried in the arms of a giant rather than being allowed to walk with dignity to the doctor's house, and he had not enjoyed having a bent nail from a donkey shoe extracted from his shoulder without anaesthetic. He had not enjoyed being held down by the giant as the doctor worked, since he had been quite capable of enduring the pain on his own. Nor had it been convenient or economic to have to cease fishing for two weeks whilst the wound healed.

What he thanked Megalo Velisarios for was that in the doctor's house he first set eyes on Pelagia, the doctor's daughter. At some indefinable moment he had become aware that he was being bandaged, that there was a young woman's long hair tickling his face, and that it smelled of rosemary. He had opened his eyes, and found himself gazing into another pair of eyes that were alight with concern. 'At that moment,' he liked to say, 'I became aware of my destiny.' It was true that he only said this when somewhat in his cups, but he meant it nonetheless.

Up on Mt Aenos, on the roof of the world, Alekos had heard the boom of the weapon, and wondered if it meant the start of another war.

4

L'OMOSESSUALE (1)

I, CARLO PIERO Guercio, write these words with the intention that they should be found after my death, when neither scorn nor loss of reputation may dog my steps nor blemish me. The circumstance of life leaves it impossible that this testament of my nature should find its way into the world before I have drawn my last breath, and until that time I shall be condemned to wear the mask decreed by misfortune.

I have been reduced to eternal and infinite silence, I have not even told the chaplain in confession. I know in advance what I will be told; that it is a perversion, an abomination in the sight of God, that I must fight the good fight, that I must marry and lead the life of a normal man, that I have a choice.

I have not told a doctor. I know in advance that I will be called an invert, that I am in some strange way in love with myself, that I am sick and can be cured, that my mother is responsible, that I am an effeminate even though I am as strong as an ox and fully capable of lifting my own weight above my head, that I must marry and lead the life of a normal man, that I have a choice.

What could I say to such priests and doctors? I would say to the priest that God made me as I am, that I had no choice, that He must have made me like this for a purpose, that He knows the ultimate reasons for all things and that therefore it must be all to the good that I am as I am, even if we cannot know what that good is. I can say to the priest that if

God is the reason for all things, then God is to blame and I should not be condemned.

And the priest will say, 'This is a matter of the Devil and not of God,' and I will reply, 'Did God not make the Devil? Is He not omniscient? How can I be blamed for what He knew would occur from the very commencement of time?' And the priest will refer me to the destruction of Sodom and Gomorrah and tell me that God's mysteries are not to be understood by us. He will tell me that we are commanded to be fruitful and multiply.

I would say to the doctor, 'I have been like this from the first, it is nature that has moulded me, how am I supposed to change? How can I decide to desire women, any more than I can suddenly decide to enjoy eating anchovies, which I have always detested? I have been to the Casa Rosetta, and I loathed it, and afterwards I felt sick. I felt cheapened. I felt I was a traitor. I had to do it to appear normal.'

And the doctor will say, 'How can this be natural? Nature serves its interests by making us reproduce. This is against nature. Nature wants us to be fruitful and multiply.'

This is a conspiracy of doctors and priests who repeat the same things in different words. It is medicinal theology and theological medicine. I am like a spy who has signed a covenant of perpetual secrecy, I am like someone who is the only person in the world that knows the truth and yet is forbidden to utter it. And this truth weighs more than the universe, so that I am like Atlas bowed down forever beneath a burden that cracks the bones and solidifies the blood. There is no air in this world that I am fated to inhabit, I am a plant suffocated by lack of air and light, I have had my roots clipped and my leaves painted with poison. I am exploding with the fire of love and there is no one to accept it or nourish it. I am a foreigner within my own nation, an alien in my own race, I am as detested as cancer when I am as purely flesh as any priest or doctor.

According to Dante my like is confined to the third ring of the Seventh Circle of Nether Hell, in the improbable company of usurers. He gives me a desert of naked spirits scourged by flakes of fire, he makes me run in circles, perpetually and in futility, looking for the ones whose bodies I've defiled. You see how it is; I have been driven to search everywhere just to find myself mentioned. I am mentioned almost nowhere, but where I find myself, I find myself condemned. And how remarkable it is, you doctors and priests, that Dante pitied us when God did not. Dante said, 'It makes me heartsick only to think of them.' And Dante was right, I have always run in circles, futilely, looking for the warmth of bodies, scorned by God who created me, and all my life has been a desert and a rain of flakes of flame.

Yes, I have read everything, looking for evidence that I exist, that I am a possibility. And do you know where I found myself? Do you know where I found out that I was, in another vanished world, beautiful and true? It was in the writings of a Greek.

Ironical. I am an Italian soldier oppressing the only people whose ancestors bestowed upon my kind the right to embody a most perfect form of love.

I joined the Army because the men are young and beautiful, I admit it. And also because I got the idea from Plato. I am probably the only soldier in history who has taken up arms because of a philosopher. You see, I had been searching for a vocation in which my affliction could be of use, and I had been ignorant of the love of Achilles and Patroclus, and other such ancient Greekeries. In short, I read *The Symposium*, and found Aristophanes explaining that there were three sexes; the men and women who loved each other, the men who loved men, and the women who loved women. It was a revelation to conceive that I was of a different sex, it was an idea that made some sense. And I found Phaedrus explaining that 'if there were only some way of contriving that a state or an army should be made up of lovers and their loves, they would be the very best governors of their own city, abstaining from all dishonour, and emulating one another in honour; and when fighting at one another's side, although a mere handful, they would overcome the world. For what lover would not choose rather to be seen by all mankind than by his beloved, either when abandoning his post or throwing away his arms? He

28

would be ready to die a thousand deaths rather than endure this. Or who would desert his beloved or fail him in the hour of danger? The veriest coward would become an inspired hero, equal to the bravest, at such a time; Love would inspire him. That courage which, as Homer says, the god breathes into the soul of heroes, Love of his own nature infuses into the lover. Love will make men dare to die for their beloved – Love alone.'

I knew that in the Army there would be those that I could love, albeit never touch. I would find someone to love, and I would be ennobled by this love. I would not desert him in battle, he would make me an inspired hero. I would have someone to impress, someone whose admiration would give me that which I cannot give myself; esteem, and honour. I would dare to die for him, and if I died I would know that I was dross which some inscrutable alchemy had transmuted into gold.

It was a wild idea, romantic and implausible, and the odd thing is that it worked. But finally it brought me incalculable grief.

5

THE MAN WHO SAID 'NO'

PRIME MINISTER METAXAS slumped forlornly in his favourite armchair in the Villa Kifisia and reflected bitterly upon the two imponderable problems of his life: 'What am I going to do about Mussolini?' and 'What am I going to do about Lulu?' It would be difficult to say which one caused him the most bewilderment and pain, for both were in unequal parts personal and political. Metaxas reached for his journal and wrote, 'This morning I attempted to reach an understanding with Lulu. Up to a certain point it went quite well, but then we argued all over again. She just doesn't understand me. I know exactly who it is that is egging her on and deceiving her. I even forgot my meeting with the British minister. I stayed with her till noon. I am so sorry for her. And what a tragic girl she is. Lulu, Lulu, my most beloved daughter. We threw ourselves into each other's embrace and wept together over our fate.'

With Lulu he never quite knew what the truth was; it seemed that Athens buzzed with more improbable legends about her than it had with stories of Zeus in ancient times. There was the story about the policeman who had lost his trousers and his cap, both of which were found at the top of a lamppost. There was the story about the young man with the Bugatti and the wild trips to Piraeus, and then that account of her playing an English game called 'sardines', a kind of hide-and-seek in which the seekers had to cram themselves into the same space as the hunted; it seemed that Lulu had been found inextricably entwined with a young man in a cupboard. Some people said that she smoked opium and became blisteringly drunk. She knew all those fast American dances, like the tango (so inelegant and vulgar, an alleged 'dance' from the brothels of Buenos Aires), and the quickstep, and the samba, and dances with untranslatable and idiotic names, like the jitterbug, that involved frenetic flapping of the hands and legs. It was a sort of indecency. It reeked of immodesty and intemperance. Young people were so impressionable, so prone to fads and fashions from immature civilisations like America, so averse to discipline and the dignity that accompanies a natural sense of amour propre. What could one do? She always denied everything, or, worse, dismissed his concerns with a laugh and a wave of the hand. God knows, one is only young once, but in her case it was once too often.

And she openly disavowed and controverted his policies in public. It was a Judas touch. It was this that hurt so much, this exhibition of filial disloyalty. She loved him, she said. Indeed, he knew that she did, so why did she ridicule his National Youth Organisation? Why did she laugh at jokes about his diminutive stature? Why was she so damned individualist? Did she not realise that to be a kind of female playboy brought into question all those things that he wished for Greece? How could he lambast the plutocrats when his own daughter was consorting, frolicking with the worst of them? How could he commend discipline and self-sacrifice?

Thank God he had muzzled the press, because every journalist in the land had a pet 'Lulu' story. Thank God his ministers were too discreet to mention it, thank God he had not yet lost respect through contagion. But that didn't prevent people like Grazzi smiling in their oily way and asking, 'And how is your dear daughter, Lulu? I hear that she is a mischievous little thing. Ah, what we fathers have to suffer!' Couldn't he just hear the sniggers and the whispers? That he controlled all of Greece and could not control his own daughter? It seemed that even the secret police were too embarrassed by the whole thing to report her escapades in any detail. It was said that people holding parties would implore their guests, 'Don't bring Lulu.' The grief and shame were too much to take.

Outside, the tranquillity of the pines and the white glare of the floodlights conspired to exacerbate his sensation of having become a prisoner behind his own iron gates; he had fulfilled the requirements of classical tragedy by creating the circumstances of his own entrapment. All Greece had shrunk to this modest pseudo-Byzantine villa and its bourgeois furniture, for the very simple reason that he held the fate and the honour of his beloved country in the palm of his hand. He looked down at his hands and reflected that they were small, like himself. He wished briefly that he had chosen to retire on a colonel's pension and live quietly in some anonymous corner, a place in which to live and die blamelessly.

Dying had much preoccupied him recently, for he had realised that his body was failing him. It was nothing specific, there was no catalogue of tell-tale symptoms, it was merely that he felt exhausted enough to die. He knew that a kind of detached and passive grief overtakes those on the threshold of death, a resigned composure, and it was this detachment and composure which was rising up in him at the same time as circumstances were obliging him to summon up a strength, purpose, and nobility such as he had never required before. Sometimes he wanted to pass the reins of state to other hands, but he knew that fate had selected him as protagonist in the tragedy and that he had no choice but to grip the hilt of the sword and draw it. 'There are so many things I should have done,' he thought, and suddenly it was borne in upon him that life could have been sweet if only he had known thirty years ago what the results of the doctors' analyses would be at this far-distant point of the future that had rolled slowly but maliciously towards him and become the inescapable, arduous, and insupportable present. 'If I had lived my life in the consciousness of this death, everything would have been different.'

He cast his mind back over the impossible vicissitudes of his career, and wondered whether history would show him any charity. It had been a long journey from the Prussian Military Academy in Berlin; it seemed that it must have been in another life that he had learned to admire the teutonic sense of order, discipline, and seriousness, the very qualities that he had tried to instil in his native land. He had even commissioned the very first grammar of the demotic tongue and made it compulsory in schools, because of the theory that learning grammar promotes logicality and would therefore curb the wild, irresponsible individualism of the Greeks.

He recalled the fiasco of the Great War, when Venizelos had wanted to join the Allies and the King had wanted to remain neutral. How he had argued that Bulgaria would take the opportunity to invade if Greece were to join in; how nobly he had resigned his post as Chief-of-Staff, how nobly he had accepted exile. Better forget the attempted coup in 1923. And now it looked as though Bulgaria might invade indeed, grasping the opportunities granted this time by Italy in its attempts to fill the vacuum left by the Turks.

He remembered his defeat of the striking tobacco workers in Salonica; twelve dead. On the strength of that disorder he had persuaded the King to suspend the constitution in order to thwart the Communists; he had persuaded the King to appoint him Prime Minister even though he was the leader of the most marginal right-wing party in the country. But why had he done it? 'Metaxa',' he said to himself, 'history will say that it was opportunism, that you could not succeed by democratic means. There will be no one near to say the truth on my behalf, which is that there was a slump and that our democracy was too effeminate to cope with it. It is easy to say what should have been, harder to acknowledge the inexorable force of necessity. I was the embodiment of necessity, that's all. If it hadn't been me, it would have been someone else. At least I didn't allow the Germans any influence, though God knows they nearly got the economy. At least I kept up the links with Britain, at least I tried to meld the glories of the mediaeval and the ancient civilisation into a new force. No one can ever say that I acted without regard to Greece. Greece has been my one true wife. Perhaps history will remember me as the man who forbade the reading of the funeral oration of Pericles and who alienated the peasantry by putting limits on the number of goats that ruin our forests. O God, perhaps I have been nothing but an absurd little man.

'But I have done my best, I have done everything to prepare for this war that I still work to avoid. I have built railways and fortifications, I have called up the reserve, I have prepared the people by way of speeches, I have pursued diplomacy to the point of ridicule. Let history say that I was the man who did everything possible to save his native land. Everything ends in death.'

But there was no doubt that he had been too much obsessed by an historical sense, with the idea that there was a messianic mission which had been chosen for him to fulfil. He had thought that there could have been no other man, that he was the one to take the Greek nation by the neck and drag it, kicking and expostulating, towards the rightful goal. He had felt himself a doctor who inflicts necessary pain, knowing that after the curses and protests of the patient, there would come a time when he would be crowned with the flowers of the grateful. He had always done what he knew to be right, but perhaps in the end it was vanity that had impelled him, something as simple and disgraceful as megalomania.

But now his spirit had been cast into the fire, and he knew that his temper was being assayed in the furnace of destiny. Was he going to be the man who saved Greece? The man who could have saved Greece, but did not? The man who could not have saved Greece, but who strove with the utmost effort to save her honour? That was it; it was a question above all of personal and national honour, because the important thing was that Greece should come through this trial without the slightest imputation of turpitude. When soldiers are dead, when a country is devastated and destroyed, it is honour that survives and endures. It is honour that breathes life into the corpse when evil times have passed.

Was it not a form of irony to be so mocked by fate? Had

he not selected for himself his role as 'The First Peasant', 'The First Worker', 'The National Father'? Had he not surrounded himself with the pompous trappings of a modern Fascist? A 'Regime of the Fourth Of August 1936'? A Third Hellenic Civilisation to echo Hitler's Third Reich? A National Youth Organisation that held parades, waved banners, just like the Hitler Youth? Didn't he despise Liberals, Communists, and Parliamentarianism, just as did Franco, Salazar, Hitler, and Mussolini? Hadn't he sowed discord amongst the leftists, according to the textbook? What could have been easier, given their ludicrous factionalism and their eagerness to betray each other on the grounds of false consciousness and any one of a plethora of ideological impurities? Didn't he denounce the plutocracy? Didn't the secret police know the exact aroma and chemical composition of every subversive fart in Greece?

So why had his international brothers deserted him? Why did Ribbentrop send him anodyne assurances that could not be believed? Why was Mussolini fabricating border incidents and diplomatic impasses? What had gone wrong? How had it occurred that he had risen to such heights by catching the currents of the times, only to find himself confronted by the greatest crisis in the modern history of the fatherland, a crisis engineered by the very people whom he had taken as his exemplars and mentors? Wasn't it an irony that nowadays he could rely only upon the British – the Parliamentarian, Liberal, democratic, plutocratic British?

Prime Minister Metaxas wrote down on a piece of paper the differences between himself and the others. He was not a racist. That's not much. He was struck by a thought that should have been obvious; the others wanted empires and were engaged in building them, whereas he had only ever wanted the union of all the Greek peoples. He wanted Macedonia, Cyprus, the Dodecanese, and, by the Grace of God, Constantinople. He did not want North Africa, like Mussolini, or the whole world, like Hitler.

So perhaps the others looked at him and considered that he lacked ambition, that he lacked the urge to greatness, that this indicated the absence of that essential Will-to-

Power of the Übermensch, that he was a poodle amongst wolves. In the new world where the strongest had the right to rule because they were strongest, where strength was the indicator of natural superiority, where natural superiority gave one the moral right to subsume other nations and lesser breeds, he was an anomaly. He only wanted his own nation. Greece was a natural target, then. Metaxas wrote down the word 'poodle', and then crossed it out. He looked at the two words 'racism' and 'empire'. 'They think that we are inferior,' he muttered, 'they want us in their empire.' It was disgusting and outrageous, it was exasperating. He enclosed the two words in a bracket and wrote the word 'NO' beside it. He stood up and went to the window to look out at the peaceful pines. He leaned on the sill and reflected upon the sublime ignorance of those dreaming trees, silvered by the moon. He shivered and then stood erect. He had made a decision; it would be another Thermopylae. If three hundred Spartans could hold out against five million of the bravest Persians, what could he not achieve with twenty divisions against the Italians? If only it were so easy to prepare oneself for the terrible and infinite solitude of death. If only it were so easy to deal with Lulu.

6

L'OMOSESSUALE (2)

I, CARLO PIERO Guercio, testify that in the Army I found my family. I have a father and mother, four sisters, and three brothers, but I have not had a family since puberty. I had to live among them secretly, like one who conceals leprosy. It was not their fault that I was made into a thespian. I had to dance with girls at festas, I had to flirt with girls in the playground of the school and when taking the evening passeggiata in the piazza. I had to answer my grandmother when she asked me what kind of girl I would like to marry and whether I wanted sons or daughters. I had to listen with delight to my friends describing the intricacies of the female pudenda, I had to learn to relate fabulous histories of what I had done with girls. I learned to be more lonely than it ought to be possible to feel.

In the Army there was the same gross talk, but it was a world without women. To a soldier a woman is an imaginary being. It is permissible to be sentimental about your mother, but that's all. Otherwise there are the inmates of the military brothels, the fictitious or unfaithful sweethearts at home, and the girls at whom one catcalls in the streets. I am not a misogynist, but you should understand that to me the company of a woman is painful because it reminds me of what I am not, and of what I would have been if God had not meddled in my mother's womb.

I was very lucky at first. I was not sent to Abyssinia or North Africa, but to Albania. There was no fighting to speak of and we were blissfully oblivious to the notion that

37

the Duce might order us to invade Greece. It seemed more likely that we would eventually become involved in Yugoslavia, and that they would be as useless and cowardly as the Albanians. It was common knowledge that the Yugoslavs hated each other more than they could ever hate a foreigner or an invader.

It soon became clear that everything was in chaos. No sooner had I settled down and made friends in one unit than I was transferred to help make up numbers in another, and then I was transferred again. We had almost no transport and we were made to march from the Yugoslav border to the Greek one and back again, seemingly at a whim of the High Command. I think I must have been in about seven units before I was finally settled in the Julia Division. There were a lot of reasons why the Greek campaign was a fiasco, but one of them was that personnel were moved around so much that there was no possibility of developing any esprit de corps. Initially I did not have time to make anyone a Jonathan to my David.

But with the Julia Division I enjoyed every moment. No civilian can comprehend the joy of being a soldier. That is, quite simply, an irreducible fact. A further fact is, that regardless of the matter of sex, soldiers grow to love each other; and, regardless of the matter of sex, this is a love without parallel in civil life. You are all young and strong, overflowing with life, and you are all in the shit together.

You come to know every nuance of each others' moods; you know exactly what the other is going to say; you know exactly who will laugh and for how long over which particular type of joke; you acquaint yourself intimately with the smell of each man's feet and perspiration; you can put your hand on someone's face in the dark, and know who it is; you recognise someone's equipment hanging on the back of a chair, even though his is the same as everyone else's; you can tell whose stubble it is in the washing bowl; you know precisely who will swap you a carrot for your potato, a packet of cigarettes for your spare pair of socks, a postcard of Siena for a pencil. You become accustomed to seeing each other frankly, and nothing is hidden. Unless your desires are the same as mine.

We were all young together. We would never be more handsome, we would never be more lean and strong, we would never again have such water-fights, we would never again feel so invincible and immortal. We could march fifty miles in one day, singing battle songs and lewd songs, swinging along together or trudging, limbs in unison, the cockerel feathers of our helmets black and glistening, tossing. We could piss together on the wheels of the Colonel's car, as drunk as cardinals; we could shit unashamed in each others' presence; we could read each others' letters so that it seemed that every son's mother wrote to all of us; we could dig a trench all night in solid rock in the pouring rain and march away at dawn without ever having slept in it; on live-firing exercises we could lob mortar bombs at rabbits without permission; we could bathe naked and beautiful as Phoebus and someone would point at someone's penis and say, 'Hey you, why haven't you handed that in to the armoury?' and we all would laugh and make nothing of it, and someone else would say, 'Watch out or there'll be a negligent discharge,' and the victim of the joke would say, 'No such luck.'

We were new and beautiful, we loved each other more than brothers, that's for sure. What spoiled it always was that none of us knew why we were in Albania, none of us had an easy conscience about this rebuilding of the Roman Empire. We often had fights with the members of the Fascist Legions. They were vainglorious and useless and stupid, and many of us were Communists. No one minds dying in a noble cause, but we were haunted behind the eyes by the strange pointlessness of loving a life that had no reasonable excuse. My point is that we were like gladiators, prepared to do our duty, prepared to be stoical, but always perplexed. Count Ciano played golf, Mussolini conducted vendettas against cats, and we were in an unmapped waste, wasting time until the time ran out and we were thrown into mismanaged battle against a people that fought like gods.

I am not a cynic, but I do know that history is the propaganda of the victors. I know that if we win the war there will be shocking stories of British atrocities, volumes written to show the inevitability and justice of our cause, irrefutable evidence compiled to reveal the conspiracies of Jewish plutocrats, photographs of piles of bones found in mass graves in the suburbs of London. Equally I know that the reverse will be true if the British win. I know that the Duce has made it clear that the Greek campaign was a resounding victory for Italy. But he was not there. He does not know what happened. He does not know that the ultimate truth is that history ought to consist only of the anecdotes of the little people who are caught up in it. He ought to know that the truth is that we were losing badly until the Germans invaded from Bulgaria. He will never acknowledge this because the 'truth' belongs to the victors. But I was there, and I know what was happening in my part of the war. For me that war was an experience that shaped the whole course of my thought, it was the deepest personal shock that I have ever had, the worst and most intimate tragedy of my life. It destroyed my patriotism, it changed my ideals, it made me question the whole notion of duty, and it horrified me and made me sad.

Socrates said that the genius of tragedy is the same as that of comedy, but the remark is left unexplained in the text because the people to whom it was addressed were either asleep or drunk when he said it. It sounds like the kind of thing that aristocrats say to each other at parties, but I can illustrate its perfect truth simply by relating what befell during that campaign in northern Greece.

Let me begin by saying that I, Carlo Piero Guercio, upon joining the Julia Division, fell in love with a young married corporal who accepted me as his best friend without ever once suspecting that he constituted the entire population of my most fevered dreams. His name was Francesco and he came from Genoa, complete with a Genoese accent and an understanding of the sea that was of no possible use in Epirus. There was no doubt at all that he should have been in the Navy, but the skewed logic of the times decreed that he should volunteer for the Navy, get posted to the carabinieri, but find himself in the Army. He had arrived via a regiment of Alpini and a regiment of Bersaglieri, not counting two days with the Grenadiers.

He was an entirely beautiful boy. His skin was darker than mine, like that of a southerner, but he was slender and smooth-skinned. I recollect that he had only three hairs in the centre of his chest and that his legs were completely hairless. You could see every sinew of his body, and I used to wonder particularly at those muscles that one only sees on particularly fit individuals; the parallel tracks down the back of the forearm, the ones at the side of the abdomen that curve and taper to the groin. He was like one of those elegant, lanky cats that give the impression of immense but casual strength.

I was attracted most of all to his face. He had a black and misbehaving forelock that fell about his eyes. These were very dark, set in the slavic fashion above prominent bones. His mouth was wide, composed into a permanent, ironical, and lopsided smile, and he had an Etruscan nose that seemed inexplicably to have fallen a little crooked at the bridge. His hands were large, with slender spatulate fingers that I could only too easily imagine lingering upon my body. I saw him mend a tiny link on a filigree gold chain once, and I can testify that his fingers had all the immaculate precision of an embroiderer. He had the most delicate fingernails imaginable.

You will understand that we men were often naked together in one context or another and that I knew and memorised every last detail of every part of him; but I rebel against the charges of perversion and obscenity that would be made against my memory, and I will keep these recollections to myself. To me they are not obscene; they are precious, exquisite and pure. In any case, no one would know what they mean. They are for the private museum that each of us carries in our heads, and to which not even the experts or the crowned heads of Europe are permitted access.

Francesco was a man of impetuosities, ludicrous jests, and complete irreverence. He made no secret of respecting no one, and could entertain us by mimicking the cockerel antics of the Duce and the antic Prussianisms of Adolf

Hitler. He could reproduce the gestures and intonations of Visconti Prasca and deliver absurd speeches in the Prasca manner, full of extravagant optimism, wild plans, and obsequious references to the hierarchy. Everybody loved him, he never got promotion, and nor did he care. He adopted a wild mouse and called it Mario; part of the time it lived in his pocket, but when we were on route marches we used to see it poking its whiskers out of the top of his backpack and washing its face. It used to eat the peel of fruit and vegetables and was annoyingly fond of leather. I still have a little round hole at the top of one of my boots.

We soldiers knew next to nothing about what was going on in the centres of power. We received so many orders and counter-orders that there were times when we did not obey any of them at all, knowing that they were likely to be countermanded almost immediately. Albania was a sort of holiday camp without any amenities, and we assumed that these orders had the sole purpose of attempting to keep us busy and were of no serious import.

However, it seems clear in retrospect that an invasion of Greece must have been the ultimate intention; there were clues everywhere, if only we had seen them. In the first place there was all that propaganda about the Mediterranean being the 'Mare Nostrum' and the fact that all our road-building, which was supposedly for the benefit of the Albanians, produced nothing but highways towards the Greek border. In the second place the troops started singing battle songs of unknown provenance and anonymous composership, with words like 'We'll go to the Aegean Sea, we'll seize Piraeus, and if things go right we'll have Athens too.' We used to curse the Greeks for sheltering the ruritanian King Zog, and the newspapers were always full of alleged British attacks on our shipping from Greek waters. I say 'alleged' because nowadays I don't believe they really happened. I have a friend in the Navy who told me that as far as he knew none of our ships had been lost.

I also don't believe any more that story that the Greeks killed Daut Hoggia. I think that we did it and tried to blame it on the Greeks. This is a terrible thing for me to say because it shows how much I have lost my patriotic faith, but the fact is that I now know the Greek version of the events, which I got from Dottore Iannis when I went to see him about a bad toenail. It turns out that the man Hoggia was not an Albanian irredentist patriot at all. He had been convicted over twenty years of the murder of five Muslims, cattle-theft, brigandage, extortion, attempted murder, demanding money with menaces, carrying forbidden weapons, and rape. And this is the man that they tried to fool us into thinking of as a martyr. We were never told that the Greeks had arrested two Albanians for this man's murder, and were waiting for an extradition request. In any case I wonder now how the entire Italian nation could have been so naïve, and I wonder why we were supposed to be so concerned about the Albanians when we had just taken their country and it had become obvious to all of us that they were only interested in murdering each other. The two men who murdered the 'patriot' Hoggia apparently poisoned him and then cut off his head, which is mild indeed by Albanian standards.

A great many things caused me to lose faith, and I commit to paper here an account involving Francesco and myself which demonstrates clearly that it was our side that started the war, and not the Greeks. If we win the war these facts will never come to light, I know, because these papers will be suppressed. But if we lose there may be a chance that the world will learn the truth.

It is hard enough to live at peace with yourself when you are a sexual outsider, but it is even harder when you know that in the line of duty you have carried out the most abominable and filthy deeds. Nowadays I frequently have intimations of impending death, and below you will find my confessions of a guilt for which I have already received absolution from a priest, but which will never be forgiven either by the Greeks or by the families of the Italian soldiers concerned.

7

EXTREME REMEDIES

FATHER ARSENIOS RUMINATED bitterly behind the iconostasis; how was he supposed to go out amongst the people, comforting the sick and the dying, arbitrating in disputes, disseminating the Word of God, advocating the reunion of Greece, when it seemed indubitable that he no longer had any respect? He pondered briefly the romantic possibility of disappearing; he could go to Piraeus and work as a clerk; he could become a fisherman; he could go to America and make a new beginning. He entertained an ephemeral image of himself, liberated from his grotesque folds of lard, singing bawdy rebetika in the brothels of Athens, swigging kokkinelli and chárming the young girls. Conversely he envisaged himself retiring to a hermitage in the mountains of Epirus, being fed by the ravens, and attaining a splendid sainthood. He thought about the miracles that might be performed in his name, and hit upon the unpleasant notion that he might become the patron saint of the obscenely fat. Perhaps he could write great poetry instead, and become as famous and respected as Kostis Palamas. But why stop there? He might be another Homer. Behind the iconostasis he began to rumble in his deep bass voice, 'It vexes me to see how mean are these creatures of a day towards us Gods, when they charge against us the evils (far beyond our worst doomings) which their own exceeding wantonness has heaped upon themselves.' He faltered and stopped, furrowing his brow; was the next bit about Aegisthus, or was it the bit about Athene having a conversation with Zeus? 'My child,' protested Zeus, the cloud-compeller, 'what sharp judgements you let slip between your teeth . . .'

He was interrupted by a discreet cough from the main body of the church. Hastily he gathered his wits together, felt extreme embarrassment paint his ears and neck, and sat completely still. He had been caught in an unselfconscious act of declamatory daydreaming, and now the villagers would be saying that he was demented. He heard the shuffle of departing footsteps, and peeked round the corner of the screen to see that someone had left him a loaf of bread. He found himself smacking his lips and wishing for some cheese to accompany it. There were more footsteps, and he hid himself quickly, like a child at play. The feet departed, and he peered through a small hole to see that someone had left a large, soft, and succulent cheese. 'A miracle,' he said to himself. 'Thanks be to God.' He wished venially for some aubergines and a bottle of oil, only to be rewarded not with another miracle, but with a pair of slippers. 'My God, my God,' he said, looking up at the ceiling, 'how perverse thou art.'

Gradually the entrance to the building filled up with gifts as the villagers left their tokens of apology. Father Arsenios watched through the hole with naïve cupidity as fish were followed by vegetables and embroidered handkerchiefs. He began to notice that a large amount of Robola was accumulating, and he expostulated to himself, 'What? Do they all think I'm a drunk?' He began to work out how long the supply would last if he drank two bottles per diem. Then how long if he drank three. For mathematical amusement and intellectual challenge he started to compute the results of three and five-eighths each day, but became confused and was obliged to recommence.

As the pile continued to grow he became urgently aware of a need to urinate. He shifted uncomfortably and began to perspire. It was a most terrible dilemma; either he went out of the church, in which case people might be deterred from leaving the gifts in his presence, or else he would have to sit there in augmenting desperation until such a time that he could be sure that the flow of penitent presents had ceased. He began to regret vehemently the bottle he had drunk before coming out; 'This is the retribution of God against the bibulous,' he thought, 'I will never touch another drop.' He prayed to St Gerasimos for relief.

Upon conclusion of the prayer he was visited by inspiration. Out in the church was a large supply of bottles. He listened intently for the approach of footsteps, heard none, and nipped out as quickly as his girth would permit. He waddled rapidly to the entrance, leaned down painfully for a bottle, and then retreated to his concealment behind the screen. He pulled the cork with his teeth and considered the next problem; in order to be able to employ the bottle it would have to be empty. What could he do with the wine? It seemed a shame to waste it. He tipped back the bottle and poured it down his throat. Rivulets of the sweet liquid runnelled down his beard and onto his cassock. He inspected the bottle, found one or two drops left, and shook them with a flourish into his mouth.

Father Arsenios peeped through the hole to ensure that he would not be heard, lifted his cassock, and released a formidable stream of urine into the bottle. It hammered against the glass of the bottom, and then splashed and hissed as the bottle filled. He noted with alarm that as the neck of the vessel narrowed, it filled at an exponential rate. 'They should make bottles uniformly cylindrical,' reflected the priest, and was promptly taken by surprise.

He rubbed the splashback into the dust of the floor with his foot, and realised that he would have to wait in the church until the damp patches on his robes had dried. 'A priest,' he thought, 'cannot be seen to have pissed himself.' He put the bottle of urine down and reseated himself. Someone came in and left him a pair of socks.

A quarter of an hour passed, and Velisarios came in, hoping to apologise in person. He looked in the campanile and in the main body of the church, and was about to leave when he heard a long and gurgling belch emanate from behind the screen. 'Patir?' called Velisarios. 'I have come to apologise.'

'Go away,' came the petulant reply, and then, 'I am trying to pray.'

'But Patir, I want to apologise and kiss your hand.'

'I can't come out. For various reasons.'

Velisarios scratched his head, 'What reasons?'

'Religious ones. Besides, I don't feel well.'

'Do you want me to fetch Doctor Iannis?'

'No.'

'I apologise, Patir, for what I did, and to make amends I have left you a bottle of wine. I will pray to God to forgive me.' He left the church and returned to the doctor's house to see how Mandras was getting on, finding him gazing at Pelagia with positively canine adoration. He went to tell the doctor that the priest was unwell.

Father Arsenios was finding that his solution to the problem of a distended bladder was itself the cause of further distension. After Velisarios' departure he had emptied another bottle, and refilled it with the transmogrified produce of the previous one. This time his aim, his balance, and his judgement of the right moment at which to stop all lacked even the suspect precision of the earlier enterprise. There was further mess to be rubbed into the dust with his foot, and more dampening of the robe. Arsenios reseated himself blearily, and began to feel nauseous. He slipped heavily off the stool, bruising his coccyx, and was woken twenty minutes later by the urgent need to empty and refill another bottle. He vowed to stop before the narrowing neck could create another venturi effect, but was so oppressed by now with high pressure that once more his judgement failed. Dismally.

Dr Iannis walked to the church in the transparent light of the afternoon. On weekdays he wore the kind of clothes that peasants wore on holidays and church days; a bedraggled black suit with shiny patches, and a collarless shirt, black shoes embellished with dust and scuffs, and a wide-brimmed hat. He was twirling his moustache, sucking pensively upon his pipe, and had divided his attention in two so that he was thinking simultaneously about the sacking of the island by crusaders and of what he was going to say to the priest. He envisaged the following scene:

He would say, 'Patir, I regret deeply the indignity inflicted upon you this morning,' and the priest would say, 'I find this surprising in an irreligious man,' and he would reply, 'But I do believe that a priest should be treated with respect. A village needs a priest as an island needs the sea. Please come and eat with us tomorrow. Pelagia is going to do lamb with potatoes in the fourno. I will also invite the teacher. I am sorry to hear, by the way, that you are unwell. Is there anything I can do?'

But when he entered the church he was immediately apprised of the probability that this conversation was unlikely to occur. He heard groaning and retching from behind the screen. 'Patir,' he called, 'are you all right? Patir?'

There was another pitiful and wracking groan, and the doglike noise of painful vomiting. From his experience of the vomit of innumerable patients, he visualised that this would be of a predominantly yellow colour. He knocked a knuckle on the screen and called, 'Patir, are you in there?'

'O God, O God,' moaned the priest.

The doctor was presented with an intractable problem. The fact was that only the ordained might pass behind the screen. He had long ago abandoned his religion in favour of a Machian variety of materialism, but he felt nonetheless that he could not break the prohibition. Such a taboo cannot be lightly cast aside even by one who places no credence in its premise. He could not enter there any more than he could have made sexual overtures to a nun. He knocked more urgently, 'Patir, it's me, Doctor Iannis.'

'Iatre,' wailed the priest, 'I am grievously stricken. O God, wherefore hast thou made all men in vain? Help me for the love of God.'

The doctor sent a prayer of penitence up to the God in whom he did not believe, and stepped behind the screen. He beheld the supine priest, helplessly recumbent in a pool of urine and vomit. One of the man's eyes was closed and the other was streaming with tears. The doctor noted with dispassionate surprise that the vomit was more white than yellow, and that it contrasted brightly with the dull blackness of the robes. 'You've got to stand up,' he said. 'You can lean on my shoulder, but I am afraid that I cannot carry you.'

There ensued an unequal and impossible struggle in which the slight doctor contrived to raise the rotund cleric. He very quickly realised the futility of the effort, and stood upright. He noted the presence of three bottles of urine in that holy place. Out of professional curiosity he held one of the bottles up to the light and inspected it for the tell-tale mucal streaks that indicate urethral infections. It was clear. He realised that he had some vomit on his hands. He looked at them for a moment; he was damned if he was going to wipe them on his trousers, and even more damned if he was going to do so on the back of the screen. He stooped down and cleaned them on the priest's robe. He went to fetch Velisarios.

So it was that Velisarios' penance for submitting the priest to the indignity of the morning was that he should be obliged to carry the colossal weight of him to the doctor's house. It was possibly the most titanic feat of strength and determination that he had ever had to perform. He staggered twice and nearly fell once. Afterwards his arms and his back felt as though he had borne up the entire universe, and he understood how St Christopher must have felt after carrying Our Lord across the river. He sat sweating in the shade, panting, and experiencing a most alarming galloping of the heart whilst Pelagia plied him with lemon juice sweetened with honey, and she in turn was plied with smiles by Mandras, who had turned on his side in order to watch her. Pelagia felt his gaze as though it were a hot caress, finding that it had the disconcerting effect of making her trip over her own feet, and that it seemed to cause her hips to sway more than usual. In truth it was the attempt to control her hips that had caused the difficulty with her feet.

Inside the house the doctor forced the priest to drink jar upon jar of water, this being the only sensible cure for alcoholic poisoning of which he was aware. He found himself waxing unbecomingly censorial with respect to his patient, for he was unravelling in his mind an internal monologue along the lines of: 'Surely a priest should set a better example than this? Surely it is shameful to become inebriated so long before evening? How can this man hope to retain any stature in these parts when he is greedy and drunken? I do not remember any priest as bad as this, and we've had some bad ones, God knows . . .' He frowned and tutted as he swabbed the vomit from the man's robes, and transferred his irritation to Pelagia's goat, which had entered the room and leapt up onto the table. 'Stupid brute,' he shouted at it, and it looked at him impudently with its slotted eyes, as if to say, 'I, at least, am not drunk. I am merely mischievous.'

The doctor left the patient to his stupor and sat at his desk. He tapped his pen on the table and wrote, 'In 1082 an infamous Norman baron named Robert Guiscard attempted to conquer the island and was resisted with extreme determination by bands of guerrillas. The world was relieved of his obnoxious presence by a fever that killed him in 1085, and the sole trace of him on earth is the fact that Fiskardo is named after him, although history does not relate how the G transformed itself into an F. Another Norman, Bohemund, whilst flaunting the piety freshly culled from a recent crusade, sacked the island with the most extreme and inexcusable cruelty. The reader should be reminded that it was crusaders and not the Muslims who originally sacked Constantinople, which should have caused perpetual scepticism about the value of noble causes. Apparently it has not, as the human race is incapable of learning anything from history.'

He leaned back in his chair and twirled his moustache, and then he lit his pipe. He saw Lemoni pass the window and called her in. The tiny girl listened with wide-eyed seriousness as the doctor asked her to go and fetch the priest's wife. He patted her on the head, called her his 'little koritsimou' and smiled as he watched her skipping erratically away along the street. Pelagia had been just as sweet when she was small, and it made him feel nostalgic. He felt a tear rise to his eye, and he banished it forthwith by writing another sentence excoriating the Normans. He leaned back again and was interrupted by the entrance of Stamatis, who was holding his hat in his hands and kneading the brim. 'Kalispera, Kyrie Stamatis,' he said, 'what can I do for you?'

Stamatis shuffled his feet, looked with concern at the round mound of priest upon the floor, and said, 'You know that . . . that thing in my ear?'

'The papilionaceous and exorbitant auditory impediment?'

'That's the one, Iatre. Well, what I want to know, is . . . I mean, can you put it back?'

'Put it back, Kyrie Stamatis?'

'It's my wife, you see.'

'I see,' said the doctor, releasing a rank cloud from his pipe. 'Actually I don't see. Perhaps you would explain.'

'Well, when I was deaf in that ear I couldn't hear her. Where I sit, you see, I had my good ear on the other side, and I could sort of take it.'

'Take it?'

'The nagging. I mean before it was sort of like the murmuring of the sea. I liked it. It helped me to doze off. But now it's so loud, and it won't stop. It just goes on and on.' The man waggled his shoulders in imitation of an irritated woman, and mimicked his wife: 'You're no good for anything, why don't you bring in the wood, why haven't we ever got any money, why do I have to do everything round here, why didn't I marry a man, how come you only ever gave me daughters, what happened to the man I married? All that stuff, it's driving me crazy.'

'Have you tried beating her?'

'No, Iatre. Last time I struck her she broke a plate across my head. I still have the scar. Look.' The old man leaned forward and indicated something invisible upon his forehead.

'Well, you shouldn't beat her anyway,' said the doctor. 'They just find more subversive ways of getting at you. Like oversalting the food. My advice is to be nice to her.'

Stamatis was shocked. It was a course of action so inconceivable that he had never even conceived of conceiving it. 'Iatre . . .' he protested, but could find no other words.

'Just bring in the wood before she asks for it, and bring her a flower every time you come back from the field. If it's cold put a shawl around her shoulders, and if it's hot, bring her a glass of water. It's simple. Women only nag when they feel unappreciated. Think of her as your mother who has fallen ill, and treat her accordingly.'

'Then you won't put back the . . . the, er . . . disputatious and pugnacious extraordinary embodiment?'

'Certainly not. It would be against the Hippocratic oath. I can't allow that. It was Hippocrates, incidentally, who said that "extreme remedies are most appropriate for extreme diseases."'

Stamatis appeared downcast: 'Hippocrates says so? So I've got to be nice to her?'

The doctor nodded paternally, and Stamatis replaced his hat. 'O God,' he said.

The doctor watched the old man from his window. Stamatis went out into the road and began to walk away. He paused and looked down at a small purple flower in the embankment. He leaned down to pick it, but immediately straightened up. He peered about himself to ensure that no one was watching. He pulled at his belt in the manner of girding up his loins, glared at the flower, and turned on his heel. He began to stroll away, but then stopped. Like a little boy involved in a petty theft he darted back, snapped the stem of the flower, concealed it within his coat, and sauntered away with an exaggeratedly insouciant and casual air. The doctor leaned out of the window and called after him, 'Bravo Stamatis,' just for the simple but malicious pleasure of witnessing his embarrassment and shame.

8

A FUNNY KIND OF CAT

LEMONI RAN INTO the courtyard of Dr Iannis' house just
as he was departing for the kapheneion for breakfast; he
had been planning to meet all the mangas there and argue
about the problems of the world. Yesterday he had been
disputing vehemently with Kokolios about Communism,
and during the night he had come up with a splendid argument which he had been rehearsing in his head so much that
it had prevented sleep, obliging him to get up and write a
little more of his history, a little diatribe about the Orsini
family. This was his speech to Kokolios:

'Listen, if everybody is employed by the state, it's obvious
that everyone gets paid by the state, yes? So all the tax that
comes back to the state is money that came from the state
in the first place, yes? So the state only ever gets back maybe
one third of what it paid out last week. So this week the
only way to pay everyone is to print more money, no? So it
follows that in a Communist state the money very soon
becomes imaginary, because the state has nothing for that
money to represent.'

He envisaged Kokolios riposting thus: 'Ah, Iatre, the
missing money comes from profits,' and then, quick as a
flash, he would come back with, 'But look, Kokolio', the
only way the state can get a profit is by selling the goods
abroad, and the only way that this can happen is if the
foreign states are capitalist and have a surplus from their
taxes to buy things with. Or else you've got to sell to capitalist companies. So it's obvious that Communism cannot

survive without capitalism, and this makes it self-contradictory, because Communism is supposed to be the end of capitalism, and moreover it is supposed to be internationalist. It follows from my argument that if the whole world went Communist, the entire economy of the globe would grind to a halt within the space of a week. What do you say to that?' The doctor was practising the dramatic gesture with which he would conclude this peroration (the return of his pipe to the clenched position between the teeth) when Lemoni caught at his sleeve and said, 'Please, Iatre, I've found a funny kind of cat.'

He looked down at the diminutive girl, caught her earnest expression, and said, 'Oh, hello, koritsimou. What was that you said?'

'A funny kind of cat.'

'Hmm, yes, what about a funny kind of cat?'

The little girl rolled her eyes in exasperation and wiped a filthy hand across her forehead, leaving a grimy streak. 'I've found a funny kind of cat.'

'How clever of you. Why don't you go and tell your Papa?'

'It's ill.'

'What kind of ill?'

'It's tired. It might have a headache.'

The doctor hesitated. A cup of coffee was calling him, and he had a conclusive refutation of Communism to deliver to the assembly. He felt a twinge of childish disappointment at the thought of having to forgo their admiration and applause. He looked down at the consternation on the face of the little girl, smiled with noble resignation, and took her hand. 'Show it to me,' he said, 'and bear in mind that I don't like cats. Also I don't know anything about curing headaches in cats. Especially funny ones.'

Lemoni led him impatiently down the road, urging him to make haste at every step. She obliged him to climb over a low wall and duck beneath the branches of the olives. 'Can't we go round the trees?' he demanded. 'Remember I'm taller than you.'

'Straight is quicker.' She took him to a patch of briar and

scrub, fell to her knees, and began to crawl on all fours through a tunnel that had been forged by some wild animal for its own use. 'I can't go through there,' protested the doctor, 'I'm much too big.' He beat his way through with his cane, following the retreating backside as best he could. Painfully he imagined Pelagia's displeasure at being asked to repair the rents in his trousers and do something about the tangled loops of thread. He felt his scratches beginning to itch already. 'What on earth were you doing in here?' he asked.

'Looking for snails.'

'Did you know that childhood is the only time in our lives when insanity is not only permitted to us, but expected?' asked the doctor rhetorically. 'If I went crawling around for snails I would be taken to Piraeus and locked up.'

'Lots of big snails,' observed Lemoni.

Just when the doctor was feeling exasperation and heat overcome him, they came into a small clearing that had been divided at some distant time into two by a sorry and sagging barbed-wire fence. Lemoni jumped to her feet and ran to the wire, pointing. It took some moments for the doctor to realise that he was supposed to follow, not the line of the mucky finger (which was directed obtusely towards the sky) but the general line of her arm. 'There it is,' she proclaimed, 'it's the funny cat, and it's still tired.'

'It's not tired, koritsimou, it's got caught on the wire. God knows how long it's been hanging there.' He went down on his knees and peered at the animal. A small pair of very bright black eyes blinked back at him with an expression that bespoke an infinity of despair and exhaustion. He felt moved in a manner that struck him as quite strange and illogical.

It had a flat, triangular head, a sharp snout, a bushy tail. It was a deep chestnut colour, except for the throat and breast, which was of a shade that had settled at some indefinable point between yellow and creamy white. The ears were rounded and broad. The doctor peered into the eyes; the suspended creature was quite obviously near to death. 'It's not a cat,' he said to Lemoni, 'it's a pine marten. It could have been hanging here for ages. I think it would be best to kill it, because it's going to die anyway.'

Lemoni was overcome with indignation. Tears rose to her eyes, she stamped, she jumped up and down, and, in short, forbade the doctor to kill it. She stroked the head of the animal and stood between it and the man to whom she had entrusted its salvation. 'Don't touch it, Lemoni. Remember that King Alexander died of a monkey bite.'

'It's not a monkey.'

'It might have rabies. It might give you tetanus. Just don't touch it.'

'I stroked it before and it didn't bite. It's tired.'

'Lemoni, it's got a barb through the skin of its stomach, and it could have been there for hours. Days. It's not tired, it's dying.'

'It was tightrope walking,' she said. 'I've seen them. They walk along the wire and they go up that tree, and they eat the eggs in the nests. I've seen them.'

'I didn't know we had any down here at all. I thought they stayed in the trees on the mountains. It just goes to show.'

'Show what?'

'Children see more than we do.' The doctor knelt down again and examined the marten. It was very young, and he imagined that it had only opened its eyes a few days before. It was exceedingly pretty. He decided, for Lemoni's sake, to rescue it and then kill it when he got home. No one would thank him for saving an animal that killed chickens and geese, stole eggs, ate garden berries, and even rifled bee-hives; he could tell the little girl that it had died on its own, and perhaps he could give it to her to bury. He peered round and saw that it had not only impaled itself on a barb, but that it had actually managed to wind itself around the wire twice. It must have struggled relentlessly, and it must have endured an excruciating torment.

Very carefully he grasped it behind its neck and rotated the body. Hand over hand he unwound it from the wire, conscious of Lemoni's head right next to his own as intently she watched him. 'Careful,' she advised.

56

The doctor winced at the thought of the lethal bite that might leave him foaming at the mouth or lying in bed with his jaw locked. Imagine it, risking one's own life for the sake of vermin. The things that a child could make one do. He must be mad or stupid or both.

He held the animal belly upwards and inspected the wound. It was solely in the loose skin of the groin and would have done no muscular damage. It was probably merely a question of acute dehydration. He noted that it was a female and that its smell was sweet and musky. It reminded him of a woman sometime during his maritime days, a smell to which he could not fit a face. He showed it to Lemoni and said, 'It's a girl,' to which she replied, inevitably, 'Why?'

The doctor put the kitten in the pocket of his coat and took Lemoni home, promising to do his best. He then proceeded to his own house, only to find that Mandras was in the yard, engaging Pelagia in animated conversation as she attempted to sweep it. The fisherman looked up shame-facedly and said, 'O, kalimera, Iatre. I was just coming to see you, and as you weren't here, I have been talking to Pelagia, as you see. I have been having some trouble with the wound.'

Dr Iannis eyed him sceptically and experienced a surge of annoyance; no doubt the suffering of the little animal had upset him. 'There's nothing wrong with your wound. I suppose you are going to tell me that it has been itching.'

Mandras smiled ingratiatingly and said, 'That's exactly it, Iatre. You must be a magician. How did you know?'

The doctor twisted his mouth laconically and heaved a mock sigh. 'Mandras, you know perfectly well that wounds always itch when they are in the process of healing. You also know perfectly well that I know perfectly well that you have only come here to flirt with Pelagia.'

'Flirt?' repeated the young man, affecting both innocence and horror.

'Yes. Flirt. There's no other word for it. Yesterday you brought us another fish and then flirted with Pelagia for one hour and ten minutes. Well, you'd better get on with it, because I'm not wasting time on a perfectly healthy wound,

I haven't had breakfast, and I've got a funny kind of cat in my pocket that I have to look at indoors.'

Mandras attempted not to appear bemused, and was inspired by unwonted boldness: 'Then I have your permission to talk to your daughter?'

'Talk, talk, talk,' said Dr Iannis, waving his hands with irritation. He turned on his heel and went inside the house. Mandras looked at Pelagia and remarked, 'Your dad's a funny fellow.'

'There's nothing wrong with my father,' she exclaimed, 'and anyone who says otherwise gets a broom in the face.' She prodded at him playfully with the implement and he caught it and twisted it out of her grasp. 'Give it back,' she said, laughing.

'I'll give it back . . . in return for a kiss.'

Dr Iannis placed the expiring animal carefully on the kitchen table and contemplated it. He took off one of his boots, grasped it by the toe, and raised it above his head. Such a small and fragile skull would be very easy to crush. There would be no suffering involved. It would be the best thing to do.

He hesitated. He couldn't give it back to Lemoni for burial with a smashed skull. Perhaps he should break the neck. He picked it up with his right hand, placing the fingers behind the neck and the thumb under the chin. It was simply a question of pressing back with the thumb.

He contemplated the deed for a few moments, exhorted himself to the act, and felt his thumb begin to move. The marten was not only very pretty, but also charming and inconceivably pathetic. It had barely lived as yet. He put it down on the table and went to fetch a bottle of alcohol. He bathed the wound carefully and put a single stitch in it. He called Pelagia.

She entered, convinced that her father had seen her kissing Mandras. She was preparing an obdurate defence, her face was flushed, and she fully expected an explosion. She was entirely amazed when her father did not even look up. He demanded, 'Did we get any mice in the traps today?'

'We got two, Papakis.'

'Well, go and dig them out of wherever you threw them, and grind them up.'

'Grind them up?'

'Yes. Mince them. And bring me some straw.'

Pelagia hurried out, both perplexed and relieved. She said to Mandras, who had been nervously kicking stones round the olive tree, 'It's all right, he only wants me to mince some mice and find him some straw.'

'Jesus, I said he was a funny fellow.'

She laughed: 'It only means he's got some new project. He's not really a madman. You can go and find the straw if you like.'

'Thanks,' he said, 'I just love looking for straw.'

She smiled archly, 'There might be recompense.'

'For a kiss,' he said, 'I would lick a pigsty clean.'

'You don't honestly think I'd kiss you after you'd licked a pigsty?'

'I'd kiss you even if you'd licked the slime from the bottom of my boat.'

'I believe you. You're a lot madder than my father.'

Inside, the doctor filled an eyedropper with goat milk and began to drip it into the back of the marten's throat. It filled him with immense medical satisfaction when eventually it urinated on the knee of his trousers. This indicated healthy renal functioning. 'I'll kill it when I come back from the kapheneion,' he decided, stroking the rich brown fur of its forehead with one finger.

Half an hour later his patient was fast asleep on a bed of straw and Pelagia was in the yard chopping the mice with an hachoir. Inexplicably, Mandras was perched on a branch of the olive tree. Dr Iannis swept past them on his way to the kapheneion, once more rehearsing his devastating critique of Communist economics and imagining the confounded expression that was shortly to appear on the face of Kokolios. Pelagia ran to catch her father up and tugged at his sleeve just as Lemoni had done. 'Papakis,' she said, 'don't you know you're going out with only one boot on?'

9

AUGUST 15TH, 1940

ON HIS WAY to the kapheneion Dr Iannis encountered Lemoni, who was engaged in prodding the nose of a rangy brindled dog with a stick. The animal was leaping about in a frenzy of barking, and was attempting to snap at the piece of wood, its cloudy intellect darkened further by a question whose solution seemed to lie in a decision to bark ever more wildly; was this a game or a genuine provocation? He sat back on his haunches, threw back his head, and howled like a wolf.

'He's singing, he's singing,' cried Lemoni gleefully, and joined in; 'A-ee-ra, a-ee-ra, a-ee-ra.'

The doctor put his fingers into his ears and protested, 'Koritsimou, stop, stop at once, the day is already too hot, and this noise is making me sweat. And don't do that to the dog, or it will bite you.'

'No, it won't, it only bites sticks.'

The doctor reached out to pat the animal on the head, and remembered that he had once sewn up a gash in one of its pads. He winced as he recalled extracting some pieces of broken glass. He knew that everyone thought that he was odd on account of his compulsion to heal, and indeed he himself also believed it peculiar, but he also knew that every man needs an obsession in order to enjoy life, and it was so much the better if that obsession was constructive. Look at Hitler and Metaxas and Mussolini, those megalomaniacs. Look at Kokolios, preoccupied with the redistribution of other people's wealth, or Father Arsenios, a slave to appetite, or Mandras, so much in love with his daughter that he even swung about in the olive tree, imitating an ape for Pelagia's pleasure. He shuddered as he remembered a chained monkey he had seen in a tree in Spain; it had been masturbating and eating the results. O God, just imagine Mandras doing that.

'You shouldn't pat it,' said Lemoni, glad of an opportunity to break his reverie and show off her wisdom to an adult, 'it's got fleas.'

He removed his hand quickly and the dog placed itself behind him in order to avoid the little girl with the stick. 'Have you decided on a name for the pine marten?' he asked.

'Psipsina,' she announced. 'It's called Psipsina.'

'You can't call it that, it isn't a cat.'

'Well, I'm not a lemon, and I'm called Lemoni.'

'I was there when you were born,' the doctor told her, 'and we didn't know whether you were a baby or a lemon, and I nearly took you into the kitchen and squeezed all the juice out.' Lemoni's face contorted sceptically and the dog quite suddenly shot between the doctor's legs, took the stick from her hand, and ran off with it to a heap of rubble where he proceeded to tear it to slivers. 'Clever dog,' commented the doctor, and left the little girl staring with astonishment at her empty hands.

When he entered the kapheneion he saw that it was full of the usual mangas: Kokolios with his splendidly exuberant and masculine moustache; Stamatis, evading the reproachful glares and the nagging tongue of his wife; Father Arsenios, spherical and perspiring. The doctor collected his tiny cup of grainy coffee and his tumbler of water, and sat next to Kokolios as he always did. He took a deep draught of the water, and quoted Pindar, also at he always did: 'Water is best.'

Kokolios took a deep suck on the nargiles, blew out a cloud of blue smoke, and asked, 'You've been a sailor, Iatre, have you not? Is it true that Greek water tastes more like water than that of any other country?'

'Undoubtedly. And Cephallonian water tastes even more like water than any other in Greece. We also have the best wine and the best light and the best sailors.'

'When the revolution comes we'll have the best life as well,' announced Kokolios with the intention of provoking the assembly. He pointed to the portrait of King George on the wall, adding 'And that fool's mugshot will be replaced by that of Lenin.'

'Scoundrel,' said Stamatis, under his breath. The deposal of the pea from his ear had exposed him not only to the irritations of marriage, but to Kokolios' shockingly unpatriotic anti-monarchism. Stamatis slapped his palm with the back of his hand to indicate the degree of Kokolios' stupidity, and added, 'Putanas yie.'

Kokolios smiled dangerously and said, 'Son of a whore, am I? Well, you can just drink my fart.'

'Ai gamisou. Theh gamiesei.'

The doctor bridled at these insults and these invitations to fuck off, and he slapped his glass down on the table. 'Paidia, paidia, this is enough. We have this unpleasantness every morning. I have always been a Venizelist; I am not a monarchist, and I am not a Communist. I disagree with both of you, but I cure Stamatis' deafness and I burn out Kokolios' warts. This is how we should be. We should care for each other more than we care for ideas, or else we will end up killing each other. Am I not right?'

'You can't make an omelette without breaking eggs,' quoted Kokolios, looking at Stamatis significantly.

'I don't like your omelette,' said Stamatis. 'It's made with bad eggs, it tastes foul, and it makes me shit.'

'The revolution will plug your backside,' said Kokolios, adding, 'a fair share of what little we have, the means of production in the hands of the producers, the equal obligation of all to work.'

'You don't work any more than you have to,' commented Father Arsenios in his slow bass voice.

'You don't work at all, Patir. You grow fatter every day. Everything is given to you for nothing. You are a parasite.'

Arsenios wiped his plump hands on his black robes, and the doctor said, 'There is such a thing as an indispensable parasite. There are parasitic bacteria in the gut that aid digestion. I am not a religious man, I am a materialist, but even I can see that priests are a kind of bacteria that enable people to find life digestible. Father Arsenios has done many useful things for those who seek consolation; he is a member of every family, and he is the family for those who don't have one.'

'Thank you, Iatre,' said the priest. 'I never thought I would hear such praise from such a notoriously godless man. I have never seen you in church.'

'Empedocles said that God is a circle whose centre is everywhere and whose circumference is nowhere. If that is true, then I don't need to go to church. And I don't need to believe the same things as you to see that you have a purpose. Now let's smoke and drink our coffee in peace. If we can't stop arguing in here, then I am going to start having breakfast at home.'

'The doctor is thinking of becoming a heretic indeed, though I agree with him that our priest is a great comforter of widows,' said Kokolios, grinning. 'I couldn't have some of your tobacco, could I? I am running out.'

'Kokolio', since you maintain that all property is theft, it follows that you should give us all a fair share of what little you have. Pass over your tin and I shall finish it for you. Fair's fair. Be a good Communist. Or is it only other people who have to share their property in utopia?'

'When the revolution comes, Iatre, there will be a sufficiency for everyone. In the meantime, pass me your pouch, and I shall return the favour another time.'

The doctor passed over his tobacco and Kokolios stuffed his nargiles contentedly. 'What's the news of the war?'

The doctor twisted the ends of his moustache and said, 'Germany is taking everything, the Italians are playing the fool, the French have run away, the Belgians have been overrun whilst they were looking the other way, the Poles have been charging tanks with cavalry, the Americans have been playing baseball, the British have been drinking tea and adjusting their monocles, the Russians have been sitting on their hands except when voting unanimously to do whatever they are told. Thank God we are out of it. Why don't we turn on the radio?'

The large British radio in the corner of the kapheneion was switched on, its valves began to glow through the brass mesh, its whistles, crackles and hisses were reduced to a minimum by the judicious twiddling of knobs and the careful turning back and forth of the set, and the company settled down to listen to the broadcast from Athens. They were fully expecting to hear about the latest parade of the National Youth Organisation before Prime Minister Metaxas; there might be something about the King, and perhaps something about the most recent Nazi conquest.

There was an item about Churchill's new alliance with the Free French, another about a revolt in Albania against Italian occupation, another about the annexation of Luxemburg and Alsace-Lorraine, and at that point Pelagia appeared at the door of the kapheneion, beckoning urgently to her father, and embarrassed by the knowledge that the presence of a female anywhere near to such a place was a worse sacrilege than spitting on the tomb of a saint.

Dr Iannis stuffed his pipe into his pocket, sighed, and went reluctantly to the door. 'What is it, kori, what is it?'

'It's Mandras, Papakis. He's fallen out of the olive tree and he fell on a pot, and he's got some shards of it . . . you know . . . in his seat.'

'In his backside? What was he doing up the tree? Showing off again? Monkey impressions? The boy's a lunatic.'

Pelagia was both disappointed and strangely relieved when her father forbade her to enter the kitchen whilst he extracted crumbs and morsels of terracotta from the smooth and muscular backside of her suitor. She stood outside, her back to the door, and shuddered in sympathy every time that Mandras yelled. Inside, the doctor had the fisherman lying face down on the table with his trousers about his knees, and was reflecting on the general idiocy of love. How could Pelagia fall for a whippersnapper as accident-prone, charming, and unformed as this? He remembered the things he had done to show off to his own wife before they were affianced: he had climbed onto her roof, lifted a tile, and told her every Turkish joke he knew; he had pinned 'anonymous' verses to the jamb of her door at night, detailing her

64

loveliness; just like Mandras, he had made exceptional efforts to court her father. 'You're an idiot,' he told the patient.

'I know,' said Mandras, wincing as another shard came out.

'First of all you get shot accidentally, and now you fall out of a tree.'

'I saw a Tarzan film when I was in Athens,' explained Mandras, 'and I was just giving Pelagia an idea of what it was about. Ow. With respect, Iatre, be careful.'

'Wounded in the cause of culture, eh? Young fool.'

'Yes, Iatre.'

'Stop being so polite. I know what you're up to. Are you going to ask her to marry you, or not? I warn you, I'm not giving away a dowry.'

'No dowry?'

'Does that put you off? Would that be too novel for your family? No one is going to marry my daughter just for the expectation of wealth. Pelagia deserves better than that.'

'No, Iatre, it's not a question of wealth.'

'Well, that's good. Are you going to ask my permission?'

'Not yet, Iatre.'

The doctor adjusted his spectacles: 'Best to be cautious. You have too many high spirits, altogether too much kefi, to be a good husband.'

'Yes, Iatre. Everyone says there's going to be a war, and I don't want to leave a widow, that's all. You know how everyone treats a widow.'

'They end up as whores,' said the doctor.

Mandras was shocked: 'Pelagia would never come to that, I trust to God.'

The doctor swabbed away a trickle of blood, and wondered whether his own buttocks had ever been that beautiful. 'You shouldn't trust to God for anything. These things are ours to ensure.'

'Yes, Iatre.'

'Stop being so polite. I take it that you will be replacing the pot that you have so liberally redistributed about your own flesh?'

'Would a fish be acceptable, Iatre? I could bring you a bucket of whitebait.'

It was six hours before the doctor returned to the kapheneion, because, quite apart from the performance of surgery, he had had to reassure his daughter that Mandras would be all right apart from some bruising and some permanent terracotta spots in his backside, he had had to help her catch her goat, which had somehow found its way onto the roof of a neighbour's shed, he had had to feed minced mice to Psipsina, and, above all, he had had to take refuge from the insufferable heat of August. He had taken a siesta, and had been awakened by the evening concert of the crickets and sparrows, and by the gathering of the villagers for the celebration of the Feast of the Dormition of the Virgin Mary. He set out on his peripato, the evening walk that was broken inevitably by a stop in the kapheneion and then was resumed in the expectation that Pelagia would have cooked something by the time that he returned. He was hoping that she would have prepared an unseasonable kokoretsi, as he had noted the presence of liver and intestines on the table where previously he had been performing his surgery. It had occurred to him that some spots of Mandras' blood might end up in the meal, and he wondered idly if that might amount to cannibalism. This had prompted the further speculation as to whether or not a Muslim might consider the taking of Holy Communion to be anthropophagous.

As soon as he entered the kapheneion he knew that something was amiss. Solemn martial music was emanating from the radio, and the boys were sitting in a grim and ominous silence, clutching their tumblers, their brows furrowed. Dr Iannis noted with astonishment that both Stamatis and Kokolios had the glistening tracks of tears down their cheeks. To his astonishment, he saw Father Arsenios stride by outside, his arms raised prophetically, his patriarchal beard thrust forward, crying, 'Sacrilege, sacrilege, howl ye ships of Tarshish, behold, I will raise up against Babylon, and against them that dwell in the midst of them that rise up against me, a destroying wind. Cry ye daughters of Rabbah, clothe ye with sackcloth, woe, woe, woe . . .'

'What's going on?' he asked.

'The bastards have sunk the *Elli*,' said Kokolios, 'and they've torpedoed the wharf at Tinos.'

'What? What?'

'The *Elli*. The battleship. The Italians sank it at Tinos, just when all the pilgrims were setting off to the church to see the miracles.'

'The icon wasn't on board was it? What's going on? I mean why? Is the icon all right?'

'We don't know, we don't know,' said Stamatis. 'I wish I was still deaf so that I could not have heard it. Nobody knows how many were killed, I don't know if the icon's all right. The Italians attacked us, that's all, I don't know why. On the Feast of the Dormition, it's an unholy thing.'

'It's an outrage, all those sick pilgrims. What is Metaxas going to do?'

Kokolios shrugged; 'The Italians say it wasn't them, but they've already found bits of Italian torpedo. Do they think that we have no balls? The bastards say it was the British, and no one saw the submarine. No one knows what will happen.'

The doctor put his hands to his face and felt his own tears fighting to appear. He was possessed by all the furious and impotent rage of the little man who has been bound and gagged, and forced to watch whilst his own wife is raped and mutilated. He did not stop to try to understand why he and Kokolios should both be sick with horror over the violation of an icon and a holy day, when one was a Communist and the other a secularist. He did not stop to question whether or not war was inevitable. These were not things that needed to be examined. Kokolios and Stamatis stood up and came out together when he said, 'Come on boys, we're all going to the church. It's a question of solidarity.'

IO

L'OMOSESSUALE (3)

A GUILTY MAN wishes only to be understood, because to be understood is to appear to be forgiven. Perhaps in his own eyes he is guiltless, but it is enough for him to know that others consider him culpable and he feels the need to be explained. In my case, however, no one knows that I am guilty, and nonetheless I wish to be understood.

I was picked for the mission because I am a big man, because I had acquired a reputation for endurance, because I am reasonably intelligent (Francesco used to say that in the Army 'intelligent' means 'doesn't usually fuck anything up'), and because I was 'soldierly', which means that I kept my men in order, polished my boots when they were not too wet, and knew the meaning of most of the acronyms that customarily reduce our military documents to impenetrable code.

I received an order by motorcycle messenger asking me to report to Colonel Rivolta, bringing with me one other reliable man. Naturally I chose Francesco; I think I have already explained that it was my intention to use my vice as a means to becoming a good soldier. With him at my side I felt that I was capable of anything. As we were not at war it did not occur to me that I would be leading him into danger by taking him with me, and little was I to know that very soon I was to have the opportunity to demonstrate to him the quality of my heroism.

To receive an order is one thing and to obey it is another. At that time we had only about twenty-four lorries per ten thousand troops. Colonel Rivolta was fifteen miles away. To reach him we had to run five miles, ride a pair of mules for another five, and finally hitch a lift on the back of a tank that was going for repair with only the reverse gear operating. We went by going backwards, a veritable motto for the whole of the impending campaign.

Rivolta was an exorbitantly portly man who had clearly risen in the ranks by knowing the right people. He was a prodigal mine of fashionable slogans like 'A book in one hand and a gun in the other', and he displayed the consummate heroism of one who sites his HQ fifteen miles away from his troops in an abandoned villa so that he can use the lawns for receptions. We in the Alpini are notorious for having fisticuffs with the Blackshirts, and this may have been a reason why I was picked for the mission; it would not have mattered very much if I was killed, since I was not automatically in line for preferral. Those who wonder why our soldiers have been ineffective compared to their fathers in the 1914 war should bear in mind that this time around it was impossible to become a senior officer by merit alone; it was done by browning the tongue.

Rivolta was short, fat, bored, and the owner of several medals from the Abyssinian campaign even though everybody knew that he and his men had stayed in one place and done nothing at all; this had not prevented him from sending home lurid reports of successful operations. They were fabulous and highly imaginative works of fiction and it was commonly said by the soldiers that his medals were for literary prowess. Also, his tongue was busy and almost perfectly brown.

When we marched into that noble, high-ceilinged room and saluted, Rivolta responded with the Roman salute. It occurred to both of us that perhaps he was mimicking the Duce, and Francesco giggled. Rivolta glared at him and probably made a mental note to have him transferred to latrine duty.

'Gentlemen,' said Rivolta dramatically, 'I trust that your courage can be relied upon and that your discretion is complete.'

Francesco raised an eyebrow and glanced at me sideways. I said, 'Yes, sir. Absolutely, sir,' and Francesco made an unmistakable gesture with his tongue that fortunately was not observed.

Rivolta beckoned us over to a map that was spread upon a large and exquisitely polished antique table, and leaned over it. He pointed with a fat finger to a spot that was in the valley next to the one where we were bivouacked, and said, 'At 0200 hours tomorrow night you two will go under cover of darkness to this point here and . . .'

'Excuse me, sir,' interrupted Francesco, 'but that is in Greek territory.'

'I know, I know. I am not stupid. That is beside the point. There are no Greeks there and so they will not know.'

Francesco raised his eyebrows again and the colonel said, sarcastically, 'I presume you have heard of such a thing as operational necessity?'

'Are we at war, then?' asked Francesco, and the colonel probably made a mental note to double the length of the latrine duty. The mouse Mario took the opportunity at that point to emerge from Francesco's breast pocket, and had to be pushed back down before Rivolta noticed. This added to the irreverence of my friend's mood, and he smiled idiotically whilst the colonel continued:

'There is a watchtower there, a wooden one, and it has been taken over by a band of local brigands who have killed the guards and adopted their uniforms. They look like our soldiers but are not.' He paused to let this information sink in, and continued, 'It will be your task to take this tower. You will be armed and equipped by our quartermaster here, who has special supplies for you. Any questions?'

'We have two companies of Bersaglieri in that valley, sir,' I said. 'Why can't they do it?'

Francesco chipped in with, 'If they are merely brigands then this is a matter for the carabinieri, is it not?'

The colonel puffed himself up with indignation, demanded, 'Are you questioning my orders?' and, quick as a flash, Francesco came back with, 'You did ask for questions, sir.'

'Operational questions, not questions of policy. I have

had quite enough of your impertinent attitude, and I must warn you to give respect where it is due.'

'Where it is due,' repeated Francesco, nodding his head vigorously, and thereby courting further reproof. The colonel said, 'Good luck lads, and I wish I was coming with you.' Sotto voce, but clearly audible to me, Francesco muttered, 'I bet you do, shithead.'

Rivolta sent us packing with the promise of medals in the event of success and a thick packet of orders that also contained maps, a precise horary, and a photograph of Mussolini taken from low profile in order to emphasise the jut of his chin. I think that this was intended to fire us up and lend rigidity to our moral backbone.

Outside the villa we sat on a wall and went through the papers. 'This is fishy business,' said Francesco. 'What do you think it's really about?'

I looked into his beautiful dark eyes and said, 'I don't care what it is. It's just orders, and we have to assume that someone knows what it's all about, don't we?'

'You assume too much,' he said. 'I think it's not only fishy, but dirty.' He took his pet from his pocket and said to it, 'Mario, this is not a good thing for you to be involved in.'

We could hardly believe it when the stores that we drew from the quartermaster turned out to consist of British military uniforms and Greek weapons. It seemed to make no sense at all, and there were no instructions for using the Hotchkiss light machine-gun. We worked it out for ourselves, but later on we concluded that perhaps we were not intended to have done so.

Francesco and I were saved by the weather in a most curious fashion. We were well prepared in advance, and crept out of our own lines at ten o'clock in the evening. Across the border we changed into our British uniforms as instructed, and then found our way over the escarpment into the next valley. At this point Francesco and I were caught up in a turmoil of conflicting moods.

I do not think that a person who has never seen action can truly understand what whirlwinds revolve inside the head of a soldier in the hours of combat, but I shall try to explain. In this case we were both proud to have been chosen for a serious military mission. It made us feel very special and important. But neither of us had ever done anything like this before, and so we were deeply afraid, not only of the physical danger but of the heavy responsibility and the possibility that we would make a mess of it. We kept making foolish jokes to conceal this fear. The soldier also always has the fear that the authorities know more than he does and that he does not know what is really happening. He knows that sometimes the High Command will sacrifice him for some greater interest without informing him of the fact, and this makes him contemptuous and suspicious of authority. It also augments his fear.

The uncertainty of outcome makes him superstitious and he will cross himself continually or kiss his lucky charm, or put his cigarette case in his breast pocket in order to deflect bullets. Francesco and I developed the superstition that neither of us should employ the word 'certamente'. We never said it once either on that mission or during the war afterwards. Francesco seemed to feel the constant necessity for confiding in his mouse, and he would cradle it in his hands and talk nonsense to it whilst the rest of us were chainsmoking, pacing up and down, gazing at dogeared photographs of our loved ones, or rushing off to the latrines every five minutes.

We found that there is also a wild excitement when the tension of waiting is done with, and that sometimes this transforms itself into a kind of demented sadism once an action is commenced. You cannot always blame soldiers for their atrocities, because I can tell you from experience that they are the natural consequence of the inferno of relief that comes from not having to think any more. Atrocities are sometimes nothing less than the vengeance of the tormented. Catharsis is the word I was looking for. A Greek word.

Lying in the scrub in front of that nocturnal tower I felt Francesco at my side and knew that Phaedrus was right in believing that a lover is more valourous with his beloved at his side. I wanted to protect Francesco and prove to him that I was a man. I found that my love for him was increased by the thought that soon we might lose each other to a bullet.

It was just before midnight, the owls were shrieking, and in the distance I heard the mellow chiming of goatbells. It was intensely cold, and a freezing wind had sprung up from the north. We called that wind by a lot of names, but 'ball-shrinker' was probably the most apt.

At midnight Francesco looked at his watch and said, 'I can't stand much more of this. My fingers are dropping off, my feet are like ice, and I swear it's going to rain. For Christ's sake let's get this over with.'

'We can't,' I said. 'The order is not to attack until two o'clock.'

'Come on, Carlo, what does it matter? Let's do it now and go home. Mario's pissed off and so am I.'

'For you, home is Genoa. You can't go there. Look, it's a question of discipline.'

I lost the argument because in truth I agreed with Francesco and I didn't want to die of exposure in that god-forsaken spot just because we had arrived early on account of efficiency and enthusiasm.

The order had been to use the machine-gun on the brigands, but out there in the night in that lethal temperature it no longer seemed a very good idea. It was so cold to the touch that it hurt the fingers, and besides, we were not sure that we could operate it in the dark. We decided to scout nearer the watchtower.

They had a lamp up there, and we were astonished to see that there were at least ten men. We had expected three at the most. We also saw that there were four machine-guns perched on the outer railings. Francesco whispered, 'Why did they only send the two of us? If we fire on them, we're dead. I tell you, it's fishy business. Since when did brigands have machine-guns?'

There was the sound of singing from the tower, and it seemed that they must have been a little drunk. It gave me the confidence to crawl forward and do a close reconnaissance, trying to ignore the pine cones that scratched my hands and the little sharp rocks that seemed to cut through to my bones. I discovered that there was a large heap of kindling and a drum of kerosene under the tower, where it would be protected from the rain. All the watchtowers had wood-burning stoves and oil-lamps, and naturally the supplies were always kept underneath them.

That is why Francesco and I not only began the attack two hours early, but did it by overturning the drum and setting fire to it. The tower went up like a torch, and we filled it with machine-gun bullets from almost directly underneath. We fired and fired until we had used a complete belt. If there were screams we could not hear them. We were only aware of that leaping gun, the clenching of our own teeth, and the horrible madness of desperate action.

When the belt ran out there was a horrifying silence. We looked at each other and smiled. Francesco's smile was weak and sorrowful, and I should think that mine was the same. It was our first atrocity. We felt no triumph. We felt exhausted and tainted.

It was Francesco who fell over the body of Captain Roatta of the Bersaglieri, who had tumbled over the railings of the tower and broken his neck. The body lay spreadeagled and twisted, as though it had never contained a life. It was Francesco who found the orders that had instructed the captain to take nine men to the tower in anticipation of an attack by the Greek Army, which Intelligence expected at 0200 hours.

Francesco sat next to me beside that body and looked up at the stars. 'These aren't British uniforms at all,' he said at last. 'The Greeks wear the same uniform as the British, don't they?'

I too looked at the stars. 'We were supposed to be killed. That's why we were told to go without identification discs. We are Greeks attacking the Italian Army, and we're supposed to be dead. That's why they only sent two of us, to make sure that we couldn't win.'

Francesco stood up slowly. He raised his hands in a small gesture of anguish, and then let them drop to his side. He said bitterly, 'It looks as though some stupid bastard wants to provoke a little war with Greece.'

74

I I

PELAGIA AND MANDRAS

PELAGIA (SITTING IN the privy after breakfast): It's so nice that whoever built this place left a gap at the top of the door. I could just sit here for hours watching the clouds unfolding about the summit of the mountain. I wonder where they come from? I mean, I know that it's water vapour, but they just seem to gather together out of nothing, quite suddenly. It's as if every drop has a secret to share with its brothers, and so they rise up out of the sea and huddle together and drift along in the breeze, and the clouds change shapes as the drops hurry from one confidante to another, whispering. They are saying, 'I can see Pelagia down there, sitting on the privy, and she doesn't even know that we're talking about her.' They are saying, 'I saw Pelagia and Mandras kissing. What will come of it? She would blush if she knew.' O, I am blushing. I am stupid. And why do the clouds travel more slowly than the wind that drives them? And why, sometimes, does the wind blow one way and the clouds travel in another? Is Papakis right when he says that there are several different layers of wind, or is it that the clouds have some means of travelling against it? I must cut up some more clouts, I have those pains in my stomach and my back, and it's about time. I saw the new moon last night, and that means I'm due. Auntie says that the only good thing about being pregnant is that you don't have to worry about bleeding. Poor little Chrysoula, poor little girl, what a terrible thing to happen. Papas coming home late at night, shaking with rage and distress, all because Chrysoula got to the age of fourteen and no one had ever told her that one day she would bleed, and she is so horrified, she thinks that she has some loathsome secret disease, and she can't tell anyone, and she takes rat-poison. And Papas is so angry that he takes Chrysoula's mother by the neck and shakes her like a dog shakes a rabbit, and Chrysoula's father just goes out with the boys as usual and comes home drunk as if nothing has happened, and underneath Chrysoula's bed is a pile of paper as thick as a bible, full of her prayers to St Gerasimos for a cure, and the prayers are so sad and desperate that they make you weep. Well, I can't sit here all day, thinking about clouds and menstruation, and anyway it's beginning to get a bit hot, and there'll be a stench setting in. I'll stay here a little longer though, because Papas won't be coming back from breakfast for another ten minutes, and the important thing is to look busy when he turns up. I suppose they had to leave a gap in the top of the door, or else it would be completely dark in here.

MANDRAS (loading his nets onto the boat): St Peter and St Andrew grant me a good catch. It's going to be another scorching day, I just know it, I just know all the fish will hide in the rocks and go to the bottom. God should have made them with sunglasses for the sake of us poor fishermen. Let the clouds on Mt Aenos shift across the sun, Lord, let me catch a fine mullet for Doctor Iannis and Pelagia, let me see some dolphins or some porpoises so that I know where the fish are, let me see some gulls so that I can find some whitebait, and Pelagia can cover them in flour and fry them in oil and squeeze lemon juice all over them and she'll ask me to eat with them, and I can touch Pelagia's leg with my foot under the table whilst the doctor goes on about Euripides and the Napoleonic occupation, and I'll say, 'How interesting, I never knew that, is that so?' Let me catch a bream for my mother, and a seabass, and a fine big octopus to cut up into rings so that mother can cook them and I'll eat them tomorrow, cold, covered with thyme and oil, on a thick white piece of bread. I shouldn't go out on a Tuesday, there's never any luck on a Tuesday, but a man has to live, and maybe there'll be a smile for me amongst the numberless smiles of the waves. That's something I learned from the doctor; 'The innumerable smiles of the waves,' a line by Aeschylus, who obviously never went to sea in winter. Innumerable drenchings and infinite cold, more like. But it's a pretty day today, as pretty as Pelagia, and if I drop a line onto the bottom, I'll probably get a flatfish, and if I get salt water into these cuts in my backside, it's going to sting like fuck.

PELAGIA (drawing water from the well): Papakis says that Mandras is going to have specks of terracotta in his backside for the rest of his life, and it's going to look as though someone's sprinkled it with red pepper. I like his backside, God forgive me, even though I've never seen it. I can just tell that I like it. That I would like it. It's very small. When he bends down I can see that it's like two halves of a melon. I mean, the curves seem to be in a proportion according to God's original design for fruit. When he kisses me I want to reach round him and take a buttock in each hand. I never have. I wouldn't. What would he say if I did? I have such sluttish thoughts. Thank God no one reads my mind, I'd be locked up and all the old women would throw stones at me and call me a whore. When I think of Mandras I get a picture of his face, grinning, and then I get a picture of him bending over. Sometimes I wonder if I'm normal, but the things the women say when we're all together and the men are in the kapheneion. If the men only knew, what a shock! Every woman in the village knows that Kokolios' penis is curved sideways like a banana and that the priest has a rash on his scrotum, and the men don't know. They don't have a clue what we talk about, they think we talk about cooking and babies and sewing up rents in our clothes. And when we find a potato that looks like a set of men's equipment we pass it round and laugh about it. I wish there was some way of bringing water to the house without having to

77

carry it. Every jar is heavier than the last, and I always get wet.

They say that the Normans used to poison the wells by throwing down corpses, and you had no choice except to die of thirst or die of foul water. It's a miracle, an island without streams or rivers, blessed with clean water from the ground even in August. I'm going to rest a while when I get home; I hate the sticky prickling feeling in the back of my neck when I start to sweat. What I want to know is, why did God make it too hot in the summer and too cold in the winter? And where is it written down that women have to carry water when men are stronger? When Mandras asks me to marry him, I am going to say, 'Not unless you agree to fetch the water.' He'll say, 'Fine, if you do the fishing,' and I won't know what to say. What we need is an inventor to come and put in a pump to take the water to the house. I could kill Papas. What does he mean, telling Mandras that I won't have a dowry? Who marries without one? Papas says that it's a barbarism, and they don't do it in any civilised country he knows of, and you should marry for love as he did, and that it's an obscenity to make it a trans-action, and that it implies that a woman is not worth marry-ing unless she carries property on her back. Well, then, I'll be forced to marry a foreigner if he thinks like that. I said to him, 'Papakis, if you think about it, it's foolish to wear clothes in hot weather. Do you want me to be the only woman in Greece who wears no clothes in the summer?' and he kisses me on the forehead and says, 'You're almost clever enough to be my daughter,' and goes out. I've a good mind to be naked when he comes home, I really have. You can't go against the custom, you just can't, even if the cus-tom's stupid, and what will Mandras' family say? How am I supposed to bear the shame? All I have is a goat. Am I sup-posed to go off to his father's house with nothing but a goat and a pack of clothes? And who says they'll want my goat? Well, I'm not going if I can't take the goat, and that's that. Who else is going to breathe up his nose and scratch behind his ears? Papakis won't. And I wish Papas would stop pee-ing on the herbs, it makes me wince when I have to use

Pelagia it's as though I'm twelve again; one minute I'm up the olive tree being Tarzan, and the next minute I'm pretending to have a fight with the goat. It's showing off, that's what it is, but what else am I supposed to do? I can't see myself saying, 'Come on Pelagia, let's talk about politics.' Women aren't interested in that sort of thing, they want you to entertain them. I've never talked to her about my vision of things. Perhaps she thinks I'm a fool as well. I'm not in her class, I know that. The doctor taught her Italian and a bit of English, and their house is bigger than ours, but I'm not inferior. At least, I don't think I'm inferior. They're not a typical family, that's all. Unconventional. The doctor says what he likes. I don't really know where I stand a lot of the time. It would have been easier to fall in love with Despina or Polyxeni. Perhaps if I'd had my period of exiteia I would be more worldly-wise. I mean, the doctor's sailed all over the world, he's even been to America. And where have I been? What do I know? I've been to Ithaca and Zante and Levkas. Big deal. I don't have any stories and souvenirs. I've never tried French wine. He says that in Ireland it rains every day and that in Chile there's a desert where it has never rained at all. I love Pelagia, but I know that I will never be a man until I've done something important, something great, something I can live with, something to be esteemed. That's why I hope there's going to be a war. I don't want bloodshed and glory, I want something to get to grips with. No man is a man until he has been a soldier. I can come back in my uniform and no one will say, 'Mandras is a likeable lad, but there's nothing to him.' I'll be worth a dowry then. Ah, dolphins. A bit of rudder, throw the jib over. No, no, don't come to me, I'm coming to you. I hope you weren't just playing. Ah, I do believe it's dolphin Kosmas, dolphin Nionios, and dolphiness Krystal. Kalimera, my smiling friends. Out of the way, I'm reeling out the net, and don't take too many fish from the mesh this time. Fuck it, I'm too hot, I'm coming in the water. Clothes off, drop the anchor. Watch out you dolphins, I'm coming in. Jesus it's lovely. Is there anything as good as seawater on the bridge of an overheated groin? Anything as good as scudding away with one hand on the fin of a dolphin? Swim, Krystal, swim. Shit, that stings.

PELAGIA (at siesta): It's too hot. The door's moving. Who's that? Mandras? No, don't be stupid, you can't make some- one come just by thinking of them. They say that there is such a thing as a ghost of the living. O, it's you, Psipsina. O no, O no. Why can't we have a dog like everyone else? Even a cat? We've got to have a mad pine marten that doesn't take siestas. Get off. How much bigger do you think you can grow? I can't sleep with half a ton on my chest. Stay still. Mmm, why do you always smell so sweet, Psipsina? Been stealing eggs and berries again? Why can't you catch your own mice? I'm sick of grinding up mice. Why can't you use the floor like everyone else? What's the pleasure in fly- ing about the room without touching the floor? Mmm, how sweet you are, I'm glad Lemoni found you. Really, I am. I wish you were Mandras. I want Mandras lying on my chest. God, it's hot. How can you stand that fur coat, Psipsina? I wish you were Mandras. I wonder what he's doing? Out in the breeze at sea, I suppose. I wonder how his backside is. Papakis said it was a very splendid backside. Full of terra- cotta. 'The arse of a classical statue, a very fine arse,' he said. If I close my eyes and hold out my arms, and pray to St Gerasimos, perhaps when I open them it'll be Mandras on my chest instead of Psipsina. No luck. No luck, Psipsina. He's so beautiful. And he's so funny. He made my stomach ache with laughing before he fell out of the tree. That's when I knew that I loved him, it was the fear I felt when he fell on the pot. I'll hug Psipsina as if it was him, and perhaps he'll feel it. I hope you haven't got fleas. I don't want red spots up my arms. My ankle was itching yesterday and I was thinking of blaming you, Psipsina, but I think I must have brushed a thorn with it. When will he ask me to marry him? He says that his mother is not very nice. What a thing to say about one's own mother. I wish I could remember Mitera. Poor Mitera. Died like a skeleton coughing up blood. She looks nice in the photograph, so young and contented, and the way she has her hand on his shoulder, you can tell that she loved him. If she was still alive I would know what to do about Mandras, she'd change Papakis' mind about the dowry. Mandras doesn't seem to mind. He's not a serious fellow, and it gives me doubts. He's so funny, but I can't talk to him about anything. You have to be able to discuss things with a husband, don't you? Everything's a joke with him. He is witty, and that shows that he's not stupid, I hope. I say, 'Is there going to be a war?' and he just grins and says, 'Who cares? Is there going to be a kiss?' I don't want there to be a war. Let there not be war. Let there be Mandras standing at the entrance of the yard with a fish in his hands. Let there be Mandras every day with a fish. I'm a bit sick of fish, to tell the truth. Have you noticed, Psipsina? Every time he brings a fish, a bit more of it ends up in your bowl?

MANDRAS (mending his nets at the harbour): Yesterday British Somaliland fell to the Italians. How long before they attack us from Albania? It was tanks against camels, it seems. I feel so useless and insignificant here on this island. This is a time for men to be about their business. Arsenios wrote a letter for me to the King, saying that I wanted to volunteer, and I've got a letter from the office of Metaxas himself saying that I will get my call-up if I'm needed. Well, tonight I'm going to get him to write again and say that I want my call-up immediately. How am I going to tell Pelagia? I know one thing, I'm going to ask her to marry me before I leave, dowry or not. I'm going to ask her father's permission, and then I'm going to go down on one knee and ask her. With no jokes. I'm going to make her understand that in defending Greece I will be defending her and every woman like her. It's a question of national salvation. Everyone has the duty to do his utmost. And if I die, then it's too bad, I won't have died for nothing. I'll die with the name of Pelagia and the name of Greece equally on my lips, because it amounts to the same thing, the same sacred thing. And if I live, I'll walk with my head held high for the rest of

82

my life, and I'll come back to my dolphins and my nets, and everyone will say, 'That's Mandras, who fought in the war. We owe everything to people like him,' and not Pelagia, and not her father, will be able to look at me and call me a fool and an idiot, and I'll always be more than a nobody-fisherman with terracotta shards in his arse.

PELAGIA (taking kleftico from the communal oven): Where's Mandras? He's usually here by now. I want him to come. I can hardly breathe, I want him to come so much. My hands are shaking again. I'd better take this silly smile off my face, or everyone'll think that I'm mad. Come, Mandras, please come, and I won't give my share of the fish to Psipsina. Only the guts and the tail and the head. Stay for dinner, and stroke my shin with your feet, Mandras. Isn't Psipsina big enough by now to tear up mice for herself? I'm so stupid, doing things by habit, without necessity. Stay for dinner.

12

ALL THE SAINT'S MIRACLES

NOTHING ON THE island had changed, there had been no portents of war; God Himself had remained unperturbed by the megalomania and destruction visited upon the world. On August 23rd the sacred lily before the icon of Our Lady at Demountsandata had erupted punctually from its desiccated state and blossomed reassuringly, renewing the wonder and confirming the piety of the faithful. In the middle of the month a horde of non-venomous snakes, unknown to science, embellished with black crosses upon their heads and skin like velvet, had wriggled out of apparent nothingness at Markopoulo. They had filled the streets with their writhing and creeping, had approached the silver icon of the Virgin, had installed themselves upon the bishop's throne, and at the end of the service had disappeared as quietly and unaccountably as they had come. In the great ruined castle of Kastro, high above Travliata and Mitakata, the martial spectres of Romans demanded passwords of Normans and French, and the shades of British redcoats played at dice with those of Turks, Catalans and Venetians amongst the dank and unmappable labyrinth of subterranean cisterns, tunnels and mines. In the fallen Venetian town of Fiskardo the roaring ghost of Guiscard strode the ramparts, braying for Greek blood and treasure. At the northern tip of Argostoli the sea poured down the sink-holes of the shore as ever, vanishing inexplicably into the bowels of the earth, and at Paliki the rock known as Kounopetra ceaselessly moved to its own unalterable rhythm. The villagers of

Manzavinata, as predictable as the rock, never failed to inform all who would listen that once a fleet of British warships had slung a chain about Kounopetra, and had not moved it; it was one small Greek rock that had resisted the power and the scientific curiosity of the greatest empire ever known to man. Perhaps even more worthy of note, an expedition of Frenchmen had once more failed to find the bottom of Lake Akoli, and a puzzled zoologist from Wyoming had confirmed the report of the eminent historian, Iannis Kosti Laverdos, that the wild hares and some of the goats on Mt Ayia Dinati had gold and silver teeth.

Ever since the time when the Goddess Io had been instrumental in the killing of Memnon by Achilles and had precipitated the accidental shooting of Procris by her own unsuspecting husband, the island had been a prodigy of wonders. This itself was no wonder, for the island possessed a saint unique to itself, and it was as if his numinous power was too great and too effulgent to be contained within himself.

St Gerasimos, withered and blackened, sealed inside his domed and gilded sarcophagus by the reredos of his own monastery, dead for five centuries, rose up at night. Decked in scarlet and golden robes, precious stones and ancient medals, he rattled and creaked his way discreetly amongst his flock of sinners and the sick, visiting them in their homes, sometimes even going abroad to his native Corinthia, there to visit the bones of his fathers and wander amongst the hills and groves of his youth. But the dutiful saint had always returned by morning, obliging the garrulous nuns who attended him to clean the mud from the golden brocade of his slippers and resettle his emaciated and mummified limbs into a posture of peaceful repose.

He was a real saint, a genuine holy man with nothing in common with the imaginary and doubtful saints of other faiths. He had not blemished the world, like St Dominic with his inquisition, he had not been an eighteen-foot giant with cannibal proclivities, like St Christopher, and he had not accidentally killed the spectators at his death, like St Catherine. Neither was he an incomplete saint, like St

Andrew, who had succeeded in leaving only the sole of his right foot in the convent near Travliata. Like St Spiridon of Corfu, Gerasimos had lived an exemplary life and left his entire mortal shell as an inspiration and as evidence.

He had gone for a monk at the age of twelve, spent the same number of years in the Holy Land, had dwelt for five years in Zante, and had finally settled in a cave at Spilla, thence to reorganise the monastery at Omala, where he had planted the plane tree and dug the well with his own hands. He was so beloved of the normally cynical islanders that he had two feast days to himself, one in August and one in October; sons by the dozen were named after him, he was believed in more fervently than the Lord Himself, and from his throne in heaven he had had to become used to folk cursing and swearing in his name. On the two feast days he tolerantly averted the eyes of his soul as the entire population of the island waxed outlandishly drunk.

It was on the eighth day before Metaxas rejected the ultimatum of the Duce, yet it might have been any feast day of the last hundred years. The cruelty had gone out of the sun and the day was gloriously warm without being oppressive. A light breeze from the sea wandered in and out of the olives, rustling the leaves so that each one flashed an intricate semaphore of silver and dark green. Poppies and daisies swayed amid grass that was still sere from the summer but was now beginning to freshen, and the bees made the most of the flowers, as if aware of the onset of autumn; their numerous hives dripped with the clear dark honey that the islanders confidently knew to be the best in the world. High on Mt Aenos the Egyptian vultures searched for the corpses of unfortunate or clumsy goats, and down in the briars of the plains the small black Sicilian warblers flitted and squabbled. Innumerable hedgehogs rooted and snuffled beneath them, providently arranging nests of grass and leaves in anticipation of some cold days ahead, and the beaches were strewn with what appeared to be minor shipwrecks, half-dismantled boats drawn up out of the water for inspection and recaulking. Tropical plants in the south of the island began to appear less exuberant, as though drawing in their sap or holding their breath, and the fig trees displayed heavy purple fruit amid the green youngsters that would ripen in the subsequent year, the year in which they would become officially the fruit of the Fascists of Rome.

At dawn Alekos stroked the stock of his antiquated rifle and decided to leave it behind; there were always too many casualties at the feast of the saint, and this detracted from the miracles. He wrapped the weapon in his blankets and walked out into the mist to see if the goats were well; he was planning to leave them to themselves for one day, but he was sure that the saint would protect them. All through the long walk down from Mt Aenos he knew that he would be able to hear the plangent tones of their bells; he would play a game with himself in which he identified the sound of each. He felt an almost unbearable excitement as he imagined in advance the spectacle of the saint curing epileptics and the mad. Who would he choose?

At the village, Father Arsenios poured a bottle of Robola down his throat and wiped his eyes blearily, unaccustomed to the hardship of early rising, and Pelagia and her father chained up the goat to the olive tree and locked Psipsina in a cupboard where she would find nothing to tear to pieces. Kokolios struggled very briefly with his Communist beliefs about the opiate of the masses, and then put on his wife's clothes anyway. Stamatis glued a conical paper hat together, and tried it for size whilst his wife cut up lumps of cheese, wrapped up rozoli and mantola sweetmeats, and remembered things to complain about. Megalo Velisarios loaded his culverin onto the back of a sturdy bull that he had borrowed from a third cousin, and dreamed of winning the race. He had loaded the cannon with scraps of silver and gold foil, and looked forward to the sighs of admiration of the crowd as the sparkling ammunition shot up into the sky and then fluttered down like a rain of metallic butterflies.

At the monastery the rubicund little nuns awakened the many guests and pilgrims in their tidy guestrooms, filled the garish washbowls and waterjugs, plumped up the embroidered pillows, replaced the luxurious towels, and swept out the dust. They themselves lived in spartan little rooms with nothing but a shredded mat, a creaky truckle bed, and dark icons upon the wall. Their pleasure lay in catering for others, listening with exquisite prurience to their tales of woe and betrayal, and constructing a jigsaw image of the outside world from what they had heard. It was better to hear of it than to have to inhabit it, of that they were convinced.

In the adjacent madhouse, other nuns dressed the inmates in clean robes and wondered which one would be cured by the aura of the saint. There were very few occasions when he had withheld a cure, and no doubt his great charity (and perhaps his vanity) was in itself a guarantee of some unfortunate's restoration. Would it be Mina, who squawked and gibbered, recognised no one, and exposed herself to the unwary? Would it be Dmitri, who smashed windows and bottles and ate the glass? Maria, who thought that she was Queen of America and made even the doctors approach her on their knees? Socrates, who was so much a victim of neurasthenia that the mere lifting of a fork was an unsustainable responsibility that could make him weep and tremble? The nuns believed that to live near the saint was itself a gentle form of remedy, and in their lucid moments the mad wondered when their turn would come. The saint selected his cures with no apparent logic or consistency, and some died after waiting for forty years, whilst others arrived one year with a record of atheism and reprehensible behaviour and were away the next.

Outside in the beautiful meadows of the valley and amongst the plane trees that lined the road from Kastro, pilgrims and corybants had been arriving for two days, some of them from distant parts indeed. The relatives of the mad had already kissed the hand of the saint and had prayed together in the church for the healing of their loved ones, whilst the nuns polished the golden ornaments, filled the building with flowers, and lit the gigantic tapers. The pews were filled with distant acquaintances renewing their friendship by means of the animated and voluble conversation that non-Greeks mistakenly construe as irreverence. Outside, the pilgrims unloaded animals laden with feta, melons, cooked fowl, and Cephallonian meat pie, shared it with their neighbours, and composed epigrammatic couplets at each others' expense. Groups of laughing girls strolled about, arm in arm, smiling sideways at potential husbands and possible sources of flirtation, and the men, pretending to ignore them, stood about in knots, gesticulating and waving bottles as they solved the outstanding problems of the world. Priests swarmed together like bees, discussing theological points with immense gravitas, their grey beards augmenting the patriarchal effect of their shining black shoes and flapping robes, and endured the flattering interruptions of the faithful, who could never think of any sensible pretext for conversation other than to enquire whether or not this or that bishop was likely to attend.

But in truth the scenes of pastoral merriment and ecclesiastical dignity were a disguise for the growing anxiety in the hearts of everyone there, the anxiety of anticipation, the fear of witnessing the mechanically inexplicable, the trepidation that afflicts those who are about to be witnesses to the breaking of the veil between this world and the next. It was a species of nervousness that swelled into a tightening of the chest and a susceptibility to tears as soon as the bell began to toll for the commencement of the service.

There was a sudden buzz of chatter and activity as the people began to press into the church, packed it beyond capacity, and compressed themselves together in the courtyard outside. Some people went to stand in the priests' cemetery. At different points in the crowd Alekos, Velisarios, Pelagia, Dr Iannis, Kokolios, and Stamatis all strained their heads sideways to hear the distant intonations of the priest. When the folk inside the church crossed themselves, those at the door did so a moment afterwards, and then those behind them, and then those at the back, so that a ripple of gestures passed through the crowd like that of a stone tossed into a pool.

The sun climbed higher and the people, crammed together, began to perspire. The sticky heat was just becoming intolerable when the service drew to a resounding close, and the people began a reverse process of shuffling and jostling, in which those who had been the unlucky ones with respect to a place in the church suddenly found their fortunes changed as they became the first to reach the site of the miracles beneath the plane tree of the saint.

Inside the church the saint's body was taken up by the bearers, and beneath the tree the happy nuns arranged and rearranged the unpredictable and erratic gathering of the mad, most of whom had become both subdued and terrified, overwhelmed by the impression of a chaos of unfamiliar faces pressing all about them. The glass-eater began to howl. The Queen of America, thrilled by the arrival of her subjects, composed herself into a posture of supreme regality, and Socrates stared abjectly at his right foot, which it had become too much of an ordeal to move. He summoned up an effort of will which, to his consternation, moved one of his forefingers. He tried to make the effort of will to stop it, but could not make the effort of will to make the effort of will. Locked into an infinite regress of incapacity, he stood absolutely still and retreated into the kaleidoscope of unconnected images behind his eyes. One of the nuns wiped a tear from his face, and hurried on to quiet the glass-eater. Others joined her in order to cajole the patients into lying or sitting.

Mina sat beneath the mighty tree and put her arms about her knees. Despite the throng of people and despite the palpable curtain that separated her world from theirs, she felt something like a mood of calm cut through the gibbering of her thoughts. She looked at the glaring whitewash of the church and realised that it was a church. 'Turtles' eggs,' she thought, and then remembered a snatch of a nonsense rhyme from her childhood. She stood up suddenly and began to lift her robe, but was forced down gently by a nun. She accepted it, and listened vaguely to the turmoil of voices inside her own chest. Sometimes the voices shouted and screeched, and she could not get rid of them even by crouching in corners or beating her face against a wall. Sometimes they made her do things by threatening not to go away until she did what she was told. Sometimes they made her itch all over until she was in a frenzy of ripping her own flesh with her nails, and

90

sometimes they told her to stop breathing. In a whirling of panic she would feel her lungs stop and her heart slow towards a heavy halt. Sometimes the gap between herself and the world would yawn so wide that she would look down and see an infinite void beneath her feet; those were the times when she would run wildly, trying to find the ground, crashing into invisible things that made her bruise and bleed. Sometimes, overwhelmed with fear, she would sweat so much that she became too slippery for the nuns to restrain, and she would slide on the floor of the asylum, weeping and hawking. The worst thing was when she could see the faces of the people around her, knew that they were looking at her, knew that they were planning to kill her, and lifted her skirts to hide her own face, as though by this magic she could prevent them from seeing her. Whenever she did this, hands appeared from nowhere and dragged her skirts down again, so that she was forced to struggle with all the strength of her desperation to raise them up. Hunted and wounded, Mina sat on the grass and cowered as an unintelligible shadow approached and passed over her.

Dr Iannis and Pelagia had found themselves at the front of the crowd, and watched with mounting excitement as the ornamented body of the saint was carried over the recumbent madmen. Never had a body been handled with greater solicitude, nor with so much respect; it must not be jostled in its bier, nor disarranged. Its bearers stepped carefully between the limbs of the mad, and anxious families restrained the flailing and convulsing of their afflicted relatives. The glass-eater's eyes rolled, and his mouth foamed with epileptic spume, but he remained still. He had no family to constrain him, and he drew power from the saint to constrain himself. He saw a pair of embroidered slippers pass by his nose.

As the saint was borne away, the people, in an agony of suspense, scrutinised the patients in order to see if there had been any change. Someone spotted Socrates and pointed. He was shaking his shoulders like an athlete about to throw a javelin, and he was staring with amazement at his hands, moving his fingers in order one by one. He looked up suddenly, saw that everyone was watching him, and waved shyly. An unnatural howl went up from the crowd, and Socrates' mother fell to her knees, kissing her son's hands. She stood up, threw up her arms to the wide sky, and called, 'Praise to the saint, praise to the saint,' so that in no time at all the whole assembly was hysterical with exhilarated awe. Dr Iannis pulled Pelagia away from the impending crush, and wiped the sweat from his face and the tears from his eyes. He was trembling in every part of his body, and so, he saw, was Pelagia. 'A purely psychological phenomenon,' he muttered to himself, and was struck suddenly by the sensation of being an ingrate. The bell of the church began to peal out wildly as nuns and priests decorously fought each other for a tug of the wire.

The carnival began, impelled as much by general relief and the need to dispel goosepimples as by the natural propensity for celebration that was shared by the islanders. Velisarios permitted Lemoni to put a match to the touchhole of his cannon, there was a mighty roar, and a glittering shower of foil fluttered down like the golden flakes of Zeus. Socrates walked in a daze of bliss amongst the flurry of hands that clapped him on the back and the hurricane of kisses that descended upon the back of his palm. 'Is this the feast of the saint?' he asked. 'I know it's stupid, but I can't remember coming at all.' He was drawn into a dance, a syrtos of the young people of Lixouri.

A small improvised band consisting of askotsobouno bagpipes, a panpipe, a guitar, and a mandolin was winding itself into harmony from different points of the musical compass, and a fine baritone, a quarryman, was inventing a song in honour of the miracle. He sang one line, repeated by the dancers, which gave him time to draw out the next, until a complete song emerged with its own melody:

'On a fine young day I came to see the girls and dance
I came as a heathen comes with thoughts of wine and
   food.
But the saint has washed my doubting eyes,
And shown that God is good . . .'

92

A line of pretty girls holding hands stepped from side to side at the back, and in front of them a row of young men flicked one leg behind them with their heads twisted backwards, leaping as lightly as crickets. Socrates took the red kerchief of the leading dancer, and to the delight of the spectators performed the most athletic and spectacular tsalimia that any of them had ever seen. As his legs crossed and tipped above the level of his own head, as the words of the song sprang out of his mouth, he knew for the first time the true meaning of exhilaration and relief. His body jumped and spun without the least effort of will, muscles whose existence he had long forgotten snapped like steel, and he could almost feel the sun itself glittering upon his teeth as his face cracked in an enormous, insuppressible grin. The waul of the bagpipe vibrated inside his head, and suddenly he looked up at the clouds on Mt Aenos, and was struck by the thought that he must have died and entered paradise. He kicked his legs still higher, and his heart sang like a choir of birds.

A troupe from Argostoli with its own band began to dance a divaratiko, inviting negative criticisms from Lixourians and positive ones from Argostolians, and on the far side of the meadow a posse of the fishermen known as tratoloi began to open bottles and sing lustily all the songs that they had been perfecting for weeks in the tavernas of Panagopoula after they had shared the day's profit, teased each other, quarrelled over the takings, eaten olives and pretza, and finally arrived at the point where singing was both natural and inevitable.

They sang together a cantada:

'The garden where you sit
Has never a need of flowers,
For you are the blossoms
And only a fool or the blind
Would fail to know it.'

The rapid arpeggios of the guitar tailed away, and the tenor began an arietta. His voice ululated at the top of its range,

93

above the chattering of the crowd and even the crash of Velisarios' cannon, until his friends joined in and wove a harmony intricate and polyphonic about the melody that he had created, arriving at the end together on exactly the right tone and in the right key, the brotherhood of the sea thus producing conclusive proof of their metaphysical unity.

Amid the songs and dances the little nuns wove a path, leaving in their wake a plenitude of wine and food. Those who were drunk already began to mock each other, and in places mockery turned itself into insult, and from thence to blows. Dr Iannis left his cheese and melons to staunch bleeding noses and cuts from broken bottles. The women and the more sensible men moved their rugs to places more distant from those who threatened to become unruly. Pelagia moved nearer the monastery and sat on a bench.

She watched as new dancers brought the traditions of the carnival to the panegyri. Men were turning up dressed absurdly in tight white shirts, white kilts, white gloves, and extravagant paper hats. They were draped in red silk ribbons, clusters of tiny bells, gold jewellery and chains, photographs of sweethearts or the King, and they were accompanied by short little boys garbed satirically as girls. All of them sported masks, hilarious and grotesque, and amongst them was Kokolios, decked in his protesting wife's most precious clothes. Near the road some youths in fantastic costume and daubed faces began to enact babaoulia, the comic skits in which not even the saint could escape the fate of being lampooned. A swirl of competing polkas, lancers, quadrilles, waltzes and ballos threw the crowd into a chaos of falling bodies, shrieks and insults. Pelagia spotted Lemoni solemnly attempting to set fire to the beard of a capsized priest, and her heart jumped a little when she saw Mandras throwing firecrackers amongst the feet of some dancers from Fiskardo.

She lost sight of him, and then felt a tap on her shoulder. She looked up and beheld Mandras, his arms thrown back in a mock embrace. She smiled, despite his drunken state, and suddenly he fell to his knees and intoned dramatically,

'Siora, will you marry me? Marry me or I die.'

'Why do you call me Siora?' she asked.

'Because you speak Italian and sometimes wear a hat.' He grinned stupidly, and Pelagia said, 'Nonetheless, I am hardly an aristocrat and I must not be called Siora.' She looked at him a moment, and a silence flowered between them, the kind of silence that obliged her to answer his proposal. 'Of course I'll marry you,' she said quietly.

Mandras leapt into the air, and Pelagia noticed that the knees of his breeches had darkened where he had knelt down in a puddle of wine. He pirouetted and cavorted, and she stood up, laughing. But she could not stand; an invisible force seemed to have glued her to the seat. She sat down hastily, examined her skirts, and realised that Mandras had pinned them to the bench. Her new fiancé threw himself backwards upon the grass and howled with mirth, until suddenly he sat up, composed his face into an expression of extreme seriousness, and said, 'Koritsimou, I love you with all my heart, but we can't get married until I come back from the Army.'

'Go and speak to my father,' said Pelagia, and, her heart seeming to choke her in the throat, she wandered numbly amongst the revellers in order to digest this contradictory miracle. Then, troubled by the curious way in which she did not feel as happy as she ought, she wended her way back to the church in order to be alone with the saint.

The day wore on, and Mandras failed to find the doctor before drink overcame him. He slept seraphically in a pool of something foul but unidentifiable, whilst nearby Stamatis drew a monarchist knife on Kokolios and threatened to remove his Communist balls, before throwing himself about his neck and swearing eternal brotherhood. Elsewhere a man was stabbed to death over a property dispute that had wrangled on for nearly a hundred years, and Father Arsenios incurred such blurred vision that he mistook Velisarios for his dead father.

The evening gathered itself together out of the seemingly intractable anarchy of the afternoon when the time arrived for the concluding race. Little boys bestrode fat billy goats, a tiny girl was attached to a large dog, contented inebriates sat themselves backwards upon donkeys, abused and emaciated horses hung their heads as overweight tavern-keepers scrambled up their flanks, and Velisarios seated himself astride the placid bull that he had borrowed.

There was a false start which it was impossible to remedy, and a delightful stampede commenced before the starter had even had time to raise his kerchief. The little girl on the large dog careered at a tangent towards a fallen joint of lamb, the boys on the billy goats were bucked up and down whilst making progress neither forwards nor backwards, the donkeys trotted obligingly towards places other than the finishing line, and the horses refused to budge at all. Only the bull and its Herculean load plodded in a straight line towards the far end of the meadow, preceded solely by an excited but riderless pig. Velisarios, a popular winner, arrived at the finishing line, dismounted, and, to the amazement and applause of the spectators, took the bull by the horns and with one mighty heave wrestled it to the ground. It lay bellowing with incomprehension and stupefaction as Velisarios was borne away upon the shoulders of the crowd.

Parties of the intoxicated began to drift away, singing raucously at the tops of their voices:

'We're leaving the panegyri boys,
In a fine old fighting mood.
We went as pilgrims
And staggered back drunk
According to the Holy custom.
The saint smiles down,
And we honour him
By dancing and falling over.'

Pelagia and the doctor found their way home, Father Arsenios took advantage of the hospitality of the monastery, Alekos slept half way up the mountain in a stone shelter, and Kokolios and Stamatis became lost in the maquis of Troianata whilst searching for their respective wives.

Back in the madhouse, Mina sat on her bed and wondered where she was. She blinked her eyes and looked down at her legs, noticing that her feet were very dirty. Her uncle came in to say goodbye for another year, and to his astonishment she smiled brightly: 'Theio, have you come to take me home?' Her relative stood dumbfounded, cried out incredulously, wheeled about with his clenched fists raised in the air, performed three steps of a kalamatianos for sheer joy, and then rocked her in his arms exclaiming 'Efkharisto, efkharisto,' over and over again. She had recognised him, she was no longer gibbering, she no longer felt the compulsion to raise her skirts, she was sane and, at twenty-six, still marriageable – with a dowry and a bit of luck. He blew kisses towards the heavens, and promised the saint that he would find her a dowry even if it killed him.

It seemed that Gerasimos had performed two miracles that year, and had modestly decided to make one of them less immediately sensational than the other. The glass-eater and his unfortunate fellows dolefully watched her leave, and poignantly wondered how long the saint would make them wait.

13

DELIRIUM

MANDRAS PUT IN no appearance for two days after the feast of the saint, leaving Pelagia to ferment in an agony of agitation. She could not think what could have happened to him, and she invented one reason upon another for his absence, which she felt as a growing lack that was threatening to become more real than the obligations and objects of everyday life.

She had walked back from the feast with her father, and had deduced that the levity of his conversation was due to a combination of drink and the fact that Mandras had not found him. At every step she had wanted to interrupt his flow of remarks about the psychological nature of the miraculous and his surprisingly coarse observations about what had been going on at the periphery of the feast; she was bursting with an insupportable admixture of anxiety and happiness, and wanted nothing so much as to mention Mandras' proposal. It was information that weighed more than the entire world, and she needed her father to share it, so that it might be lightened. The doctor had not noticed her flushed cheeks, her erratic attention, her tendency to trip over stones, the overemphatic gestures of her hands, and the slight strangulation of her voice; he had achieved precisely that stage of inebriation where high spirits teetered on the edge of nausea and unsteadiness, and decided to withdraw. His was a happiness that precluded any sensitivity to the state of his daughter's mind, and she had still not imparted her news by the time that they had reached home, where the doctor had gathered the philosophical Psipsina in his arms and waltzed about the yard before urinating on the mint and retiring to bed, malodorous and fully clothed.

Pelagia went to her own bed and could not sleep. A gibbous moon slid filaments of eerie silver light through the slats of the shutters, and this conspired with the energetic carpentry of the crickets to keep her lying on her back with her eyes wide open. She had never felt more awake. Her mind looped interminably as it replayed the events of the day; the miracle, the songs and dances, the fights, the race, the proposal. It always came back to that; every train of memory twisted on its track and returned to that handsome boy on his knees by the bench where she sat, Mandras on his knees in a pool of wine, Mandras, so beautiful, luminous, and young; Mandras, as exquisite as Apollo. Perspiration broke out on her limbs as she imagined herself entwined in his embrace, transformed him into an incubus, moved her arms and legs, caressed his back and experienced in absentia the soft curl of his tongue on her breasts and the lithe pressure of his weight.

'I love you,' she declared, at the same time as doubts assailed her like an invasion of tiny invisible devils. Marriage was such a big thing, it meant giving up one life for another. It meant leaving her father's house, it meant childbirth and relentless work in place of this gentle idyll with its mock contretemps, its tranquil routines, and its congenial eccentricities. She bridled at the thought of accepting orders and decisions from anyone but her own father, whose commands, however brusque and peremptory, were really requests ironically disguised. What would Mandras be like? How much did she really know him? What evidence did she have that he was patient and humane? He brought gifts, that was sure, but would the gifts not stop when the bargain was secured? Wasn't he too young and too full of impulses? There was something too decisive about his movements, his unconsidered responses; can you trust someone who replies immediately, without thought? Someone whose actions and words are poetic rather than solidly cogitated? She was frightened by the suspicion that there was something adamantine about the structure of his heart. 'Could he be a romoi,' she wondered, 'without even knowing it himself?' And how do you tell the difference between desire and love? She listened to the tinny buzz of a mosquito as she compared her fiancé to her father. She adored the latter; yes, that was love. But what did it have in common with her feelings for Mandras? Was it conceivable that service to him would feel so much like liberty? Was it just that there were different kinds of love? If it were not love that she felt for Mandras, then why this breathlessness, this bottomless and perpetual longing that furred her tongue and gave her palpitations? Why, like God or a dictator, did this emotion command her without reason, irresistibly? Why, like the arbitrations of Patir Arsenios, did it seem to have the force of law without the law's formality? The moon shifted behind the olive tree, casting a ceaseless motion of leaves upon the wall, the melancholy bells of the goats of Mt Aenos rang through the gentle chill of the night, and outside Psipsina could be heard foraging in the yard. 'Catching her own mice,' thought Pelagia, as she lay listening to the palpable hunger of her body. She thought of the capricious joie de vivre of the pine marten, its innocence and its complete absorption in the business of being itself, and realised quite suddenly that she had exchanged the carelessness of youth for something very like unhappiness. She imagined that Mandras had died, and as the tears came she was shocked to discover that she also felt relief. She banished the image sternly, and told herself that she was vile.

In the morning she betook herself to the yard and created tasks for herself that would cause her to see him as soon as he came around the curve of the road, the same curve where he had been shot by Velisarios. She inspected the ruminating goat for ticks, burned them off with a hot needle, and then burrowed through the coarse hair all over again. She looked up repeatedly to see if it was Mandras who came. Her father went to the kapheneia for breakfast, and it occurred to her that Psipsina might also have ticks. She set the animal on the wall, even closer to the road, and with her fingers brushed the fur against its natural lie. Pelagia buried her nose in the soft fur of its stomach, and felt at once sad-dened and comforted by the sweetness of the smell. Psipsina wriggled and squeaked with pleasure as the busy fingers found two fleas and broke them between the nails of thumb and forefinger. Unwilling to leave the wall, Pelagia brushed the marten vigorously and pulled out the matted knots of fur. She draped Psipsina about her neck and decided to fetch water, which would take her round the curve alto-gether. Psipsina slept as Pelagia sat by the well and engaged the other women in conversation; but she forgot every detail of the scandals that were discussed, and her eyes kept flicking away. She began to feel a little sick. She drew more water than she knew how to use, and decided to irrigate the herbs. Wearied with waiting, she sat in the shade of the olive with her arm about the scrawny neck of her goat, which indifferently continued to chew as though there were no other world than its own. Longing turned to impatience, and thence to irritation. In order to spite Mandras, Pelagia decided to go for a walk. It would serve him right if she were not there when he came. She walked along the road in the direction that he would come, sat on a wall until the day grew too hot, and then wandered into the maquis, where she came across Lemoni, who was looking for crickets.

Pelagia sat on a rock and watched as the little girl hurried from one patch of scrub to another, closing her plump fin-gers over thin air as the crickets took evasive action. 'How old are you, koritsimou?' Pelagia asked suddenly.

'Six,' said Lemoni. 'Just. After the next feast I am going to be seven.'

'Can you count to ten yet?'

'I can count to thirty,' said Lemoni, who then proceeded to demonstrate. 'Twenty-one, twenty-two, twenty-thirty.'

Pelagia sighed. She reckoned that before the elapse of two more feasts, Lemoni would be set to work in the house, and that would be the end of hunting for small creatures in the maquis. It would be a question of lapsing into the monot-ony of spoiling the menfolk and only being allowed to dis-cuss important things with other women, when the men were not listening or were in the kapheneion playing backgammon when they ought to be working. For Lemoni there would be no freedom until widowhood, which was precisely the time when the community would turn against her, as though she had no right to outlive a husband, as though he had died only because of his wife's negligence. This was why one had to have sons; it was the only insurance against an indigent and terrifying old age. Pelagia wished that there was something better for Lemoni, as though it were idle to wish better things for herself.

Lemoni wailed suddenly, startling Pelagia out of her reflections. It was a sound very like that of a wauling cat. Tears started from Lemoni's eyes, and she clutched a forefinger, doubled over, and rocked back and forth. Pelagia ran forward and uncurled the little girl's fingers, saying, 'What happened, koritsimou? What hurt you?'

'It bit me, it bit me,' she cried.

'O dear, o dear. Didn't you know that they bite?' She put her fingers next to her mouth and waggled them, 'They've got big jaws with pincers. It'll stop hurting in a minute.'

Lemoni clutched her finger again. 'It stings.'

'If you were a cricket, wouldn't you bite people who pick you up? The cricket thought you were going to hurt it, and that's why it hurt you. That's the way it is. When you're older, you'll find that people are very much the same.'

Pelagia pretended to do a special spell for curing cricket bites, and led the placated Lemoni back to the village. There was still no Mandras, and everything was unusually quiet as people crept about, nursing their hangovers and inexplicable bruises. A donkey brayed ridiculously and at length, receiving a ragged chorus of 'Ai gamisou' from the dark interiors of the houses. Pelagia set about the preparation of the evening meal, thankful that tonight it would not be fish. Later, as she sat with her father after the customary peripato, he said quite unexpectedly, 'I expect he hasn't come because he's feeling as sick as everyone else.' Pelagia felt herself flood with a kind of gratitude, and she took his hand and kissed it. The doctor squeezed her hand and said sadly, 'I don't know how I'll manage when you've gone.'

'Papakis, he's asked me to marry him . . . I told him that

he'd have to ask you.'

'I don't want to marry him,' said Dr Iannis. 'It would be a much better idea if he married you, I think.' He squeezed her hand again. 'We used to have some Arabs on one of my ships. They always said "inshallah" after every sentence; "I'll do it tomorrow, inshallah." It could be very annoying, because they seemed to expect God to do things when they couldn't be bothered themselves, but there is some wisdom in it. You will marry Mandras if that is what providence decrees.'

'Don't you approve of him, Papakis?'

He turned and looked at her gently. 'He's too young. Everyone is too young when they marry. I was. Also, I have not done you a favour. You read the poetry of Cavafy, I have taught you to speak Katharevousa and Italian. He isn't your equal, and he would expect to be better than his wife. He is a man after all. I have often thought that you would only ever be able to marry happily with a foreigner, a dentist from Norway or something.'

Pelagia laughed at the incongruous thought, and fell silent. 'He calls me "Siora",' she said.

'I was afraid of something like that.' There was a long pause whilst they both gazed at the stars over the mountain, and then Dr Iannis asked, 'Have you ever thought that we should emigrate? America or Canada or something?'

Pelagia closed her eyes and sighed. 'Mandras,' she said.

'Yes. Mandras. And this is our home. There isn't any other. In Toronto it is probably snowing, and in Hollywood no one would give us a part.' The doctor stood up and went inside, re-emerging with something in his hand that gleamed metallically in the semi-darkness. Very formally he handed it to his daughter. She took it, saw what it was, felt its ominous weight, and dropped it into the lap of her skirts with a small cry of horror.

The doctor remained standing. 'There's going to be a war. Terrible things happen in wars. Especially to women. Use that to defend yourself, and if necessary use it against yourself. You may also use it against me if that is what circumstances demand. It's only a little derringer, but . . .' he

103

waved his hand across the horizon, '. . . a terrible darkness has fallen across the world, and every one of us must do what we can, that's all. Maybe you don't know it, koritsimou, but it might happen that your marriage will have to wait. We must make sure first that Mussolini does not invite himself to the wedding.' The doctor turned on his heel and went into the house, leaving Pelagia to the fear that was growing in her breast, and to a most unwelcome solitude. She remembered that in the mountains of Souli, sixty women had gone to one of the peaks, danced together, and thrown their children and themselves over the precipice rather than surrender to the slavery of the Turks. After a few moments she went to her room, put the derringer under her pillow, and sat on the edge of her bed, absently caressing Psipsina and imagining once again that Mandras was dead.

On the second day after the feast Pelagia repeated the same slow ballet of pointless tasks that failed to counterbalance the absence of her lover, but became instead a kind of frame to it. Everything – the trees, Lemoni playing, the goat, the antics of Psipsina, the self-important, cumbersome waddle of Father Arsenios, the distant hammering of Stamatis as he made a wooden saddle for a donkey, Kokolios' raucous rendition of the 'Internationale' with half the words missing – all was nothing but a sign of what was missing. The world retreated and gave place to a pall of hopelessness and dejection that seemed to have become a property of things themselves; even the lamb with rosemary and garlic that she prepared for dinner embodied nothing other than a poignant lack of fish. That night she felt too exhausted and dispirited to cry herself to sleep. In her dreams she accused Mandras of cruelty and he laughed at her like a satyr, and danced away across the waves

On the third day Pelagia went down to the sea. She sat on a rock and watched an enormous warship steam portentously away to the west. It was most probably British. She thought about war and felt her heart grow heavy, reflecting that in the old days men were the playthings of the gods, and had advanced no further than to become the toys of other men who thought that they themselves were gods. She played with the euphony of words; 'Hitler, Attila, Caligula. Hitler, Attila, Caligula.' She found no word to accompany 'Mussolini' until she came up with 'Metaxas'. 'Mussolini, Metaxas,' she said, and added, 'Mandras.'

As though answering her thoughts, a movement caught the corner of her eye. Below, to the left, a body was diving about in the waves like a human dolphin. She watched the brown fisherman with a pleasure that was entirely aesthetic, until she realised with a small shock that he was completely naked. He must have been a hundred metres away, and she knew that he was arranging a buoyed net with a mesh tiny enough to catch whitebait. He was diving for long moments, arranging his net in a crescent, and all about him the gulls wheeled and plunged for their share of the harvest. Guilefully, but without guilt, Pelagia crept closer in order to admire this man who was so sleek, so at one with the sea, so much like a fish, a man naked and wild, a man like Adam.

She watched as the net was curled about the shoal, and, as he stood glistening on the beach, hauling hand over hand, his muscles tightening and his shoulders rhythmically working, she realised that it was Mandras. She put her hand over her mouth to suppress her shock and a sudden access of shame, but she did not creep away. She was still transfixed by his beauty, by the harmony and strength of his work, and could not resist the idea that God had given her a chance to look over what was hers before she took possession of it; the slim hips, the sharp shoulders, the taut stomach, the dark shadow of the groin with its mysterious modellings that were the subject of so much lubricious female gossip at the well. Mandras was too young to be a Poseidon, too much without malice. Was he a male seanymph, then? Was there such a thing as a male Nereid or Potamid? Should there not be a sacrifice of honey, oil, milk, or a goat? Of herself? It was difficult to witness Mandras slipping through the water and not believe that such a creature would not, as Plutarch said, live for 9,720 years. But this vision of Mandras possessed a quality of eternity, and

Plutarch's imputed span of life seemed too arbitrary and too short. It occurred to Pelagia that perhaps this same scene had been enacted generation after generation since Mycenean times; perhaps in the time of Odysseus there had been young girls like herself who had gone to the sea in order to spy on the nakedness of those they loved. She shivered at the thought of such a melting into history.

Mandras reeled in his net and bent over to busy himself with extracting the tiny fish from the mesh, throwing them into a line of buckets arranged in a neat row upon the sand. The silver fish flashed in the sun like new knives, transforming their asphyxiation into a display of beauty as they flicked and leapt against each other and died. Pelagia noticed that his shoulders had peeled raw, and had not hardened to the sun despite an entire summer's exposure. She was surprised, even disappointed, for it revealed that the lovely boy was made only of flesh, and not of imperishable gold.

He stood up, placed two fingers in his mouth, and whistled. She saw that he was looking out to sea, waving his arms in a slow semaphore above his head. Vainly she tried to descry the object of his attention. Puzzled, she raised her head a little higher above the rock behind which she had concealed herself, and glimpsed three dark shapes curving in unison through the waves towards him. She heard his cry of pleasure and watched him wade towards them with three larger fish in his hands. She saw him throw the fish high into the air, and the three dolphins leap and twist to catch them. She saw him grasp a dorsal fin and sweep out to sea.

She ran down to the edge of the sand and furrowed her brow in a desperate attempt to exclude the scintillating and shifting darts of light that the sun threw from the water, but could see nothing. Surely Mandras was drowned? She remembered suddenly that it was terribly bad luck to see a nymph naked; it caused delirium. What was happening? She wrung her hands and bit her lip. The sun burned her forearms with an intensity that amounted to vindictiveness, and she clasped them anxiously to her chest. She hovered for a few more moments on the shore, and then turned and ran home.

In her room she hugged Psipsina and wept. Mandras was drowned, he had gone away with the dolphins, he was never going to come again, it was the end of everything. She complained to the pine marten about the injustice and futility of life and submitted to the rasping tongue as it relished the saltiness of her tears. There was a discreet knock on the door.

Mandras stood, smiling diffidently, in his hand a bucket of whitebait. He shifted from one foot to another, and spoke all in a rush: 'I'm sorry I didn't come sooner, it's just that I was ill the day after the feast, you know, it was the wine, and I wasn't very well, and yesterday I had to go into Argostoli to get my call-up papers, and I've got to go to the mainland the day after tomorrow, and I've spoken to your father in the kapheneion, and he's given his consent, and I've brought you some fish. Look, some whitebait.'

Pelagia sat on the edge of her bed and went numb inside; it was too much happiness, too much desolation. Officially engaged to a man who was going to wrestle with fate, to a man who should have drowned in the sea, a man who jumbled a marriage together with whitebait and war, a man who was a boy who played with dolphins and was too beautiful to go away to die in the snows of Tsamoria. He seemed suddenly to have become a dream-creature of frightening and infinite fragility, something too exquisite and ephemeral to be human. Her hands began to shake; 'Don't go, don't go,' she pleaded, and remembered that it was bad luck to see a nymph naked, that it brought about delirium, and occasionally death.

14

GRAZZI

I HAVE HAD many regrets in my life, and I suppose that everyone else can say the same. But it is not as if I regret little things, childish things, things like arguing with my father or flirting with a woman who was not my wife. What I regret is having had to learn a most bitter lesson about the way in which personal ambitions can lead a man, against his will and against his nature, into playing a part in events that will cause history to heap him with opprobrium and contempt.

I had a very nice job, and it was pleasant to be the Italian Minister in Athens, for the very simple reason that Colonel Mondini and I had no idea until the war started that there was going to be a war at all. You would think that Ciano or Badoglio or Soddu would have told us, you would think that they would have given us a month or two to prepare, but no, they let us carry on with the normal pleasantries of diplomacy. It infuriates me that I was attending receptions, going to plays, organising joint projects with the Minister of Education, reassuring my Greek friends that the Duce had no hostile intentions, telling the Italian community that there was no need to pack, and then find that no one had ever bothered to tell me what was going on, so that I had no time to pack myself.

All I had was rumours and jokes to go on. At least, I thought they were jokes. Curzio Malaparte, that idiotic snob with the ironic and twisted sense of humour and the lust for wars to fuel his journalism, came to see me, and he said, 'My dear friend, Count Ciano, told me to tell you that you can do what you like, because he's going to make war on Greece all the same, and that one day soon he's going to lead Jacomoni's Albanians into Greek territory.' It was the way he said it, wryly and mocking, that made me think it was a joke, as well as the fact that this cockatoo will say anything whatsoever, however ridiculous, untruthful, or inconsequential, as long as it contains something to indicate that he is a personal friend of Ciano.

The only other thing that I had to go on was when Mondini was called to the airport to meet an intelligence officer, who told him that war was going to break out within three days, and that Bulgaria would invade at the same time. He told Mondini that all the Greek officials had been bribed. Naturally I telegraphed Rome and I also spoke to the Bulgarian ambassador. Rome did not reply, and the Bulgarian ambassador (rightly as it turned out) told me that Bulgaria had no intention whatsoever of declaring war. I was reassured, but I think now that Ciano and the Duce were just trying to confuse me or keep their own options open. Perhaps they were trying to confuse each other. Colonel Mondini and I sat in my office, oppressed by the deepest gloom imaginable, and we discussed the idea of returning to private life.

Things became increasingly incomprehensible. For example, Rome asked me to send a member of my legation for 'Urgent confidential instructions', but Ala Littoria wasn't providing any flights, so nobody could go. Then the Palazzo Chigi telegraphed to say that a courier was coming by special flight, and whoever it was never arrived. Everyone in the diplomatic community in Athens was making representations to me to do something about preventing a war, and all I could do was blush and stammer, because I was in the untenable position of being an ambassador who didn't have a single notion of what was happening. Mussolini and Ciano humiliated me, and I will never forgive them for forcing me to rely on the propaganda of the Stefani Agency as my sole source of information. Information? It was all lies, and even the Greeks knew more about the impending invasion than I did.

What happened was this; the Greek National Theatre put on a special show of *Madama Butterfly*, and they invited Puccini's son and his wife as guests of the government. It was a wonderful gesture, a typically noble and Greek thing to do, and we issued invitations to a reception on the night of October 26th, after midnight. Receptions after midnight are a Greek habit I never quite adjusted to, I must confess.

Metaxas and the King did not come, but it was a very fine party all the same. We had an enormous gateau with 'Long Live Greece' iced onto it, and we had the tables laid with the Greek and Italian flags, intertwined to symbolise our friendship. We had poets, playwrights, professors, intellectuals, as well as representatives of society and the diplomatic community. Mondini looked splendid in his full dress uniform covered with medals, but I noticed that as the telegrams began to flood in from Rome he was growing pale and seemed visibly to shrink inside his tunic until it looked as though he had disavowed it or borrowed it from someone else.

It was a horrible situation. The people with the telegrams had to pretend to be guests, and as I read them, one after another, my heart sank to my boots. I had to make small-talk with people as I became steadily overwhelmed by a wave of horror and disgust. I felt ashamed for my government, I felt anger at having been kept in ignorance, I felt embarrassment before my Greek friends, and over and over again I heard the same sentence repeating itself in my head – 'Don't they know what war is?' A novelist asked me if I was quite well, because I had turned very pale and my hands were shaking. I looked from face to face and saw that everyone in our legation had experienced the same reaction; we were dogs who had been commanded to bite the hand that fed us.

The first part of the Duce's ultimatum arrived last, and I did not know exactly what was transpiring until five o'clock in the morning. I was tired and sick, and I don't know if I was relieved or pained by the instruction not to deliver it until 3 a.m. on the 28th, and wait for a reply until 6 a.m. It seemed that the 'Unsleeping Dictator' (who, I happen to know, used to sleep rather a lot) was determined not only to unleash havoc, but to keep us from our beds.

On the 27th the Greek Chief-of-Staff summoned Mondini in order to deny that the border incidents and the explosion at Santi Quaranta were anything to do with Greece. Mondini came back very depressed and told me that Papagos had humiliated him by asking a single pertinent question: 'By what miracle do you know that we did these things when no one knows who it was and no one has ever been caught?' Mondini tried to placate him by saying that it was probably the British, whereupon Papagos laughed and said, 'I suppose you are aware that every yard of the border is guarded by Greek patriots who will fight to the last drop of blood?' Mondini shared my sense of shame and impotence; Badoglio had not kept him informed. Badoglio later told me that he himself was not informed, despite being our Chief-of-Staff at home – was there ever another war when the Commander-in-Chief did not know that there was going to be one? Mondini and I discussed resignation again, whilst outside the Athenians went about their usual clamorous business. It was a beautiful, warm, splendidly autumnal day, and Mondini and I both knew that soon this beauty and this peace were going to be torn apart by sirens and bombs; it was too revolting, even sacrilegious, to contemplate. We began to receive ashen-faced delegates from the Italian community in Athens, who feared internment and persecution in the event of war. I was obliged to lie to them, and I sent them away with my heart bleeding. As it turned out, the Greeks very honourably tried to evacuate them, and at Salonika they were bombed by mistake by our own air force.

My interview with Metaxas was the most painful occasion of my life, and afterwards I was repatriated, but I didn't see Ciano until November 8th. You see, the campaign was already a fiasco, and Ciano didn't want me to say 'I told you so'. He didn't really want to see me at all, and he kept interrupting and changing the subject. In my presence he telephoned the Duce and told him that I had said things that I had not, and then he told me that the Albanian campaign would be over in two weeks. Later on, when I had started to make a fuss about the truth of the matter, he sent Anfuso to advise me to go on a holiday, and I suppose that that was the end of my career.

You want to know about my interview with Metaxas? Isn't that famous enough already? I don't like to talk about it much. You see, I admired Metaxas, and the truth is that we were friends. No, it's not true that Metaxas just said 'No.' O, all right, I'll tell you.

We had a Greek chauffeur, I can't remember his name, and we sent him home so that it was Mondini who drove us to the villa at Kifisia. De Santo came along to interpret, though he wasn't needed in the event. We left at 2.30 a.m., with stars shining like diamonds above us, and it was so mild that I didn't even have to button my coat. We arrived at the villa, a modest little place in the suburbs, at about 2.45, and the commander of the guard got muddled – he must have mistaken our Italian tricolor for the French one – and he telephoned Metaxas to say that the French ambassador wanted to see him. It would have been comical on any other occasion. As I waited I listened to the rustling of the pines and tried to spot the owl that was hooting in one of the trees. I felt sick.

Metaxas came to the service door himself. He was very ill, you know, and he looked quite small and pathetic, he looked like a little bourgeois who has come out to collect the newspaper or call the cat. He was wearing a nightgown that was covered in a pattern of white flowers. Somehow one expects the night attire of the eminent to be more dignified. He squinted up into my face, saw that it was me, and exclaimed with pleasure, 'Ah, monsieur le ministre, comment allez-vous?' I can't remember what I said in reply, but I knew that Metaxas suspected that I had come to give him the kiss of Judas. He was dying by then, as I expect you know, and the burden on his soul must already have been unimaginably great.

We went to a little sitting-room that was full of cheap furniture and those little gewgaws that every middle-class Greek seems to love. Metaxas was an honest politician, you

112

see. He was never accused of corruption even by his enemies, not even by the Communists, and it was obvious from his house that state funds had never contributed towards its embellishment. There could not have been a man more different from the Duce.

He put me in a leather armchair. I heard later that Metaxas' widow never let anyone sit in it again. He sat on a couch that was covered in cretonne. We spoke entirely in French. I told him that I had been commanded by my government to hand over an urgent note. He took it, and read it very slowly, over and over again, as though it were intrinsically unbelievable. He made that click of the tongue that Greeks employ to signify refusal, and he began to shake his head.

The note said that Greece had openly sided with the British, that she had violated the duties of neutrality, that she had provoked Albania . . . and it concluded with these words that I shall never forget:

'All this cannot be tolerated by Italy any further. The Italian government has therefore decided to ask the Greek government, as a guarantee of Greek neutrality and of Italian security, for permission to occupy some strategic areas on Greek territory for the duration of the present conflict with Great Britain. The Italian government asks the Greek government not to oppose such occupation and not to place obstacles in the way of the free passage of troops that are to carry out this task. These troops do not come as enemies of the Greek people, and by the occupation of some strategic points, dictated by contingent and purely defensive necessities, the Italian government in no way intends to prejudice the sovereignty and independence of Greece. The Italian government asks the Greek government immediately to give the orders necessary to enable this occupation to take place in a peaceful manner. Should Italian troops meet with resistance, such resistance would be broken by force of arms, and the Greek government would assume responsibility for the consequences that would ensue.'

Metaxas' spectacles misted over, and behind them I could see tears. It is a hard thing to see a powerful man, a dictator, reduced to this state. His hands shook a little; he was a hard man, but passionate. I sat there opposite him, my elbows on my knees, and I was bitterly ashamed of the folly and injustice of this escapade in which I had become embroiled. I too wanted to weep. He looked up at me and said, 'Alors, c'est la guerre.'

So you see, he didn't say 'okhi' as the Greeks believe; it was not as simple as 'No,' but it meant the same. It had the same resolve and the same dignity, an identical finality.

'Mais non,' I said, knowing that I was lying, 'you can accept the ultimatum. You have three hours.'

Metaxas raised an eyebrow, almost with sympathy, because he knew that I was not cut out for dishonour, and replied, 'Il est impossible. In three hours it is impossible to awaken the King, summon Papagos, and get orders to every outpost on the border. Many of them have no telephone.'

'Il est possible, néanmoins,' I insisted, and he shook his head; 'Which strategic parts do you wish to occupy?' He placed a sarcastic emphasis upon the word 'strategic'. I shrugged my shoulders in embarrassment, and said, 'Je ne sais pas. Je suis désolé.'

He looked at me again, this time with a trace of amusement in his eyes: 'Alors, vous voyez, c'est la guerre.'

'Mais non,' I repeated, and told him that I would wait until 6 a.m. for his final answer. He accompanied me to the door. He knew that we intended to occupy all of Greece whatever his reply, and he knew that if he fought us he would finish by having to fight the Germans. 'Vous êtes les plus forts,' he said, 'mais c'est une question d'honneur.'

It was the last time that I ever saw Metaxas. He died on January 29th of a phlegmon of the pharynx that had turned into an abscess and led to toxaemia. He died wishing that the British had been able to send him five divisions of armour, without which he had nonetheless succeeded in transforming our Blitzkrieg into an ignominious retreat.

I had left him standing there in his flowery gown, a little man who was ridiculous in the eyes of most of the world, a little man, accursed with a notorious and intransigent daughter, unelected, who had just spoken to me with the voice of the entire people of Greece. It was Greece's finest hour and my country's most disgraceful. Metaxas had earned his place in history amongst liberators, caesars and kings, and I was left diminished and ashamed.

There, I have told you what happened. I hope you're satisfied.

15

L'OMOSESSUALE (4)

WE DID NOT report back to Colonel Rivolta because we had not been instructed to. We were expected to be dead. But the dispatches were full of accounts of 'border incidents' perpetrated by the Greek 'lackeys of the British'. The Army was gripped by a grim sense of outrage, and everyone except Francesco and me was straining at the leash. We kept quiet. We thought it miraculous that we had not been given a machine-gun that would jam after the first shot.

But we often talked to each other, and our complicity deepened our sense of mutual isolation. We felt a terrible sense of betrayal long before it became the foremost emotion in the breast of every one of our soldiers in the mountains of Epirus. We received medals for what we had done and were ordered not to wear them. We were ordered not to tell anyone that we had won them. We had been tricked into becoming accomplices to murder, and we would not have worn them anyway. Francesco and I made a pact that one day one of us would put a bullet through the brain of Colonel Rivolta.

I wanted to desert, but I did not want to leave my beautiful beloved. In any case it was a physical impossibility, since I would have had to have trekked across mountain ranges, through uninhabitable wastes. I would have had to find my way across the sea to Italy. And then what? Be arrested? The only path I considered seriously was crossing the border into Greece. I would have become the first of the many Italian soldiers who joined the anti-Fascist alliance.

My plans were pre-empted by events. Our unanticipated success had obviously impressed somebody, because Francesco and I were temporarily withdrawn from our unit and sent to a top-secret training camp near Tirana. We arrived there after a journey much of which was again on foot, in the expectation of being trained for commando operations. I will admit that both of us were excited by this prospect, as any young man would have been in our situation.

Imagine our consternation and disbelief when we turned up and found that we were instructors. Imagine the immensity of our misgivings when we were told to train one hundred and fifty Albanians in the art of sabotage. Imagine our incredulous hilarity when we got drunk and talked the situation over. How could it happen to us? We had done one operation and were supposed to be experts. These Albanians were outrageous and hyperbolical Balkan brigands, and not one of them spoke a word of Italian. We did not speak Albanian. We had about a week in which to train them.

The project was under the control of Jacomoni himself, and we were now fully party to an official conspiracy to create 'Greek' incidents which would give the Duce reasonable excuse to declare war. It was as cynical as that. No doubt the Duce thought that Greece would be an easy conquest that would supply him with something to set against the Blitzkrieg of Adolf Hitler.

The Albanian would-be commandos were all overweight, they all seemed to have enormous moustachios, they were all inebriates, they were all murderous, lecherous, rapacious, and incapable of work or honesty. They were nominally Muslims, which meant having to stop for prayer at inconvenient moments, but Francesco and I rapidly came to the conclusion that they had succeeded in remaining entirely untouched by religious or humane sentiments of any kind.

We took them on route marches, and Francesco and I were the only ones to arrive at the end. We taught them only to fire brief bursts from machine-guns, but they emptied entire belts at a time and buckled the barrels from over-

117

heating. We taught them unarmed combat, only to have knives drawn on us if we appeared to be winning. We taught them how to live off the land, only to find them sloping away to visit taverns in the middle of the night. We taught them how to destroy telegraph poles and telephone installations; one of them electrocuted himself in the penis by urinating on a transformer. We taught them how to eliminate watchtowers; we made them build one, and then they refused to practise destroying it because it had taken so much trouble to erect it in the first place. We taught them how to encourage a local population to rebel; the local populations rebelled only against our Albanians. The only things we successfully taught were how to assassinate generals, and how to create confusion by opening fire behind the lines; they proved this by shooting one of the camp guards and then shooting up a brothel with the intention of robbing the pimps. At the end of the training these commandos were paid very large sums of cash and released into Greek territory in order to begin the process of destabilising it. Without exception they disappeared with the money and were never heard of again. Francesco and I received more medals for our 'outstanding contribution', and were posted back to our unit.

A few more things happened. One of our own aircraft dropped 'Greek' pamphlets on us, encouraging the Albanians to revolt against us and join the British. We identified the aircraft as one of ours almost immediately, and some of our more stupid soldiers could not understand why we were encouraging our own people to defect. More of our frontier posts were attacked by our own people dressed as Greeks, and some Albanians had potshots taken at them to make them think that they needed us to protect them. Some Albanians actually shot at us as well, and we announced that they had been Greeks. The Governor-General arranged to have his own offices blown up so that the Duce could finally and definitively declare war. He duly did so, shortly after he had ordered a demobilisation that left us with too few troops and no reasonable expectation of reinforcements.

I have related these things as though they were amusing, but really they were acts of lunacy. We had been told that the Greeks were demoralised and corrupt, that they would desert to fight on our side, that the war would be a Blitzkrieg that would be over in seconds, that northern Greece was full of disaffected irredentists who wanted union with Albania; but we only wanted to go home.

I only wanted to be in love with Francesco. We were sent off to die, with no transport, no equipment, no tanks worthy of the name, an air force that was mainly in Belgium, insufficient troops, and no officers above the rank of colonel who knew anything about tactics. Our commander refused reinforcements because he would get more credit for a victory with a small army. Another idiot. I did not desert. Perhaps we were all idiots.

It fills me with incalculable bitterness and weariness to describe that campaign. Here in this sunny, secluded island of Cephallonia with its genial inhabitants and its pots of basil, it seems inconceivable that much of it ever happened. Here in Cephallonia I lounge in the sun and watch dancing competitions between the inhabitants of Lixouri and those of Argostoli. Here in Cephallonia I fill my dreams with reveries of Captain Antonio Corelli, a man who, full of mirth, his mind whirling with mandolins, could not be more different from the vanished and beloved Francesco, but whom I love as much.

How wonderful it was to be at war. How we whistled and sang as frantically we prepared to move, as motorcycle couriers sped back and forth like bees, how exhilarating it was to cross a foreign border unopposed, how flattering it was to conceive of ourselves as the new legionaries of the new empire that would last ten thousand years. How gratifying it was to think that soon our German allies would hear of victories to equal theirs. What strength was gathered inside us as we boasted of our part in the famous Pact of Steel. I marched at Francesco's side, watching his limbs swing and the clear droplets of sweat run down the side of his face. From time to time he looked at me and smiled. 'Athens in two weeks,' he said.

The night of October 28th. With five days' worth of ammunition and carrying our own supplies for lack of mules, we were sent eastward to take the Metsovon pass. How indescribably light we felt when we took those packs from our backs at night! How we slept like babies, and how grindingly stiff were our limbs in the early light of morning! We heard that there would be no reinforcements because the sea was too rough and the British were sinking our ships. We sang songs about winning against all possible odds. We were reassured by the idea that we were under Prasca's direct command.

How wonderful it was to be at war, until the weather turned against us. We slogged through mud. Our aeroplanes were grounded by cloud. We were ten thousand men soaked to the bone. Our twenty heavy guns subsided into the morass, and our poor abused and beaten mules struggled unavailingly to extract them. We were assured that the Duce had decided on a winter campaign in order to avert the risk of malaria; we were not assured of winter clothing. The Albanian troops sent with us began to vanish into thin air. It became clear that the Bulgarians were not to fight on our side, and the Greeks brought in reinforcements from the Bulgarian border. Our lines of communication and supply became inoperable before a shot had even been fired. The Greek soldiers did not desert. My rifle began to rust. I was supplied with the wrong ammunition. We heard that we would get no air defence, and that a bureaucrat had ordered our Fiat 666 trucks back to Turin by mistake. It didn't matter. The trucks bogged down the same as the guns. Heels that once had clicked smartly in salute now came together with a sticky thud, and we began to yearn for the stinging yellow dust of October 25th. We trudged on, convinced of easy victory, still singing about being in Athens in two weeks. We had not yet fired a round.

We thought that the Greeks were not opposing us because their forces were weak and cowardly, and it elated us, in spite of everything. It occurred to none of us that they had foreseen our strategy and had gone into an elastic defence in order to concentrate their force. We clambered

120

through the inexorable rain and the clinging mud whilst above us the mist swirled about the titanic Mt Smolikas and the Greeks patiently waited.

How I hate puttees. I have never understood the purpose of them. I hated having to wrap them precisely in the regulation manner. Now I hated them for the way that they accumulated glutinous clods of yellow earth and filtered the freezing water down into my boots. The skin of my feet turned white and began to peel away. The hooves of the mules softened and flaked, but still they kicked up the slush that beslimed us from head to foot. Francesco and I entered a house with a photograph of King George and General Metaxas on the wall. We looted a raincoat and dry pairs of socks. There was a half-finished meal, still warm, and we ate it. Afterwards we spent hours worrying over whether or not it might have been poisoned and left deliberately. There were no Greeks, we were winning without fighting. We forgot about how some of us had used to shout anti-war slogans at the Fascist militiamen and beat them up whenever we encountered them in the dark.

We reached the River Sarandaporos and found that we had no bridge-building equipment and no engineers. It was a swollen torrent laden with a flotsam of blown-up bridges and the carcasses of mountain sheep. Francesco saved my life by coming after me when I was swept away during an attempt to get a gun across. It was the first time that he held me in his arms. We heard that someone had spotted some Greek troops vanishing into the forest. 'Cowards,' we laughed. We repeated the hell of the River Sarandaporos at the River Vojussa. Francesco said, 'God is against us.'

I hate puttees. At one thousand metres of altitude the water in them froze solid. When water freezes, it expands. This is an unremarkable commonplace, no doubt, but in the case of puttees the effect is twofold. The ice weighs pounds. The ice constricts the legs and the flow of blood to the feet is cut off. All sensation is lost. We longed for the squalid hovels that we had left behind us in Albania. We realised that our heavy guns had fallen miles behind and would probably never catch up. 'Athens in two months,' said

Francesco, twisting the corners of his mouth in the spirit of irony.

War is wonderful, until someone is killed. On November 1st the weather improved and a sniper shot our corporal. There was a crackling sound from the trees, and the corporal stepped back and flung up his arms. He pivoted towards me on one heel and fell back into the snow with a bright glistening spot in the centre of his forehead. The men threw themselves into prone positions and returned fire whilst a platoon circled up into the pines to find an enemy which had already disappeared. A mortar snapped, there was a whoosh as the bomb fell amongst us, a scream as the shrapnel tore through the legs of a poor conscript from Piedmont, and a terrible silence. I realised that I was covered with gory scraps of human flesh that were already freezing fast to my uniform. We gathered about the wounded and realised that we had no way to get them back behind the lines. Francesco put his hand on my shoulder and said, 'Shoot me through the head if I am wounded.'

The misprised Greeks had manoeuvred us into positions where we could be surrounded and cut off, and yet we very rarely saw them. We were trapped in the roads and tracks at the valley floors, and the Greeks flitted like spectres amongst the upper slopes. We never knew when we would be attacked, or from where. The mortar shells seemed at one moment to come from behind, at another to come from the flank or in front. We whirled like dervishes. We fired at ghosts and at mountain goats.

We were confounded by the heroism of the invisible Greeks. They rose out of dead ground and fell on us as though we were the rapists of their mothers. It shocked us. On Hill 1289 they terrified our Albanians so greatly that the latter fled, firing on the carabinieri who attempted to stop them. Ninety percent of that Tomor Battalion deserted. Our whole line was swivelled anti-clockwise with us as the pivot, cut off from both arms of our front. No air support. Greek soldiers in their British uniforms and Tommy helmets machine-gunned us, mortared us, and made themselves invisible. 'Athens in two years,' said Francesco. We were completely alone.

The Greeks took Samarini and were behind us. We ate nothing but dry biscuits that flaked like scrofula. Our horses began to die, and we began to eat them. The little Greek horses carried their cavalry above us, and were too tough to die. We were ordered to retreat to Konitsa and had to fight our way backwards through the soldiers that had encircled us.

We had become anonymous. We grew immense beards, we were buried in storms of sleet, our bloodshot eyes sank deep into our heads, our uniforms disappeared beneath an encrustation of icy clag, our hands were torn as though by cats, and our fingers curled up into leaden clubs. Francesco looked the same as me, and I looked like everyone else; our life was neolithic. Within the space of a few days we had become skeletons, rooting for food like pigs.

We saw an Italian bomber at long last. We waved to it, it circled, and it dropped a bomb that narrowly missed us, but killed three of our mules. We cut off their flesh in strips, and ate them raw whilst they were yet warm and quivering with life. The radios packed up. It became clear that the Greeks were massing their troops in the very places where we were most weak. They began to pick off isolated detachments and take them prisoner. 'Lucky bastards,' said Francesco, 'I bet it's hot in Athens.' At night he and I slept huddled up together for warmth. I was too exhausted for lust. We all slept like that. I wanted only to protect him.

Our commander was sacked and replaced by General Soddu, whom, inevitably, we nicknamed 'General Sodomia'. Visconti Prasca then lost his post commanding the Eleventh Army. How the mighty are fallen! He was a meteor who had turned out to be an incandescent fart. All our commanders were incandescent farts, starting with Mussolini who picked them.

We retreated towards Konitsa like a wounded giant tormented by wild packs of infuriated dogs. It was an inferno of machine-guns and artillery, mortars and ice. The civilian population hunted us with sporting rifles and slings. An entire week passed without food or respite. Battles at point-blank range were fought for eight hours at a time. We lost hundreds of comrades. The mountains became a congregation of the dead. We fought on, but we lost our hearts. A great darkness had settled across the land. Francesco talked to his mouse even during the ambushes and sudden enfilades, and all of us were on the verge of madness. We reached our old position at Perati bridge, having sacrificed in vain a fifth of our number. I looked around and felt the palpable horror of the irrecoverable absence of the men that I had come to love and whose indomitable courage nobody should ever doubt or carelessly impugn. War is a wonderful thing. In movies and in books. Gladiators, Wellingtons and Blenheims began to appear in the sky over our heads, and so the British added their strength to the Greek daggers twisting in our wounds. General Soddu inspected us and compared us to granite. 'Does granite bleed,' asked Francesco, 'on Golgotha?'

16

LETTERS TO MANDRAS AT THE FRONT

(1)

Agapeton,

I have heard nothing from you for such a long time, you have not written since that sad day that I saw you off from Sami. I have written to you every day, and I am beginning to suppose that you never got my letters, or that your replies do not reach me on account of the war. Yesterday I wrote the best one, that said everything perfectly, and believe it or not, the goat ate it. I was furious and I beat it on the head with my shoe. It would have made a funny picture, and I know that you would have laughed if you had seen it. All the time I see things, and wish that you were here to see them with your own eyes. I try to see things for you, and remember them, and I have a fantasy that if I concentrate hard enough I can send them to you so that you might see them in your dreams. If only life could be like that.

I am so terrified that I am not getting letters from you because you have been wounded or taken prisoner, and I have nightmares that you are dead. Please, please write to me so that I can breathe again and so that my heart can find some peace. Every day I wait for people to come back from Argostoli with the post for the village, and I run out, and every day there is nothing, and I feel desperate and helpless, and I am burning my brains with worry. Now that it is December the days here have turned very cold, there is no sun, and it rains almost every day, so that I fancy that the sky weeps as I weep. I shudder to think how cold it must be in the mountains of Epirus. Did you get the socks that I made for you, and the fisherman's sweater, and the scarf? Did you think it clever of me to dye them khaki? Or was I stupid not to make them white? I hope that you got the coffee and the jar of honey and the smoked meat. My poor darling, how you must suffer in that cold, in that place so far away and wild that it is almost a foreign country. How you must miss your boat and your dolphins; did you realise that I knew about your dolphins, who have no friend to feed fish to them until you return?

Everything here is much the same, except that we are beginning to go short of things. Yesterday I couldn't get oil for the lamps, and last week there was no flour to make bread. My father has made lamps by threading a wick through a cork and floating it in a bowl of olive oil, which he says was what we did in ancient times, but the light is poor, they are very smokey, and the smell unpleasant. Who would have thought that one could get nostalgic for kerosene?

Everyone comments on how silent and dismal the place is now that all the young men have gone, and we all wonder how many will return. I have heard that Dimos was killed and that Marigo's fiancé was taken prisoner. Whenever I hear such things I thank God that it wasn't you, even though it's a terrible thing to wish that misfortune should choose to fall on others. I couldn't bear it if you were killed. I think that I would die myself. I think that I would make an offer to God to take me in your place, if only you might live. We women are ashamed that we can make no sacrifice comparable with yours, but each one of us would take up a rifle and join you if only it were possible or permitted. Papakis has given me a small pistol, and I sleep with it under my pillow at night, and have it in the pocket of my apron by day. If this island is invaded, there are women and old men here who would fight to the death with broomsticks and kitchen knives, and already we are accustomed to doing those things that used to be done by the men. The only thing we don't do is sit around in the kapheneion and play backgammon. We go to church quite a lot, and Father Arsenios has made many fine and moving speeches to us. He tells us that an icon of the St John appeared all by itself outside a cave that was used by Gerasimos, and it has been declared a genuine archeiropoieton. Even God, it seems, sends us messages and shows that we are in the right. Somebody pointed out to me the other day that we are the only country still fighting, apart from the British Empire. When I think of this, I take heart, because it is the biggest empire that the world has ever seen, and, if this is so, how can we lose? I often see the British warships, and they are so big that you would think that it was not possible to sail them. I know that we will win.

All the news from the front is so good that our victory seems already assured. Every day we hear of more Italian armies driven back or defeated, and we feel the jubilation of David with Goliath dead at his feet. Who would have believed it only two months ago? It seemed an impossibility. We sent you away to resist them for the sake of honour, but without hope of success, and now we wait to welcome you home as conquering heroes. All of Greece is bursting with pride and gratitude for our men who are greater than Achilles and Agamemnon put together. There is talk that you have won back all the land that was disputed in past times and that the Italians have been virtually expelled from Albania. How great you are, your names will live eternally in the hearts of Greeks, and the world will remember forever what happens when anyone dares to wound us. We are so proud, my Mandras, so proud. We walk with our heads high and remember the glorious past that was taken away from us by Romans and Turks, and which you and your comrades have returned to us at last. The day will come when we and the British Empire will stand together and say to the world, 'It was we who made you free,' and the Americans and the

Russians and the other Pontius Pilates like them will hang their heads and feel ashamed that all the glory came to us.

Everybody here has been moved by the spirit of the war. Papas, who hated Metaxas so much, and Kokolios, who is a communist, and Stamatis, who is a monarchist, are all united in acclaiming Metaxas as the greatest Greek since Pericles or Alexander, and all are united in praising the military success of Papagos. They work together to collect parcels for the troops, and my father even offered to go to the front to be a doctor. They turned him down when they found that he had learned everything on ships and has no qualifications on paper. You should have seen his fury. He stamped about the house, and I have never heard him say 'heston' so much or with so much venom. I am glad that he cannot go, but it is unfair, because even the rich people come to him instead of going to college doctors. He has a gift of healing like the saint, he only has to touch a wound and it begins to cure.

Mandras, you would be amused by the outbreak of fortune-telling that has occurred since the war began. Everyone consults their coffee cup to find out whether and when their cousins, brothers and sons will return, it has turned into an industry. Kokolios' wife read my cup and told me that someone would come from far away and change my life forever, and she said it so seriously, as if she didn't know that I know that she knows that I am waiting for you to return from far away.

There have been bad things happening to the Italian families on the island, and the authorities have had to intervene to prevent house-burnings and other such stupid acts of violence. Some hotheads in Lixouri even beat up an old man who has lived here for forty years and who hung our flag from his window. Why are people such animals?

You will be glad to know that Psipsina and the goat are both well. I'm glad anyway, and since we soon will be one, that means that you must be glad too. I hope that you will be glad to know that I have decided to make my own dowry. I think that my father has no sense of shame, and sometimes I feel very angry with him for refusing the very thing that is normal for every other girl. He is not fair because he is too rational. He thinks that he is a Socrates who can fly in the face of the custom, but I feel embarrassed every time that I meet a member of your family, and I cannot allow it to be thought that you are disapproved of, even though you aren't. I began to crochet a big cover for our marriage bed, but I had to unpick it because it went wrong and began to look like a dead animal. I am no good at womanly things because my mother died when I was too young, and now I am having to try to learn all the things that I should have grown up with. I am beginning with things for the bed, because that is where our life will begin, but afterwards I will make other things for the house to use on feast days and for when we have visitors. I get very bored with the crochet, but my comfort is that when you return you will find all the evidence of my love before you. I am thinking that it would be a fine thing if I made you a waistcoat embroidered with gold thread and flowers made in feston and fil-tiré so that you flash in the sunlight when you dance.

On Christmas Day the Italians bombed Corfu, and even my father was shocked by their godlessness. On the radio we hear that the British have sunk many of their ships. I hope it is so, but I hate to hear of such things nonetheless, because I cannot bear the waste of life and because my heart is heavy when I think of all the old whose children go to the grave before them. I have seen your mother in the agora, and she tells me that she has had no news of you either. She is so worried and her face is more lined than it was before. Please write to her, even if you do not write to me. I believe she suffers more than I do, if such a thing is possible.

Mandras, we haven't had fish since you left, and I am beginning to miss it. We eat nothing but beans, like the poor. My father says that they are very good for you, but they make the belly swell. On Christmas Day we had to do without kourabiedes and christopsomo and loukoumades, and it was a bleak occasion even though we did our best. Father Arsenios surprised us all by not getting drunk.

Remember that there are those here who love you and pray for you, and that all of Greece marches with you wherever you may be. Come back to us after the victory, so that things might be as they were before. Your dolphins wait for you, and your boat, and your island, and I wait for you too, who loves you so much and misses you as though you were a limb of my body that has been cut off. My darling, without you nothing is complete, and even when I feel happy my happiness hurts me.

Your loving fiancée, Pelagia, who kisses you with these words.

(2)

On St Basil's Day

Agapeton,

Still no word of you, and strangely enough I am beginning to get stoical about it. Panayis came back from the front with a hand missing, and he told me that it is too cold at the front for it to be possible to hold a pen at all. He says that he hasn't seen you, but I suppose that that is entirely unsurprising, since you aren't in the same unit. He is petitioning the King for the right to return to the front and carry on fighting, as he says that anyone can use a rifle with one hand. The potter on the road to Kastro says that he will make Panayis a new hand in clay that will look better than the original one and will be very strong, and Panayis told him to make it frostproof for when he returns to the battle. In fact he asked for two versions of the hand, one as a bunched fist for fighting with, and the other with the fingers curled so that he can use it to hold a glass. It wouldn't surprise me if he asks for a third one with a bayonet-fitting, he has such spirit.

This St Basil's Day has been better than Christmas. My

father gave me a book of poems and political writings by Andreas Laskaratos, saying that it was good for my soul to read things by someone who was excommunicated. I quoted that proverb to him 'mega biblion, mega kakon' (big book, big evil) and he threatened to take it away and give me a smaller one. I gave him a nice clasp-knife. We counted the seeds of a pomegranate to see whether or not this year would be plentiful. Not too bad, it seems. I managed to make a vasilopeta by swapping some ingredients with your mother, and my father gave me an English gold sovereign to put in it. He was very pleased when it didn't turn up in the slice for Christ or the one for St Basil, because he doesn't like to give money to the church. It turned up in mine, and so I get all the good luck for this year. Isn't that wonderful? I am hoping that it means that you will return.

I have started the waistcoat for you, but I have had to unpick the bedcover again because it was coming out even worse than before. I don't know what's wrong with me.

Nothing but good news from the front, everyone is so pleased that Mussolini is being cut down to size by our boys, he has learned 'me kinei Kamarinan' the hard way, has he not? We have heard that our boys are digging Italian tanks out of the snow and mud, and using them against their former owners. Bravo for us. And we hear that we have taken Argyrokastro, Korytsa and Aghioi Saranda, but we keep hearing sad rumours that Metaxas is not well.

Have you seen the new poster that is going up everywhere? In case you haven't, it shows one of our men striding forward with the hand of the Virgin guiding him by the elbow. She has exactly the same expression as the soldier, and the writing says: 'Victory. Freedom. The Virgin is with him.' We all think it's terribly good.

Father is making his moustache more patriotic by allowing it to get bushy. I am glad that he is not waxing it anymore, as it used to feel hard and spiky when I kissed his cheek. Now it tickles. I expect that you have grown a beard by now, just to keep your face warm.

131

Mandras, you really must write to your mother, she is so anxious. It is as much a question of philotimo as fighting for your country. Honour has many faces, and being good to your mother is one of them, I think. But I'm not criticising, I just think that perhaps you need reminding.

Your loving betrothed, Pelagia.

(3)

In the week of Apokrea

Agapeton,

This is my hundredth letter to you, and still we have heard nothing. Papakis says that no news is neither good nor bad news, and so I don't know whether to feel sad or reassured. I thank God that your name has never appeared in the list of the dead that is posted in Argostoli. You will be sorry to know that Kokolios has lost two of his sons (Gerasimos and Yanaros) and he has taken it very badly. His lip trembles when he talks, there are tears in his eyes, and he has taken to working so much that he even works after dark. He says that he doesn't blame the Italians but the Russians, who have not done their duty in opposing the Fascists. He says that Stalin cannot be a true Communist, and ever since the British Empire threw the Italians out of Somaliland and captured 200,000 in Libya, he has been walking around kissing a picture of Winston Churchill that he cut from a newspaper. The other day, when Papas heard about Hitler's ultimatum to us to stop fighting the Italians, he cut off his moustache altogether because even a big bushy patriotic moustache is too much like Hitler's. Ever since Metaxas died, Papas has worn a black armband, and he swears that he will not remove it until the war is over. We are all still very grieved by the old man's death, but we are resolved not to let it weaken us. We have the utmost faith that Papagos will lead us to

132

victory.

Well, there isn't much of a carnival this year, with all the young men gone, and it is as if we were in Lent already. We are all fasting whether we like it or not, and I can't see that Easter will be much of a feast either. It just won't be the same without dyed eggs and tsoureki and kokoretsi and mayeritsa and a lamb roasting on the spit. I expect we'll have the eggs, but apart from that we'll probably have to eat shoe-leather with avgolemono sauce. It makes my mouth water just thinking about all the things that we can't have, and I can't wait for everything to be normal again.

We have been having some awful tempests ever since December, and it has been very cold and windy. I have nearly finished your waistcoat, and although it is not as beautiful as I had hoped, it will be handsome enough. The foul weather gives me plenty of time to work at it, though it is not easy when one's hands are blue with cold. I got half way through the bedcover, but then Psipsina was sick on it, and I had to wash it. It didn't shrink, thanks be to God, but when I laid it out to dry the goat ate three mouthfuls from the middle. I was so angry that I actually beat it with a broomstick, and then Papas came out and found me in a storm of tears. I hit him too. You should have seen the look on his face. Anyway, I unpicked it yet again, and saved as much wool as I could, but I'm beginning to think that fate wants me to make something else.

I hope that you are well and cheerful, and I'm still looking forward to having you back, as are we all.

All my love, your Pelagia, who still misses you.

17

L'OMOSESSUALE (5)

THE BARI DIVISION took over from us in order to allow us to rest and regroup, but the Greeks came in with a curtain of flame and caught them before they had had time to bring up their artillery. We in the Julia Division were called back into the line to save them. It was as though a portion of my mind had disappeared, or as though my soul had diminished to a tiny point of grey light. I could think of nothing at all. I fought doggedly, I was an automaton without emotion or hope, and if I had any worry at all, it was that Francesco was becoming stranger. He had become convinced that he would one day be shot through the heart, and had therefore moved the mouse Mario from his breast pocket to a pocket on the sleeve of his shirt. He was concerned that the mouse would be shot when he was, and he made me promise to look after it when he was killed.

Our units became muddled up. Portions of other divisions were sent to ours. No one knew the exact hierarchy of local command. A novice battalion of partially trained boys from the country arrived at the wrong map reference and was annihilated by the Greeks. On November 14th the Greeks commenced an offensive whose ruthless fury we could not possibly have imagined in advance.

We were dug in with the Mrava Massif behind us. This means nothing unless you know that it was uninhabited, a savage place of ravines and chasms, crude and monstrous crags, roadless, a place through which our supplies could not be brought. We were in a land that the Greeks had always considered theirs by right, and which they had twice ceded by treaty. Now they wanted it back. We were wrapped in mist, enveloped in snow, and an accursed Arctic wind sprang up from the north that flung itself upon us like the bunched fist of a Titan.

They cut deep notches into our lines and we lost contact with other units. We had to retreat. There was nowhere to retreat to. The Brandt mortars of the enemy cut out entire platoons at a time. We had no bandages or field hospitals. A weeping chaplain extracted shrapnel from my arm without anaesthetic on the kitchen table of a roofless and ruined cottage. I was too cold to feel the knife dividing my flesh or the needle piercing my skin. I thanked God that I had been wounded and not Francesco, and was sent straight back into the fray. I found that the men from the mule trains had abandoned their animals and were fighting alongside us. Our officer had been killed and replaced by a major from the supply service. 'There are no supplies,' he told us, 'and so I have come to do my duty. I am relying on you for your good advice.' This admirable and honourable man, accustomed to stacking blankets and making inventories, lost his entrails in a bayonet attack that he was leading heroically with an empty pistol in his hand. We were utterly defeated.

I don't just hate puttees. I hate my entire uniform. The threads rotted and it fell apart. The cloth hardened like cardboard, and stiffened into adamantine inflexibility. It garnered the cold like a refrigerator and forced it into my flesh. It grew heavier and more abrasive by the day. I shot a goat and clothed myself in its uncured pelt. Francesco skinned a shattered mule and did the same. Koritsa was abandoned to the enemy, and we now had less territory than we had possessed when we started. We left behind our heavy equipment. It was worn out anyway. We became accustomed to the horrible ulceration and rank stench of gangrene. Whilst Koritsa was evacuated we in the Julia Division held on in Epirus. We were not so easily defeated. But then we retreated along the same roads by which we had advanced. The Centauro Division, for the sake of speed, left behind the tanks that had been sucked into the mud. The Greeks found these sad little rusty hulks, dug them out, repaired them, and used them against us. We were reinforced by a battalion of Customs Guards. For God's sake. We held a bridgehead at Perati. Pointlessly.

A small miracle; the Greeks allowed us a couple of days' rest. No doubt they thought that we must have mined the roads. Then we heard that we had lost Pogradec because the enemy had infiltrated the line by following the path of a mountain stream whilst our defences had been organised to defend the tracks. 'What's the use?' asked Francesco. 'We do our best, and everyone else fucks it up.' Then someone else's manoeuvre exposed our right flank and we were cut off from the Modena Division. Our General Soddu, who had replaced Prasca, was now replaced by Cavallero. It looked as though our glorious conquest of Greece was going to finish ignominiously with a Greek conquest of Albania. The snow fell relentlessly and we discovered that we could warm our heads by cutting out the brains of dying mules and putting them in our helmets. We realised that the only way to prevent continuous attack from above was to hold the high ground. The high ground was whipped by vicious winds that carried before them a stinging shield of crystals. My boots fell apart and I itched and squirmed with lice. I think it must have been Christmas when we finally understood that we were as broken as our boots.

Waking up in the morning, ten degrees below zero. The first question: who has frozen to death now? Who has slipped from sleep to death? The second question: how many swollen fords must we cross today, with the frost-fettering water gripping our testicles until they ache and scream? How many miles of waist-deep slush on the 'roads' today? The third question: how do the Greeks know to attack us when it is twenty degrees below and the slides of our rifles have jammed solid? The fourth question: why are the 'friendly' Albanians acting as guides to the Greeks? The fifth question: which unit has become so infinitely weary today that it has chosen to surrender to an inferior force? Not the Julia. Not us. Not yet. Francesco has stopped talking to me altogether. He talks only to his mouse. Another attack upon us by our own planes, a flight of SM79s; twenty dead. We hear that the officers of the Modena Division have received an order stating that those among them who do not show sufficient leadership will be shot. My own Colonel Gaetano Tavoni has been killed on Mali Topojanit, leading us in attack after sixty days without rest. God rest his soul and reward his care for us. The women of Italy begin to send us knitted gloves that soak up the water and freeze to our skin so that we cannot take them off. Francesco has received a panettone from his mother and is sharing it with the mouse Mario. He chips portions of it off with a bayonet. We hear that Ciano and the Fascist hierarchs have joined up and have patriotically chosen to go on bombing jaunts to Corfu, where there are no air defences.

How I hate puttees. These are the days of the white death. Undrained trenches. The ice expanding in the cloth, the blood cut off. We do not hate the Greeks, we fight them for reasons unclear and without honour, but we do hate the white death.

To be sure, there is no pain at first. Above the puttees the legs swell, and below the puttees the foot falls asleep. The legs turn lurid colours: shades of lilac, hints of purple, ebony black. Because I am a very big man I spend days carrying our afflicted boys back behind the lines. I am exhausted, bewildered by their cries of agony. I have replaced my puttees with the skin of cats rubbed on the inside with gun oil. I have impregnated my boots with candlewax. The water still penetrates and I live in fear of the white death. In the tents I hear the unearthly shrieks of amputation. I inspect my feet every few hours and massage them with goat-fat unfrozen over the heat of a match. I hear that in Africa Graziani has been defeated. We have thirteen thousand victims of the white death. Even the Greeks are petrified by cold; the attacks have abated. Francesco is undoubtedly mad. His mouth works continually, his beard has become a stalactite of ice, his eyes roll in his head and he does not recognise me. He shits himself deliberately in order to savour the momentary heat. All my love turns to pity. I make him mittens from a brace of rabbits, leaving the fat on the inside of the skin. He eats the fat. We have been reduced to one thousand men with fifteen machine-guns and five mortars. We have lost four thousand men. There is nothing in our lines but the white death, the bitter absence of our friends, the desolation of the wilderness.

In Klisura the wild and angry Greeks come against us. We who are exhausted and full of sorrow. Francesco talks to the mouse Mario: 'Athens in two weeks, a place in history for the mouse of Albania. The mouse who deposed a king. Mario the mouse. Mousey mousey mousey.' We can no longer stand and the Julia is beaten, our troops maddened and gangrenous, our bodies severed from our souls. The Lupi di Toscana Division come to help us and are defeated; they turn from wolves to hares and we call them the Lepri di Toscana. If the veterans of the Julia cannot win, what chance for the amateurs? They were sent without food into unknown places which did not correspond to the maps. They had no officer. They were attacked immediately. Sacrifice, sacrifice. Nothing but calvary upon calvary. They were sent to save us, and we saved them.

A counterattack. Failure. Loss of Klisura. A desperate message from Cavallero: 'Make this last attempt, I beg you in the name of Italy. I should come and die with you.' Fuck the name of Italy. Fuck the generals who never come and die with you. Fuck your confidence and your mendacious promises of reinforcements. Fuck your defeats which you snatch from the jaws of victory. Fuck this frivolous war we did not want and do not understand. Long live Greece if it means an end to this, this white death and this snow incarnadine, this ungrateful lethal cold, these trails of entrails, these shattered bones, these bellies void of food and torn by mortars and ripped by bayonets, these fingers paralysed, these model 91 rifles jammed, these young men broken, these innocent minds made mad.

We live in a perpetual daze. The snow has made everything unrecognisable so that we never know where we are. Is this the escarpment we were told to take? Is that a stream in that valley floor, somewhere six feet below the shimmering cloak of white? What mountain is that? Someone strip away the cloud, for the love of God, so that we can tell. Is this a road we are floundering upon, or a river? Don't worry, we'll know when we reach the source. Don't worry, if we go to the wrong place we might be captured, with any luck. Radio back to HQ that we've taken the objective; I don't know where this place is, but it's as good as any other. What does it matter? 'HQ on the radio, sir. They want a map reference.' 'Tell them to give me a map that corresponds to something on the ground, and I'll give them the reference. No, just pretend the radio's packed up.' 'Yes, sir.' 'What are you doing now, Corporal?' 'Pissing on my helmet to take the shine off, sir. It's camouflage, sir. You piss on it and rub it with mud.'

The Greeks march on Tepeleni and we in the Julia are sent to support the Eleventh Army. They give us nine thousand untrained reservists to bring us up to strength, and two hundred officers with no experience, plus some old retired officers who have forgotten their tactics and who do not understand the working of their weapons. These old warhorses huff their way up the slopes and die the same as anyone, coughing to death, face down in the mud, red bubbles frothing at their lips. The Greeks are fanatical but cool, wild yet full of purpose. They take the Golico, Monastery Hill, and Mt Scialesit, but we stop them before they invest Tepeleni. The Duce comes to visit us and receives the acclaim that has been demanded of us. I sit with Francesco and do not come out to cheer him. An offensive is begun which has the express purpose of forming a spectacle for our Duce, who stands at Komarit and preens himself whilst he watches his soldiers being sent, wave by wave, towards certain death. Vanity is the mother of perdition, Signor Duce.

Francesco writes a letter for me to give to his mother in the event of his death, believing that it would not pass the censors if sent by military mail:

Beloved Mother,

This letter comes by the hand of Carlo Guercio, who is a

139

true friend of mine and an old comrade who has gone with me through the gates of hell. Do not be frightened by how big he is, because he is a good and gentle man. His jokes have always made me laugh when times were hard, his hand has steadied me at times when I was afraid, and his arms have carried me when I was exhausted. I would like you to think of him as your own son, so that not everything will have been lost. He is loyal and true, there has never been a finer man, and he will make a better son to you than I did.

Dear Mother, I came into this war in a state of innocence, and I leave it so utterly wearied that I am contented to die. After this there could not be any life to speak of. I have come to understand that God did not make this world a garden, that the angels are not in charge of it, and that the body can be disowned. I feel that I have been dead for months, but that my soul has yet to find a time to leave. I kiss you and each of my sweet sisters, and I love you with all my strength. Tell my wife that I think of her always and carry her in my heart like a constant flame. Do not be sad. Francesco.

O, the things I do not tell Francesco's mother on that melancholy day in April when I deliver the letter.

that he was thinking about Pelagia and Mandras.

Ever since the latter had so abruptly departed, he had watched his daughter evolving through a series of emotions, all of which struck him as unhealthy and worrying. At first she had been in a whirl of panic and anxiety, and then in storms of tears. The tempests had given way to days of ominous and nervous calm, where she would sit by the wall outside as though expecting him to arrive at the bend of the road where he had been shot by Velisarios. Even when it was very cold she might be seen there with Psipsina curled up on her lap as she caressed the soft ears of the animal. Once she had even sat out there in the snow. Later on she had taken to remaining silently in the room with him, her hands motionless on her lap as tears followed each other silently down her cheeks. Suddenly she would be seized by a mood of compulsive optimism and activity, and would work furiously on a coverlet that she was making for her marriage bed, and then, just as abruptly, she would spring to her feet, cast her work to the ground, kick it, and proceed to dismantle it with a ferocity that amounted to violence.

As day succeeded day it became clear that not only had Mandras not written, but that he never would. The doctor scrutinised his daughter's face, and realised that she was becoming bitter, as though inferring with increasing certainty that Mandras could not love her. She permitted herself to be imprisoned in apathy, and the doctor diagnosed the evident symptoms of depression. He broke a lifetime's habit, and took to making her accompany him on his medical visits; he found her to be full of happy chatter one minute, and profoundly silent the next. 'Unhappiness conceals itself in sleep,' he told himself, and he sent her to bed early and let her sleep in the mornings. He sent her on improbable errands to places that were unfeasibly distant in order to ensure that physical tiredness would be a prophylactic against the inevitable insomnia of the young and miserable, and he made a point of telling her the funniest stories that he could remember from his years of listening to garrulous men in the kapheneion and in the wardrooms of ships. He perceived shrewdly that Pelagia's state of mind was such that she considered it both logical and dutiful that she should be sad, passive, and remote, and so he made a point not only of making her laugh against her will, but also of provoking her to fits of rage. He persistently took the olive oil from the kitchen in order to treat cases of eczema, and deliberately failed to replace it, considering it to be a triumph of psychological science when her exasperation led her to flail at his chest with her fists whilst he restrained her by grasping her shoulders.

Curiously, he felt a sense of shock when his treatment began to work, and he considered the resumption of her normal cheerful equanimity to be a sign that she had given up her passion for Mandras altogether. On the one hand he would have been glad of this, since he did not truly believe that Mandras would make a good husband, but on the other hand Pelagia was already betrothed, and the breaking of a betrothal would cause much shame and disgrace. The awful possibility occurred to him that Pelagia might finish up by marrying out of a sense of obligation to a man she no longer loved. The doctor found himself hoping guiltily that Mandras would not survive the war, and this led him to the uncomfortable suspicion that he was not as good a man as he had always deluded himself into believing.

All this was bad enough, but the war had caused any number of difficulties that he could not have foreseen. He could put up with the loss of supplies of things like iodine and calamine lotion, since there were alternatives that worked just as well, but there had been no supply of boracic acid ever since the outbreak of the war, since that particular substance had always come from the volcanic steam of Tuscany; it was the best drug he knew of for coping with infections of the bladder and foulness of the urine. Far worse than this, there were cases of syphilis that required bismuth, mercury, and novarsenobenzol. This latter had to be injected once a week for twelve weeks, and no doubt all the supplies had been diverted to the front. He cursed the singular pervert who had first contracted the disease by copulating with a llama, and the hispanic brutes who had brought it back from the New World after cutting a swathe of rape through the territories that they had subjugated.

Fortunately the excitement of the war had diminished the number of those with imaginary diseases, but nonetheless he had found himself running repeatedly to his medical encyclopaedia in order to find out how to cope without all those things upon which he had always relied. He had found his *Complete and Concise Home Doctor* (two massive volumes, cross-indexed, fifteen hundred pages, including everything from ptomaine poisoning to beauty tips on the care and shaping of the eyebrow) in the Port of London, and had even learned English in order to understand it. He had memorised it from front to back with even more enthusiasm and dedication than a Muslim learns the Koran in order to become a Hafiz. Even so, his memory of it had by now diminished somewhat, since he had only ever had to employ parts of it regularly and had come to the realisation that most afflictions pass away by themselves, regardless of anything that he might do. Mostly it was a question of turning up and looking suitably solemn whilst performing the rituals of inspection. Most of the exotic and thrilling afflictions that he had read about with so much morbid curiosity had never turned up at all in his part of the island, and he had realised that whereas Father Arsenios was a priest to the soul, he himself was little more than a priest to the body. Most of the truly interesting ailments seemed to occur in animals, and it always gave him the greatest pleasure to diagnose and cure the problems of a horse or an ox.

The doctor had not failed to notice that the war had had the effect of increasing his own importance, as it had that of Father Arsenios. In the past he had grown accustomed to his status as a fount of wisdom, but the questions had often been philosophical – Lemoni's father had once sent her to ask him why it was that cats cannot talk – but nowadays people not only wanted to know all about the politics and progress of the conflict, but needed urgently to ask his opinions about the optimum size and disposition of sandbags. He had not elected himself as a leader of the community, but had become one by a process of invisible franchise, as though an autodidact such as himself must possess uncommon common sense as well as recondite knowledge. He had become a kind of Aga to replace the Turkish ones that the island had once briefly possessed, except that, unlike the Ottoman headmen, he had no particular interest in lying about on cushions all day in between filling the orifices of pretty little catamites who would eventually grow up with similarly unnatural predilections for buggery, narcotics, and prodigious extremes of idleness.

The doctor heard Pelagia singing in the kitchen and took up his pen. He reached a finger to twirl his moustache, experienced a peculiar irritation when he remembered that he had shaved it off as a gesture of defiance against Hitler, and then looked down at the black armband that he had worn ever since the death of Metaxas. He sighed and wrote:

'Greece lies on both a geographical and cultural faultline that separates east from west; we are simultaneously a battleground and a site of cataclysmic earthquakes. If the islands of the Dodecanese are eastern, however, Cephallonia is undoubtedly western, whereas the mainland is simultaneously both without being entirely either. The Balkans have always been the instruments of the foreign policy of the Great Powers, and have failed since ancient times to reach even a resemblance to advanced civilisation because of the natural indolence, fractiousness and brutality of their peoples. It is true to say that Greece has fewer of the Balkan vices than other nations to the north and east, however, and it is also undoubtedly the case that, of all the Greeks, Cephallonians have the greatest reputations as wits and eggheads. Readers will remember that Homer came from these parts and that Odysseus was famed for his cunning. Homer also describes us as fierce and ill-disciplined, but we have never been accused of cruelty. There are occasional deaths due to disputes over property, but we possess little of the bloodlust that is the characteristic defect of neighbouring slavic peoples.

'The reason for our occidental orientation is that the island was occupied by the Turks for only twenty-one years, between 1479 and 1500, when they were expelled by a combined Spanish and Venetian force. They returned only for one raid, in 1538, when they left with thirteen thousand Cephallonians to be sold into slavery. The short period of their stay, combined with their genius for torpor and inertia, ensured that they left behind them no permanent legacy in cultural terms.

'Apart from this brief period, the island was Venetian from 1194 until 1797, when it was taken by Napoleon Bonaparte, the notorious warmonger and megalomaniac, who promised the island union with Greece, and then perfidiously annexed it.

'The reader will readily see that to all intents and purposes the island was Italian for about six hundred years, and this explains a great many things that may puzzle the foreigner. The dialect of the island is replete with Italian words and manners of speech, the educated and the aristocratic speak Italian as a second language, and the campaniles of the churches are built into the structure, quite unlike the usual Greek arrangement whereby the bell is within a separate and simpler construction near the gates. The architecture of the island is, in fact, almost entirely Italian, and is highly conducive to a civilised and sociable private life on account of the shady balconies, courtyards, and external stair-cases.

'The Italian occupation ensured that much of the development of the people was along western rather than eastern lines, even including the habit of poisoning inconvenient relatives (Anna Palaiologos killed John II in this way, for example), and our rulers were mainly ebullient and dishonest eccentrics in the authentic Italian mould. The first Orsini used the island for piracy, and repeatedly deceived the Pope. Under his tutelage the Orthodox bishopry was abolished, and to this day there is much animosity here towards Roman Catholicism, an animosity compounded by that faith's historical arrogance and its deplorable preoccupation with sin and guilt. There were installed the Italian customs of levying taxes in order to raise money for substantial bribes, of hatching plots and machinations of labyrinthine complexity, of arranging catastrophically inappropriate marriages of convenience, of merciless in-fighting, of family feuding, of swapping the island between one Italian despotate and another (so that for a while we were part of Naples), and finally, in the eighteenth century there was such a prodigious outbreak of violence between the leading families (the Aninos, Metaxas, Karoussos, Antypas, Typaldos, and Laverdos) that the authorities deported all the agitators to Venice and hanged them. The islanders themselves remained above all these quaint Italian perversities, but there was much intermarriage, and we lost the habit of wearing traditional dress long before this occurred in the rest of Greece. The Italians left us a European rather than an eastern outlook on life, our women were considerably freer than elsewhere in Greece, and for centuries they gave us an aristocracy that we could both lampoon and imitate. We were immensely pleased when they left, unaware that there were worse things in store, but on account of the length of their stay they were undoubtedly, along with the British, the most significant force that shaped our history and culture; we found their rule tolerable and occasionally amusing, and, if we ever hated them, it was with affection and even gratitude in our hearts. Above all, they had the inestimable merit of not being Turks.'

The doctor put down his pen and read over what he had just written. He smiled wryly at his last remarks, and reflected that under present circumstances it was unlikely that the gratitude was likely to survive. He went into the kitchen and moved all the knives from one drawer into another, so that Pelagia's anger would find a new occasion for catharsis.

It was easier to be a psychologist than to be an historian; he realised that he had just covered several hundred years in a couple of pages. He really would have to take it more slowly and relate the events at a properly scrupulous pace. He went back to his desk, gathered up the small sheaf of papers, went out into the yard, sniffed the air for intimations of impending spring, and stoically and resolutely fed the sheets one by one to Pelagia's goat. The doctor was distressed by its philistine capacity for digesting literature. 'Accursed ruminant,' he muttered, and decided to go to the kapheneion.

19
L'OMOSESSUALE (6)

FRANCESCO'S MOTHER WAS a small grey woman with a mole on one cheek and a brushing of black down upon her upper lip. She wore black, and all the time that I talked to her she twisted a duster in her hands. I could see that once she had been beautiful and that my beloved Francesco had inherited his looks from her; the same slavonic eyes, the same olive skin, the same jeweller's fingers. Francesco's wife was there too, but I could hardly bear to look at her; she had known the pleasure of his body in a way that I could never know. She sobbed in a corner whilst her mother kneaded the duster and questioned me.

'When did he die, Signor? Was it a good day?'

'He died on a fine day, Signora, with the sun shining and the birds singing.'

(He died on a day when the snow was melting and when, from beneath that carapace, there were emerging a thousand broken corpses, knapsacks, rusted rifles, water-bottles, illegible unfinished letters drenched in blood. He died on the day when one of our men realised that he had entirely lost his genitals to frostbite, put a rifle barrel into his mouth, and blew away the back of his head. He died on the day when we found a corpse with its trousers down, squatting against a tree, frozen solid in the act of straining against the intractable constipation of the military diet. Beneath the fundament of the dead man lay two tiny nuggets of blood-streaked turd. The cadaver wore bandages

148

in the place of boots. He died on a day when the buzzards came down from the hills and began to tear the eyes from those long dead. The Greek mortars were coughing over the bluff, and we were buried in the hail of mud. It was raining.)

'He died in action, Signor? Was there a victory?'
　'Yes, Signora. We charged a Greek position with bayonets and the enemy were expelled.'

(The Greeks had repelled us for the fourth time with a barrage of mortar fire. They had four machine-guns above us where they could not be seen, and we were being cut to pieces as we fell back. Eventually we received a command rescinding the order to take the position, since it was of no tactical significance.)

'Did he die happy, Signor?'
　'He died with a smile on his lips, and told me that he was proud to have done his duty. You should be pleased to have had such a son, Signora.'

(Francesco limped up to me in the trench with a wild expression in his eyes. He spoke to me for the first time in weeks. 'Bastards, bastards,' he shouted. He said, 'Look,' and he rolled up his trousers. I saw the purple ulcers of the white death. Francesco touched the rotting flesh with a glow of wonder in his eyes. He rolled his trouser back down again and said to me, 'It's enough, Carlo. It's too much. It's all over.' He clasped me in his arms and kissed me on both cheeks. He began to sob. I felt him trembling in my arms. He took the mouse Mario from his pocket and gave it to me. He took up his rifle and clambered up over the lip of the trench. I grabbed at his ankle to prevent him, but he struck me on the side of the head with the butt of his weapon. He advanced slowly on the enemy position, stopping to fire at every five paces. The Greeks perceived his heroism and did not return fire. They preferred to capture courageous men rather than to shoot them. A mortar shell fell next to him, and he disappeared beneath a shower of yellow clay. There was a long silence. I saw something stir where Francesco had been.)

'He died quickly, didn't he, Signor? He was not in pain?'
   'He died very quickly of a bullet through the heart. He can have felt nothing.'

(I put down my rifle and climbed out of the trench. The Greeks did not shoot at me. I reached Francesco and saw that the side of his head had been blown away. The pieces of skull looked grey and were coated in membrane and thick blood. Some of the fluid was bright red, and some of it was crimson. He was still alive. I looked down at him and my eyes were blinded with tears. I knelt and gathered him into my arms. He was so emaciated from the winter and the hardship that he was as light as a sparrow. I stood up and faced the Greeks. I was offering myself to their guns. There was a silence, and then a cheer came from their lines. One of them shouted hoarsely, 'Bravissimo.' I turned and carried the limp bundle back to my lines.

   In the trench Francesco took two hours to die. His gore soaked into the sleeves and flanks of my tunic. His shattered head was cradled in my arms like a little child and his mouth formed words that only he could hear. Tears began to follow each other down his cheeks. I gathered his tears on my fingers and drank them. I bent down and whispered into his ear, 'Francesco, I have always loved you.' His eyes rolled up and met mine. He fixed my gaze. He cleared his throat with difficulty and said, 'I know.' I said, 'I never told you until now.' He smiled that slow laconic smile and said, 'Life's a bitch, Carlo. I felt good with you.' I saw the light grow dim in his eyes and he began the long slow journey down into death. There was no morphia. His agony must have been indescribable. He did not ask me to shoot him; perhaps at the very end he loved his vanishing life.)

'What were his last words, Signor?'
   'He recommended himself to you, Signora, and he died

with the name of the Virgin on his lips.'

(He opened his eyes once and said, 'Don't forget our pact to kill that bastard Rivolta.' Later on, in a great spasm of pain, he grasped my collar with his hands. He said, 'Mario.' I took the little mouse from my pocket and placed it in his hands. In the ecstasy of his own death he clenched his fist so tightly that the little creature died with him. To be precise, its eyes came out.)

'Signor, where is he buried?'
   'He is buried on the side of a mountain that in spring is covered with tulips and receives the first light of the sun. He was buried with full military honours, and shots were fired over his grave by his comrades.

(I buried him myself. I dug a deep hole in our trench that filled instantly with ochre water. I loaded him with stones so that his corpse would not rise to the surface of the earth. I buried him in a place inhabited by gigantic rats and tiny goats. I stood over his grave and beat to death with a shovel the rats that arrived to dig for his corpse. I put the mouse Mario in his breast pocket, above his heart. I took his personal effects. They are in this bag that I shall leave with you. It contains a lucky stone from Epirus, a letter from his wife, the insignia of the 9th Regiment of Alpini, three medals for valour, and the wing feather of an eagle that he was delighted with when it fell in his lap on the way to Metsovon. It also contains a photograph of me that I did not know that he possessed.)

'Signor, as long as he did not die for nothing.'
   'Signora, we now have mastery of Greece with the help of our German allies.'

(We lost the war and were saved only when the Germans invaded from Bulgaria and opened a second front that the Greeks had no resources to defend. We fought and froze and died for the sake of an empire that has no purpose.

151

When Francesco died I held his broken head and kissed him on the lips. I sat there with tears of rage falling upon his atrocious wounds and vowed that I would live for both of us.

I took no part in the dismembering of Greece or in the shameful triumphalism of a conquest that was a victory only in name. The valiant Greeks fell before eleven hundred German panzers, which they faced with less than two hundred light tanks, many of them captured from us, and our glorious Italian advance consisted merely in following them as they retreated in a vain attempt to avoid the German encirclement.

I took no part in that iniquitous charade because, the day after I buried Francesco, I took a pistol that I had removed from a wounded Greek, and in a moment of cold calculation I shot myself through the flesh of the thigh.)

20

THE WILD MAN OF THE ICE

PELAGIA RETURNED FROM the well with a jar upon her shoulder, set it down in the yard, and came through the door, singing. The bad news that had set the island buzzing had only served to increase her appreciation of momentary beauties, and she had just seen her first butterfly of the year. She was feeling strong and whole, and had been enjoying having the house to herself whilst her father was up on the mountain checking both Alekos and his herd of goats; nothing was ever wrong with either of them, the advantage to Alekos being that he could catch up with the news, enjoy some human company, hear words whose use had vanished from his interior monologue, and to the doctor that he would return with a plentiful supply of dried meat that made scratching and crackling noises in his haversack as he walked. Additionally the doctor believed that the pleasure of homecoming was more than recompense for the pains of setting out, and that therefore it was always worth departing.

When Pelagia entered the kitchen she stopped singing abruptly, and was seized with consternation. There was a stranger seated at the kitchen table, a most horrible and wild stranger who looked worse than the brigands of childhood tales. The man was quite motionless except for the rhythmic fluttering and trembling of his hands. His head was utterly concealed beneath a cascade of matted hair that seemed to have no form nor colour. In places it stuck out in twisted corkscrews, and in others it lay in congealed pads like felt; it was the hair of a Nazarene or of a hermit demented by the glory and solitude of God. Beneath it Pelagia could see nothing but an enormous and disorderly beard surmounted by two tiny bright eyes that would not look at her. There was a nose in there, stripped of its skin, reddened and flaked, and glimpses of darkened, streaked and grimy flesh.

The stranger wore the unidentifiable and ragged remains of a shirt and trousers, and a kind of surcoat cut out of animal skins that had been tacked together with thongs of sinew. Pelagia saw, beneath the table, that in place of shoes his feet were bound with bandages that were both caked with old, congealed blood, and the bright stains of fresh. He was breathing stertorously, and the smell was inconceivably foul; it was the reek of rotting flesh, of suppurating wounds, of dung and urine, of ancient perspiration, and of fear. She looked at the hands that were clasped together in the effort to prevent their quivering, and was overcome both with fright and pity. What was she to do?

'My father's out,' she said. 'He should be back tomorrow.'

'You're happy, anyway. Singing,' said the man in a cracked and phlegmy voice that Pelagia recognised as that of someone whose damaged lungs were filling with mucus; it could be tuberculosis, the onset of pneumonia, or perhaps it was the voice of a man whose throat had filled with polyps or contracted in the grip of cancer.

'Ice,' said the stranger, as though he had not heard her, 'I'll never be warm again. The obscenity of ice.' His voice cracked and she realised that his shoulders were heaving. 'O God, the ice,' he repeated. He held his hands before his face and accused them: 'Bastards, bastards, leave me alone, for the love of God, be still.' He wrapped his fingers together, and his whole body seemed to be fighting to suppress a succession of spasms.

'You can come back tomorrow,' said Pelagia, appalled by this gibbering apparition, and completely at a loss.

'No crampons, you see. The snow is whipped away by the wind, and the ice is in ridges, sharper than knives, and when you fall you are cut. Look at my hands.' He held them

154

up to her, palm outwards in the gesture that would normally be an insult, and she saw the horrendous cross-tracking of hard white scars that had obliterated every natural line, scored away the pads and calluses, and left seeping cracks across the joints. There were no nails and no trace of cuticles.

'And the ice screams. It shrieks. And voices call to you out of it. And you look into it and you see people. Mating like dogs. They beckon and wave, and they mock, and you shoot into the ice but they don't shut up, and then the ice squeaks. It squeaks all night, all night.'

'Look, you can't stay,' said Pelagia, adding, as though to excuse herself, 'I'm on my own.'

The wild man ignored her. 'I saw my father, my father who died, and he was stuck under the ice, and his eyes were staring at me, and his mouth was open, and I hacked with my bayonet. To get him out. And when I got him out it was someone else. I don't know who it was, the ice deceived me, you see. I know I'll never be warm, never.' He hugged himself with both arms and began to shiver violently. 'Pathemata mathemata, pathemata mathemata; so sufferings are lessons, are they? Don't go out in the cold, don't go out in the cold.'

Pelagia's perplexity was growing into an acute anxiety as she wondered what on earth she was supposed to do on her own with a mad vagrant ranting in her kitchen. She thought of leaving him there and running out to fetch Stamatis or Kokolios, but was paralysed by the thought of what he might do or steal in her absence. 'Please leave,' she pleaded, 'my father will be back tomorrow, and he can . . .' she paused, torn between the naming of any number of medical procedures that would be necessary, '. . . see to your feet.'

The man responded to her for the first time, 'I can't walk. I walked from Epirus. No boots.'

Psipsina entered the room and sniffed the air, her whiskers twitching as she sampled the strong and unfamiliar smells. She ran across the floor in her fluid and elliptical manner, and leapt up onto the table. She approached the neolithic man and burrowed in the remains of a pocket, emerging triumphantly with a small cube of white cheese that she demolished with evident satisfaction. She returned to the pocket and found only a broken cigarette, which she discarded.

The man smiled, revealing good teeth but bleeding gums, and he petted the animal about the head. 'Ah, at least Psipsina remembers me,' he said, and silent tears began to follow each other down his cheeks and into his beard. 'She still smells sweet.'

Pelagia was astounded. Psipsina was afraid of strangers, and how did this ghastly ruin know her name? Who could have told him? She wiped her hands on her apron for the lack of any sense of what to think or do, and said, 'Mandras?'

The man turned his face towards her and said, 'Don't touch me, Pelagia. I've got lice. And I stink. And I shat myself when a bomb fell next to me. I didn't know what to do, and I came here first. All the time I knew I had to get here first, that's all, and I'm tired and I stink. Do you have any coffee?'

Pelagia's mind became void, decentred by a babble of emotions. She felt despair, unbearable excitement, guilt, pity, revulsion. Her heart jumped in her chest and her hands fell to her side. Perhaps more than anything else, she felt helpless. It seemed inconceivable that this desolate ghost concealed the soul and body of the man she had loved and desired and missed so much, and then finally dismissed. 'You never wrote to me,' she said, coming up with the first thing that entered her head, the accusation that had rankled in her mind from the moment of his departure, the accusation that had grown into the angry, resentful monster that had eaten out the bowels of her devotion and left it empty.

Mandras looked up wearily, and said, as though it were he that pitied her, 'I can't write.'

For a reason that she did not understand, Pelagia was more repelled by this admission than by his filth. Had she betrothed herself to an illiterate, without even knowing it? For the sake of something to say she asked, 'Couldn't someone else have written for you? I thought you were dead. I thought you . . . couldn't love me.'

Mandras looked up, an infinity of fatigue in his eyes, and shook his head. He tried to steady his cup to drink, failed, and put it down on the table. 'I couldn't dictate to a comrade. How could I let everyone know? How could I have my feelings discussed by the boys?' He shook his head again, and futilely attempted another sip at the coffee, which ran into his beard and onto the skins. He glanced up again so that at last she recognised his eyes, and said, 'Pelagia, I got all your letters. I couldn't read them but I got them.' He fumbled inside his clothing and drew out a huge and bedraggled packet bound together with tripwire. 'I kept them where they would keep me warm, knowing they were there. I thought that you could read them to me. Read them to me, Pelagia, so that I know everything.' He added, with resignation rather than conscious pathos, 'Even if it's too late.'

Pelagia was horrified. Mandras would perceive without fail the steady diminution of endearments, the greater concentration on the factual as the order of the letters proceeded. He would perceive it with a clarity far greater than if he had read them over successive months. 'Later,' she said.

Mandras sighed heavily and fondled Psipsina's ears, talking as though he was addressing the pine marten rather than his fiancée. 'I carried you in here,' he said, thumping his chest with his fist. 'Every day, all the time, I was thinking of you, talking to you. I kept going because of you. I was not a coward because of you. The bombs, the shells, the ice, the night attacks, the bodies, the friends I lost. I had you instead of the Virgin, I even prayed to you. Yes, I even prayed to you. I had you in my mind, singing in the yard, and I saw you at the feast, when I pinned your skirts to the bench and asked you to marry me. I would have died a thousand times, but I had you before my eyes like a cross, like a cross at Easter, like an icon, and I never forgot, I remembered every second. And it burned in my heart, it burned even in the snow, it gave me courage, and I fought for you more than I fought for Greece. Yes, more than Greece. And when the Germans came from behind I got through the lines, and all I could think of was Pelagia, I've got to get home to Pelagia,

21

PELAGIA'S FIRST PATIENT

MANDRAS' MOTHER WAS one of those perplexing creatures as ugly as the mythical wife of Antiphates, of whom the poet wrote that she was 'a monstrous woman whose ill-aspect struck men with horror', and yet she had married a fine man, borne a child, and become widely loved. Some said that she had prospered through witchcraft, but the truth was that she was an amiable and good-natured woman whom fate had deprived of a pretext for becoming vain in her youth, and consequently she had not become embittered as her girth and her hairiness increased. Kyria Drosoula was descended from a family of 'ghiaourtovaptismenoi', the 'baptised in yoghurt', which is to say that her family had been expelled from Turkish territory with nothing to carry away except sacks containing the bones of their ancestors.

The Lausanne settlement had seen nearly half a million Muslims translated to Turkey in return for over a million Greeks, and was an example of racial cleansing which, though necessary for the prevention of further wars, had brought with it a profound legacy of bitterness. Drosoula had known only how to speak Turkish, and she and her mother had been roundly despised by the Old Greeks at the same time as they wept with nostalgia for their life in the lost homelands. Drosoula's mother buried the bones of her father and her husband, and for fear of being ridiculed for her Pontos accent, elected to become dumb, leaving all responsibilities to her fifteen-year-old daughter, who, within the space of three years, had learned to speak the Cephallonian dialect and had married a shrewd fisherman who knew a faithful wife when he saw one. Like so many of the oar-loving islanders, he had lost his life in a squall that sprang up suddenly from the east, leaving a son to take up his trade and a formidable widow who sometimes dreamed in Turkish but had forgotten how to speak it.

During Mandras' absence Pelagia had found her way down to Kyria Drosoula's house almost every day, enraptured by tales of the imperial city of Byzantium and of life on the Black Sea amongst the infidels, and in that small, fishy, but immaculate house by the quayside they had comforted each other with words that, however deeply meant, had by now become clichés in every household in Europe. As the ever-changing sea slopped on the stones outside, they had cried and hugged each other, repeating that Mandras must be all right, because they would have heard if he wasn't. They practised for the eventuality of having to hit an Italian over the head with a shovel, and they laughed behind their hands at some of the appallingly coarse jokes that Drosoula had learned in Turkey from the Muslim boys.

It was to this admirable and hirsute amazon that Pelagia ran, leaving her fiancé at the kitchen table, lost in his world-girdling oceans of fatigue and his terrible memories of comrades who had become the spoil and booty of the carrion birds. The two women returned, breathless, to find him in the same position, still absently caressing Psipsina's ears.

Intending to gather her son into her arms, Drosoula flung herself into the kitchen with a cry of joy, and then performed a double-take that in other circumstances might have been comical. She looked about the kitchen as if to see whether or not there was any other there than that dishev-elled apparition, and glanced at Pelagia questioningly.

'It is him,' said Pelagia. 'I told you he was in an awful state.'

'Jesus,' she exclaimed, and without further ado she took her son by the shoulder, raised him out of his seat, and led him outside, despite Pelagia's protests and the evident wreckage of his feet. 'I'm sorry,' said Drosoula, 'but I'm not having my son sitting in a respectable house in that state. It is too much shame.'

Out in the courtyard Kyria Drosoula inspected Mandras as though he were an animal whose purchase she was contemplating. She peered into his ears, disgustedly lifted his locks of matted hair, made him show his teeth, and then announced, 'You see, Pelagia, what a state these men get into when there are no women to look after them. It's disgraceful and there's no excuse for it, no there isn't. They're just babies who can't manage without their mothers, that's what, and I don't care if he's been to war. Go and put a big pot to boil, because I'm going to wash him from head to foot, but first of all I'm getting rid of all this awful mop, so bring me some scissors, koritsimou, and if I catch his fleas and lice I'm going to flay him alive, I'm itching from just looking at him, I can hardly bear to be on the same island, and the stench, phew, it's worse than pigs.'

Mandras sat passively as his mother ardently and disapprovingly cut away the ropes and pads of his head and beard. She tutted and grimaced at every glimpse of a louse, and carried away the rank locks in the blades of the scissors so that they and their cargo of nits could burn foully in the charcoal of the brazier, shrivelling and spitting, releasing a thick and stinking smoke vile enough to banish demons and disturb the dead.

Pelagia grimaced as much as her future mother-in-law as she witnessed the scurrying of the grey-bodied parasites and as the septic excoriations and the eczema were revealed; the scalp was pitted with inflamed scratches that glistened with fluid, and, most worrying of all, the glands of the neck were finally revealed to be enlarged and suppurating. She felt sickened where she knew that she should feel compassion, and she hurried indoors to look for the oil of sassafras. As she reached for it she realised for the first time, and with a small shock, that she had learned enough from her father over the years to become a doctor herself. If there was such a thing as a doctor who was also a woman. She toyed with the idea, and then went to look for a paintbrush, as though this action could cancel the uncomfortable sensation of having been born into the wrong world.

161

When she emerged into the spring sunlight with the jar of aromatic and pungent oil, she found Mandras completely shorn, and she offered the jar to Drosoula. 'You paint it on quite thick, and it even kills ringworm if he's got that too. Then you cover his head with a cloth and tie it round with string. I'm afraid it's an irritant, and you have to rub olive oil in when the lice have gone, but oil of paraffin takes about two weeks to work, so I thought we'd better use this.'

Kyria Drosoula looked at her admiringly, sniffed the liquid, said, 'Pooh,' and began to slop it about on her son's head. 'I hope you know what I'm doing,' she commented. Mandras spoke for the first time: 'It stings,' whereupon his mother said, 'O, you're in there, are you?' and continued to paint.

When the head was bound up in linen, the two women stepped back and admired their work. Mandras' face was as emaciated as that of the saint in his sarcophagus, and looked as hollow-eyed and pale as that of someone recently dead but already cold. 'Is it really him?' asked Drosoula, with genuine doubt in her mind, and then she asked why it was that the scratches on the head became infected. 'It's because the excrement of the lice is rubbed into the scratches,' said Pelagia, 'it's not actually the lice that cause it.'

'I always told him not to scratch,' said Drosoula, 'but until now I didn't know why. Shall we do the rest of him?'

The two women exchanged glances, and Pelagia flushed. 'I don't think. . .' she began, and Drosoula winked and grinned broadly. 'Don't you want to see what you're getting? Most girls would kill for the chance. I won't tell anyone, I promise, and as for him,' she nodded in her son's direction, 'he's so far gone he won't even know.'

Pelagia thought three things all at once: 'I don't want to marry him. I've already seen him, but I can't say so, and it was a time when he was beautiful. Not like now. And I can't say anything because I've got so fond of Drosoula.'

'No, really, I can't.'

'Well, you help me with everything else, and you'll have to tell me what to do with the other bits from the other side

162

of the door. Is the water hot? I'll tell you confidentially, I can't wait to see what kind of a man I've produced; do you think I'm terrible?'

Pelagia smiled, 'Everyone thinks you're terrible, but no one thinks any the worse of you for it. They just say "O, there's Kyria Drosoula for you."'

With his clothes removed Mandras shivered no more than he had done with them on. He was so pathetically reduced that Pelagia felt no shame in remaining with him even when he was naked, and she did not have to resort to delivering instructions from the far side of a door. His muscle was gone, and the skin hung about his bones in flaccid sheets. His stomach bulged, either from starvation or parasites, and his ribs protruded as sharply as the bones of his spine. The shoulders and back seemed to have bent and crumpled, and the thighs and calves had shrunk so disproportionately that the knees seemed hugely swollen. The worst of it was what they beheld when they peeled off the encrusted bandages upon the feet; Pelagia was reminded of the story of Philoctetes, erstwhile Argonaut and suitor to Helen, abandoned by Odysseus upon the island of Lemnos because of the insupportable decay of his foot, with only his great bow and the arrows of Hercules for company. Pelagia would later recall that the conclusion to this story was that he was cured by Aesculapius and had helped to bring down the Trojans, and would reflect that she herself had been the healer, whilst the Italians had aptly supplied the place of their own forebears.

She did not feel very much like a healer when she saw those feet, however; they were unrecognisable as such. They were a necrotic, multi-hued pulp. A shell of pus and scab lay upon the inner windings of the abandoned bandages, and yellow maggots writhed and squirmed in flesh that was all but dead. 'Gerasimos!' exclaimed Drosoula, clutching her son's withered shoulders for support as she tried not to faint away. The stench was inconceivably stupefying, and at last Pelagia felt herself flood with the sacred compassion whose absence had previously so appalled her. 'Wash him all over,' she said to Drosoula, 'and I'll do the feet.' She looked

163

up at Mandras with tears brimming in her eyes and said, 'Agapeton, I'm going to have to hurt you. I'm so sorry.'

He returned her gaze, and spoke for the second time: 'It's the war. We beat them hollow, we had them running. We beat the wops. You can hurt me if you want, but we couldn't fight the Germans. It was the tanks, that's all.'

Pelagia forced herself to look at the feet until in her own mind they had become a problem to be solved rather than ghastly suffering to be abhorred. Gently she plucked out the maggots, throwing them over the wall, and then gathered her wits together to decide whether or not the rot had spread into the bones. If it had, it was a case of amputation, and she knew that things would have to be left to others; probably her own father would not be willing to do it. What worse could any physician do to a fellow being? She shuddered, she wiped her hands on her apron, she closed her eyes, and she picked up the right foot. She turned it this way and that, felt its textures and decided to her own surprise that there was no granulation and that no bone had died away and separated itself. 'There's no sequestrum,' she said; thinking, 'But I've only ever done this on a dog,' and Drosoula replied, 'There's plenty of dirt, though.' Pelagia found the flesh of the foot dry, and sighed as if a burden had been lifted away; it was the moist gangrene that was worse. She saw that there was no red line of demarcation between healthy and infected areas, and concluded that it wasn't gangrene at all. She inspected the other foot and came to the same conclusions. She fetched a bowl of clean water, salted it heavily, and as gently as she could she washed the terrible mess. Mandras flinched as he stung, but said nothing. Pelagia found that the most gruesome patches fell away as she washed them, and that there was living flesh beneath.

She felt a sense of elation and triumph as she stood in the kitchen and pounded five fat heads of garlic in the mortar. The powerful domestic smell comforted her, and she smiled as Drosoula's voice wafted in from the yard. She was scolding her son as though he had not spent months in the snow, as though he was not a hero who had, like all his comrades, carried hardship far beyond the call of duty and beaten off a superior force that had been defeated by those same hardships. With a knife she spread the garlic onto two long bandages, and she carried them outside. She said to Mandras, 'Agapeton, this will sting even worse than the salt.' He winced as she wound the poultice about his feet, and took in his breath sharply, but he did not complain. Pelagia wondered at his fortitude, and remarked, 'I'm not surprised we won.'

'We haven't, have we?' retorted Drosoula. 'The wops couldn't do it, so Attila did it instead.'

'Hitler. But it doesn't matter, because the British Empire is on our side.'

'The British have gone home. We're in God's hands now.'

'I don't believe it,' said Pelagia resolutely. 'Think of Lord Napier, Lord Byron. They'll come back.'

'What's all this?' enquired Drosoula, indicating the generality of scars, inflamed pits, and scarlet patterns on the body of her son. Pelagia scrutinised the sorry body, freshly washed, and diagnosed every parasite she had ever encountered in the company of her father. 'On the shoulder it's favus. You see, it smells of mice. You need sulphur and salicylic acid for that. It's a kind of honeycomb ringworm. It's lucky it didn't get into the hair, because he would have lost it. These red punctures are body lice. We've got to burn all his clothes, and we've got to shave him all over – you can do that – to get the eggs off his hairs. Or we can wash him in vinegar. And we cover him with eucalyptus oil and paraffin emulsion. The rashes on his legs and arms are bêtes rouges, and we can get rid of them with ammonia and zinc ointment. They go away on their own anyway. This patch is pityriasis, you see, it's coffee-coloured. The things we use for the other troubles will cure that too. If you shave him, you know, down there, it'll get rid of any crab lice. I won't look if you don't mind. And he's got terrible eczema on his arms and calves. We'll have to paint the cracks with iodine, if I can find any, and they'll heal up, and then we just cover him with calamine lotion, if we can find any of that, and we keep covering him with it until it's cured. It might take weeks. We could use olive oil, I suppose, but not in the groin. You shouldn't put anything greasy in the groin. And these maroon prickmarks are flea bites.' Pelagia paused, looked up, and saw that Drosoula was smiling down at her in amazement. 'Koritsimou,' said the gigantic creature, 'you are astonishing. You are the first woman I have ever known who knows anything. Give me a hug.' Pelagia blushed with pleasure, and, to distract attention from herself, she embraced Drosoula and told her, 'I know you're wondering about all the horrible red lumps on his belly and his . . . equipment. They're in between his fingers as well, but don't worry, it's only scabies. The other treatments will treat that too, especially the zinc and sulphur. At least, that's what I think, but we'd better ask my father,' she concluded modestly.

Drosoula gestured towards her much-diminished son, 'He's not much of a bargain is he?'

Pelagia cursed herself inwardly and said, 'You fall in love with the person, not the body.'

Drosoula laughed: 'Romantic claptrap. Love enters by the eyes and also leaves by the eyes, and in case you're wondering why my husband fell for me, ugly as I am, it was because he had strange tastes, thank God and the saint. Otherwise I would still be a maid.'

'I don't believe it for a moment,' said Pelagia, who, like everyone else, had always wondered how Drosoula had succeeded in finding a husband.

The following morning Dr Iannis returned exhausted from the mountain (via the kapheneion), and not only found a corpselike man asleep in his daughter's bed, but found the latter and a craggy and repulsive woman asleep in his own. The house stank of garlic, soap, ammonia, iodine, sulphur, sick flesh, vinegar, burned hair, in short, it smelled of a busy medical practice. He shook his daughter awake and demanded, 'Daughter, who is that old man in your bed?'

'It's Mandras, Papakis, and this is his mother, Kyria Drosoula. You've met her before.'

'Not in my bed,' he retorted, 'and that isn't Mandras. It's some terrible old man with scabies and bandaged feet. I've already looked.'

Later that morning Dr Iannis listened to Pelagia's account of everything that she had done, snorting and sucking on his pipe at every tentative diagnosis and prognostication. When she had finished she blushed, construing her father's attitude as indicating strong reproof for her presumptuousness. Then he went and examined the patient scrupulously, paying particular attention to the feet.

He said nothing until he reached for his battered hat to go out. Pelagia nervously kneaded her duster and awaited his fury. 'If I could cook,' he said, to her astonishment, 'I would exchange jobs with you. In fact, I might retire. Well done, koritsimou, I have never been so prodigiously proud.' He kissed her on the forehead and swept out dramatically, scrutinising the skies for the anticipated invasion. He had a meeting of the Defence Committee to attend, in the kapheneion.

Drosoula smiled down at Pelagia, who was so overwhelmed with relief and gratification that her hands were shaking. 'I always wanted a daughter,' said Drosoula. 'You know what men are, they only want sons. You're lucky to have a father like that. Mine was a complete dog as far as I can remember, always drunk on raki. I pray to the saint that Mandras gets well, and then you will be a daughter.'

'As soon as we can,' said Pelagia, taking her arm, 'we should get him into the sunlight and down to the sea. In cases like this it's the mind that makes a difference.'

Drosoula noted that Pelagia had judiciously ignored her remarks, but forgave her for it. It was enough to see the young woman blooming with that peculiar beauty that derives from a sudden sense of vocation.

22

MANDRAS BEHIND THE VEIL

THEY TALK ABOUT me as if I were not there, Pelagia, the doctor, and my mother. They talk about me as though I were senile or unconscious, as though I were a body without a mind. I am too tired and too sad to resist the indignity. Pelagia has seen me naked and my mother washes me intimately as though I were a baby, and they cover me with unguents and lotions that sting and soothe and stink, so that I am like a piece of furniture that is treated with oil and wax, whose worm-holes are filled, and whose cushions are plumped up and repaired. My mother inspects my stools and talks about them to my betrothed, and they feed me with a spoon because they have no patience to see me struggle with the trembling of my hands, and I ask myself if there is any sense in which I can be considered to exist.

I suppose that I don't. Everything has become a dream. There is a veil between me and them, so that they are shadows and I am dead, and the veil is perhaps a shroud that dims the light and blurs the vision. I have been to war, and it has created a chasm between me and those who have not; what do they know about anything? Since I encountered death, met death on every mountain path, conversed with death in my sleep, wrestled with death in the snow, gambled at dice with death, I have come to the conclusion that death is not an enemy but a brother. Death is a beautiful naked man who looks like Apollo, and he is not satisfied with those who wither away in old age. Death is a perfectionist, he likes the young and beautiful, he wants to stroke our hair

168

and caress the sinew that binds our muscle to the bone. He does all he can to meet us, our faces gladden his heart, and he stands in our path to challenge us because he likes a clean fair fight, and after the fight he likes to befriend us, clap us on the shoulder, and make us laugh at all the pettiness and folly of the living. At the conclusion of a battle he wanders amongst the dead, raising them up, placing laurels upon the brows of those most comely, and he gathers them together as his own children and takes them away to drink wine that tastes of honey and gives them the sense of proportion that they never had in life.

But he didn't take me and I don't know why. I was brave enough certainly. I never avoided danger, and I continued even when my body was already destroyed. I think I lived because our commanders were too clever, I think I lived because death loved the Italians. Death told them to advance in line abreast against our strongest points, and we mowed them down like corn. But our generals made us outflank, out-manoeuvre, ambush, disappear and reappear. Our generals made it difficult for Death, and so, instead of striking me with bullets, he made my body rot as much in a few months as with others he causes in sixty years. It was the cold, mud, parasites, starvation, grief, fear, blizzards of crystals sharper than glass, rain so dense that fish could have swum in it, all the things that there is no point in explaining because a civilian cannot even imagine it.

Do you know what kept me going? It was Pelagia, and a sense of beauty. For me, Pelagia meant home. You see, I wasn't fighting for Greece, I was fighting for home. I was getting it over with so that I could come back. Unfortunately my dream of Pelagia was better than Pelagia herself. I can see and hear that she is disgusted with her returning hero, and I knew before I went that I was not good enough for her. It means that if she loves me then she is being patronising, making a sacrifice, and I cannot stand it because it makes me hate her and despise myself. I am going to go away again when I am well so that I can reclaim the dream of Pelagia and love her without bitterness as I did in those mountains when I fought for her and the idea of home, and when I return I shall be remade and renewed, because next time I am going to make sure that I have done things so great that even a queen would beg to be my bride. I don't know what they are, but they shall be the glory and the wonder of the world, they shall robe me about, as rich and gorgeous as the jewels of the saint.

Also I have to go away again because I should not have come home in the first place. I came home because it was possible, and because coming home is like iced water after a day at sea in August when there has been no wind. I needed to wash myself in the rustling of olives, the clang of goatbells, the chaffering of crickets, the taste of Robola, and the smell of salt. I needed the strength, my bare feet on the soil I sprang from, that's all.

The fact is that my unit was wiped out by the Germans near Mt Olympus. I was the only survivor, and as I sat there amongst the bodies of my friends Pelagia came to me in a vision. Malnutrition causes these things, they say, and great strain, but to me it was as if she stood in front of me and smiled. If she had not done this I would have joined up with another unit and fought the Germans all the way to Thermopylae, but suddenly I knew that I had to get home even though I didn't know the way. I looked amongst the corpses and found the best pair of boots, a pair whose soles were coming away, but better than mine. I put them on and I walked south-west.

Every night I noted where the sun set, and in the morning where it rose. I divided the semicircle, chose a landmark, and walked. At midday I checked that I was walking to the left of the sun. The roads were clogged with the chaos of retreat – the dying donkeys, the abandoned vehicles, the knapsacks and weapons, the victims of the Stukas – and so I walked across the land, through the infinite wilderness that I now know to be the greater part of Greece. It was at first a wilderness of thorns, and stunted trees just bursting into bud, but somewhere past Elasson the land rose and it became an inhuman waste of pines, gorges, cataracts, ravines, a land of hawks and bats. There were marshes full of peaty water and barbarous flowers, mountainsides slippery with shale and scree, and goat-paths that ended suddenly and inexplicably on the edge of an abyss. My new boots gave out, and that was when I wrapped my feet in bandages. At night Pelagia lay next to me as I froze in caves, and in the morning she walked before me to the south. I could see her skirts sway about her hips, I saw her stoop to pluck the flowers, and she smiled and waited for me when I fell.

In that land there are bears and there are wild dogs that might be wolves, there are lynxes and deer. There were times that I tore the raw flesh off abandoned prey with my teeth, and once an eagle dropped a pigeon near my feet and plummeted down after it so that its talons scraped my hands as I dived for its victim. There are also people who live in those desolate places, people who are a kind of animal. Some of them are blond and it is impossible to understand them, they speak so strangely. They live in small stone houses or houses made of wood, and they dress in rags, living off outrageous stews that are made of meat and roots, cooked in ancient pots whose cracks are sealed with mud. These people threw stones at me, but when I knelt and pointed with my finger to my mouth, they took me in and fed me as gently as a child. It was one of them who gave me my jerkin made of skins.

As I travelled I began to suspect that my body was falling apart and that I was becoming mad. I no longer knew exactly what was happening. I not only saw Pelagia, but strange monsters that threatened me with their maws filled with rows of teeth. There was a place where I was passing by a waterfall, a waterfall so high that it tumbled with a roar like that of the sea in a wild storm. It fell into a pool whose waters whirled and rotated, swallowing up anything that passed by it, and I saw no way of going south-west except by swimming past it. On my left was a cliff that jutted outwards so that nothing might climb it, not even a goat, and it seemed to me that there was a creature on it with three heads that intended to devour me. I stood there with nothing in my mind but the battle between my homeward desperation and the fear of the pool and the monster.

171

I saw Pelagia walk ahead, seemingly across the water like Our Lord, and I realised that there was a ledge beneath the water at the base of the cliff, so that I passed as easily as if I was wading out to a boat in the shallows of the bay of Assos.

When I knew that I was going mad I also knew that I had to stop, if only for a day, and I came to a stone hovel in the trees, at a place where the ground rose at the feet of a mountain and the pine needles lay on the ground as soft and thick as a blanket. There was no one inside, and I was unsure whether or not it was inhabited, and so I went in and lay down against the wall, and fell asleep, except that I dreamed I was in a bombardment.

I woke up when somebody poked me with their foot. When I saw that it was an old hag, I wondered whether my dream had simply changed, but it hadn't. She was small and withered, and she had tied her few strands of hair behind her head. Her back was bowed and bent, her dress was in tatters, and her cheeks were hollow, her chin sharpened, because there was not one tooth in her head.

One day, when I have the strength to speak, I will tell this story in the kapheneion to make the boys laugh, because the truth is that this old scarecrow took a fancy to me. I forgot to tell you that she had only one eye. The other one was closed up and shrivelled.

She knew only one word, 'Circe', which I suppose was her name – she kept pointing to herself and saying it, so that I had to say 'Mandras' and point to my own self – and her voice was like the croak of a raven. Her one eye lit up every time she saw me, and she fed me on pigmeat from the herd that she kept near a stand of oak so that they could feed on the acorns. I was repelled and horrified by her, but I could see that she was a simple soul to whom God had given a kind heart.

On the third night that I was there, I slept more peacefully than for many months, and because my body was healing itself thanks to the hogmeat I did not dream of bombs and corpses, but of Pelagia. In my dream she frowned and became impatient because of my delay, and for the first time

172

in all my visions I ran to her and kissed her. She melted in my arms and returned my passion, so that very soon we were rolling together on the floor of the forest. She clasped me to her and ran her hands about my body so that I became inflamed, and her lips were as hot as fire. She bit my lip and squirmed, and I tore her clothes away, so that my hands knew her breasts and her thighs, and I trembled with the winds of Dionysus, and entered her. In no time at all I felt the surge in my loins, and it was as I wrenched with the supreme moment that I awoke.

Beneath me the ancient vixen writhed and groaned and croaked, her one mad eye half-closed with ecstasy. For a second I lay above her, perplexed and confused, and then I sprang to my feet with a cry of horror and rage, for I knew that she had crept beneath my skins and seduced me in Pelagia's form. 'Witch, witch,' I cried, kicking her, and she sat up and shielded herself, her dugs falling to her waist and her body seeping with sores to equal mine. She waved her arms and twittered like a bird in the jaws of a cat, and it was at that point that I recognised the madness in us both and in the very manufacture of the world. I threw back my head and laughed. I had lost my virginity to an antique, loveless, solitary crone, and it was all just one small part of the way in which God had turned His face away and consigned us all to the malice and caprices of the dark. The world looked the same, but beneath the surface it had broken out with boils. I laid back down next to her, and we slept together like that until morning. I had realised that we humans are blameless.

She tried to stop me leaving, kneeling at my feet and weeping and howling as she clutched my knees. It was pitiful, but I remember thinking that since nothing mattered any more, it did not matter if she too shared in this suffering that has taken the world by storm and laid it all to waste.

I reached Trikkala and managed to cadge a lift on a truck that was returning from the front with a cargo of the wounded. The driver looked at the blood of my feet and the shreds of my uniform, and agreed that I too was wounded, and so I took the place of another who had died. At Lipson I rode another truck through Agios Nikolaos to Arta and Preveza, and from there it was simple to go to Levkas with a fellow fisherman who was taking mail to the island. I took another fisherman's boat to Ithaca, and yet another to get home. I walked to Pelagia's house all the way from Sami.

All I got when I arrived was a horror equal to my reaction to the old woman in the woods, and I was recognised only by a small dumb animal, Psipsina. The disappointment, after so many dreams and so much fighting and wandering with Pelagia as my light, snuffed out the flame inside me, and the fatigue came over me like a fog that encloses a boat in October in the Strait of Zante. I closed my eyes and fell into the shadows, like the spirits of the dead.

I said it was Pelagia and the sense of beauty that got me home, but I have said nothing about the sense of beauty. Once, near the Metsovon pass, in December, when it was twenty degrees below zero because there was no cloud, the Italians sent up a starshell. It exploded in a cascade of brilliant blue light against the face of the full moon, and the sparks drifted to earth in slow motion like the souls of reluctant angels. As that small magnesium sun hovered and blazed, the black pines stepped out of their modest shadows as though previously they had been veiled like virgins but had now decided to be seen as they are in heaven. The drifts of snow pulsed with the incandescence of the absolute chastity of ice, a mortar coughed disconsolately, and an owl whooped. For the first time in my life I shivered physically from something other than the cold; the world had sloughed away its skin and revealed itself as energy and light.

It is my wish to get well so that I can go back to the lines and experience, perhaps for only one more time, that immaculate moment when I saw the face of Gabriel in an instrument of war.

23

APRIL 30TH, 1941

THERE IS A story that in the Royal Palace, which was so vast and empty that the Royal Family travelled within it on bicycles, and so derelict that its water-taps spewed cockroaches, a White Lady appears as an omen of disaster. Her footsteps make no sound, her face blazes with malevolence, and once, when two aides-de-camp attempted to arrest her for attacking the grandmother of Prince Christopher, she vanished into thin air. If she had wandered the palace on this day, she would have found it occupied not by King George, but by German soldiers. If she had gone outside into the city, she would have found the swastika flying from the Acropolis, and she would have had to travel to Crete to find the King.

The Cephallonians needed no such malicious ghosts to warn them. Two days before, the Italians had taken Corfu under farcical circumstances which were to be repeated identically today, and there was no one on the island who did not anticipate the worst.

It was the waiting that was tormenting. A great nostalgia rose up like a palpable mist; it was like making love for the last time to someone who is adored but is leaving forever. Every last moment of freedom and security was rolled about on the tongue, tasted, and remembered. Kokolios and Stamatis, the Communist and the monarchist, sat together at a table cleaning the components of a hunting rifle that had gathered dust on a wall for fifty years. They were without ammunition, but, as it was to everyone on the island, it seemed important to be engaged upon some gesture of resistance. Their busy fingers sought to calm the storms of anxiety and speculation in their minds, and they talked in low voices with a mutual affection that belied their years of vehement ideological difference. Neither of them knew any more how long their lives would be, and they had become precious to each other at last.

Families embraced more than had been the habit; fathers who expected to be beaten to death stroked the hair of pretty daughters who expected to be raped. Sons sat with their mothers on doorsteps and talked gently of their memories. Farmers took their barrels of wine with the glint of sunlight in it, and buried them in the earth so that no Italian would have the pleasure of their drinking. Grandmothers sharpened their cooking knives, and grandfathers remembered old deeds, persuading themselves that age had not diminished them; in the privacy of sheds they practised the 'shoulder-arms' with shovels and sticks. Many people visited their favourite places as if for the last time, and found that stones and dust, pellucid sea and ancient rock, had taken on an air of sadness such as one finds in a room where a beautiful child is lying at the door of death.

Father Arsenios knelt in his church, attempting to find words to a prayer, perplexed by a novel sensation of having been let down by God. He had become so accustomed to the idea that he was condemned forever to be the one who let down God, that he found himself lost for a formula that was not full of reproaches, and even insults. He resorted to his habitual, 'Lord Jesus, Son of God, have mercy on me, a sinner,' and reflected that even after all these years its repetition had failed to enter his heart. In his youth he had believed that one day this prayer would reveal the Vision of Divine and Uncreated Light, but he knew now that it had become a formula, a barrier between himself and the God who was speechless and evasive. 'Lord Jesus, Son of God,' he prayed at last, 'what the hell do you think you're doing? What was the point of Golgotha if the Devil was not defeated? I thought you said you'd banished sin. Did you die for nothing, then? Are you going to let us all die for nothing? Why don't you do something? I know that you are invisibly manifest at the Eucharist, but if you are invisible, how do I know that you are there?' His fat jowls vibrated with emotion; he felt like a boy who has come to man's estate and discovered that his father has left him no inheritance. 'Lord Jesus, Son of God,' he prayed. 'If you're not going to do anything, I will.'

At his desk Dr Iannis read once more the famous open letter to Hitler that Vlakhos had published in the *Kathimerini*. Moved by its noble, grandiloquent exposition of the right to national independence, he cut it out of the paper, stood up and stuck it onto the wall with a thumbtack, unaware that every other literate man in Greece had done the same; it would remain there until 1953, growing dry and yellow, curling at the corners, its sentiments freshening and deepening with every passing year.

The doctor removed Psipsina from his desk, sat down and wrote, 'It is our custom to compare the many nations that have usurped this island to the Turks. Thus the Romans and the Normans were worse than the Turks, the Catholics were worse, the Turks themselves were probably not as bad as we like to imagine, and so, paradoxically, were not as bad as themselves. The Russians were infinitely better, and the French were marginally better. The latter enjoyed constructing roads, but could not be trusted – the Turks never promised us anything, and therefore were by definition incapable of perfidy – and the British were worse than the Turks for some of the time, and the best of all of them for the rest. The general Greek bitterness against the British arose because they brazenly sold Parga to Ali Pasha, but in this island it was caused initially by the governor, Sir Thomas Maitland, who was an unmitigated tyrant. However, Charles de Bosset, a Swiss serving in the British Army, built our invaluable bridge across the Bay of Argostoli. Lord Napier built the magnificent courtroom at Lixouri with its arcaded market underneath (the Markato) and was so popular that the population raised a subscription for a commemorative statue after he left. Lord Nugent became so well-liked that our parliament issued him with a vote of thanks. Frederic Adam, Stewart McKenzie, and John Seaton appear to have been more philhellenic than we ourselves, but General Howard Douglas was outrageously and scandalously despotic. And so it goes on. What does this teach us?

'It teaches us that to be associated with the British is to be offered the choice of one of two bags tied at the neck with string. One contains a viper, and the other a bag of gold. If you are lucky you will choose the bag of gold, only to find that the British have reserved the right to exchange it for the other without notice. Conversely, ill luck might cause you to pick the bag with the viper, whereupon the British will wait until you have been bitten and then say, "We didn't mean it; have this other bag."

'We don't know what to think about the British. With the Turks we knew that our sons would be taken for janissaries, our daughters to harems. We knew that we would be exempt from military service, that we would be forbidden to ride horses, and that our sultans were voluptuaries and lunatics. With the British you can be sure of nothing except that they will treat you despicably and then make up for it a hundredfold. At one time we loved them so much that we asked for Prince Alfred as our King – and we still have a cult of Lord Byron – and at other times they have kicked us in the teeth. It is with a heavy heart that I record here the fact that they have abandoned us to our fate because they have judged that the war will not be decided in Greece.

'I wait despondently, in the knowledge that Corfu has fallen and that this may be the last thing I ever write. I commend my memory to posterity, and that of my beloved daughter Pelagia, and I beg that whoever finds these papers and my unfinished history should preserve them intact. I pray that the British have not abandoned us irrevocably, and I pray that they may win through to victory even if I am dead. I believe that I have led a good and useful life, and if it were not for the daughter who may not live and the grandchildren I may never see, I am content to die in the hope that, as Plato says, death might be ". . . a change, a migration of the soul from one place to another". I have never believed this to be so, but the imminence of invasion convinces me that life can be a sad and weary thing, and that death might conceivably be a time when I will rest once more with my wife in whatever place she might have gone. Solon said that one should call no man happy until he dies, because until then he is at best fortunate. But I have been both happy and fortunate; happy in my marriage and fortunate in my daughter. Let it not have been for nothing.'

The doctor reached for a top shelf and took down a black tin box. Into it he placed the sheaves of his history and this final piece, which, as usual, had started on one subject and finished on another, and then he turned the key. He put the box under one arm, lifted the mat beneath the table, and opened the trapdoor, exposing the large cavity that had been made there in 1849 for the concealment of the Radicals whom the British had first persecuted and then put into government. Into this hole that had once concealed the fugitive Joseph Momferatos and Gerasimos Livadas, the doctor placed his literary remains. He returned to his desk, took down his two massive volumes of *The Complete and Concise Home Doctor*, and began to revise the sections that dealt with 'bleeding; dressings; shock; tourniquet; bullet wounds; burns; cuts; stabs; asepsis; drainage and irrigation of wounds; lockjaw; pus; trepanning for the relief of depressed fractures of the skull.'

In Drosoula's house, to which Mandras had been transferred, the doctor's daughter sat in an agony of shame; she had begun to suspect that Mandras was torturing her deliberately.

His physical ills had abated considerably. The red nodules, the eczema, the skin on his feet, had all begun to cure themselves. His face had filled out a little, his ribs had hidden themselves beneath new flesh, his hair was beginning to grow, and the insane gleam in his eyes had dimmed to a feeble glimmer that the doctor did not think was an improvement. 'It's a shame,' he had said, 'that he was not actually wounded. It would have given him something concrete to concern himself with.' Pelagia had been startled and angered by this remark, but at this moment she wanted

179

nothing so much as to take her little derringer from her apron and shoot her fiancé in the head. The fact was that Mandras had devolved to a state more unmanageable than infancy, and she was convinced that he was doing it on purpose as an act of vengeance or a punishment. She believed that he wanted her to be desperately worried, and she was.

The doctor had diagnosed his behaviour at different times as anergic stupor, melancholic stupor, resistive stupor, and katatonic stupor. The odd way in which it was all of these at different times indicated to him that it was none of them, but he was at a loss as to any other interpretation. 'War shock' did not entirely fit the bill either, and like Pelagia he had begun to feel the temptation to ascribe the condition to a pathological need to enslave others by means of manoeuvring himself into a condition of complete dependency. 'He thinks that nobody wants him,' said Dr Iannis, 'and he's doing this in order to force us to demonstrate that we do.'

'But I don't want him,' thought Pelagia, over and over again, as she sat near his bed crocheting the matrimonial bedspread that had never grown beyond the size of a towel.

Mandras had begun his exile into inaccessibility by dramatising the idea of death. As though he had frozen into rigor mortis he lay in his bed, utterly rigid, his arms held into the air in a contorted position that no ordinary person could have sustained for a single minute. Saliva dribbled from his mouth, down his chin, across his shoulder, and soaked into the bed. Drosoula placed a cloth to soak it up, and when she returned she found that he had shifted and that the saliva was dripping from the other shoulder. Because of the position of his arms she had had the most intractable difficulty with dressing and undressing him. The doctor had tested him for katatonia by sticking pins into him; he had made no reaction, and had not closed his eye when the doctor made to prick that too. He had been fed with soup poured down a tube into his gullet, and he had neither urinated nor defecated for days until the very time that Drosoula stopped trying to make him do it. Then he had soiled the sheets so copiously that she had had to run outside and gag in the street.

On March 25th Mandras had got out of bed to celebrate National Day, had dressed himself and gone out, returning drunk and exhilarated at three o'clock in the morning. Drosoula and Pelagia held hands and danced together in circles, whirling and laughing from pleasure and relief.

But the next day he was back in bed, passive and speechless. His rigidity had gone, to be replaced by a condition in which he seemed to have disowned his body. The doctor had raised his arm, and it had fallen back to the bed as though it were a stocking loosely stuffed with rags. His temperature fell and his lips swelled and turned blue, his pulse raced, and he breathed so shallowly that it seemed that he spurned the air.

On the day after that Mandras mimicked the condition of the day before, except that now he struggled wildly yet expertly against every attempt to move him or feed him. Drosoula called in Kokolios, Stamatis, and Velisarios, and not even the two tough old men and the giant could make him open his mouth and eat. It seemed that he was determined to starve himself and die. Kokolios suggested whipping him, the traditional cure for the mad, and demonstrated its efficacy by slapping the patient hard across the face. Mandras sat up suddenly, put a hand to his cheek, said, 'Shit. I'll get you, you bastard,' and sank back into the sheets. Everyone present was by that time so enraged and frustrated that the idea of whipping him did not seem such a bad one.

Mandras continued his policy of resistance and starvation until the evening of April 19th, when he recovered miraculously, in time for the great celebrations of Easter. On Holy Thursday the lambs had been killed and hung, the eggs had been painted red and polished with olive oil, and he had nearly succumbed to the traditional lentil soup. On Good Friday the island had drifted with the aroma of the women's Easter bread, and on Saturday the men had roasted the lambs on spits, teased each other, and become indecently drunk whilst the women laboured to make soup and sausage. During all of this Mandras had lain motionless in bed, shitting himself and pissing whenever Drosoula had just changed the sheets.

But on Saturday night he got up, and then, dressed in black, bearing an unlit black candle, he joined the sombre procession of the icons to the monastery at Sissia. He seemed to be completely normal; when Stamatis wished him a good recovery he replied, 'From your lips to the ear of God,' and when Kokolios clapped him on the back and congratulated him on his sudden appearance amongst the living, Mandras had grinned his old grin and replied with the proverb, 'I am a Greek, and we Greeks are not subject to the laws of nature.'

In the absolute darkness and silence of the church Mandras waited with growing anticipation. The suspense was unbearable, and the lowering war had already rendered that Easter a poignant one; does Christ still rise when Greeks fall? There were many there who wondered whether this might not be the last of their passiontides upon earth, and they held the hands of their children with an extra strength and a deeper emotion. Those with watches noticed that minutes were longer than they used to be, and people craned their necks to get a better view of the iconostasis.

At last the priest appeared with his lighted candle, and his voice boomed: 'Christos anesti, Christos anesti.'

A great shout of joy arose from the pilgrims, who answered him, 'Alithos anesti, alithos anesti,' and set about lighting each other's candles. 'Christ is risen,' exclaimed Drosoula, embracing her son. 'Risen indeed,' he cried, and kissed Pelagia on the cheek. Shielding her flame with her hand, Pelagia wondered, 'Mandras anesti? Is Mandras risen?' She caught Drosoula's eye, and realised that they had both been having the same thought. The bells rang out all over the island, the people shouted and leapt in triumph, the dogs howled, the donkeys brayed, and the cats wauled; a surge of exhilaration and faith lightened the heart, and people greeted each other, 'Christos anesti,' never tiring of hearing 'alithos anesti' in reply. The fasting of the last week was over (a fast that in truth had been obligatory for months) and there was about to be a new miracle of the feeding of the five thousand as people brought out the feasts that they had saved for and improvised, feasts to be interpreted as a poke in the eye for the Duce, as acts of defiance and resistance.

All through their midnight feast and the eating of the lamb on Sunday, Mandras seemed to be his old self. The mayeritsa soup with its avgolemono sauce disappeared into his maw as if he had just returned from a day's fishing, and the lamb, sprinkled with oregano and pierced with abundant slivers of garlic, was crammed down his throat with a ravenous appetite worthy of a Turk. But on Sunday evening he undressed and, inevitably, betook himself once more to bed.

This time he managed not only to emulate death, but to do so with every appearance of the most extreme spiritual pain. He would neither move nor speak, his pulse softened, his breathing diminished to the minimum for life, and his facial expression was eloquent of the most acute and extraordinary misery. The doctor explained to Drosoula that he had probably lost the power of volition, and was promptly confounded when Mandras sat up and asked to see a priest.

Father Arsenios found the small door of the house impossible to negotiate, and so Mandras was carried outside by his redoubtable mother and left on the quayside to talk with the clergyman.

'I've done terrible things,' he said, 'things so terrible that I cannot name them.' He spoke with enormous effort, struggling painfully to enunciate the words, his voice emerging almost inaudibly.

'Name them anyway,' said Arsenios, who was still perspiring on account of his long walk from the village and had always found situations such as this abysmally unnerving.

'I committed adultery,' said Mandras, 'I fucked the Queen.'

'I see,' said Arsenios. There was a long silence.

'I fucked Queen Circe because I thought she was someone else.'

'The Queen isn't called Circe, so that's all right,' said Arsenios, wishing that he had not agreed to come.

183

'God help me, I'm not fit to live,' continued Mandras, his voice a hoarse and confidential whisper. 'And I've got this punishment.'

'Punishment?'

Mandras tapped his knee: 'See? I can't move my legs, and do you know why?'

'I just saw you move your legs.'

Mandras turned his head slowly, with a mechanical motion that resembled the rotation of a wheel of cogs: 'They're made of glass.'

Father Arsenios stood up and returned to where Pelagia and Drosoula were standing discreetly apart. 'I know what's wrong with him,' he said.

'What is it, Patir?' asked Drosoula, her voice replete with maternal anxiety and hope.

'He's completely mad. You should send him to the madhouse at the monastery of the saint, and wait for the miracle.' The fat priest waddled slowly back up the hill, leaving the two women to exchange shakes of the head. To their surprise Mandras stood up and walked over to them, his hips rigid, woodenly moving his legs only from the knees. He stopped in front of them, wrung his hands with remorse, tore a sheet of skin from the remaining eczema on his leg, waved it in their faces, fumbled with the buttons of his nightshirt, and croaked, 'Made of glass.'

He returned to his bed, and two days later there began a period of hysterical rage. It began with shouting, proceeded to a bizarre episode in which he attempted to amputate his leg with a spoon, continued to a stage in which he lashed out at Pelagia and Drosoula, and concluded on April 30th with a terrifyingly lucid wrath in which he appeared to have recovered his sanity completely, and insisted that Pelagia should read to him her letters. It was this that had reduced her to an extreme and anxious state of embarrassment and shame.

She had begun with the first ones, the ones in which the love and the sense of separation had spilled out of her and overflowed onto the page in lyrical crescendos worthy of a romantic poet: ' "Agapeton, agapeton, I love you and miss

184

you and worry for you, I can't wait for you to come back, I want to take your dear face in my hands and kiss you until my spirit flies with the angels, I want to take you in my arms and love you so that time stops and the stars fall. Every second of every minute I dream of you, and every second I know more clearly that you are life itself, more dear than life, the only thing that can life can mean . . ." '

She felt her cheeks flush with irritation, she was aghast at these geysers of emotion that seemed to be those of another, lesser self. She cringed in the same way as she did when her aunt reminded her of something winsome that she had done or said as a child. The loving words now stuck in her throat and left a taste of bitterness on her tongue, but every time that she paused, Mandras would glare at her, his eyes flashing, and would demand that she continue.

It was with a sense of relief that almost made her feel sick that she reached the letters in which news gradually started to preponderate. Her voice lightened, and she began to relax. But Mandras suddenly yelled, and hammered at his thighs with his fists, 'I don't want that, I don't want those bits, I don't want to hear about how upset everyone is that I don't write. I want the other bits.' His voice, as querulous as that of a spoiled child, irked her, but she feared his strength and his vindictive madness, and she continued to read the letters, excising all but the parts in which she named the variety and quality of her affection.

'The letters are getting too short,' he shouted, 'they're too short. Do you think I don't know what it means?' He grabbed the last of the letters from the bottom of the pile, and waved it in her face. 'Look at this,' he exclaimed, 'four lines, that's all. Do you think I don't know? Read it.'

Pelagia took the letter and read it silently to herself, knowing already what it said: 'You never write to me, and at first I was sad and worried. Now I realise that you cannot care, and this has caused me to lose my affection also. I want you to know that I have decided to release you from your promises. I am sorry.'

'Read it,' demanded Mandras.

Pelagia was appalled. She fumbled with the sheet of paper

and smiled appeasingly, 'My handwriting is terrible, I'm not sure I can make sense of it.'

'Read it.'

She cleared her throat, and with a tremor in her voice she improvised: ' "My darling, please come back to me soon. I miss you so much and long for you more than you can imagine. Keep safe from the bullets, and . . ." ' she halted, sickened by the necessary duplicity of her part in the charade. She surmised that this was what it must be like to be violated by a stranger.

'And what?' insisted Mandras.

' "And I don't know how to tell you how much I love you," ' said Pelagia, closing her eyes in desperation.

'Read the letter before that.'

It was a letter that began with 'Yesterday I thought I saw a swallow, and that means that spring is returning. My father' . . . but she hesitated and began to improvise again: ' "My darling, I think that you are like a swallow that has flown away, but will one day return to the nest I have made for you in my heart . . ." '

Mandras made Pelagia read all the letters, handing them to her one by one, so that, with tears in her eyes, her voice quavering, she endured a purgatorial hour of utter panic, each letter a torment of Sisyphus, the sweat pouring down her face and stinging her eyes. She begged to stop, and was denied. She felt herself deaden inside as desperately she invented endearments for this man she had grown first to pity and then to hate.

She was saved by the rhythmic drone of planes. Drosoula ran inside, shouting, 'Italians, Italians. It's the invasion.'

'Thank God, thank God,' thought Pelagia, realising almost immediately the absurdity, the bizarreness of her relief. She ran outside with Drosoula, standing arm in arm with her as the pot-bellied Marsupials lumbered overhead, disgorging their long trails of tiny black dolls that were jerked upwards into the air as their parachutes opened, parachutes that looked as clean and pretty as fresh mushrooms in a field of autumn dew.

Nothing was as anyone had anticipated. Those who had

thought that they would be filled with rage were afflicted instead by sensations of wonder, curiosity, or apathy. Those who knew that they would be terrified felt an icy calm and a rush of grim determination. Those who had long felt a terrible anxiety became calm, and there was one woman who was visited by an almost venial apprehension of salvation.

She ran up the hill to be with her father, following the ancient instinct that decrees that those who love each other must be united when they die. She found him standing in his doorway, as everyone else stood in theirs, his hand shielding his eyes against the sun as he watched the paratroops descend. Out of breath, she flew into his arms, and felt him tremble. Could he be afraid? She glanced up at him as he stroked her hair, and realised with a small shock that his lips moved and his eyes gleamed, not with fear, but with excitement. He looked down at her, straightened his back, and waved one hand to the skies. 'History,' he proclaimed, 'all this time I have been writing history, and now history is happening before my very eyes. Pelagia, my darling daughter, I have always wanted to live in history.' He released her, went indoors, and returned with a notebook and a sharpened pencil.

The planes disappeared and there was a long silence. It seemed as though nothing was to happen.

Down in the harbours the men of the Acqui Division disembarked apologetically from their landing craft and waved cheerfully but diffidently to the people in their doorways. Some of them shook their fists in return, others waved, and many made the emphatic gesture with the palm of the hand that is so insulting that in later years its perpetration was to become an imprisonable offence.

In the village, Pelagia and her father watched the platoons of paratroopers amble by, their commanders consulting maps with furrowed brows and pursed lips. Some of the Italians seemed so small as to be shorter than their rifles. 'They're a funny lot,' observed the doctor. At the back end of one line of soldiers a particularly diminutive man with cockerel feathers nodding in his helmet was goose-stepping satirically with one finger held under his nose in imitation

187

of a moustache. He widened his eyes and explained, 'Signor Hitler,' as he passed Pelagia by, anxious that she should perceive the joke and share it.

In front of his house Kokolios defiantly raised a Communist salute, his arm outstretched, his fist clenched, only to be confounded completely when a small group without an officer cheered him as it passed by and returned the salute, con brio and with exaggeration. He dropped his arm and his mouth fell open with astonishment. Were they mocking him, or were there comrades in the Fascist army?

An officer looking for his men stopped and questioned the doctor anxiously, waving a map in his face. 'Ecco una carta della Cephallonia,' he said, 'Dov'è Argostoli?'

The doctor looked into the dark eyes set in a handsome face, diagnosed a terminal case of extreme amiability, and replied, in Italian, 'I don't speak Italian, and Argostoli is more or less opposite Lixouri.'

'You speak very fluently for one who doesn't,' said the officer, smiling, 'so where is Lixouri?'

'Opposite Argostoli. Find one and you find the other, except that you must swim between them.'

Pelagia nudged her father in the ribs, fearful on his behalf. But the officer sighed, lifted his helmet, scratched his forehead, and glanced sideways at them. 'I'll follow the others,' he said, and hurried away. He returned a moment later, presented Pelagia with a small yellow flower, and disappeared once more. 'Extraordinary,' said the doctor, scribbling in his notebook.

A column of men, much smarter than most of the others, marched by in unison. At their head perspired Captain Antonio Corelli of the 33rd Regiment of Artillery, and slung across his back was a case containing the mandolin that he had named Antonia because it was the other half of himself. He spotted Pelagia 'Bella bambina at nine o'clock,' he shouted, 'E-y-e-s left.'

In unison the heads of the troops snapped in her direction, and for one astonishing minute she endured a march-past of the most comical and grotesque antics and expressions devisable by man. There was a soldier who

188

crossed his eyes and folded down his lower lip, another who pouted and blew her a kiss, another who converted his marching into a Charlie Chaplin walk, another who pretended at each step to trip over his own feet, and another who twisted his helmet sideways, flared his nostrils, and rolled his eyes so high that the pupils vanished behind the upper lids. Pelagia put her hand to her mouth.

'Don't laugh,' ordered the doctor, sotto voce. 'It is our duty to hate them.'

24

A MOST UNGRACIOUS SURRENDER

I DID NOT arrive in Cephallonia until the middle of May, and I was only transferred there, to the 33rd Regiment of Artillery, Acqui Division, because the damage to the muscles in my thigh left me temporarily useless for anything except garrison duty. By that time I was so disillusioned by the Army that I would have gone anywhere just for a tranquil life where I could revolve my memories and scratch my wounds. I was experiencing the kind of abject depression that comes to soldiers who have realised that they have been fighting on the wrong side, expending an infinity of effort and draining the sources of courage and sanity until it seems that there is nothing inside; in truth I was feeling that my head was hollow and that the cavity of my chest was a vacuum. I was still dumb with sorrow about the death of Francesco, and I was still shocked by my own stupidity in failing to foresee that my dreams of turning my vice to advantage had rested on an incomplete assumption; it was true that my love for Francesco had inspired me to great things, but I had forgotten the possibility that he would be killed. I had gone into the war a romantic, and had come out of it desolate, dismal and forlorn. The word 'heartbroken' occurs to me, except that this is inadequate to describe the sensation of being utterly broken in both body and soul. I knew that I wanted to escape – I felt envious of our soldiers in Yugoslavia who had changed sides and joined the Garibaldi Division – but finally it is impossible to escape those monsters that devour from the inner depths, and the only ways to vanquish them are either to wrestle with them like Jacob with his angel or Hercules with his serpents, or else ignore them until they give up and disappear. I did the latter, and this was made more easy by a small miracle whose name was Captain Antonio Corelli. He became my source of optimism, a clear fountain, a kind of saint who had no repellent trace of piety, a kind of saint who thought of temptation as something to play with rather than something to be opposed, but who remained a man of honour because he knew no other way to be.

I first met him in the encampment outside Argostoli, in the days before the quartermasters had arranged billets with local Greeks. It was the middle of spring, when the island is at its most serene and beautiful. Earlier in the year the weather can be most tempestuous, and later on it can become quite insufferably hot, but in spring the weather is balmy, there is a light breeze and gentle rain in the night, and there are wild flowers blooming in impossible places. After the torments of war it seemed that I had stepped off a boat into Arcadia; the impression of peace was so overwhelming that it left me feeling tearful, grateful and incredulous. It was an island where it was physically impossible to be morose, where vicious emotions could not exist. By the time that I arrived the Acqui Division had already surrendered to its charms, had sunk back into its cushions, closed its eyes, and become enclosed in a gentle dream. We forgot to be soldiers.

The first thing that struck me was the painful clarity of the light. I suppose that it would be ridiculous to maintain that the air in Cephallonia has no density, but the light is so pellucid, so pure, that one is temporarily blinded and overwhelmed, and yet one feels no pain. I walked about for two or three days with my eyes screwed up against it. I found that in Cephallonia the night falls without the intervention of twilight, and that before it rains the light is like mother-of-pearl. After it rains, the island smells of pines, warm earth, and the dark sea.

The second thing that struck me, curiously enough, was the incredible size and antiquity of the olive trees. They were blackened and gnarled, twisted and stout, they made me feel strangely ephemeral, as though they had seen people like us a thousand times, and had watched us depart. They had a quality of patient omniscience. In Italy we cut down our old trees and plant fresh ones, but here it was possible to place one's hand on that antique bark, look up at the fragments of sky that glittered through the canopy, and feel dwarfed by the sensation that others might have done this very thing under this very tree a millennium before. The Greeks keep them alive by judicious pruning, generation upon generation, and perhaps the trees become accustomed to a family in the same way as a house or a flock of sheep.

The third thing that struck me was the quiet, resolute dignity of the islanders, and I was to discover that our soldiers had also been impressed by this. Many of our boys were the rowdy and uncouth sort that you find in any kind of army, the criminal type who have serendipitously happened upon a legitimate way of being a bastard, and some of them were drunken and base enough to act as though conquest had given them rights over the populace, but the fact is that the islanders made it quite clear from the start that they were not going to take any nonsense, whether we had weapons or not. Fortunately the officers of the division were honourable men, and if it were not for this fact, I am quite sure that the islanders would soon have gone into insurrection, as they very quickly did in those places occupied by the Germans.

I will illustrate the pride of the populace by retailing what happened when we asked them to surrender. I had this story from Captain Corelli. He was prone to dramatic exaggeration in the telling of a story because everything about him was original, he was always larger than his circumstance, and he would say things for the sake of their value as amusement, with an ironic disregard for the truth. Generally he observed life with raised eyebrows, and he had none of that fragile self-pride that prevents a man from telling a joke against himself. There were some people who thought him a little mad, but I see him as a man who loved life so much that he did not care what kind of impression he made. He adored children, and I saw him kiss a little girl on the head and whirl her in his arms whilst his whole battery was standing at attention, awaiting his inspection, and he loved to make pretty women giggle by snapping his heels together and saluting them with a military precision so consummate that it came over as a mockery of everything soldierly. When saluting General Gandin the action was sloppy to the point of insolence, so you can see what kind of man he was.

I first came across him in the latrines of the encampment. His battery had a latrine known as 'La Scala' because he had a little opera club that shat together there at the same time every morning, sitting in a row on the wooden plank with their trousers about their ankles. He had two baritones, three tenors, a bass, and a counter-tenor who was much mocked on account of having to sing all the women's parts, and the idea was that each man should expel either a turd or a fart during the crescendos, when they could not be heard above the singing. In this way the indignity of communal defecation was minimised, and the whole encampment would begin the day humming a rousing tune that they had heard wafting out of the heads. My first experience of La Scala was hearing the Anvil Chorus at 7.30 a.m., accompanied by a very prodigious and resonant timpani. Naturally I could not resist going to investigate, and I approached a canvas enclosure that had 'La Scala' painted on it in splashes of blanco. I noticed an appalling and very rank stench, but I went in, only to see a row of soldiers shitting at their perches, red in the face, singing at full heart, hammering at their steel helmets with spoons. I was both confused and amazed, especially when I saw that there was an officer sitting there amongst the men, insouciantly conducting the concert with the aid of a feather in his right hand. Generally one salutes an officer in uniform, especially when he is wearing his cap. My salute was a hurried and incomplete gesture that accompanied my departure – I did not know the regulation that governs the saluting of an officer in uniform who has his breeches at half-mast during a drill that consists of choral elimination in occupied territory.

193

Subsequently I was to join the opera society, 'volunteered' by the captain after he had heard me singing as I polished my boots, and had realised that I was another baritone. He handed me a piece of paper filched from General Gandin's own order-pad, and on it was written:

TOP SECRET

By Order of HQ, Supergreccia, Bombardier Carlo Piero Guercio is to report for operatic duty at every and any whim of Captain Antonio Corelli of the 33rd Regiment of Artillery, Acqui Division.

Rules of engagement:
1) All those called to regular musical fatigues shall be obliged to play a musical instrument (spoons, tin helmet, comb-and-paper, etc.).
2) Anyone failing persistently to reach high notes shall be emasculated, his testicles to be donated to charitable causes.
3) Anyone maintaining that Donizetti is better than Verdi shall be dressed as a woman, mocked openly before the battery and its guns, shall wear a cooking pot upon his head, and, in extreme cases, shall be required to sing 'Funiculi Funicula' and any other songs about railways that Captain Antonio Corelli shall from time to time see fit to determine.
4) All aficionados of Wagner shall be shot peremptorily, without trial, and without leave of appeal.
5) Drunkenness shall be mandatory only at those times when Captain Antonio Corelli is not buying the drinks.
Signed; General Vecchiarelli, Supreme Commander, Supergreccia, on behalf of His Majesty, King Victor Emmanuel.

The captain's story about the capitulation of Cephallonia was that the commanders at the time of the landing had gone to the town hall of Argostoli in order to receive the surrender of the town's authorities.

They had stood outside, accompanied by a squad of armed troops, and sent in a message requiring the handing over of the building and of authority. Out comes a message that simply says 'Va fanculo'. Much consternation and shock amongst our officers. This is not the language of diplomacy, and hardly an appropriate response from those who are supposedly cowering under the heel of conquest. They send in another message, threatening the storming of the building. Out comes a note stating that any Italian demanding surrender will be shot forthwith. Additional consternation caused by speculation as to whether or not those inside really have any arms. The officers are embarrassed by the idea that they might actually have to plan a siege. They send in another message, demanding clarification, and out comes another that says 'If you don't know what "fuck off" means, then come in here and we'll show you.' 'O shit,' say the officers, standing about in the sunlight. There is a delay of about half an hour whilst the confusion mounts, and then another note comes from inside that says 'We refuse categorically to surrender to a nation that we have utterly routed, and we demand the right to surrender to a German officer of significant rank'. Eventually a German officer is flown in from Zante or Corfu or somewhere, and the authorities emerge triumphantly from the town hall, having humiliated and vanquished us on our first day of conquest.

That is what Corelli told me, and I am sure that in some of the details it is somewhat embellished. But it is true that the authorities flatly refused to surrender to us, and eventually we did have to fly in a German. Corelli thought that this story was hilariously amusing, and he liked to relate it over and over again, multiplying the number of messages and insults, whilst the rest of us sat listening to him with our ears burning.

I think that Corelli was able to find it so funny because music was the only thing he considered serious, until he met Pelagia. As for me, I grew to love him as much as I had loved Francesco, but in an entirely different way. He was like one of those saprophytic orchids that can create harmony and wonder even as it grows and blossoms on a pile of shit, in a place of skulls and bones. He let his rifle rust, and even lost it once or twice, but he won battles armed with nothing but a mandolin.

25

RESISTANCE

ALL OVER THE island there was a burgeoning of graffiti that took merry or malicious advantage of the fact that the Italians could not decipher the Cyrillic script. They mistook Rs for Ps, did not know that Gs can look like Ys or inverted Ls, had no idea what the triangle was, thought that an E was an H, construed theta as a kind of O, did not appreciate that the letter in the shape of a tent was the same as the one that looked like an inverted Y, were baffled by the three horizontal strokes that could also be written as a squiggle, knew from mathematics that pi meant 22 divided by 7, were unaware that E the wrong way round was an S, that the Y could also be written as a V and was in fact an E, were confused by the existence of an O with a vertical stroke that was actually an F, did not understand that the X was a K, failed utterly to find anything that might be meant by the elegant trident, and found that the omega reminded them of an earring. Ergo, conditions were ideal for the nocturnal splashing of white paint in huge letters on all available walls, especially as the quirks of an individual's handwriting could render the letters even more completely inscrutable. ENOSIS fought for space with ELEPHTHERIA, 'Long Live The King' cohabited without apparent anomaly with 'Workers Of The World Unite', 'Wops fuck off' abutted with 'Duce, Eat My Shit'. An admirer of Lord Byron wrote, 'I dream'd that Greece might still be free' in wobbly Roman letters, and General Tsolakoglou, the new quisling leader of the Greek people, appeared everywhere as a cartoon figure, committing various obscene and unpleasant acts with the Duce.

In the kapheneia and fields the men related Italian jokes: How many gears does an Italian tank have? One forward and four in reverse. What is the shortest book in the world? *The Italian Book of War Heroes*. How many Italians does it take to put in a light-bulb? One to hold the bulb and two hundred to rotate the room. What is the name of Hitler's dog? Benito Mussolini. Why do Italians wear moustaches? To be reminded of their mothers. In the encampments the Italian soldiers in their turn asked, 'How do you know when a Greek girl is having a period?' And the answer would be 'She is wearing only one sock.' It was a long interlude during which the two populations stood off from each other, defusing by means of jokes the guilty suspicion on the one side and the livid resentment on the other. The Greeks talked fierily in secret about the partisans, about forming a resistance, and the Italians confined themselves to camp, the only signs of activity being the setting up of batteries, a daily reconnaissance by amphibious aircraft, and a mounted curfew patrol that jogged about at dusk, its members more anxious to exercise charm on females than to enforce an early night. Then a decision was made to billet officers upon suitable members of the local population.

The first thing about it that Pelagia knew was when she returned from the well, only to find a rotund Italian officer, accompanied by a sergeant and a private, standing in the kitchen, looking around with an appraising expression, and making notes with a pencil so blunt that he was obliged to read what he had written by casting the indentations against the light.

Pelagia had already stopped fearing that she was going to be raped, and had become accustomed to scowling at leers and slapping at the hands that made exploratory pinches of the backside; the Italians had turned out to be the modest kind of Romeo that is resigned to being rebuffed, but does not abandon hope. Nonetheless, she felt a momentary leap of fear when she came in and found the soldiers, and, but for a moment of indecision, she would have turned tail and fled. The plump officer smiled expansively, raised his arms in a gesture that signified, 'I would explain if I could, but I don't speak Greek,' and said, 'Ah,' in a manner that signified, 'How delightful to see you, since you are so pretty, and I am embarrassed to be in your kitchen, but what else can I do?' Pelagia said, 'Aspettami, vengo,' and ran to fetch her father from the kapheneion.

The soldiers waited, as requested, and soon Pelagia reappeared with her father, who was anticipating the encounter with some trepidation. There was a lurch of dread waiting to surge into his heart and weaken it, but also a cold and detached courage that comes to those who are determined to resist oppression with dignity; he remembered his advice to the boys in the kapheneion – 'Let us use our anger wisely' – and squared his shoulders. He wished that he had retained his moustache with the waxed tips, so that he might twist its extremities balefully and censoriously.

'Buon giorno,' said the officer, holding out his hand hopefully. The doctor perceived the conciliatory nature of the gesture and its lack of conqueror's hubris, and much to his own surprise he reached out and shook the proffered hand.

'Buon giorno,' he replied. 'I do hope that you enjoy your regrettably short stay on our island.'

The officer raised his eyebrows, 'Short?'

'You have been expelled from Libya and Ethiopia,' the doctor said, leaving the Italian to extrapolate his meaning.

'You speak Italian very well,' said the officer, 'you are the first one I have come across. We are very badly in need of translators to work with the populace. There would be privileges. It seems that no one here speaks Italian.'

'I think you mean that none of you speak Greek.'

'Just so, as you say. It was only an idea.'

'You are very kind,' said Dr Iannis acidly, 'but I think you will find that those of us who do speak Italian will suddenly lose our memory when required to do so.'

The officer laughed, 'Understandable under the circumstances. I meant no offence.'

'There is Pasquale Lacerba, the photographer. He is an

Italian who lives in Argostoli, but perhaps even he would not like to co-operate. But he is young enough not to know better. As for me, I am a doctor, and I have enough to do without becoming a collaborator.'

'It's worth a try,' said the quartermaster, 'most of the time we don't understand anything.'

'It's just as well,' observed the doctor. 'Perhaps you could tell me why you're here?'

'Ah,' said the man, shifting uneasily, aware of the unpleasantness of his position, 'the fact is, I am sorry to say, and with great regret, that . . . we shall be obliged to billet an officer on these premises.'

'There are only two rooms, my daughter's and my own. This is quite impossible, and it is also, as you probably realise, an outrage. I must refuse.' The doctor bristled like an angry cat, and the officer scratched his head with his pencil. It was really very awkward that the doctor spoke Italian; in other houses he had avoided this kind of scene and left it to the unfortunate guests to explain the situation, by means of grunts and gesticulations, when they turned up unannounced with their kitbags and drivers. The two men looked at one another, the doctor tilting his chin at a proud angle, and the Italian searching for a form of words that was both firm and mollifying. Suddenly the doctor's expression changed, and he asked, 'Did you say that you are a quartermaster?'

'No, Signor Dottore, you seem to have worked it out for yourself. I am a quartermaster. Why?'

'So do you have access to medical supplies?'

'Naturally,' replied the officer, 'I have access to everything.' The two men exchanged glances, divining perfectly the train of the other's thought. Dr Iannis said, 'I am short of many things, and the war has made it worse.'

'And I am short of accommodation. So?'

'So it's a deal,' said the doctor.

'A deal,' repeated the quartermaster. 'Anything you want, you send me a message via Captain Corelli. I am sure you will find him very charming. By the way, do you know anything about corns? Our doctors are useless.'

'For your corns I would probably need morphia, hypodermic syringes, sulphur ointment and iodine, neosalvarsan, bandages and lint, surgical spirit, salicylic acid, scalpels, and collodion,' said the doctor, 'but I will need a great deal, if you understand me. In the meantime get a pair of boots that fits you.'

When the quartermaster had gone, taking with him the details of the doctor's requirements, Pelagia took her father's elbow anxiously and asked, 'But Papas, where is he to sleep? Am I to cook for him? And what with? There is almost no food.'

'He will have my bed,' said the doctor, knowing perfectly well that Pelagia would protest.

'O no, Papas, he will have mine. I will sleep in the kitchen.'

'Since you insist, koritsimou. Just think of all the medicine and equipment it will mean for us.' He rubbed his hands together and added, 'The secret of being occupied is to exploit the exploiters. It is also knowing how to resist. I think we shall be very horrible to this captain.'

In the early evening Captain Corelli arrived, driven by his new baritone, Bombardier Carlo Piero Guercio. The jeep skidded to a halt outside, generating clouds of dust and much noisy alarm amongst the chickens that were scratching in the road, and the two men came in by the entrance of the yard. Carlo looked at the olive tree, amazed by its size, and the Captain looked around, appreciating the signs of a quiet domestic life. There was a goat tied to the tree, washing hanging on a line from the tree to the house, a vivid bougainvillaea and a trailing vine, an old table upon which there lay a small heap of chopped onions. There was also a young woman with dark eyes, a scarf tied around her head, and in her hand was a large cooking knife. The captain fell to his knees before her and exclaimed dramatically, 'Please don't kill me, I am innocent.'

'Don't worry about him,' said Carlo, 'he is always being foolish. He can't help it.'

Pelagia smiled, against her will and against her resolutions, and caught Carlo's eye. He was huge, as big as

201

Velisarios. Two ordinary men might have fitted inside one leg of his breeches, and she could have made two shirts for her father from the one that he wore. The Captain sprang to his feet. 'I am Captain Antonio Corelli, but you may call me maestro if you wish, and this . . .' he took Carlo by the arm '. . . is one of our heroes. He has a hundred medals for saving life, and none for taking it.'

'It's nothing,' said Carlo, smiling diffidently. Pelagia looked up at the towering soldier, and knew intuitively that, despite his size, despite his enormous hands that might fit about the neck of an ox, he was a soft and saddened man. 'A brave Italian is a freak of nature,' she said sourly, remembering her father's instructions to be as unaccommodating as possible.

Corelli protested. 'He rescued a fallen comrade in the open field, under fire. He is famous all over the Army, and he refused promotion too. He is a one-man ambulance. What a man he is. He has a Greek bullet in his leg to show for it. And this . . .' he tapped a case in his hand ' . . . is Antonia. Perhaps we will make more formal introductions later on. She is very anxious to meet you, as am I. By what name do men know you, may I ask?'

Pelagia looked at him properly for the first time, and realised with a start that this was the very same officer who had commanded his platoon of comedians to march past at the eyes left. She blushed. At the same moment Corelli recognised her, and he bit his lower lip in mockery of himself. 'Ah,' he exclaimed, and slapped himself on the wrist. He fell to his knees once more, hung his head in sly penitence, and said softly, 'Forgive me, Father, for I have sinned. Mea culpa, mea culpa, mea maxima culpa.' He beat his breast and wiped away an imaginary tear.

Carlo exchanged glances with Pelagia, and shrugged his shoulders. 'He's always like this.'

Dr Iannis came out, saw the captain on his knees before his daughter, caught her bemused expression, and said, 'Captain Corelli? I want a word with you. Now.'

Startled by the authority in the older man's voice, Corelli stood up, abashed, and held out his hand. The doctor withheld his own, and said crisply, 'I want an explanation.'

'Of what? I have done nothing. You must excuse me, I was only joking with your daughter.' He shifted nervously, unhappily conscious of the possibility that he had made a bad start.

'I want to know why you have defaced the monument.'

'The monument? Forgive me, but . . .'

'The monument, the one in the middle of the bridge that de Bosset built. It has been defaced.'

The captain knitted his brows in perplexity, and then his face lightened, 'Ah, you mean the one across the bay at Argostoli. Why, what has happened to it?'

'It had "To The Glory Of The British People" inscribed on the obelisk. I have heard that some of your soldiers have chipped away the letters. Do you think you can so easily erase our history? Are you so stupid that you think that we will forget what it said? Is this how you wage war, by the chipping away of letters? What kind of heroism is this?' The doctor raised his voice to a new note of vehemence, 'Tell me how you would like it if we defaced the tombstones in the Italian cemetery, Captain.'

'I had nothing to do with it, Signor. You are blaming the wrong man. I apologise for the offence, but . . .' he shrugged his shoulders '. . . the decision was not mine, and neither were the soldiers.'

The doctor scowled and raised his finger, stabbing the air, 'There would be no tyranny, Captain, and no wars, if minions did not ignore their conscience.'

The captain looked to Pelagia, as though in expectation of support, and suffered the unbearable sensation of having been sent back to school. 'I must protest,' he said feebly.

'You cannot protest, because there is no excuse. And why, will you tell me, has the teaching of Greek history been prohibited in our schools? Why is everyone being obliged to learn Italian, eh?'

Pelagia smiled to herself; she could not have calculated how often she had heard her father divagating upon the absolute necessity and perfect reasonableness of having compulsory Italian in schools.

The captain felt himself wanting to squirm like a little boy who has been caught stealing sweets from the tin reserved for Sundays. 'In the Italian Empire,' he said, the words tasting bitter on his tongue, 'it is logical that everyone should learn Italian . . . I believe that that is the reason. I am not responsible for it, I repeat.' He began visibly to perspire. The doctor shot him a glance that was intended to be, and was, deeply withering. 'Pathetic,' he said, and turned on his heel. He went indoors and sat down at his desk, very satisfied with himself. He leaned forward, annoyed Psipsina by tickling her whiskers, and confided to her, 'Got him on the run already.'

Outside in the yard Captain Corelli was dumbfounded, and Pelagia was feeling sorry for him. 'Your father is . . .' he said, and the words failed him. 'Yes, he is,' confirmed Pelagia.

'Where am I to sleep?' asked Corelli, glad of anything that might be a distraction, all his good humour having dried to dust.

'You will have my bed,' said Pelagia.

Under normal circumstances Antonio Corelli would have asked brightly, 'Are we to share it then? How hospitable,' but now, after the doctor's words, he was appalled by this information. 'It's out of the question,' he said briskly. 'Tonight I shall sleep in the yard, and tomorrow I shall request alternative accommodation.'

Pelagia was shocked by the feelings of alarm that arose in her breast. Could it be that there was something inside her that wanted this foreigner, this interloper, to stay? She went inside and relayed the Italian's decision to her father. 'He can't go,' he said. 'How am I supposed to browbeat him if he isn't here? And anyway, he seems like a personable boy.'

'Papakis, you made him feel like a flea. I almost felt sorry for him.'

'You did feel sorry for him, koritsimou. I saw it in your face.' He took his daughter's arm and went back out with her. 'Young man,' he said to the captain, 'you are staying here, whether you like it or not. It is quite possible that your quartermaster will decide to impose someone even worse.'

'But your daughter's bed, Dottore? It would not be . . . it would be a terrible thing.'

'She will be comfortable in the kitchen, Captain. I don't care how bad you feel, that is not my problem. I am not the aggressor. Do you understand me?'

'Yes,' said the captain, overpowered, and not entirely grasping what was happening to him.

'Kyria Pelagia will bring water, some coffee, and some mezedakia to eat. You will find that we do not lack hospitality. It is our tradition, Captain, to be hospitable even to those who do not merit it. It is a question of honour, a motive which you may find somewhat foreign and unfamiliar. Your sizeable friend is welcome to join us.'

Carlo and the captain uneasily partook of the tiny spinach pies, the fried baby squid and the dolmades stuffed with rice. The doctor glowered at them, inwardly delighted with the successful inauguration of his novel project for resistance, and the two soldiers avoided his gaze, commenting politely and inconsequentially upon the beauty of the night, the impossible size of the olive tree, and any and every irrelevance that occurred to them.

Carlo drove gratefully away, and the captain sat on Pelagia's bed miserably. It was the time for an evening meal, and despite the plates of appetisers his stomach growled from force of habit. The thought of more of that wonderful food left him feeling weak. The doctor came in once and told him, 'The answer to your problem is to eat a lot of onions, tomatoes, parsley, basil, oregano, and garlic. The garlic will be an antiseptic for the fissures, and the other things, taken together, will soften the stools. It is very important not to strain at all, and if you eat meat, it must always be accompanied by a great deal of fluid and a sideplate of vegetables.'

The captain watched him leave the room, and felt more humiliated than he had ever thought possible. How could the old man possibly have known that he suffered from haemorrhoids?

In the kitchen the doctor asked Pelagia whether or not she had noticed that the captain walked very carefully and occasionally winced.

Father and daughter sat down to eat, both of them clattering the cutlery on the plates, and waited until they were sure that the Italian must be dying of hunger and feeling like a ragamuffin boy who has been sent to Coventry at school, and then they invited him to join them. He sat with them and ate in silence.

'This is Cephallonian meat pie,' said the doctor in an informative tone of voice, 'except that, thanks to your people, it doesn't have any meat in it.'

Afterwards, when the curfew patrol had already passed, the doctor announced his intention to go for a walk. 'But the curfew . . .' protested Corelli, and the doctor replied, 'I was born here, this is my island.' He gathered up his hat and his pipe, and swept out.

'I must insist,' he called vainly after the doctor, who prudently circled about the house and waited a quarter of an hour as he sat upon the wall, eavesdropping on the conversation of the two young people.

Pelagia looked at Corelli as he sat at the table, and felt the need to comfort him. 'What is Antonia?' she asked.

He avoided her eyes, 'My mandolin. I am a musician.'

'A musician? In the Army?'

'When I joined, Kyria Pelagia, Army life consisted mainly of being paid for sitting about doing nothing. Plenty of time for practice, you see. I had a plan to become the best mandolin player in Italy, and then I would leave the Army and earn a living. I didn't want to be a café player, I wanted to play Hummel and Conforto and Giuliani. There's not much demand, so you have to be very good.'

'You mean you're a soldier by mistake?' asked Pelagia, who had never heard of any of these composers.

'It was a plan that went wrong; the Duce got some big ideas.' He looked at her wistfully.

'After the war,' she said.

He nodded and smiled, 'After the war.'

'I want to be a doctor,' said Pelagia, who had not even mentioned this idea to her father.

That night, just as she was drifting off to sleep beneath her blankets, she heard a muffled cry, and shortly afterwards the captain appeared in the kitchen, a little wide-eyed, a towel wrapped about his waist. She sat up, clutching the blankets about her breasts.

'Forgive me,' he said, perceiving her alarm, 'but there appears to be an enormous weasel on my bed.'

Pelagia laughed, 'That's not a weasel, that's Psipsina. She is our pet. She always sleeps on my bed.'

'What is it?'

Pelagia could not resist essaying her father's mode of resistance: 'Haven't you heard of Greek cats?'

The captain looked at her suspiciously, shrugged his shoulders, and returned to his room. He approached the pine marten and stroked it on the forehead with a tentative forefinger. It felt very soft and comforting. 'Micino, micino,' he cooed speculatively, and fondled her ears. Psipsina sniffed at the wiggling digit, did not recognise it, surmised that it might be edible, and bit it.

Captain Antonio Corelli snatched his hand away, watched the beads of blood well out of his finger, and fought against the shamingly childish tears that were rising unbidden to his eyes. He attempted by force of will to suppress the mounting sting of the bite, and knew for certain that he had been pierced through to the bone. Never, in all his life, had he felt so unloved. These Greeks. When they said 'ne' it meant 'yes', when they nodded it meant 'no', and the more angry they were, the more they smiled. Even the cats were from another planet, and moreover could have no possible motive for such malice.

He lay abjectly upon the hard cold floor, unable to sleep, until at last Psipsina missed Pelagia, and went off to look for her. He climbed back into the bed and sank gratefully into the mattress. 'Mmm,' he said to himself, and realised that he was savouring a lingering, vanishing smell of young woman. He thought about Pelagia for a while, remembering the clean scoop of white flesh as the neck became the breast and shoulder, and finally fell asleep.

He woke in the night, suffering from the sensation that his neck was abominably hot and that his chin was ticklish. As he emerged into awareness it became horribly evident that the Greek cat had wrapped itself about his neck and was fast asleep. Horrified and afraid, he tried to move a little. The animal growled sleepily.

He lay paralysed for what seemed like hours, sweating, resisting the itching and the unnatural warmth, listening to the owls and the unholy noises of the night. At some point he noticed that the encumbrance across his neck smelled consolingly sweet. It was an aroma that mingled pleasantly with the smell of Pelagia. He drifted away at last, and for some reason dreamed irrelevantly of elephants, bakelite, and horses.

26

SHARP EDGES

THE HOUR SHORTLY after dawn found Captain Antonio Corelli waiting in vain at the entrance to the yard for Carlo to come and fetch him away. The latter had broken a shackle on the suspension of his jeep, and was engaged in kicking the tyres and swearing at the profound potholes in the road that had undone his early start. He already possessed a deep horror of letting down the captain, a horror shared by all the men who served under him, and his fractious ill-temper was exacerbated when he tried to light a cigarette, only to find that the desiccated rod of powdery tobacco slid out of its tube of paper and smouldered insolently in the dust, leaving him with a piece of scorchingly hot paper that stuck tenaciously to his lower lip. He pulled the paper away, and it removed a tag of skin. He licked the stinging wound, touched it with his finger, and cursed the Germans for their success in monopolising the supplies of the best tobacco. A thin old peasant mounted sidesaddle on a donkey passed him by, saw the broken state of the vehicle as it sagged to one side, smiled with satisfaction, and raised a hand in a gesture of casual greeting. Carlo gritted his teeth and smiled. 'Fuck the war,' he said, since one greeting was as good as another to a Greek. It looked as though there would be no La Scala that morning, unless the opera society could manage the Soldiers' Chorus on its own. He abandoned the jeep and began to trudge towards the village.

Velisarios passed him, and the two men looked at one another with something like recognition. However thin and bedraggled he had become since he had gone to the front, Velisarios was still the biggest man that anyone had ever seen, and Carlo, despite his equivalent experiences on the other side of the line, was also the biggest man that anyone had ever seen. Both of these Titans had become accustomed to the saddening suspicion within themselves that they were freaks; to be superhuman was a burden that had seemed impossible to share and impossible to explain to ordinary people, who would have been incredulous.

They were both astonished, and for a moment forgot that they were enemies. 'Hey,' exclaimed Velisarios, raising his hands in a gesture of pleasure. Carlo, stumped for an exclamation that would make sense to a Greek, aimed inaccurately for a failed compromise that sounded very like 'Ung'. Carlo offered one of his atrocious cigarettes, Velisarios took one, and they gesticulated and made sour faces to each other as they drew on the smoke that was sharp as needles. 'Fuck the war,' said Carlo, by way of farewell, and the two went on their opposite ways, Carlo beginning to feel very content. A kilometre away, Velisarios came across the crippled jeep, paused in thought, and went to fetch a friend. He returned, lifted the vehicle at each corner in turn, and his companion removed the wheels. Then he drained the water from the radiator, and refilled it with petrol from the jerrycan strapped to the back.

Corelli continued to wait. The doctor passed by on his way to the kapheneion, in an anticipatory state of annoyance on account of the fact that the coffee being served these days tasted of river mud and tar, and was becoming more expensive by the second. 'Buon giorno,' called the captain, and the doctor turned. 'I trust that you slept badly,' he said.

The captain smiled resignedly, 'For some reason I dreamed about animals made of bakelite. They were like dolphins with sharp edges, and they were leaping about. It was very disturbing. Also, your cat bit me.' He held out the wounded finger, and the doctor inspected it. 'It's very swollen,' he said, 'and it will probably go septic. Pine martens can have a nasty bite. If I were you I would show it to a doctor.' With that he went on his way, leaving the

210

captain to repeat foolishly, 'Pine martens?' He realised that Pelagia had only made a small joke at his expense, but, curiously, it left him feeling let down and very gullible.

When Pelagia came out she found the usurper of her bed throwing Lemoni up and down in the air by the armpits. The child was whooping and laughing, and it appeared that what was transpiring was a lesson in Italian. 'Bella fanciulla,' the captain was saying. He was waiting for Lemoni to repeat it. 'Bla fanshla,' she giggled, and the captain threw her up, exclaiming, 'No, no, bella fanciulla.' He dwelt lovingly upon the doubled L, waited for Lemoni to descend, and raised an eyebrow as he awaited her next attempt. 'Bla flanshla,' she said triumphantly, only to be launched skyward again.

Pelagia smiled as she watched, and then Lemoni saw her. The captain followed the cast of her glance, and straightened up, a little embarrassed, 'Buon giorno, Kyria Pelagia. It seems that my driver has been delayed.'

'What's it mean, what's it mean?' demanded Lemoni, whose faith in the omniscience of adults was such that she was sure that Pelagia would be able to tell her. Pelagia patted her cheek, cleared the strands of hair from her eyes, and told her, 'It means "pretty puss", koritsimou. Off you go now, I'm sure that someone is missing you.'

The little girl skipped away in her usual capricious and erratic manner, waving her arms and chanting, 'Bla, bla, bla. Bla, bla, bla.'

Corelli reproached Pelagia, 'Why did you send her away? We were having a wonderful time.'

'Fraternisation,' answered Pelagia. 'It's indecent, even in a child.'

Corelli's face fell, and he scuffed the toe of his boot in the dust. He looked up the sky, dropped his head, and sighed. Without looking at Pelagia, he said with heartfelt sincerity, 'Signorina, in times like this, in a war, all of us have to make the most of what little innocent pleasure there is.'

Pelagia saw the resignation and weariness in his face, and felt ashamed of herself. In the silence that followed, both of them reflected upon their own unworthiness. Then the captain said, 'One day I would like a pretty puss like that, for my own,' and without awaiting a reply he set off in the direction from which he expected Carlo to come.

Pelagia watched him leave, thinking her own thoughts. His retreating back had about it a poignant air of solitude. Then she went inside, took down the two volumes of *The Complete and Concise Home Doctor*, opened them out on the table, and guiltlessly read the sections about reproduction, venereal infections, parturition, and the scrotum. She proceeded at random to read about cascarilla, furred tongue, the anus and its disorders, and anxiety.

Fearing the return of her father from the kapheneion, she finally replaced the books on their shelf, and began to think of reasons for delaying her necessary trip to the well. She chopped some onions, unclear as to what recipe she was intending them to be a part of, but anxious that her father should be able to perceive some concrete evidence of activity, and then she went outside to brush her oblivious goat. She found two ticks and a small swelling in the loose skin of the haunch. She worried about whether or not she should be worried about this, and then began to think about the captain. Mandras caught her dreaming.

He had climbed out of bed, cursing and completely cured, on the day of the invasion. It was as if the advent of the Italians had been something so important, so weighty, that it precluded the luxury of indulging in his illness. The doctor had affected to be unsurprised, but Drosoula and Pelagia had agreed that there was something suspicious about an affliction that could be switched off with such a virtuoso flourish. Mandras had gone down to the sea and swum with his dolphins as though he had never been away, and had returned refreshed, the salt water drying in his tousled hair, a smile upon his face, the muscles in his torso uncontracted, and had climbed the hill with a mullet to present to Pelagia. He had ruffled Psipsina's ears, swung briefly in the olive tree, and had left the impression on Pelagia of being madder in his new sanity than he had been when he was mad. She felt guilty now, whenever she saw him, and deeply uncomfortable.

She started when he tapped her on the shoulder, and despite the effort to force a radiant smile he did not fail to see the flicker of alarm in her eyes. He ignored it, but would remember it later. 'Hello,' he said, 'is your father in? I've still got some bad skin on my arm.'

Glad of something objective upon which to focus her attention, she said, 'Let me look at it,' whereupon he said brightly, 'I was hoping to see the organ-grinder rather than the monkey.'

Mandras had heard this metaphor at the front, had liked it, and had waited a long time for an opportunity to use it. It had struck him as witty, and he had thought that what was witty was also likely to be charming. He wanted nothing so much as to be able to charm Pelagia back into the affection that he unhappily feared that he had lost.

But Pelagia's eyes flashed fire, and Mandras' heart sank. 'I didn't mean it,' he said, 'it was a joke.' The two young people looked at one another, as though sharing an appreciation of all that was gone, and then Mandras said, 'I'm going to join the partisans.'

'Oh,' she said.

He shrugged, 'I haven't any choice. I'm leaving tomorrow. I'll take my boat to Manolas.'

Pelagia was horrified, 'What about the submarines? And the warships? It's madness.'

'It's worth the risk if I go at night. I can sail by the stars. I was thinking of tomorrow night.'

There was a long silence. Pelagia said, 'I won't be able to write.'

'I know.'

Pelagia went inside a moment and came out bearing the waistcoat that she had so devotedly made and embroidered whilst her fiancé had been at the front. She showed it to him diffidently, saying, 'This is what I was making for you, to dance at feasts. Do you want to take it now?'

Mandras took it and held it up. He cocked his head to one side and said, 'It doesn't quite match up, does it? I mean, the pattern is a little different on each side.'

Pelagia felt a pang of disappointment that tasted of

213

betrayal. 'I tried so hard,' she exclaimed piteously, in a rush of emotion, 'and I can never please you.'

Mandras smote his forehead with the heel of his palm, screwed up his face in self-criticism, and said, 'O God, I am sorry. I didn't mean it the way it came out.' He sighed and shook his head. 'Ever since I went away, my mouth and my heart and my brain don't seem so well connected. Everything is upside down.'

Pelagia took back the waistcoat and told him, 'I'll try to put it right. What does your mother say?'

He looked at her appealingly, 'I was hoping that you could tell her. I couldn't bear to hear her weeping and pleading if I tell her myself.'

Pelagia laughed bitterly, 'Are you such a coward, then?'

'I am with my mother,' he confessed. 'Please tell her.'

'All right. All right, I will. She has lost a husband and now she loses a son.'

'I'll be back,' he said.

She shook her head slowly, and sighed, 'Promise me one thing.' He nodded, and she continued, 'Whenever you are about to do something terrible, think of me, and then don't do it.'

'I'm a Greek,' he said gently, 'not a Fascist. And I will think of you every minute.'

She heard the touching sincerity in his voice, and felt herself wanting to cry. Spontaneously they embraced, as though they were brother and sister rather than two betrothed, and then they gazed for a moment into each other's eyes. 'God go with you,' said Pelagia, and he smiled sadly, 'And with you.'

'I shall always remember you swinging in the tree.'

'And me falling on the pot.'

They laughed together a moment, and then he looked at her longingly for one last moment, and began to leave. A few paces away he paused, turned, and said softly, with a catch in his voice, 'I shall always love you.'

A long way down the road, Carlo and the captain, both of them covered in fine beige dust, ruefully inspected their vehicle. It had no wheels and the interior was piled high with a smoking stack of manure.

That evening the captain noticed an exquisitely embroidered waistcoat hanging over the back of a chair in the kitchen. He picked it up and held it against the light; the velvet was richly scarlet, and the satin lining was sewn in with tiny conscientious threads that looked as though they could only have been done by the fingers of a diminutive sylph. In gold and yellow thread he saw languid flowers, soaring eagles, and leaping fish. He ran his finger over the embroidery and felt the density of the designs. He closed his eyes and realised that each figure recapitulated in relief the curves of the creature it portrayed.

Pelagia came in and caught him. She felt a rush of embarrassment, perhaps because she did not want him to know why she had made the article, perhaps because she had been rendered ashamed of its imperfections. He opened his eyes and held out the waistcoat to her. 'This is so beautiful,' he said, 'I have never seen anything as good as this that wasn't in a museum. Where does it come from?'

'I made it. And it's not so good.'

'Not so good?' he repeated disbelievingly. 'It's a masterpiece.'

Pelagia shook her head, 'It doesn't match up properly on both sides. They're supposed to be mirror images of each other, and if you look, this eagle is at a different angle to that one, and this flower is supposed to be the same size as that one, but it's bigger.'

The captain clicked his tongue disapprovingly, 'Symmetry is only a property of dead things. Did you ever see a tree or a mountain that was symmetrical? It's fine for buildings, but if you ever see a symmetrical human face, you will have the impression that you ought to think it beautiful, but that in fact you find it cold. The human heart likes a little disorder in its geometry, Kyria Pelagia. Look at your face in a mirror, Signorina, and you will see that one eyebrow is a little higher than the other, that the set of the lid of your left eye is such that the eye is a fraction more open than the other. It is these things that make you both attractive and beautiful, whereas . . . otherwise you would be a statue.

215

Symmetry is for God, not for us.'

Pelagia pulled a sceptical expression, and prepared impatiently to dismiss his allegation that she was beautiful, but at that point she noticed that his nose was not perfectly straight. 'What is this?' asked the captain, pointing to an eagle, 'I mean, how is it done?'

Pelagia pointed with her finger, 'This is fil-tiré, and that is feston.' He was able to appreciate the articulateness of her forefinger and the smell of rosemary in her hair, but he shook his head, 'I'm none the wiser. Will you sell it to me? How much do you want for it?'

'It's not for sale,' she said.

'O please, Kyria Pelagia, I will pay you in anything you want. Drachmas, lire, tins of ham, bottled olives, tobacco. Name a price. I have some British gold sovereigns.'

Pelagia shook her head; there was little reason now why she should not sell it, but the captain had made her proud enough of it to induce her to want to keep it, and besides, selling it to him would have been, in some indefinable way, quite wrong.

'I am very sorry,' said the captain, 'but that reminds me; how much rent do you want?'

'Rent?' said Pelagia, almost dumbfounded.

'Did you think I intended to live here for nothing?' He reached into his pocket and produced a large chunk of salami, saying, 'I thought you might like to borrow this from the Officers' Mess. I have already given a slice to the "cat", and I think that now we are friends.'

'You've turned Psipsina and Lemoni into collaborators,' observed Pelagia wryly, 'and you'd better ask my father about the rent.'

A week later, after it had been reclaimed and given a new set of wheels, the engine of the jeep would explode spectacularly as it was being driven up the hairpin bends of the hill to Kastro. The driver was a very young lance-bombardier who had been a tenor in Corelli's opera society, and had been waiting for the war to end so that he could marry his childhood love in Palermo.

By that time Mandras was in the heart of Peloponnisos, widowmaking and rebuilding his dream of Pelagia.

27

A Discourse on Mandolins and
a Concert

THE DOCTOR AWOKE at his usual hour, and departed for the kapheneion without awaking Pelagia; he had looked at her, curled up in her blankets upon the kitchen floor, and had not had the heart to disturb her. It did offend his sense of the natural decency of arising promptly upon the hour, but on the other hand she worked hard for him, and had already become exhausted by the difficulties of coping with the war. Besides all that, she looked very fetching with her hair disarrayed upon the bolster, the blanket pulled over her nose, and only one small ear completely exposed. He had stood over her, appreciating the paternal emotions that arose in his breast, and then had not been able to prevent himself from leaning down and peering into the ear in order to check that it was in good condition; there was one very small flake of skin suspended upon the tip of a gossamer hair at the junction of the auricle and the external auditory meatus, but the overall impression was one of perfect health. The doctor smiled down upon her, and then made himself miserable by reflecting that one day she would grow old, bent, and wrinkled, the sweet beauty would desiccate and disappear like dry leaves so that no one would know that it had ever been there. Seized by an impression of the preciousness of the ephemeral, he knelt down and kissed her on the cheek. He went to the kapheneion in a tragic mood that sat oddly with the serenity of a cloudless morning.

The captain, awakened by a sharp twinge from a haemorrhoid, came out into the kitchen, saw Pelagia fast asleep, and did not know what to do. He would have liked to have brewed himself a cup of coffee and eaten a piece of fruit, but he too was captivated by the appealing tranquillity of the sleeping girl, and felt that it would have been a desecration to awake her by clattering about. In addition he did not want to cause her any embarrassment that might arise from being in his presence in night-clothes, and, besides, it was terrible to be reminded of the shame of having displaced a rightful owner from her own bed. He looked down upon her and experienced the urge to crawl in beside her – nothing could have seemed more natural – but instead he returned to his room and took Antonia out of her case. He began to practise fingerings with his left hand, sounding the notes minimally by hammering on and pulling off with his fingers rather than by using a plectrum. Tiring of this, he took a plectrum and laid the side of his right hand across the bridge so that he could mute the strings and play 'sordo'. It made a sound very like a violin playing pizzicato, and with great concentration he set himself to playing a very difficult and rapid piece by Paganini that consisted entirely of that effect.

Half way between sleep and waking, Pelagia's lucid dream took on the distant rhythm of the piece. She was remembering the day before, when the captain had actually arrived at the house on a grey horse that he had borrowed from one of the soldiers who performed the curfew patrol each night. This capricious beast had been trained to caracole, and his owner had taken to impressing girls by making the beast execute this pretty trick whenever he saw one. The horse had soon cottoned onto the idea, and now readily did it unbidden whenever he came across a human in skirts who had long hair and bright eyes. All the soldiers were very envious of this animal, and its rider was always prepared to lend it to officers on the understanding that advantageous adjustments would be made to duty rosters. On the day that the captain borrowed it, its rider would be excused from latrine fatigues.

When Corelli had arrived at the entrance of the yard and Pelagia had looked up from brushing her goat, the horse

219

had pricked up its ears and caracoled. The captain had raised his cap, smiling broadly, and Pelagia had felt a dart of pleasure such as she had seldom experienced before. It was the kind of pleasure that one feels when a dancer who has been kicking his legs impossibly high suddenly somersaults backwards, or when an apple rolls off a shelf, strikes a spoon, and the spoon spins up into the air and lands in a cup, scoop downwards, and comes tinkling to a rest as though it had been tossed there on purpose. Pelagia had beheld Corelli and the exhibitionist horse, and she had smiled and clapped spontaneously whilst Corelli's face had split from ear to ear in an enormous grin like that of a little boy who has at last been given a football after years of whining and begging.

In her dream the horse caracoled to the tempo of Paganini, and its rider at one moment had the face of Mandras, and at another that of the captain. She found this annoying, and made a mental effort to reduce the faces to a single one. It became Mandras, but she found this unsatisfactory, and changed it to Corelli. Had there been anybody in the room, they would have seen her smiling in her sleep; she was reliving the jingle of brass, the creak of leather, the sharp sweet smell of horse's sweat, the intelligent pricking of its ears, the tiny sideways motion of the hooves as they struck the dust and stones of the road, the tensing and relaxing of the muscles in the haunches of the horse, the grand gesture of the smiling soldier as he swept off his cap.

Sitting on the bed, Corelli became so absorbed in his practising that he forgot the sleeping girl, and he began to work on getting his tremolo up to speed; it was deeply annoying to him that every day he would have to play for at least a quarter of an hour before he could make it steady and continuous, and he commenced the exercise by mechanically clicking the plectrum backwards and forwards at half speed across the top pair of trebles.

Pelagia awoke ten minutes later. Her eyes flicked open, and she lay there for a second, wondering if she was still asleep. There was a most beautiful noise coming from somewhere in the house, as though a thrush had adapted its

220

song to human tastes and was pouring out its heart on a branch by the sill. A shaft of sunlight was breaking through the window, she felt too hot, and she realised that she had overslept. She sat up, wrapped her arms about her knees, and listened. Then she picked up her clothes from where they lay beside her pallet, and went to dress in her father's room, still attending to the trilling of the mandolin.

Corelli heard the metallic clatter of a spoon in a pan, realised that she had risen at last, and, still clutching the mandolin, came out into the kitchen. 'Sewage?' she asked, offering him a cup of the bitter liquid that nowadays passed for coffee. He smiled and took it, realising that he was still very sore from riding that horse, and that he was still very relieved that he had not suddenly fallen off; it had been a near thing when it had started to dance like that. His thighs ached and it was painful to walk, so he sat down. 'That was very beautiful,' commented Pelagia.

The captain looked at his mandolin as though he was blaming it for something, 'I was only practising tremolando scales.'

'I don't care,' she replied, 'I still liked it, it made waking up very easy.'

He looked unhappy, 'I'm sorry I woke you up, I didn't mean to.'

'That's very beautiful,' she said, pointing at the instrument with a spoon, 'the decoration is wonderful. Does all that improve the sound?'

'I doubt it,' said the captain, turning it around in his hands. He himself had forgotten how exquisite it was. It was purfled about the rim of the soundbox with trapezia of shimmering mother-of-pearl, and it had a black strikeplate in the shape of a clematis flower, inlaid with multicoloured blossoms that were purely the result of an exuberant craftsman's imagination. The ebony diapason was marked at the fifth, seventh, and twelfth frets with a pattern of ivory dots, and the rounded belly of it was composed of tapering strips of close-grained maple, separated skilfully by thin fillets of rosewood. The machine heads were finished in the shape of ancient lyres, and, Pelagia noted, the strings themselves

221

were decorated at the silver tailpiece with small balls of brightly coloured fluff. 'I suppose you don't want me to touch it,' she said, and he clutched it tightly to his chest.

'My mother dropped it once, and for a moment I thought I was going to kill her. And some people have greasy fingers.'

Pelagia was offended, 'I don't have greasy fingers.'

The captain noted her aggrieved expression, and explained, 'Everyone has greasy fingers. You have to wash and then dry your hands before you touch the strings.'

'I like the little balls of fluff,' said Pelagia.

Corelli laughed, 'They're stupid, I don't even know why they're there. It's traditional.'

She sat down opposite him on the bench and asked, 'Why do you play it?'

'What an odd question. Why does one do anything? Do you mean, what led me to start?'

She shrugged her shoulders, and he said, 'I used to play the violin. A lot of violinists play one of these because they're tuned the same, you see.' Contemplatively he ran a fingernail across the strings to illustrate his point, a point which Pelagia, for the sake of simplicity, pretended to see. 'You can play violin music on one of these, except that you have to put in tremolos where a violin would have one sustained note.' He executed a quick tremolo to illustrate this second point. 'But I gave up the violin because, however much I tried, it just came out sounding like cats. I'd look up and the yard would be full of them, all yowling. No, seriously, it was like a tribe of cats or even worse, and the neighbours kept complaining. One day my uncle gave me Antonia, which used to belong to his own uncle, and I discovered that with frets on the fingerboard I could be a good musician. So there you are.'

Pelagia smiled, 'So do cats like the mandolin?'

'This is a little known fact,' he said in a confidential manner, 'but cats like anything in the soprano range. They don't like things that are alto, so you can't play a guitar or a viola to a cat. They just walk out with their tails in the air. But they do like a mandolin.'

222

'So the cats and the neighbours were both happy with the change?'

He nodded happily, and continued, 'And another thing. People don't realise how many of the great masters wrote for the mandolin. Not just Vivaldi and Hummel, but even Beethoven.'

'Even Beethoven,' repeated Pelagia. It was one of those mysterious, awesome, mythical names that implied the ultimate possibilities of human achievement, a name that in fact meant nothing at all specific to her, since she had never knowingly heard a single piece of his music. She knew simply that it was the name of an almighty genius.

'When the war's over,' said Corelli, 'I am going to become a professional concert player, and one day I am going to write a proper concerto in three movements, for mandolin and small orchestra.'

'You're going to be rich and famous then?' she said teasingly.

'Poor but happy. I'd have to take another job as well. What do you dream about? Being a doctor, you said.'

Pelagia shrugged, distorting her lips into an expression of resignation and scepticism. 'I don't know,' she said at last. 'I know I want to do something, but I don't know what it is. They don't let women become doctors, do they?'

'You can have bambinos. Everyone should have bambinos. I'm going to have thirty or forty.'

'Your poor wife,' said Pelagia disapprovingly.

'I don't have one, so I might have to adopt.'

'You could be a teacher. That way you could be with children in the daytime and have time for music in the evening. Why don't you play me something?'

'O God, whenever people ask me to play something I forget what pieces I know. And I always depend on having the music in front of me. It's very bad. I know, I'll play you a polka. It's by Persichini.' He positioned the mandolin, and played two notes. He stopped, explaining, 'It slipped. That's the trouble with these roundbacks from Naples. I often think I should get a Portuguese one with a flat back, but where does one get one of those in times of war?' He

223

followed this rhetorical question with the same two notes, ritardando, played four quaver chords, then a bar which disrupted one's expectations by the introduction of a rest and a pair of semiquavers, and very shortly broke into cascades of chorded and unchorded semiquavers that left Pelagia open-mouthed. She had never before heard such elaborate virtuosity, and never before had she found a piece of music to be so full of surprises. There were sudden, flashing tremolos at the beginning of bars, and places where the music hesitated without losing its tempo, or sustained the same speed despite appearing to halve or double it. Best of all, there were places where a note so high in pitch that it could barely be sounded descended at exhilarating pace down through the scale, and fell upon a reverberant bass note that barely had had time to ring before there came a sweet alternation of bass and treble. It made her want to dance or do something foolish.

She watched wonderingly as the fingers of his left hand crawled like a powerful and menacing spider up and down the diapason. She saw the tendons moving and rippling beneath the skin, and then she saw that a symphony of expressions was passing over his face; at times serene, at times suddenly furious, occasionally smiling, from time to time stern and dictatorial, and then coaxing and gentle. Transfixed by this, she realised suddenly that there was something about music that had never been revealed to her before: it was not merely the production of sweet sound; it was, to those who understood it, an emotional and intellectual odyssey. She watched his face, and forgot to attend any more to the music; she wanted to share the journey. She leaned forward and clasped her hands together as though she were at prayer.

The captain repeated the first part, and concluded it suddenly on a spread chord that he muted immediately so that Pelagia felt deprived. 'There you are,' he said, wiping his forehead with his sleeve.

She felt excited, she wanted to jump up and perform a pirouette. Instead she said, 'I just don't understand why an artist like you would descend to being a soldier.'

He frowned, 'Don't have any silly ideas about soldiers. Soldiers have mothers, you know, and most of us end up as farmers and fishermen like everyone else.'

'I mean that for you it must be a waste of time, that's all.'

'Of course it's a waste of time.' He stood up and looked at his watch, 'Carlo should have been here by now. I'll just go and put Antonia away.' He looked at her with one eyebrow raised, 'By the way, Signorina, I couldn't help noticing that you have a derringer in the pocket of your apron.'

Pelagia's heart sank, and she began to tremble. But the captain continued, 'I understand why you should want to have it, and in fact I haven't seen it at all. But you must realise what would happen if someone else saw it. Especially a German. Just be more discreet.'

She looked up at him, appealing with her eyes, and he smiled, touched her shoulder, tapped the side of his nose with his forefinger, and winked.

After he had gone the thought occurred to Pelagia that by now they could have poisoned the captain a hundred times over if they had ever wanted to. They could have extracted aconite from monkshood, they could have gathered hemlock, or stopped his heart with digitalis, and the authorities would never have known why he had died. She slipped her hand into the pocket of her apron and slid a finger round the trigger with that familiar motion that she had practised a hundred times. She weighed it in her hand. It was good of the captain to let her know that he respected her need for safety, for the reassurance and the defiance that proceeded from the ownership of a weapon. And you don't poison a musician, not even an Italian; it would have been as abominable as smearing excrement upon the tombstone of a priest.

That evening the doctor himself demanded a concert, and he and Pelagia found themselves outdoors in the yard whilst the captain spread a sheet of music upon the table, and both illuminated it and prevented it from being carried away by the breeze by placing a lantern on its upper edge. Solemnly he sat down and began to tap the striking plate with the plectrum.

The doctor raised his eyebrows in perplexity. This tapping seemed to go on for a very long time. Perhaps the captain was trying to establish a rhythm. Perhaps this was one of those minimalist pieces he had heard about, which was all squawks and squeaks and no melody, and perhaps this was the introduction. He looked at Pelagia, and she caught his glance and raised her hands in incomprehension. There was more tapping. The doctor peered at the captain's face, which was rapt in deep concentration. The doctor always found that in incomprehensible artistic situations like this his backside inevitably began to itch. He shifted his seat, and then lost patience, 'Excuse me, young man, but what on earth are you doing? This is not quite what my daughter led me to expect.'

'Damn,' exclaimed the captain, his concentration utterly destroyed, 'I was just about to start playing.'

'Well, about time too, I should think. What on earth were you doing? What is it? Some ghastly modern twaddle called "Two Tin Cans, a Carrot, and Dead Harlot?"'

Corelli was offended, and spoke with a distinct tone of lofty disdain, 'I am playing one of Hummel's Concertos for Mandolin. The first forty-five and a half bars are for the orchestra, allegro moderato e grazioso. You have to imagine the orchestra. Now I've got to begin all over again.'

The doctor glared at him, 'I'm damned if I'm going to sit through all that tapping again, and I'm damned if I can imagine an orchestra. Just play your parts.'

The captain glared back, clearly indicating his conviction that the doctor was a complete philistine. 'If I do that,' he said, 'I'll start getting confused about when I'm supposed to come in, and that, in a concert hall, would be a disaster.'

The doctor stood up and waved his arm about to take in the olive tree, the goat, the house, the night sky above. 'Ladies and gentlemen,' he bawled, 'I apologise for disrupting the concert.' He turned to Corelli, 'Is this a concert hall? And do my eyes deceive me, or is there not one orchestra present? Do my eyes perceive a single trombone? The smallest and most insignificant violin? Where, pray, is the conductor, and where are the royalty draped in jewellery?'

The captain sighed in resignation, Pelagia looked at him sympathetically, and the doctor added, 'And another thing. Whilst you are tapping away and imagining your orchestra, you are exchanging one stupid expression for another. How are we supposed to concentrate in front of such a gallery?'

28

LIBERATING THE MASSES (1)

WHEN THE GERMANS withdrew from North Africa, they established their centre of operations for the region in Peloponnisos, which meant that Mandras and his small group of andartes were obliged to move across the Corinth Canal into Roumeli.

In Peloponnisos Mandras had done very little. He had joined up with one man, and then two others, and they had conceived neither plan nor purpose. All they knew was that they were driven by something from the very depths of the soul, something that commanded them to rid their land of strangers or die in the attempt. They set fire to lorries, and one of their number garrotted an enemy soldier and sat afterwards, shaking with retrospective fear and revulsion, whilst the others comforted and praised him. They dwelt on the outer fringe of a forest in a cave, living off supplies brought by the priest of a neighbouring village, who brought bread, potatoes, and olives, and took away their clothes to be washed by a local woman. One day they chopped down the legs of a wooden footbridge that constituted part of a footpath leading to a local garrison. In reprisal for having to get their feet wet in a stream, the enemy burned down four houses in the village, and the priest and the school-master begged them to leave before anything worse could happen. The four householders, now homeless, joined them.

In Roumeli there was a small British team of enthusiastic amateurs, none of whom spoke Greek, who had trained for one day before dropping in by parachute, using an innovative type of parachute which had supplies and radios tied into the upper cords, which struck the soldiers resoundingly upon the head when they landed on the ground. These Britons had been co-ordinating guerrilla groups, with the intention of blowing up the viaducts of the single-track railway that was the main supply route that led eventually from Piraeus to Crete, and thence to Tobruk. They assumed that naturally the autonomous groups would be delighted to be commanded by British officers, and the Greeks were so impressed by this confident assumption that they fell for it almost immediately.

There was one group, however, called ELAS, which was the military wing of an organisation called the EAM, which in turn was controlled by a committee in Athens whose members belonged to the KKE. Intelligent people realised immediately that any group with such credentials must have been Communist, and that the purpose of having such attenuated chains of control was to disguise from ordinary citizens the fact that they were a Communist organisation. Initially their recruits came from all walks of life, and included Venizelist republicans and Royalists, as well as moderate socialists, Liberals and Communists, all of whom were easily duped into believing that they were a part of the national liberation struggle, and not part of some convoluted hidden agenda which was more to do with seizing power after the war than beating the Axis. The British armed them, because no one believed the assertion of the British officers on the ground that this was merely storing up trouble for later, and no one believed that swarthy foreigners could make much trouble for the British anyway. Brigadier Myers and his officers shrugged their shoulders and just got on with the job, whilst ELAS only helped or obeyed them when it felt like it. The task of Myers and his officers was impossible, but they achieved all that they had set out to do by means of a combination of grit, patience, and élan. They even recruited two Palestinian Arabs who had somehow got left behind in the general muddle of 1941.

Mandras might have joined EKKA, or EDES, or EOA, but it happened by chance that the first andartes he came across in Roumeli belonged to ELAS, and the commander who first took him into his particular band was proudly and overtly Communist. He was astute enough to see that Mandras was a lost soul, a little embittered without knowing why, young enough to be impressed and delighted by the attaching of resonant names to lofty concepts, lonely and sad enough to be befriended.

Mandras hated the mountains. There were mountains at home, of course, but ringed to infinity by the churning open masses of the sea. It was not just that these mountains of Roumeli abolished the horizon and enclosed him like the embrace of an enormous, ugly, and effusive aunt, it was also that they reminded him of the war on the border of Albania that had cost so much of his sanity, his comrades, and his health. They oppressed him and punished him, even though he knew their ways before he had seen them. He knew already how it was to roast one's thighs and belly before a fire whilst one's back and backside froze to the bone, how it was to undress and wade naked in winter, holding one's clothes above the head, through torrents that snatched the breath from the throat and stunned the flesh like a bruise. He knew already that to defeat the Italians you had to calculate upon needing roughly half their number, and he knew how to load and fire a Mannlicher when the other hand was bleeding and being used to staunch another wound. He knew already how it was to create a life out of dreaming of Pelagia and fraternising in the cups with beloved comrades who might die upon the night.

Mandras joined ELAS at first because he had no choice. He and his fellows were lounging in a small shelter of brush with leaves for bedding, when they were surprised by ten men who surrounded them. All of these men were garbed in the remnants of uniform, were draped in bandoliers, had knives stuffed into their belts, and were so bearded as to look almost exactly alike. Their leader was distinguished by a red fez that would have been poor camouflage had it not been so faded and filthed.

Mandras and his friends looked up into the barrels of a semicircle of light automatics, and the man with the fez said, 'Come out.'

Reluctantly the men stood up and came out, fearing for their lives, their hands upon the backs of their heads, and one or two andartes entered the shelter and threw out their weapons, which rattled together on the ground with that curious sound of dense metal muffled by wooden stocks and oil.

'Who are you with?' demanded the fez.

'With no one,' replied Mandras, confused.

'Are you with EDES?'

'No, we are on our own. We have no name.'

'Just as well,' said the fez, 'now go back to your villages.'

'I have no village,' said one of the prisoners, 'the Italians burned it.'

'The deal is, that either you go back to your villages and leave us your weapons, or you fight it out with us and we kill you, or you join us under my command. This is our territory and no one else muscles in, especially not EDES, so which is it to be?'

'We came to fight,' explained Mandras. 'Who are you?'

'I am Hector, not my real name, which no one knows, and this . . .' he indicated his troop, '. . . is the local branch of ELAS.' The men grinned at him in a very friendly fashion, quite at odds with the dictatorial mien of the fez, and Mandras looked from one of his men to the others. 'We stay?' he asked, and they all nodded in agreement. They had been too long in the field to give it up, and it was good to have found a leader who might know what ought to be done. It had been demoralising to wander like Odysseus from place to place, far from home, improvising a resistance that never seemed to amount to anything.

'Good,' said Hector. 'Come with us, and let's see what you're made of.'

Still disarmed, the small column was led three kilometres to a tiny village which seemed to consist of nothing but rangy dogs, a few sagging houses whose stones had lost their mortar and were held together only by gravity and habit, and a pathway that had widened temporarily and optimistically into a dusty street. There was one house guarded by an andarte, and to this man Hector signalled, 'Bring him out.'

The partisan went inside and, kicking and pushing, propelled an emaciated old man into the sunlight, where he stood trembling and blinking, naked to the waist. Hector handed Mandras a length of knotted rope, and, pointing to the old man, said, 'Beat him.'

Mandras looked at Hector in disbelief, and the latter glared at him ferociously. 'If you want to be with us, you've got to learn to administer justice. This man . . .' he pointed '. . . has been found guilty. Now beat him.'

It was loathsome, but it was not impossible to beat a collaborator. He struck the man once with the rope, lightly, out of deference for his age, and Hector impatiently exclaimed, 'Harder, harder. What are you? A woman?' He struck the old man once more, a little harder. 'Again,' commanded Hector.

It was easier at each stroke. In fact it became an exhilaration. It was as if every rage from the earliest year of childhood was welling up inside him, purging him, leaving him renewed and cleansed. The old man, who had been yelping and jumping sideways at every blow, spinning and cowering, finally threw himself to the ground, whining piteously, and Mandras suddenly knew that he could be a god.

A young woman, perhaps no more than nineteen years old, ran forward, escaping the grasp of one of the andartes, and threw herself at Hector's feet. She was gasping in fear and desperation. 'My father, my father!' she exclaimed. 'Mercy on him, have mercy, he is an old man, o my poor father.'

Hector placed the sole of his foot upon the side of her shoulder and pushed her over. 'Shut up, Comrade, stop your whining, or I won't answer for the consequences. Somebody take her away.'

She was dragged away, pleading and weeping, and Hector took the rope from Mandras. 'You do it like this,' he said, as though explaining some abstruse point of science. 'You start at the top . . .' he slashed a wide cut across the man's shoulders '. . . then you do the same across the bottom . . .' he cut another bloody swathe across the small of the back '. . . and then you fill in between in parallel lines, until the skin is all gone. That is what I mean when I say "beat him".'

Mandras did not even notice that the man had stopped moving, had stopped screaming and whining. With tight-lipped determination he filled in the gap between the lines, going back over the ones that might have left a suspicion of pink skin. The muscles of his own shoulders ached and screamed, and finally he stopped to mop his brow with his sleeve. A fly settled on the pulp of the back, and he crushed it with one more stroke. Hector stepped forward, took the rope from his hand, and placed a pistol in his grasp, 'Now kill him.' He placed a forefinger against his own temple, and used his thumb to convey the impression of an imaginary hammer.

Mandras knelt down and placed the barrel against the old man's head. He hesitated, appalled with himself some-where in the back of his mind. He could not do it. In order to make it look as though he was doing something, he clicked back the hammer and took up first pressure. He could not do it. He closed his eyes tightly. He could not lose face. It was a question of being a man in front of other men, a question of honour. Anyway, it was Hector who was the executioner and he was only the hand. The man had been sentenced to death, and was going to die anyway. He looked a little like Dr Iannis, with his thin grey hair and prominent occipital bone. Dr Iannis, who didn't think him worth a dowry. Who cares about one more useless old man? Mandras clenched together the muscles of his face, and pulled the trigger.

Afterwards he looked not at the bloody mess of bone and brain, but in disbelief at the smoking orifice of the barrel of the gun. Hector took it from him and gave him back his car-bine. He patted Mandras on the back and said, 'You'll do.' Mandras tried to struggle to his feet, but was too weary, and Hector crooked an elbow under his armpit to lift him. 'Revolutionary justice,' he said, adding, 'historical necessity.'

As they left the village along the dust and jagged stone that had once more shrunk to a path, Mandras found that he could not look anyone in the face, and he stared vacantly down into the dirt. 'What did he do?' he asked finally.

'He was a dirty old thief.'

'What did he steal?'

'Well it wasn't exactly stealing,' said Hector, removing his fez and scratching his head, 'but the British drop supplies to us and to EDES. We've given strict instructions to the people round here that every drop must be reported to us, so that we can get there first. Only reasonable under the circumstances. That man went and reported the drop to EDES, and after he did that, he opened one of the canisters and took a bottle of whisky. We found him lying under the parachute silk, drunk as a Turk. It was theft and disobedience.' He replaced the fez, 'You have to be firm with these people, or they start doing what they like. They're full of false consciousness, and it's just something that we have to get out of them, in their own interests. You won't believe this, but half of these peasants are Royalists. Just imagine! Identifying yourself with the oppressors!'

It had never occurred to Mandras to be anything other than a Royalist, but he nodded in agreement, and then asked, 'Was it a drop for EDES?'

'Yes.'

Behind them in the village a lifequelling wail expanded through the stillness. It rose and fell like a siren, echoing from the cliff above them across the valley to the opposite rocks, returning and mingling with the later variations of its own sound. Mandras blocked from his mind the precisely clear picture of what must have been happening – the keening weeping girl, black-haired and youthful like Pelagia, rocking and moaning over the mangled and aborted flesh of her own father – and concentrated on the ululation. If you didn't think about what it was, it sounded weirdly beautiful.

234

29

ETIQUETTE

ON A BRIGHT morning early in the occupation, Captain Antonio Corelli woke up feeling guilty as usual. It was an emotion that struck him each morning and left the taste of rancid butter in his mouth, and it was caused by the knowledge that he was sleeping in somebody else's bed. He felt his self-esteem ratchet lower by the day as he struggled with the idea that he had displaced Pelagia, that she was sleeping, wrapped up in blankets, on the cold flags of the kitchen floor. It was true that Psipsina would creep in beside her on colder nights, and it was also true that he had brought her two Army bedrolls to place one above the other to form a mattress, but he still felt himself unworthy, and he wondered whether she would forever regard her bed as contaminated. It also worried him that she had been obliged to get up very early so that she would be decent, her bed rolled away, by the time that he came into the kitchen. He would find her yawning, her finger following the difficult English of the medical encyclopaedia, or else working vindictively at a crocheted blanket that never seemed to get any larger. Every day he would raise his cap and say, 'Buon giorno, Kyria Pelagia,' and every day it would strike him as ludicrous that he knew the Greek for 'Miss' but did not know how to say 'Good morning'. Nothing delighted him so much as to see her smile, and for this reason he resolved to learn the Greek for 'Good morning', so that he could say it to her casually as he passed on his way to where Carlo was waiting to take him away in the jeep. He asked Dr Iannis for guidance.

This latter was in a testy mood for no other reason than that it had appealed to him to be in that particular mood on that particular morning. His acquaintance with the fat quartermaster had made his practice very much easier to run than it had been even in peacetime, and since the latter was undoubtedly a hypochondriac, he had seen him often enough to ensure a continuous flow of essential supplies. Curiously enough, just when at last he had enough to get by, the islanders stopped getting ill. The communal deferral of illness in straitened times was a phenomenon of which he had heard but never previously witnessed, and every time that he was apprised of an Allied success he had set to worrying about the inevitable flood of maladies that would occur after the liberation. He had begun to resent the Italians for diminishing his usefulness, and it was for this reason perhaps that he informed Corelli that the Greek for 'good morning' was 'ai gamisou'.

'Ai gamisou,' repeated Corelli three or four times, and then he said, 'now I can say it to Pelagia.'

The doctor was horrified, and thought quickly. 'O no,' he said, 'you can't say that to Kyria Pelagia. To a woman who lives in the same house you say "kalimera". It's just one of those strange rules that some languages have.'

'Kalimera,' repeated the captain.

'And if someone greets you,' continued the doctor, 'you have to say "putanas yie" in reply.'

'Putanas yie,' practised the captain. On his way out he proudly said, 'Kalimera, Kyria Pelagia.'

'Kalimera,' said Pelagia, pulling the stitches out of her futile crochet. Corelli waited for her to be surprised or to smile, but there was no response. Disappointed, he left, and after he had gone, Pelagia smiled.

Outside, Corelli found that Carlo had not yet materialised, and so he practised his new greeting on the villagers. 'Ai gamisou,' he said cheerfully to Kokolios, who glared at him, scowled darkly, and spat into the dust.

'Ai gamisou,' he said to Velisarios, who promptly swerved in his direction and released a torrent of invective that the captain fortunately failed to understand. Corelli only avoided being struck by the enormous and wrathful man by offering him a cigarette. 'Maybe I just shouldn't speak to Greeks,' he thought.

'Ai gamisou,' he said to Stamatis, who had recently been coping with his marriage by practising the pretence that his deafness was recurring. 'Putanas yie,' mumbled the old man as he passed.

In Argostoli that evening the captain proudly tried out his new greeting on Pasquale Lacerba, the gawky Italian photographer who had been pressed into working as a translator, and was appalled to find, after some misunderstandings, that the doctor had misled him. He found himself sitting in a café near the town hall, more miserable than angry. Why did the doctor do that? He thought that they had established some kind of mutual respect, and yet the doctor had told him how to say 'Go fuck yourself' and 'Son of a whore', and he been making a fool of himself all day, raising his cap and smiling, and saying those terrible things. For God's sake he had even said them to a priest, a friendly dog, and a little girl with a dirty but touchingly innocent face.

30

THE GOOD NAZI (1)

ONE OF THE many curiosities of the old British administrative classes was that they clearly perceived what had gone wrong at home, and never put it right. Instead, they applied these lessons to their possessions abroad. Thus, in his 'Treatise Concerning Civil Government' of 1781, the philosopher Josiah Tucker noted that London was grossly over-represented in Parliament, and unfairly engrossed with advantages which ought to be common to all. More importantly, he wrote:

'AGAIN; All over-grown Cities are formidable in another View, and therefore ought not to be encouraged by new Privileges, to grow ftill more dangerous; for they are, and ever were, the Seats of Faction and Sedition, and the Nurferies of Anarchy and Confufion. A daring, and defperate Leader, in any great Metropolis, at the Head of a numerous Mob, is terrible to the Peace of Society, even in the moft defpotic Governments . . .

'Once more, if a man has any senfe of Rectitude and good Morals, or has a Spark of Goodnefs and Humanity remaining, he cannot wifh to entice men into great Cities by frefh Allurements. Such places are already become the bane of mankind in every Senfe, in their Healths, their Fortunes, their Morals, religion, &c. &c. &c. And it is obfervable of London in particular, that were no frefh Recruits, Male and Female, to come out of the Country, to fupply thofe Devaftations which Vice, Intemperance, Brothels, and the gallows are continually making, the whole human Species

238

in that City would be foon exhaufted; for the Number of Deaths exceed the Births by at leaft 7,000 every Year.'

Philosophers who have only one idea and propound it in barbarous neologisms in thirty successive volumes have a guaranteed future in the universities, but the unfortunate Josiah Tucker, so influential in his own day, has been lost to modern departments of philosophy because he was insufficiently obscure, did not propound theories mad enough, and rooted his thought in concrete examples. In Britain, instead of sensibly moving the capital to York, London was allowed to grow into the vilest human cesspit in the history of the world. But in Cephallonia the British authorities noticed that Argostoli was growing too big, took Tucker's advice, and set about constructing the exquisite town of Lixouri.

In Lixouri there was a spacious agora rimmed with trees, and a splendid courthouse constructed with a market beneath it, neatly coalescing the related benefits of commerce, justice, and sociable shade from the blows of sun and rain. To this day Lixouri and Argostoli regard each other as aberrant and eccentric, and compete doggedly in dance, music, trade, and civic pride, but in 1941 a new and ominous kind of rivalry was imposed by newly parasitic foreign powers. The Italians garrisoned Argostoli, and the Germans garrisoned Lixouri.

The German detachment was small and unassuming, and there is no doubt that it was only there at all because the Nazis knew perfectly well that the Italians were not to be trusted, and wanted to keep them under observation. It is true that Hitler had described Mussolini as 'The Great Man beyond the Alps', but by then he also knew that the Duce and his henchmen were the only genuine Fascists left in Italy. He knew that their generals were old-fashioned and uninspired, he had seen for himself that the soldiers were ill-disciplined, fractious, and had minds of their own, and in North Africa he had ensured that they were always kept away from the front line during engagements that mattered. Like God setting his rainbow in the sky to remind the Israelites who was boss, Hitler sent to Lixouri three thousand grenadiers of the 996th Regiment, under Colonel Barge.

Nobody liked them, although relations between Germans and Italians were superficially friendly and co-operative. The Germans thought of the Italians as racially inferior negroids, and the Italians were perplexed by the Nazi cult of death. The belts and uniforms grimly embellished with skulls and bones struck them as pathological, as did their iron discipline, their irrational and irritating uniformity of views and conversation, and their incomprehensible passion for hegemony. The Italians, who were inveterately inclined to putting their arms across each others' shoulders, did not feel likewise inclined when in the company of a German, as though they would have received an electric shock, as though their arm might have turned to ice or been lost in the void. In the evenings one could hear 'Lili Marlene' drifting out of the messes, the convivial chatter, the roars of laughter, the high jinks, but this was a private world. In the daytime the Germans were serious, did not understand irony, took polite offence, and were coldly and brutally efficient in their dealings with the local population. Captain Corelli made friends with one of them, a boy who spoke some Italian, and discovered that he only became truly human when he shed his uniform, put on his swimming trunks, and splashed about in the sea.

Günter Weber desperately wanted to be blond, and it was for this reason that he frequented the sunlit beaches in the hours away from duty, hoping that the sun would bleach his hair. But there was nothing he could do to transform his brown eyes to an unsuspiciously Aryan blue. It was on the beach of Lepada Bay that he made the acquaintance of the man who became his friend and whom he was destined to betray with a Judas kiss that consisted of a maelstrom of bullets that opened scarlet and bleeding mouths in the bodies of the companions he had grown to love.

Lepada Bay is found near Lixouri, beneath the monastery where Anthimos Kourouklis conversed with God, overlooked by the ruined Corinthian hill-city of Pale, where in classical times there flourished an innocent cult of Persephone. The beach curves elegantly, and at one tip there is a striated rock that has every appearance of a listing, ruined galleon. It is a stone ideally designed by nature for sitting on in the sun, or for peering over the edge into the ungarnered sea at the hundreds of tiny fish that dart amid the weed.

It was on the sterncastle of this petrified ship that Günter Weber was sitting when he heard the Italian truck arrive beyond the fringe of stiffened grasses and disgorge its merry cargo of songsters and whores.

One would have described these whores as fresh from North Africa, were it not for the egregious inaccuracy of the term 'fresh'. Having been devoured by stinging insects and obliterated by the unfeasibly dry heat of the grey desert, this party of stale but amiable pussycats had recently arrived in their new island paradise, and still could not believe their good fortune. In skimpy dresses, their faces plastered with powder and rouge, their lips fashioned into caricatures of the Cupid's bow, they adored the manner in which the mouths of old peasants dropped open as they flounced by with their parasols. They adored the fresh taste of the water, the silky feel of the sea as they swam shamelessly naked, the miraculous way in which the sun cured blemishes of the skin, and the companionable lethargy of their idle moments in the military brothel, when they lay about painting their nails and complaining about men in general and in particular. Most of all they adored it when they caught diseases that would oblige the military doctors to order periods of recovery that could allow them weeks off at a time. It was a break from getting up early and being transported like cattle from one base to another, only to come home to further bouts of thrusting athletics and unvarying repertoires of grunts. Their existence was nothing but friction (no wonder their skins were smooth) and an eternity of ceilings.

Like the young German grenadier, the whores all wanted to be blonde, but they achieved with violent peroxide the end that he pursued by means of the sun. The inch of black roots at the parting of their brittle, coarsened hair gave them a disappointed and disappointing air, as if they had lacked, like a talented but unmotivated artist, that final impulse that might have consummated the illusions of artifice.

241

The beauty of these jaded but heliotropic flowers was entirely self-generated and self-perpetuated. Their gossamer gloss of youth and loveliness seemed to shimmer upon them like the loose glamour of a tentative spell, but was in truth created by their own efforts, efforts conscientiously made, more the product of perseverance than of hope. Theirs was a vanity in which they struggled to believe. The dutiful exercise of their profession kept their bodies slim and lithe, but there were ineradicable lines at the corners of their eyes, little pouches beneath their breasts where they had begun almost imperceptibly to sag. Their teeth were white and clean, but their smiles were automatic even when sincere. Their legs and armpits were shaven, they smelled of a greenhouse crammed with hyacinth, and they trimmed and shaped their pubic hair so religiously that soldiers who liked to burrow and disappear into a good, abundant, honest muff would come away feeling flat and cheated, as though penetration had not occurred. The women were scrubbed and shining, and Corelli and his opera club sometimes took them to the beach in a lorry because he thought it would cheer them up. The women, well-versed in the varieties of male idiosyncrasy, came along because life had always washed over them and propelled them hither and thither like weed at the edge of tide, and men were the browsing fish that ate them.

Günter Weber watched from his rock as the party of Italian soldiers opened their bottles of wine and began to wave their arms about and sing. He watched the naked nymphs separate themselves and run into the sea, squealing and splashing each other inefficiently, and he smiled with superiority as he reflected that all Italians were mad. It was agreed in the mess, agreed by the whole nation of the reunited German peoples, that the Italians were like children who would eventually be sent home at the end of a party, clutching a balloon and a lollipop in their sticky fingers. They'd get Albania and anything else that the Führer could not see any point in having.

Weber was twenty-two years old and had never seen a naked woman before; he was not one of the diehard and compulsive immolatory rapists such as the Croats and the

German Czechs who had joined up, and in any case military rape did not require the removal of a woman's clothing; its brutality was perfunctory, and it was concluded with a killing. Weber was still a virgin, his father was a Lutheran pastor, and he had grown up in the Austrian mountains, capable of hating Jews and gypsies only because he had never met one. He wandered over to the group of Italians, motivated by a desperate desire, disguised as unconcern, to see a naked woman.

Corelli looked up at the open young face, and liked it. It was ingenuous and friendly. 'Heil Hitler,' said Weber, and held out his hand. 'Heil Puccini,' said Corelli, extending his own.

'I am Leutnant Günter Weber, with the Grenadiers at Lixouri. I saw your party, and I thought that I would come and introduce myself.'

'Ah,' said Carlo, winking, you wanted to come and look at the women.'

'It is no such thing,' lied Weber stiffly. 'Naturally one has seen such things before.'

'I am Antonio Corelli,' said the captain, 'and naturally, one cannot see enough of such things if one is a man.'

'Just so,' lied Carlo, who found the presence of the women a cause of deep spiritual discomfort and perplexity. He was still remembering Francesco and hanging a new loyalty onto the captain, certain that with the captain it was bound to be an affection that would have to constitute its own reward. He had never been entirely sure of this with Francesco, even though Francesco had been married and had expressed vehement aversion to homosexuals. Carlo was glad that Corelli was not an aficionado of the brothel, and had not, as others had, ever pressed him into visiting it. Carlo knew that Corelli had fallen for Pelagia before even Corelli knew it for himself, and this, along with his love of music and his adoration of children and his mandolin, was promiscuity enough for one man.

'You wouldn't be descended from the great composer?' asked Corelli, and the German replied, 'I said "Weber", not Wagner.'

The captain laughed, 'Wagner is not a great composer. Too overblown, too windy, too pompous and overbearing. No, I mean Carl Maria Von Weber, the one who wrote "Der Freischütz", and the two clarinet concerti, and the Symphony in Doh major.'

Weber shrugged his shoulders, 'I regret, Signor, that I have never heard of him.'

'And you are supposed to ask me if I am descended from the great composer,' said Corelli, smiling with anticipation. Weber shrugged again, and the captain supplied, 'Arcangelo Corelli? The "Concerti grossi"? You are not a music lover?'

'No, I like . . .' the lieutenant paused, unable to think of anything that he did like. 'You forgot to tell me your rank.'

'I am the breve, Carlo here is the semibreve, he is the crotchet, he is the quaver, and that lad in the sea is a semi-quaver, and little Piero here is a demi-semiquaver. In the opera club we have our own ranking system, but otherwise I am a captain. Thirty-Third Regiment of Artillery. Please join us, we have plenty of wine, but the girls are off-duty, and I'm sure you've got your own. By the way, your Italian is excellent.'

Günter Weber settled himself in the sand, wary of all these dark jovial foreigners, and replied, 'I come from the Tyrol. Many of us speak Italian.'

'You're not German then?'

'Of course I am a German.'

Corelli looked puzzled, 'I thought the Tyrol was in Austria.'

Weber felt his temper beginning to fray; it was bad enough having to hear slurs on the reputation of Wagner, one of the greatest of proto-Fascists. 'Our Führer is Austrian, and nobody says that he is not a German. I am German.'

There was a difficult silence, which Corelli broke by handing him a bottle of red wine. 'Drink,' he said, 'and be happy.'

Günter Weber drank, and was happy. The wine, the cor-uscating heat of the sun and the mitigating balm of the breeze, the smell of aloes, the rousing choruses, the ever-incredible nakedness of the girls, the Morse code of virgin light glancing after the perpetual motion of the waters, conspired together and unknitted the dry bones in his heart.

He permitted Adriana to fire a round from his Luger, he fell asleep, he was thrown from the rock into the sea, he basked in the admiration of the naked girls who loved his golden tan and his blond hair, and he was delivered to base that evening, his uniform sandy and askew, a fully paid-up member of the opera club, having drunkenly agreed that if ever he should express admiration for Wagner he would be shot, without trial, and without leave of appeal. He was the only one who could not sing a note, and his rank was dotted demi-semiquaver rest.

31

A PROBLEM WITH EYES

PELAGIA TREATED THE captain as badly as she could. If she served him food she would set the plate before him with a great clatter that sent the contents of the bowl splashing and overflowing, and if by any chance it did spill onto his uniform, she would fetch a damp clout, omit to wring it out, and smear the soup or the stew in a wide circle about his tunic, all the time apologising cynically for the terrible mess. 'O, no, please Kyria Pelagia, this is unnecessary,' he would protest futilely, and eventually she noticed that he had acquired the habit of not drawing in his chair until she had already slopped the food onto the table.

His failure to remonstrate with her, and his complete reluctance to come up with the kind of threats that one might expect from an officer of an occupying force, only succeeded in irritating her. She would have liked him to shout, to command her to cease from her insolence, because her anger was so deep and bitter that only a confrontation seemed sufficient to purge it. She wanted to give it an airing, to throw her arms about like a protestant preacher; but he was bent, it seemed, upon frustrating her. He remained submissive and polite, and she would find herself practising in private all the narrowings of the eyes and hard pursings of the lips that would eventually accompany the hypothetical tempest of recrimination and contempt that every day she looked forward to heaping upon his head. After two months of passing her nights sleepless with rage, curled up in her blankets upon the kitchen floor, she had perfected several versions of the impromptu and vitriolic speech with which she intended to confound him. But when would the opportunity to deliver it arise? How does one explode with righteous rancour when the target of it remains circumspect and diffident?

The captain did not seem to her to be a typical Italian. It was true that he sometimes came home a little inebriated, and that occasionally he suffered bursts of incorrigibly high spirits; sometimes he burst in and fell to his knees, presenting her with a flower which she would accept and then feed pointedly and conspicuously to the goat; sometimes he would suddenly grasp her about the waist with his right hand, and her right hand with his left, and whirl her vertiginously a couple of times as though executing a waltz, but this only occurred when his battery won a football match. So he was impulsive like a typical Italian, and he seemed to have not a care in the world, but on the other hand he appeared to be a very thoughtful character who was a master at disguising it. Quite often she would see him standing by the wall of the yard with his hands behind his back like a German, his feet apart, deep in contemplation either of the mountains or of some matter for which they were nothing more than a peaceful occupation for his eyes. She thought that he had a sadness that was very like nostalgia, without actually being it. 'If only,' she thought, 'he was like the other Italians who hiss when I walk by, or try to pinch my backside. Then I could swear at him and hit him, and say "Testa d'asino" and "Possate muri massa," and I would feel very much better.'

One day he left his pistol on the table. She thought how easy it would be for her to purloin it, and perhaps blame it on an opportunistic thief. It came to her that she could actually shoot him when he came through the door, and then run away to join the andartes with it. The trouble was that he was no longer just an Italian, he was Captain Antonio Corelli, who played the mandolin and was very charming and respectful. In any case, she could have shot him with the derringer by now, she could have cracked his pate with a frying pan, and the temptation had not arisen. In fact the very idea was sickening, and it would in any case have been pointless and counter-productive; it would lead to horrendous reprisals, and it would hardly win the war. She decided to immerse the pistol in water for a few minutes so that its barrel went rusty up its inside and the mechanism would seize up.

The captain came in and caught her red-handed just as she was lifting it out. She was standing with her forefinger through the trigger guard, moving the surprisingly heavy deadweight of it up and down so as to shake off the drips. She heard a voice behind her and was so startled that she dropped it back into the bowl.

'What are you doing?'

'O God,' she exclaimed, 'you frightened me!'

The captain looked down at his immersed pistol with an expression of scientific objectivity, raised his eyebrows, and said, 'I see you're engaged in a bit of mischief.'

This was not what she had expected, but nonetheless her heart galloped painfully with fear and anxiety, and a sensation of extreme dread rendered her momentarily speechless; 'I was washing it,' she said feebly at last. 'It was terribly oily and greasy.'

'I had no idea you were so touchingly ignorant,' said the captain laconically. Pelagia flushed with a very curious emotion indeed, an emotion arising from his sarcasm, and his ironic imputation that she was a sweet and silly girl who did stupid things because she was too sweet and silly to know any better. He was pretending to be patronising, and that was easily as galling as actually being patronised. She was also still frightened, still apprehensive about what he would do, and still, far back in her mind, angry that she could not succeed in provoking him.

'You are not disingenuous enough to be a good liar,' he said.

'What do you expect?' she demanded, only to find herself immediately wondering what she had meant.

The captain seemed to know, however: 'It must be very difficult for you all to have to put up with us.'

'You have no right . . .' she began, employing the first

248

words of her well-rehearsed speech, and immediately for-getting the rest of it.

He fished the pistol out of the bowl, sighed, and said, 'I suppose you have done me a favour. I should have dis-mantled it for cleaning and oiling a long time ago. Somehow one forgets, or puts it off.'

'Aren't you angry, then? Why aren't you angry?'

He looked down at her quizzically, 'What's anger got to do with cadenzas? Do you really believe I've got nothing important to think about? Let's just think about important things, and leave one another in peace. I'll leave you alone, and you can leave me alone.'

This idea struck Pelagia as novel and unacceptable. She did not want to leave him alone, she wanted to shout at him and strike him. Suddenly overwhelmed, and cynically aware that she would herself come to no harm by it, she slapped him stingingly with all her force, right across his left cheek.

He had tried to step back in time, but was too late. A little dazed and perplexed, he steadied himself and touched a hand to his face, as though comforting himself. He held out the pistol. 'Put it back in the water,' he said, 'I might find it less painful.' Pelagia was now enraged by this new trick, perfectly designed for the instantaneous annulment of her rage. Frustrated beyond human ability to suffer, she raised her eyes to heaven, clenched her fists, gritted her teeth, and strode out. In the yard she kicked a cast-iron pot with all her might, grievously injuring her big toe in the process. She hopped about until the pain subsided, and then threw the offending pot over the wall. She limped back and forth a little, with great vehemence and bitterness, and plucked an unripe green olive from the tree. It was satisfying and con-soling, so she wrenched off a few more. When she had suf-ficient for a good handful she returned to the kitchen and threw them hard at the captain, who had turned to face her. He ducked futilely as the hard fruits bounced harmlessly off him, and shook his head in bemusement as Pelagia once more disappeared. These Greek girls, such spirit and fire. He wondered why no one had ever set an opera in modern Greece. Perhaps they had, come to think of it. Perhaps he should write one himself. A tune entered his mind and he began to hum it, but it kept turning into the 'Marseillaise'. He struck the side of his head in order to expel the intruder, and the tune perversely transformed itself into the 'Radetzky March'. 'Carogna,' he shouted, in extreme annoyance. Outside, Pelagia heard him, feared a delayed reaction, and hurried away down the hill to escape to Drosoula's house until he cooled down.

As the months went by Pelagia noticed that she was losing her anger, and this puzzled and upset her. The fact was that the captain had become as much a fixture in the house as the goat or her own father. She was quite used to seeing him seated at the table, scribbling furiously, or rapt in concentration with a pencil stuck between his teeth. Early in the morning she anticipated with a small and familiar domestic pleasure the moment when he would emerge from his room and say, 'Kalimera, Kyria Pelagia. Is Carlo here yet?' and in the evening she would actually begin to become concerned if he were a little late, sighing with relief as he came through the door, and smiling very much against her will.

The captain had some engaging traits. He tied a cork to a piece of string, and sprinted about the house with Psipsina in hot pursuit, and in the evening at bedtime he would go out and call her, because normally the pine marten judiciously and fair-mindedly began the night with him and concluded it with Pelagia. He was often to be found on his knees with one hand clamped about Psipsina's stomach as he rolled her back and forth on the flags whilst she pretended to bite him and rake him with her claws, and if the animal happened to be sitting on a piece of his music, he would go away and fetch another sheet rather than disturb her.

Moreover, the captain was possessed of a deep curiosity, so that he could sit with unnerving patience watching Pelagia's hands doing the formal dance of the crochet, until it seemed to her that his eyes were radiating some strange and potent force that would give her fingers the cramps and cause her to lose a stitch. 'I'm wondering,' he said one day, 'what a piece of music would be like if it sounded the way

250

your fingers look.' She was deeply puzzled by this apparently nonsensical remark, and when he said that he did not like a certain tune because it was a particularly vile shade of puce, she surmised either that he had an extra sense or that the wires of his brain were connected amiss. The idea that he was slightly mad left her feeling protective towards him, and it was this that probably eroded her scruples of principle. The unfortunate truth was that, Italian invader or not, he made life more various, rich and strange.

She found a new irritation to replace the old, except that this time it was an irritation against herself. It seemed that she just could not help looking at him, and he was always catching her.

There was something about him, sitting at the table as he waded through the mountains of paperwork demanded by the Byzantine military bureaucracy of Italy, that made her look up at him regularly, as though by conditioned reflex. No doubt his mind was on sorting out the family problems of his soldiers; no doubt he was tactfully suggesting to a bombardier's wife that she go to a clinic for a check-up; no doubt he was signing requisition forms in quadruplicate; no doubt he was trying to work out why a consignment of anti-aircraft shells had mysteriously turned up in Parma, and why he had received in their place a crate of government-issue combinations. No doubt; but all the same, every time she looked up his eyes would flick to hers and she would be caught in his steady and ironic gaze as surely as if he had grasped her by the wrists.

For a few seconds they would look at one another, and then she would grow abashed, her cheeks would flush a little, and she would return her attention to her crochet, knowing that perhaps she had slighted him by so breaking away, but cognisant also of the brazenness of holding his regard for one moment longer. A few seconds later she would look up furtively, and at that exact instant he would return her glance. It was impossible. It was infuriating. It was so embarrassing as to be an humiliation.

'I've got to stop doing this,' she would resolve, and, convinced that he was deep in his tasks, would look up and get caught again. She tried to control herself rigidly, saying to herself, 'I won't look at him for another half hour.' But all to no avail. She would sneak a glimpse, his eyes would flicker, and there she would be again, imprisoned by an amused smile and a raised eyebrow.

She knew that he was playing a game with her, that she was being teased and taunted so gently that it was impossible to protest or to bring it out into the open in order to make an issue of it. After all, she never caught him looking at her, so it was all her fault, obviously. Nonetheless, it was a game of which he was in absolute command, and in that sense she was its victim. She decided to change her tactics in this war of eyes. She decided that she would not be the one to break the impasse; she would wait for his spirit to fail, she would wait until it was he who broke away. She composed herself, summoned up every last spark of resolution, and looked up.

They looked at one another for what seemed like hours, and Pelagia wondered absurdly if it was considered technically legitimate to blink. His face fell out of focus, and she concentrated on the bridge of his nose. It too began to blur, and she switched back to his eyes. But which eye? It was like the paradox of Buridan's ass: an equal choice yields no decision. She concentrated upon his left eye, which seemed to grow into an immense and wavering void, and so she changed to the right eye. Its pupil seemed to transfix her like an owl. How strange, that one eye should be a bottomless chasm and the other a weapon as honed as a lance. She began to feel a terrible vertigo.

He did not look away. Just as her giddiness was about to confound her, he set himself to pulling faces, all the while holding her in his gaze. He flared his nostrils rhythmically, and then waggled his ears. He bared his teeth like a horse, and started to move the tip of his nose from side to side. He leered horribly, like a satyr, and then grimaced.

A smile began to tug at the corners of Pelagia's mouth, and then tugged harder. Finally it pulled irresistibly, and suddenly she laughed aloud and blinked. Corelli sprang dancing to his feet, capering ridiculously and crying, 'I won,

I won,' and the doctor looked up from his book, exclaiming, 'What? What? What?'

'You cheated,' protested Pelagia, laughing. She turned to her father, 'Papas, he cheated. It's not fair.'

The doctor looked from the corybantic captain to his primly smirking daughter, adjusted his spectacles, and sighed. 'Whatever next?' he demanded rhetorically, knowing full well what was next, and working out in advance how best to deal with it.

32

LIBERATING THE MASSES (2)

'HEY, HEY, WHAT are you doing? Get out of here. Leave
my sheep alone.'

Hector did not drop the young sheep that he had draped
across his shoulder. To Mandras he looked just like the pictures of the Good Shepherd in the religious instruction
books that the Catholic missionaries used to hand around
in Orthodox villages, and like the Jesus of the Bible. Hector
was so inspirational, so clear in all his explanations. He was
a man who understood everything. He had a book called
What Is To Be Done? and he knew exactly where to look in
it for guidance. It was an old book, very well-used, falling
apart, but it was by a man called Lenin who was even more
important than Jesus. Mandras was overwhelmingly impressed by the way that Hector could look at all those contorted black worms of print, and turn them into words.
Hector had promised to teach him to read, along with
several others who were illiterate, and they were going to be
a Workers' Self-Education Caucus. Mandras had already
learned the alphabet, and had given a talk about the art of
fishing in the sea. Everyone had applauded. He had learned
from Hector that he was not a fisherman, but a worker, and
he had learned that what he and a carpenter and a man in a
factory had in common was that the capitalists got all the
profit from their work. Except that profit was called surplus
value. He did not understand yet how it was that any of his
surplus value went to someone else, but it was only a matter of time. He felt very angry against the King for making

it that way, and he had learned to scowl or laugh sarcastically every time that someone mentioned the British or the Americans. It was what everyone else did. He could make people laugh by calling his rifle 'bourgeois' when it wasn't working properly. Clerks and shipowners, and any farmer who employed other people were bourgeois, and so were doctors. He thought of all the fish he had given to Dr Iannis in payment for treatment, and felt bitter. The doctor was richer than he was, and in a fair world it should be the doctor whose surplus value came to him. What he should have done was to get together with the other fishermen, and refuse to sell any fish at all unless it was a good price. It was all obvious now.

Mandras was beginning to feel enlightened and knowledgeable, and he worshipped Hector, that stronger and older man who had been in the thick of the fight at Guadalajara and routed the Italian Fascists. Where is Guadalajara? In Spain. Well, where exactly is Spain? We'll have a geography lesson sometime, don't worry. A pat on the back. Thank you, Comrade. This was an adult world, here there was no sir or madam, just comrade. Soldierly, reassuring, inclusive, virile. Comrade. A warm word that was full of solidarity.

Hector smiled at the irate smallholder and said, 'We're taking this sheep on the orders of Allied High Command in Cairo.'

The peasant heaved a sigh of relief, and said, 'And I thought you were thieves.'

Hector laughed, and so Mandras laughed also. The man held out his hand. Hector looked at the horny, grimy palm, and a frown crossed his face. 'One gold sovereign,' explained the farmer.

'Get lost,' said Hector. 'Are you a Fascist yourself, or something?'

'The British always pay one gold sovereign for a sheep,' said the man. 'It's the standard payment. Aren't you with EDES? Surely you know that?'

'We're ELAS, and we don't consider the loss of a sheep much of a hardship when you consider what we're trying to do on your behalf. We'll pay you later. Now do as I say and get lost. The new order from the British is that we take the sheep, and they pay you later.'

The peasant looked down at his boots, 'EDES gave me a gold sovereign this morning for another sheep.'

'If I hear you've been selling supplies to EDES, you're dead,' said Hector, 'so just shut your mouth. Don't you know they've been collaborating with the Fascists?'

'They blew a bridge yesterday,' persisted the unfortunate man.

'For God's sake,' exploded Hector, 'are you so stupid that you don't know a cover operation when you see one?'

As they walked away, the appropriated sheep bleating in distress across the andarte's shoulders, and the man scratching his head in bewilderment, Mandras giggled and said, 'That showed him.' He paused, regretted the silence, however comradely, and added a little hesitantly but with suitable contempt, 'Fascist stooge.'

33

A PROBLEM WITH HANDS

IT WAS A Stygian night. Outside the rain drifted in drapes and an east wind was gusting, causing unknown objects to clatter past in the road and leaving the doctor anxious for the health of the roof, whose pantiles could be heard scraping against each other as they lifted and settled and moved. The three of them were sitting in the kitchen, Pelagia unravelling her ever-diminishing blanket, the doctor reading a book of poems, and the captain composing a sonata in the style of Scarlatti. Pelagia was fascinated by the way in which he seemed to be able to hear the music in his head, and now and then she went to inspect the progress of the incomprehensible squiggles on the page. At one moment she stood with her hand on his shoulder because it seemed the most natural and inevitable pose, and it was only after a couple of minutes that she realised what she was doing.

She looked at her hand in surprise where it rested on the man's body, as though remonstrating with it for behaving so wilfully in the absence of proper adult supervision. She wondered what to do. If she plucked it away, it would seem rude, perhaps. Perhaps it would betray the fact that she had put it there unconsciously, and he would surmise that it bespoke feelings on her part that she would not like to have avowed either to him or to herself. Perhaps if she just left it there as though it belonged to someone else she would be able to disown responsibility for its actions. But what if he suddenly noticed where it was? If she moved it, he would instantly realise by virtue of where it had been that it had in fact been upon his shoulder; and if she did not move it, then he might realise that it was there, and make something of the fact that it had not been moved. She scowled at her hand, and felt anxiety obstructing her understanding of his explanatory monologue about phrasing and harmony. She decided on balance that the best thing to do was to leave her hand where it was and pretend that it belonged to someone else. She leaned forward and adorned her face with an expression intended to convey the most extreme intellectual seriousness that had in it not a trace of natural affection or physical attraction. 'Mmm, how interesting,' she said.

Psipsina scratched at the door, squeaking plaintively, and with relief Pelagia ran to let her in, at which point the captain became aware that a hand had been lightly resting for some minutes upon his shoulder. The absence of its weight was quite palpable, and its former presence most retrospectively pleasant and consoling. He smiled with discreet pleasure, and a note of triumph would have entered his voice if he had had occasion to speak.

His pleasant musings were most horribly interrupted by Psipsina, whose soggy weight in his lap entirely displaced any pleasure or triumph that he might have been entertaining. Psipsina's policy in rainstorms was always to get as wet as was feasible and then leap into the nearest and warmest lap so as to dry herself as efficiently as possible, and this time the captain had fallen victim, since the doctor had very wisely and presciently stood up to prevent it from happening to him. Corelli looked down in horror at the sodden bundle of fur, and felt the water soaking into his groin. 'Aaah,' he cried, throwing his hands into the air.

Pelagia laughed in malicious glee, and swept the bedraggled animal from his lap. He felt the swift brush of her fingers on his thighs, and knew a momentary thrill of surprise, which was augmented almost to infinity when she started to sweep at his breeches with her hands, saying, 'O what a mess, you poor thing, look at all this grit and muck . . .' He looked down in astonishment as the hands worked, and then realised that she had noticed his expression. She stood up quickly, shot him a withering and accusing look, and returned haughtily to her unravelling, whereupon the persistent Psipsina leapt once more into his lap. As the water in his groin warmed up beneath the weight of the pine marten, he felt that odd glow of satisfaction that he had once experienced as a little boy when he had urinated by mistake in his sleep, imagining that he was doing it against a wall. It was the same comforting warmth that one had before waking up in horror and shame. He forgot Scarlatti and thought about Pelagia's hands. Such slender fingers, such pink nails. He imagined them engaged upon amorous and nocturnal things, and realised that he was disturbing Psipsina. He tried to suppress his lubricious imagination by thinking about Vivaldi.

This was a mistake, because he immediately recalled that Vivaldi had taught young girls in a convent. His wayward brain conjured up images of a whole class full of winsome little Pelagias, all of them licking the tips of their pencils suggestively and luring him with their glowing dark eyes. It was a lovely image. He imagined all of them standing at his desk, bending over him as he explained something, with his finger moving along the lines of a text whilst their black hair tickled his cheeks and filled his nostrils with the scent of rosemary.

One of them put her hand inside his shirt, and another one began to stroke his hair and the nape of his neck. Very soon there were dozens of identical slender hands, and in a flash his mind pictured himself stark naked on a vast table, with every one of the miraculously unclothed Pelagias crawling all over him, engaged upon a delicious assault of breasts, hands, and hot, wet, nuzzling lips. He began to breathe heavily and perspire.

Psipsina decided that she could stand no more of this pressing disturbance from below, and jumped off his lap. His beautiful reverie turned to panic. If Pelagia happened to look up, she would see only too clearly that he had a pyramidal protuberance at a particular spot in his breeches, for which only one explanation could have been adequate or convincing.

He tried desperately to think of something deeply

unpleasant, and meanwhile he swivelled in his chair to face away from her a little more. He put his papers in his lap and pretended to study them in that position. In safety now, his thoughts returned to all the Pelagias on the table, their many hands running up and down his body, their many ripe breasts pressing to his mouth like cool and succulent fruit.

The real Pelagia sighed, realising that she was tired of crochet. At her feet lay a tangled heap of unravelled wool that had kinked and interwound upon itself in an attempt to resume the knotted configurations of its former state. Pelagia did not understand why wool should be nostalgic in this way, but it was certainly irritating. She began to gather it up, and became confounded by its intransigence. 'Captain,' she said, 'could you spare me a moment? I need a pair of hands to wind this wool on.'

It was a supreme moment of crisis; the captain had been so far lost in fairyland that he was at that precise moment making love to each of his naked Pelagias in turn. Her voice cut through his dream of Elysium like a knife through a melon. He almost physically heard the susurration of the knife as it sliced, and the hollow knock as it struck the chopping board below and the melon fell in two. 'What?' he asked.

'Lend me a hand,' she said. 'I'm all tangled up in wool.'

'I can't. I mean I've just got to a crucial point. In the sonata. Could you hang on a minute?' It was a desperate situation; he could not possibly stand up now without betraying his tumescent state. He disciplined himself to think about his grandmother, a freezing swim in the sea, a fly-blown horse dead at the side of the road after a battle. The erection dipped its head a little, but not enough.

There was nothing for it; it was very lucky that she was so used to him behaving idiotically from time to time. He dropped to his knees and went over to her on all fours. He wagged his backside like a dog, lolled his tongue, and looked up at her with an expression of extreme canine loyalty. With any luck he would be able to gain some time with this charade, until he was ready to straighten up. She looked down at him and pulled a wry expression. 'You are a very silly man,' she said.

'Wuf,' he said, and waggled his backside again. He presented his two hands as though they were begging paws, and Pelagia straightened them authoritatively, placing them a few centimetres apart, so that she could begin to use them to wind her wool. She was desperately trying not to smile.

The captain lolled his tongue with even greater exaggeration, and gazed up into her face with such doggy adoration that she stopped her winding and said, 'Look, how am I supposed to do this properly if you keep making me laugh? Lunatic.'

'Wuf,' he said again, so embroiled by now in his comic masquerade that he had already forgotten why he had had to embark upon it, the problem having disappeared. He whined, as though asking to be let out, and then began to bark sharply at the wool as though convinced that it was a dangerous and incomprehensible enemy. 'Stupid dog,' said Pelagia, smacking him gently on the nose.

'Do you have any idea how foolish you two look?' expostulated the doctor. 'For God's sake, it's embarrassing. If only you could see yourselves.'

'I can't help it,' said Pelagia reprovingly, resenting this interruption to their very infantile enjoyment, 'he's a madman, and it's contagious.'

The captain threw back his head and howled to the tune of 'Sola, Perduta, Abandonnata'. The doctor winced and shook his head, and Psipsina went to the door and scratched at it, preferring to be let out into the drifting rain than to remain in the room and endure that frightful lament; real dogs were bad enough. Pelagia got up, took a peach from the table, returned to her seat, and just when the captain had thrown his head back for a most plaintive howl, she jammed the peach into his mouth. His expression of astonishment, pop-eyed and disproportionate, was a pleasure to behold. 'Do you know how silly you look?' she enquired. 'Down on your knees, all tied up with wool, and a peach in your mouth?'

'Invaders should behave with more dignity,' said the doctor, his sense of historical aptness somewhat offended.

'Ung,' said the captain.

Pelagia was distracted, understandably, and when she had finished winding the skein, it transpired that she had been doing so with a steadily increasing pressure. The captain stood up, and realised that his nose was becoming blocked just because he could not breathe through his mouth. He bit into the peach and let the remainder of it drop upon the floor, where Psipsina investigated it with some interest before running off with it. He struggled to extract his hands, and failed. 'A plot,' he cried, 'a treacherous Greek plot against their Italian liberators.'

'I'm not going to unwind it again,' said Pelagia, 'it took long enough as it is.'

'Tied up for life,' said the Captain, and spontaneously their eyes met. She smiled coyly, and for no good reason at all lowered her eyes again and said, 'Bad dog.'

34

LIBERATING THE MASSES (3)

IT WAS AN humiliation and an embarrassment to be car-
peted by Lt-Col Myers, but it had happened to Hector and
to Aris, his commander, so many times that it had become
almost a game. All you had to do was profess ignorance or
indignation or penitent horror every time your andarte
group was reported to the British for misdemeanours and
atrocities, and then say that you could not sign any agree-
ments without permission from the committee in Athens,
and for that you would have to send a runner who might
take two weeks to get back. You could always say that the
runner had been caught and killed by the Italians, or the
Germans, or one of the other resistance groups, or you
could even blame the British, saying that they obviously
favoured EDES. You could even blame the Greek villagers
whom the Germans had armed so that they could defend
their chickens against the relentless requisitioning of the
patriotic ELAS guerrillas. This had the advantage of being
occasionally true, and nearly always unverifiable.

Hector adjusted his red fez, and stood before Lt-Col
Myers, feeling like a naughty schoolboy. He had left
Mandras outside, unwilling that he should be a witness to
his discomfiture. Mandras watched the British Liaison
Officers coming and going, and was once again struck by
their great height, their red and peeling noses, and the great
pleasure they took in banter. Some of them were New
Zealanders, and Mandras guessed that this must be a
special place somewhere in Britain where soldiers were bred

specially for the purpose of parachuting out of Liberators and blowing up viaducts. They always had colds, but were capable of incredible endurance, and they made incomprehensible jokes whose irony was completely lost in translation. They made sincere efforts to learn Romaic Greek, but delighted in mispronunciation; if a woman was called Antigone, they all called her 'Auntie Gonie', and Hector himself was known as 'My Sector'. Mandras could not have known that this was because 'This is my sector' was the standard ripost of his mentor when confronted with his double-dealings, his dishonesty, and his barbarity.

'This is my sector,' said Hector to Myers, 'and my orders come from Athens, not from you. Are you Greek, to be giving us orders all the time?'

Myers heaved a patient sigh. He was not trained in diplomacy, had not been told that ninety percent of his job would be the prevention of internecine war amongst the Greeks, and was longing for a simple life in which all one had to do was fight the Germans. He had nearly died of pneumonia, and was still very thin and tired, but nonetheless he had the moral authority of someone who refuses to compromise an ethical principle in the name of an ideal. All the ELAS leaders hated him for making them feel like worms, and yet they never dared to defy him too much because he was the source of all the weapons and gold sovereigns that they were storing up for the revolution, after the Germans had gone. They had to keep him quiet by going along with some of his plans, by occasionally performing minor warlike acts against the Axis troops, and by enduring the lectures that he always delivered with blazing eyes and unanswerable certainty.

'It was agreed from the beginning that all andarte groups would be under the control of Cairo. Kindly do not oblige me to repeat the same things every time I see you. If there is any continuation of your present counter-productive behaviour, I shall not hesitate to arrange for your supplies to be cut off. Is that understood?'

'You give us nothing, all the supplies go to EDES. You have not been fair to us.'

'The same nonsense,' expostulated the colonel. 'How many times must I tell you what you already know? We have always been strictly proportionate.' The colonel straightened up, 'How many times have I got to remind you that in this war we have a common enemy? Does it ever even cross your mind that we are fighting the Germans? Do you really think it's enough to have blown up the Gorgopotamos viaduct? Because that was the last useful thing that ELAS ever did, and that was the last time you ever co-operated with EDES.'

Hector flushed, 'It's Aris you should talk to. I get my orders from him, and he gets his orders from Athens. It's no use going on at me.'

'I have talked to Aris. Again and again and again. And now I am talking to you. Aris told me to talk to you, because he says that the responsibility for these latest outrages is yours.'

'Outrages? What outrages?'

The colonel felt a surge of contempt, and wanted to strike the duplicitous andarte, but he restrained himself. As he talked he enumerated his points on his fingers. 'Firstly, last Friday there was a drop to EDES, which, let me remind you, has been the only major group that actually fights the enemy. You and your men attacked EDES, drove them away, and stole the entire drop.'

'We did not,' maintained Hector, 'and anyway we wouldn't have had to if you supplied us fairly. No one was killed.'

'You killed five men of Zervas' group, including a British Liaison Officer. Secondly, we have supplied you with plenty of money, and yet you never pay the peasants for what you take. Are you so stupid that you can't see that you're driving them into the arms of the enemy? I have had endless complaints, I have had peasants walking fifty miles in order to come and demand recompense. You have burned out three villages whose members resisted your thieving, on the pretext that they were collaborators. You killed twelve men and five women. I have seen the bodies, Hector, and I am not blind. What is the purpose of castration, tearing out eyes, and slitting the mouth so that they die smiling?'

'If they will not supply us, then obviously they are collaborators, and if you will not supply us, what else are we supposed to do? If they are collaborators, I cannot blame my men for getting carried away, can I? And in any case, who says it was us?'

Myers was almost fit to explode. He nearly said, 'The villagers,' but realised that this would invite further Communist reprisals. Instead he said, 'One of our officers saw it.'

Hector shrugged, 'Lies.'

Myers went cold, 'British officers don't lie.' He ruefully regretted the necessary hypocrisy. He glared with patrician disdain at the andarte leader; the trouble with these red Fascists was that they were not gentlemen. They had no sense of personal honour whatsoever. 'Thirdly,' he continued, 'you have been preventing villagers from high in the mountains from entering EDES areas in order to buy wheat, without which they will starve. Is this patriotic? You are not letting them through unless they join ELAS first, and then you are doling out the death penalty for "deserters", even though you do not have the authority. Fourthly, you have brought reprisals against a village by taking potatoes already requisitioned by the Italians. Fifthly, you personally misdirected one of our Liaison Officers when he was looking for Aris with the intention of complaining about your actions. Sixthly, you have been following a policy of disarming other andarte bands, and murdering their officers.'

Hector was adept at diversions, and he counter-accused: 'We know the British policy. Do you think we are stupid? You are going to bring back the King without asking the people.'

Myers slammed the side of his fist into the table-top, sending a glass tumbler toppling to the floor. 'Seven,' he roared, 'you kidnapped and murdered a chief of gendarmerie who was arranging a mass defection of his own men to EDES, and you made them defect to you on pain of death. Eighth, you have proclaimed that anyone not joining ELAS is a traitor to Greece, and will be shot. Ninth, you are giving the funds we give you to EAM, who give it to the

KKE in Athens, and instead of payment you are giving empty promissory notes to the peasants. Tenthly, some men of your unit disgracefully attacked an EDES unit on the flank when they were engaged in a pitched battle with a unit of the SS. This is a blot on the good name of Greece, an infamy that must never be repeated. Is that clear?' The colonel paused and took up a piece of paper from his desk. 'I have here an agreement which has been signed by EDES and EKKA and the EOA, who have all agreed to adopt it as a code of practice. I am going to get Aris to sign it, and I want you to read it and give me your word of honour as a gentleman that you will abide by it. If not, we will have to consider cutting off your supplies.'

Hector looked back defiantly. The colonel had tried this tactic a hundred times. 'I cannot, and Aris will not sign anything unless we have orders from the committee in Athens. We will have to send a runner. Who knows how long it will take?'

'Those are the terms,' said Myers, handing him the piece of paper. Hector took it, saluted with lazy disrespect, and left.

'What was all that about then?' asked Mandras as they descended the precipitous and slippery goatpath that wound downwards into the valley from the cave that Myers had been using as his local Headquarters.

'A load of shit,' answered Hector. 'What you've got to understand about the British is that they are Fascists, and they just want Greece for their empire, and people like Zervas and his lackeys in EDES are helping them to do it. That's why he's got all the supplies and we haven't.'

'We've got tons of stuff,' said Mandras. 'We've got enough to blow up every Nazi in Greece.'

Hector ignored him; he was young and would learn. He said, 'Those villagers reported us to Myers. I think we should go and teach them some lessons. Collaborating bastards.'

'There were some nice women,' said Mandras, smiling.

'We'll teach them a thing or two as well,' replied Hector, and the two men laughed in conspiratorial pleasure. These villagers were all petit-bourgeois sympathisers, Royalists, republicans who only pretended to be opposed to the king that everyone contemptuously referred to as 'Glucksburg'. They were all Fascist fellow-travellers, and all of them spat on scientific socialism. It was good to get those traitor women screaming and squirming underneath you, and you didn't have to trouble your conscience about it because it was the least they deserved; a new and better Greece was about to be built, and you did what you liked with inferior bricks that were going to be discarded anyway. Likewise, when you made an omelette you threw away the shells.

Up in his cave Myers thought again about requesting to be evacuated. Cairo ignored everything he told them about ELAS and did not seem to understand that sooner rather than later the Communists were going to start a civil war. He was just wasting his time. He mopped his brow with his handkerchief and ran his fingers through the itching beard that was still a novelty to him. Tom Barnes came in, having trekked for five days after destroying a bridge with the aid of Zervas' men. He sat down heavily on the old wooden chair, took off his boots, and inspected the raw blisters on the soles of his feet and on his toes. Myers questioned him with one raised eyebrow, and Barnes looked up and smiled. 'Top-hole explosion,' he said in his New Zealand drawl, 'absolutely ripping. Cantilevers all over the shop. It'll keep the wops and jerries busy for weeks.'

'Splendid,' said Myers. 'Cup of tea? I've just had that Hector here. He's almost as ghastly as Aris, an absolutely bloody swine, through and through.'

'That's the trouble with bad hats,' said Barnes, 'they always jolly well end up at the head.'

35

A Pamphlet Distributed on the Island, Entitled with the Fascist Slogan 'Believe, Fight, and Obey'

ITALIANS! LET US celebrate together the life and achievements of Benito Andrea Amilcare Mussolini, Who from unpromising beginnings has led us to perdition.

In His infancy He was thought to be dumb, but later proved to be incorrigibly garrulous and more full of wind than all the herds of cows that browse the pastures of the Alps. As a boy He blinded captive birds with pins, plucked the feathers of chickens, was deemed uncontrollable, and pinched little girls in school in order to make them cry. He led gangs, started fights, sought quarrels without provocation, and refused to pay up on bets that He lost. At the age of ten He stabbed a boy at supper, and then stabbed someone else shortly after. He let it be known that He was at the top of His class, when He was not, and at the onset of puberty took to visiting the brothel at Farti on Sundays. Amid what clouds of glory did He therefore begin His life!

He committed a rape against a virgin in a stairwell, and when she wept for her honour He reproached her for mounting an insufficient resistance. Misanthropic and eremitic, He was scruffy, ill-mannered, unemployable, and only went out after dark. How splendidly did He continue to develop His talents!

As a schoolteacher He was known as 'the tyrant' but

could not control His classes. He took to alcohol and cards, undertook an adulterous affair with the wife of a soldier who was away on duty, stabbed her, and acquired a knuck-leduster. In order to escape from His debtors, His affairs, and military service, He fled to Switzerland, where He declined to work. Instead He began to beg with menaces, and upon being arrested as a vagabond, protested to the police that He hated other tramps, and therefore could not be one of them. In this He displayed the gift for reasoned oratory which has since become so well known to us.

He went to work for a wine merchant, but was sacked for drinking all the stock. His official version of this story is that He was at the time having meetings with Lenin, who professed the profoundest admiration of His qualities. In 1904 He began to encourage Italian soldiers to desert the Army, which was entirely consistent with His later demand (with which all of us are presently familiar), that all desert-ers must be shot.

He moved to Paris, where He earned a living by telling fortunes. He affected an interest in philosophy, and has more recently disclosed that He studied at Geneva and Zürich Universities. This is of course true, even though there is no record of His attendance or enrolment. It is also true that He did not abandon his mother to a death in penury, or His father to imprisonment. As we all know, the DUCE believes His own propaganda, and so, therefore, do we.

He took another teaching post and was sacked after one year for holding riotous parties in cemeteries. He also con-tracted syphilis during an adulterous affair. This cannot be accepted as a reason for His current insanity however, since He was already mad when He contracted it. It was at this time that He wrote His superb history of philosophy which He says was torn up by a jealous lover, but which all our professors know to have been a work of genius, even with-out ever having seen it. He was dismissed from another teaching post, and discovered a new political ideology, con-sisting of the notion that one should act first, and think up the reasons afterwards, this being the only way in which His doctrines conflict with those of Stalin, who has always known in advance what he was intending to achieve.

The DUCE took to pulling His hat down over His eyes in order to avoid having to recognise anyone and converse with them, deliberately crumpling His clothes and using foul language, and wrote an excellent novel in the manner of Edgar Allan Poe, which was inexplicably refused publication by all the publishing houses to which He sent it. It was a work of genius, and was possibly too sophisticated for their tastes. Shortly afterwards He became a sub-editor of *Il Popolo*, and discovered that he could economise on journalists by concocting the news Himself. Ten editions were confiscated for libel, and He was arrested for defaulting on a fine. Originality has always thus been persecuted.

The DUCE gained much notoriety by accusing Jesus Christ of copulating with Mary Magdelen and by penning a pamphlet entitled 'God Does Not Exist', and shortly afterwards was imprisoned for encouraging sedition within the Army. He married His own half-sister, she being the illegitimate child of His own father, thus adding incest to the list of His accomplishments, and then fathered an illegitimate child in Trent. Dutiful sons should always so emulate their fathers, and in this way will one generation be a light that shines in perpetuity to every other. At this time it was said of Him that He could not look people in the eye when in conversation, possessed no sense of humour, was delinquent and paranoid, and was known by all as 'The Madman'. This, of course, is not true, even though everyone who knew Him in those days remembers it perfectly. In 1911 He opposed the war on Libya, and on achieving power in later years followed a policy of bestial oppression in that same country, thus displaying His extraordinary adaptability in the face of an unchanging situation.

Whilst editor of *Avanti* He began an affair with Ida Dalser, who had His child and allowed Him to live off her money. He abandoned her and later imprisoned her in a mental institution, in this way displaying His incredible capacity for loyalty. Similarly He made Margherita Sarfatti his mistress, and later had her imprisoned under anti-Jewish legislation. It should be noted that every single one of His scores of mistresses has been extraordinarily hideous, and no doubt the DUCE has been indulging His charitable impulses by consorting with them. Beauty is in the eye of the beholder, and possibly the DUCE is astygmatic. At this point we should note that Leda Rafanelli declined to become one of His women on the grounds that He was a madman and a liar, and for this slander He later subjected her to police harassment that was entirely justified and had nothing to do with petty and vindictive motives connected with revenge.

The DUCE refined His ideology into one wherein He agreed completely with the last person to whom he had spoken, and in 1915 tried to avoid conscription into the war which at different times he had both opposed and advocated. He was unaccountably rejected for a commission, and claimed that the Austrians had specially shelled the hospital where He was being treated for shrapnel wounds with the single intention of eliminating Him, since He was the most important man in Italy. By this time His newspaper was being funded entirely by advertisements from arms manufacturers, which had nothing to do with His sudden conversion to the allied cause.

The DUCE diverted funds intended for the Fiume adventure, and used them for His own election campaign. He was arrested for the illegal possession of arms, sent parcel bombs to the Archbishop of Milan and its mayor, and after election was, as is well-known, responsible for the assassination of Di Vagno and Matteoti. Since then He has been responsible for the murders of Don Mizzoni Amendola, the Roselli brothers, and the journalist Piero Gobetti, quite apart from the hundreds who have been the victims of His squadristi in Ferrara, Ravenna and Trieste, and the thousands who have perished in foreign places whose conquest was useless and pointless. We Italians remain eternally grateful for this, and consider that so much violence has made us a superior race, just as the introduction of revolvers into Parliament and the complete destruction of constitutional democracy have raised our institutions to the greatest possible heights of civilisation.

Since the illegal seizure of power, Italy has known an average of five acts of political violence per diem, the DUCE has decreed that 1922 is the new Annus Domini, and He has pretended to be a Catholic in order to dupe the Holy Father into supporting Him against the Communists, even though He really is one Himself. He has completely suborned the press by wrecking the premises of dissident newspapers and journals. In 1923 he invaded Corfu for no apparent reason, and was forced to withdraw by the League of Nations. In 1924 He gerrymandered the elections, and He has oppressed minorities in the Tyrol and the North-East. He sent our soldiers to take part in the rape of Somalia and Libya, drenching their hands in the blood of innocents, He has doubled the number of the bureaucracy in order to tame the bourgeoisie, He has abolished local government, interfered with the judiciary, and purportedly has divinely stopped the flow of lava on Mt Etna by a mere act of will. He has struck Napoleonic attitudes whilst permitting Himself to be used to advertise Perugina chocolates, He has shaved His head because He is ashamed to be seen to be going bald, He has been obliged to hire a tutor to teach Him table manners, He has introduced the Roman salute as a more hygienic alternative to the handshake, He pretends not to need spectacles, He has a repertoire of only two facial expressions, He stands on a concealed podium whilst making speeches because He is so short, He pretends to have studied economics with Pareto, and He has assumed infallibility and encouraged the people to carry His image in marches, as though He were a saint. He is a saint, of course.

He has (and who are we to disagree?) declared Himself greater than Aristotle, Kant, Aquinas, Dante, Michelangelo, Washington, Lincoln, and Bonaparte, and He has appointed ministers to serve Him who are all sycophants, renegades, racketeers, placemen, and shorter than He is. He is afraid of the Evil Eye and has abolished the second person singular as a form of address. He has caused Toscanini to be beaten up for refusing to play 'Giovinezza', and He has appointed academicians to prove that all great inventions

273

were originally Italian and that Shakespeare was the pseudonym of an Italian poet. He has built a road through the site of the forum, demolishing fifteen ancient churches, and has ordered a statue of Hercules, eighty metres high, which will have His own visage, and which so far consists of a part of the face and one gigantic foot, and which cannot be completed because it has already used up one hundred tons of metal.

Everything in His speeches is contradicted somewhere by another speech, since He has acutely observed that we Italians only pick up the points with which we ourselves agree, and in this manner He has made Himself all things to all men. He has burned books and doctored the texts of our schools, He has persecuted the philosopher, Benedetto Croce, He has appointed revolutionary courts with the power to pass sentence of death, and He has turned idyllic islands into prisons where His opponents can be tortured. He has made us all swear oaths of obedience at the age of eighteen, so that only the insincere hypocrites and the terminally stupid may make progress, and He has tried to turn us all into puritans by telling us that it is virile to remain unsmiling except when expressing extreme sarcasm.

He has violated the islands of the Dodecanese, even effacing the tombstones of Greeks, He has opened a school in Parma to teach terrorism to Croats and Macedonians, He has subverted the League of Nations by infiltrating its administration, He has blocked peace negotiations between Albania and Yugoslavia, He has re-armed Germany, Belgium, and Austria, leaving His own army to fight scandalously unjustifiable wars without weapons, and yet has signed the Kellogg pact that outlawed the use of force as an instrument of foreign policy.

This Promiscuous Syphilitic has made the transfer of syphilis an imprisonable offence, this Father of Innumerable Stunted Bastards has made contraception illegal, this Foul-Mouthed Peasant has proscribed swearing and has regulated dancing and the consumption of alcohol in an attempt to make us more serious. He has legislated to make women into battery hens, He has suppressed all freedom of religion,

274

He has caused all pronouns referring to Himself to be capitalised, and the word DUCE to be printed in newspapers in the upper case, He has set up concentration camps in Libya, and He has at one time or another decided to invade France, Yugoslavia, French Somaliland, Ethiopia, Tunisia, Corsica, Spain, and Greece. The DUCE has said 'Better one day as a lion than one hundred years as a sheep,' and therefore He has become a cardboard lion and we Italians have become the sheep who follow Him into the slaughter house and tell each other that we too are lions. He has said 'The more enemies, the greater the honour,' and so we have created enemies out of thin air and gone out to fight them without boots on our feet, and in armoured cars whose barrels are made of wood.

This Ludicrous Buffoon, owner of a thousand florid uniforms covered with spurious medal ribbons for acts of valour that he has never performed, has caused us to take photographs of our own babies dressed in black shirts, He has made us rehearse the applause at His speeches by means of prompt-cards and bells, He has inaugurated a 'move towards youth' that has placed thugs and the disastrously inexperienced in positions of power. Against the Catholic doctrine of the Holy Church He has introduced sterilisation for the 'racially inferior', He has signed non-aggression pacts with the USSR and Britain, with both of whom we are now at war for no obvious reason, He has made military training compulsory at the age of eight so that our children are turned into toy soldiers. He has named Hitler as a 'tragic clown', 'a horrible sexual degenerate', and 'disloyal and untrustworthy', and yet this is the man from whom He takes His orders. He has let it be known that His name is to be used as an anaesthetic in hospitals prior to operations, and, as though His own intellect were anaesthetised, He has foolishly declared that the British are too decadent to oppose us. The British have since then decadently sunk half our fleet, which is why we have everywhere been left to starve, and they have defeated us in North Africa, where our coloured troops have unanimously defected. We invaded Ethiopia at the cost of 5,000 Italian lives, an entire year's revenue, and the equivalent of the equipment of 75 divisions, and in this way directly caused the decadent British to re-arm with the very weapons that are now being used against us.

This Moral and Intellectual pygmy has caused the Felix Mater prayer to be addressed to His own dead mother, He has caused us to lose 6,000 troops in the civil war in Spain, for no return whatsoever. Because we have been lions led by a donkey, we were defeated by an army of amateurs at Guadalajara, and worse than this, He has blotted our name forever by ordering the massacre of Spanish prisoners in Majorca. Equally shamefully He has ordered the torpedoing of neutral ships and refused permission for survivors to be picked up, He has entered an alliance with Japan and ordered the newspapers to refer to them as 'Aryans', He has made us the lackeys of Germany by forcing us to march at the goose-step, He has performed the semantically impossible feat of appointing both Himself and the King as 'First Marshal', He has persecuted Italian Jews in order to please Hitler, and He has declared that we cannot lose against the British because they effeminately carry umbrellas.

Soldiers! We have no uniforms to wear because the DUCE has ordered that they must be worn by all teachers and government employees, we have been abandoned in North Africa for lack of transport, having marched 600 kilometres across the desert in full summer. We have lost one-third of our merchant marine because He forgot to order them home before declaring war, we have been persuaded that halving the size of a division means that we have double the number of divisions, we have been made to invade Greece from the north in the rainy season, without winter clothing, having been demobilised, through ports in the Adriatic where it was impossible to disembark, without the knowledge of the Army Chief-of-Staff, who first heard about it on the radio. All our Albanian soldiers immediately deserted, and we only know what is happening to us by listening to the BBC. Our Navy, for lack of air cover and aircraft carriers, has been annihilated at Taranto and Cape Matapan, for the loss of one British plane, and in North

Africa our 300,000 troops have been defeated by 35,000, because we have no Air Force, our light tanks are made of paper, and our motorised units have no motors. Whilst we die for nothing the DUCE has set up His Headquarters near the Vatican, so that it will not be bombed.

Soldiers! We have been made to invade an innocent country of brave people, knowing that we could never feed them in the event of victory, so that their starvation is worse than ours. Against all rules of war and conscience, the DUCE has ordered us to kill twenty of them for each of ours that is lost, and to our eternal credit, most of us have ignored Him.

Soldiers! Let us weep for what has happened at home, where 350,000 of us have been transported as slave labour to Germany, where the DUCE has created the impossible condition of there being unemployment during a war, where there is hopeless inflation and where three-quarters of food is obtainable only on the black market that is run by His own officials, where ration cards are forged without restraint, and where there are forty distribution agencies with overlapping functions that ensure that nothing can ever happen.

Let us weep for our country, where medals are awarded for the imaginary sinking of non-existent British ships, where we are obliged to stand and salute during radio news bulletins, where the speeches of a lunatic are treated as sacred texts and a million copies printed, where the Lunatic in question is like a conductor Who Himself attempts to play simultaneously all the instruments of the orchestra, Who is like a power station connected to a single broken bulb, Who has had Himself filmed winning tennis matches against professionals in games umpired by the Minister for Propaganda, Who is the Most Disobeyed Man in History because everyone knows that every order will be shortly countermanded.

Soldiers! This is the Man who commanded us to use mustard gas and phosgene against savages armed with spears. This is the Ridiculous Man whose malicious blackshirted bandits and arsonists run away in battle but kill our fathers, mothers, and uncles by making them drink castor oil laced with petrol. This is the Man who has destroyed the economy and has made us ashamed forever.

Soldiers! It has been well said that every nation gets the leader it deserves. VIVA IL BUFFONE. VIVA IL BALORDO. VIVA L'ASSASSINO. VIVA IL DUCE.

his hallowed copy of *What Is To Be Done?* under his arm. An owl hooted in the distance, as though in mockery of his discourse, and the night grew colder as a northern wind stirred the branches of the pines. Behind them the peak of the mountain sat brooding between two brightly pulsing stars, oppressing and overhanging that limitless forest, with its strangely intermuddled population of heroes, pine martens, boars, brigands, and thieves.

'Now, comrades, I want to speak to you because I think that many of you have not learned yet that without revolutionary theory there can be no revolutionary movement, and that the role of vanguard fighter can only be fulfilled by a party that is guided by the most advanced theory. The point is that many of you have no clear idea of how to understand our historical experience, and this leads to narrow ameliorism, economism, concessionism, and democratism. Now, it's true that this kind of bourgeois socialism, bourgeois social reformism and opportunist-socialism is consciousness in an embryonic form, but it completely fails to take account of the necessary and irreconcilable antagonism between the interests of the proletariat and the interests of reactionary obscurantism. It fails to understand the dialectic of social contradiction. You see, the interests of the proletariat are diametrically opposed to the interests of the bourgeoisie. It's not only theory, but praxis that reveals this, and it hardly needs me to try and prove it, because it's so obvious. What we have constantly to keep before the eyes of our understanding is that the world-historical significance of the struggle demands the direct intervention of the proletariat in social life, and not just some kind of parliamentarian republicanism or military semi-absolutism. The point is that Communism is always to be found in advance of all others in furnishing the most revolutionary appraisal of any given event, and is always the most irreconcilable in the struggle against all defence of backwardness. And I don't want you to go thinking that we can expose and repudiate the revisionist and eclecticist historico-ideologues of the ruling classes just by arranging strikes and forming into unions, because the trade-unionist

280

politics of the working class is nothing more than precisely a petit-bourgeois politics of the working-class. We go far, far beyond that.

'It is absolutely scientifically true that what we are about is the political and economic emancipation of the masses, but we know only too well that the proletariat must be led by an intelligentsia with sufficient education and leisure to theorise; Marx, Engels, Plekhanov, Lenin, they were all bourgeois intellectuals who sacrificed their own interests in order to raise the consciousness of the world-proletariat who still do not fully understand the nature of the structures that have to be put in place. What we are aiming at is the effacement of all distinctions between workers and intellectuals, and so we need sufficiently trained, developed and experienced leaders to guide the spontaneously awakening masses away from erroneous theories that deviate from the perception of the necessary and inevitable nature of the materialist conception of history.

'We need leaders who are not susceptible to tailism, leaders who do not give in to working-class aspirations, but who help them to form correct aspirations. With the right leaders it is not necessary to bring the workers up to the level of intellectuals, because all they have to do is place their faith and trust in the leaders who will provide the stable organisation that will maintain continuity and reach a scientific understanding of the concrete conditions prevailing.

'I know that some of you have been complaining about the fact that we don't submit decisions to democratic vote, but what you've got to understand is that we have so many revanchist, recidivist, chauvinist, reactionary forces ranged against us that it is vital for our leadership to remain secret. And if it's got to be secret, how can it possibly be democratic? Democratic implies an openness that would be suicidal. It's obvious, isn't it? So let's have no more of this votism. It's a useless and harmful toy.

'And another thing. It's clear to anyone with any brains that leadership is a functional specialisation, and that therefore it inevitably presupposes centralisation. So stop moaning that we're not fighting the Germans enough, and stop moaning about having to fight EDES and EKKA. The central leadership knows exactly what it's doing. It sees the whole picture whilst we only see a tiny corner of it, and that's why we absolutely must not go around acting on our own initiative; there might be some bigger plan that we mess up if we start to be opportunist. Opportunism means a lack of definite and firm principles. There must be complete, comradely, mutual confidence amongst revolutionaries, and we must stand undeviatingly together in the decisive struggle. And if you're going to complain any more about opposing the reactionary and fascist so-called guerrillas in EDES, just let me remind you that a bad peace is not better than a good quarrel. They say that they are fighting the same enemy as us, but they weaken us by taking recruits that should have come to us and by inculcating in them a false consciousness of the real nature of the world-historical struggle. It is our absolute historical duty to purge them because a party always becomes stronger by purging itself.

'This means that we must at all times preserve solidarity and iron discipline, and that is why it is in accordance with the strictest demands of justice that the leadership has decided that anyone who deviates earns himself a sentence of death. Since I am the representative of that leadership hereabouts, it all boils down to the single requirement that you should obey me, without questioning. At this moment in history there is no room whatsoever for doubters and hangers-on and false-humanitarians. We must keep our eyes fixed solely upon the single goal, because to do anything else is to betray not only Greece and the working classes, but History itself. Any questions?'

Mandras raised his hand deferentially, 'I didn't understand all of it, Comrade Hector, but I want to say that you can count on me.' One day he might be able to read that book of Hector's himself. He might hold it in his hands as though it were printed upon sheets of diamond. At night he might kiss its covers and sleep with it beneath his head, as though its inconceivable wisdom might seep by capillary action into his brain. One day he would be an intellectual, and neither the doctor nor Pelagia would ever be able to say otherwise. He imagined himself as a schoolteacher, with everyone calling him 'daskale' and listening avidly to his opinions in the kapheneion. He imagined himself as the mayor of Lixouri.

Mandras never did read that book, and was spared the disappointment of discovering that it was an immensely tedious and irrational tirade against a rival Communist newspaper. But there would come a time when he understood every word that Hector said, and would drink in his intoxicating visions of the dictatorship of the proletariat as though they were the revelations of a saint.

But on that evening, one of the Venizelists who was about to risk his life by defecting to EDES came up to him later in the darkness, sympathetically offering him a cigarette, and explaining, 'Look, you don't have to understand all that jargon from our sesquipedalian friend, because all it boils down to is that you've got to do just as he says, or he'll cut your throat. It's really that simple.' The man, a lawyer in civilian life, patted him on the shoulder, and, as he turned away, said enigmatically, 'I feel sorry for you.'

'Why?' called Mandras after him, but received no reply.

37

AN EPISODE CONFIRMING PELAGIA'S BELIEF THAT MEN DO NOT KNOW THE DIFFERENCE BETWEEN BRAVERY AND A LACK OF COMMON SENSE

A GREAT VOICE boomed out behind him, and Captain Corelli, absorbed in reading the pamphlet, nearly died of shock.

'Those that seek my soul to destroy it shall go to the lower parts of the earth, they shall fall by the sword, they shall be a portion for foxes, God shall shoot at them with an arrow and suddenly they shall be wounded.'

Corelli leapt up and found himself face to face with the patriarchal beard and flaming eyes of Father Arsenios, who was glaring at him over the wall, having lately taken to startling unsuspecting Italian soldiers by means of thunderous improvisations upon Greek biblical texts. The two men stared at one another, Corelli with his hand over his heart and Arsenios waving his home-made crozier. 'Kalispera, Patir,' said Corelli, whose grasp of Greek etiquette was improving, whereupon Arsenios spat into the dust and declared, 'Thou shalt make them as a fiery oven in the time of thine anger, thou shalt swallow them up in the time of thy wrath, and the fire shall devour them. Their fruit shalt thou destroy from the earth, and their seed from among the children of men, for they have imagined a mischievous device which they are not able to perform.'

The priest's eyes rolled prophetically, and Corelli said placatingly, 'Quite so, quite so,' despite not having understood any of it. Arsenios spat again, rubbed the saliva into the ground with his foot, and pointed at the captain to signify that he would be milled into the dust in the same way. 'Quite so,' repeated Corelli, smiling politely, whereupon Arsenios waddled away in a manner intended to convey disgust and absolute certainty.

The captain returned to his reading, only to be disturbed by the doctor and Pelagia returning from a medical expedition, and Carlo Guercio arriving in the jeep. Hastily he hid the document in his jacket, but not before the doctor had caught a glimpse of it.

'Ah,' said the doctor, 'I see that you've got a copy too. Amusing, isn't it?'

'Fuck the war,' said Carlo gaily as he came through the entrance to the yard with his customary greeting. He struck his forehead on a lower branch of the olive where Mandras had used to swing, and momentarily stunned himself. He grinned sheepishly, 'I'm always doing that. You'd think I'd know it was there by now.'

'You shouldn't be so tall,' said the doctor, 'it shows lack of foresight and good judgement. There was a king of France who died from doing something like that.'

'I appear to be alive,' said Carlo, touching the incipient bruise with an index finger. 'Have you seen the pamphlet?'

Corelli shot him an angry glance, but Pelagia said, 'It seems to have appeared all over the island during the night.'

'In fact the captain is trying to conceal one at this very moment,' said the doctor gleefully.

'British propaganda,' said the captain, feigning a great lack of interest.

'There weren't any planes last night,' said Carlo. 'When they come over everything rumbles and shakes, but there was nothing.'

'Can't be British then,' said the doctor happily, 'I think you've got someone here with access to a press and an excellent delivery service.' He saw Carlo flushing and looking at him angrily, and realised that it was better not to talk. 'As you say, just British propaganda,' he added lamely, shrugging his shoulders.

'It must be somebody who knows a lot,' said Pelagia, 'because everything in it is true.'

Corelli flushed with anger and stood up abruptly. She feared for a second that he was tempted to strike her. He removed the leaflet from his jacket and dramatically tore it in half, throwing the pieces to the goat. 'It's nothing but a heap of shit,' he declared, and strode into the house.

The remaining three exchanged glances, and Carlo made a grimace that mockingly expressed fear and trembling. Then he became very serious and said to Pelagia, 'Please excuse the captain, and do not tell him that I said this, but you must understand that in his position . . . he is an officer, after all.'

'I understand, Carlo. He wouldn't admit it was true even if he wrote it himself. Do you think it could have been written by a Greek?'

The doctor scowled. 'What a stupid idea.'

'I just thought . . .'

'How many Greeks could know all that, and how many Greeks here can write Italian, and how many Greeks have transport, that they can leave it lying about the whole island? Don't be silly.'

But Pelagia warmed to her hypothesis, 'Lots of the Rs were written as Ps, and that's a natural Greek mistake, so an Italian could have given all the information to a Greek, they could have composed it and printed it, and then the Italian could have delivered it everywhere on a motorcycle or something.' She smiled triumphantly, and raised her hands to show how simple it all was. 'And anyway, everyone knows that people listen to the BBC.' In the presence of Carlo she deemed it imprudent to mention that the men of the village listened to it, smoking furiously as they crammed themselves together inside a large cupboard in the kapheneion, and then emerged choking and spluttering, to bring the news home to their wives, who in turn passed it on to each other at the well and in their kitchens. She was not to know that the Italian soldiers did much the same thing in their barracks and billets, which would have explained why everybody on the island knew the same jokes about Mussolini.

286

Carlo and the doctor looked at one another, fearing that if Pelagia could work it out, someone else might. 'Don't get too clever,' said the doctor, 'or your brains might squeeze out of your ears.' It was a childhood formula.

Pelagia saw the unease of her father and Carlo, remembered that before the war Kokolios had been given a small hand-turned press by the Communist Party, for the purpose of turning out party propaganda, and recalled that Carlo had access to a jeep. She shook her head as if to drive these speculations out of her mind, and then it occurred to her to wonder where they might have got hold of sets of Roman letters. Her momentary sense of relief was vanquished when she recalled that her father had some quid pro quo arrangements with the fat hypochondriac quartermaster with the intractable corns. She looked from Carlo to her father and felt a pang of anger strike her in the throat; if it was them, and it was a conspiracy, then just how stupid and irresponsible could they get? Did they not know the danger? 'The trouble with men . . .' she began, and followed the captain into the house, without completing the sentence. She swept Psipsina from the kitchen table, as though cuddling the animal might abate her sense of peril.

Carlo and the doctor raised their hands, and let them fall, standing together in a moment of self-conscious and eloquent silence. 'I should have brought her up stupid,' said the doctor at last. 'When women acquire powers of deduction there's no knowing where trouble can end.'

38

THE ORIGIN OF PELAGIA'S MARCH

ONE DAY IT happened that Captain Corelli did not go into work because an earthquake was vibrating in his head. He lay in Pelagia's bed, attempting not to open his eyes and not to move; the slightest shard of light pierced his brain like a poignard through the eye, and when he moved he had the distinct certainty that his cerebellum had become loose and was sloshing about on the inside of his skull. His throat was as dry and stiff as leather, and there was no doubt that someone had been stropping razors in it. Periodically a tide of nausea welled in his gullet, rippling equally towards his stomach and his lips, and he fought disgustedly to restrain the bitter torrents of bile that seemed determined to find their way to an exit and decorate his chest. 'O God,' he groaned. 'O God have mercy.'

He opened his eyes and held them open with his fingers. Very slowly, so as not to perturb his brain too much, he looked about the room, and suffered a disturbing hallucination. He blinked; yes, it was true that his uniform was lying on the floor and was moving about on its own. He checked groggily that its movement was independent of the circular motion of the room, and closed his eyes again. Psipsina emerged from inside the tunic, and jumped up on the table in order to curl up inside his cap, which had been her favourite resting place ever since she had discovered the joys of contortionism; she filled it and overflowed from it in such a tangle and jumble of whiskers, ears, tail and paws that it was impossible to tell which part of her was which,

288

and she slept in it because it reminded her of gifts of salami and chicken skins. The captain opened his eyes and saw that his rumpled uniform was now rotating in harmony with the rest of the world, and felt reassured that he was getting better, until some demented and metaphysical percussionist began to play the kettledrum in his temples. He screwed up his face and pressed the palms of his hands to the sides of his head. He realised that he needed to empty his bladder, but also recognised with resignation that it was going to be one of those occasions when he would need to be supported, would sway backwards and forwards, would be unable to exercise voluntary release, and would finally and inexplicably find himself simultaneously pissing on his own foot and falling over. He felt infinitely oppressed by intimations of mortality, and wondered whether it might not be better to die than to suffer. 'I want to die,' he groaned, as though the articulation of the thought might give it greater precision and dramatic force.

Pelagia entered, bearing a pitcher of water, which she set down at the side of the bed with a tumbler. 'You've got to drink all this water,' she said firmly, 'it's the only cure for a hangover.'

'I haven't got a hangover,' said the captain pathetically, 'I'm very ill, that's all.'

Pelagia filled the tumbler and administered it to his lips. 'Drink,' she ordered him. He sipped at it suspiciously and was astonished by the cleansing effect of it upon his physical and psychological state. Pelagia refilled the glass. 'I've never seen anyone so drunk,' she remonstrated, 'not even at the feast of the saint.'

'O God, what did I do?'

'Carlo brought you back at two in the morning. To be exact, he crashed the jeep into the wall outside, carried you inside like a baby in his arms, tripped over, hurt his knees, and woke everyone who was not already awake by shouting and swearing. Then he lay on the table in the yard and went to sleep. He's still there, and during the night he wet himself.'

'Really?'

'Yes. And then you woke up and you knelt down in front of me and waved your arms about and sang "Io sono ricco e tu sei bella", at the top of your voice and completely out of tune, and you forgot the words. Then you tried to kiss my feet.'

The captain was completely appalled, 'Out of tune? I never forget the words of anything, I am a musician. What did you do?'

'I kicked you, and you fell over backwards, and then you declared eternal love, and then you were sick.'

The captain closed his eyes despairingly and ashamedly, 'I was drunk. My battery won the football match, you see. It doesn't happen every day.'

'Leutnant Weber called round early this morning. He said that your side cheated, and that the match was delayed for half an hour in the middle because two little boys stole the ball when it went over a fence.'

'It was sabotage,' said the captain.

'I don't like Leutnant Weber. He looks at me as though I'm an animal.'

'He's a Nazi; he thinks that I'm an animal as well. It can't be helped. I like him. He's only a little boy, he'll grow out of it.'

'And you're a drunk. It seems to me that you Italians are always drunk, or stealing, or chasing local girls, or playing football.'

'We also swim in the sea and sing. And you can't blame the boys for chasing the girls, because they can't do it at home, and anyway, some of the girls do very well out of it. Give me some more water.'

Pelagia frowned; there was something about the captain's remarks that struck her as offensive, and even cruel. Besides, she was in just the right mood for an argument. She stood up, emptied the pitcher over his face, and said vehemently, 'You know perfectly well that they are bullied into it and driven into it out of necessity. And everyone is ashamed to have your whores here. How do you think we feel?'

The captain's head throbbed too much for quarrelling; it

even throbbed too much to allow a reaction to being suddenly drenched by an angry maiden. Nonetheless, he became abruptly subject to a great sense of injustice. He sat up and told her, 'Everything you say and do is because you want me to apologise, in every look I see nothing but reproaches. It's been the same ever since I came. How do you think I feel? Why don't you ask yourself that? Do you think I'm proud? Do you think I have a vocation for suppressing the Greeks? Do you think I am the Duce that I commanded myself to be here? It's shit, it's all shit, but I can't do anything about it. OK, OK, I apologise. Are you satisfied?' He slumped back into the pillows.

Pelagia put her hands on her hips, taking advantage of the superiority implicit in the fact that she was standing and he lying down. She pulled a wry face and said, 'Are you seriously saying that you are a victim, as much as us? Poor little boy, poor little thing.' She walked over to the table, noticed Psipsina's somnolent presence in the captain's cap, and smiled to herself as she gazed out of the window. She was deliberately frustrating the intended effect of any response of the captain's, by ensuring that he would not be able to look into her eyes whilst he made it. She did feel sorry for him, she could not remain hostile to a man who permitted a pine marten to sleep in his hat, but she was not going to let her fondness show when there were principles at stake.

No answer came. Corelli looked at her silhouette against the light of the window, and a tune came into his head. He could visualise the patterned patrol of his fingers on the fretboard of the mandolin, he could hear the disciplined notes ringing from the treble, singing the praise of Pelagia as they also portrayed her wrath and her resistance. It was a march, a march of a proud woman who prosecuted war with hard words and kindnesses. He heard three simple chords and a martial melody that implied a world of grace. He heard the melody rise and swell, breaking into a torrent of bright tremolo more limpid than the song of thrushes, more pellucid than the sky. He realised with some irritation that it would require two instruments.

39

ARSENIOS

FATHER ARSENIOS WAS saved by the war, as though the entire cycle of his life had been nothing but a curve through purgatory that had finally broken through an invisible carapace and brought him to his mission. His agonies of self-revulsion fell away, his greed and indolence, his alcoholic excesses, followed one another into the graveyard of the past, and it was as if a cubit had been added to his height. His theology wound subtly around itself like a snake, and transformed his soul, so that whereas in the past he knew that he had failed his God, he now knew that God had failed the holy land of Greece. It came to him, as a man, that he might surpass the God that made him, and do for Greece what God had not. He discovered within himself the gift of prophecy.

It occurred to him that he should acquire a large dog and train it to bite Italians, and to this end he bought an animal from Stamatis that was guaranteed to be patriotic, since its own sire already had achieved a long and honourable record of biting at the calves of soldiers. His own mongrel however, misinterpreting his teaching as commands to bite the tyres of passing military trucks, passed prematurely beyond the veil, and Arsenios adopted another, less excitable dog. He set out on foot, laden with nothing but a scrip and an olivewood cross that would serve him as a staff.

Arsenios walked and preached. His blubbery thighs chafed against each other, bringing rashes and sores to his groin; in the height of summer the perspiration poured from his brow and the pits of his arms so that his black robes blossomed with sodden darker rings whose circumference was marked by wide irregular rims of fine white salt, and his beard glistened and dripped like the Arethusa spring. The leather soles of his black boots abraded away into contiguous holes until he walked on bare feet shod only by the uppers, trailing long strands of cobbler's thread behind him that left tracks in the pale dust like the marks of hair-thin snakes. In winter Arsenios discovered that any man will be warm who preserves himself in motion, and he leaned his weight against the callous wind and the inordinate rain whilst his abject dog followed behind him, soaked to the skin, its tail between its legs, its head hanging dolefully, the very picture of unwise and unquestioning fealty.

From the lentisk bushes and the cypress of the north to the shingle sands of Skala in the south, from the underground lakes of Sami in the east to the vertiginous slopes of Petani in the west, Arsenios trudged and sermonised. As he walked, his head as lowered as that of his dog, he constructed phrases of righteous rage that would emerge as wild tirades outside the encampments of Italians. At the German garrisons he was ignored or rudely driven away with the butts of rifles, not because they were cruel, but because they did not share their ally's love of drama. To the Teutons he was an irritation rather than an entertainment, but to the Italians he was welcome relief from interminable card games and watching out for British bombers. They looked forward to his visitations with as much anticipation as they awaited the truck of whores, Arsenios being all the more welcome for the unpredictability of his arrivals and departures.

When he came the soldiers would gather round him, mesmerised by the operatic gestures of the weatherbeaten priest and the thunderous roll of biblical Greek, of which they understood not one word. Arsenios would look from one smiling and delighted face to another, knowing that their incomprehension was absolute, but would still persist because it seemed to him that he had no choice. There were

293

words piling up inside him, words of supernatural strength, and it seemed to him that the hand of the Virgin pushed him on, that the grief of Christ had been poured into him, that it overflowed his soul and must be given to the land:

'Schismatics of Rome, brothers lost to us, children of Christ who weeps for thee, sacrificial lambs, pawns of tyrants, ye who are unjust, ye who are filthy, ye who are unrighteous, ye who are dogs and whoremongers, sorcerers and idolaters, ye whose hearts are unlit by the sun, ye that have no temple within, ye of a nation that shall not be saved, ye who work abominations, ye who defile the Virgin, ye that thirst for truth and cannot drink it; ye are corrupt and have done nothing good, ye have done iniquity, ye have eaten my people as they eat bread, ye have not called upon God, ye have encamped against our cities, ye have been put to shame and God has despised thee and scattered thy bones. Behold, the Lord shall give ear to the words of my mouth, for He is my helper, He is with them who uphold my soul, He shall reward evils unto mine enemies, he shall cut them off in His truth, for strangers are risen up against my people, oppressors seek after our trees of olive and our maidens, wickedness is in the midst of them. My soul is amongst lions, and I lie even with them that are set on fire, even the sons of men, whose teeth are spears and arrows, and their tongue a sharp sword.

'Yea, in heart ye work wickedness, ye weigh the violence of your hands upon the earth, ye are estranged from the womb, ye go astray as soon as ye be born, speaking lies, thy poison is like the poison of the serpent, ye are like the deaf adder that stoppeth her ear.

'But we are like the green olive in the House of God, and we shall trust in the mercy of God for ever and ever, for God has stretched forth His hand and God has spoken with the word of His mouth and behold I have heard him speaking in a great wind and in the midst of storms, in the stones of Assos and the caves of mountains. He hath strewn His salt in the lake of Melissani, He hath stored up iron in the skies of Lixouri.

'Schismatics of Rome, the Lord hath prepared a pit, He

hath laid up a net for thy steps, and calamities shall overpass thee, for Satan shall be loosed from his prison, and Gog and Magog shall go out to deceive the nations that are in the four quarters of the earth, to gather them together in battle; the number of whom is as the sand of the sea. And fire shall come out of heaven above the beloved city, and devour thee, and thou shalt be cast, yea, even the innocent and those as pure as babes, into the lake of oil and brimstone where the beast and the false prophet are, and thy flesh shall be divided from thy bones, for ye have not been found written in the book of life and shall be cast into the flame.

'And the Lord God shall wipe away all tears from the eyes of my people, and there shall be no more tears nor crying, and neither shall there be any more pain, for the former things shall pass away, and He that sits upon the Throne shall make all things new, and He shall give to my people that are athirst to drink of the water of the fountain of life freely. For He shall take the Beast and the false prophet and the armies gathered together against us that wrought miracles before them, and He shall smite them, and the fowls of the air shall be filled with their flesh, and they shall be cast alive into the lake of fire burning with brimstone, and the remnant shall be slain.'

The soldiers provided Arsenios and his dog with bread and water, scraps and olives, and in monasteries as far apart as those of Agrilion and Kipoureon he was cared for by nuns and monks. But the hard nights in caves, the meagre diet, the two years of relentless tramping, caused his ample flesh to fall away until his vast black robes flapped about a body that had become a skeleton stretched with skin and burned with sores. His vivid eyes burned forth from above hollow cheeks, the parchment of his hands and face grew dark as teak, and for the first time in his life he found peace within himself and was happy. It is true that he neglected his parish completely, but it is probable that, had he lived, Arsenios might have become a saint.

40

A PROBLEM WITH LIPS

THEY PASSED EACH other at the door, she going out, and he returning from work. Unselfconsciously she put one hand up to his left cheek and, in passing, kissed him on the other.

He was astonished, and, by the time that she reached the entrance to the yard, so was she, because it was not until then that she suddenly realised what she had done. She stopped dead, as though having walked straight into a metaphysical but palpable stone wall. She felt her blood rising to the roots of her hair, and realised that she did not dare look back at him. Undoubtedly he too would be rooted to the spot. She could almost feel his eyes travelling from her feet to her head, finally settling upon the back of her head in the expectation that she would turn around. He called out, as she knew he would, 'Kyria Pelagia.'

'What?' she demanded curtly, as though an effort to be short with him could cancel out the hideously simple way in which she had betrayed her affection without even thinking about it.

'What's for dinner?'

'Don't tease me.'

'Would I tease you?'

'Don't make anything of it. I thought you were my father. I always kiss him like that when he comes in.'

'Very understandable. We are both old and small.'

'If you are going to tease me, I shall never speak to you again.'

He came up behind her and around her, and threw himself upon his knees before her. 'O no,' he cried, 'anything but that.' He bowed his head to the ground and moaned piteously, 'Have mercy. Shoot me, flog me, but don't say you'll never speak to me.' He grasped her about the knees and pretended to weep.

'The whole village is looking,' she protested, 'stop it at once. You are so embarrassing, get off me.'

'My heart is broken,' he wailed, and he grasped her hand and began to smatter it with kisses.

'Stupid goat, you are deranged.'

'I am tormented, I am burning, I am broken into pieces, my eyes spout forth with tears.' He leaned back and gestured poetically with his fingers to portray the extraordinary cascade of invisible tears that he intended her to envisage. 'Don't laugh at me,' he continued, having struck upon a new tack. 'O, light of my eyes, do not mock poor Antonio in his affliction.'

'Are you drunk again?'

'Drunk with sorrow, drunk with agony. Speak to me.'

'Did your battery win another football match?'

Corelli leapt to his feet and spread his arms with delight, 'Yes. We beat Günter's company by four goals to one, and we injured three of them, and then I came in and you kissed me. A glorious day for Italy.'

'It was a mistake.'

'A significant mistake.'

'An insignificant mistake. I am very sorry.'

'Come inside,' he said, 'I've got something very interesting to show you.'

Relieved by this abrupt change of subject, she followed him through the door, only to find that he was passing her on his way out again. He clamped his hands upon either side of her head, kissed her lingeringly and flamboyantly on the forehead, exclaimed, 'Mi scusi, I thought it was the doctor, don't make anything of it,' and then sprinted away across the yard and down the street. She put her hands on her hips and stared after him in amazement, shaking her head and making every effort not to laugh or smile.

41

SNAILS

THE DOCTOR GLANCED out of the window and saw Captain Corelli creeping up on Lemoni in order to give her a surprise. At the same time Psipsina leapt foursquare onto the page he was writing about the French occupation, and this combination of circumstances inspired him with a wonderful idea. He set down his pipe and his pen, and ventured out into the incandescent sunlight of the early afternoon.

'Fischio!' exclaimed the captain, and Lemoni squealed.

'Excuse me, children,' said the doctor.

'Ah,' said Corelli, straightening up sheepishly, 'kalispera, Iatre. I was just . . .'

'Playing?' He turned to the small girl, 'Koritsimou, do you remember when you found Psipsina when she was very little and was hanging on the fence? And you made me come along to rescue her?'

Lemoni nodded importantly, and the doctor asked, 'Are all the snails still there?'

'Yes,' she said. 'Lots. Big ones.' She pointed at Corelli, 'Bigger than him, even.'

'When is the best time to find them?'

'Early and late.'

'I see. Can you come round this evening and show me again where they were?'

'After dark's best.'

'We can't go out after dark, there's a curfew.'

'Before dark,' she agreed.

'What was all that about?' asked the captain, when

298

Lemoni had departed.

Stiffly the doctor said, 'Thanks to you there's almost no food. We're going out this evening to find snails.'

The captain bridled, 'The blockade is British. They have the idea that they can best help you by starving you. As you know very well, I have done my best to help.'

'Your borrowings at the expense of the Army are very much appreciated, but it's a pity that the situation even arises. We need the protein. You can see what we've been reduced to.'

'At home snails are an expensive luxury.'

'And here they are a regrettable necessity.'

The captain wiped the perspiration from his forehead and said, 'Permit me to come and help.'

So it was that in the evening, an hour before the setting of the sun and shortly after the cooling of the day, Pelagia and her father, Lemoni and the captain, found themselves crawling through the impossible tangle of animal runs and briars, having climbed the crumbling wall and negotiated their way beneath the branches of ancient and neglected olives.

The doctor was crawling behind Lemoni, and suddenly she stopped and looked round at him. 'You said,' she reproached him, 'you said that if you went round looking for snails, you'd be taken somewhere and locked up.'

'Piraeus,' said the doctor. 'I said I'd be taken to Piraeus. Anyway, we're all locked up nowadays.'

It became apparent in that dingy light that upon the undersides of the lower leaves there were legions of fat snails, competing with each other for variegation of design. There were tawny snails with almost invisible markings, there were light snails with whorls of stripes, there were snails of ochre yellow and bright lemon, and snails of red speckles and black dots. In the upper branches the Sicilian warblers cocked their heads and flitted about, listening to the dull clacks and pings as the harvest was gathered and dropped into the buckets.

The child and the three adults became so absorbed in their task that they did not notice themselves becoming separated. The doctor and Lemoni vanished down one tunnel, and the captain and Pelagia down another. At some point the captain found himself on his own, and paused for a second to reflect upon the curious fact that he could not remember ever having felt so contented. He carelessly deplored the state of the knees of his breeches, and squinted up at the reddening sun as its crimson light softened amongst the twigs and leaves. He breathed deeply and sighed, relaxing back upon his heels. He poked with a fore-finger at a snail that was attempting to crawl out of the bucket. 'Bad snail,' he said, and was relieved that there was no one near to hear him utter such inanities. In the distance an anti-aircraft gun cracked, and he shrugged his shoulders. It probably was nothing.

'Ow, o no,' came a voice nearby that was undoubtedly Pelagia's. 'O, for God's sake.'

Horrified by the terrible thought that perhaps she had been struck by falling shrapnel, the captain fell to his hands and knees, and crawled quickly back along his tunnel towards the place from which the exclamations had come.

He found Pelagia, apparently paralysed into a contorted posture that had left her neck ricked backwards. She was on her hands and knees, a long thin streak of blood was beading diagonally across her cheek, and she was clearly in a state of extreme irritation. 'Che succede?' he asked, crawling towards her. 'Che succede?'

'I got my hair caught,' she replied indignantly. 'A thorn scraped my cheek, and I jerked my head away, and I caught my hair on these briars, and I can't untangle it. And don't laugh.'

'I'm not laughing,' he said, laughing. 'I was afraid you'd been wounded.'

'I am wounded. My cheek stings.'

Corelli reached into his pocket for a handkerchief, and dabbed at the graze. He showed her the blood and said lightly, 'I'll treasure this forever.'

'If you don't untangle me, I'll murder you. Just stop laughing.'

'If I don't untangle you, you'll never catch me to murder me, will you? Just hold still.' He was obliged to reach his

300

hands over her shoulders and peer past her ear in order to see what he was doing. She found her face pressing into his chest, and she took in the rough texture and dusty aroma of his uniform. 'You're squashing my nose,' she protested.

Corelli sniffed appreciatively; Pelagia always smelled of rosemary. It was a young, fresh scent, and it reminded him of festive meals at home. 'I might have to cut this,' he said, pulling futilely at the black strands that had wound themselves about the thorns.

'Ow, ow, stop pulling it about, just be careful. And you're not cutting it.'

'You're in a very vulnerable position,' he remarked, 'so just try to appear grateful.' He tugged it out, piece by piece, ensuring that he let no hairs slide between his fingers to cause her any pain. His arms began to ache from being held so much in a stretched and horizontal position, and he rested his elbows on her shoulders. 'I've done it,' he said, pleased with himself, and began to draw back. She shook her head with relief, and as the captain's lips passed by her cheek, he kissed it gently, before the ear, where there was an almost invisible, soft down.

She touched her fingertips to the site of the kiss, and reproached him, 'You shouldn't have done that.'

He knelt back and held her gaze with his own. 'I couldn't help it.'

'It was taking advantage.'

'I'm sorry.' They looked at one another for a long moment, and then, for reasons that even she could not fathom, Pelagia began to cry.

'What's the matter? What's the matter?' asked Corelli, his face furrowing in consternation. Pelagia's tears rolled down her cheeks and fell into the bucket amongst the snails. 'You're drowning them,' he said, pointing. 'What's the matter?'

She smiled pitifully, and set once more to crying. He took her in his arms and patted her back. She felt her nose begin to run, and became anxious that she might leave mucus on the epaulette of his uniform. She sniffed hard in order to preclude this eventuality. Suddenly she blurted out, 'I can't stand it any more, not any of it. I'm sorry.'

301

'Everything is lousy,' agreed the captain, wondering if he too might yield to the temptation to cry. He took her head gently in his hands and touched at the tears with his lips. She gazed at him wonderingly, and suddenly they found themselves, underneath the briars, in the sunset, flanked by two buckets of escaping snails, their knees sore and filthy, infinitely enclosed in their first unpatriotic and secret kiss. Hungry and desperate, filled with light, they could not draw away from each other, and when finally they returned home at dusk, their combined booty shamefully and accusingly failed to reach the quota reached by Lemoni on her own.

42

How like a Woman is a Mandolin

HOW LIKE A woman is a mandolin, how gracious and how lovely. In the evening when the dogs howl and the crickets chirr, and the huge moon hoists above the hills, and in Argostoli the searchlights search for false alarms, I take my sweet Antonia. I brush her strings, softly, and I say to her, 'How can you be made of wood?' just as I see Pelagia and ask without speaking, 'Are you truly made of flesh? Is there not here a fire? A vanishing trace of angels? A something far estranged from bone and blood?' I catch her eye in passing, her gaze so frank and quizzical, holding mine. Her head turns, a smile, an arch and knowing smile, and she has gone. I see her go for water, and then she comes, the urn upon her shoulder, a living caryatid, and as she passes she permits a splash upon my epaulettes. She apologises, laughing, and I say 'Accidents will happen', and she knows that I know it was no chance. She did it because I am a soldier and an Italian, because I am the enemy, because she is funny, because she likes to tease, because it is an act of resistance, because she likes me, because it is contact, because we are brother and sister before she is Greek or I am invader. I notice that her wrists remind me of the slender necks of mandolins, and her hand broadens from the wrist like the head that holds the pegs, and the place where the heel swells to meet the soundbox gives the same contour as her line of neck and chin, and glows the same with the soft polish of youth and pine.

At night I dream of Pelagia. Pelagia comes, undressing,

and I see her breasts are the backs of mandolins moulded in Napoli. I cup them in my hands and they are cold like wood and warm like yielding mother's flesh, and she turns about and I see that each buttock is the rounded pear-shaped singing mandolin, swelling in tapered segments, purfled in pearl and slivers of ebony. I am confused because I am caught between looking for strings and the pain of the loins' longing, and I wake up moistened by my own lust, clutching Antonia, pricked by the scratching ends of strings, sweating. I put Antonia down and say, 'O Pelagia,' and I lie awake awhile, thinking of her before I force myself asleep because then it will be morning sooner, and I will see Pelagia.

I think of Pelagia in terms of chords. Antonia has three chords that live together in the first three frets, *doh*, *re*, and *sol*, and they all need two fingers apiece to stop them. I play *sol*, and I move it one space across and I make the *doh*, and they ring in each others' aftermath like soprano and alto in the same key in a Tuscan song. I play the *re*, twisting my hand, making a double space, and it belongs with the other two, but it is sad and incomplete, it is like a virgin unfulfilled. It begs me 'Take me back where I can find my peace', and I return to *sol*, and all's complete, and I feel like God Himself who made a woman and found His world perfected by a final and a consummating touch.

Pelagia shares these simple, merry chords. She plays with a cat and laughs, and it is *sol*. She raises an eyebrow when she catches me observing, and pretends to reproach me and reprove me for the guilt of admiration, and it is *doh*. She asks me a question, 'Haven't you anything useful to do?' and it is like *re*, requiring resolution. I say, 'Il Duce and I are conquering Serbia today,' and she laughs and all is brought back and clarified. She throws back her head and laughs, her white teeth sparkling, and she knows she is beautiful and that I find her so. I am reminded of sparkling white-washed houses on a distant hill in Candia. She is glad and proud and withholding, everything has circled back upon itself. She has returned to *sol*. I find myself laughing also; we are octaves apart, laughing in octaves together, mandola

304

and mandolin, and far away a gun roars at imaginary British planes, there is a spurious rattle of machine-guns, and behold, there is our timpani.

Pelagia hears the guns and frowns. We were happy together, sitting on this balcony shaded by bougainvillaea visited by bees, but now it is the war; the war has returned, and Pelagia knits her brow and frowns. I want to say, 'I am sorry Pelagia, it was not my idea, it was not me who stole Ionia. I was not inspired to take your goats and burn your olive trees for fuel. I am not a natural parasite.' But I can say no such thing, as Pelagia knows. And she understands why I cannot say it, but still she blames me for a lack of will. She has heard me talking of the new *pax Romana*, the reconstitution of the ancient sway that brought order and peace to all, the longest period of civilisation known to man, and she frowns.

When Pelagia frowns at distant guns, it is like a chord of *mi* minor seventh with a flattened fifth; strike it hard and it is martial and angry, a chord for guerrillas and partisans. But stroke it softly, and it is a chord of infinite, yearning gloom. Pelagia is sad, and I pick up Antonia and play *re* minor. She looks up and says, 'That was exactly how I was feeling. How did you know?' and I would have liked to have said, 'Pelagia, I love you, and that is how I know,' but instead I say, 'Because you are wistful and waiting.'

'Waiting for what?' she asks, and I say, 'You tell me, Pelagia,' but I know that she will never tell me that she is waiting for a new world where a Greek may love an Italian and think nothing of it.

'I am composing a march for you,' I say, 'listen,' and I play *re* minor, one two, and then *doh* major, one-and-two-and-, and back to *re* minor, one two . . . and I tell her, 'The trouble is that I need another player to put a Greek melody over the top, perhaps a rebetiko of some sort. Maybe I can find someone in the battalion with a mandolin, and I can play the chords an octave lower on a mandola. I think that would sound very good.'

'Someone must have a guitar,' offers Pelagia, and I tell her, 'A chord or a tune that sounds one way on the mandolin will sound completely different on a guitar; it's one of the inexplicable facts of musical life. Those two chords sound banal beyond belief on a guitar, without drama of any kind, unless played by a Spaniard.'

Pelagia smiles, and I know that she doesn't understand a word of what I have been saying, but it doesn't matter. I start to think of a melody in tremolo to dance above the chords. Pelagia loves it when I play tremolo; she says it is a most moving and exquisite sound.

But it offends her to be moved by an invader and an occupier, someone who requisitions cheese and Robola wine, and suddenly she stands up and I see that her soul is on fire. She points a wavering finger at me and begins to shout through gritted teeth, 'How can you be like this? What's the matter with you? How can you, a musician, an educated man, come here with your mandolin and make beautiful tunes to a Greek, when all around you the island is pillaged and despoiled? And don't give me any of that shit about the restoration of the Roman Empire. If you really want to know, it was Greece that educated Rome, and we didn't do it by conquest either. What's the matter with you? How can you stand to be here? Orders? Orders from whom? A vain megalomaniac with a silver tongue who was given Cephallonia by a mad brute of another black-haired megalomaniac who wants everyone except himself to be blond? It's you who's mad, don't you know that? Don't you know that you're being used? Do you think that Hitler's going to let you keep your new Roman Empire when he's finished everyone else? How can you sit on a bomb, playing the mandolin? Why don't you take your guns and leave? Don't you know who the enemy is?'

And Pelagia runs down the Venetian steps and out into the sun. She stops and looks back up at me, her eyes welling with tears of rage and bitterness, and I know that she hates me because she loves me, because she loves me and I am a man who lacks the courage to take an evil by the throat and throttle it. I am ashamed. I play a diminished chord because I am diminished. My flirtation and my attempt at charm have exposed me. I am a dishonourable man.

The rounded, breasted belly of the mandolin slips in its place above my belt, as it always does, and as always I think, 'Maybe I need a flatbacked Portuguese mandolin that doesn't slip,' but I suppress such stupid thoughts; where does one get a flatbacked Portuguese mandolin in times of war? Instead I think again, 'How like a woman is a mandolin, how like Pelagia is a mandolin, how gracious and how lovely,' and I have the further thought, a paradox worthy of Xeno himself, that it was the war that brought us together and the war that prises us apart. The British call it 'giving with one hand and taking away with the other'. What have I got against the British that I have had to come to Greece? Pelagia is right, but who will be the first to say it? So far only Antonia has said it, ringing with 'Pelagia's March', singing beneath my fingers.

43

THE GREAT BIG SPIKY RUSTBALL

PELAGIA DID NOT greatly enjoy the preparation of snails. For one thing, she had received much conflicting advice about the proper technique for rendering them palatable, and she detested the feeling of insecurity engendered by her own confusion; she dreaded the idea of serving up something that would turn out to be slimy and repulsive, and was fearful that if she cooked a bad meal she might be lowered in the captain's estimation. The warm and jubilant glow which she felt after the discovery of their mutual love was now being threatened not only by the furtive guilt of it, but also by the appalling thought that if she did the wrong thing with the snails she would at best revolt him, and at worst perpetrate a poisoning.

Drosoula told her emphatically that what you had to do was leave the snails overnight in a pot full of water, with the lid on to prevent escape, and in the morning you had to wash them thoroughly. Then you heated them alive in water, and waited for froth and scum to appear on the surface. At this precise moment you had to throw in some salt and begin to stir them clockwise ('If you stir them anti-clockwise they'll taste horrible'). After fifteen minutes you had to pierce a hole in the back of each shell, 'to let the devil out and the sauce in', and then you had to rinse them clean in the water in which they had boiled. She did not explain to Pelagia how it was supposed to be possible, when performing this operation, to dip one's fingers into water that was still boiling hot. Drosoula also maintained that you could only eat snails that had been feeding on thyme, and Pelagia, whilst not believing this for a moment, became yet more anxious nonetheless.

Kokolios' wife told her at the well that this was all nonsense, because she remembered how her grandmother had done it: 'You don't want to listen to that Drosoula. The woman's almost a Turk.' No, what you had to do was pinch each snail, and if it moved it was alive. 'But how do I pinch it when it's gone inside?' asked Pelagia.

'Wait for it to come out,' replied Kokolios' wife.

'But if it comes out, then obviously it's alive, and so I don't have to pinch it.'

'You still pinch it. It's best to be sure. Then you take a pointed knife and clean around the mouth of the shell, and then you take clean water and wash each snail twenty-one times. No more because that will wash away the flavour, and no less because then they will still be dirty, and then you leave them to drain for half an hour, and then you put salt in the mouth of the shell and all this disgusting yellow bubbly slime starts to come out, and that's how you know they're ready. Then you fry them one at a time in oil, with the mouth downwards, and then you add wine and boil them for two minutes, no more no less. And then you eat them.'

'But Drosoula says you ought to . . .'

'Don't listen to that old witch. Ask anyone who knows and they'll tell you the same as I did, and if they tell you anything otherwise, then they don't know what they're talking about.'

Pelagia asked Arsenios' wife, and she asked Stamatis' wife. She even looked up 'snails' in the medical encyclopaedia, and found no entry for it. She felt like throwing them down onto the floor of the yard and stamping on them. In fact she felt so frustrated that she wanted to cry or shout. She had been told five different ways of preparing the gastropods themselves, and had heard four different recipes: boiled snails, fried snails, Cretan snail stew, and snails pilaf. There was no rice, so the pilaf was out. At the memory of rice her mouth began to water, and she wished all over again that the war would end.

309

But how do you know how many snails to use? Drosoula said a kilo for four people. But was that with the shells or without them? And how on earth were you supposed to get them out of their shells anyway? And how did you weigh them without getting slime on the scales? The kind of slime that would not even wash off with hot water and soap, and just transferred itself to everything you touched it with, as though it had some mystical ability to multiply itself to infinity.

Pelagia looked down at her shiny cargo of mucilaginous animals, and poked them with her finger when they tried to crawl out of the pot. She began to feel terribly sorry for them. They were not only very grotesque, with their erectile horns and their helplessly slow weaving of the body when you held them upside down, but they were also deeply pathetic in their sad and pitiful faith in the safety of their carapace. She was reminded of herself as a child, when she had honestly believed that if she closed her eyes, then her father would not be able to see her doing something naughty. Prodding at the snails, she was saddened by the cruelty of a world in which the living can only live by predation on creatures weaker than themselves; it seemed a poor way to order a universe.

Her practical and ethical quandaries were broken by an excited cry of, 'Barba C'relli, Barba C'relli,' and she smiled as she recognised the voice of Lemoni in a state of high excitement and pleasure. The little girl had taken to calling the captain 'Old Man' and coming every evening to relate to him in breathless and childish Greek every event of the day. 'Barba' Corelli would listen patiently, failing to understand any of it, and then he would pat her on the head, call her 'koritsimou', and begin to throw her up and down in the air. Pelagia could not see what possible pleasure there was in this for either of them, but some things are inexplicable, and Lemoni's piercing shrieks of joy were a conclusive testament to the improbable. Pelagia, glad of a distraction, went out into the yard.

'I saw a great big spiky rustball,' Lemoni informed the captain, 'and I climbed all over it.'

'She says that she saw a great big spiky rustball and she climbed all over it,' translated Pelagia.

Carlo and Corelli exchanged glances, and blanched. 'She's found a mine,' said Carlo.

'Ask her if it was on the beach,' said Corelli, appealing to Pelagia.

'Was it on the beach?' she asked.

'Yes, yes, yes,' said Lemoni gleefully, adding, 'and I climbed on it.'

Corelli knew enough Greek to recognise the word for 'yes', and he stood up suddenly, and then just as suddenly sat down. 'Puttana,' he exclaimed, taking the little girl into his arms and hugging her tightly, 'she could have been killed.'

Carlo put it more realistically; 'She should have been killed. It's a miracle.' He rolled his eyes and added, 'Porco dio.'

'Puttana, puttana, puttana,' chanted Lemoni inconsequentially, her voice muffled by the captain's chest. Pelagia winced, and said, 'Antonio, how many times have I told you not to use bad words in front of the child? What do you think her father will say when she comes home talking like that?'

Corelli looked at her shamefacedly, and then grinned; 'He will probably say, "What figlio di puttana taught my little girl to say puttana?"'

There was no one in the village who could resist joining the long straggle of the inquisitive that wound its way down the cliffs to the sand. When they saw it they pointed and cried, 'There it is, there's the mine,' and there indeed it was, perched with a deceptive air of aptness and innocence at the very edge of the peacock sea. It was a sphere the height of a man, a sphere that was a little squatter than it was tall, studded with blunt spikes that made it look like an unnaturally gigantic horse chestnut, or like a vast sea urchin whose spines had freshly emerged from an encounter with a military barber.

They gathered about it at a respectable distance, and the captain and Carlo went in close in order to inspect it. 'How much explosive, do you think?' asked Carlo.

311

'God knows,' answered the captain. 'Enough to blow a battleship out of the water. We'll have to cordon it off and explode it. I wouldn't know how to make it safe.'

'Magnificent,' exclaimed Carlo, who, despite the horrors of Albania, loved explosions from the bottom of his heart and had never lost his boyish delight in harmless destruction.

'Go back to base and get some dynamite, a command wire and one of those electrical plunger things. I'll stay here and get the villagers organised.'

'It's Turkish,' said Carlo, pointing to the swirling characters that were still barely visible amongst the great flakes and pits of rust. 'It must have been floating about for twenty years or more, ever since the Great War.'

'Merda, that's incredible,' said Corelli, 'truly a freak. I expect that all the explosive has decayed by now.'

'Won't it be a big bang then?' asked Carlo ruefully.

'It will be if you get enough dynamite, testa d'asino.'

'I get the hint,' said Carlo, and he began to walk back up the beach towards the village.

Corelli turned to Pelagia, who was still gazing wonderingly at the immense and ancient weapon, 'Tell Lemoni that if she ever finds anything, anywhere, that's made of metal and she doesn't know what it is, then she mustn't ever, ever, touch it, and she's got to run and tell me about it straight away. Tell her to tell all the other children the same thing.'

Corelli asked Pelagia to translate for him, and gestured to the villagers to gather round. 'First of all,' he told them, 'we are going to have to explode this device. It might be a very big explosion indeed, and so when the time comes I want you all to go back to the top of the cliff and watch from there, because otherwise there could be a serious accidental massacre. Whilst we're waiting for the dynamite, I need some strong men with spades to dig me a trench about fifty metres from this thing, over there, where I can get down in safety whilst I detonate the device. It has to be about the same size as a grave. Any volunteers?' He looked from face to face, and the eyes in those faces were averted. It was not a good thing to help an Italian, and, whilst everybody wanted to see the big bang, it would have been a matter of shame to be the first to volunteer. Corelli saw those truculent faces, and flushed. 'There'll be a chicken to share between you,' he announced.

Kokolios held up two fingers and said, 'Two chickens.'

Corelli nodded in agreement, and Kokolios said, 'I will do it with Stamatis, and we want two chickens each.'

Pelagia translated, and the captain grimaced, 'Each?' He rolled his eyes in exasperation and muttered, 'Rompiscatole,' under his breath.

And so it was that Kokolios and Stamatis, the Royalist and the Communist but two old friends nonetheless, and united in hunger and entrepreneurial acumen, returned to their houses and came back with spades. In the place indicated by the captain they began to dig a rectangular hole, piling up the sand on the mine side of it to form a protective rampart. When it was only four feet deep it began to fill with water, and the captain looked down at the ochre slush with some disapprobation and dismay. 'It's filling up with water,' he remarked unnecessarily to Pelagia, who was standing with everyone else watching the labour of the two old men. She looked at him and laughed, 'Everyone knows that if you dig a hole in a beach it fills up with water.'

Corelli frowned, and began to have reservations about this whole idea, which only made him more determined to carry it through.

Carlo returned, not only with the dynamite and the other equipment, but with an entire truckload of troops, all of them heavily armed and wonderfully eager to witness the forthcoming spectacle. Corelli was annoyed: 'Why didn't you tell Hitler too, and invite the entire German Army?'

Carlo was impenitent and aggrieved: 'They made me bring all these men because it's against regulations to transport explosives without an escort. It's because of the partisans, so don't blame me.'

'Partisans? What partisans? You mean those bandits that loot the villages when we're not looking? Don't make me laugh.'

'This hole is in the wrong place,' interrupted a small man in the uniform of an engineer.

'This hole is where I put it,' cried the captain, growing increasingly annoyed at the prospect of having his recreational escapade removed from his control.

'It's too close,' persisted the engineer, 'the shock wave will pass straight over this hole and suck your eyes and brains out, and then we'll have to dig you out, unless it's your wish to rest there in peace.'

'Listen Corporal, let me point out to you that I am a captain and you are a corporal. I am in charge around here.'

The soldier was undeterred, 'And let me point out to you that I am a sapper and you are a mad son of a bitch.'

Corelli's eyes opened at first with surprise, and then opened yet wider with rage. 'Insubordination!' he shouted. 'I'm putting you up on a charge.'

The sapper shrugged his shoulders and smiled, 'You can do what you like, because a dead man can't press charges. If you want to die, OK, I'll watch.'

'Carogna,' spluttered Corelli, and the soldier repeated, 'Mad son of a bitch,' and strolled away. Disowning the entire proceeding, he went to the top of the cliff, lit a cigarette, and squinted against the lowering sun as he watched the preparations below. It was lovely. The sea was a multitude of shades of aquamarine and lapis lazuli, and he could see the dark mounds of rocks and the swaying tresses of weeds beneath the waves. He was looking forward to seeing what was going to happen to that idiot officer.

Corelli placed a charge of dynamite beneath the mine, and unreeled the command wire, which was just long enough to reach his soggy trench. Then, anxious that what the sapper had said might just be true, but determined nonetheless to complete his purpose, he and the excitable troop of soldiers piled a thick wall of sand about the mine so that most of the blast would be directed upwards, until eventually it looked like the exact opposite of a doughnut, an excavated ring containing at its centre a column of sand, domed by a forlorn-looking bristle of rusty and truncated spikes. Drosoula was not the only woman who reflected that it looked very like a megalithic penis in repose.

'Avanti,' cried the captain at last, and the soldiers and

spectators wound their way back up the slopes of the cliff, perspiring and panting even though the evening sun had by now lost most of its heat. Down below, Corelli looked little larger than a mouse. The soldiers settled down and argued about whether or not it would be a good beach for playing football. The engineer corporal expatiated vehemently and acidly upon the lunacy of the officer, and offered to take wagers upon his survival. Pelagia began to feel deeply worried, and she noticed that Carlo was sweating with anxiety. She saw him cross himself repeatedly, and mutter prayers. He caught her eye and shot her an imploring glance, as if to say, 'You are the only one to stop him.'

Down in his trench, Corelli peeped over the rim of his bunker, and was struck by the implausible propinquity of the mine. The more he looked, the closer and larger it grew, until it actually seemed to be twenty metres high and sitting in his very lap like a grotesque, enormous, and unwelcome whore in a brothel that one has naïvely mistaken for a bar. He decided not to look at it. His bowels churned up in a most disconcerting fashion, and he realised that he was soaked up to the knees and that his boots had filled with irritatingly gritty and startlingly wet water. He put both hands upon the T-piece of the plunger, and depressed it a couple of times in order to accustom it to the idea of producing a discharge. Then he connected the terminals.

Concerned about the vivid possibility of having his eyes and brains sucked out, he practised in his imagination the swift manoeuvre of depressing the plunger and immediately transferring his hands to the sides of his head whilst simultaneously screwing his eyes shut. He raised his gaze to heaven, crossed himself, composed himself, and smartly thrust the plunger down.

There was a sharp crack, an almost infinitesimal pause, and then a basso profundo roar. The folk on the cliff saw a vast column of debris ascend with majestic certainty and grace past their eyes and up into the sky. With awe in their faces they discerned slowly revolving dark plates of steel, effulgent gouts of water glistening with momentary rainbows, sloppy and distended clods of wet sand, powder

315

storms of dry sand, and billowing efflorescences of black smoke and orange flame.

'Aira!' cried the exhilarated Greeks, and, 'Figlio di puttana di stronzo d'un cane d'un culo d'un porco d'un pezzo di merda!' cried the soldiers. Quite suddenly the shock wave swept upon them and bowled them flat on their backs like the impotent mortals who in ancient times were swatted by the hand of cloud-compelling Zeus. 'Putanas yie!' muttered the stupefied Greeks, and, 'Porco cane!' the soldiers. They were just beginning to struggle to their feet when they looked up and saw that the seemingly inexhaustible ascent of materials had ceased. In fact it had not only ceased but was flowering inexorably sideways, spinning out in a magisterial and all-encompassing arc. Horrified and mesmerised, the people on the cliff watched and craned their necks ever backward as the perilous but beautiful dark cloud spread above their own heads. Pelagia, like Carlo and so many of the others, was overcome by an icy and paralysed calm, a terrible and helpless dismay, and then, like them, she flung herself face down upon the thorny turf of the cliff and buried her face in her arms.

A malicious and gigantic pat of wet sand slapped her stingingly across the back, knocking the breath out of her body, and a white-hot shard of metal shot into the soil next to her head, audibly singeing its way to the rock beneath. A splinter snapped into the sole of her shoe, neatly separating it from the heel. Burning motes of rust settled upon her clothes, charring tiny pepper-holes that tormented her flesh and made her squirm from sharp darts of pain that stung and then lingered and mushroomed like the venom of hornets and wasps. Her mind emptied of anything but the vacuum of resignation that afflicts the hopeless in the imminence of death.

It ended, after an eternity, with a gentle and tenderly consoling rain of dry sand that drifted down out of the sky and pattered softly all upon and about them, piling up in symmetrical cones on the backs of their heads, sticking like icing sugar to the irregular splashes and streaks of wet sand, insinuating itself with insidious skill down behind the collars of

316

their clothes and inside the uppers of their shoes. It was warm and almost metaphysically pleasant.

Tremulous and weak as kittens, the people began to stagger to their feet. Some people fell over as soon as they were almost upright, and others fell over because someone nearby had reached out a hand to steady themselves. It was a festa of standing up and falling over, a festa of groping and blundering, a carnival of inexplicably weakened knees and looming pallid faces streaked with congealed or dripping gloops and glots of sand. It was a solemn and stately lumbering of incredibly and bizarrely modified coiffure and unrecognisably tattered clothing, an otherworldly and Stygian celebrazione of lurching bodies, and staringly virgin eyes anomalously inserted into nigger-minstrel faces.

The calming drizzle of sand was unrelenting; it powdered them, it settled like tiny yellow mites upon their lashes and brows, it clung with tenacious electrostatic force to the hairs within their noses, it ingratiated itself horribly into the saliva of their mouths, it found its way obscenely into the underclothes and horrified the women, it attached itself gratefully to the perspiration of their armpits, and fortuitously it rejuvenated the old by filling up their wrinkles.

The people clung wordlessly together, dazed with astonishment, watching the spectacular black cloud of filthy smoke massively growing and spreading, blotting the sun and sky and aborting the light. They wiped the sand from their faces with their sleeves, succeeding only in replacing one streak with another. One or two of them began to inspect their cuts and watch with fascination as the crimson-welling blood rose up beneath their dusting of sand, darkened, and congealed.

No one could recognise anybody else, and Italian and Greek peered into one another's faces, denationalised by coughing, by grime, and by mutual amazement. Suddenly a choking voice cried out.

As though galvanised, the people gathered around the corpse of the smug engineer, his neatly severed head smiling seraphically up through its white powdering of sand. The body lay nearby, chest downwards, guillotined by a smoking

317

disc of rusty and jagged steel that was buried to its radius in the turf. 'He died happy,' came a voice that Pelagia recognised as that of Carlo, 'you can't ask more than that. But he won't be collecting any bets.'

'Puttana,' came a tentative and trebly little voice that must have been that of Lemoni. Somebody began to retch, and five or six caught the contagion, adding the noise of painful gagging to the general plague of coughing.

Abruptly seized by dread, Pelagia ran to the edge of the cliff and peered through the falling sand with panic in her heart. What had happened to the captain?

She saw a crater thirty metres wide that had already been filled by the curious sea. There were tangled ribbons of metal scattered for hundreds of metres, variously shaped satellitic craters and mounds, but of the captain and his trench there was not a single sign. 'Carlo!' she howled, and clutched at her chest. Stunned by grief she sank to her knees and began to weep.

Carlo ran down the path to the beach, as much emptied by horror as Pelagia, but more accustomed to the duty of overwhelming it. His mind expanded with the remembrance of the pietà of Francesco, with his shattered head, dying in his arms in Albania, and nothing but running could forestall the hurricane of mourning that was about to burst his heart.

He came to the point where he guessed the trench had been, and stopped. There was nothing. It was all obliterated and unrecognisable. He raised his arms as though reproaching God, and was about to start pounding at his own temples when there was a movement at the corner of his eye.

Corelli was indistinguishable from the wet sand because he was perfectly covered in it. The blast had concussed him, and the updraught had sucked him high into the air and then flung him down upon his back. He was now lying face up, modelled perfectly into the beach by a chamfering and moulding of precipitated sand. Floundering and failing to sit up, he looked very like a monster from a film. Carlo laughed out loud, but at the same time his hilarity was tempered by the anxiety that this man whom he so much loved might yet be terribly injured. He could think of nothing else he could do but pick him up in his arms and carry him into the sea; it brought back once again the memory of carrying Francesco from where he had fallen between the lines, and he heard again the gallant cheering of the Greeks.

In the waves Carlo washed his Captain down, and found him wildly disorientated, but apparently uninjured. 'Was it good?' asked Corelli. 'I missed it.'

'It was a real sporcaccione of an explosion,' said Carlo, 'absolutely better than anything I've ever seen.'

Corelli saw his lips move, but heard no sound at all. In fact he could hear nothing but the prolonged bonging of the biggest bell in the world. 'Speak up,' he said.

Of the aftermath of this episode there is much to be said. Corelli was deaf for two days, and suffered the most extreme mortification at the thought of losing his music forever. For the rest of his life he would suffer periods of tinnitus, an enduring souvenir of Greece. He was put on a charge by General Gandin because of the death of the engineer and for causing the immediate mobilisation of all Axis troops on the island, an unexpected invasion by the Allies having been adduced from that terrific blast and regal mushroom cloud. He was very nearly demoted, but General Gandin concluded that since the Germans were paying the salaries of the Italian garrison, no material benefit would accrue to Italy. In any case, it was already a cause for friction that the Germans would not allow the Italians to promote anyone because of the expense to the chancellery, and the general was not about to present them with even a minimal saving. He charged Corelli for acting on his own initiative without permission, for not handing over the responsibility to the qualified authority, for reckless endangerment, and for conduct unbecoming to an officer. He was sentenced to a severe reprimand that would rest on his file for the length of his military career. Corelli flamboyantly and ingeniously presented the general's desirable secretary with a red rose and a box of contraband Swiss chocolates, and the reprimand disappeared mysteriously from the file after smouldering ominously therein for only three days.

The captain enjoyed the luxury of being pampered and fussed over by Pelagia as never before, and she expressed her relief by means of bombardments of kisses, tender words and promises that easily outshowered the rain of sand. Günter Weber brought over his wind-up gramophone and sat by his bed teaching him the words to 'Mein Blondes Baby' and 'Leben Ohne Liebe', and Carlo came in and out reporting the steady and saddening erosion of the crater by the sea. Lemoni called in, from now on an unparalleled expert in the finding of pieces of rusty metal, and forced him to get out of bed to come and identify an old ploughshare, the nosecone of an expended anti-aircraft shell, and a squashed tin can. Her disappointment at the realisation that none of them could be blown up surpassed adult understanding by a measure that might accurately be described as infinite.

But on the evening of that splendid event, the enraged doctor emerged from the kitchen, intending to find Pelagia and give her a piece of his mind, when not only his daughter but an entire crowd of inconceivably filthy, exhausted and ragged folk turned up at the yard. An unrecognisable man as large as Carlo, who later turned out to be Carlo, was bearing in his arms the raving body of someone who later turned out to be the captain. A young woman who looked like some mad and irredeemable slut from the most iniquitously impoverished quarter of Cairo turned out to be Pelagia. A tiny thing that could have been either a boy or a girl dug from an early grave turned out to be Lemoni. He would be busy all night cleaning cuts, and he would earn a spectacular profit in aubergines, which at that time were just coming into season.

But at that moment, confronted by the sorry crowd of disorientated and beggarish soldiers and Greeks, all he could think of was the repellent and astounding spectacle he had just encountered in the kitchen. 'Who,' he roared rhetorically, 'has had the audacity to fill my house with snails?'

It was true. There were snails everywhere. They were on the windows, under the rims of tables, perpendicularly sideways on the walls and on Psipsina's bowl, in the water jug, glued inadvisedly to the mats, proceeding with determination towards the vegetable basket, and clinging with quixotic relish to the stem of the doctor's pipe and the glasses of the spectacles that in all innocence he had left upon the sill.

Pelagia put her hand to her mouth in guilty horror, and Lemoni, perceiving the silvery, meandering, crisscrossing, glistening trails, and the delightfully random distribution of the beasts themselves, clapped her hands together in joy. 'Porca puttana,' she said, and a man who must have been her father clipped her sharply about the side of the head.

44

THEFT

KOKOLIOS WAS AWOKEN in the middle of the night by sounds of avine distress. His first thought was that the pine marten owned by the doctor had got in amongst his fowls; he had always said that it was antisocial to keep such a notorious bird-thief as a pet, and he had already twice caught it carrying away his eggs. He swore, and then leapt out of bed; he was going to give that little robber a sound thwack over the head with a baton, and that would put an end to the issue whether Dr Iannis liked it or not.

He pulled on his boots and reached for the cudgel that he had kept over the lintel ever since the outbreak of war. It was a heavy and knotted piece of thorn from the maquis, and he had drilled a hole through the thinner end, to take a loop of leather thong. He slipped the thong over his wrist and pulled open the door of his house, scraping the bottom of it in an arc along the flags. He had been meaning to rehang the door for ten years. Fortunately the sound of it was drowned by the frenzied clucking and screeching of the hens, and he stepped out into the night.

It was very dark because a heavy cloud had interposed itself between earth and moon, and the noise was atrocious because the crickets had caught the contagion of excitement from the chickens and were sawing at double forte. Kokolios squinted into the darkness, and distinctly heard the sound of muttered oaths. Perplexed, he peered even harder. He saw two small Italian soldiers scurrying about the pen, desperately trying to grab at the poultry.

Seized by rage, he acted without thinking. Despite the rifles slung across their backs, Kokolios uttered a fearful war-cry and threw himself into combat.

The two men had endured the Albanian campaign and had acquitted themselves with courage, but they were no match in the dark for some ferocious, naked, and demonic creature that rained blows about their backs and heads, kicked at their legs, and uttered unearthly shrieks. 'Puttana!' they cried, and shielded their heads with their hands, only to find their knuckles and elbows cracked by further crushing blows. They fell to their knees and with pitiful cries held out their hands and implored him to stop.

Kokolios knew not one word of Italian, but he knew a defeated enemy when he saw one. Throwing down his cudgel he seized the two thieves by the collar and dragged them to their feet. Kicking their backsides at every step, he frog-marched the both of them towards the doctor's house, periodically cracking their skulls together like a demented schoolmaster.

Outside the doctor's house, still shaking and kicking them, he set himself to yelling, 'Iatre! Iatre!'

Dr Iannis appeared shortly, clad in his nightgown, as did the captain and Pelagia. They beheld, by the newly disclosed illumination of the moon, Kokolios, stark naked apart from his heavy boots, shaking with rage, with one vanquished soldier dangling from each hand. Most curiously, both soldiers still had their carbines slung across their backs. 'Go inside at once,' said Dr Iannis to his daughter, concerned for her modesty in the presence of that enraged and unclothed man with bandy legs and barrel chest. Obediently she retreated to the kitchen in order to enjoy the spectacle from the shadow of the window.

Kokolios pointed at Corelli but shouted at the doctor, 'Tell that wop son of a bitch officer that his men are chicken-thieves, nothing but chicken-thieves, do you understand?'

Dr Iannis relayed this information to Corelli, who stood for a moment as though making up his mind. He disappeared back into the house, and the doctor said to

323

Kokolios, 'I think it would help if you calmed down a little.' Whilst the officer was inside, Dr Iannis took the opportunity to tease his neighbour. 'I thought that you were a Communist,' he observed.

'Of course I'm a Communist,' retorted Kokolios shortly.

'Forgive me,' said the doctor, 'but if I remember rightly, all property is theft. So, if you own the chickens, you too are a thief.'

Kokolios spat into the dust, 'The property of the rich is theft, not the property of the poor.'

This philosophical debate was cut short when the captain reappeared with his revolver, and for one awful moment both Pelagia and her father thought that he was intending to shoot Kokolios down. She wondered desperately whether she ought to go and find her derringer, but could not move. Kokolios looked at the captain with an expression that combined horror, defiance, and righteous rage. He held out his chest proudly, as though willing to die for the right of Greek chickens to live unmolested even in occupied territory.

To everyone's surprise the captain pointed his pistol straight into the face of one of the culprits and commanded him to lie down in the dust. The thief smiled ingratiatingly, and Corelli clicked back the hammer. The man dropped to the ground with comical promptitude and began to whine his excuses, which Corelli ignored. He motioned to the other man to do the same.

Corelli took Kokolios' arm and moved him a metre or so. He nudged both of the supine men with his foot, and commanded, 'Now crawl.'

The men looked at one another in surmise. 'I said "crawl,"' shouted the captain, exploding from calm anger to disgusted fury. One of the men rose to his hands and knees, and the captain put one foot in the small of his back and brutally forced him down, 'On your bellies, you sons of whores.'

They writhed forward with the motion of snakes, until they were level with Kokolios' boots. 'Lick them,' ordered the captain.

It was useless to protest. The captain whipped one of them across the side of the head, and the doctor closed his eyes, wincing for the bodily damage that he feared was about to ensue. Pelagia put her hand to her mouth in shock, and her heart went out to the grovelling crooks; she had never dreamed that her captain could have been so cruel, so remorseless. Perhaps a musician could be a soldier after all.

The two men licked Kokolios' boots. The latter stared down at them in mute amazement, and it was not until his eye caught the fleshy protuberances of his private parts glimmering palely in the light of the moon that he remembered that he was without his clothes. His mouth fell open, he placed both hands rapidly over his most precious possessions, and he scampered away back to his house.

Inside her kitchen, Pelagia could not help but laugh, but the captain was in no mood for levity when he came back in. 'Southerners!' he shouted. 'Camorra and mafiosi! Renegades!' The thieves sat at the table whilst the captain slapped them about the head at each epithet. They looked very small and pathetic, and the doctor moved his hand to stay the captain's blows. The latter lifted them by the collar as Kokolios had done, dragged them to the door, and propelled them out into the night. They sprawled on the paving stones, picked themselves up, and ran.

He re-entered, his eyes blazing with fury. He glared at Pelagia and her father as if something had been their fault, and shouted, 'We're all hungry!' He raised his hands into the air as though appealing to God, shook his head, beat his fist on his chest, and exclaimed incredulously, 'The dishonour!' before striding into his room and slamming the door.

Two days later Pelagia went out into the yard and was struck by the absence of something familiar. She looked around but could not see anything. And then she realised. The captain came out and found her weeping into her hands.

'They've taken my goat,' she wailed, 'my beautiful goat.' She could imagine its slaughter, its being dismembered for meat, and it was too appalling to bear.

The captain put his hand on the shoulder of the sobbing

45

A Time of Innocence

THEY BECAME LOVERS in the old-fashioned sense, and made love in the old-fashioned sense. Their idea of making love was to kiss in the dark under the olive tree after curfew, or sit on a rock watching for dolphins through his binoculars. He loved her too much to jeopardise her happiness, and she in turn had too much sense to throw her caution to the winds. She had seen again and again the misery of girls with an unreckoned child, and again and again she had seen the septicaemia, the protracted poisoned deaths of girls who underwent the lethal curettage of crochet hooks and wires. She attended them with her father, and later attended them with priests, and she knew that the captain understood that they did not lie together, not because it was undesired, but because in fact there was no choice.

They made the most of stolen time, and it became easier when Günter Weber organised a motorcycle for Corelli, 'borrowed' from the Wehrmacht in return for Parma ham, Chianti, and mozzarella cheese. It had been officially written off in a spurious accident, and Weber had simply had it repaired and delivered to his friend.

The first that Pelagia knew of it was when, outside the yard, there came the sound of a popping exhaust, an engine throbbing, a backfire, and a silence. Psipsina came running in and hid under the table. Pelagia went outside and found Corelli, complete with flying hat and goggles, his face dark with dirt, coughing up dust on the seat of a black machine. He saw her coming and raised his goggles. She laughed at him because he had two pale rings about his eyes, set in a grey and grimy face, and his lips looked unnaturally pink, as though he had been applying a cosmetic. He grinned, believing that she was merely glad to see him, and said, 'Vuole fare un giro?'

She crossed her arms and shook her head, 'I've never been on one. In fact I've never been in a car either, and I'm not starting now.'

'I've never been on one either,' he said, 'but it's very easy. And isn't she a beautiful machine?'

'It's only got two wheels, it's bound to fall over. It's obvious. You've got to be mad to go around on that.'

He looked up at her, 'I agree that it ought to fall over, but it doesn't. It just doesn't go in a straight line all the time. But I'm getting the hang of it. And just listen to this.' He clambered off, jumped on the kickstart, revved the engine, and then fiddled with the advance-retard until it was ticking over happily. 'Just listen,' he cried, 'it's metronomic. And you could play a tune to it. That tempo, it's perfect, not a beat missed, not a hesitation. It's a musical machine, bubble, bubble bubble, and the exhaust, it sings. Look, it's a BMW vertical single-cylinder shaft drive. No chain to break or fall off, and it pulls up these mountains as though they don't exist. Come for a ride. It's the best feeling there is. Wind in your hair.'

'Muck all over your face,' said Pelagia sceptically. 'You look like a monkey. Anyway, somebody might see us.'

The captain considered this problem. 'OK, tomorrow I'll bring you a helmet and goggles and a big leather coat, and then you won't be recognised. Is that a deal?'

'No.'

But the next day they met around the bend of the road, and Pelagia hurriedly put on her disguise. The captain found it almost impossible to control the machine with the extra weight, and to begin with they wove about and went into the stony grass verges. They fell off twice, without injury, and then they established that she should try not to move about when she was seated behind him. She clung to his waist, white-knuckled with terror, her face buried between his shoulder-blades, the machine thundering in her groin with a sensation that was at once deeply pleasant and thoroughly disturbing. After they had arrived at Fiskardo she had clambered off, shaking, and realised that she couldn't wait to get back on. He was right, it was glorious to ride a motorcycle. The captain was exhilarated.

They went to places where Pelagia could not have been known, and to places that were deserted. She would thread her arm through his and walk beside him, leaning her weight upon his shoulder, always laughing. With him she would always remember that she laughed. Sometimes they took a bottle of Robola, and that would make her laugh much more, though it left the coming home a hazardous adventure; he did not drive very straight even when sober, and more than once they took an unintended fork for lack of time for slowing down to turn. That was how they discovered the ruined shepherd's hut.

It was so old that the floor had sunk into the earth, and there was nothing in there but a rusty pan and two green bottles. The laths had cracked and slipped, and the tiles bowed dangerously. It smelt of moss and honeysuckle and old men's clothes, and the light fragmented between the stones in places where the mortar had long since disappeared. They referred to it as 'Casa Nostra', and sometimes swept its floor with sheaves of twigs, happy to share it with a small colony of discreet bats and three families of swallows. In this secret house they would spread a rug and lie embracing, kissing and talking, and now and then he would play his mandolin.

He played her sentimental songs from forgotten times, usually in a melodramatic and ironic style; he was conscious that his voice was not a strong one, and he wanted merely to make her laugh:

'Alma del core, spirito dell'alma,
Sempre constante, t'adorero.
Saro contento nel mio tormento,
Se quel bel labro baciar potro . . .'

When she was feeling frivolous and light with wine he would sing:

'Danza, danza, fanciulla, al mio cantar;
Danza, danza, fanciulla gentile, al mio cantar,
Gira legera, sotile al suono, al suono del'onde del mar . . .'

And indeed in the distance came the sound of the sea, and Pelagia waltzed satirically about the hut, pirouetting and giggling, throwing pouts at him to burlesque the military whores she had seen so often, making faces and blowing kisses at the men as they rattled by in their trucks.

Sometimes Corelli became depressed and sentimental, reflecting upon the eternal impossibility of their devotion, and his light tenor voice would take on a tragic mien that brought tears to his own eyes, if not to Pelagia's. It would be a time to make lament, and he would sing 'Donna non vidi mai . . .' not because it was sad, which it was not, but because it was sung andante lento and had plenty of scope for maximum expression con anima in that refrain of 'Manon Lescaut me chiamo'.

All their lovers' talk began with the phrase 'After the war'.

After the war, when we are married, shall we live in Italy? There are nice places. My father thinks I wouldn't like it, but I would. As long as I'm with you. After the war, if we have a girl, can we call her Lemoni? After the war, if we have a son, we've got to call him Iannis. After the war, I'll speak to the children in Greek, and you can speak to them in Italian, and that way they'll grow bilingual. After the war I'm going to write a concerto, and I'll dedicate it to you. After the war I'm going to train to be a doctor, and I don't care if they don't let women in, I'm still going to do it. After the war I'll get a job in a convent, like Vivaldi, teaching music, and all the little girls will fall in love with me, and you'll be jealous. After the war, let's go to America, I've got relatives in Chicago. After the war we won't bring up our children with any religion, they can make their own minds up when they're older. After the war, we'll get our own

330

motorbike, and we'll go all over Europe, and you can give concerts in hotels, and that's how we'll live, and I'll start writing poems. After the war I'll get a mandola so that I can play viola music. After the war I'll love you, after the war I'll love you, I'll love you forever, after the war.

46

BUNNIOS

AT THE SUMMIT of Mt Aenos, Alekos rose from his bed of skins at dawn, and reminded himself that he had better milk a few nanny goats if he was going to make any cheese. But first of all it was time to go out with his rifle and check if all of his charges were still there. Just recently there had been people who called themselves 'andartes', who appeared from nowhere and tried to steal his goats. He had already shot two of them and left their flesh for the Egyptian vultures.

He did not understand it. This kind of thing had not happened since his great-grandfather's time, in the days when these andartes were called·klefts. Well, never mind, he had acquired two new rifles and a lot of ammunition thanks to the goat-thieves, and he doubted very much if they would ever return. It took a man of incredible tenacity and stamina to climb that mountain, and he had probably shot the only two who had been sufficiently strong in leg and lung.

Perhaps it was something to do with the war. He had noticed early on that there must be a war, because sometimes at night the whole sky was lit up with distant searchlights, and very often he saw flashes of gunfire followed by distant rumbles. It was a lovely and entertaining thing to sit outside his hut at night, watching the fireworks and eating cheese dunked in olive oil and thyme. It made him feel very much less alone, and he hoped wistfully that the war would not end before the festival of the saint. When the doctor had come up the mountain, he had confirmed that indeed there was a war, saying that some people were starving so piti-fully that tiny children had grown straight into little old men with wispy beards and stooping backs. It seemed that their stomachs had told them that there was no point in bothering to be young, and it seemed that before long Mother Nature would see to it that babies came out of their mothers already nailed into a box.

When the Liberator growled overhead, he did not pay very much attention, because they flew frequently and in pairs or threes, disappearing like noisy bats in the general direction of the mainland.

But this time he looked up, perhaps from instinct, and beheld a particularly pretty sight. A sort of white mush-room was drifting down with a tiny man suspended under-neath, and what was marvellous about it was that the rising sun was glinting from the silk before it had had time to become more than a suspicion of a glow upon the horizon. Alekos stood up and watched it with fascination. Perhaps it was an angel. It was certainly garbed in white. He crossed himself and struggled to remember a prayer. He had never heard of an angel that floated about below a mushroom, but you never knew. And it seemed that the angel had a big rock, perhaps a package, hanging from his feet on a rope.

The angel tugged hard at one side of the strings that attached it to the mushroom, and at the last minute it seem-ed to be coming down so fast that it was bound to crash. Alekos felt some satisfaction in having been right when indeed the angel came down with a thud, fell over sideways, cracked its head on a rock, and was dragged along the ground, the crosswind billowing out the silk. He seized one of his rifles and ran over to it; it was best to be sure, and per-haps even the angels were so famished nowadays that they had taken to stealing goats.

It was a very red-faced angel, and it was terribly tangled up in strings and the fabric of the diaphanous mushroom. Alekos cocked the rifle and pointed it straight into the angel's face. It opened its eyes, looked at him politely, said, 'What ho,' and went straight to sleep.

It took Alekos some time to disentangle the angel from its

webbing and cords, and he decided that the wondrous cloth of the mushroom would make a most luxurious sheet. It also had an ingenious hole in the middle through which one could place one's head, thereby allowing the mushroom to be worn as a robe. Alekos decided that he would wear it to the feast of the saint, if the angel would give it to him and allow him to cut off the strings.

He moved the heavenly visitor into his hut, and went to open the large packet that had fallen with him; it contained a heavy metal box with dials, and a small engine. Alekos was by no means stupid, and he concluded that the angel was probably bringing in the engine so that he could build himself some kind of vehicle.

For two days he fed it on honey and yoghurt, and other dainties that he thought suitable for such a creature from another world, and was delightedly pleased when it began to sit up, rub its head, and talk.

The trouble was that he could not make head or tail of what it was saying. He did recognise some of the words, but the rhythm of angel-speech was quite foreign to him, the words did not seem to fit together, and it spoke as if it had a pebble in its throat and a bee up its nose. The angel was obviously very annoyed and frustrated at not being understood, and it made Alekos feel fearful and guilty even though it was not his fault. They had to resort to communicating by signs and facial expressions.

The most intriguing thing about the angel was that when it wanted to speak to God or one of the saints, it fiddled about with the metal box and made lots of interesting whines and hisses and crackles. And then God would speak back in angel-speech, sounding so far away and stilted that Alekos realised for the first time how difficult it was for God to get himself heard by anyone. He began to recognise words that were repeated often, like 'Charlie' and 'Bravo', and 'Wilco', and 'Roger'. Another odd thing about the creature was that it carried a pistol, a light automatic, and a number of very heavy khaki-coloured iron pine cones with metal levers that he was not allowed to touch. All the angels he had ever seen in pictures carried swords or spears, and it seemed odd that God had seen fit to modernise.

After four days the angel showed clear signs of wanting to go somewhere, and Alekos, having struggled with his reluctance to leave his goats to the andarte thieves, tapped his chest, smiled, and indicated that the angel should follow him. It accepted with gratitude and gave him chocolate, which he ate in one go, feeling slightly sick afterwards. However, it did not want to go in daylight, and Alekos had to wait until dusk. It also wanted to exchange its webbing packs for a large goatskin. As far Alekos was concerned, this was the best deal that had ever come his way, and he accepted with alacrity, despite a small twinge of guilt over having diddled an angel, albeit involuntarily and by consent. It consigned its metal box and small engine to the goatskin, bound it up with cord, and slung it over its shoulder.

Alekos knew that the only person who might have a chance of understanding angel-speech was Dr Iannis, and accordingly it was to that house that he took the angel. It took four days of travelling at night with what Alekos considered to be quite unnecessary stealth, and it took three days of hiding in the maquis in the outrageous heat, being bitten to death by mosquitoes and trying to talk in whispers. It seemed quite likely that God had expelled this particular angel from heaven on the grounds of insanity. But Alekos was not going to protest; it had very fair hair, was outstandingly tall, had indefatigable powers of endurance, and possessed all of its teeth, giving it a very engaging smile. It also scowled fiercely when Italian or German soldiers were nearby, and from this Alekos deduced that God was undoubtedly fighting for the Greeks.

Dr Iannis was awoken at three o'clock in the morning by a gentle tapping on his window. He lay still for a moment, wondering with irritation how a branch could be doing such a thing when there was not any tree. Finally he rolled out of bed and unbolted the shutters. He saw Alekos, which was surprising enough, but he also saw a very tall fair-haired man dressed in the fustanella of an evzone. Alekos perceived the expression of perplexity on the doctor's face, raised his hands, shrugged, said, 'I've brought you an angel,' and departed before he could become involved in any arguments about responsibility for it.

The angel smiled and held out his hand, 'Bunnios,' he said, 'I cleped am.'

The doctor shook the proffered hand through the window, and said, 'Dr Iannis.'

'Sire, of youre gentillesse, by the leve of yow wol I speke in pryvetee of certeyn thyng.'

The doctor knitted his brows in bewilderment, 'What?'

The strange man signalled that he wanted to come in, and the doctor sighed impatiently, reckoning upon telling him to go around to the door. But as soon as he nodded the man put one hand up to the frame of the window and bounded through. He dumped his skin full of equipment upon the floor, and shook the doctor's hand all over again. Pelagia came in blearily, having heard the sounds, and beheld a man dressed in the tasselled cap, the white kilt and hose, the embroidered waistcoat, and the slippers with pompoms that was the festival dress of some people on the mainland. It was very grubby, but unmistakably new. She looked up at him in amazement, and put her hand over her mouth. Wide-eyed, she demanded of her father, 'Who's this?'

'Who's this?' repeated the doctor. 'How am I supposed to know? Alekos said it was an angel and then ran off. He says he's called Bunnios, and he talks Greek like a Spanish cow.'

The outlandish man bowed politely and shook Pelagia's hand. She let it go limp in his, and could not conceal her astonishment. He smiled charmingly and said, 'I preise wel thy fresshe beautee and age tendre, I trow.'

'I am Pelagia,' she said, and then she asked her father, 'What's he speaking? It's not Katharevousa.'

'Of course it isn't. And it certainly isn't Romaic.'

'Do you think it's Bulgarian or Turkish or something?'

'Greek of th'olde dayes,' said the man, adding, 'Pericles. Demosthenes. Homer.'

'Ancient Greek?' exclaimed Pelagia, disbelievingly. She stepped back for fear of being in the company of a ghost. She had heard from childhood all about the Marble

Emperor who had been carried by an angel to a cave, whence he would return one day to drive out the oppressors. But this man seemed more flesh than marble, and it was only a silly legend. There was another tale about fair-haired strangers from the north who would bring deliverance. Who knows?

The doctor tapped his forefinger to his forehead, and looked up triumphantly. 'English?' he asked.

'Engelonde,' agreed the man. 'Natheless, I prithee, by my trouthe . . .'

'Of course we won't tell anyone. Please may we speak English? Your pronunciation is truly terrible. It hurts my head. Pelagia, bring a glass of water and some spoon sweets.'

The Englishman smiled with what was obviously an enormous relief; it had been an awful burden to be speaking the finest public school Greek, and not be understood. He had been told that he was the nearest thing to a real Graecophone that could be found under the circumstances, and he knew perfectly well that modern Greek was not quite the same as the Greek of Eton, but he had had no idea that he would be found quite so incomprehensible. It was also very clear that someone in Intelligence had contrived a completely aberrant notion of what was worn in Cephallonia.

'We are having an Italian officer asleeping in a room,' said the doctor, whose English was not as good as he liked to believe, 'so we are being very quiet, please.'

The Englishman unbound his goatskin and removed a revolver. Pelagia was horrified. As far as she was concerned, no one was going to shoot Antonio. The man saw her consternation and said, 'A precaution. I wouldn't want to bring about reprisals unless I jolly well had to.'

'A spy?' asked the doctor. 'Espionage?'

The man nodded, and said, 'Very hush-hush. Do you have any clothes I could have? I would be most frightfully grateful.'

The doctor indicated the fustanella; 'Is not our cloths of Cephallonia.' He pointed to a framed picture on the wall of a young man in knee-length breeches, a white sash about his waist, a white floppy cap upon his head, and a waistcoat with two rows of broad silver buttons. 'Is our cloths,' he explained, 'but only feast. We dress same as you. I bring you cloths, you give me fustanella, OK?'

The doctor had always wanted a set of fustanella and had never been able to afford it. Whilst fetching some ordinary clothes he said, 'Thank you Wiston Tzortzil,' raising his eyes to heaven as though Churchill were the deity. One day he would astonish everybody at a celebration. He chuckled with anticipative delight. The mangas in the kapheneion would think he had given up being a Europeanised alafranga and turned into one of those traditionalist fustanellophoroi. He wondered where he could find one of those elaborate traditional pipes, a tsibouki, to complete the picture.

It was far from easy to get the spy into the garments of a smaller man, but it was a small consolation that they both required an identical size of hat. The trussed Englishman departed for Argostoli at dawn, the turn-ups of his trousers half way up his pink calves and the jacket unfastenable, bearing his equipment in a hessian sack, also provided by the doctor, who would not let him depart without imparting some sound advice.

'Look, OK? You accent terrible-terrible. Not to talk, understand? You are quiet until you learning. Also, you watch out andartes. They thieves, not soldiers, they say Communist, but they thieves. They not interested fighting, understand? Italians OK, Germans not good, see?'

And so it was that Lieutenant 'Bunny' Warren, seconded to the SOE from the King's Dragoon Guards, with astounding initiative and outstanding cheek, set up his home in a large house in which four Italian officers were already billeted. He perplexed and confounded them by trying to communicate in Latin, and every week he trekked to the deserted shack where he had installed his radio and his recharging engine. He reported in great detail to Cairo, informing them of troop movements and numbers, just in case the Allies should decide to invade Greece instead of Sicily.

It was a lonely life, and it was galling to be considered mad, but then madness was perhaps the best disguise. With his bodybelt full of gold sovereigns he covered Cephallonia on foot, memorising everything, and once or twice he climbed Mt Aenos to pay his respects to his first host, who was never entirely convinced that he had not been an angel. He sometimes joined up with the conveniently peripatetic Father Arsenios, and passed for another prophetic religious fanatic.

His radio never let him down once. It was a Brown B2. It had only two Loctal valves, it had an aerial that looked exactly like a washing-line, it ran from the mains or by a six-volt battery, and, weighing in at a paltry thirty-two pounds, it was a miracle of miniaturisation.

47

DR IANNIS COUNSELS HIS DAUGHTER

DR IANNIS PACKED his pipe with the lethally acrid mixture that passed for tobacco in those days of occupation, tamped it down, lit it, and sucked unwisely hard. The sharp smoke struck him at the back of the throat, and his eyes bulged. He spluttered, clutched at his neck with one hand, and coughed violently. He threw the pipe down and muttered, 'Faeces, nothing but faeces. What has the world come to when I am reduced to smoking coprolite? Well, that's it, I will never smoke again.'

The pipe had recently brought him more pain than consolation. For one thing it was impossible to obtain pipe cleaners, and he had been reduced to scouring the garden for wing feathers. He had even bribed little Lemoni to go down to the beach and find them, and this had involved inducing Pelagia to make the little honey-pastries that Lemoni loved. It threatened to become an infinite and unmanageable regress of corruption. He had attempted to cut the Gordian knot by giving up the cleaning of his pipe, but this had resulted in the inhalation of indescribably repellent, ferociously bitter, and appallingly slimy gobbets of cold dottle. It made him feel as nauseated as a maladapted dog that had eaten chilli peppers soaked in gasoline, and all this just so that he could smoke tobacco that was no less than the equivalent of an amateur tonsillectomy. He felt betrayed and irritable. His pipe was a St Claude that he had bought in Marseilles, and it was supposed to be an old friend. Agreed, it had burned away about

340

the rim and the stem was yellowed and bitten, but it had never before attacked him with such malice. He left it on the floor and returned to his writing:

'Because the island is a jewel it has since the time of Odysseus been the plaything of the great, the powerful, the plutocratic, and the odious. The unphilosophical Romans, unenlightened in any of the arts except for that of managing slaves and that of military conquest, sacked the city of Sami and massacred its population after an heroic resistance that had endured for four months. There began a long and lamentable history of its being passed from hand to hand as a gift, at the same time as it was repeatedly being raided by corsairs from all the many corners of the malversated Mediterranean Sea. Thus was an island plundered in perpetuity, an island whose celebrated musician Melampus had won the prize for Cithara at the Olympic Games as long ago as 582 BC. From the time of the Romans the only prize for us was survival.'

The doctor paused and picked up his pipe from the floor, forgetting that moments before he had renounced it forever. It was the same old problem; it was not so much a history as a lament. Or a tirade. Or a Philippic. He was struck suddenly by the illuminating idea that perhaps it was not that it was impossible for him to write a history, but that History Itself Was Impossible. Satisfied with the profundity of the implications of this thought, he rewarded himself with a deep draw on his pipe that once again reduced him to helpless paroxysms of agonising sneezes and coughs.

Seized with fury, he stood up and contemplated breaking the pipe in half. He was on the point of doing so when he was vanquished by a sense of pre-emptive panic. The fact was that Giving Up Smoking was as Inconceivable as History. It was clear that there was going to have to be some kind of accommodation between himself and his pipe. He called in Pelagia, who had been carefully spooning the coffee grounds out of that morning's cups so that they could be used again. The coffee situation was as dire as the tobacco crisis.

'Daughter,' he said, 'I want you to melt a little honey in

341

some brandy, and then mix this tobacco in it. It is simply insufferable as it is. It is most unpleasantly sternutatory.'

Pelagia looked at him wryly and took the proffered tin. She was on the point of going when her father added, 'Don't go yet, there's something I have to talk to you about.'

The doctor was surprised. 'What do I want to talk to her about?' he asked himself. It was as if he had gleaned some impressions, some impressions that needed to be discussed, but which had not yet congealed into a set of ideas.

Pelagia sat down opposite him, removed some stray hairs that had fallen about her face by force of habit, and asked, 'What is it, Papakis?' He looked at her sitting there, her hands folded on her lap, an expectant expression playing about her eyes, and a demure smile upon her lips. Her appearance of pretty innocence reminded him of what he had wanted to say. Anyone, and especially a daughter, who could appear so virginal and sweet was quite obviously involved in mischiefs and misdemeanours.

'It has not escaped my notice, Pelagia, that you have fallen in love with the captain.'

She flushed violently, looked perfectly horrified, and began to stammer. 'The captain?' she repeated foolishly.

'Yes, the captain, our uninvited but charming guest. He who plays the mandolin in the moonlight and brings you Italian confectionery that you do not always see fit to share with your father. This latter being the one whom you presume to be both blind and stupid.'

'Papakis,' she protested, too taken aback to add any kind of articulate coda to this interjection.

'Even your neck and your ears have gone red,' observed the doctor, enjoying her discomfiture and deliberately heaping more coals upon it.

'But Papakis . . .'

The doctor waved his pipe expansively. 'Really, this point is not worth denying or discussing, because it is all very obvious. The diagnosis has been made and confirmed. We should be discussing the implications. By the way, it is clear to me that he also is in love with you.'

'He has said no such thing, Papas. Why are you trying to

vex me? I am beginning to be very annoyed. How can you say such things?'

'That's the spirit,' he said with satisfaction, 'that's my daughter.'

'I am going to hit you, really I am.'

He leaned forward and took one of her hands. She looked away and flushed even more deeply. It was so typical of him to make her utterly indignant and then to deflate her with a gentle gesture. He was an unmanageable father, a farrago of peremptory orders one minute, sly and wheedling the next, lofty and aristocratically detached the minute after that.

'I am a doctor, but I am also a man who has lived a lot of life and who has observed it,' said the doctor. 'Love is a kind of dementia with very precise and oft-repeated clinical symptoms. You blush in each other's presence, you both hover in places where you expect the other to pass, you are both a little tongue-tied, you both laugh inexplicably and too long, you become quite nauseatingly girlish, and he becomes quite ridiculously gallant. You have also grown a little stupid. He gave you a rose the other day, and you pressed it in my book of symptoms. If you had not been in love and had had a little sense, you would have pressed it in some other book that I did not use every day. I think it very fitting that the rose is to be found in the section that deals with erotomania.'

Pelagia suspected the imminent collapse of a thousand pretty dreams. She remembered the confidential advice of her aunt: 'For a woman to obtain success, she is obliged either to weep, to nag, or to sulk. She must be prepared to do this for years, because she is the disposable property of the men of the family, and men, like rocks, take a long time to wear down.' Pelagia tried to weep, but was physically prevented by a mounting sense of panic. She stood up suddenly, and just as abruptly sat down again. She foresaw an abyss opening at her feet and an army of Turks, in the form of her father, preparing to push her over the precipice. His dry dissection of her heart seemed already to have banished the magic from her imagination.

But Dr Iannis squeezed her hand, repenting already of his

rude humour, and inspired to compassion by no more than the undeniable fact that it was another beautiful day. He rotated the end of his forefinger in one extremity of his moustache, and detachedly observed his daughter's attempts to produce a tear. He commenced a lengthy monologue:

'It's a fact of life that the honour of a family derives from the conduct of its women. I don't know why this is, and possibly matters are different elsewhere. But we live here, and I note the fact scientifically in the same way that I observe that there is snow on Mt Aenos in January and that we have no rivers.

'It's not that I don't like the captain. Of course he is a little mad, which is quite simply explained by the fact that he is Italian, but he is not so mad as to be completely risible. In fact I like him very much, and the fact that he plays the mandolin like an angel makes up in great measure for him being a foreigner.' At this point the doctor wondered whether or not it would be constructive to reveal his suspicion that the captain suffered from haemorrhoids; the revelation of physical imperfections and infirmities was often a powerful antidote to love. Out of respect for Pelagia, he decided against it. One should not, after all, place dogshit in Aphrodite's bed. He continued:

'But you must remember that you are betrothed to Mandras. You do remember that, don't you? Technically the captain is an enemy. Can you conceive the torment that would be inflicted upon you by others when they judge that you have renounced the love of a patriotic Greek, in favour of an invader, an oppressor? You will be called a collaborator, a Fascist's whore, and a thousand things besides. People will throw stones at you and spit, you know that, don't you? You would have to move away to Italy if you wanted to stay with him, because here you might not be safe. Are you ready to leave this island and this people? What do you know of life over there? Do you think that Italians know how to make meat pie and have churches dedicated to St Gerasimos? No, they do not.

'And another thing. Love is a temporary madness, it

erupts like volcanoes and then subsides. And when it subsides you have to make a decision. You have to work out whether your roots have so entwined together that it is inconceivable that you should ever part. Because this is what love it. Love is not breathlessness, it is not excitement, it is not the promulgation of promises of eternal passion, it is not the desire to mate every second minute of the day, it is not lying awake at night imagining that he is kissing every cranny of your body. No, don't blush, I am telling you some truths. That is just being "in love", which any fool can do. Love itself is what is left over when being in love has burned away, and this is both an art and a fortunate accident. Your mother and I had it, we had roots that grew towards each other underground, and when all the pretty blossom had fallen from our branches we found that we were one tree and not two. But sometimes the petals fall away and the roots have not entwined. Imagine giving up your home and your people, only to discover after six months, a year, three years, that the trees have had no roots and have fallen over. Imagine the desolation. Imagine the imprisonment.

'I say to you that to marry the captain is impossible until our homeland is liberated. One can only forgive a sin after the sinner has finished committing it, because we cannot allow ourselves to condone it whilst it is still being perpetrated. I admit this possibility, indeed I would be happy with it. Perhaps you do not love Mandras any more. Perhaps there is an equation to be balanced, with love on one side and dishonour on the other. No one knows where Mandras is. He may not be amongst the living.

'But this means that you have a love that will be indefinitely delayed. Pelagia, you know as well as I do that love delayed is lust augmented. No, don't look at me like that. I am not ignorant or stupid, and I was not born yesterday. Also I am a doctor and I deal not in impossible moral commands but in demonstrable facts. No one can tell me that just because someone is young, good-looking, well-educated and sensible, they are not also inflamed. Do you think I don't know that young girls can be eaten by desire? I am even resigned to the possibility that my dear little daughter may be in such a state. Don't hang your head, you should not be ashamed. I am not a priest, I am a doctor, my attitude is anthropological, and besides, when I was young . . . well, that's enough of that. Suffice it to say that I am not prepared to be a hypocrite or to affect a sudden and amenable amnesia.

'But this gives us even more problems, doesn't it? When we are mad we lose control of ourselves. We become driven. This is why our forefathers chose to control the natural madness of the young by tarring it with shame. This is why in some places they still hang out the blotted sheet on the bridal morning. I saw one in Assos last week when I was called to that broken arm, remember? If we were not made ashamed of this beautiful thing then we would do nothing else. We would not work, we would be inundated with babies, and because of this there would be no civilisation. In short we would still be in the caves, mating relentlessly and without discrimination. If we had not reserved a time and a place, and forbidden it in other times and places, we would be living like dogs, and life would possess little beauty or peace.

'Pelagia, I am not telling you to be ashamed. I am a doctor, not a maker of civilisations who wants people to stop enjoying themselves so that a village might be built. But imagine if you got pregnant! Stop pretending to be shocked, who knows what one might do in a moment of passion? These things are possible, they are natural consequences of natural things. What do you think would happen? Pelagia, I would not help you to abort a child, even though I know how. To speak plainly, I would not be a party to the murder of an innocent. What would you do? Go to one of these midwives or wise-women who kill half their clients and leave the rest permanently sterile? Would you have the child, only to find that no man would ever marry you? Many such women finish up as prostitutes, take my word for it, because suddenly they find that they have nothing left to lose and no way to keep body and soul together. But Pelagia, I would not abandon you as long as I live, even under such circumstances. But imagine if I should die. Don't grimace, we all owe a death to nature, it can't be helped. And what if the captain could not marry you because the Army forbids it? What then?

'And are you aware that there are foul diseases attendant upon improvident actions in this regard? Can you be completely sure that our captain has not been visiting that brothel? Young men are infinitely corruptible in this one matter, however honourable they may be otherwise, and the Army has made it easy by supplying a brothel. Do you know what syphilis can do? It makes the body disintegrate and the brain go mad. It causes blindness. The children of syphilitics are born deaf and cretinous. What if the captain goes there and closes his eyes and imagines that it is you in his arms? Such a thing is very likely, although it pains me to say so, young men being what they are.'

Pelagia wept real tears. She had never felt so crushed and humiliated. Her father had reduced all her rosy reveries to common sense and medical sordidities. She looked up at him through her tears and found him looking at her with enormous sympathy. 'You're in a fix,' he said simply, 'you've put us both in a fix.'

'You make everything squalid,' she reproached him bitterly. 'You don't know how it is.'

'I went through a lot of this with your mother,' he replied. 'She was betrothed to someone else. I do know how it is. That is why I am talking to you as one person to another, and that is why I am not striding up and down shouting at you and forbidding everything, as a father should.'

'You don't forbid everything then?' she asked hopefully.

'No, I don't forbid everything. I say you must be very mindful of what you do, and you must act honourably with respect to Mandras. That is all. You must look at the good side of this. The longer you know the captain, the better you will be able to decide whether or not you have roots that may grow together under the ground. Don't give in to him at all. Deny yourself. Because then your eyes will not be clouded by a madness that you cannot control, and then you will be able to learn to see him as he is. Do you understand?'

'Papakis,' she said softly, 'the captain has never tried to compromise me.'

'He is a good man. He knows that he is in a bad position. Pray for the liberation of the island, Pelagia, because then everything becomes possible.'

Pelagia stood up and took the tin of tobacco. 'Honey and brandy?' she asked quietly, and her father nodded. He said, 'Don't let anything I have said diminish you. I did not intend to upset you. I was young once.'

'Not everything was different in your day, then,' she said tartly as she left the room. Her father smiled with satisfaction at this Parthian shot, and sucked very tentatively on the pipe; he had judged that a pert response signifies an undiminished daughter. It was probably easier to be a father than to be an historian. He turned to his sheaf of papers and wrote, 'The island passed into the hands of the Byzantine Empire, which had the merit of being Greek and the demerit of being Byzantine.'

48

La Scala

'IT'S TRUE, ANTONIO, some of your men are running a racket, and in my opinion and the opinion of my brother officers, it reflects very badly on you. Not you personally, but on the Army of Italy. It's as scandalous as that pamphlet about the Duce that everyone's reading. It's part of the same disease.'

Corelli turned to Carlo, 'Is this true, as Günter says?'

'Don't ask me. You'd have to ask a Greek.'

'Iatre,' called Corelli, 'is it true?'

The doctor came out of the kitchen, where he had been carefully sharpening the blades of old scalpels on a whetstone, and asked, 'Is what true?'

'That some of our soldiers are buying goods from the hungry with ration cards, and then some other people come in and confiscate the cards back again because they were acquired illegally.'

'It's not "some other people",' said the doctor, 'it's just the other half of the same gang. It goes round in a perfect circle. Stamatis got stung like that last week. He lost a valuable clock and two silver candlesticks, and ended up with no ration cards, and a belly as empty as before. Very ingenious.' The doctor turned to go, and then stopped, 'And another thing, your soldiers are stealing from people's vegetable patches. As if we were not all dying of hunger.'

'We Germans do not do this,' said Günter Weber smugly, enjoying a little schadenfreude at Corelli's expense.

'Germans can't sing,' riposted Corelli irrelevantly, 'and

349

anyway, I'll get this investigated, and I'll put a stop to it. It's too bad.'

Weber smiled, 'You are very famous for defending the rights of Greeks. I wonder sometimes if you understand why you are here.'

'I'm not here to be a bastard,' said Corelli, 'and to be perfectly frank, I do not feel good about it. I try to think of it as a holiday. I don't have your advantages, Günter.'

'Advantages?'

'Yes. I don't have the advantage of thinking that other races are inferior to mine. I don't feel entitled, that's all.'

'It's a question of science,' said Weber. 'You can't alter a scientific fact.'

Corelli frowned, 'Science? The Marxists think they are scientists, and they believe the exact opposite of you. I don't care about science. It's an irrelevance. It's a moral principle that you can't alter, not a scientific fact.'

'We disagree,' said Weber amiably, 'it's obvious to me that ethics change with the times as science does. Ethics have changed because of the theories of Darwin.'

'You're right, Günter,' interjected Carlo, 'but no one has to like it. I don't like it, and neither does Antonio, that's all. And science is about facts, and morality is about values. They are not the same thing and they don't grow together. No one can find a value on the slide of a microscope. It might be true that Jews are evil or inferior, for instance, how would I know? But how does that mean that we should treat them with injustice? I don't understand the reasoning.'

'Do you remember,' said Weber, leaning back in his chair, 'how you pulled a pistol on me when I was going to club that pine marten for its skin? I didn't kill it. I didn't know it was a pet in any case. I couldn't argue with a pistol. That is the new morality. Strength needs no excuses and doesn't have to give reasons. It is Darwinism, as I said.'

'It has to leave reasons to history,' said Corelli, 'or else it stands condemned. It's also a question of being at ease with oneself. Do you remember when that bombardier tried to rape that girl who was cured by the supposed miracle? Mina, that was her name. Do you know why I did that?'

350

'You mean when you made him stand to attention in the sun with nothing on except a tin helmet and a haversack?'

'A haversack full of rocks. Yes. I did it because I imagined that woman was my sister. I did it because when he was well-cooked I felt a lot better. That is my morality. I make myself imagine that it's personal.'

'You're a good man,' said Günter, 'I admit it.'

'By the way, I stopped you from clubbing Psipsina in order to save your life,' said Corelli. 'If I hadn't stopped you, Pelagia would have killed you.'

'Aaaaaagh,' spluttered Weber, pretending to strangle himself. 'Where is Pelagia? I thought she liked our singing.'

'She does, but it's embarrassing for her to be the only woman in a bunch of boys. I expect she's listening in the kitchen.'

'No I'm not,' she called.

'Ah,' said Weber, 'there you are. Antonio was just saying that we ought to bring some of the girls from the Casa Rosetta, to balance the numbers. What do you think of that?'

'My father would throw La Scala out, and you'd have to go back to singing in the latrines.'

'We could bring two armoured cars, and come anyway,' said Weber. He looked around at the faces that were not smiling at his remark, and said, 'Only a little joke.'

'Our armoured cars wouldn't be able to get up the hill,' said one of the baritones, 'we'd have to borrow one of yours.'

'Lies and slanders,' replied one of the tenors, 'they go very well if you take the armour off. Come on, let's sing something.'

'"La Giovinezza,"' suggested Weber enthusiastically, and all the rest of them groaned. 'OK, OK, I'll get my gramophone from my vehicle, and we can all sing with Marlene.'

'And afterwards we can sing love songs,' said Corelli, 'because tonight is a beautiful night, and everything is peaceful, and we should be thinking about being romantic.'

Weber went to his jeep, proudly and proprietorially returning with his gramophone. He set it on the table, and

351

twisted down the needle. There was a sound very like the stirring of a distant sea, and then the first martial bars of 'Lili Marlene'. Dietrich began to sing, her voice full of languid melancholy, worldliness, the sadness of knowledge, and the longing for love. 'O,' exclaimed Weber, 'she is the incarnation of sex. She makes me melt.'

Some of the boys joined in the song, and Corelli began to pick up the melody on his mandolin. 'Antonia likes this,' he said, 'Antonia is going to sing.' He began to introduce grace notes, and then rapid sections of fingerwork that filled in the scale between the notes. On the last verse he broke into a tremolo that soared above the music in a descant, embellished it with sly glissandos, rests and ritardandos, climbed ambitiously towards the highest and thinnest pitch of the instrument, and then fell back deliciously upon the sonorous middle range of the third and second strings. In the village the people stopped what they were doing and listened to Corelli fill the night. When the music stopped they sighed, and Kokolios said to his wife, 'The man's mad, and he's a wop, but he's got nightingales in his fingers.'

'It's better than listening to you snorting and farting all night,' she said.

'A proletarian fart is greater music than a bourgeois song,' he said, and she grimaced and said, 'You wish.'

Pelagia left the kitchen, her slender silhouette ghostlike in the dim light of the candle from the kitchen. 'Please play that again,' she requested, 'it was so beautiful.' She came out and stroked the polished wood of Weber's gramophone. The machine was another wonder of the modern world, like Corelli's motorbike, that had escaped the world of Cephallonia until the war years came. It was something fine and glorious amid the loss and separation, the deprivation and fear.

'Do you like it?' asked Weber, and she nodded wistfully. 'All right,' he continued, 'when I go home after the war, I'll leave it with you. You can have it. It would please me very much, and you will always remember Günter. I can easily find another in Vienna, and you can accept it as an apology to Psipsina.'

Pelagia was touched, almost overjoyed. She looked at the smiling youngster with his smart uniform, his clipped blond hair and his brown eyes, and she was filled with pleasure and gratitude. 'You're so sweet,' she said, and kissed him very naturally on one cheek. The boys of La Scala cheered, and Weber blushed, hiding his eyes with his hand.

49

THE DOCTOR ADVISES THE CAPTAIN

THE DOCTOR AND the captain were sitting indoors at the kitchen table, the latter removing a broken string from his mandolin, and lamenting the fact that new strings were impossible to obtain.

'How about surgical wire?' enquired the doctor, leaning forward and inspecting the defunct string through his spectacles, 'I think I've got some of the same gauge.'

'It's got to be right,' replied Corelli. 'If it's too thick, you have to tighten the string beyond the capacity of the instrument, and it just folds in half. If it's too thin, then it's too slack to have a decent tone and it rattles on the frets.'

The doctor leaned back and sighed. Suddenly he asked, 'Are you and Pelagia planning to be married? As her father I think I have a right to know.'

The captain was so taken aback by the frankness of the question that he was utterly stumped for an answer. Things had only been able to proceed on the basis that no one ever brought the issue out into the open; things could only work at all on the understanding that it was a dark secret that everybody knew. He looked at the doctor in dismay, his mouth working wordlessly like an improvident fish that a wave has tossed unsuspectingly upon a spit of sand.

'You can't live here,' said the doctor. He pointed at the mandolin. 'If you want to be a musician this is the last place to be. You would have to go home, or to America. And I don't think that Pelagia could live in Italy. She is a Greek. She would die like a flower deprived of light.'

'Ah,' said the captain, for the lack of any intelligent remark that came immediately to mind.

'It's true,' said the doctor. 'I know you have not thought about it. Italians always act without thinking, it's the glory and the downfall of your civilisation. A German plans a month in advance what his bowel movements will be at Easter, and the British plan everything in retrospect, so it always looks as though everything occurred as they intended. The French plan everything whilst appearing to be having a party, and the Spanish . . . well, God knows. Anyway, Pelagia is Greek, that's my point. So can it work? Even disregarding the obvious impracticalities?'

The captain unwound the tangle of wire at the tuning pegs, and replied, 'It's not the point, with respect. It is a more personal thing. Let me confide in you, Dottore. Pelagia has said to me that you and I are very alike. I am obsessed by my music, and you are obsessed with your medicine. We are both men who have created a purpose for ourselves, and neither of us cares very much for what anyone else may think of us. She has only been able to love me because she learned first how to love another man who is like me. And that man is you. So being a Greek or an Italian is incidental.'

The doctor was so touched by this hypothesis that a lump arose in his throat. He quelled it and said, 'You don't understand us.'

'Of course I do.'

Dr Iannis became a little riled, and therefore a little vehement, 'But you don't. Do you think you're going to get a nice amenable girl and that every path will be strewn with petals? Don't you remember asking me why it is that Greeks smile when they are angry? Well, let me tell you something, young man. Every Greek, man, woman, and child, has two Greeks inside. We even have technical terms for them. They are a part of us, as inevitable as the fact that we all write poetry and the fact that every one of us thinks that he knows everything that there is to know. We are all hospitable to strangers, we all are nostalgic for something, our mothers all treat their grown sons like babies, our sons all

355

treat their mothers as sacred and beat their wives, we all hate solitude, we all try to find out from a stranger whether or not we are related, we all use every long word that we know as often as we possibly can, we all go out for a long walk in the evening so that we can look over each others' fences, we all think that we are equal to the best. Do you understand?'

The captain was perplexed, 'You didn't tell me about the two Greeks inside every Greek.'

'I didn't? Well, I must have wandered off the point.' The doctor stood up and began to walk about, gesturing eloquently with his right hand and clutching his pipe with his left. 'Look, I've been all over the world. I've seen Santiago de Chile, Shanghai, Stockholm, Addis Ababa, Sydney, all of them. And all the time I've been learning to be a doctor, and I can tell you that no one is more truly themselves than when they are sick and injured. That's when the qualities come out. And I've nearly always been on ships whose crews were mainly Greek. Do you understand? We are a race of exiles and sailors. I'm saying that I know more than most people what a Greek is like.

'I'll tell you about the Hellene first. The Hellene has a quality that we call "sophrosune". This Greek avoids excess, he knows his limits, he represses the violence within himself, he seeks harmony and cultivates a sense of proportion. He believes in reason, he is the spiritual heir of Plato and Pythagoras. These Greeks are suspicious of their own natural impulsiveness and love of change for the sake of change, and they assert discipline over themselves in order to avoid spontaneously going out of control. They love education for its own sake, do not take power and money into consideration when assessing someone's worth, scrupulously obey the law, suspect that Athens is the only important place in the world, detest dishonourable compromise, and consider themselves to be quintessentially European. This is from the blood of our ancient ancestors that still flows in us.' He paused, puffed on his pipe, and then continued:

'But side by side with the Hellene we have to live with the

Romoi. Perhaps I can point out to you, Captain, that this word originally meant "Roman", and these are the qualities that we learned from your ancestors, who never made a single technological advance in hundreds of years of dominion, and who enslaved entire nations with the utmost disregard for morals. The Romoi are people very like your Fascists, so that you should feel at home with them, except that it seems to me that you personally share none of their vices. The Romoi are improvisers, they seek power and money, they aren't rational because they act on intuition and instinct, so that they make a mess of everything. They don't pay taxes and only obey the law when there is no alternative, they look on education as a way of getting ahead, will always compromise an ideal for self-interest, and they like getting drunk, and dancing and singing, and breaking bottles over each others' heads. And they have a viciousness and brutality that I can only convey to you by saying that it compares very unfavourably with your gassing the natives in Ethiopia and your bombing of the field hospitals of the Red Cross. The only point of contact between the two sides of a Greek is the place that bears the label "patriotism". Romoi and Hellene alike will die gladly for Greece, but the Hellene will fight wisely and humanely, and the Romoi will use every subterfuge and barbarity, and happily throw away the lives of their own men, rather like your Mussolini. In fact they calculate their glory by the number that were sent to their death, and a bloodless victory is a disappointment.'

The captain was very sceptical, 'So what are you saying? Are you saying that Pelagia has a side that I don't know and which would be very shocking to me if I knew it?'

The doctor leaned forward and stabbed the air with his finger, 'That is exactly it. And another thing; I have that side too. You've never seen it, but I have it.'

'With respect, Dottore, I don't believe it.'

'I'm very glad that you don't. But in my better moments I know what the truth is.'

There was a silence between the two men, and the doctor sat down at the table to relight his unco-operative pipe, with its repellent mixture of coltsfoot, rose petals, and other herbs that failed even to approximate to tobacco. He coughed and spluttered violently.

'I love her,' said Corelli at last, as though this were the answer to the problem, which to him it was. A suspicion struck him: 'You wouldn't be reluctant to lose her, would you? Are you trying to discourage me?'

'You'd have to live here, that's all. If she went to Italy she would die of the homesickness. I know my daughter. You might have to choose between loving her and becoming a musician.'

The doctor left the room, more for rhetorical effect than for any other purpose, and then came back in. 'And another thing. This is a very ancient land, and we've had nothing but slaughter for two thousand years. Sacrifices, wars, murders, nothing but bad deaths. We've got so many places full of bitter ghosts that anyone who goes near them or lives in them becomes heartless or insane. I don't believe in God, Captain, and I'm not superstitious, but I do believe in ghosts. On this island we've had massacres at Sami and Fiskardo and God knows where else. There'll be more. It's only a question of time. So don't make any plans.'

Beaufighters and canoes, transforming the Iron Ring into an Iron Cage. In Lesbos the Communists took over and declared an independent republic. At Khios a Gestapo house was discovered where people had been forced to spend a night with a skeleton in a cellar. The German commander had been strafed to death whilst making love to his mistress. At Inousia the British found an island where every single person spoke fluent English, and where everyone was called either Lemmos or Pateras. Raiders killed the commanders at Nisiro, Simi, and Piscopi, and Patrick Leigh-Fermor and Billy Moss abducted the commander of Crete. At Thira the raiders killed two-thirds of the garrison for the loss of two men. In Crete, again, they destroyed two hundred thousand gallons of fuel. On Mikonos and Amorgos the wireless stations were destroyed, and seven prisoners taken by five men. On Khios a few Royal Marines destroyed two destroyers, even though the local andartes failed to turn up as agreed, having 'lost interest'. They hated to join attacks that anyone else had planned, and refused to take part if even another of their number had had the idea. On Samos one thousand Italians surrendered to Maurice Cardiff and twenty-three men, and then sat down to have breakfast; Cardiff discovered that for some inexplicable reason all the local doctors spoke French. At Naxos the German commander surrendered by mistake; he had rowed out to greet a boat that he thought was flying the red flag of the swastika, but was in fact flying the Red Ensign. He fell into such a deep depression and wept so bitterly that the crew had to cheer him up by teaching him to play ludo. At that time one pound sterling was worth two thousand million drachmas, and one cigarette cost seven and a half million. The people of Lesbos enterprisingly offered an advantageous rate of exchange, and every single coin and note from the whole region flew there, seemingly of its own accord, leaving no money at all in any other place. At Siros a party of Germans was seen running away without any trousers. The Communists got into the habit of demanding twenty-five percent of everything as tax, and in many places the people resigned from the party. Later on in Crete, and

Samos, they would turn on the Communists and defeat them. There is a story that the Cretans demanded British rule, but that the latter turned them down on the grounds that it was bad enough trying to govern Cyprus. All in all, for the loss of nineteen dead, four hundred men of the special forces held down forty thousand Axis troops, paying three hundred and eighty-one visits to seventy separate islands. The German sense of the proper way of doing things was so confounded by such randomised plagues of sliced throats and inexplicable explosions that they became completely helpless, and the Italians, who had never seen any sense in fighting in the first place, surrendered courteously and with pleasure.

On Cephallonia the Italian soldiers listened to their radios and charted the course of Allied progress up the spine of their homeland, whilst the German garrison seethed with disgust. Corelli and his brother officers sensed ice in the air, and fraternal visits between the bases of the two allies diminished. When Weber turned up at the meetings of La Scala, he seemed very quiet and distant, and his regard was interpreted as reproachful.

One day, in the midst of these events, Pelagia found Corelli absently stroking Psipsina on the wall, and when he turned to face her, his look was troubled. 'What happens,' he asked her, 'when we have to surrender before the Germans do?'

'We'll get married.'

He shook his head sadly, 'It's going to be a complete mess. There's no chance of the British coming. They're going straight for Rome. No one will save us unless we save ourselves. All the boys think we should disarm the Germans now, whilst their garrison is small. We've sent deputations to Gandin, but he doesn't do anything. He says we should trust them.'

'Don't you trust them?'

'I'm not stupid. And Gandin is one of those officers who has risen to the top by obeying orders. He doesn't know how to give them. He's just another of our typical donkey generals who's got no brains and no balls.'

'Come inside,' she said, 'my father's out, and we can have a cuddle. He's got lots of tuberculosis to deal with these days.'

'A cuddle would only make me sad, koritsimou. My mind is just a blank that's filled with worry.'

Father Arsenios passed by, accompanied by Bunny Warren, both of them battered, tattered, and dusty, and Pelagia said quickly, 'Antonio, I must go and ask them something, I'll be right back.'

Arsenios stood by the well and waved his crozier. His abject little dog slumped on the shady side of the stones, and began to lick itself. It had blood on the pads of its paws.

'How is the gold become dim! How is the most fine gold changed! The tongue of the sucking child cleaveth to the roof of his mouth for thirst; the children ask bread, and no man breaketh it unto them. They that did feed delicately are desolate in the streets, and they that were brought up in scarlet embrace dunghills . . .' began Arsenios, and Pelagia took Warren's elbow and led him to one side.

'Bunnio', when are the British coming? I've got to know. What's going to happen to the Italians when they surrender? Please tell me.'

'That I cannot tell,' he said. 'For I know it not myself, and neither doth any man.'

'Your Greek has improved an awful lot,' she said, amazed, 'but your accent is still . . . strange. Please tell me. I'm worried. Have the Germans brought in any more soldiers? It's important.'

'Nay, I think not.'

Pelagia left him, and heard him exclaiming 'Amen' at intervals. Perhaps the British were really a nation of actors and impostors. She returned to Corelli and said, 'Don't worry, everything will be all right.'

'Are you serious? You go and ask the opinion of a religious madman, and you expect me to believe it?'

'O ye of little faith. Come on, come inside. Psipsina caught a mouse and let it go under the table. I think you ought to catch it for me. It was last seen running behind the cupboard.'

362

'After the war, when we're married, you can catch the mice yourself. I'm not going to be chivalrous after I'm thirty.'

Whilst Corelli poked behind the cupboard with a broomstick, Arsenios' mantic voice and Bunny Warren's wild amens drifted musically through the windows: '. . . Our inheritance is turned to strangers, our houses to aliens. We are orphans and fatherless, our mothers are as widows . . . Our necks are under persecution, we labour and have no rest . . . Servants have ruled over us and there is none that doth deliver us out of their hand . . . our skin was black like an oven because of the terrible famine . . . Wherefore dost thou forget us for ever, and forsake us so long a time?'

'That priest has a wonderful bass voice,' remarked Corelli, releasing out of the window the mouse he had caught by the tail. 'And that reminds me, I went down to the harbour to listen to the fishermen. They had some really strange instruments I've never seen before, and the singing, it was fantastic. I wrote down some of the tunes.'

'They make them up as they go along, you know. Never the same twice.'

'Incredible. And there was one tune they sang a few times. I made them teach it to me . . .' he hummed a solemn and martial air, waving his fingers to conduct it, and only stopped when he saw Pelagia laughing. 'What's so funny?'

'It's our national anthem,' she said.

363

5 1

PARALYSIS

WE IMAGINE THE shade of Homer, writing: 'For wreaking havoc upon a strong man, even the very strongest, there is nothing so dire as the sea. But there was no unspeakable waste of salt water, no rude arrogance of land-shaking waves, no winged scavenging of the wind, as desolating in its results as the paralysis of General Gandin. He was impelled to inaction by the burden of his pains, and in the fertility of his expedients he was less endowed than a wilderness or a lake of salt. He was the daunted one, the vaguest-willed of any man born to death, a man of instant vanishment into blind silence. He bore the unappeasable pain of being obliged to make decisions, and in his confusion he was as helpless as those in my own times who watched multitudes of birds fly hither and thither in the bright sunshine, not knowing which ones might bear messages from heaven.

'If he had an impulse that quickened the seeds of his inactivity, it was foolish hope and the desperate need to spare the blood of the hapless men he loved. He took a sightless road and shortly condemned them to a grisly doom, failing to see in the Nazi promises so thick a mask of falsehood that by trusting them he condemned his beautiful youngsters to abandon their bones to dogs and birds of prey to pick, or to lie shrouded in the deep sand of the never-ceasing ocean after the fishes of the sea had stripped them. Sallow with fright, disguising a ruffled heart by means of witless negotiation and a tempest of orders transparent in their absurdity, he appointed the due time for his warriors to quit not only the lovely island but life itself.' So the sightless bard might have written, for it was certain that General Gandin lacked the clear eyes of the wily Odysseus, and neither did Athene, goddess of the limpid eyes, guide him. Rome issued contradictory orders, and from Athens Vechiarelli issued orders that were illegal. Gandin was given no place to stand, and therefore could not move the earth.

But it all happened slowly. It began with the radio. Anglo-American flights overhead were rattling the windows, and Carlo was fiddling in a desultory fashion with the dials of a machine that for so long had broadcast nothing from home but frustrating whistles and batsqueaks. In Sicily the Italian soldiers had surrendered in joyous relief, and it was an open secret that Badoglio intended to end the war. On July 19th, the United States had dropped one thousand tons of high explosives on Rome, destroying railways, airfields, factories, and government buildings, leaving hundreds dead, but sparing the antiquities and the Vatican. The Pope advised the fractious populace to be patient. On July 25th, King Victor Emmanuel had imprisoned his improbable cockerel of a prime minister and appointed the venerable Marshal Badoglio in his place, the same who had opposed all plans to invade Greece, and, despite being Chief-of-Staff, had not been informed of it even when it had already occurred. On July 26th, Badoglio had declared a state of emergency to prevent civil war. On the 27th, he had asked the suspicious Allies for terms, and outside in the streets the populace had waxed delirious with joy as they celebrated the miraculous and wondrously abrupt downfall of Benito Mussolini. On the 28th, Badoglio abolished the Fascist Party, on the 29th, he released political prisoners who had been rotting in jail without charge, some of them for more than a decade, but the war dragged on. The Germans reinforced heavily, and fought the British and the Americans with astonishing bravery whilst their Italian allies yielded. British soldiers remember that the Italian units acquired the habit of changing sides according to their perception of who was about to win, and that the local populations threw flowers over whichever side was advancing, gathering up the blossoms to use again and again in areas where battles went to and fro.

On September 3rd Badoglio signed a secret armistice with the Allies, but the Germans had seen it coming, and in one forgotten theatre of the war they had already landed troops. It was on the island of Cephallonia, the place that travellers describe as looking like a dismasted man-o'-war, and the town where they landed was Lixouri. They came on August 1st, giving themselves a month for preparation, and the Italians a month in which to watch them preparing whilst Gandin ordered no counter-preparations.

On the other side of the bay at Argostoli the Italian troops had fallen silent ever since the invasion of Sicily. La Scala did not meet any more at the doctor's house, and in the town square the music of the military band became ragged and mournful. The military police still misdirected the traffic with shrill blasts of their whistles, but there were very few German officers walking about and drinking in cafés with their longstanding Italian friends. Günter Weber stayed at his quarters, vitriolic with anger over the daily news of further Italian betrayals. He had never felt so let down, even though the troops on the island itself had done nothing disgraceful. He thought of his friend Corelli, and began to despise him. Nowadays he even despised the inmates of the Italian brothel, the sad and empty-headed girls with beautiful bodies and artificial faces who still frolicked naked in the waves as though nothing had happened. He was so angry that whereas before he had wanted to buy them, now he wanted only to rape them. He was very glad when the cavalcade of motorcycles and trucks appeared from Lixouri; the Italians needed someone to show them how to fight, how not to waver, how to face death rather than embrace dishonour.

Corelli came home to the doctor's house less often, because he did drills by day and night with his battery. Bringing up the limbers, loading, slamming the breach, aiming, firing, rangefinding, changing target, removing the limbers in the event of air attacks so that their own shells would not destroy the guns after a direct hit. His men worked hard in the apocalyptic heat of August, sweating in heavy trickles that washed erratic runnels through the grime of their faces and arms. The flesh of their shoulders bubbled and burst, leaving patches of crimson sunburn that oozed and itched for lack of skin and the opportunity to heal, but they did not complain. They knew that the captain was right to practise.

He himself stopped playing the mandolin; there was so little time for it that when he picked it up it felt foreign in his fingers by comparison with a gun. He had to play a great many scales before his fingers got up to speed, and his tremolo became ragged and sluggish. He went home to Pelagia on his motorbike at times when her father was likely to be out, and he brought her bread, honey, bottles of wine, a photograph signed on the back with the words 'After the War . . .' written on it in his elegant and foreign-looking hand, and he brought her his tired grey face, his saddened and fatalistic eyes, his air of quiet dignity and vanished joy. 'My poor carino,' she would say, her arms about his neck, 'don't worry, don't worry, don't worry,' and he would draw back a little and say, 'Koritsimou, just let me look at you.'

And then came the time when Carlo was listening to the radio, trying to find a signal. It was September 8th, and the evenings had become considerably cooler than they had been before. It was now possible to sleep a little less feverishly at night, and sometimes the breeze from the sea was more invigorating. Carlo had recently been thinking a great deal about Francesco and about the horror of Albania, and now more than ever he knew that it had all been nothing but a waste, and that his time in Cephallonia had been an interlude, a holiday from a war that was circling like a lion and was about to pounce once more. He wished that there was some law of nature that forbade the possibility of a man's voyaging through Hades more than once. He found a voice and quickly twisted back the dial to find it. '. . . all aggressive acts by Italian Armed Forces against the forces of the British and the Americans will cease at once, everywhere.

They must be prepared to repel any possible attacks from any other quarter.'

Outside the bells of the island began to ring, the Venetian campaniles reverberating with the impossible hope of peace, just as in Italy they had once rung in the exhilarating pride of war. The clamour spread; Argostoli, Lixouri, Soulari, Dorizata, Assos, Fiskardo. Across the straits of Ithaca the bells rang out in Vathi and in Frikes, and they rang far away in Zante, Levkas, and Corfu. Up on Mt Aenos, Alekos stood and listened. It could not be a feast day, so perhaps the war was over. He cupped his hand over his eyes and looked out over the valleys; it was what it must sound like in heaven when God brought all his goats to fold at night.

Carlo listened to the text of Marshal Badoglio's announcement, and then there was a message from Eisenhower himself: '. . . All Italians who now act to help eject the German aggressor from Italian soil will have the assistance and support of the Allies . . .' He ran out and found Corelli just lurching to a halt, a great cloud of blue smoke behind him. 'Antonio, Antonio, it's all over, and the Allies have promised to help us. It's over.' He threw his enormous arms about the man he loved and picked him up, dancing in a circle. 'Carlo, Carlo,' the captain reproached him, 'put me down. Don't get so excited. The Allies don't care about us. We're in Greece, remember? Merda, Carlo, you don't know your own strength. You half killed me.'

'They'll help us,' said Carlo, but Corelli shook his head. 'If we don't act now, we're fucked. We've got to disarm the Germans.'

That night the Italian warships in the harbours of the island slipped anchor and fled for home. There were minesweepers, torpedo boats, and a battleship. They did not tell anyone they were going, and they did not take with them a single Italian evacuee. Not one soldier, not one helpless military whore. They took with them their formidable firepower, and left only the damp and sulphurous stench of cowardice and burning coal. The German soldiers sneered, and Corelli's men smelled treachery. Corelli waited at the telephone for orders, and when none came he fell asleep in his chair after posting a doubled guard at his battery. He dreamed about Pelagia and about the mad priest who preached that all of them would be thrown into the fire. During his sleep the radio broadcast appeals from the Allies to fight against the Germans. The telephone rang, and someone from the general's office told the captain not to attack and to stay calm. 'Are you mad?' he shouted, but the line was already dead.

Leutnant Günter Weber also dozed intermittently in his chair, awaiting orders. He felt abysmally tired and all his confidence had gone. He missed his friends, and, worse than that, he missed the certainties that had accrued from so much past success. The Master Race was losing in Italy and Yugoslavia, the Russian front was collapsing, Hamburg destroyed. Weber no longer felt invincible and proud; he felt inferior and humiliated, so foully turned upon and betrayed that, were he a woman, he would have wept. He thought of the motto of his regiment, 'God With Us', and wondered whether it was only Italy who had betrayed him. In any case, all the sums were wrong; it was a whole Italian division against only three thousand of the 996th Grenadier Battalion, and even with God's help he didn't stand a chance. He tried to pray, but the Lutheran words turned bitter in his mouth.

In the morning, Colonel Barge, commander of the German troops, moved some armoured cars from Argostoli to Lixouri, and General Gandin tried in vain to contact both the new government in Brindisi and the old High Command in Greece. He had not slept all night, and was too well-trained to know what to do.

Pelagia and her father organised all their medical equipment and tore old sheets into strips so that they could boil them and roll them into bandages. They had a vague idea that there might be some Greeks caught in any crossfire, and in any case, they had to do something just to ease the tension. Corelli called by on his motorbike, pleading with them to let him know how to contact the partisans. But they genuinely did not know how it could be done, and he left, disconsolate, speeding away towards Sami. Perhaps the partisans might at last come out of their long and venial repose, and be of some help in holding down the Germans.

In Sami he did not even know where to start, and the local Greeks did not know him. It was a wasted journey. He stopped his motorcycle on the way back and sat on the verge by a ramshackle wall, beneath the shade of an olive. He thought about going back to Italy, about surviving, about Pelagia. The truth was that he had no home, and that was why he had never talked about it. The Duce had made his family move to Libya as part of the colonisation, and there they had died at the hands of the rebels whilst he was in hospital with dysentery. Of all the relatives' houses where he had stayed, which one was home? He had no family except his soldiers and his mandolin, and his heart was here in Greece. Had he borne so much pain, so much loneliness, had he finally found a place to be, only to have it wrested away? He tried to remember his parents, and their image was as thin and indefinite, as wavering as that of a ghost. He recalled a friendly little Arab boy with whom his parents had forbidden him to play. They used to throw stones at rows of bottles, and he always seemed to come home with sunstroke and diarrhoea. He had been prohibited from eating pomegranates in case he caught jaundice. It was poignant to remember so much and yet so little, and for the first time he began to feel nostalgic for Pelagia, as if she were already past. He remembered the doctor's tale about the Lotos eaters, wandering folk who ate Lotos once, and lost their longing for home. He was one of them. He thought about dying and wondered how long Pelagia would weep. It seemed a shame to mar her lovely flesh with tears; it was pitiful to imagine it. He wanted to reach out from beyond the grave and comfort her, even though he was not yet dead.

When eventually he returned to his battery he found his men in revolt. An order had come from Supergreccia to surrender to the Nazis in the morning.

52

DEVELOPMENTS

(1)

I AM SO full of rage that I can hardly speak. Antonio says to me, 'Carlo, calm down, we've got to be clever, because it's no use being angry, OK?' But I am tired of being the toy of lunatics, incompetents, and fools, idiots who think it's still the Great War, when everything was done in line abreast and there was still honour between enemies.

It's unbelievable. The Germans are flying in more reinforcements, the sky is full of Junkers, and Colonel Barge has gone to Gandin to demand surrender in accordance with the orders of Supergreccia, and Gandin does absolutely nothing except consult his chaplains and his senior officers. Isn't he the General? Isn't it for him to decide and to act quickly? How is he qualified to decide my fate? I who have lived through months of ice and agony in Albania, I who have held the body of a man I loved as he died in my arms in a trench of rats and freezing slime. Doesn't Gandin listen to the radio? Is he the only one who doesn't know that the Germans are looting and slaughtering in Italy? Doesn't he know that only a day or two ago they crowded one hundred into one room, and blew them up with landmines? Hasn't he heard that for one German death they have shot eighty policemen and twenty civilians in Aversa? Doesn't he know that disarmed soldiers are being transported God-knows-where in cattle trucks?

I am crazy with anger. The commanders, all except two, have agreed to surrender. We are ten thousand and they are

371

three. What madness is this? Hasn't the government ordered us to take the Germans and disarm them? What's the problem? Why does he want to obey the fascists, whose party has been abolished, and ignore the will of the Prime Minister and the King?

(2)

'Colonel Barge? I have withdrawn the 3rd Battalion of the 317th Infantry from Kardakata, in token of good will. As you know, the island is indefensible without that position, and I therefore hope that you will accept that we have no hostile intentions, and that you will not insist upon the disarming of the troops.'

'My dear General, I must insist. I have undertaken that the troops will be sent straight home to Italy, and I have no intention of going back on my word. They must be disarmed, however, or their weapons may well be turned against us when they get home. You must see that from our point of view this is only common sense. I appeal to you as an old friend.'

'Colonel, I am still awaiting clarification of orders. I hope you will understand my position. It is very difficult.'

'General, you have had your orders from Supergreccia, and whatever orders you receive from Italy itself are invalid, since that government is illegitimate. We are soldiers, General, and we must obey orders.'

'Colonel, I will let you know as soon as I can.'

Colonel Barge put down the telephone and turned to one of his majors; 'I want you to take a company of men and occupy Kardakata. The idiot Italians have just abandoned it, so there shouldn't be any problem.'

(3)

I have been to see Pelagia and the doctor. I asked them to look after my Antonia, and Pelagia wrapped it in a blanket and put it under the hole in the floor where political refugees used to hide in the time of the British. They told me

372

that Carlo had also been, and had left a thick wad of writings with them, which they were not to read unless he was dead. I wonder what he has been scribbling? I did not know that he had authorial inclinations. You don't expect it in such a big and muscular man. Pelagia looks very thin and almost ill, and we decided that we couldn't go to our little hideaway, because there might be orders for my battery at any moment. She stroked my cheek so wistfully that I almost did not know how to prevent some tears. She has tried to contact the partisans through someone that she calls Bunnios, without success.

(4)

Leutnant Weber dismantled and oiled his gun. He felt a little apprehensive without the panzers that had accompanied his odyssey across Europe. It was a relief that so many munitions had been pouring into Lixouri, but it was worrying that so far there were not many reinforcements. It was well known that the colonel had delivered a final ultimatum to General Gandin, and had asked him some embarrassing questions about his loyalties and his intentions. There were eight hours left. He thought about Corelli and wondered what he was doing, and then he removed the silver crucifix that hung about his neck, and just looked at it. General Gandin had refused complete surrender, demanded freedom of movement for his troops, and asked for written guarantees of the safety of his men. Weber smiled and shook his head. Someone was going to have to teach them a lesson.

(5)

'Gentlemen, what should I do?' asked General Gandin, and the chaplains looked from one to the other, enjoying their newfound importance, relishing this rare opportunity to become strategists consulted by a general. It was vastly more intoxicating than to hear confessions from men who did not, in the ultimate analysis, take them very seriously,

and it was a very saintly sensation, this business of expressing peaceable sentiments with immense gravitas and moral
authority.

'Lay down our arms with written guarantees,' said one,
'and then, by God's will, we will all be going home.'

'I disagree completely,' declared only one of them, 'in my
opinion it would be profoundly misguided.'

'We can disarm them,' said the general, 'but we could not
cope with the Luftwaffe afterwards. We must think about
the Stukas. We would be without air or sea support, and we
would undoubtedly be exterminated.' The general had an
obsession with Stukas. The thought of those crook-winged
howling birds of destruction made his stomach churn with
dread. Possibly he did not know that from a military point
of view they were one of the most ineffective weapons of
war ever devised; it was true that they were terrifying, but
it was shellfire that caused casualties. He had far more guns
than the Germans, and could have obliterated them within
hours.

'Ah, the Stukas,' agreed the chaplains, who also did not
know anything about it, but were adept at nodding wisely
with the air of men of the world.

(6)

'So we're going to lay down our arms and go home?' asked
one of the boys.

'Yes, my son,' said the unit's chaplain. 'Thanks be to
God.'

Carlo came running in, 'Listen, lads, the garrison on St
Maura surrendered, and the Germans took them prisoner
and shot Colonel Ottalevi.'

'Puttana,' exclaimed Corelli, drawing his pistol and slapping it down on the table. 'That's it. Let's take a vote.'

'It's probably only a rumour,' suggested the chaplain.

'We should have a vote in the whole division,' said Carlo,
ignoring the cleric. He had never had any time for the
Church and its representatives, since realising that in his
absence he had been condemned to hellfire for being born

374

as he was.

'Right, boys,' said Corelli, 'I am going to talk to every battery officer I can find, and we'll get a vote organised. Agreed?'

'What about Gandin?' asked a young lad from Naples.

The men looked from one to the other, and all had the same thought. 'If we have to,' said Corelli, 'we'll arrest him.'

(7)

In the morning General Gandin sat on his hands. He gave no orders, even though a command had come from Brindisi to take the Germans prisoner. He spent the day going through his paperwork and looking out of the window with his hands behind his back. His mind seized up, and all he could think about was what he should have done instead of being a soldier. He cast his mind back over the halcyon days of his youth, and realised that even they had not amounted to anything much. He felt like an octogenarian who looks back upon an empty life and wonders if any of it was worth the while.

Colonel Barge, on the other hand, had been struck by a most excellent brainwave. He knew that the Italians did not trust him, and he therefore set out to divide them by affecting some exemplary behaviour. At dusk he sent an Oberleutnant and a company of grenadiers to surround an Italian battery in secrecy. Captain Aldo Puglisi had no choice except to surrender peacefully as soon as he realised what had happened. His men were disarmed and sent away without the firing of a shot. On their way they passed the military brothel, but did not have the heart to enter. A wave of optimism and relief, of home-talk and peace-talk, passed through the ranks of the Acqui Division, just as the colonel had planned. It was a deception, a confidence-trick, of masterly proportions.

On the following morning an Italian sergeant shot his own captain, who had wanted to surrender, and Tiger tanks appeared out of nowhere and sat like ominous monsters at the crossroads, their hulls perspiring with the inhuman smell of oil and heated steel. Many of the Italian battery commanders ignored them as though they were anachronistic pelagic rocks that had appeared fortuitously and might just as arbitrarily disappear, but others, like Captain Antonio Corelli, traversed some of their guns away from the sea and retrained them, having grown tired of waiting for orders that never came.

(8)

For the attention of Colonel Barge; Direct Order from the Führer; Enclosed is the code word upon whose receipt by telegraph in encrypted form you will begin the assault on, and total liquidation of, all Italian anti-Fascist forces in Cephallonia. In the meantime, continue negotiations in such a way as to gain their confidence. All bodies to be disposed of thoroughly, preferably by means of barges ballasted and sunk at sea. Since there has been no formal declaration of war by Italy, all opposing Italian forces are to be treated as francs-tireurs, and not as prisoners of war.

(9)

General Gandin seemed visibly to have aged in the space of a few days: 'Gentlemen, the situation is this. I have before me Memorandum OP44, of September the 3rd. It instructs us that we are to act against the Germans only if we are attacked. I also have order no. N2 of the 6th, which states that we are to make no common cause with any forces resisting the Germans. This last order contradicts the terms of the armistice signed by Castellano, so what are we to make of it?'

'General, it means quite simply that the Allies will not trust us. The order is foolish. Are we aware of any Allied preparations to help us?'

'No, Major. They have had over forty days and have done nothing, and neither has the War Office. There is reason to suspect that they know of the Germans' intentions and have not informed us. There are apparently no plans for co-operation.'

'But General, the Germans have hundreds of planes on the mainland, and we have nothing. Why have the Allies abandoned us?'

'A good question. Furthermore, I have this order, no. 24202, which says that we must negotiate with the Germans to gain time, and that German requests for us to move should not be regarded as hostile acts. As you know, we have co-operated in this, but the result is that they now have all the most important strategic and tactical positions. Do you think that we should cease to obey this order, on our own initiative?'

'Is the order legal, General? Doesn't it contradict order no. OP44?'

'But which one takes precedence? I can't get clarification. With the relocation of the War Office from Rome to Brindisi, everything is in a state of confusion. And now we have this order from Vecchiarelli to lay down our arms. It says that General Lanz will repatriate us after fourteen days, but I cannot get confirmation of this from Brindisi. So what do we do? Vecchiarelli believes General Lanz, but do we?'

'I for one do not, General. In any case the men are one hundred per cent against it. They have had a vote, and three officers who recommended it to their men have been shot. It would be most unwise. In any case we have the order from the War Office last night, telling us to treat the Germans as enemies.'

'For that reason I telegraphed Vecchiarelli that we could not obey the order. By the way, it is my duty to inform you that I have been offered command of Mussolini's little army in his new so-called "republic". I have declined the offer, as my prime loyalty is to the King. I trust I have done the correct thing.'

'The correct thing, General, is to avoid confrontation with the Germans. They were our allies until a few days ago, and it is an intolerable dishonour to the Armed Forces to be obliged to turn against them. Many of them are our personal friends. I also think that the Allied insistence upon unconditional surrender is to them just as dishonourable as the German insistence upon the same thing. It is better to die than to submit to either of these demands.'

'I agree with you entirely, Major, and I have demanded that Colonel Barge be replaced by a full general in our negotiations. It will give us valuable time until General Lanz arrives, and if the worst comes to the worst it will save us the dishonour of ceding our arms to a mere colonel.'

(10)

'I say, chaps, the order has come through from Berlin for the show to begin in Cephallonia. Sergeant, be a stout fellow and take this through to Jumbo.'

General Jumbo Wilson read the message through, and decided not to do anything. He had plenty of men, ships, planes, and matériel at his disposal, all ready to go. But it wouldn't do to let Johnny Kraut know that he knew how to decode their messages, would it?

53

FIRST BLOOD

THE ACQUI DIVISION voted to resist the Germans but had no time to set in place an effective leadership to co-ordinate its actions. After battle had already begun, orders finally began to arrive from General Gandin, and some obeyed them and some did not. Of the exact order of events little is known, but two things are certain. One is that the Communist andartes of ELAS took no part, seeing no reason to shake themselves out of their parasitic lethargy, and the other is that the Italian resistance owed nothing to the military hierarchy. It was a spontaneous blossoming of courage and determination in the hearts of individual men who knew obscurely that the time had finally arrived for them to do something right.

Who knows what it was that truly motivated Captain Fienzo Appollonio to open fire without orders on a flotilla of German landing craft?

Perhaps he was an honourable man who could no longer bear to play an ignoble and acquiescent part in the history of a half-baked and fallen empire. Perhaps he felt a genuine sympathy for the Greeks with whom he had lived so long, and wanted now to expunge the shame he felt at their subjugation and the deprivation that he had helped to inflict. Perhaps he was ashamed of the dismal military record of the army in which he had served, and now wanted to wrest control of his little portion of it out of the hands of the complacent incompetents and sycophants who, from the safety of their bunkers, had led it to so many sanguine and pointless calamities, who, time and again, had snatched defeat from the jaws of victory. Perhaps it was merely that he saw only too clearly that there was no choice but to fight for survival.

Whatever the emotions and thoughts that circled upon themselves in the recesses of his mind, his men shared his conclusions. They had already loaded and aimed the howitzers whilst he was still watching the landing craft cutting clumsily through the swell with their cargo of vehicles and palefaced soldiers. He noted the superfluous but strangely meaningful discipline in the manner that they bore their weapons exactly alike, slung vertically upon a shoulder so that they bristled together like the spikes arranged in the bottom of a trap. The captain squinted through his binoculars and divided the intervening space of sea into units of a hundred metres. He accounted for the hidden ground between his battery and the sea, and with a confidence that he did not feel, he ordered the gun nearest to him to set the range he had determined and to fire a single shell.

With a metallic crash the gun leapt backwards, its base hopping on its bed like an excited dog jumping for a titbit. After all these years Captain Appollonio had still not adjusted to the painful ringing of metal in his ears, and he winced as he watched that tiny black dot wing at an incredible and incalculable speed, so fast that he wondered whether or not he had really seen it, high into the air. He lost it, and then seconds later saw the plume of water rise up from the sea not fifty metres from the place he had estimated that it would fall. There was a frenzy of activity on the boats that struck him as almost comical, and then he ordered an exact range and gave the command to fire at will.

The men were exhilarated. At last they had a leader, someone whose courage would mysteriously flow into the ground beneath his own feet, travel subterraneously, and spring up as if by miracle in their own hearts, filling them with the wild freedom of men who have at last discovered that they are soldiers after all. The men smiled at each other, their eyes glowing with pleasure, with a pride that they had never felt before, and they watched in wonder as spectacular spouts of water obliterated the regular and somnolent patterns of the waves. The air grew heavy with the sweet stench of cordite and the ineffably virile and infernal smell of red-hot barrels and smoking, aromatic oil. The creases in the palms of their hands filled up with grime, and their faces blackened so that their lips seemed oddly pale and pink where they had wetted them with their tongues. The sweat of their turbulent excitement drenched the hair beneath their caps, and they threw down the half-finished cigarettes that formerly had been a comfort but were now an impediment to action and to breath.

Stunned by their own success, by the incredible and unprecedented efficacy of their bombardment, the men of the battery stopped firing as the last of the landing craft disappeared beneath the waves. They clenched their fists in satisfaction as they watched two rescue launches put out from Lixouri and make their way towards the carnage and the flotsam of the dismembered and splintered boats. None of them felt like firing on a rescue operation, and they began to shake each others' hands and embrace. They would always remember this day, they told each other. It had been a rite of passage, like being confirmed or getting wed.

A seaplane flew out over the ridge towards Argostoli, laying an indiscriminate but lethal stick of bombs that blew out the roofs of one humble and innocent house after another in a perfectly straight line. Machine-guns and anti-aircraft guns opened fire as other commanders spontaneously ignored their orders and threw themselves into battle. In the streets of Argostoli Italian infantrymen, some without their officers, advanced behind the shelter of light tanks towards the Panzers, inspired by a heroism that they had never shown when fighting for the Fascists and the ludicrous dictator.

The Panzers opened fire on the battery, and their thunderous noise echoed round and round the confines of the narrow streets, shaking the walls and causing flakes of loose distemper to rain down as dust in the interiors of the houses. Appollonio's gunners retrained their barrels, and not far off the battery of Captain Antonio Corelli also opened fire. The tanks advanced, their feeble and unnecessary camouflage of brushwood falling from their flanks like the clothes of a drunken whore. Their engines roared and whined, they lurched at each change of speed, and black clouds of exhaust belched out of them as though already struck by shells.

Shells fell amongst the Panzers, raising gouts of red earth and white dust, and they all stopped dead, as though their occupants were too amazed at finding themselves opposed, as though it were inconceivable that Italians should resist. Incredibly, a German armoured car appeared on the old British bridge that ran across the shallows of the bay, and above its turret there fluttered a large white flag. The bombardiers of the batteries were triumphant, vindicated; perhaps the Germans were going to go and ask Gandin for the terms of surrender.

The troops waited and smoked in the sunset, the oil of their fingers impregnating itself acridly but somehow appropriately into the paper of their cigarettes. A large flight of Junkers flew overhead, bringing reinforcements for the Nazis, and Captain Appollonio threw his hands into the air with exasperation, 'Why don't the anti-aircraft batteries fire? What's wrong with those cretins?' He had not risked so much, only to lose everything through the vacillation of others. Vainly, but to his own satisfaction, he fired a carbine at the distant and disappearing planes, the crackling of the shots sounding oddly polite and diffident by comparison with the recent salvoes of the guns.

The field telephone rang. General Gandin, instead of opportunely demanding a surrender, had agreed to a truce. Appollonio rolled his eyes in disbelief, and yelled so loudly at the operator that it was some time before he realised that he was cursing down a closed line. 'Mad son of a bitch,' he shouted, as he slammed down the receiver, and he was consoled only a little when a runner arrived bearing a message from Captain Antonio Corelli: 'If you are court-martialled, I shall demand the honour of being tried alongside you.'

54
CARLO'S FAREWELL

Antonio, my Captain,

We find ourselves in bad times, and I have the strongest feelings that I shall not survive them. You know how it is, how a cat creeps away to die, or a man sees the ghost of his own mother beside his bed when he is sick, or even meets the ghost of himself coming the other way at a crossroads.

You find with this letter all my writings that I have done since I came to this island, and if you read them you will discover what kind of man I am. I hope you are not disgusted, and I hope that, because you have a big and generous heart, you will be able to forgive me and remember me without contempt. I hope that you will remember all the times that we have embraced as comrades and brothers, and that you will not shudder with retrospective horror because they were the caresses of a degenerate. I have always tried to show you the affection that I have felt, without taking anything from you and without giving you anything that you did not want.

When you read these pages you will see that in Albania I was desolated by the loss of my comrade Francesco, and I wish to tell you here that the wound that I received in that war was a wound that I inflicted on myself. I am not ashamed. I did what was right. When Francesco died, I

383

wanted to die too. All the beauty went out of my life and everything was meaningless, but I lacked the unnatural courage that a man needs to blow away his own brains. I came to this beautiful island with nothing but a grey fog in my mind and an aching and empty heart that was inconsolable, bursting with grief and bitterness. What is a man who has a chest full of medals but a heart beneath it too disconsolate to beat?

My dear Antonio, I want you to know that in return for your inextinguishable laughter, your great music, your incomparable spirit, I have loved you with the same surprise and gratitude that I see in your own eyes when you are with Pelagia, and I shall remember you always, even when I am dead. You removed the sorrow from my breast and made me smile, and I have accepted and rejoiced in your friendship, always conscious of my own unworthiness, always struggling against any impulse to debase it, and I trust that for this you will not despise me as some might think that I deserve.

Antonio, I have so many memories of these few short months, it makes me weep to think of them now that they are gone. So many happy memories. Do you recall how you nearly blew yourself up with that mine, and I carried you back to the doctor's house? I knew then that if you had died I would have gone mad, and I now thank God that I shall die before you, so that I shall not have to bear the grief.

Antonio, I speak to you from beyond the grave, in seriousness. I have loved you with all my shameful heart, as much as I once loved Francesco, and I have conquered any envy that I might have felt. If a dead man may have a wish, it is that you should find your future with Pelagia. She is beautiful and sweet, there is no one who deserves you more, and no one else worthy of you. I wish that you will have children together, and I wish that once or twice you will tell them about their Uncle Carlo that they never saw. As for me, I hoist my knapsack on my shoulders and buckle the webbing, I put my arm through the sling of my rifle, and I open the veil to march into the unknown as soldiers always will. Remember me.

Carlo.

55

VICTORY

DESPITE THE UNEQUIVOCAL demand of his men that the Germans should be forced to surrender and their arms confiscated, General Gandin played the saint and agreed with Colonel Barge that his Italian soldiers should be allowed to keep their arms and evacuate the island. There were no ships with which to evacuate them, however, a point which did not seem to strike him as significant. In Corfu the Germans had agreed in the most gentlemanly way to provide the troop transports themselves, and whilst the soldiers were wading out to them through the surf, had machine-gunned them all, every one of them, and left their bodies floating. The incomparably courageous Colonel Lusignani, entirely abandoned by the British, held out against impossible odds for several days. All of his men who survived to find their way onto German transports were killed when the British bombed them at sea. Those who managed to leap into the water were machine-gunned by the Germans, and their bodies left to float.

In Cephallonia the Germans had now had fourteen days' grace in which to organise themselves and to bring in reinforcements and extra weapons, whilst the bemused Italians, for want of any leadership, had acted or not according to the initiative of individual officers. Some, like Appollonio and Corelli, had prepared their men to the last degree, but others, intoxicated and blinded by the prospect of going home, had drifted vapidly away into a suicidal and optimistic lethargy that had left their men seething with irritation and dismay;

they foresaw transportation to labour camps in cattle wagons with no light, sanitation, or sustenance – did not everybody know that this had been happening to the Greeks for months? – and they foresaw massacres. Some sank into a fatalistic depression, and others set their jaws with determination, gripping the stocks of their rifles so hard that their knuckles blenched.

The Greeks, Pelagia and Dr Iannis amongst them, looked at one another with haunted eyes, their hearts churning with omens, and the pitiful whores of the military brothel forgot their cosmetics and drifted helplessly from room to room in their dressing-gowns like the underworld's grieving, senseless shades, opening the shutters, looking out, closing them again, and pressing their hands against their palpitating hearts.

When the formation of Stukas arrived early in the afternoon, tipped their wings, banked in formation, and howled vertically down upon the Italian batteries, it was almost a relief. Now everything was clear; it was at last obvious that the Germans were perfidious, that every soldier would have to fight for his life. Günter Weber knew that he would have to turn his weapons on his friends, Corelli knew that his musician's fingers, so well accustomed to the arts of peace, must now tighten about the trigger of a gun. General Gandin knew too late that in his radical indecision and his consultations with epicene priests he had condemned his men to die; Colonel Barge knew that he had successfully gulled his former allies into a disadvantageous position; the whores knew that men who had formerly stolen their happiness were now to leave them to the crows, and Pelagia knew that a war that had always really been somewhere else was now about to settle upon her home and blast its stones to dust.

The men of the batteries, demented and disorientated by the mechanical scream of the Stukas, the hail of machine-gun fire, and the sticks of bombs that fell amongst their guns and showered them with earth and exiguous shreds of the flesh of their comrades, struggled to remove their limbers and prevent the detonation of their ammunition. Then, before the battery commanders could set up any returning fire, the Stukas bobbed away like starlings and turned on a column of troops arriving in Argostoli on the far side of the sportsground, where in the past the Italian soldiers had passed their military service in raucous and emotional games of football, and where at night Italian soldiers in love with Greek girls had arranged assignations that were hardly private even in the dark.

To Corelli and to Appollonio, to Carlo and to the members of La Scala, it was obvious that the Germans were trying to paralyse Argostoli because that was where the most Italian troops were concentrated; the enemy was attempting to protect its scattered and undermanned emplacements at the outposts of the island. This was not obvious to Gandin, however, and he brought his troops into the city in increasing numbers, where it would be easier for the Germans to isolate and cut them down. He himself was reluctant to leave his splendid offices in the fine municipal building. He set up observation posts in the most amateurishly obvious places, the Venetian spires of the churches, and thereby provided the Germans with the most admirable opportunities for rangefinding and target practice. He omitted to provide these posts with radios or field telephones, and they were forced to communicate with their own gunners by means of motorcycle messengers, and runners who were easily winded after such a lazy war. Dripping with blood, their flesh burned and studded with fragments of shrapnel, bullets clanging against the bells and ricocheting about their heads in the confined spaces, the observers held their posts as long as they could, knowing that when darkness fell the Stukas must depart.

That night Alekos watched the fireworks from the top of Mt Aenos, wrapped luxuriously in his robes of parachute silk. On the hill above Argostoli he saw tracer bullets arcing gracefully towards the German positions, and he heard the crump and double-crump of falling shells, a noise very like a drummer tapping softly with a muffled stick upon the skin of an old bass drum. He saw two brilliant beams of light incandesce across the bay, and he tugged the sleeve of the man next to him, the man he had once mistaken for an angel, and who was now talking rapidly into his radio. Bunny Warren took up his binoculars and saw that an invasion flotilla of improvised barges had set out from Lixouri and been caught in the searchlights like an improvident rabbit held in the dazzling headlights of a car. 'Bravo!' he exclaimed, as the Italian batteries opened fire and sank the barges one by one, and Alekos admired the beautiful flashes of orange flame that sparkled like fireflies upon the hill above the town. 'These wops have balls after all,' said Warren, whose Greek had now improved to the point of becoming demotic. Once more he tried to impress his superiors with the paramount importance of providing the beleaguered Italians with air and sea support, and the efficient voice at the other end of the line told him, 'Dreadfully sorry, old boy, can't be done. Chin-chin. Over and out.'

Dr Iannis and his daughter sat side by side at their kitchen table, unable to sleep, holding each others' hands. Pelagia was weeping. The doctor wanted to relight his pipe, but out of respect for his daughter's despair he allowed his hands to stay in hers, and he repeated, 'Koritsimou, I am sure he is all right.'

'But we haven't seen him for days,' she wailed. 'I just know he's dead.'

'If he was dead someone would have told us, someone from La Scala. They were all nice boys, they would think to let us know.'

'Were?' she repeated. 'You think they're all dead? You think they're dead too, don't you?'

'O God,' he said, a little exasperated. There was a knock at the door, and Stamatis and Kokolios came in together. Dr Iannis looked up, and both men removed their hats. 'Hello boys,' said the doctor.

Stamatis shifted on his feet and said, as though it were a confession, 'Iatre, we have decided to go out and shoot some Germans.'

'Ah,' said the doctor, unsure as to what he was supposed to do with this information.

'We want to know,' said Kokolios, 'if we can have your blessing.'

389

'My blessing? I am not a priest.'

'Next best thing,' explained Stamatis. 'Who knows where Father Arsenios is?'

'Of course you have my blessing. God go with you.'

'Velisarios has dug up his cannon, and he's coming too.'

'He has my blessing also.'

'Thank you, Iatre,' continued Kokolios, 'and we want to know . . . if we are killed . . . will you see to our wives?'

'I will do my best, I promise. Do they know?'

The two men exchanged glances, and Stamatis confessed, 'Of course not. They would only try to stop us. I couldn't stand all that screaming and crying.'

'Me neither,' added Kokolios.

'I also wanted to thank you, for curing my ear. I will need it now, for hearing the Germans.'

'I am glad it turned out to be useful,' said the doctor. The two men hesitated a moment, as though to add something, and then left. The doctor turned to his daughter, 'Look, two old men are going out to fight for us. Have courage. As long as we have men like that, then Greece is never lost.'

Pelagia turned her tearstained face to her father and sobbed, 'Who cares about Greece? Where is Antonio?'

Antonio Corelli was walking in the dark through the ruins of Argostoli. The pretty town seemed to be nothing but sagging walls, dwellings that had been opened like dolls' houses, exposing complete floors that still had pictures on the walls and cheerful cloths upon the tables. All about him were heaps of rubble. From one of them a hand protruded, its fingers languid and relaxed. It was a very dirty hand, but it was diminutive and young. He scrabbled at the lumps of rock, stones that had enclosed and protected people picturesquely since Venetian times, and he found the crushed head of a little girl, about the same age as Lemoni. He looked at those pale lips, the lovable face, and he did not know whether to choke with rage or with tears. With a sense of tragedy in his heart such as he had never known before, he carefully arranged the child's hair so that it would fall more naturally about her cheeks. 'I am sorry, koritsimou,' he confided to the corpse, 'if we had not been

390

here, you would have lived.' He was exhausted, long past the point of fear, and his weariness had made him philosophical. Little girls as innocent and sweet as this had died for nothing in Malta, in London, in Hamburg, in Warsaw. But they were statistical little girls, children he had never seen himself. He thought of Lemoni, and then of Pelagia. The unspeakable enormity of this war suddenly broke his heart, so that he gasped and fought for breath, and at the identical moment he also knew with absolute certainty that nothing was more necessary than to win it. He touched his lips to his fingers, and then his fingers to the dead lips of the foreign child.

There was so much to be done. Refugees from villages razed and machine-gunned by the Germans were flooding into the town, and at the same time the citizens of the town were clogging the streets with handcarts as they attempted to flee to the villages. It was almost impossible to move the guns and troops, and, to make it worse, soldiers from outlying areas were pouring in on Gandin's orders, making themselves an easy target and severely exacerbating the congestion. There was nowhere to put them, the chain of command was breaking up, and there was in everyone the tacit knowledge that no ships or planes would come to help them. Cephallonia was an island of no strategic importance, its little children need not be saved, its ancient and buckled buildings need not be preserved for posterity, its blood and flesh were not precious to those conducting a war from easy and Olympian heights. For Cephallonia there was no Winston Churchill, no Eisenhower, no Badoglio, no squadrons of ships or flights of planes. From the sky there fell only the hyperbolical snowfalls of German propaganda containing false promises and lies, on the radio there came from Brindisi only messages of encouragement, and at the exquisite white bay of Kyriaki there landed two battalions of fresh Alpine troops under the command of Major Von Hirschfeld.

At dawn the next morning a marmoreal Oberleutnant and his men overran a somnolent camp consisting of a field kitchen and a company of muleteers. After they had all surrendered the Oberleutnant had them shot, and kicked their bodies into a ditch. From there he led his men up to the pine-clad ridge at Daphni, and waited until eight o'clock, when the new Alpine troops of Major Von Hirschfeld would certainly be arriving from the other side to complete the encirclement. Again the Italians were caught unprepared, and again they had to surrender. The Oberleutnant marched them to Kourouklata and then became bored with them, so he took them to the edge of a ravine and shot the entire battalion. Out of academic interest he had the bodies dynamited, and was impressed by the results. The region was famous for a blood-red wine called 'Thiniatiko'.

Unhampered by his prisoners he proceeded to Farsa, an attractive village which the Alpine troops had already reduced to rubble by means of mortars, and where the Italian soldiers were mounting a fierce and successful resistance. Attacked now on both sides, they fought and fell until there was only a very small number of them left to be herded into the piazza and shot. At Argostoli, wave after wave of black-winged bombers progressively demolished the batteries until all the guns fell silent.

It was on the morning of September 22nd that Captain Antonio Corelli of the 33rd Regiment of Artillery, knowing that the white banner was about to be raised over the HQ at Argostoli, having had no sleep for three days, mounted his motorcycle and sped towards Pelagia's house. It was then that he threw himself into her arms, rested his burning eyes upon her shoulder, and told her, 'Siamo perduti. We have run out of ammunition, and the British have betrayed us.'

She begged him to stay, to hide in the house, in the hole in the floor, along with his mandolin and Carlo's papers, but he took her face in his hands, kissed her without the tears that he was too tired and too resigned to weep, and then rocked her in his arms, squeezing her so tightly that she thought her ribs and spine would crack. He kissed her again and said, 'Koritsimou, this is the last time I shall ever see you. There has been no honour in this war, but I have to be with my boys.' He hung his head, 'Koritsimou, I am going to die. Remember me to your father. And I thank God I have lived long enough to love you.'

He drove away upon his motorcycle, the dust-cloud mantling higher than his head. She watched him go, and went inside. She gathered Psipsina into her arms and sat at the kitchen table with a cold talon of dread clutching at her heart. Men are sometimes driven by things that to a woman make no sense, but she did know that Corelli had to be with his boys. Honour and common sense; in the light of the other, both of them are ridiculous.

She nuzzled the fur behind the marten's ears, comforted by the warm sweet smell, and smiled. She was remembering that recent, distant time, when she had fooled the captain into believing that it was a special kind of Hellenic cat. She sat smiling wanly as one memory after another, connected only by the romantic, receding figure of the captain, pirou-etted spectrally through her head. She listened to the ominous silence of the morning, and realised that it was more consoling to listen to the barrages and thunderbolts of war.

56

THE GOOD NAZI (2)

'O MY FATHER, if it be possible, let this cup pass from me.' How many times had he heard his own father recite these words in the little church at home? Every Easter since his childhood days, excluding the years of the war.

Leutnant Günter Weber stood rigidly to attention before the major, and, his face set with determination, said, 'Herr Major, I must request that this mission be assigned to someone else. I cannot in all conscience carry it out.'

The major raised an incredulous eyebrow, but somehow failed to feel any anger. The truth was that in this position he would like to think that he would have done the same. 'Why ever not?' he asked. It was an unnecessary question, but one which formality required.

'Herr Major, it is against the Geneva Convention to murder prisoners of war. It is also wrong. I must request to be excused.' He remembered another sentence from the story, and added, 'Their blood will be upon our heads, and on our children.'

'They are not prisoners of war, they are traitors. They have turned against their own legitimate government, and they have turned against us, their allies by legally constituted treaty. To execute traitors is not against the Geneva Convention, as you well know. It never has been.'

'With respect,' persisted Weber, 'the Italian government may be established or repealed by the King. The King has established Badoglio in government, and Badoglio has declared war. Therefore the Acqui Division are prisoners of war, and therefore we cannot execute them.'

'For God's sake,' said the major, 'don't you think they are traitors?'

'Yes, Herr Major, but what I think and the legal position are not the same thing. I believe it is against the military code for a senior officer to command a junior one to perform an illegal act. I am not a criminal, Herr Major, and I do not wish to become one.'

The major sighed, 'War is a dirty business, Günter, you ought to know that. We all have to do terrible things. For example, I like you, and I admire your integrity. Never more than at this moment. But I must remind you that the penalty for refusing to obey an order is execution by firing squad. I don't state this as a threat, but as a fact of life. You know this as well as I do.' The major walked to the window and then turned on his heel, 'You see, these Italian traitors are all going to be shot anyway, whether you do it or not. Why add your own death to theirs? It would be a waste of a fine officer. All for nothing.'

Günter Weber swallowed hard, and his lips trembled. He found it hard to speak. At last he said, 'I request that my protest be recorded and put in my file, Herr Major.'

'Your request is granted, Günter, but you must do as you are ordered. Heil Hitler.'

Weber returned the salute and left the major's office. He leaned against the wall outside and lit a cigarette, but his hands shook so much that he immediately dropped it. Inside the office the major reasoned with himself that since the order came originally from the top, it was Colonel Barge's responsibility, or perhaps that of someone in Berlin. Ultimately, of course, it was down to the Führer. 'That's war,' he said aloud, and decided not to enter Leutnant Weber's protest in his record. There was no point in messing up his career for the sake of some laudable scruples.

'Let's sing, boys,' said Antonio Corelli as the truck they were in lurched from one rut to another. From the passionless faces of the German guards, he looked up and down the truck at his men. One of them was already gibbering and tearful, others were praying, their heads bowed down to their knees, and only Carlo was sitting bolt upright, his massive chest thrust forward as though no bullet in the world could break it. Corelli felt strangely euphoric, as though drunk on fatigue and the infallible excitement of certainty. Why not smile in the face of death? 'Let's sing, boys,' he repeated. 'Carlo, sing.'

Carlo fixed him with eyes full of infinite sorrow, and began very softly to sing an Ave Maria. It was neither Schubert's version nor Gounod's, but was something that came trickling out of his own soul, and it was beautiful because it was docile and lyrical. The men stopped praying, and listened. Some of them recognised notes from a lullaby, remembered from infancy, and others heard snatches from a love song. Carlo twice repeated, 'Pray for us sinners now and at the hour of our death,' and then stopped and wiped his eyes with his sleeve. One of the tenors of La Scala began the 'Humming Chorus' from *Madama Butterfly*, and soon others joined in or dropped out, as the catch in their throats permitted. There was something soothing and appropriate in that lulling melody; it suited the exhausted men, all of them filthy and ragged, all of them at the door of death, all of them too oppressed with misery even to look upon the beloved faces of comrades they were shortly due to lose. It was easy to hum whilst thinking of their mothers, their villages, their boyhood in the vines and fields, the embrace of their fathers, the first kiss of an adored fiancée, the wedding of a sister. It was easy to sway almost indiscernibly to that tune and contemplate this island, the scene of so many drunken nights, rowdy games, and beautiful girls. It was easier to hum than to dwell on death; it gave the heart something to do.

When the truck arrived at the pink walls of the brothel, Günter Weber's knees began to buckle. Almost before it had arrived, it seemed that he had known that fate had called him to the killing of his friends.

He had not expected them to arrive singing, humming the very tune that he and La Scala had sung together late at night at the doctor's house, when they were too far gone to remember or pronounce the words of anything else. He had not expected them to jump so lightly from the truck, he had thought they would be pushed and toppled from it by means of bayonets and rifle-butts. He had not expected Antonio Corelli to recognise him and wave. Perhaps he had thought that a man's face changes when he becomes an executioner. He designated a sergeant to herd his friends against the wall, lit another cigarette, and faced away. He watched his own soldiers milling about in silence, and decided to wait in case there was news of a reprieve. He knew it would never come, but nonetheless he waited.

Finally he turned on his heel, knowing that some tiny shred of decency must be salvaged, and he approached the Italians. More than half of them were praying, kneeling in the soil, and others wept like children at a death. Antonio Corelli and Carlo Guercio were embracing. Weber reached for his packet of cigarettes, and approached them. 'Cigarette?' he asked them, and Corelli took one, Carlo refusing. 'The doctor said it was bad for my health,' he said.

Corelli looked at his former protégé and said, 'Your hands are trembling, and your legs.'

'Antonio, I am very sorry, I tried . . .'

'I am sure you did, Günter. I know how it goes.' He took a deep lungful of smoke and added, 'You lot always did get the best tobacco. It annoyed the doctor.'

'Così fan tutte,' said Weber, giving a short and hollow laugh. He coughed, and jerkily applied his hand to his mouth.

'Don't give us a cold,' said Carlo.

Weber's face trembled with suppressed tears and desperation, and at last he said suddenly, 'Forgive me.'

Carlo sneered, 'You will never be forgiven.' But Corelli put his hand up to silence his friend, and said quietly, 'Günter, I forgive you. If I do not, who will?'

Carlo made a sound of disgust in his throat, and Weber held out his hand. 'Goodbye, Günter,' said Corelli, taking it. He let his hand linger in the palm of his former friend, shook it briefly one final time, and released it. He linked an arm through Carlo's, and smiled up at him. 'Come,' he said, 'we two have been companions in life. Let us go together to paradise.'

It was a beautiful day to die. A few soft inverted clouds idled on the summit of Mt Aenos. Nearby a goatbell clanged and a flock bleated. He realised that his own legs were shaking and that there was nothing he could do to prevent it. He thought about Pelagia, with her dark eyes, her vehement nature, her black hair. He thought of her framed in the doorway of Casa Nostra, laughing as he took her photograph. A succession of images: Pelagia combing Psipsina and talking to her in a squeaky voice apposite to animals; Pelagia chopping onions, wiping tears from her eyes and smiling; Pelagia striking him when her goat was stolen (he realised that he had never replaced it as he had promised – perhaps he should ask for a delay of execution?); Pelagia being delighted that first time he had played Pelagia's March; Pelagia kissing Günter Weber on the cheek at the offer of the gramophone; Pelagia crocheting a blanket that actually grew smaller every day; Pelagia embarrassed by the asymmetry of embroidery on the waistcoat; Pelagia screaming in his ear when the brakes failed on the motorcycle and sent them hurtling down a mountain; Pelagia arm in arm with her father, returning from the sea. Pelagia, who had been so pert and rounded, now so pale and thin.

The sergeant approached the Leutnant. He was a Croatian, one of those thuggish fanatics more national socialist than Goebbels himself, and considerably less endowed with charm. Weber had never understood how such a man could have found his way into the Grenadiers. He said, 'Herr Leutnant, more will be arriving. We can't delay.'

'Very well,' said Weber, and he closed his eyes and prayed. It was a prayer that had no words, addressed to an apathetic God.

The carnage had none of the ritual formality of such occasions that film and paintings might suggest. The victims were not lined up against the wall. They were not blindfolded, faced away, or faced forward. Many of them were left on their knees, praying, weeping or pleading. Some lay on the grass as though they had already fallen, tearing at it with their hands, burrowing in desperation. Some fought their way to the back of the pack. Some stood smoking, as casually as at a party, and Carlo stood to attention next to Corelli, glad to die at last, and resolved with all his heart to die a soldier's death. Corelli put one hand in the pocket of his breeches to steady the shaking of his leg, unbuttoned his jacket, and deeply breathed the Cephallonian air that held Pelagia's breath. He smelled eucalyptus, goat-dung, and the sea. It occurred to him suddenly that to die outside a brothel was a little picaresque.

The German boys heard the command to fire, and fired in disbelief. Those of them whose eyes were open aimed wide or high, or aimed such as not to cause a death. Their guns leapt and clattered in their hands, and their arms numbed and cramped from panic and vibration. The Croatian sergeant aimed to kill, firing in short and careful bursts, as intent as any carpenter, or a butcher carving joints.

Weber's head reeled. His former friends, wheeling and dancing in the horizontal rain, were crying out. They fell to their knees, their hands flailing, their nostrils haunted by the stench of cordite, searing cloth and oil, their mouths filling with the dry and dusty tang of blood. Some stood up again, holding out their arms like Christ, baring their chests in the hope of a quicker death, a shorter route through pain, a consummation to their loss. What no one had seen, not even Weber, was that at the order to fire Carlo had stepped smartly sideways like a soldier forming ranks. Antonio Corelli, in a haze of nostalgia and forgetfulness, had found in front of him the titanic bulk of Carlo Guercio, had found his wrists gripped painfully in those mighty fists, had found himself unable to move. He stared wonderingly into the middle of Carlo's back as ragged and appalling holes burst through from inside his body, releasing shreds of tattered flesh and crimson gouts of blood.

Carlo stood unbroken as one bullet after another bur-rowed like white-hot parasitic knives into the muscle of his chest. He felt blows like those of an axe splintering his bones and hacking at his veins. He stood perfectly still, and when his lungs filled up with blood he held his breath and counted. 'Uno, due, tre, quattro, cinque, sei, sette, otto, nove . . .' He decided in the arbitrariness of his valour to stand and count to thirty. At every even number he thought of Francesco dying in Albania, and at every odd number he tightened his grip on Corelli. He reached thirty just as he thought that he might be failing, and then he looked up at the sky, felt a bullet cave the jawbone of his face, and flung himself over backwards. Corelli lay beneath him, paralysed by his weight, drenched utterly in his blood, stupefied by an act of love so incomprehensible and ineffable, so filled with divine madness, that he did not hear the sergeant's voice.

'Italians, it's all over. If any of you are living, stand up now, and your lives will be spared.'

He did not see the two or three stand up, their hands clutched over their wounds, one of them with his groin ripped out. He did not see them stagger, but he heard the renewed clatter of the automatic as the sergeant cut them down. Then he heard the single shots as the trembling hand of Weber, who, intoxicated with horror, was wandering amongst the dead, ensured their despatch with a spurious coup de grâce. Next to his head he saw Weber's jackboot, and he saw Weber bend down and look directly into his eyes where he lay entrapped beneath that weight and bulk. He saw the wavering barrel of the Luger approach his face, he saw the unfathomable sorrow in Weber's brown eyes, and then he saw the gun withdrawn, unfired. He tried to breathe more freely, and realised that he was having diffi-culty not merely because of Carlo's weight, but because the bullets that had passed with such destruction through his friend had also struck himself.

57
FIRE

CORELLI LAY BENEATH his friend for hours, their blood intermingling in the soil, in their uniforms, and in their flesh. It was not until the evening that Velisarios came across that tangled heap of tragic remains, and recognised the man as big as himself who had once reached a hand across the barriers of hostility and offered him a cigarette. He looked down into the vacant and staring eyes, shuddered at the smashed and dislocated jaw, reached down a hand, and tried to close the lids. He failed, and was struck by the indecency of leaving such a brother to the flies and birds. He knelt down and reached his arms beneath that massive torso and those treelike legs. With a mighty effort he lifted Carlo from the ground, nearly toppled with the strain, and looked down. He saw the mad captain who was staying at the doctor's, the one whose secret and elaborately surreptitious love for Pelagia was known and discussed by everyone on the island. The eyes were not vacant, and they flickered. The lips moved; 'Aiutarmi,' they said.

Velisarios propped Carlo against the pink and bullet-pitted wall, and returned to kneel beside the captain. He looked at the hideous wounds and the dark lake of blood that was already turning black, and wondered whether it might not be a kindness just to kill him. 'Iatro,' said the dying man, 'Pelagia.' The strongman carefully picked him up, felt how light he was, and set off across the stony fields to save his life.

Nobody knows the exact number of the Italian dead that

lay upon the earth of Cephallonia. At least four thousand were massacred and possibly nine thousand. Was it 288,000 kilos of butchered human meat, or 648,000? Was it 18,752 litres of bright young blood, or 42,192? The evidence was lost in flame.

At the summit of Mt Aenos, Alekos looked down over his native land and wondered for one wild moment whether it was June 24th. Was St John's Day in September? Had somebody moved it? Enormous fires were springing up at regular intervals, at places where the fires were never held for the saint. He smelt olive wood and pine, kerosene, dry thorn, resin, oil, and charring flesh; he sniffed with disgust. The Italians never could cook meat. He smelt the vile odour of burning hair and bone, even at that enormous height, and watched with dismay as dirty smoke blacked out the stars. Perhaps it was the end of the world.

Down in the valleys the Germans competed with historical truth, destroying the evidence, displaying abundant knowledge of their guilt by converting flesh to smoke. They ran truckload after truckload of fuel. Soldiers hacked down olives a thousand years old and stacked them about heaps of lolling corpses so high that it became impossible to stack them higher. Contemptuously they pointed to individual dead, saying, 'This one pissed himself,' or 'This one stinks of shit,' but few could laugh. Abdominal slime and blood found their way onto their hands and uniforms, a sweet and sticky smell of fresh meat affected their heads like drink, and sweat poured down their temples as they slung one defunct boy after another across their shoulders, and tipped them upon the pyres. They worked until their legs weakened and the flames became too hot to approach, but there seemed to be no ending to the work. More cadavers arrived, frozen in reproach and ghoulish in that flickering light. They came in on trucks, in jeeps, slung across armoured cars and mules, once or twice on stretchers.

There was no priest but Arsenios. He had prophesied for months that these very boys would finish in the flames, and was felled by horror when it happened. Indeed, he felt responsible. On that evening when all the Greeks were hiding in their homes behind their shutters, peeping out into the night, Father Arsenios arrived with his little dog at the fire at Troianata, the largest one of all, not far from the monastery of the saint, and beheld a scene from Armageddon. As though invisible he walked amongst the pallid faces of the dead, reminded of Catholic depictions of the last day. All around him the dark and frantic silhouettes of German soldiers laboured and grunted like pigs as they hurled one corpse after another upon the flames. Not far away he heard a strangled and heart-stopping scream as a boy who was not yet entirely dead thrashed and struggled in the sharp agony of his cremation.

Father Arsenios felt the spirit move within him, and he spread his arms wide and cried out, his voice competing with the shouts of the soldiers and the hissing and crackling of the flames. Brandishing his crozier of olivewood he threw back his head: 'I have considered the days of old, the years of ancient times. I call to remembrance my song in the night: I commune with mine own heart.

'Will the Lord cast off forever? and will he be favourable no more? Is his mercy clean gone forever? doth his promise fail for evermore? Hath God forgotten to be gracious? hath he in anger shut up his tender mercies?

'Woe to thee that spoilest, when thou wast not spoiled! Woe to thee that dealest treachery, and they dealt not treachery to thee! When thou hast ceased to spoil, then shalt thou be spoiled!

'Woe unto thee, for the indignation of the Lord is upon all nations, and his fury upon their armies; he hath utterly destroyed them, he hath delivered them to the slaughter! The slain also shall be cast out, and their stink shall come out of their carcasses, and the mountains shall be melted with their blood!

'Woe unto thee, for the streams of the land shall be turned into pitch, and the dust thereof into brimstone, and the land thereof shall become burning pitch! It shall not be quenched night or day, the smoke thereof shall go up for-ever; from generation unto generation it shall lie waste, and none shall pass it through!'

Unaware that no one had heard him, fired by apocalyptic rage, Father Arsenios grasped his staff in both hands, roared, 'I shall uncover thy nakedness, yea, thy shame shall be seen. I will take vengeance, and I will not meet thee as a man. Thou hast polluted mine inheritance,' and flung himself into battle. Swinging the crozier he set about the shoulders and heads of the German soldiers. A helmet clanged, tired shoulders jolted with determined blows, hands were raised to protect heads, only to have their fingers crushed. The men who had efficiently slaughtered thousands seemed at a loss as to what to do. There were cries of, 'Shit, for God's sake get him off!' and from the bystanders who had with relief stopped to watch, comments such as, 'Look at that crazy priest!' They prodded each other and laughed, enjoying the discomfiture of the afflicted. In that orange glow Arsenios looked like some cadaverous bat, his voluminous black robes fluttering, and his prophetic beard, wildly glittering eyes, and tall and tattered hat with its flat top merely served to increase the impression of a madness percolated from another world. His small dog danced and skipped about him, barking senselessly with excitement and snapping at the calves of his chosen victims.

It ended only when one solider was on the ground and in danger of a fractured skull and broken hands. An officer of the Grenadiers drew his automatic pistol, came up behind Arsenios, and fired a single shot upwards through the nape of his neck, exploding his brains and the plates of his skull outwards through the front of his head. Arsenios died in a brilliant flash of white light that he took to be the revelation of the face of God, and his emaciated and skeletal remains were flung on the pyre, along with the young boys whose fate he had foreseen, but which he had not known that he would share.

His dog whimpered, frightened of the flames and the strange men, attempting to approach its burning master, but having repeatedly to withdraw. It expressed its incomprehension by raising first one paw and then another, and remained there until the soldiers left and the sickened Greeks arrived, to find it singed and howling.

Men and women and the few Italian soldiers who had escaped approached the fires as closely as the heat permitted. Without consulting each other they began to pull away the bodies they could reach at the periphery as the changing wind allowed. There were many of them still lying in distorted and toylike postures in places where no flames had reached. All of the toiling people thought the same things: is this what it will be like under the Germans? How many of these boys could there have been? How many of these boys did I know? Can I imagine the horror of their death? Can I conceive how it is to die of bleeding, slowly? Is it, as they say, like the kick of a horse when a bullet smashes bone?

It seemed that everyone had trembling hands and tearfilled eyes. People spoke as little as possible because it was hard to speak when choking either from the vile smoke of sizzling flesh or with such tormenting grief. In pairs and threes they carried bodies away to caves and crannies, to hastily dug but massive graves, to holes where in the past one hid one's goods and money from taxmen and the customs. Parties went out to places where there had been battle, and recovered those that the Nazis had not found. Orthodox prayers were said hastily over Catholic souls, and it was noted that none of them wore rings or carried cash. The bodies had been looted, their fingers hacked away, their gold teeth pulled, their silver chains with crucifix removed.

At dawn a black and viscous cloud hung over the land and blotted out the sun, and the people returned to their houses and locked the doors until dark. General Gandin's smoke had mingled with that of his boys in the Cephallonian sky, one of the first to die, an honourable, chivalrous old soldier of the ancient school, who trusted his enemies and had tried to save his men. He died straight-backed and unflinching, in the knowledge that his frequent changes of mind and his conscientious delays had killed them as surely as the fusillades that now splashed his blood upon the rocks. Soon the remainder of his officers would be taken away from the Mussolini barracks in Argostoli, and they too would spit and shrivel in the flames.

That night the Greeks emerged once more, pulling bodies from the seawells and sinks, noting once again that no one had a watch, a pen, a single coin. They found photographs of laughing girls, loveletters, pictures of families standing in a line and smiling. They found that many of the soldiers, acknowledging the imminence of extinction but determined to speak even from the far side of the grave, had scribbled addresses upon the backs of cards and photographs, in the poignant hope that there might be someone who would write a letter, someone to convey the news. On many letters the ink had run as though a few large drops of rain had caught the reader in the open air.

They did not know that, having quickly learned the lesson of the previous night, the Germans were now economising on physical effort by forcing the officers to carry their own dead to the trucks, and shooting them only when the work was done. They did not know that there was a Leutnant Weber who was not the only Nazi maddened and broken by his own dutiful atrocities. But again they saw the same fires, shook their heads as the same foul concoction of stenches impregnated their houses and clothes, and once more they did their best to salvage the dead amid a night that was made sepulchral by the attenuated and dancing shadows of trees and men that were cast out by the leaping orange pyres.

On the following day a rumour began, to the effect that St Gerasimos had wandered out in the darkness and then returned to his catafalque, the nuns purportedly finding him in the morning with the traces of tears upon the black leather of his shrivelled cheeks, and crimson blood upon the gilt and satin of his shoes.

58

SURGERY AND OBSEQUY

WHEN THE DOOR was suddenly kicked open just as it was getting dark, Pelagia's first thought was that it was the Germans. She knew that all the Italians were dead.

Like everybody else she had heard first the sounds of battle – the mechanical yattering of machine-guns, the snap of rifles, the short bursts of automatics, the muffled bass timpani of shells – and she had heard afterwards the unending crackling of the firing squads. Through the shutters she had seen truck after truck pass by, laden either with triumphant grenadiers or lolling corpses of Italians with the blood trickling from the corners of their mouths and their eyes fixed upon infinity. At night she had gone out with her father, whose cheeks were trembling with tears of rage and pity, and gone to look for lives to save amongst those bodies scattered and abandoned by those monstrous fires.

It had left her inarticulate, not with fear or sorrow, but with emptiness.

So life was already over. She knew that young and pretty women were transported by the Germans, since their brothels did not run on volunteers. She knew that they were full of terrorised and tortured girls from every place from Poland to Slovenia, and that the Nazis shot them at the first signs of resistance or disease. She had been sitting at her table, her mind preoccupied with memories, occasionally looking all about her and taking in for the last time the mundane details of a life; the knots on the leg of the table, the dinted pans she had scoured so thin, the inexplicable discoloration of one of the tiles of the floor, the illegal picture of Metaxas on the wall that her father had placed there even though he was an implacable Venizelist. She had her hand in the pocket of her apron, and when the Germans came she would shoot one of them, so that they would have to shoot her in return. The little derringer seemed insufficient to the task, but at least her father had an Italian pistol and fifty rounds that someone, perhaps a member of La Scala, had left outside their door to be a bleak inheritance.

So when the door flew open she was startled, but it had about it the narrative inevitability of a well-thumbed book. She stood up swiftly, her hand tightening upon the weapon, her face drained of colour, and beheld Velisarios, panting like a dog, his lower body runnelled with blood, his eyes glowing with the supernatural strength with which it was his fortune to be born. 'I ran,' he said, and advanced to the table, gently placing upon it the pathetic bundle that was as limp, relaxed, and peaceful as any other of the thousand dead that in the last nights she had seen. 'Who is it?' asked Pelagia, wondering why the strongman had concerned himself with one amongst so many.

'He's alive,' said Velisarios. 'It's the mad captain.'

She bent down swiftly, horror and hope wrestling and boxing in her heart. She did not recognise him. There was too much gore, too many tiny scraps and flakes of flesh, too many holes in the tunic of his chest that still seeped blood. His face and hair were glistening and caking. She wanted to touch him, but withdrew her hand. Where does one touch a man like this? She wanted to embrace him, but how does one embrace a man so broken?

The corpse opened its eyes, and the mouth smiled. 'Kalimera, koritsimou,' it said. She recognised the voice. 'It's the evening,' she said idiotically, for lack of any words with which to be profound.

'Kalispera, then,' he murmured, and closed his eyes.

Pelagia looked up at Velisarios, her eyes wide and desperate, and told him, 'Velisario', you have never done a greater thing. I'm going to get my father. Stay with him.'

It was the first time that a woman had ever entered the

kapheneion. It was not the place it once had been, but it was still a sacred place for males, and when she burst in and pulled open the door of the huge cupboard where all the men were listening to the BBC (the entire Venezia Division of the Italian Army had joined with Tito's partisans) the detonation of disapproval was more than palpable. A cloud of cigarette smoke billowed from the interior, and there were her father and four men, all bolt upright in that cramping space, glaring at her with a shock that amounted near to hate. Kokolios roared at her, but she pulled her father's hand and dragged him protesting from the shop.

The doctor looked at the body and knew that he had never seen anything worse. There was enough blood to fill the arteries of a horse, enough mites of flesh to feed the crows for months. For the first time in his medical career he felt defeated and useless, and his hands dropped to his sides. 'It would be kinder to kill him,' he said, and before Velisarios could say, 'I thought so too,' Pelagia was beating her father on the chest with both hands, lashing at his shins with her feet, outraged and incensed. Velisarios came forward, placed one arm about her waist, and hoisted her to the usual position occupied by his cannon, resting her upon the natural ledge of his hip, where she flailed at his thighs and howled.

And so it was that water was set to boil and the shreds of the captain's uniform were gently clipped away. Pelagia frantically tore in strips not only her own sheets but those of her father. Afterwards she fetched every bottle of spirit that her father had concealed, and for good measure his cherished stock of island wine.

Dr Iannis complained as he cleaned away the blood. 'What am I supposed to do? I am not qualified. I am not a proper surgeon. I have no gown, no cap, no gloves, none of this penicillin I've heard about. No X-ray machine, no sterile water, no serum, no plasma, no blood . . .'

'Shut up, shut up, shut up,' Pelagia was shouting, her heart now racing with both panic and determination, 'I've seen you pin a fracture with a ten-centimetre nail. Just shut up and do it.'

409

'Jesus,' said the intimidated doctor.

Because the doctor was unaware that most of the blood and flesh had belonged to the broad back of Carlo Guercio, it seemed to him that perhaps it was a miracle of the saint that Antonio Corelli was as little wounded as he was. Once he was cleansed, and a pile of bloody rags collected from the floor and set to boil, it was clear that the victim had six bullets in his chest, one in the abdomen, one through the outer flesh of his right arm, and an ugly but insignificant crease across his cheek.

But it still seemed hopeless. The doctor knew too much to be an optimist, and not enough to relieve his pessimism. There would be fragments of uniform in those holes, pockets of air punched inward by the bullets. There would be splinters of rib that he would not be able to locate, osteomyelitis setting in from the infection of a myriad of microbes that would spread their poison through the marrow to the veins, causing death by septicaemia. The doctor knew that bullets might be lodged in places where to touch them would cause a welter of bleeding, but where not to touch them would cause unconquerable infection. There might already be haemothorax, the spreading of blood in the spaces between the chest wall and the lung. Before too long there might be gas gangrene. There would be sequestra to remove whose location he could not conceivably deduce. The doctor opened one of the bottles of raki, took a deep swig, and passed it to Velisarios, who out of solidarity did the same. He remained there, spellbound by the whole proceeding.

Dr Iannis gathered his wits together and realised that it was no use jumping to conclusions. A surgeon explores first and thinks afterwards. With the taste of aniseed in his mouth and the tot of alcohol burning consolingly in his guts, he reached for a probe and inserted it gently into each wound until he felt it reach a bullet. He noted that the holes were surprisingly wide and that each one was surrounded by a yellow ring of bruising. Why were the holes so wide?

He stood up, amazed. The holes were not even deep. He realised suddenly that in reality the bullets should have passed clean through, leaving craters in the victim's back that should be spewing blood. 'Daughter,' he said, 'I swear by all the saints that this man's flesh is made of steel. I think he'll live.' He reached for his stethoscope and listened. The heart was weak but regular. 'Antonio,' he called, and Corelli opened his eyes. He attempted to smile. 'Antonio, I'm going to operate on you. I haven't got much morphia. Can you drink? It'll thin your blood, but it can't be helped.'

'Pelagia,' said Corelli. Velisarios held up the captain's head and Pelagia poured a cup of raki down his throat whilst the doctor prepared three-quarters of a gram of morphia. He would inject the same amount every half hour if it was necessary, and every half hour the captain would swallow raki, if that was also required. 'I want maximum light,' said the doctor, and Pelagia removed every lamp from every room, whilst Velisarios lit them in the kitchen. Outside it was dark, and the owls hooted amid the metallic scrapings of the crickets and all the natural sounds of that duplicitous and deceptive peace. Psipsina entered with the first of her nocturnal mice clamped in her teeth, and Pelagia shooed her out.

Into one arm the doctor injected morphia, and into the other, for good measure and for no precise reason other than intuition, he injected 10cc of sugar and saline solution that Pelagia had mixed up in a jug. She did not like to see the body of the man she loved pricked and probed, but she knew that shortly she would see it hacked and cut. But, looking at that pale and penetrated body with its blood, as helpless as a worm, she knew that it was not precisely a body that one loved. One loved the man who shone out through the eyes and used its mouth to smile and speak. She held the musician's fingers in her hand and looked at the carefully trimmed nails. At least the cuticles were pink. She did not adore the hands, but the man who made them move upon the frets. How often had she imagined them moving on her breasts? The doctor saw her reverie, and said, 'Don't just sit there. Do the wounds on his face and arm. Clean them up, cut away the shreds, disinfect them, and sew them up. Do you want to be a doctor or not? And we'll need more

411

boiling water, lots of it. And wash your hands, especially under the nails.'

She stood up and blinked, her hands at her sides, 'Are you sure he's unconscious? I don't want to hurt him.'

'I'm going to hurt him a lot more than you.' He slapped Corelli's face and shouted, 'Antonio, your mother's a whore.' There was no reaction, and the doctor said, 'He's out.'

'His mother is dead,' said Pelagia reproachfully. 'Don't drink any more raki if it makes you speak like that.'

Outside a German armoured car rumbled past, and all three stood stock still until it had gone. 'Bastards,' said Velisarios.

Pelagia discovered in that hour the exact enormity of what she had asked her father to do. Her hands trembled, and she could hardly bring herself to touch those wounds. At first she dabbed at them tentatively, horrified when looking up to see her father actually cutting wide holes around the bullet wounds. 'It's called debriment,' he told her, 'and I don't like it either, but it works, so if you don't like it, don't watch. I'm taking away all the damaged flesh. You should do the same.' Pelagia fought back the impulse to vomit, and Velisarios walked backwards and sat on the floor with his back against the door. He would watch them working, but he would spare himself the details.

The doctor started on the bullet in the abdomen, since he needed something to do that was relatively undangerous, to boost his confidence. He found it not far beneath the surface of the skin, picked it out with his forceps, and marvelled at its flattened and distorted shape. 'It's a miracle,' he said, showing it to Pelagia, who was snipping away a tattered morsel with some flatsided surgical clippers. 'How do you account for this?'

'He was behind that big man, the one as big as me,' offered Velisarios. 'The big man was holding him from behind, like this.' He stood up and put his hands behind his back to demonstrate how one could grip another's wrists. 'He was still holding the mad captain when I picked him up. I thought he was too heavy at first. I think he was trying to save this man.'

'Carlo,' said Pelagia, suddenly bursting into tears. Her father thought of comforting her, but realised that he would only smear her head with blood. Carlo was the first of the boys of La Scala who they now knew certainly to be dead. 'No man who dies like that has died for nothing,' said the doctor, choking on the words. He fought back his own need for tears, and, by way of distracting himself, removed and scrutinised a scrap of burned cloth from inside the wound before him. Pelagia wiped her eyes on the sleeve of her dress and said, 'Antonio always said that Carlo was the bravest in the Army.'

'All wasted,' commented the doctor, unwittingly contradicting his earlier sentiment. 'Velisario', is the man's body still there? We would like to bury it and not see it burned.'

'It's after the curfew, Iatre,' said the strongman, 'but I'll go if you want. On the way I might kill a German, who knows?' He departed, happy to be out of that grisly workshop where emotions were too high and the sights were enough to make one ill. He breathed the cool autumnal air for a few seconds, and then headed off once more across the fields.

The doctor finished cleaning out the wound, rinsed it with alcohol, and filled it up with sulphonamide powder. He had got it from the hypochondriac quartermaster with the corns. No doubt by now his soul had fled along with all his imaginary ills, and no doubt his cheerful folds of fat had been untimely rendered on the fire. There was a boundless cloud of sadness hanging in the air for anyone to feel it if they chose. It was better to concentrate on the captain. He cut a flap of flesh, rotated it, and covered the hole he had made. 'When you've done that,' he said to his daughter, 'embroider this together. There's parachute cord in my bag, so just unravel it into threads. There's nothing better.'

Pelagia's sense of outrageous unreality grew. There she was, stitching up her lover with an accuracy and care that she owed to an asymmetrical waistcoat and the patient instruction of an aunt, and there was her father next to her, carefully extracting splinters of rib and flattened bullets from the same man's chest, talking at the same time all about crepitus, facies hypocratica, and any number of other potential problems whose meaning was too obscure for their prospect to be appalling. She moved to the captain's face and cleaned out the bullet crease. She wondered whether to let it heal on its own or whether to sew it up. 'It depends,' said the doctor, preparing another injection of morphia, 'whether you want him with a crooked smile or not. It's a choice between that or a wide scar. Either of them may be charming, who knows?'

'A scar can be romantic,' said Pelagia.

'These scars,' said the doctor, indicating the chest with his scalpel, 'will be pretty horrible. If he lives.'

Velisarios buried Carlo Guercio's remains that night in the yard of the doctor's house. Struggling across the walls and fields, accompanied by that sticky smell of death, his hands slimy and slipping, he had felt like Atlas burdened by the world. It had not taken him long to discover that his load was too heavy to carry in his arms as he had carried the captain, and finally he staggered along with that great weight across his shoulders, as though it were a mighty sack of wheat.

In the darkness he bound up Carlo's shattered jaw with a strip of sheet, and then he hacked downwards, chopping through the olive's roots, unearthing ancient layers of stones and fires, tossing out shards of pottery and the ancient shoulder-blades of sheep. He did not know it, but he buried Carlo in the soil of Odysseus' time, as though he had belonged there from the first.

Just before dawn, when the surgery on the captain was complete at last, and father and daughter were both unutterably exhausted, they came out to say farewell to that heroic flesh.

Pelagia combed the hair and kissed the forehead, and the doctor, naturally a pagan and always moved by ancient ways, placed a silver coin over each eye and a flask of wine in the grave. Velisarios stood below and brought the body down. He straightened up, and a thought occurred to him. From his pocket he took a crushed pack of cigarettes, removed one, straightened it out, and placed it in the dead man's lips. 'I owed him one,' he said, and clambered out.

The doctor made an oration, with Pelagia beside him weeping and Velisarios kneading his hat in his hands.

'Our friend,' he said, 'who arrived as an enemy, has passed over the meadows of asphodel. We found him fuller of the knowledge of goodness than any other mortal man. We remember that his many decorations were for saving lives, not for destroying them. We remember that he died as nobly as he lived, valiant and strong. We are creatures of a day, but his spirit will not dim. He made an eager grace of life and was arrested in mid-path by blood-boltered men whose name will live in infamy down the passage of the years. These also will pass away, but unlamented and unforgiven; the meed of death is common to us all. When death comes to these men they shall become spirits drifting useless in the dark, for man's day is very short before the end, and the cruel man, whose ways are cruel, lies accursed and is a byword after death. But the spirit of Carlo Guercio shall live in the light as long as we have tongues to speak of him and tales to tell our friends.

'It is said that of all things that creep and breathe upon her, the earth breeds no feebler thing than man. It is true that Carlo was made by misfortune to roll around the world, but in him we found no feebleness. In him there was no rude arrogance, he was no nefarious ruffian to misuse another's home. In him we found combined the softness of a maiden and the massive strength of rock, the perfect figure of the perfect man. He was one who could have said, "I am a citizen, not of Athens or of Rome, but of the world." He was a man of whom we would say, "Nothing can harm a good man, either in life or after death."

'Remember these sayings that have come down to us from old:

'"Whom the gods love, die young."
'"Man is a dream of a shadow."
'"Even the gods cannot change the past."
'"Men in their generations are like the leaves of the trees.

415

The wind blows and one year's leaves are scattered to the ground; but the trees burst into bud and put on fresh ones when the springtime comes."

'I remember also that the poet tells us that surely there is a time for long-speaking and a time for sleep. Sleep long and well. You will not be curbed by age, you will not grow weak, you will not know sorrows nor infirmity. As long as we remember you, you will be remembered fair and young. Cephallonia has no greater honour than to count itself the guardian of your bones.'

Leaning upon each other, the doctor and his daughter returned inside, listening to Velisarios, the stony scrape of the shovel, the patter of falling earth. Carefully they carried Corelli to Pelagia's bed, and outside the first birds sang.

59

THE HISTORICAL CACHETTE

IT WAS ONLY a short time before the Germans had consolidated their positions and begun to take an interest in loot. Not only did the doctor have to hide his valuables, which was the common lot and nothing to be wondered at, but he found himself embarrassed by an Italian officer immobile in his daughter's bed. Pelagia made up bedding for him at the bottom of the cachette beneath the floor of the kitchen, and once more Velisarios was called in to carry him, neither the doctor nor Pelagia having the strength to move him without injury. There he was reunited with his mandolin, and Carlo's papers were temporarily removed. In the interests of Corelli's health the lid of the hiding-place was left open unless troops were in the vicinity, propped up by a piece of broomstick that could be quickly kicked away before the mat was replaced and the table realigned. Thus there was to come a time when he and Pelagia huddled helplessly in the darkness of the hole as the family's glasses and plates were stolen and the doctor was assaulted and abused.

For the first day after his operations he slept obliviously, but when he first awoke it was in the knowledge that his pain was terrible and his bowels had moved. He, however, could not move at all. He felt as if he had been beneath a stampede of oxen, or crushed by that mediaeval torture whereby weights were piled upon a door. 'I can't breathe,' he told the doctor.

'If you couldn't breathe you couldn't speak. The air passes from the lungs through the voicebox.'

'The pain is unbearable.'

'You have several broken ribs. I broke some myself to get the bullets out.' The doctor paused, 'I owe you an apology.'

'An apology?'

'I used some of your mandolin strings to link the bones. There wasn't anything else. I believe you made the treble strings out of my surgical wire, and I was obliged to take it back. When the bones have reknitted, there will have to be an operation to remove the wires.'

The captain winced.

'If the pain is very bad, Antonio, you should remember that, if you are a man, it is not pain that you should feel, but grief. All your friends are dead.'

'I know. I was there.'

'I am sorry.' The doctor hesitated, 'It appears that Carlo saved you.'

'It doesn't "appear". I know he did. Of all of us, he died the best, and he's left me to remember it.'

'You shouldn't weep, Captain. We are going to get you well, and then get you off the island.'

'I stink, Dottore. Don't let Pelagia see it.'

'I'll do the nursing if you wish. The space down here is very cramped, isn't it? But we'll manage. There have been many great libertarians down this hole, so consider it an honour to lie amid such history. I have to tell you that, however much it hurts, you must change position as often as possible or you'll get pressure sores. They can kill you if they rot, as surely as a bullet. Sleep as much as you can, but you must move. If the pain is unbearable I can give you morphia, but there's very little left, and with these Germans here I'm bound to need it all. If it's all right with you, I'd prefer you to be drunk. Also I have some valerian and feverfew that Pelagia gathered in the spring. I must ask you to bear the pain as best you can. I can assure you that a lot of pain during an illness will leave you feeling doubly well when you recover. It will increase your sense of gratitude.'

'Dottore, nothing could increase my gratitude.'

'You could still die,' said the doctor bluntly. He leaned down and asked in a confidential manner, 'I have been meaning to ask you if your haemorrhoids got better. Forgive me for not enquiring sooner. I thought it indiscreet.'

'I followed your advice,' said the captain, 'and it worked.'

'You will get little exercise and a poor diet in here,' said the doctor, 'although we'll do our best. You will undoubtedly get constipated, and I may be obliged to wash your bowels out. I don't want to use the tube of my stethoscope, but I might have to. If we don't do this, your haemorrhoids will return from all the straining later. I apologise for the indignity.'

The captain put his hand on the doctor's sleeve, 'Don't let Pelagia see.'

'Of course not. And another thing. You will grow a beard like a Greek. Start to think like a Greek. I will begin to teach you Greek, and so will Pelagia. I don't know where to get some papers and a ration card; we might have to do without.'

'When I am better you must move me from the house, Dottore. I don't want you in danger. If I am caught, I should die alone.'

'We can move you to your secret house where you used to go with Pelagia. Don't look so surprised. Everybody knew. There's no old woman who gossips like a goatherd. It's the loneliness. It makes them garrulous. And you may not get better, remember that. If I didn't clean you out enough, if there is a fistula somewhere letting through some liquid, if there is air . . . you must let me know at once if you get any sensation of pressure. I will have to make a hole in you and let it out.'

'Madonna Maria, Dottore, please tell me some lies.'

'I am not Pinocchio. The truth will make us free. We overcome by looking it in the eyes.'

The captain relapsed into a fever two days later, and Pelagia stayed in the cachette with him, sponging his brow to reduce his temperature, and listening to the gabble of his nightmares. She changed his dressings and sniffed him for the toxic smell of pus. Her father reassured her that toxins made a man's skin take on the yellow shade of cream, but privately he doubted for the captain's life. He had no confidence that he had done the operations well, but he continued

419

at intervals to inject him intravenously with saline sugar solution. He showed his daughter how to use cushions to vary his position and relieve the monotony of pressure that corrupts the flesh, but he made her leave the room for all those tasks which would normally fall to the lot of a woman, and which show the greatest love.

The fever came to a crisis on its fourth day, and Corelli was babbling and perspiring so much that both the doctor and Pelagia began to despair for his life. Carefully Dr Iannis inserted a thick veterinary needle into each of his wounds in case there was an abscess with poison to draw off (he called it 'subcutaneous crepitation'), but he found nothing and was left mystified as to the causes of the ill. Pelagia placed the neck of Antonia, his beloved mandolin, into the fingers of his left hand. They closed about it, the captain smiled, and her father noted privately that she had demonstrated thereby a true doctor's touch.

Two days later the fever left, and the patient opened his eyes with wonder, as though perceiving the fact of his existence for the first time. He felt weaker than it ought to be possible to feel, but he drank goatmilk laced with brandy and found that at last he could sit up a little on his own. By the same evening he was able to stand with the doctor's help and let himself be washed. His legs were thin as sticks, and trembling, but the doctor made him walk upon the spot until he was exhausted and overcome by nausea. His ribs hurt more than ever, and he was informed that they would probably be a torment for months, at every inhalation. He should use his stomach muscles to breathe, he was informed, and when he tried it, it hurt the wound in his abdomen. Pelagia fetched a mirror and showed him the livid scar across his face and his incipient and Hellenic beard. It itched and bothered him almost as much as his scars, and it gave him a brigand's air. 'I look like a Sicilian,' he said.

That night he was fed his first solid meal. Snails.

reminded of those tattered roses that manage to survive the autumn and cling to their residual beauty until December, as if sustained by a certain dispensation of a fate that was nostalgic for the past but intent upon destruction at the last. Now that there was no shamefaced Italian officer to steal them rations, and no fat quartermaster to inveigle, the doctor was reduced to trapping lizards and snakes, but was as yet disinclined to experiment with cats and rats. Things were not as bad as in Holland, where cats were served as 'roof rabbit', nor nearly as severe as on the mainland. There was always the sea, the source of Cephallonia's being, but also the source of all its turbid past and the strategic significance which was now a curious memory, the same sea that in future times would cause new invasions of Italians and Germans who would lie roasting on the sands together and leaving films of moisturising oil upon the water, tourists puzzled by the empty and surmising gaze of elderly Greeks in black who passed without acknowledgement or a word.

As soon as Corelli could walk, he went in the company of the doctor and Velisarios to Casa Nostra at the dead of night, whilst Pelagia remained at home, hiding in the cachette to which had been restored the mandolin, the doctor's History, and Carlo's papers. As long as the rapists were on the island she barely left the house, and in that hole beneath the floor she revolved her memories, crocheted and unpicked her blanket, and thought about Antonio. He had given her his ring, too big for any of her fingers, and she turned it in the lamplight, looking at the demi-falcon rising, with an olive branch in its mouth, and underneath the words 'Semper fidelis'. She feared in her heart that back home he would dismiss her, that the words would apply to her only, that she would be left forever, faithful and forgotten, waiting like Penelope for a man who never came.

But Antonio said otherwise. He came frequently, after dark, complaining that their hideaway was cold and draughty, and relating hair-raising stories of evasion and near capture, only some of which were true. His new beard scratched her cheeks as they lay face to face and fully clothed upon her bed, wrapped in each other's embrace and talking of the future and the past.

'I will always hate the Germans,' she said.

'Günter saved my life.'

'He slaughtered all your friends.'

'He had no choice. It wouldn't surprise me if he shot himself afterwards. He was trying not to cry.'

'There is always a choice. Whatever the body gets up to, it's the mind's fault. That's what we say.'

'He wasn't brave like Carlo. Carlo would have refused to shoot us, but Günter was a different kind of man.'

'Would you have refused?'

'I hope so, but I can't say. Perhaps I would have taken the easy way. I am only a man, but Carlo was like one of those heroes in our old stories, like Horatius Cocles, or whoever it was who held the bridge of Porsenna against a whole army. Only one in a million is made like that, you mustn't blame poor Günter.'

'Still, I'll always hate the Germans.'

'A lot of the Germans aren't Germans.'

'What? Don't be silly.'

'You can't tell by the uniforms, you know. They recruited in Poland, the Ukraine, Latvia, Lithuania, Czechoslovakia, Croatia, Slovenia, Romania. You name it. You don't know it, but on the mainland they've got Greeks they call "Security Battalions".'

'It's not true.'

'It is. I am sorry, but it is. Every nation has its share of shits. All those thugs and nonentities who want to feel superior. Exactly the same thing happened in Italy, they all joined the Fascists to see what they could get. All sons of clerks and peasants who wanted to be something. All ambition and no ideals. Don't you see the appeal of an army? If you want a girl, rape her. If you want a watch, take it. If you're in a sour mood, kill someone. You feel better, you feel strong. It feels good to belong to the chosen people, you can do what you want, and you can justify anything by saying it's a law of nature or the will of God.'

'We have a proverb: "Give courage to a peasant and he'll jump in your bed."'

'I like that other one you told me.'

'"Bean by bean the sack fills"? What's that got to do with it?'

'No, no, no. "If you sleep with babies you'll be pissed on." I've been pissed on, koritsimou, and I wish I'd never joined the Army. It seemed like a good idea at the time, but look what's happened.'

'Antonia's lost her strings and you're all wired up. Do you miss the boys? I do.'

'Koritsimou, I loved those boys, they were my children. How is Lemoni? When we have a daughter we'll call her Lemoni. After the war.'

'If we have two sons, the second one must be Carlo. His name should live, we should be reminded every day.'

'Every minute.'

'Carino, do you believe in God and heaven, and all of that?'

'No. Not after this, it doesn't make any sense. If you were God, would you allow all this?'

'I asked because I want Carlo and the boys to be in paradise. I can't help it, so perhaps I do believe.'

'Tell God when you see him that I want to punch him in the nose.'

'Kiss me, it's nearly dawn.'

'I must go. Tomorrow I'll bring you a rabbit. I've found a burrow, and if I lie above it I can grab one as it comes out. And I'll find us some more snails.'

'Psipsina catches rabbits, but she won't let us have them. She growls and runs away.'

'If it was spring I could look for eggs.'

'Hug me.'

'Santa Maria, my ribs.'

'I'm sorry, I'm sorry, I keep forgetting.'

'I wish I could. Merda. Nonetheless, I love you.'

'Forever?'

'In Sicily they say that eternal love lasts for two years. Fortunately, I am not Sicilian.'

'Greek men love themselves and their mothers forever. Their wives they love for six months. Fortunately I am a woman.'

'Fortunately.'

'You will come back? After the war?'

'I will leave Antonia as a hostage. That way you will know you can trust me.'

'You could get another.'

'She is irreplaceable.'

'Aren't I irreplaceable?'

'Why don't you trust me? Why do you look at me like that? Don't cry. How could I pass by the opportunity to have such a good father-in-law?'

'Bastard.'

'Ow. My ribs.'

'O, carino, I am so sorry.'

'I've got to go. Tomorrow night. Kiss me. I love you.'

Out into the night he would go, creeping from hedge to wall, jumping at the slightest sound, and dawn would find him dreaming beneath his blankets, the clouds of calcium beneath his flesh forming gradually into bone, the memory of tenderness populating his reverie with images of Pelagia and his operatic boys. In the early afternoon he would wake and search for berries, perform exercises to keep his fingers nimble, and scrabble in the undergrowth for snails. Not only did the doctor make him eat the things, but he had to grind the shells in a mortar and pestle, and the whole family would drink the gritty pieces down in wine, for it was Dr Iannis' intention that no one should be without a splendid skeleton, however thin and tired; it was no worse than the ancient stores of desiccated beans that kept the belly full but gave a man the gripes.

Pelagia was torn. She wanted to keep her captain on the island, but knew that she would kill him if she did. There were people who for bread would brook any betrayal, and it could only be a matter of time before the Nazis became aware of his furtive presence in their lives. Furthermore the weather was turning foul, the roof of Casa Nostra leaked, and the captain had no warmth against the slashing wind or the vindictive cold. There was less and less to eat for her father and herself, and sometimes she found herself looking

425

longingly at spiders on the walls. She told Kokolios and Stamatis to look out for the madman who used to go round with Arsenios, and to tell him to call on her if he could.

For some time now Bunny Warren had been following the British policy, implemented by means of gold sovereigns, of encouraging the owners of boats to deny their use to the Germans, and there were not a few surviving Italian soldiers who had found themselves bound at night for Siracusa, Bianco, or Valletta, in vessels which seemed to be made of matchsticks but in which their owners expressed the most incorrigible and optimistic faith. From trough to crest they bounced their nomadic way past E-boats and searchlights, battleships and mines, their sailors singing lustily and their passengers wide-eyed, frozen, and tormented by nausea, eventually to arrive upon dry land and discover that its stillness made them sick.

Therefore it was all in a day's work for Warren to arrange the captain's departure. He called at Pelagia's house at three in the morning, tapping softly on the window outside her own room, and when she had disentangled herself from Corelli's embrace, she opened the shutters and saw the man whose help she had both sought and dreaded. 'What ho,' he said, as he came in through the door, adding, 'Kalimera, Kyria Pelagia.' Very formally he shook her hand and made a comment about the weather.

Bunny Warren's Greek was now colourful and colloquial, but he still spoke with a perfectly upper-class English accent, managing to turn the Greek for 'Let's go' into 'In taxi', which suited his English ears, made sense to him, and was also comprehensible to Greeks. Since his normal range of adjectives and adverbs was untranslatable, he still punctuated his speech with English words such as 'spiffing' and 'simply ripping' and 'absolutely ghastly', whose effect was disorientating and redundant rather than nonsensical.

'Who is this?' asked Corelli, who for a moment had been fearing a visit from the Germans.

'Bunnio',' said Pelagia, without answering his question, 'this is an Italian soldier, and we have to get him out.'

Warren smiled and extended his hand. 'Ave,' he said, not

426

having had as much opportunity to modernise his Italian as he had his Greek. Corelli felt that his hand had been almost crushed, and he was left with an exaggerated impression of the general strength of the British. He did not know that in England an attempt to break another's fingers signifies both virility and bonhomie. He was also stupefied by the man's lankiness and height, and disturbingly reminded of a German by the blue and very nordic eyes.

It turned out that a caïque was leaving for Sicily the following night, weather permitting, and that it would be perfectly easy to put the captain on board, 'Though we might have to kill one or two of those rotten bounders.' It was simply a case of going to the bay at one o'clock in the morning with a shielded lamp, and flashing it out to sea in answer to the signals from the boat. Warren promised to be there, assuring them that everything would go swimmingly and end up top-hole and ticketyboo.

61

EVERY PARTING IS A FORETASTE
OF DEATH

CORELLI DID NOT go back to Casa Nostra before dawn, but stayed with Pelagia in the house by the doctor's consent. If it was at such short notice to be their last day together, then it seemed only humane to tolerate the risk, and in any case Corelli looked exactly like a Greek in his peasant clothes and his splendid beard that yet exposed the livid cicatrice across his cheek. Moreover he now spoke Greek well enough to fool a German who would know no Greek at all, and he even slapped the back of his hand to indicate someone's stupidity, as well as tossing his head back and clicking his tongue to signify a negative. From time to time he dreamed in Greek, a terrible frustration for his sleeping soul because this necessarily slowed the pace of his dreams' narrative, and he discovered that when speaking it his personality was different from when he spoke in Italian. He felt a fiercer man, and, for some extraordinary reason which had nothing to do with his beard, much hairier.

The three of them sat in that familiar kitchen, saddened and apprehensive, talking quietly and shaking their heads over all the memories.

'There are so many things I will never forget,' said Corelli, 'like pissing on the herbs. It was when I was invited to piss on them that I knew I had been accepted.'

'I wish my father would forget it,' commented Pelagia, 'it makes me anxious when I use them. I waste hours in washing them.'

'I feel guilty about leaving alive, when all my friends are

428

dead, and Carlo is buried out there in the yard.'

'In the Odyssey, Achilles says, "Put me on earth again and I would rather be a serf in the house of a landless man than king of all these dead men who have done with life," and he was right,' offered the doctor. 'When loved ones die, you have to live on their behalf. See things as though with their eyes. Remember how they used to say things, and use those words oneself. Be thankful that you can do things that they cannot, and also feel the sadness of it. This is how I live without Pelagia's mother. I have no interest in flowers, but for her I will look at a rock-rose or a lily. For her I eat aubergines, because she loved them. For your boys you should make music and enjoy yourself, doing it for them. And anyway,' he added, 'you may not survive the voyage to Sicily.'

'Papas,' protested Pelagia, 'don't say that.'

'He's right,' said Corelli philosophically. 'And one can also see things for the living. After so much time with you two, I shall see things and imagine what you would have said. I shall miss you very badly.'

'You'll be back,' affirmed the doctor. 'You've become an islander, like us.'

'In Italy I shall have no home.'

'You must get X-rayed. God knows what I left behind inside you, and you must get the mandolin strings removed.'

'I owe my life to you, Iatre.'

'I am sorry about the scars. It was the best I could do.'

'And I am sorry, Iatre, for the rape of the island. I do not suppose we will ever be forgiven.'

'We forgave the British and the Venetians. Perhaps we won't forgive the Germans. I don't know. And in any case, barbarians have always been convenient; we have usually had someone else to blame for our catastrophes. It will be easy to forgive you, because all of you are dead.'

'Papakis,' protested Pelagia again, 'don't talk like that. Do we need to be reminded, with Carlo buried in the yard?'

'It's the truth. Only the living need forgiveness, and, as you know, Captain, I must have forgiven you, or I would not have given you permission to wed my daughter.'

Pelagia and Corelli looked at one another, and the latter said, 'I never asked you specifically for permission . . . it seemed, somehow, an effrontery. And . . .'

'Nonetheless, you have it. Nothing would please me more. But there is one condition. You must allow Pelagia to become a doctor. She is not only my daughter. She is, since I have no son, the nearest to a son that I have fathered. She must have a son's prerogatives, because she will continue my life when I am gone. I have not brought her up to be a domestic slave, for the simple reason that such company would have been tedious in the absence of a son. I confess it was selfish of me; she is now too clever to be a humble wife.'

'Am I then an honorary man?' demanded Pelagia.

'Koritsimou, you are yourself alone, but nonetheless, you are as I made you. You should be grateful. In any other house you would be scrubbing the floor whilst I talked with Antonio.'

'In any other house I would be nagging you. You should be grateful.'

'Koritsimou, I am.'

'Naturally, Pelagia shall be a doctor if she wishes. A musician would never manage on his own income alone,' said Corelli, only to be tapped smartly about the back of his head by his betrothed, who exclaimed, 'You are supposed to become rich. If not, I will not marry you.'

'I was joking, I was joking.' He turned to the doctor. 'We have decided that if we have a son, we will name him Iannis.'

The doctor was visibly touched, even though this was exactly what he would have expected under the circumstances. There was a prolonged and sorrowful silence whilst all three of them pondered the imminent destruction of their mutual society, and at last Dr Iannis looked up, his eyes watering, and said simply, 'Antonio, if I have ever had a son, it was you. You have a place at this table.'

In lieu of the obvious reply, which by virtue of its obviousness would necessarily have rung hollow, Corelli stood up and approached the older man, who rose from his seat.

They embraced, clapping each other on the back, and then the doctor, by dint of having some emotion left to express, also embraced his daughter.

'When the war is over, I shall return,' said Corelli. 'Until then I am still in the Army, and it is necessary to get rid of the Germans.'

'They are losing,' said the doctor confidently. 'It will not be long.'

'Don't go back to fight!' cried Pelagia. 'Haven't you done enough? Haven't you had enough of death? And what about me? Don't you think of me at all?'

'Of course he thinks of you. He thinks of getting rid of them so that you can leave the house without being afraid.'

'Carlo would have done it. I can do no less.'

'You men are all so stupid!' she exclaimed. 'You should give the world to women, and see how much fighting there is then.'

'Many of the andartes on the mainland are women,' said Corelli, 'and many of the partisans in Yugoslavia. There would be fighting just the same, and the world has had its share of bloodthirsty queens. It is important to defeat the Nazis, and nothing could be more obvious.'

She looked up at him reproachfully and replied softly, 'It was important to defeat the Fascists, but you fought for them.'

Corelli flushed, and the doctor intervened, 'Don't let us spoil our last day together. A man makes mistakes, he gets caught up in things, he is sometimes a sheep, and then he learns by experience and becomes a lion.'

'I don't want you to fight,' she insisted, gazing steadily at Corelli. 'You are a musician. In ancient times when there was slaughtering between tribes, the bards were spared.'

The captain aimed for a compromise. 'Perhaps it won't be necessary, and perhaps they won't let me. I am sure I will not be considered fit.'

'Do something useful,' said Pelagia. 'Join the fire brigade or something.'

'When I get home,' said Corelli, after an embarrassing pause, 'I shall have a pot of basil on my sill to remind me of

Greece. Perhaps it will bring good luck.' He paced about the room, reminding himself of everything it held; not only the familiar objects, but its history of emotions. It was a place that still echoed with hopes, with shared confidences and jokes, past antagonisms and resentment, and the saving of a life. There hung about it a residual aroma of music and embraces that mingled with the scent of herbs and soap. Corelli stood, stroking the long flat back of Psipsina where she reclined along a shelf that was bare of food, and felt an unspeakable sadness well up in him that competed with the dry mouth and fluttering stomach of a man who was about to escape to sea. The doctor saw him standing, as lonely as a man awaiting execution, and then looked at Pelagia, sitting with her hands in her lap and her head bowed. 'I'll leave you two children together,' he said. 'There is a little girl dying of tuberculosis, and I should visit. It's in the spine and there's nothing to be done, but all the same . . .'

He left the house, and the two lovers sat opposite each other, lost for words, caressing each other's fingers. Finally the tears began to follow each other silently down her cheeks, and Corelli knelt beside her, put his arms about her, and laid his head against her chest. He was shocked all over again at how thin she was, and closed his eyes tightly, imagining that it was another world. 'I am so afraid,' she said. 'I think you won't come back, and the war goes on and on forever, and there's no safety and no hope, and I'll be left with nothing.'

'We have deep memories,' replied Corelli. 'Whether they make us glad or sad is up to us. I shall not forget you, and I will come back.'

'Promise?'

'I promise. I have given you my ring, and I have left you with Antonia.'

'We never read Carlo's papers.'

'Too painful. We'll read them when I return, when it's not so . . . so recent.'

She stroked his hair in silence, and said finally, 'Antonio, I wish that we had . . . lain together. As a man and woman.'

'Everything at the right time, koritsimou.'

432

'There may not be a time.'

'There will be. There will come a time. You have my word.'

'Psipsina will miss you. And Lemoni.'

'Lemoni thinks I am dead, no doubt.'

'After you've gone I'll tell her that Barba C'relli is alive. She will be very happy.'

'You must get Velisarios to throw her into the air for me from time to time.'

And so the conversation continued, circling back upon itself and reaffirming itself, until the doctor returned at curfew, as distressed as always when he had been obliged helplessly to watch a child groping its last blind steps along the path to death. He had walked home thinking the same thoughts that such occasions always provoked: 'Is it any wonder that I lost my faith? What are you doing up there, you idle God? Do you think I am so easily fobbed off with one or two miracles at the feast of the saint? Do you think I'm stupid? Do you think I have no eyes?' In his pocket he turned over the gold sovereign that the child's father had given him in payment. The British had dispensed so many of them in the funding of the andartes that they had lost their value. 'Even gold,' he reflected, 'is worth less than bread.'

That evening they shared a single scrawny leg of an old rooster that Kokolios had killed so that the rapists could not appropriate it, and Pelagia saved the bone for inclusion in a soup that also contained the bones of a hedgehog. If she cooked them long enough, they would be soft enough to chew. Afterwards she made a weak and bitter tea from the hips that she had gathered from the wild roses in the autumn, pleased to have something to do to divert her from her fears, and the three of them sat in the semi-darkness, waiting as the hours passed both too slowly and too fast.

At eleven o'clock Lieutenant Bunny Warren scratched at the window, and the doctor let him in. He entered with an air of decisive self-possession that struck Pelagia as quite unlike his usual diffident self, and there was a large and obviously well-honed knife stuck through his belt. She had heard that the British Special Forces had a positively Balkan aptitude for the silent slicing of throats, and she shuddered. It was hard to imagine Bunnios doing such a thing, and the idea that he probably did it quite frequently was discomfiting.

He sat on the edge of the table and spoke in his usual mixture of colloquial Romaic and British jargon, and it was only at this point that Corelli began to wonder how it was that Pelagia and the doctor could possibly have made the acquaintance of a British Liaison Officer. In war, so much is bizarre that one sometimes forgets to be surprised or to ask a pertinent question.

'Standard SOPs,' began Warren. 'Dark clothing only. Don't want the blighters to see us. No conversation unless absolutely necessary. Stop and listen every twenty seconds. Feet to be placed on the ground flat, ergo less crunch. Feet to descend vertically, ergo no sliding and scraping. I shall go point, doctor and Kyria Pelagia second, Corelli last. Corelli must turn and look behind at every pause.' He handed the captain a piece of wire, at each end of which was a short stick of dowel. It took some seconds for him to appreciate that this was a garrotte, and that he might be expected to use it. 'No shooting unless commanded,' continued Warren. 'In the event of one unexpected jerry, I shall top the cad myself. In the event of two, Corelli and I shall take one each. In the event of three or more, we lie still, and at my signal we jolly well retrace and circle round.' He looked from one face to another and asked, 'Clear as water or clear as mud?'

The doctor translated these instructions for Corelli's benefit, and it was generally agreed that it was all as clear as water. Warren spoke again, 'I've done a recce tonight, and jerry's lying low. Doesn't like the cold. Warm clothing essential. Understood?'

Pelagia stood up and went into her room, returning with her blankets and something else. 'Antonio,' she said, 'take this. I want you to have it.' He unwrapped the soft paper, and saw that it was the embroidered waistcoat that, so many months before, he had offered to buy. He held it up, and the gold thread glistened darkly in the half light. 'O, koritsimou,' he said, feeling the sumptuous velvet beneath his thumb and, with his forefinger, the slippery satin of the lining. He stood up, removed his jerkin, and put the waist-coat on. He buttoned it, shook his shoulders to settle it comfortably, and exclaimed, 'It fits exactly.'

'You will wear it to dance at our wedding,' she said, 'but for now it will help to warm you on the boat.'

Beyond the village of Spartia, on Cape Liaka, there is a very steep cliff that falls to the sea, and which in those days was accessible only by a long goatpath that snaked its stony way through the maquis. It sole human use was as a track for those fishermen who in the summer spread finely meshed nets for the catching of the shoals of whitebait that gathered unsuspectingly in the lee of the great rocks that jutted above the water, and its beach consisted of a strip of sand barely two metres wide in the places which were not occupied by battered stone. As rocky and perilous as it appeared, the sea bed itself consisted almost entirely of fine sand, and it was ideal for the landing of even quite large boats, since it shelved quite sharply to a good draught, and above it the cliffs projected forward, making it difficult to observe from the summit. There were German observation posts at regular intervals from Cape Aghia Pelagia to Lourdas Bay, but they were undermanned and apathetic, especially on cold December nights, and, like the Italians before them, the Germans knew very well that the real war was happening elsewhere. In the absence of officers, the sentinels would play cards and smoke cigarettes in their little wooden huts, occasionally going out to stamp their feet or urinate, looking all the while for the pole star that beckoned the direction home.

The journey to the beach did not therefore consist of the stuff of great adventures. A cold wind soughed through the thorns, and no moon was shining. A light rain threatened its onset by means of an occasional speckle of droplets, and the darkness was so entire that at times Pelagia feared she would lose contact with her father in front of her. The effect of the cold on her wasted frame rendered her doubly miserable at every one of Warren's silent stops, and the fact that her father was carrying a pistol in his hand seemed somehow more frightening and disturbing than her own tight grip on her derringer. She fought against both the void that seemed to be opening in her heart, and the same heart's fearful thumping and racing. Behind her, Antonio Corelli, although called to strength by the need to protect the fiancée in front of him, felt much the same emotions. He found himself demanding why he was involved in all of this, rebelling against it and rejecting it, but acknowledging its necessity. He was oppressed by an enfeebling sense of futility and melancholy, and almost wished that they would meet a German patrol, so that he could die, fighting and killing, ending it all in lightning and fire, but ending it now. He knew that to leave the island would be to become deracinated.

The four of them huddled together on that tiny strip of sand, out of the cold grip of the wind, waiting for the flash of a lamp that would come to them from the sea. Warren lit his own, and shielded its glow inside his cape whilst the others took turns to warm their hands beside it. Corelli walked to the waterline and saw the black waves heaving, wondering how he would ever survive it. He remembered other beaches, seeing the boys of La Scala singing and drinking together as the naked whores splashed in the shallows of a sea so calm and clear that it should have been a lake in Arcadia. In his mind's eye he saw the incredible turquoise of Kiriaki Bay seen from above in the summer on the journey back from Assos, and the beauty of the memory increased his sense of loss. He remembered what the doctor had told him about xenitia, the terrible nostalgic love of one's native land that hurts the exiled Greek, and felt it turning in his own breast like the twist of a bayonet. He had his own village now, his own patrida, and even his thought and speech had changed. He threw a black stone into the sea to charm some luck, and returned to Pelagia. In the darkness he held her face in his hands, and then embraced her. Her hair still smelled of rosemary, and he breathed the scent so deeply that it hurt his mending ribs. The aroma had been quickened by the cold fresh air, and he knew that rosemary would never smell so poignant and complete again. From now on it would smell of vanished light, and dust.

When the light flashed three times from the sea, and Warren returned the signal, Corelli shook the lieutenant's hand, kissed his father-in-law on both cheeks, and returned to Pelagia. There was nothing to be said. He knew that her mouth was working with grief, and he himself felt the constriction of the same passion in his throat. He stroked her cheek tenderly and kissed her at the eyes, as though to mitigate her tears. He heard the hollow sound of oars striking the gunwales of a skiff, the creak of wood on leather, and looked up to see the silhouette of the craft approaching, the shadows of two men labouring together. The four approached the water, and the doctor said, 'Go well, Antonio, and return.'

In Romaic the captain said, 'From your lips to the ear of God,' and for the last time he held Pelagia.

After he had plunged through the surf and clambered aboard, vanishing into the darkness like a ghost, Pelagia ran into the waves until the sea reached her thighs. She strained to see him for the last time, and saw nothing. As though by a raptor's claw, she was seized and clutched by emptiness. She put her hands to her face and wept, her shoulders heaving, her sobs of agony carried off in the wind and lost in the hiss of the sea.

62

OF THE GERMAN OCCUPATION

OF THE GERMAN occupation there is little to say, except
that it caused the islanders to love more nearly the Italians
they had lost. It seldom happens that a people can bring
themselves to learn affection for their oppressors, but hardly
since Roman times had there been any other kind of rule.
Now there were no more Italians working amid the vines
beside the farmers in order to escape the boredom of garrison life, there were no more football matches between sides
that squabbled and cheated and mobbed the referee, there
was no flirtation with girls by bombardiers whose caps were
askew, whose chins were unshaven, and who always had a
demi-cigarette smouldering at the corners of their mouths.
There were no more tenor voices to send snatches of
Neapolitan song and sentimental aria out across the pine of
the mountains. There were no more inefficient military
police to cause traffic jams at the centre of Argostoli by waving their arms and shrilling their whistles at everyone at
once, there was no unpunctual aquaplane to buzz a lazy and
half-hearted reconnaissance about the island, there were no
more flagrant military whores with painted lips and parasols
bathing naked in the sea and being driven about by a
bemused old Greek with a cart. There is no record of what
happened to the girls; possibly they were deported for slave
labour to some nameless camp of Eastern Europe, and possibly they were abused and killed, finding a grave amongst
the men they had loved for duty, or mingling their ashes with
theirs in the biblical pyres that had filled the sky with black

smoke, burned giant circles deep into the turf, and tarred the nostrils with the stench of kerosene and charring bone. Adriana, La Triestina, Madama Nina, all had disappeared.

The few remains of the Italian soldiers were gathered together after the war. A few bodies were dug intact from the Italian cemetery, they were carried back to Italy on a black-hulled ship of war, and efforts were made to identify them. It was not possible, and it is said that families were given bones and cinders that could have been those of any man at all. Therefore there were some mothers who made lamentation over the dead children of other mothers, but most were left with sons who now were melding with the soil of Cephallonia or who had scattered to the Ionian air as ash, cut off in the full exuberance of youth and lost forever to a world that had ignored their plight in life and disregarded them in death.

Gone were the charming chicken-thieves, the waggish individualists and songsters, and in their place an interregnum came that the doctor recorded in his History as the direst time of all.

The islanders remember that the Germans were not human beings. They were automata without principles, machines finely tuned in the art of pillage and brutality, without any passion except the love of strength, and without belief except in their natural right to grind an inferior race beneath the heel.

To be sure the Italians had been thieves, but their sorties at night, their strategies to avoid being caught, their shame when apprehended, had disclosed that they knew that what they did was wrong. The Germans came into any house at any time of day, kicked over the furniture, beat the occupants, however old or young, however ill, and in front of their eyes carried away whatever took their fancy. Ornaments, rings handed down in one family for generations, oil-lamps, benzene stoves, sailors' souvenirs of the East, all disappeared. It was amusing and appropriate to humiliate the negroids whose culture was so paltry. Casually they let the people starve, and made the sign of thumbs up when Greek coffins passed over the stones to tombs.

Both Pelagia and her father were beaten at different times for no apparent cause. Psipsina, for the crime of being tame, was torn from Pelagia's arms and frivolously clubbed to death with the butt of a rifle. Drosoula had cigarette stubs burned into the skin of her breasts for scowling at an officer. The doctor had all his precious medical equipment, gathered together through twenty conscientious years of poverty, smashed in his presence by four soldiers who wore the death's-head upon their belts and whose hearts were as dark and dank and empty as the Drogarati caves. In the year of the German occupation, the Holy Snakes did not appear at the church of Our Lady at Marcopoulo, and neither did the Sacred Lily flower at Demoutsandata.

When in November 1944 the invincible representatives of the master-race of the eternal Reich were ordered to withdraw, they destroyed every building for which they found the time, and the inhabitants of Cephallonia rose spontaneously against them and fought them all the way to the sea.

But the night before he left, Günter Weber, who had ashamedly stayed away from the house since the time of the massacres, brought his gramophone and his collection of Marlene Dietrich recordings, and left them outside Pelagia's door, as he had promised in more fortunate days. He left an envelope underneath the lid, and when she opened it Pelagia found a photograph depicting Antonio Corelli and the Leutnant on the beach, their arms about each others' shoulders. Corelli wore an elaborate woman's bonnet complete with artificial fruit and tattered paper roses; he was waving a bottle of wine at the camera, and Günter was wearing an Italian fore-and-aft cap sideways on his head. Their eyes were half-closed, and obviously both of them were drunk. In the distance Pelagia barely discerned the figure of a naked woman paddling at the sea's edge, wearing the peaked officer's cap of a German grenadier. Her arms were outspread in a gesture of delight, and an arc of spray had been caught by the light as she had kicked it upward with her foot. Obscurely, Pelagia felt neither surprise nor jealousy at the presence of this arresting figure; it seemed right that she should be there, appropriate to the intimations of Eden that

Corelli used to conjure from the air.

She turned the photograph over, and found four lines from Faust whose meaning she would not discover until she showed it to a diffident German tourist some thirty-five years later. It said:

'Mein Ruh ist hin,
Mein Herz ist schwer;
Ich finde sie nimmer
Und nimmermehr.'

Underneath Weber had written in Italian, 'God be with you, I will remember you always.'

The record-player was hidden in the hole in the floor, along with Antonio's mandolin and Carlo's confessional papers, and it survived the fratricide.

History repeats itself, first as tragedy, and then again as tragedy. The Germans had killed perhaps four thousand Italian boys, including one hundred medical orderlies with Red Cross armbands, burning their bodies or sinking them at sea in ballasted barges. But another four thousand had survived, and, exactly as in Corfu, the British bombed the ships that were taking them away to labour camps. Most drowned in the hulls, but those who managed to leap into the sea were machine-gunned by the Germans, and once again their bodies left to float.

63

LIBERATION

THE GERMANS LEFT and the celebrations began, but no sooner had the bells pealed out than the andartes of ELAS, now calling themselves the EAM, emerged from their state of hibernation and imposed themselves on the people with the aid of British arms, mistakenly supplied in the belief that they were to be used to defeat the Nazis. Acting, it was said, on Tito's orders, they formed Workers' Councils and Committees, and proceeded to elect themselves unanimously to every post of authority, and to extort a tax of a quarter on everything they could think of. In Zante, villages with Royalist sympathies armed themselves and fortified their houses, and in Cephallonia the Communists began to deport awkward characters to concentration camps; from a safe distance they had watched the Nazis for years, and were well-versed in all the arts of atrocity and oppression. Hitler would have been proud of such assiduous pupils. Their secret police (OPLA) identified all Venizelists and Royalists, and marked them down for Fascists.

On the mainland they seized Red Cross provisions, poisoned the wells of hostile villages with dead donkeys and the corpses of dissidents, demanded a quarter of the food landed at Piraeus for the relief of Athens, circulated a newspaper ironically entitled *Alithea* (*The Truth*), which was full of lies about their own heroism and the cowardice of everyone else, disposed randomly of anyone inconvenient on the grounds that they had been 'collaborators', hired prostitutes to lure British soldiers into their line of fire, disguised

442

themselves as British soldiers, Red Cross workers, as police or members of the Mountain Brigade, and used children carrying the white flag to work deceptions that were to lead to ambush. They fired shells at shoppers and at British soldiers ladling food out to the starving, took 20,000 innocents as hostages, shot 114 socialist but non-Communist trades union leaders, and destroyed factories, docks and railways that the Germans had left intact. Into mass graves they threw the cadavers of Greeks who had been castrated, had their mouths slashed into a 'smile', and had their eyes torn out. They created 100,000 refugees, and, worst of all, the Communists kidnapped 30,000 little children and shipped them across the border into Yugoslavia for indoctrination. ELAS soldiers captured by the British pleaded not to be exchanged for prisoners, so terrified were they of their leaders, and ordinary Greeks begged the British officers to help them. A dentist in Athens offered free false teeth to servicemen.

In all this there was both an irony and a tragedy. The irony was that if the Communists had continued their wartime policy of doing absolutely nothing, they would undoubtedly have become the first freely elected Communist government in the world. Whereas in France the Communists had earned themselves a rightful and respected place in political life, the Greek Communists made themselves permanently unelectable because even Communists could not bring themselves to vote for them. The tragedy was that this was yet another step along the fated path by which Communism was growing into the Greatest and Most Humane Ideology Never to Have Been Implemented Even When it Was in Power, or perhaps The Most Noble Cause Ever to Attract the Highest Proportion of Hooligans and Opportunists.

Of all the millions of lives irreparably blighted by those hooligans, those of Pelagia and the doctor were but two. The doctor was dragged away in the night by three armed men who had decided that since he was a republican he must therefore be a Fascist, and that since he was a doctor he must therefore be a bourgeois. They threw Pelagia into a corner and beat her unconscious with a chair. When

Kokolios emerged from his house to defend the doctor, he too was carried away, even though he was a Communist. By his actions he had betrayed the impurity of his faith, and he was supported on the arm of the monarchist Stamatis as all three were herded to the docks for transportation.

Pelagia did not know what had happened to her father or where he had been taken, and none of the authorities would tell her. Alone in the house, penniless and helpless, stricken by a second dose of inconsolable despair, she thought for the first time in her life of ending everything by suicide. She saw no future except the succession of one type of Fascism by another, on an island seemingly accursed and destined forever to be a part of someone else's game, a game whose cynical players changed but whose counters were fashioned out of bone and blood, the flesh of all the innocent and weak. When would Antonio return? The war was dragging on in Europe, and probably he was dead. It was a life where her beauty would be gnawed by poverty, her health by hunger. She wandered from room to room, her footsteps echoing in that empty, haunted house, her heart aching for herself and for mankind. The Nazis had slaughtered 60,000 Greek Jews, or so it said on the radio, and now her own people killed their brothers as if the Nazis had only been a police force whose departure had been eagerly awaited by the fratricides. She heard that the Communists had been killing off the Italian soldiers who had come to fight along-side them against the Germans. She remembered the happy boys of La Scala, she remembered saying that she would always hate the Nazis. Had the time come, finally, to always hate the Greeks? Of the nations who had broken into her house to beat her and steal her possessions, only the Italians were innocent, it seemed. She thought of how the British were too slow to come, and wondered what had happened to Lieutenant Bunny Warren. She would not have been sur-prised if she had known that shortly after the liberation he had been invited to a party by the Communists, and shot. This was the man who had told her, 'I would do anything for the Greeks. I have come to love them.' And if she hated the Greeks, to which people did she now belong? She was without father, without possessions, without food, without love, without hope, without country.

Fortunately she had a friend. Drosoula had long known that Pelagia had lost her love for Mandras, that there would be no wedding, and that in his long absence and by his long silence her son had forfeited his rights. She also knew that Pelagia was waiting for an Italian, and yet she felt no bitterness and never uttered a single word of blame. When Pelagia had limped bleeding through her door and flown into her arms after the abduction of her father, Drosoula, who had also suffered much, stroked her hair and uttered words such as a mother might for her daughter. Within a week she had closed up the doors and shutters of her little house on the quay, and moved into the doctor's house on the hill. She found his Italian pistol and its ammunition in a drawer, and kept it at her side for when the Fascist pigs returned.

Like Pelagia, Drosoula had been diminished by the war. Her great ugly moon of a face had shrunk inwards, giving her an air of ethereal soulfulness despite her thick lips and massive brows. Her cheerful rolls of fat had fallen from her thighs and hips, and the massive promontory of her maternal bosom had lapsed downwards into the space left vacant by the erstwhile exuberance of her stomach. Arthritis had begun to afflict one knee and both joints of the thigh, and she walked now with a slow dragging and jerking motion that was painful and mechanical to behold. Her new and unwonted slenderness lent dignity to her great height, however, and her grey hairs inspired respect and left her more formidable. Her spirit was unbroken, and she gave Pelagia strength.

For comfort they slept together in the doctor's bed, and by day they concocted schemes to find supplies of food and listened to each others' plaints and tales. They dug for roots in the maquis, sprouted ancient beans in dishes, lethally disturbed the hibernation of hedgehogs, and Drosoula took her young friend down to the rocks to learn to fish and turn the stones for crabs, returning with seaweed to serve in place of vegetables and salt.

But it was at an hour that Drosoula was out that Mandras returned, full of his purported glory and his new ideas, expectant of the dutiful and admiring attention of the fiancée that he had not seen for years, and intent upon exacting his revenge.

He came in through the door without knocking, dropped his knapsack from his shoulders, and propped his Lee-Enfield against the wall. Pelagia had been sitting upon her bed putting the finishing touches to the blanket that she had crocheted for her wedding, and which, miraculously, had burgeoned flawlessly from the day of Antonio's departure. It had been a way of creating their life together in his absence, and every stitch and knot had been tied in with all the labyrinthine yearning of her solitary heart. When she heard the noise in the kitchen she called out, 'Drosoula?'

A man came in that she did not recognise, except that he looked very like Drosoula had done before the war. There was the same distended belly and thighs, the same round, coarse face, the identical heavy eyebrows and thickened lips. Three years of living in idleness upon the bounty of the British and the booty stolen from peasants had turned the handsome fisherman into nothing if not a toad. In perplexity, Pelagia stood up.

Mandras also was perplexed. There was something about this frightened skinny girl that reminded him of Pelagia.

But this breastless woman had silver threads in her thin black hair, her lank skirts hung straight to the ground for lack of rounded hips, her lips were chapped and parched, her cheeks hollow. He looked quickly about the room to see whether Pelagia was there, assuming that this must be a cousin or an aunt. 'Mandras, is it you?' said the woman, and he recognised the voice.

He stood, astounded, much of his hatred knocked out of him, confused and appalled. She in her turn looked at those gross and transfigured features, and felt a pang of horror. 'I thought you must be dead,' she said at length.

He closed the door and leaned against it, 'You mean you were hoping I was dead. As you see, I am not. I am very alive and very well. Don't I get a kiss from my betrothed?'

She advanced timidly and reluctantly, and placed a kiss on his right cheek. 'I am glad you are alive,' she said.

He caught both her wrists and held them tightly, 'I don't think you are. How is your father, by the way? Is he not here?'

'Let me go,' she said softly, and he did so. She returned to the bed and told him, 'The Communists took him away.'

'Well, he must have done something to deserve it.'

'He did nothing. He healed the sick. And they beat me with a chair, and they took everything.'

'There would be reasons. The party is never wrong. Whoever is not with us is against us.'

She noticed that he was in the uniform of an Italian captain, and that he wore the red star of ELAS clumsily sewn into the front of his cap. He was a shabby caricature of the man who had replaced him. 'You're one of them,' she said.

He leaned ever more casually against the door, placing all his weight against it, increasing her sense of imprisonment and her fear. 'Not just one of them,' he said complacently, 'an important one of them.' He taunted her, 'Soon I shall be a commissar, and we will have a nice big house to live in. When shall we get married?'

She trembled and shuddered. He saw it, and it increased his rage. 'We will not be married,' she said. She looked up at him as placatingly as she could, 'We were very young and naïve, it was not what we thought it was.'

'Not what we thought? And there was I, fighting for Greece, thinking of you all day and dreaming of you all night. And when I thought of Greece, I gave her your face, and I fought harder. And now I come back at last and find a faded slut who has forgotten me. And did I say "married"? I forgot myself. I forgot that marriage is a sham.' He quoted the *Communist Manifesto*: 'Bourgeois marriage is in reality a system of wives in common.'

'What's the matter with you?' she asked.

'The matter with me?' He took from his jacket a thick bundle of tattered papers. 'This is what is the matter with me.' He tossed them towards her feet, and she picked them up slowly, her stomach churning with misgivings. She held

447

the bundle in her hands, and realised that it consisted of her letters to him at the Albanian front. 'My letters?' she said, turning them over in her hands.

'Your letters. As you know, I cannot read, so I have come back to hear you read them again. A reasonable request I think. I would like you to start with the last one, and we will work backwards from there perhaps. Go on, read.'

'O Mandras, please. Why is this necessary? It's all in the past.'

'Read,' he said, raising his hand to strike her. She cringed away, protecting her face with her hands, and then fumbled with the tripwire that bound the letters together. She found the last one, but could not read it. She pretended to be looking for it, and chose one from near the beginning. In a faltering voice she began, '"Agapeton, Still no word from you, and strangely enough I am beginning to get stoical about it. Panayis came back from the front with his hand missing, and he told me that it is too cold at the front for it to be possible to hold a pen at all . . ."'

Mandras interrupted her, 'Do you think I am stupid, slut? I said, read the last one.'

Horrified, she scrabbled through the sheets to find the last one, and realised that he was putting her through a torment identical to that which she had suffered so many months before. She looked at the stark message on her last letter, and her terror made her weak. '"Agapeton,"' she began, her voice cracking, '"I miss you so much . . ."'

Mandras roared with disgust and snatched it out of her hands. He held the paper up to the light and read, '"You never write to me, and at first I was sad and worried. Now I realise that you cannot care, and this has caused me to lose my affection also. I want you to know that I have decided to release you from your promises. I am sorry."' He smiled sardonically, a mirthless grin both sinister and menacing. 'Have you ever heard of Workers' Self-Education? Yes, I can read. And this is what I found in the letters I had been carrying next to my heart. It's strange, but when you read this letter to me once, I seem to recall that it said something different. I have been wondering how a letter might rewrite

448

itself. It almost makes me believe in angels. Peculiar isn't it? I wonder what the explanation could possibly be.'

'I didn't want to hurt you. I am sorry. But now at least you know the truth.'

'The truth,' he shouted, 'the truth? The truth is that you are a whore. And do you know what else? Do you know the first thing I hear when I arrive? I hear, "Hey Mandras, did you hear about your old fiancée? She's going to marry an Italian." So you've found a Fascist for yourself have you? Is this what I've been fighting for? Traitor slut.'

Pelagia stood up, her lips quivering, and said, 'Mandras, let me out.'

'Let me out,' he repeated satirically, 'let me out. Poor little thing's frightened is she?' He strode up to her and struck her across the face so brutally that she wheeled about before she fell. He kicked her in the region of the kidneys, and bent down to pick her up by the wrists. He flung her on the bed, and, quite against his original intentions, began to tear at her clothes.

This violation of women was something that he could not help, it seemed. It was some irresistible reflex that welled up from deep inside his breast, a reflex acquired in three years of omnipotence and unaccountability that had begun with the armed appropriation of property and ended with the appropriation of everything. It was a natural right, a matter of course, and its violence and animality was infinitely more exhilarating than the feeble stings of lust with which it ended. Sometimes one had to kill at the end of it to draw back a tiny remnant, a vestige of the prior joy. And then there was a weariness, an emptiness that whipped one on to repetition after repetition.

Pelagia fought. Her nails broke in his flesh, she flailed at him with hands and knees and elbows, she shrieked and writhed. To Mandras her resistance was both unreasonable and unwarranted, he was getting nowhere despite his weight and strength, and he sat back and slapped her repeatedly about the face, attempting to subdue her. Her head was flung from side to side at every blow, and suddenly he tried to wrench up her skirts. At the same moment her

449

apron was also flung back, and the solid weight of her der-ringer fell from its pocket and landed beside her head on the pillow. Mandras, his eyes glazed with ferocity and rage, his breath laboured, did not see it, and when the bullet cracked through his collar-bone the shock stunned him. He put a foot to the ground and staggered backwards, clutching at his wound, his gaze both astonished and accusing.

Drosoula heard the snap of the pistol-shot just as she came in through the kitchen door, and at first she did not recognise it. But then she knew it for what it was, and took the Italian pistol from beneath the pieces of stale bread for which she had fought with so many others of the hungry behind the windows of the Communist Party offices. With-out thinking, knowing that thought would make of her a coward, she pushed open the door of Pelagia's room and beheld the unthinkable.

She had thought that Pelagia might have shot herself, that there might be thieves, but when she burst in she saw the doctor's daughter leaning up on her elbows, the tiny pistol smoking in her right hand, her face pulped and bloody, her lips split, her clothes ripped, her eyes already swollen and blackening. Drosoula followed Pelagia's gaze and the finger that was now pointing, and she saw, leaning against the wall behind the door, a man who might have been her son. She ran to Pelagia's side and took her into her arms, rock-ing her and shushing her, and heard words emerge from underneath the whimpering and the terror, 'He . . . tried . . . to . . . rape me.'

Drosoula stood up, and mother and son examined each other in disbelief. So much had changed. As the fury mounted in the woman's breast, so the fire in Mandras' soul quelled and died. A wave of self-pity overthrew him, and all he wanted to do was weep. Everything had come to nothing, everything was lost. The torment of the war in the ice of Albania, the years in the forest, the deluded self-confidence of his mastery of writing and his lexicographical knowledge of the technical terms of the revolution, his new power and importance, it was all a vapour and a dream. He was a little cowering boy again, trembling before the fury of

450

his mother. And his shoulder hurt so much. He wanted to show it to her, to achieve her sympathy and attention, he wanted her to touch it and restore it.

But she pointed the pistol at him, its barrel wavering with her rage, and she spat the one word that seemed to mean the most, 'Fascist.'

His voice was pathetic and imploring, 'Mother . . .'

'How dare you call me "mother"? I am no mother, and you are not my son.' She paused and wiped the saliva from her mouth with her sleeve. 'I have a daughter . . .' she indicated Pelagia, who was now curled up with her eyes closed, panting as though she had given birth, '. . . and this is what you do. I disown you. I do not know you, you will not come back, never in my life do I want to see you, I have forgotten you, my curse goes with you. May you never know peace, may your heart burst in your chest, may you die alone.' She spat on the ground and shook her head with contempt, 'Nazi rapist, get out before I kill you.'

Mandras left his rifle leaning against the wall of the kitchen, and left his knapsack. With bright scarlet blood trickling through the fingers of his right hand where still he comforted his wound, he stumbled out into the bleak December sun, and drew breath. He looked through swimming eyes at the olive tree where once he had swung and laughed, and where, he seemed to remember, there had been a goat. It was a tree that was incomplete without Pelagia as she was, fresh and beautiful, chopping onions beneath it and smiling through the tears. It was a solitary tree that signified an absence and a loss. A wave of grief and nostalgia overwhelmed him, and his throat constricted with sorrow as he lurched his way along the stones.

It did not occur to him that he was a statistic, one more life warped and ruined by a war, a tarnished hero destined for the void. He was aware of nothing but a vanishment of paradise, an optimism that had turned to dust and ash, a joy that had once shone brighter than the summer sun, but now had disappeared and melted in the black light and frigid heat of massacre and cumulative remorse. He had struggled for a better world, and wrecked it.

There was a place, once, where all had sparkled with delight and innocence. He stood still a moment, recalling where it was. He swayed on his feet, nearly fell backwards, and the peasants in their houses looked out and wondered. They did not know him, although he seemed familiar, and they thought it better not to interfere. There had been enough soldiers, enough blood. They stared at him through their shutters, and watched him lumber past.

Mandras went down to the sea. He stood on the water-line, watching the bubbles of foam glitter and burst on his boots. Italian boots, he remembered, a man who had not died well. He kicked them off and watched them arc into the waves. With his one hand that worked he unbuttoned his breeches, let them fall, and stepped out of them. Carefully he removed his jacket and let it slip from his wounded shoulder. In wonder he watched the circle of blood soaking an ever wider circumference in his shirt around that tiny ragged hole. He unfastened his shirt's buttons and let that fall too.

He stood naked before the sea, even in that bitter cold, and looked up at the sky for gulls. They would guide him to the fish. He realised that he wanted nothing so much as to feel the sea upon his flesh, the draw of sand across his skin, the tightening and contraction of his groin upon the cold caress of salt and silky water. He felt the wind whipping, and his wound hurt less. He needed to be washed.

He remembered days in his boat with nothing to do but fish and squint against the light, he remembered his triumph when something fine was landed for Pelagia, his pleasure at her pleasure when she was given it, the kisses stolen in the evenings when the crickets sawed and the sun fell suddenly in the western skies of Lixouri. He remembered that in those days he was slim and beautiful, his muscles standing proud and keen, and he recalled that there had been three wild and exuberant creatures who had loved and trusted him. Creatures who in their grace and simplicity were unruffled about dowries and inconstancy, unconcerned about changing the world, creatures with love but without complications. 'Kosmas! Nionios! Krystal!' he cried, and

452

waded out into the sea.

The fisherman who recovered the bloated body reported that when he had found it, there had been three dolphins taking it in turns to nudge it towards the shore. But there had been stories like that from ancient times, and in truth no one knew any more whether it was merely a romantic figure or a fact of life.

64

ANTONIA

THERE HAD BEEN so many rapes and so many orphans made, that Pelagia and Drosoula were not surprised to find an abandoned bundle on their doorstep. It had been born at such a time that its father could have been a Nazi or a Communist, and its mother might have been any unfortunate girl at all. Whoever this sorrowing and dishonoured girl had been, she had cared enough about her child to leave it upon the doorstep of a doctor's house, knowing that those inside would have an inkling what to do. Such was the intractable chaos of the times that the two women could think of nothing else to do other than to try to care for it themselves, thinking that in time it could be adopted by someone childless or handed to the Red Cross.

They had taken the child inside and unwrapped it, discovering that it was a girl in the process, and also had seen straight away that she was a child whose nature was made for a better world to come. She was calm and serene, sought no pretexts for that demented howling with which some babies torment their parents, she sucked the thumb of her right hand, a habit she was never to lose even in old age, and she smiled liberally, her legs and arms pumping with delight in a motion that Pelagia called 'twittering'. She could be induced to emit a long gurgle of pleasure merely by pressing one's finger upon the tip of her nose, producing a sound so much like a slow tremolo on a bass string that Pelagia decided to name her after Captain Corelli's mandolin.

The two women, whose souls had been so continuously

tempered in the crucibles of bereavement and unhappiness, found in Antonia a new and poignant focus for their lives. There was no penury too grievous to endure that she did not make sufferable, no tragic memory that she could not efface, and she took her place in that providential matriarchy as though designed for it by fate. In all her life she never asked a question about her father, as though it had fallen to her naturally to arrive by parthenogenesis, and it was not until she was applying for a passport to take her abroad on her honeymoon that she discovered the extreme weightlessness of finding that officially she did not exist.

She did have a grandfather, however. When Dr Iannis returned after two years, shuffling into the kitchen supported upon the arms of two workers of the Red Cross, utterly broken by the continual dread of daily brutality, forever speechless and emotionally paralysed, he bent down and kissed the child upon her head before retiring to his room. Just as Antonia did not speculate about a father, so Dr Iannis did not speculate about the child. It was enough for him to understand that the world had forked along a path that was inapprehensible, alien, and opaque. It had become a mirror that reflected dimly the grotesque, the demonic, and the hegemony of death. He accepted that his daughter and Drosoula would sleep in his bed and that he would take Pelagia's, because, whichever bed it was, he would dream the same dreams of a forced march of hundreds of kilometres without his stolen boots, without sustenance or water. He would hear the cries of villagers as their houses burned, the screams of live castration and extracted eyes, and the crackle of shots as stragglers were executed, and he would witness over and over again Stamatis and Kokolios, the monarchist and the Communist, the very image of Greece itself, dying in each others' arms and imploring him to leave them in the road lest he himself be shot. His mind echoed perpetually with the ELAS hymn, a panegyric to unity and heroism and love, and the sour irony of being addressed as comrade when his back was beaten and a barrel pressed upon the nape of his neck in the false executions that struck his guards as humorous.

In his wordlessness, thinking in images instead of words, because words were too feeble and too far off the mark, Dr Iannis drew the same comfort from Antonia as he had drawn from his daughter after his own young wife had died. He would dandle the child upon his knee, arranging her black hair, tickling her ears, gazing intently into her brown eyes as if this alone was any way to speak, her every smile filling his heart with sorrow because when she was old she would lose her innocence and know that tragedy wastes the muscles of the face until a smile becomes impossible.

Dr Iannis took up medicine again, helping his daughter in a reversal of their prior roles. It alarmed her to see the shaking of his hands as silently he dealt with wounds and sores, and she knew also that he worked only in the face of his own overwhelming sense of futility. Why preserve life when all of us must die, when there is no such thing as immortality and health is an ephemeral accident of youth? She wondered sometimes at the invincible power of his humanitarian impulse, an impulse as inconceivably courageous, hopeless and quixotic as the task of Sisyphus, an impulse as noble and incomprehensible as that which inspires a martyr to cry out blessings as he burns. In the evenings she wrapped her arms about him and held him as his mind revolved upon his past, his eyes wet with sadness, and she buried her head in his chest, understanding that it was his despair that lightened hers.

She attempted to interest him in working on his History, and when she took the papers from the cachette and arranged them in front of him at his table, he seemed willing enough to work. He read through them, but at the end of a week Pelagia found that he had added only one short paragraph in a calligraphy that had transformed itself from the old firm hand into a spidery chaos of wavering spikes and attenuated loops. She read it and remembered something that her father had once said to Antonio. Diagonally across the bottom of the last page, her father had written, 'In the past we had the barbarians. Now we have only ourselves to blame.'

While she had been in the cachette, Pelagia had rediscovered Mandras' rifle, Antonio's mandolin, and Carlo's papers. The latter she read through in a single evening, beginning with the heartrending and prophetic letter of farewell, and continuing through the story of Albania and the death of Francesco. She had never once imagined that that virile and genial Titan had suffered so immensely from a secret woe that had transformed him permanently into a stranger to himself, drying up the source and springs of happiness. But at last she understood the true source of all his fortitude and sacrifice, and she understood that nothing is less obvious in a man than that which seems unquestionable. She saw that he had been as much intent on losing his life as he had been to save Corelli's, and she realised that her own adopted child at risk would have prompted the same ineffable courage in herself.

Antonia grew tall and slender, approximating daily to the classical image of the amazon athlete depicted on the vases in museums. When she walked she strode, springing lightly from the balls of her feet, and very early on she adopted white as the colour of her clothes. She was incapable of decorum, and when she sat in her grandfather's armchair she not only sucked her thumb, but dangled one leg languorously over the arm of the chair, lolling in the most unladylike fashion, and reproving her mother's and Drosoula's reproofs with laughing cries of, 'Don't be so old-fashioned.' Pelagia recognised that in a house run by eccentric women for themselves, she had only herself to blame if Antonia continued the process of becoming anomalous amongst the female sex that her father had inaugurated with herself.

Eccentric they were seen to be. The empty-headed gossips of the village transformed Drosoula, with her extreme ugliness, and Pelagia with her fearless lack of deference to men, into a pair of harridans and witches. The fact that the doctor was silent and impotent in the house was explained away by means of chemically emasculating potions and Ottoman spells, and the fact that Pelagia was driven by impecuniousness to resort to valerian and thyme rather than to sophisticated modern drugs merely served to exacerbate the certainty that their methods were suspicious and occult. Children stoned them as they passed, taunting them, and adults warned their children to keep away and encouraged their dogs to bite them. Nonetheless, Pelagia earned a living, because after darkness people would arrive furtively in the belief that her cures and lotions were infallible.

The first great crisis of this life occurred in 1950, when the women of the house failed to accumulate enough money to bribe a public health official into ignoring the fact that the doctor and Pelagia were unqualified. Forbidden to practise, it seemed that they were destined to sink into the most abject destitution, and to return to a wartime subsistence of hedgehogs, lizards, and snails.

But as though the fates were smiling upon them for the first time, a lugubrious Canadian poet who specialised in verses concerning suicide attempts and metaphysical laments, arrived on the island looking for lodgings. He was the first in the new vanguard of Western romantic intellectuals with Byronic aspirations, and he was looking for a simple house amongst simple people of the earth where he could get to grips with the truly gritty realities of life.

What he got was a simple house amongst simple people of the sea. Ashamed and apologetic, Drosoula showed him around all two rooms of her unsanitised, damp, peeling, and faintly smelly little house on the quay which had been closed for five years and become a haven for cockroaches, lizards, and rats. She was bracing herself for a contemptuous refusal when he promptly professed himself delighted, offering a rent that was nine and a half times as big as she had tentatively proposed to herself. She concluded that the man was undoubtedly rich and mad, and the man himself could not believe his good fortune in having found a house at a sum so peppercorn that even a poet could live. He even felt guilty about it and would put too much money in the envelope that he would insert through the shutters, whereupon Drosoula would honestly return it.

He stayed there for three years until the disaster of 1953, filling the rooms with neurotic bohemian blondes and fashionably Marxist novelists who expounded their conspiracy theories all night and with increasingly slurred vehemence, over bottles of coarse red wine whose alcoholic content and deleterious effect upon the intellect were significantly greater than they thought. The poet would have stayed after the disaster too, but he had come to realise with increasing clarity that relaxation, sunshine, and contentment were doing irreparable damage to his muse. It had at last become impossible to write depressing verse, and it had become a priority to return to Montreal, via Paris, where freedom was in the process of being recognised as the major source of Angst.

But Pelagia, Drosoula and Antonia revelled in the freedom of their unprecedented wealth. They ate lamb at least twice a week, and were able to buy beans that had been dried this year rather than the year before. Additionally, the daily bottle of wine had the salutary effect upon the doctor of healing his psychic wounds one by one, releasing his memories and making light of them, until at length he smiled and laughed even if he never spoke. He had taken to going for long slow walks with Antonia, watching the little girl taking delight in butterflies and skittering from one treasure to another in a fashion that reminded him of Lemoni when she had been a child. Nowadays the only complication in their lives was that they had adopted a cat.

It was not a serious complication, but a confounding one nonetheless. It seemed that cats, for a very obvious reason, had been exterminated from the island during the war, but within a few years they had bred to their former number. Once more there were fat and contented creatures waiting on the quays for offcuts of fish, and once again there were pathetic, worm-infested, skinny and stunted cats begging from house to house in expectation of nothing but blows and kicks.

It so happened that Drosoula had taken to calling Antonia 'puss', which was by no means uncommon nor unwarranted, and the name, in Greek 'Psipsina', had stuck and spread to Pelagia, until the girl had almost forgotten her real name. She had become completely accustomed to it, it suited her feline nature and her languid grace, and she was used to being called to dinner by the name. It took some time for the family to work out why, one evening and upon seven subsequent evenings, a small brindled cat leapt through the kitchen window and onto the table just after they had called Antonia in.

At first they shooed it away with snapping dishcloths and waves of the hand, but of course it persisted, and of course eventually it stayed. It meant that Antonia would hear, 'Psipsina, get off the table,' when she was innocently playing in the yard, or, 'Psipsina, dinnertime,' only to come in and find that a small and uninviting dish of raw and bloody offal had been placed upon the tiles. If there was a sudden cry of, 'Psipsina, don't do that,' she would freeze in the process of her mischief and wonder desperately whether or not it was she who had been caught. Drosoula sensibly proposed that Antonia and the cat should swap names, so that the cat became Antonia and the little girl became Psipsina, but it was tried and found unworkable.

During all this time Pelagia became convinced that Antonio Corelli was dead, and like her father she became assured beyond doubt of the reality of ghosts.

It had happened first in 1946 when, one day in October, at about the anniversary of the massacres, she was standing outside the house with the infant Antonia cradled in her arms. She was at the time making cooing noises and giving the baby her forefinger to suckle. Something made her look up, and she saw a figure dressed in black standing looking at her. He was in exactly the place where Mandras had been when he was shot by Velisarios' cannon. The figure was looking at her, poised between a hesitation and a forward pace, and her heart leapt. He had about him the melancholy atmosphere of nine thousand grieving ghosts, and sorrow emanated from his face with the same distinctness with which a light breaks through the mantle of a lamp. She was sure it was him. Thin and bearded though he was, she saw clearly the scar on his cheek and the same brown eyes, the same fall of hair, the same symmetry of his carriage. Excited beyond all joy she put the baby down in order to run to him, but when she looked up he had gone.

Her heart jumping and pounding, she ran. Around the

bend of the road she stopped and looked wildly about. 'Antonio!' she cried out, 'Antonio!' But no voice responded and no man moved towards her. He had vanished. Her hands rose to the heavens in incomprehension, and fell down again to her sides in despair. She stood, watching and calling, until her shouts hurt her throat and tears blinded her eyes. The following morning she found a single red rose on the ground above where Carlo Guercio lay.

The same ghost appeared at the same place in 1947, and every year thereafter at roughly the same time, but never exactly, and every year at some moment in October there would be a rose. It was by this that Pelagia was led to conclude that Antonio had honoured his promise to return and that it was possible to keep a vow and to continue to love even from beyond the prison of a grave. She was able to live satisfied, knowing that she had not been deserted and cast off, filled with happy reveries of being desired and cherished even in her dry and fading spinsterhood, and anticipating that her own death would restore all that had been stolen away in life.

65

1953

WHEN ZEUS WISHED to establish the exact location of the navel of the world he released two eagles from the furthest perimeters of it and made a note of where the flight of these birds crossed. They did so at Delphi, and Greece became the place where East divides from West, and North from South, the rendezvous of mutually exclusive cultures, and the crossroads of the rapacious and itinerant armies of the world.

Pelagia had taken pride in the idea that she lived at the very centre, but now, if such a thing is possible, she gave up being Greek. She had seen with her own eyes the contempt with which Drosoula was treated merely because to have become a widow is to have ceased to exist. For her own conscientious idealism in attempting to heal the sick she had acquired the reputation of being a witch, and, worse than any of this, the barbarity of the civil war had knocked out of her forever the Hellenic faith which her father had instilled in her. She could no longer believe that she was heir to the greatest and most exquisite culture in the history of the earth; Ancient Greece may have been in the same place as modern Greece, but it was not the same country and it did not contain the same people. Papandreou was not Pericles, and the King was hardly Constantine.

Pelagia pretended to herself that she was Italian, and from afar she was able to feel more a part of it precisely because distance and the fact that she had never been there permitted her never to discover that it was no more full of liberal humanist mandolin-players than Greece was. 'After all,' she told herself, 'I was to marry an Italian, I speak Italian, and I expect that in Italy I could have become a doctor.'

Accordingly she brought up Antonia to speak Italian, so that the latter learned Romaic Greek from Drosoula and never would speak Katharevousa, and she bought herself a wireless from someone who was happy to part with it for next to nothing, because something had gone wrong with its tuning mechanism and it would only pick up stations in Italy. She bought it in 1949, just after the battle of Vitsi had concluded the civil war, and was able to listen to it at the anniversary of the massacres in October. She loved it dearly, polishing its scratched veneer until it gleamed, and neglecting her obligations by sitting motionless before it for hours, not only listening to it, but watching it carefully as if expecting Antonio to seep suddenly like smoke through its bronzed mesh.

She could hardly bear to leave it, and she would sit through hours of tedious nonsense just in the hope of hearing 'Non Ti Scorda Di Me', 'Core'n Grato', 'Parlami d'Amore', or 'La Donna e Mobile'. But most of all she longed to be transported back to the days of La Scala by hearing 'Torna a Surriento', the favourite song of the club and the one they would sing the most, and she would close her eyes in the most blissful state of melancholy as she heard its melody and visualised the boys outside under the olive, scarcely aware of the melodrama of their gestures as they poured their hearts and the full lust of their voices into the grippingly beautiful mordants and grace-notes of the final phrase, after which they would sit in a moment of nostalgic silence before sighing, shaking their heads, and wiping the tears from their eyes with their sleeves. It was also because of the radio that she discovered that there were beautiful songs for women, and she sang 'O Mio Babbino Caro' at the top of her voice as she scrubbed the floor on her hands and knees, investing it with oriental microtones and adorning it with ululations, thus abnegating in the very attempt her project of becoming Italian.

She listened also and in particular for the sound of mandolins, and would remind herself that one day she must rescue that of the captain from the cachette. Once she had come in from gathering berries and could have sworn that she heard the last bars of 'Pelagia's March', but she realised that she could not have done, since the captain was dead. No, it was just that this profligate world possessed other players who could supply his place. She wondered often where he had met his fate; most probably in the sea, in that little boat, but perhaps in Italy, at Anzio, or somewhere on the Gothic Line. It filled her with a sense of the utmost bereavement to conceive of his skeleton whitening beneath the ground, the muscles and tendons that had worked such music stilled and useless, contracting into rotting thongs. The ground above him was perhaps as still and silent as that which held the dead in the maquis, or perhaps it was a thoroughfare like that above Carlo Guercio. She herself did not like to walk above Carlo's grave, and she teased herself at the ludicrous modesty of fearing that a dead man might peer through a depth of soil and see right up her skirts.

But the duplicitous soil of Cephallonia was far from still; it was like a dog who has slept in the rain and then gets up to shake away the drops.

It is said that in ancient times all lands were one, and it seems that the continents themselves profess nostalgia for that state of affairs, just as there are people who say that they belong not to their nation but to the world, demanding an international passport and a universal right of residence. Thus India pushes northwards, ploughing up the Himalayas, determined not to be an island but to press its tropical and humid lust on Asia. The Arabian peninsula wreaks a sly revenge on the Ottomans by leaning against Turkey casually in the hope of causing it to fall into the Black Sea. Africa, tired of white folk who think of it as musky, perilous, unknowable and romantic, squeezes northward in the determination that Europe shall look it in the face for once, and admit after all that its civilisation was conceived in Egypt. Only the Americas hurry away westwards, so determined to be isolated and superior that they have forgotten that the world is round and that one day perforce they will find themselves glued prodigiously to China.

It seemed obvious afterwards that it was going to happen, but there had last been such an occasion not in Cephallonia but in Levkas to the north, in 1948, when Greece had been so embroiled in savagery that no one else had noticed, and the signs and omens of the morning were considered strange rather than portentous.

The Korean War had just concluded, but French troops had just parachuted into Indochina, and it was a fine August 13th of 1953, near the Feast of the Assumption, after the harvesting of the grapes. There was a thin haze, and streaky clouds like vapour trails were draped across the skies at insouciant angles, as though placed there by an expressionist artist with an allergy to order and serious aesthetic objections to symmetry and form. Drosoula had noticed that there was an inexplicably strange smell and glow upon the land, and Pelagia had found that the water was right up to the top level of the well, even though there had been no rain. Yet minutes later she had returned with her pail and found no liquid there at all. Dr Iannis, who had been tightening the miniature screws of his spectacles, found to his amazement that they stuck to his screwdriver with implausible magnetic force. Antonia, now eight years old but as tall as a child of twelve, went to pick up a sheet of paper from the floor, and the sheet fluttered upwards and stuck to her hand. 'I'm a witch, I'm a witch,' she cried, skipping out of the door, only to find that a hedgehog with two babies was scuttling across the yard, and that a similarly nocturnal owl was inspecting her from a lower branch of the olive, flanked by rows of Pelagia's new chickens that sat roosting obliviously with their heads beneath their wings. If Antonia had looked, she would have seen not one bird flying in the sky, and if she had gone down to the sea, she would have seen flatfish swimming near the surface, and the other fish leaping as if they now wished to be birds and to swim in air, whilst many others pre-emptively turned turtle, and died.

Snakes and rats left their holes, and the martens in the Cephallonian pines gathered together in groups upon the ground and sat waiting like opera-lovers before the overture begins. Outside the doctor's house a mule tethered to the wall strained against its rope and kicked out at the stones, the thudding of its hooves reverberating in the house. The dogs of the village set up the same ungainly and enervating chorus that normally occurs at dusk, and rivers of crickets streamed purposefully across roads and yards to vanish amongst the thorns.

Curious events followed one upon another. Crockery rattled and cutlery clattered just as it had in the war when British bombers overflew. Outside in the yard Pelagia's bucket fell over, spilling its water, and Antonia denied upsetting it. Drosoula came inside, perspiring and shaking, and told Pelagia, 'I am ill, I feel terrible, something has happened to my heart.' She sat down heavily, clutching her hand to her chest, gasping with anxiety. She had never felt so weak in the limb, so tormented by pins and needles in the feet. Not since the last feast of the saint had she so much wanted to be sick. She took deep breaths, and Pelagia made her a restorative tisane.

Outside in the yard Antonia realised that she was suffering from headache, was a little giddy, and was also oppressed by that vertiginous terror that one experiences when looking over a precipice and fears that one is being drawn over it. Pelagia came out and said, 'Psipsina, come in and watch; the other Psipsina's going bonkers.'

It was true. The cat was indulging in behaviour more mysterious than any seen in any feline since the time of Cleopatra and the Ptolemies. She scratched at the floor as though burying something or unearthing it, and then rolled upon the spot as though expressing pleasure or wriggling against the pricking of her fleas. She skipped suddenly sideways, and then straight up in the air to an extraordinary height. She turned her gaze on the humans for one split second, somersaulted with a wide-eyed expression that could only have meant astonishment, and then shot out of the door and up the tree, where she ignored the chickens. A moment later she was back in the house looking for things to get into. She tried a wicker basket for size, put her head and forepaws into a brown paper bag, sat for a minute in a pan that was too small to contain her, and ran straight up the wall to perch, blinking owlishly, upon the top of a shutter that was swaying precariously from side to side and creaking with her weight. 'Mad cat,' remonstrated Pelagia, whereupon the animal leapt and skittered from one shelf to another, hurling itself dementedly round and round the room without once touching the floor, in a manner that reminded Pelagia of the cat's eponymous predecessor. She stopped abruptly, her tail fluffed out to splendid dimensions, the hair of her arching back standing straight on end, and she hissed fiercely at an invisible enemy that appeared to be somewhere in the region of the door. Then quietly she returned to the ground, slunk out into the yard as though stalking, and sat on the wall yowling tragically as though perplexed at the loss of kittens or lamenting an atrocity. Antonia, who had been clapping her hands and laughing with delight, suddenly burst into tears, exclaimed, 'Mama, I've got to get out,' and ran outdoors.

Drosoula and Pelagia exchanged glances, as if to say, 'She must have reached puberty early,' when there erupted from the earth below a stupefying roar so far below an audible pitch that it was sensed rather than heard. The two women felt their chests heave and vibrate against the restraint of sinews and cartilage, their ribs seemed to be tearing, a god seeming to be dealing mighty blows to a bass drum within their lungs. 'A heart attack,' thought Pelagia desperately, 'O God, I've never lived,' and she saw Drosoula with her hands to her stomach and her eyes bulging, stumbling towards her as though felled by an axe.

It seemed as though time stopped and the unspeakable rowling of the earth would never end. Dr Iannis plunged out of the doorway of the room that used to be Pelagia's and spoke for the first time in eight years: 'Get out! Get out!' he cried, 'It's an earthquake! Save yourselves!' His voice sounded tinny and infinitely remote behind that guttural explosion of ever-augmenting sound, and he was thrown violently sideways.

Panicked and blinded by the frantic leaping and quivering of the world, the two women lurched for the door, were

467

hurled down, and attempted to crawl. To the infernal and brain-splitting booming of the earth was added the cacophony of cascading pans and dishes, the menacing, wild, but mincing tarantella of chairs and table, the gunshot reports of snapping beams and walls, the random clanging of the church-bell, and a choking cloud of dust with the stench of sulphur that tore at the throat and eyes. They could not crawl on hands and knees for being thrown upwards and sideways, again and again, and they spread their hands and legs and writhed like serpents for the door, reaching it only as the roof began to cave.

Out into the heaving yard they went, the light obliterated from the sky, the direful clamour bursting inside their heads and breasts, dust rising slowly from the earth as though attracted by the moon. The ancient olive, before their very eyes, made obeisance to the ground and split cleanly down the centre of the trunk before springing upright and shaking its branches like a palsied Nazarene. A bubbling and filthy waterspout erupted from the centre of the street to a height of twelve metres, and then disappeared as though it had never been, leaving a pool of water that filled rapidly with dust and also disappeared. Higher up the hill, invisible because of the ascending curtains of pale and choking dust, a plate of rock and red clay split from the slope and tobogganed down, entering the road to the south side, dragging the olives in its route, and removing the field from which the crickets had migrated. Once more the unsettled giant in the bowels of the earth slammed a mighty fist vertically upwards, so that houses leapt from their foundations and solid stone walls rippled like paper in the wind, and suddenly there was a stillness like that of death. An uncanny and sepulchral silence settled upon the land, as though belatedly regretting such catastrophe, and Pelagia, hawking and filthy, filled beyond measure by a sense of impotence and tininess, began to struggle to her knees, still winded beyond measure by the last titanic blow that had struck her in the diaphragm and paralysed her lungs. She stood up, tottered on her feet, and the praeternatural stillness was suddenly broken by the wild and savage cries of the priest, who had rushed from his church and was now wheeling and spinning, his arms raised to the heavens, his eyes flashing through the grime of his face, not imploring the deity to desist, as Pelagia at first supposed, but berating him. 'You bastard!' he roared, 'You filthy dog! You son of a fleabitten bitch! You whore's disease!' The forbidden words spewed out of him, all the serenity of his pious soul transformed instantaneously to contempt, and he fell to his knees, battered the earth with his fists, and, his body incapable of enfolding his rage, he sprang once more to his feet and punched a fist towards the sky. Tears rose to his eyes and he demanded, 'Have we not loved you? Ungrateful shit! Excrement of the devil!'

At this point, as though in response, the deep growling recommenced and mounted. Once more that plutonic fist shot upwards from the profoundest depths, and once more the crust and rocks of Cephallonia jolted and danced, the peaks of the mountains rocking like the masts of boats. Thrown to the ground again, Pelagia clawed at the oscillating, thudding earth, her helplessness and terror confounding and abolishing even her desperation to survive. The whole world had shrunk to the dimensions of a dark ball of fire that seemed to be erupting in her stomach and disgorging its consuming flames into the fibres of her brain, and in this solitary inferno she writhed and choked, incredulous, astonished, beyond amazement or dismay, a plaything of the impudence and callousness of earth.

To the south, in the island of Zante, the capital town blazed beneath a rain of incandescent cinders that fell upon the flesh so tormentingly that both men and dogs went mad. A rescue worker, one who had been a witness to Nagasaki, said afterwards that this was worse. All over the Ionian islands people found themselves with nothing but whatever idiotic items they had tried to save as they disgorged from their houses; a chamber pot, a letter, a cushion, a pot of basil, or a ring. On Cephallonia the rock at Kounopetra, in Paliki, which had vibrated for centuries and which even British warships had failed to disturb, fell still and found repose amid the demolition of the land. It became just another seaside rock as the island transmogrified itself, dissolving into desolation and rehearsing Armageddon.

Clutching each other for support, Pelagia, Drosoula, and Antonia stood looking at their house during those intervals when the apoplectic Titan below was recouping its strength and conceiving new and ever more compelling grounds for malice. As the plates and seams of the rocks cracked apart with the noise of artillery and tanks, as the roads buckled and undulated and the pillars of Venetian balconies rotated and twisted, the three women tottered and staggered in disbelief and woe. Psipsina emerged from nowhere and joined them, her fur clogged with white dust and her whiskers embellished with cobwebs, and Antonia picked her up and held her.

Of the old house there was little left; walls were reduced to half their height, and what was left held nothing but rubble and the remnants of the roof. It also contained the disillusioned soul and tired old body of the doctor, who had planned his dying words for years, and left them all unsaid.

66

RESCUE

IN THOSE DAYS Great Britain was less wealthy than it is now, but it was also less complacent, and considerably less useless. It had a sense of humanitarian responsibility and a myth of its own importance that was quixotically true and universally accepted merely because it believed in it, and said so in a voice loud enough for foreigners to understand. It had not yet acquired the schoolboy habit of waiting for months for permission from Washington before it clambered out of its post-imperial bed, put on its boots, made a sugary cup of tea, and ventured through the door.

Accordingly the British were the first to arrive, the ones to stay longest, the ones to do the most, and the last to leave. Overnight HMS *Daring* loaded with water, food, medicines, spare doctors, and rescue equipment, and sailed from Malta to arrive at dawn the following day, to find the harbour of Argostoli churning, spouting and foaming with what seemed to be depth-charges and magnetic mines. A Sunderland flying-boat brought the Commander-in-Chief of Mediterranean forces, HMS *Wrangler* took supplies to Ithaca, and before long there turned up HMS *Bermuda*, the *Forth*, the *Reggio*, and the New Zealand ship, *The Black Prince*. Between them they brought 250 miles of bandages, 2,500 gallons of disinfectant, 50 Nissen huts, 6,000 blankets, bulldozers, baby bottles, 60,000 tins of milk, three meals per diem for 15,000 people for seven days, and an inordinate and prodigal two and a half tons of cotton wool and lint.

471

The Yugoslavs, whose Dubrovnik port was closest, sent nothing whatsoever to the capitalists, but soon there would appear four diffident little ships of the Israeli Navy. Italy, mindful of its shameful past and the obligations implied by it, sent its finest capital ships loaded with the élite firemen of Naples, Milan and Rome, and began the evacuation of casualties to Patras. The *Franklin D. Roosevelt* and the *Salem* arrived, loaded with earthmovers and helicopters, and shortly there would come four combat transports loaded with 3,000 US marines. The Greek Navy, hindered by bureaucratic in-fighting, turned up late but eager, and General Iatrides was appointed governor of Ionia for the duration of the emergency. The King and his family took advantage of the occasion to swerve incognito about the islands in a jeep, and the rotund little nuns of the enclosed monasteries emerged conscientiously but gleefully to take a taste of life, with its attendant chocolate and its opportunities for work and conversation.

Because of the wide streets there were few casualties in Cephallonia; the towns consisted mainly of one-storey buildings separated by courtyards and rubbish tips, and there were the usual miracles concerning people who had lost their sense of time, and emerged from beneath the rubble after nine days, believing that it had been a few hours.

The British ratings perspired and laboured in the ener-vating heat, complaining bitterly about the smell of faeces in the harbour and the sunburn peeling off their skin in sheets. As red as cardinals, they dynamited unsafe build-ings, which turned out to be all of them, so that the island seemed to have been made yet more desolate by their atten-tions, and further panicking the distraught islanders, who could not distinguish aftershocks from explosions, and whom the sailors, poor on both geography and polite cir-cumlocution, referred to jovially as 'wogs'. On their notice boards were pinned, amidst the standing orders and special instructions, the regularly updated scores of the cricket match between England and Australia.

The foreign-aid workers built cities of tents and cleared

gigantic parking lots for their jeeps and trucks. To the growling of the uneasy earth was added the stupefying clatter of helicopters and the splutter and roar of earthmovers trying to clear the landslides that cut off the remoter communities, whose people for three days believed that they had been unutterably forgotten and left to starve or die of thirst. One village in Zante was on the point of despair when an aeroplane dropped the best bread they had ever tasted, its savour remaining in their collective memory forever as a foretaste of paradise that no mortal housewife would ever be able to recreate. It was followed by corned beef and chocolate, the latter on the point of melting almost as soon as it landed, to be licked eagerly from the silver paper by the humans, and then doubly licked by dogs before they swallowed the foil itself.

The crew of the *Franklin D. Roosevelt* made seven thousand loaves a day, and delivered them in crumbled ports and upon beaches by landing craft more accustomed to howitzers, tanks and troops. An American officer with a phrasebook wandered about, repeating 'Hungry?' with an insufficiently interrogative intonation, and pointing to his mouth to reinforce the point, until some villagers took pity on him and made him a banquet with what little they could find. When the Americans left, their tents and rubbish bins were plundered, and for a decade their miraculous tinopeners no bigger than a razorblade were currency in the place of coins and penknives within the swaps and negotiations of the islands' little boys.

The Greeks themselves reacted differently according to whether or not they found a natural leader amongst themselves. Those where none appeared lapsed into melancholia, lost their sense of time, became listless and purposeless, and suffered harrowing nightmares about falling infinitely in space. They were beyond tears, and no one wept. They did not even pin up notices, as elsewhere, arranging rendezvous with relatives and friends.

During the earthquake itself, perhaps a quarter, like the doctor, had not panicked, but afterwards the remaining three-quarters remembered their desertion of their children and their aged parents, and suffered the agony of utter humiliation. Strong men felt like cowards and fools, and to the sense of having been frivolously and gratuitously struck by God was added a dire and insidious sense of worthlessness. Their hearts leapt and fluttered at the braying of a mule, the creak of a door, or the scratching of a cat.

Some enterprising Greeks took instantaneously to business, avidly and opportunistically selling government property such as stamps and licences. Others opened fruit-stalls, and a bank-manager in Argostoli set up a table before the ruins of his bank, conducting his usual transactions and enjoying his job for the first time. In Ithaca somebody hung up a sheet and opened up a cinema. Youth clubs from all over Greece poured in for working holidays, laughing and taunting each other if anyone showed fear at the pulse and breathing of the rock.

The most unlikely people emerged as saviours. Although he had always been considered slow and placid, Velisarios took command in Pelagia's village. He was now forty-two years old, and without vanity knew that he was stronger than he had ever been before, even though he lacked the immeasurable stamina of youth and all its happy dreams of remaining young forever. The earthquake somehow cleared his brain, just as it cured Drosoula's rheumatism, and it was as if a light had switched itself on amid his mind's flow of animal apperception and instinctive reflex.

It was Velisarios who threw himself into the task of the village's resurrection, and it was the grateful inhabitants who followed. With a strength that seemed greater than that of the earthquake he threw off the beams and boulders that imprisoned the crumpled body of the doctor, aware that putrefaction brought with it its diseases, and thereafter he gathered together the confused and hopeless, and ordered them into small working parties with widely varying jobs. He himself clambered down into the well and began to pass up the rubble that had filled it, working so furiously that he exhausted two fatigue parties without resting himself. It was solely because of Velisarios that no one suffered thirst.

A rumour began, to the effect that the island was sinking into the sea, and that the government had ordered the entire population to take to its boats. As the gullible and credulous ran to the ruins of their houses for anything they could salvage for the exodus, Velisarios strode from one to the other, appealing to the cupidity and common sense of the people. 'Are you stupid?' he demanded. 'This is a nonsense started by people who would be looters. Do you want to lose everything and be made a fool of? If anyone leaves, I'll change their lights, and that's a promise. Cephallonia doesn't sink, it floats. Don't be idiots, because that's what people want.' When folk scattered and screamed at every one of the thousands of small aftershocks, it was Velisarios who told them to pull themselves together and get back to work, and more than once he pulled idlers and the terrified from their hidey-holes and threatened them with broken bones and heads unless they resumed their tasks. With his shaggy grey hair, his perspiring temples, his bare chest hairier than a bear, and his legs thicker than columns of stone, there was no one whom he did not bully into sanity and work. Even Pelagia was persuaded to cover her father's corpse, and went to attend to people's wounds. She splinted and set two broken legs, even putting them into traction by means of ropes and boulders, and she smeared honey on cuts and extracted grit from babies' eyes with a feather and spittle. Drosoula, who at first had done nothing but cry hysterically, 'We have nothing left, nothing but our eyes to cry with,' was put in charge of the children so that their parents could be put to work. They played hide-and-seek in the ruins, and tag, and built pyramids of stones; their small contribution to clearing up the houses and the street. When the aid workers finally bulldozed through the landslide in the road, they found a small community living in tents of corrugated iron lashed to salvaged beams, with discreet latrines dug at a safe distance from the well, their communal olive-press repaired and in working order so that money would continue to be earned and starvation kept at bay. They found a gigantic man in charge, who into old age would be more venerated and respected than the teacher or the priest.

For three months the earth heaved, sounding as though it was breathing, holding its breath, and exhaling. Everyone lived in tents that were washed away and shredded by an untimely and freezing storm, only to be tacked together and re-erected. Through the early part of winter they shivered, sometimes fifteen to a tent for warmth, and then the wooden sheds went up, inconceivably spacious by comparison, but very near as cold. For three months Antonia went away on a holiday organised by the Queen in camps originally built for orphans of the civil war, and returned with lice and nits, and a shocking new vocabulary of oaths and names for private parts. In one year reconstruction began, and in three years it was complete. Ancient and beautiful Venetian towns re-emerged as undistinguished agglomerations of whitewashed concrete boxes. One village was rebuilt completely by a philanthropic exile who lavished his wealth on running water, sewerage, metalled streets, and wrought-iron lamp posts, and it became as charming as Fiskardo, the only town to survive intact. Pelagia's village was rebuilt further down the hill, nearer to the new road that had been built by ingenious French engineers, and her old house was abandoned, the treasures and relics in the cachette buried, it seemed, beyond recall.

Because the earthquake had consisted entirely of compression waves, very few fissures had opened in the earth. But soon after the disaster an Italian fireman found one. He had travelled up from Argostoli in a jeep borrowed from an American, and he stood before Pelagia's deserted and demolished house, looking up at it in dismay and trepidation. He walked across the yard with its sundered olive, and noticed that a crack had widened in the earth. He looked down into it and saw a skeleton, its sternum and ribs splintered, its massive skull with its shattered jaw opened as if caught in mid-speech, the tarnished silver coins in the sockets of its eyes endowing it with an expression of sadness, astonishment, and reproach.

The fireman gazed at it for a few minutes, until a new tremor stirred him. He fetched a golden poppy from amongst the stones, threw it down upon the corpse, and then he went to the jeep for a spade. No sooner had he begun the task of reburial than another judder unbalanced him, and the red earth closed once again over the colossal bones of Carlo Guercio.

67

PELAGIA'S LAMENT

THIS WAS MY place of safety, my single refuge, the substance of my memory. Here in this house my mother held me, her brown eyes shining, and in this house she died. And my grieving father gathered in his love and gave it to me only, and he brought me up and made me unpalatable, manly meals, and sat me on his knees, and he made my feet grow into the earth by telling me its stories. He talked to me with so much love, he worked for me, he let me be a child. When I was tired he picked me up and carried me, he laid me in my bed and stroked my hair, and in the darkness I would hear him saying, 'Koritsimou, if it wasn't for you, if it wasn't for you . . .' and he would shake his head because for once he had no words, his heart was too big to hold them, and I would close my eyes and go to sleep with my nostrils full of the smells of ointment and tobacco, and in my dreams there were no Turks and no monsters to scare me, and sometimes at night I thought I saw my mother passing through the door and smiling.

And in the morning he would wake me up and bring me chocolate, and say, 'Koritsimou, I'm off to the kapheneion, and make sure you're up by the time I come back,' and he was still saying that when I was twenty, and I would lie there as happy as a nun for the new day, thinking of everything I could do, and I would listen for his footsteps on the flags, and fly out of bed, and he would come in and say, 'Lazy little miss, this time I nearly caught you,' until I would say it first, and he would laugh and say, 'Right, today I am going to tell you all about Pythagoras, and then this evening you'll choose a poem to read to me, and I'll choose a poem to read to you, and then I'll tell you why I don't like yours, and you can tell me why you don't like mine, and then we can lose our tempers and have a fight.' And I would jump up and down and say, 'Let's fight now, let's fight now,' and he would tickle me until I nearly fell sick with laughing, and then he'd sit me in a chair and comb my hair, pulling it much too hard, and telling me frightful stories about Cretan abbots who burned themselves and their monks to death in their churches rather than surrender to the Turks. And he told me about islands he had seen, where women had four husbands and no one wore any clothes, and places in Africa where the people's backsides were wider than their height, and places so cold that the sea froze over and everything was white.

But it's all gone now. I come and sit in the ruins of my home and all I see is ghosts. There is nothing now but withered grass and broken stones and a severed tree. There is no table where the boys of La Scala sing, there is no Psipsina catching mice, no goat to bleat in the dawn and wake me, there is no Antonio seducing my heart with his flowers and mandolin, there is no Papas returning from the kapheneion and saying, 'Kokolios said the most ridiculous thing . . .'

All my home is nothing but sadness and silence and ruin and memory. I have been reduced, I am my own ghost, all my beauty and youth have shrivelled away, there are no illusions of happiness to impel me. Life is a prison of poverty and aborted dreams, it is nothing but a slow progress to my place beneath the soil, it is a plot by God to disenchant us with the flesh, it is nothing but a brief flame in a bowl of oil between one darkness and another one that ends it.

I sit here and remember former times. I remember music in the night, and I know that all my joys have been pulled out of my mouth like teeth. I shall be hungry and thirsty and longing forever. If only I had a child, a child to suckle at the breast, if I had Antonio. I have been eaten up like bread. I lie down in thorns and my well is filled with stones. All my happiness was smoke.

O my poor father, silent and still, wasted and lost forever. My own father, who brought me up alone and taught me, who explained everything, and took my hand and walked with me. Never again will I see your face, and in the morning you will not wake me. Never again in our ruined house will I see you sit, writing, always writing, your pipe clenched between your teeth and your sharp eyes shining. O my poor father, who never tired of healing, who could not heal himself and died without his daughter; my throat aches from the hour you died alone.

I remain upon these piles of shattered rocks and imagine it how it was. I remember Velisarios heaving away the tiles and beams as though it were his own father dead beneath them. And I remember when he brought my father out, covered in white dust, his head hanging back in Velisarios' arms, his mouth hanging open, his limbs all limp and dangling. I remember when Velisarios set him down and I knelt beside him, blind and drunk with tears, and I cradled his bloodied head in my hands and saw that his eyes were empty. His old eyes, looking not on me but on the hidden world beyond. And I thought then for the first time how small and frail he was, how beaten and betrayed, and I realised that without his soul he was so light and thin that even I could lift him. And I raised up his body and clasped his head in my breast, and a great cry came out that must have been mine, and I saw as clearly as one sees a mountain that he was the only man I've loved who loved me to the end, and never bruised my heart, and never for a single moment failed me.

68

THE RESURRECTION OF THE
HISTORY

THE EARTHQUAKE CHANGED lives so profoundly that to
this day it is still the single greatest topic of conversation.
When other families elsewhere are arguing about whether
or not socialism has a future or whether or not it was a good
idea to abolish the monarchy, Cephallonians talk about
whether there will be another earthquake and whether it
will be as vicious as the last. They live in the shadow of
apocalypse, and when they are ostensibly talking about
socialism or the monarchy, they are really thinking about
1953. It will be marked by a pause during which someone
forgets what they are saying, or a momentary interruption
in the passage of fork to mouth. Like the Ancient Mariner,
they cannot resist buttonholing strangers in order to inform
them of the facts, and tourist guides will contrive to work
them into sentences which were promising to be about the
prospects of finer weather. Old people pin down a remembered year by reference to its being before or after the earthquake, just as the custom continues of naming this year's
occasions as being before or after the feast of the saint. The
catastrophe caused people to recall the war as piffling and
inconsequential by comparison, and renewed their sense of
life. It was now possible to wake up in the morning and be
amazed and grateful to be yet alive and living in a solid
house, and to go to bed at night full of relief at having lived
a commonplace and uneventful day.

Lovers who had been procrastinating got married
immediately, and longstanding couples in unsatisfactory

marriages looked at one another in wonder at such a waste of years and immediately got divorced. Close families grew ever closer, and sibling squabblers emigrated to different lands in order to place the sea between them.

The three inhabitants of their new matriarchal house grew closer, turning their faces inwards upon each other, structuring their lives about the one pillar of Pelagia's atrocious guilt. Insomniac and occasionally hysterical, she reproached herself relentlessly for being instrumental in her father's death. 'He was seventy,' said Drosoula sensibly, 'and he owed God a death. It was better to die like that, trying to save us, and so quickly.'

But Pelagia would have none of it. She knew that in the moment of disaster her mind had been whirling with nothing but the need to save herself, and she knew that when her father had fallen she should have tried, even at the expense of her own existence, to drag him through the door before the roof fell in. Over and over she played through in her mind the manner in which she had been rendered as impotent as a blowfly in a hurricane, the way in which all rational thought had been cudgelled from her mind, the way in which the tie of blood and affection had been nullified by that awesome roaring and that leaping of the earth. But it was no good. Whatever the rationalisations and excuses, the one palpable fact remained that she had deserted her own father in his hour of greatest peril; he had saved her by galvanising her into action, and she had let him die. It was not the quid pro quo of a loving and dutiful daughter.

She fell into a morass of self-recrimination and remorse. She neglected her appearance and her household tasks, preferring instead to sit by his grave, watching the eternal flame that she tended in a red glass lamp, chewing her own lips until they bled, and wishing that she could speak to him. She could have spoken through the black marble slab with its old but smiling photograph, but felt herself unworthy to address him. With her greying hair disarrayed and her face pale, she simply sat and watched, as though expecting his shade to rise up through the earth and burden her with

482

reproaches. When there was a vile east wind in January or a raging tempest she would pull her black shawl about her head, rise up from her chair beside the stove, and bow down her head to battle against the elements, struggling up the hill on the interminably repeated pilgrimage, obsessed with the single thought that his flame should not go out. She knelt in the soughing wind, bowing over her lamp to protect it from the rain, warming her shaking hands upon the glass, transforming her life into one long penitence and apology. She was in those days capable of believing that God had taken away Antonio because in His divine foreknowledge He had known that she would one day fail her father, contriving the former as her punishment, foreseeing the latter as her sin. Drosoula lost count of the times that she and Antonia had to go to the cemetery and drag Pelagia away, anguished and beseeching, her hands fluttering and her legs seemingly unhinged at the knees.

One day Antonia and Drosoula could take no more; their sympathy had transformed itself gradually and imperceptibly into anger and irritation, and the old woman and the young girl conspired together to bring her back to her senses. 'The trouble is,' said Drosoula, 'that she lost someone she loved during the war, and this extra death has made it all boil over.'

'Is that the ghost she always talks about?'

'Yes. His name was Corelli, a musician.'

'Do you think she really sees him, or do you think she's gone mad?'

'She wasn't mad before. The thing about ghosts is that they can appear to anyone they choose, and no one else sees them. It's Grandpa's dying that's changed her bulbs.'

The little girl shuddered, 'Poor Grandpa.'

'I'm thinking of going to the priest for advice,' said Drosoula.

'But he's mad too, ever since the earthquake. What if we dress up as Grandpa's ghost and come and tell her that it wasn't her fault?'

Drosoula frowned, 'It's a good idea, but she's not stupid, even if she's mad. It's not easy to impersonate a ghost, you know. I'm too tall and you're too small, and we don't know how to talk like him at all. All those words that are three pages long if you write them down, and sentences that could cover an entire book from start to finish, and you've got to remember that it might even make it worse.'

'Why don't we just tie her to the bed and hit her?'

Drosoula sighed longingly at the satisfying image, and wondered whether or not it would work. In the old days, even when she was a child in Turkey, they had cured the crazy by beating them until they were too scared to be insane anymore. It had worked well enough back then, but there was no way of knowing how much human nature had changed in the intervening period. She suspected that in any case Pelagia's madness had about it an element of self-indulgence, a sort of masochistic egomania, and she might look upon a beating as amply deserved rather than deterrent. She held the young girl's hands in her own, kissed her on the top of the head, and her eyes brightened. 'I've had an idea,' she said.

Accordingly, at breakfast the next morning, Antonia suddenly announced, 'I had a dream about Grandpa last night.'

'That's funny,' said Drosoula, 'so did I.'

They looked to Pelagia for some kind of reaction, but the latter continued merely to tear a piece of bread into tiny pieces.

'He told me he was glad he was dead,' said Antonia, 'because now he can be with Mama's mother.'

'That's not what he told me,' replied Drosoula, whereupon Pelagia asked, 'Why are you talking as though I'm not here?'

'Because you're not,' observed Drosoula, brutally. 'You haven't been here for a long time.'

'What did he tell you, then?' enquired Antonia.

'He told me that he wants Mama to write the History of Cephallonia that got buried in the earthquake. To get it done for him. He said it spoils all the fun of being dead, knowing that it's got lost.'

Pelagia eyed them suspiciously, and the other two continued to ignore her. Antonia was discovering that this play-acting could be tremendously amusing. 'I didn't know he was writing a history.'

'O yes, it was more important than being a doctor.'

Antonia turned to Pelagia and demanded innocently, 'Are you going to write it then?'

'No point in asking her,' said Drosoula, 'she's too far gone.'

'I am here,' protested Pelagia.

'Welcome back,' said Drosoula sarcastically.

Pelagia went back to the cemetery and renewed the oil in the lamp. She stood looking at the inscription (Beloved Father and Grandfather, Faithful Husband, Friend Of The Poor, Healer Of All Living Things, Infinitely Learned And Courageous) and it occurred to her that there was indeed a way to keep his flame alive, even if all this stuff about dreams was silly nonsense. She went into Argostoli, hitching a lift on the back of a mulecart, and returned with pens and a thick sheaf of paper.

It was surprisingly easy. She had read through the manuscript so many times that all the old phrases rolled through the kitchen door and windows, made themselves heard inaudibly, and flowed down her arm and right hand, emerging from the nib of her pen and filling sheet after sheet of paper: 'The half-forgotten island of Cephallonia rises improvidently and inadvisedly from the Ionian Sea; it is an island so immense in antiquity that the very rocks themselves exhale nostalgia and the red earth is stupefied not only by the sun, but by the impossible weight of memory . . .'

Drosoula and Antonia spied on her, sitting at her table in a scholarly attitude, tapping her teeth with her pen, and occasionally staring out of the window at nothing in particular. The two conspirators crept away to a safe distance, hugged each other, and danced.

Pelagia almost became the doctor. As in the time of her distress, and just as he had done throughout his life, she did virtually nothing about the house, leaving it all to the women. Of the few souvenirs of her father, dug from the ruins, there remained his pipe, and this she stuck between

485

her teeth as he had done, inhaling the faded traces of tarry dottle, and impressing the stem with the indentations of her own teeth over the marks of his. She did not light it, but regarded it as an instrument of her mediumship, so that the old words now seemed to flow in through the empty bowl, gather in the stem, and sound directly in her brain. Tentatively she began to add a woman's touch to the male prepossessions of the text, supplying details of manners of dress and the techniques of baking in the communal fourno, the economic significance of child labour, and the cruel but traditional contempt for widows. As she wrote, she discovered her own passions surmounting those of her father, passions whose existence she had never previously suspected, and out onto the page there soared thundering condemnations and acid verdicts to rival and outvenom his.

The joy of it transformed her. Her act of filial devotion metamorphosed into a grand design involving trips to the library and earnest letters of enquiry to learned institutions, to maritime museums, the British Library, experts on Napoleon, and American Professors of The History of Imperial Power. To her amazement and gratification she discovered that all over the world there were enthusiastic people so enamoured of knowledge and its coherent explanation that they would actually spend months making enquiries on her behalf, and eventually send her much more than she had asked for, with personal notes of encouragement and lists of other experts and institutions to consult. As the piles of correspondence mounted, she began to feel in danger of finishing up by writing a 'Universal History of the Entire World', because everything connected to everything else in the most elaborate, devious, and elegant ways. Finally Pelagia compressed her sheaves of paper into a large boxfile, and wondered what to do next. It ought to be published, under the joint names of herself and her father, but it seemed an unbearable wrench to part with it, to send her intellectual baby out into the world without its mother there to defend it. She would want to be beside each reader in order to answer their objections and tell them not to skip any sections, to adduce additional proofs. Nonetheless she made tentative enquiries of four publishers, who expressed sympathy and support, advised her that such a book would have no market, and told her that the best thing to do would be to donate it to a university. 'I will when I'm dead,' thought Pelagia, and she left it on her shelf as visible evidence of the now undeniable fact that she was a substantial intellectual in the great Hellenic tradition.

The project had kept her busy right up to 1961, the year in which Karamanlis won the election from Papandreou, and at the end of it she looked through her massive document and realised that throughout its composition and compilation, a transmogrification had been unfolding within herself.

The calligraphy near the beginning was as spidery and unhinged as that of her father during the long years of his silence, but as time progressed it had become firmer and more rounded, more confident and affirmative. But more importantly than this, the process of writing had crystallised opinions and philosophical positions that she had not even known that she had held. She discovered that her basic understanding of economic processes was Marxist, but that, paradoxically, she thought that capitalism had the best ways of dealing with the problems. She considered that cultural traditions were a stronger force in history than economic transformations, and that human nature was fundamentally irrational to the point of insanity, which accounted for its willingness to embrace demagoguery and unbelievable beliefs, and she concluded that freedom and order were not mutually exclusive, but essential preconditions of each other.

Drosoula had too much common sense to listen to grand theories, and so Pelagia bludgeoned the budding Antonia with these ideas, the two of them sitting up late into the night, too intoxicated with philosophising to drag themselves away to empty bladders that were bursting with mint tea, or to go to bed and close eyes that were burning with fatigue.

Antonia, now in the most fresh and perfect stage of an adolescent's beauty and natural perversity, opposed all of her adopted mother's ideas not only for the sake of argument, but as a matter of principle, and Pelagia soon discovered the extreme delight of forcing an opponent into contradicting a position she had held the day before. It left Antonia speechless and enraged, hedging her comments carefully with qualifications and provisos that involved her either in further contradictions or in arriving at a conclusion so tempered that it amounted to no opinion at all. Pelagia exacerbated the girl's frustration and annoyance by informing her repeatedly, 'When you're my age, you'll look back and see I was right.'

Antonia had no intention whatsoever of reaching Pelagia's age, and said so. 'I want to die before I'm twenty-five,' she said. 'I don't want to get old and crusty.' She foresaw an eternity of infinite youth stretching out before her, and, with fire in her eyes, she told Pelagia, 'You old people caused all the problems in the first place, and it's up to us young ones to sort them out.'

'Enjoy your dreams,' commented Pelagia, who was not surprised but was still shocked when Antonia, at the age of seventeen, announced not only that she was going to get married, but that she was henceforth a Communist.

'I bet you cry when the King dies,' said Pelagia.

69

BEAN BY BEAN THE SACK FILLS

IT WAS AT about this time that mysterious postcards in rather truncated Greek began to arrive from all over the world. From Santa Fe came one that said, 'You would like it here. All the houses are made of mud.' From Edinburgh: 'The wind at the top of the castle knocks you off your feet.' From Vienna: 'There is a statue of a Russian soldier here, and everyone calls it "The Monument to the Unknown Rapist".' From Rio de Janeiro: 'Carnival time. Streets full of urine and heartbreakingly beautiful girls.' From London: 'Mad people; terrible fog.' From Paris: 'Found a shop that only sold trusses and hernia supports.' From Glasgow: 'Knee-deep in soot and fallen drunks.' From Moscow: 'Works of art in the metro.' From Madrid: 'Too hot. Everyone asleep.' From Cape Town: 'Nice fruit, rotten pasta.' From Calcutta: 'Buried in dust. Abysmal diarrhoea.'

Her first thought was that her father's maritime soul had taken to revisiting his favourite foreign climes, and was sending her communications from beyond the grave. But Moscow was hardly by the sea. Her second thought was that they might be from Antonio.

But he too was dead, he had not known sufficient Greek to read or write it, and for what reason would he be whirling about the world from Sydney to Kiev even if he were still alive? Perhaps these anonymous cards were from someone with whom she had corresponded during the writing of the History. Puzzled, but intrigued and pleased, she bound her collections of quirky cards together with rubber-bands, and stacked them in a box.

'You've got a secret boyfriend,' maintained Antonia, who was pleased to entertain such a possibility because it might distract attention from her own romance, which both Pelagia and Drosoula were attempting to discourage.

They had met whilst Antonia was earning a little cash by helping to serve coffee in a busy café on the plaza of Argostoli. There had been a noisy brass band from Lixouri playing in the square, and the gentleman concerned had had to rise and shout his order in the young girl's ear, at the same moment realising that it was a splendid and appealing young ear that positively cried out for nibbling at night beneath a tree in a dark street. Antonia in her turn had realised that here was a man who smelled of the exactly correct admixture of virility and aftershave, whose breath was as cool and calming as mint, and whose perpetually startled brown eyes bespoke both gentleness and humour.

Alexi idled conspicuously at the café day after day, choosing the same table for preference, his heart bursting with the longing to see the young and statuesque maiden with her perfect teeth and slender fingers that were made respectively for amorous biting and caressing. She waited for him faithfully, vehemently forbidding the other girls, the waiters, and even the proprietor himself, to serve him. One day he took her hand when she was putting down a cup, looked up at her with doglike devotion, and said, 'Marry me.' He rotated an eloquent hand figuratively in the air, and added, 'We have nothing to lose but our chains.'

Alexi was a radical lawyer who could not only prove that when a rich man evaded taxes it was a crime against society, but also that when a poor man did it, it was a valid, meritorious and powerful action against the class-oppressors, deserving not merely the support of every right-thinking citizen, but even the full approval of the law. He could reduce a judge to tears with his heartrending accounts of the unhappy childhood of his clients, and equally could bring a jury to a standing ovation with his acerbic condemnations of police who brutally and unreasonably sought to uphold the law in the course of their duties.

Pelagia saw immediately that Alexi would become an arch-conservative in later life, and it was not his political affiliations to which she objected. The fact was that she could not abide the thought of Alexi and Antonia making love. She was very tall, he was very short. She was only seventeen, and he was thirty-two. She was slim and graceful, he was plump and bald, and inclined to trip over objects that were never there when he looked. She remembered her own passion for Mandras at the same tender age, shuddered, and forbade the marriage outright, determined to obviate a sacrilege and a blasphemy.

The wedding day was nonetheless delightful. In early spring the fields and hillsides were clothed in crocus and viola, white stachys, and yellow sternbergia, and pale lilac colchicum nodded on exiguous stalks amid the already sere grass of the meadows. The couple followed the custom of having fifteen best men and women at the wedding, and Alexi even capered successfully through the dance of Isaiah without disgracing himself or falling over. Antonia, radiant and delighted, kissed even the strangers standing by to gawp, and Alexi, perspiring with alcohol and joy, made a long and poetic speech that he had composed in rhyming epigrams, much of it very wisely in praise of his mother-in-law. She would always remember the exact moment during the celebrations when she had seen suddenly what it was about him that had awakened Antonia's heart; it was when he put his arm about her, kissed her on the cheek, and said, 'We are going to buy a house in your village, with your permission.' His sincere humility and his implied doubt that she might not want him near was enough to cause her to adore him. From that time onwards she devoted many happy hours to embroidering his handkerchiefs and mending the holes in the socks that Antonia always tried to persuade him to throw away. 'My darling,' she said, 'if only you would cut your toenails, you would spare me so many scratches, and save my mother from so much pointless work.'

Pelagia waited impatiently for a grandchild, and Drosoula

immersed herself in work. In the empty space by the quay that had once been her own house, she erected a straw roof and some romantic lanterns. She begged and borrowed some ancient, rickety tables and chairs, set up a charcoal stove, and grandly founded the taverna that she would run with eccentric and erratic diligence until the day of her death in 1972.

The tourists were just beginning to ebb into Cephallonia. At first it was the rich yacht owners who passed on supercilious information to their friends about the quaintest and most ruritanian places to eat, and then it was the rucksacked spiritual inheritors of the lugubrious Canadian poet's way of life. Connoisseurs and aficionados of Lord Byron trickled in, and went. German soldiers who had turned into prosperous and gentle burghers with vast families brought their sons and daughters and told them, 'This is where Daddy was in the war, isn't it beautiful?' Italians arrived on the ferry via Ithaca, bringing with them their nauseating white poodles and their individual ability to eat entire fish that were large enough to feed the five thousand. As the owner of the only taverna in the little port, Drosoula earned enough in the summer to do nothing whatsoever in the winter.

Lemoni, who was now married, stirringly fat, and blessed with three children, helped out with the serving, and Pelagia came down ostensibly to work, but in fact to have the opportunity to speak Italian. The service was not fast; it was dilatory in the extreme. Sometimes Drosoula would send away a child on a bicycle to fetch the fish that had been ordered, and if the oven had not fired properly it was quite possible to wait two hours whilst food was prepared and baked. The guests were treated unapologetically as members of a patient family which it was her business to discipline and supervise, and quite often there was no service at all if Drosoula happened to like a particular customer with whom she was deep in conversation. She soon discovered that foreigners thought of her as exotic, and she would sit at their tables amidst the skeletons of mullet and the torn-up shreds of bread, unselfconsciously and unashamedly feeding scraps of leftovers to Psipsina's mewing and begging descendants, and concocting preposterous tales about local ghosts, Turkish abominations, and the time she had been to Australia to live amongst the kangaroos. The foreigners adored her and feared her, with her bovine eyes, her slow shuffle, her turkey's jowls, her bent back, her colossal height, and her spectacular spouts of facial hair. They never complained about her forgetfulness and her indefinite delays, and would say, 'She's so nice, poor old thing, it seems a shame to hurry her.'

Meanwhile Pelagia waited for her grandchild that never came. She forgave Antonia for taking up smoking and wearing trousers, and agreed with her that it was a good thing that dowries had been abolished. She smiled when Antonia cried in 1964 over the death of King Paul, even whilst maintaining between her sobs that the monarchy was a corrupting anachronism. She moved temporarily into Antonia's house to comfort her when in 1967 Alexi was arbitrarily but briefly locked up by the Colonels, and again in 1973 when he was imprisoned for wrestling with a policeman during the student occupation of the Law Faculty at Athens University. Later on she would withhold her doubts over Antonia's support of Papandreou's socialist government, and even concede that Antonia had a point when she insisted upon going to the mainland in order to participate indecorously in feminist demonstrations. She felt that she could not pour scorn upon such touchingly utopian and optimistic faith, and in any case it was her own fault; she was reaping the inevitable whirlwind consequent upon having taught the girl to think. In addition, she still liked the idea that she had cherished in her own youth, that everything was possible.

But she did object to Antonia's insistence that she did not have to provide a grandchild. 'It's my body,' maintained Antonia, 'and it's not fair to expect me to be constrained by an accident of biology, is it? Anyway, the world's already overpopulated, and it's my right to have a choice isn't it? Alexi agrees with me, so don't think you can go and bully him.'

'Everything is all right, isn't it?' asked Pelagia.

'Mama, what do you mean? No, I'm not a virgin, and there's isn't a problem . . . like that. It's still very good, if you must know. I don't want to be mean, but you're so old-fashioned sometimes.'

'No, I don't want to know. I'm an old woman, and I don't need to hear. I just want to be sure. Don't you think I have a right?'

'It's my body,' repeated Antonia, turning the eternal wheel of their dispute back to its original point.

'I'm getting old,' Pelagia would say, 'that's all.'

'You'll live longer than I will, Mama.'

But it was Drosoula who died first, perfectly upright in her rocking chair, so quietly that it seemed she was apologising for having lived at all. She was an indomitable woman who had lived a few short years of happiness with a husband that she had loved, a woman who had disowned her own son as a matter of principle, and lived out the rest of her days in ungrudging service to those who had adopted her by apparent accident, even earning them their bread. She had husbanded the little family like a patient shepherd, and gathered it to her capacious bosom like a mother. After she was buried in the same cemetery as the doctor, Pelagia realised with desperate clarity that she not only had another flame to tend, but that she was alone. She had no idea any more how to run a life, and it was with fear and hopelessness in her heart that she took over Drosoula's taverna and fumbled for a living.

Alexi, now completely bald and having travelled from the ideological arctic of the puritanical Communist party into the sub-tropical clime of the Socialist party, discovered with some initial anxiety and guilt that his success as a lawyer had indiscernibly precipitated him into the very class that he had professed to despise. He was a sleek bourgeois with a big Citroën, a purportedly earthquake-proof house complete with terracotta pots bursting with geraniums, four suits, and a loathing of the corruption and incompetence embodied by the party of his heart. He spoke volubly in favour of the socialists at meetings and parties, but in the ballot box he furtively marked his cross against Karamanlis, and then affected terrible despair when the latter won the vote. He hired an accountant and became as efficient in evading taxes as any other conscientious Greek with a long tradition to uphold.

Antonia held out for four years after her womb began to clamour for an occupant, seeing no reason to cave in to a body that made such unreasonable and ideologically suspect demands, until eventually she conspired with it and allowed it to cause her to forget to take her pills. There was no one, therefore, more genuinely surprised than she when her belly swelled unseasonably and a child began to form. She and Alexi started to hold hands again in public, stared dewy-eyed at babies and baby clothes, and compiled long lists of names, only to cross them out on the grounds that, 'I knew someone called that, and they were awful.'

'It's going to be a girl,' said Pelagia upon those frequent occasions when she pressed her ear to Antonia's ever-expanding belly. 'It's so quiet, it can't be anything else. Really you must call her Drosoula.'

'But Drosoula was so big, and . . .'

'Ugly? It doesn't matter. We loved her all the same. Her name should live. When this child is older, she should know how she got her name and who it belonged to.'

'O, I don't know, Mama . . .'

'I am an old woman,' declared Pelagia, who gained substantial gratification from reiterating this refrain. 'It might be my last wish.'

'You're sixty. These days that isn't old.'

'Well, I feel old.'

'Well, you don't look it.'

'I didn't bring you up to be a liar,' said Pelagia, terribly pleased nonetheless.

'I'm thirty-four,' said Antonia, 'that's old. Sixty is just a number.'

The little girl transpired without a shadow of a doubt to be a little boy, complete with a fascinatingly wrinkled scrotum and a slim penis that would undoubtedly prove serviceable in later years. Pelagia cradled the infant in her arms, feeling all the sadness of a woman who has remained a virgin and technically childless all her life, and began to refer to it as Iannis. She referred to it so often by that name that it soon seemed obvious to its parents that it could not be Kyriakos or Vassos or Stratis or Dionisios. If you called it Iannis, it smiled and blew slimy bubbles that burst and trickled down its chin, and so Iannis it was. It had a determined and obstinate grandmother who would only ever talk to it in Italian, and parents who talked earnestly about sending it to a private school, even though there was nothing really wrong with the state ones.

Alexi, driven by the suddenly self-evident notion that a man must pass something on to his son, unmediated by inheritance tax if possible, began to look around for good investments. He built a small block of holiday apartments on a barren hillside, and installed a modern kitchen and lavatories in the taverna. He persuaded Pelagia to accept the hiring of a proper cook, leaving her as the manager, and they split the profits fifty-fifty. On the distempered walls Pelagia stuck all the postcards that continued to arrive from the four corners of the globe, along with multicoloured samples of foreign currency donated by tourists grown generous and whimsical under the benign and mellowing influence of Robola and retsina.

70

EXCAVATION

BY THE TIME that he was five years old and Christos Sartzetakis was elected in place of Karamanlis, Iannis already knew how to say 'Hello' and 'Isn't he adorable?' in six different languages. This was because he spent nearly all his time at the taverna in his grandmother's care, being cooed over by pink and sentimental foreigners who loved olive-skinned little boys with black fringes over their ebony eyes, just as long as they did not grow older and come to their own countries looking for employment. Iannis delivered the baskets of bread to the tables, peering very charmingly over the tablecloth, and earned enough money in tips to be able to afford a teddy bear, a radio-controlled toy car, and a simulation in durable plastic of a World Cup football. Pelagia proudly introduced him to her guests, and he would hold out his hand confidently and politely, the very image of the perfect child that in more prosperous but less sensible countries was no longer to be found. His antique manners were a prodigious novelty, and he only grimaced when embraced and slobbered over by fat women with halitosis and adhesive red lipstick.

The reason for his continual presence at the Taverna Drosoula was that his father was building new holiday apartments with swimming pools and tennis courts, and his mother was reverting to an old-fashioned, pre-socialist feminism, that declared that a woman has equal rights to a man when it comes to capitalist enterprise. She borrowed money from her husband in order to open a shop, and

497

conscientiously paid it back at five per cent interest over four years. On Bergoti Street in Argostoli she opened a souvenir emporium that sold reproduction amphorae, worry beads, dolls dressed in the fustanella of the evzones, cassettes of syrtaki music, snorkelling equipment, statuettes of Pan playing his pipes with every evidence of concentration yet endowed with a resplendent and hyperbolical erection, owls of Minerva shaped in limestone, postcards, handmade rugs that were really made by machines in North Africa, porcelain dolphins, gods, goddesses, and caryatids, terracotta tragedians' masks, silver trinkets, bedspreads embellished with meanders, keyrings that humorously mimicked in miniature the motions of copulation, diminutive clockwork bozoukis with loose red nylon strings made of fishing line that played 'Never on Sunday' or 'Zorba the Greek', copies of Kazantzakis' novels in English, sombre icons with authentic patina depicting various saints whose names in Cyrillic were indecipherable and improbable, emollients for sunburned Britons, leather belts and handbags, T-shirts which proclaimed variations on the message of 'My Dad Went To Greece, And All I Got Was This Lousy T-shirt', tourist guides and phrase-books, harpoon guns, paracetamol, beach-bags whose handles became unstitched, raffia mats, intimate wipes, and condoms. Antonia presided over this eclectic emporium, dressed as always in clothes of sparkling white, sitting at the open till (in order to leave no clues for the taxman), with her thumb in her mouth and her long legs arranged about her in attitudes of sophisticated grace.

Shortly she opened other shops with identical stock in Lixouri, Skala, Sami, Fiskardo, and Assos, and, to salve her finer artistic conscience, she sponsored a potter who was to make genuinely beautiful garden equipment and ornament out of frostproof terracotta, in the classical style. She and Alexi visited Paris and Milan with the vague idea of opening a very expensive boutique in Athens, and these days Alexi contemptuously dismissed the arguments of those who wished to redistribute his wealth: 'Between us Antonia and I keep dozens of people in employment. By enriching ourselves we enrich our staff, so don't give me any of that outdated crap, OK? What do you want? Do you want them all to live on the dole? And have you any idea how many people there are making the stuff that we sell? Hundreds, that's how many.'

Their son grew up contentedly in his grandmother's company, dabbling his toes in the astoundingly clear water of the port and mesmerised by its flitting and impulsive shoals of fish. In the evenings the reunited family would sit together in the taverna, sometimes before the rush but more usually after it, arguing both in Italian and in Greek, whilst Pelagia, already nostalgic for Iannis' infancy, would say, 'Do you remember the time when I was changing his nappy on the wall, and suddenly he peed, whoosh, and a great golden spout came out and landed on the cat? And how the cat ran away, and it licked itself clean, ugh, and we laughed so much we thought we would burst? Those were the days. It's such a shame they've got to grow up.' And the little boy would laugh politely and wish that his granny would not embarrass him so much, and then he would go behind the wall and see how high he could spread the damp patch, leaning backwards from the knees and experimenting with the range and elevation of his interesting appendage and its wonderful golden spout. He had a friend called Dmitri who could pee higher than him, and he had some catching up to do before he took on any bets. He had a piece of chalk back there too, and he kept a score of all the beautiful foreign women who had kissed him on the cheek when they said goodbye at the end of their holiday. It was one hundred and forty-two, almost too many to imagine, and he could not remember any of their faces, only a general and blissful impression of shiny hair and big eyes, redolent scent, and spongey breasts that flattened against him fortuitously and then resumed their shape. In the evening, after he had been carried home at midnight, fast asleep in his father's arms, he would dream in a babel of languages about exquisite girls and the smell of moisturising face-cream.

When he was ten years old, in the year of the antithetical coalition between Communists and conservatives, Pelagia

499

hired a bozouki player to entertain her guests in the taverna. His name was Spiridon, he was a charismatic Corfiote, and his exuberance was inexhaustible. He played his bozouki with such vibrant virtuosity that he seemed to be playing three, and he could induce even the Germans to put their arms about each others' shoulders and dance in a circle with motions of the feet like the impatient pawings of a horse. He knew exactly how to play a piece accelerando, starting very slowly and pompously, and gradually speeding up until all the dancers were tangled hysterically in each others' flailing limbs. He knew cradle songs and fishing songs, classical tunes and new compositions by Theodorakis, Xarhakos, Markopoulos, and Hadjidakis, and he executed all of them with perfect tremolos and extraordinary syncopated improvisations that were inclined to prevent his audience from dancing because it was even better to listen.

Iannis worshipped him, with his broad shoulders, huge black beard, his wide mouth that seemed to contain a hundred flashing teeth (including a gold one), and his repertoire of prestidigitatory tricks whereby he produced eggs out of one's own ears and made coins disappear and return in a flash of the fingers. Pelagia also loved him because he reminded her so much of her vanished captain, and occasionally her heart yearned for a time-machine to take her back to the days of the only real love of her life. She thought that perhaps the captain's soul inhabited the fingers of someone like Spiridon, for it seemed that even when players died, their vagrant music moved to other hands, and lived.

Iannis' secret desire was to become a harpoon, as soon as he was old enough. These 'kamakia' were the young Greek boys who lived on a diet of perpetual sex, entertaining the unchaperoned and romantic foreign girls who arrived on the island in search of true love and multiple orgasms in the arms of any latter-day Adonis who agreed to sweep them off their feet. They considered themselves so indispensable to the tourist industry that there was even talk of forming a union to represent their interests. Charmingly and chivalrously they doled out beautiful memories and broken hearts, waiting at the airport after one girl had flown out in order to acquire another as she flew in. They hung about on their mopeds in fallow times, discussing the sexual hierarchy of merit amongst the different nationalities. Italian girls were best, and English girls were useless unless inebriated. German girls were technicians, Spanish girls uncontrollable and melodramatic, and French girls were so vain that you had to pretend to be in love with them from the very first. Iannis used to inspect his diminutive rod with its unpredictable and painful erections, and wonder if he would ever have an orgasm, whatever that was, and whether and when his particular harpoon would waken from its humid dreams and grow.

Iannis did not fail to notice that Spiridon was popular with the girls. At the end of every performance they would seize the red roses from the slender vases in the middle of their tables, and throw them at him. He noticed that Spiro would go round early in the evening, to remove the prickles from the stems, so confident was he of this floral bombard-ment. He also observed that Spiro was always having his picture taken with his arms across the shoulders of girls with shining noses, sometimes two or four of them at a time, and that on these occasions his grin spread from ear to ear as his face radiated pride and happiness. Accordingly Iannis demanded one day that Spiro should teach him how to play bozouki.

'Your arms aren't long enough yet,' said Spiro, 'it would make more sense to start with a mandolin. It's the same thing really, but small enough for you. You're ten now, and maybe when you're fourteen you should start to play bozouki. Look . . .' he placed the instrument in the boy's lap and stretched out the left arm '. . . your arm's too short and your hand isn't big enough to get round the neck. You need a mandolin.'

Iannis was a little disappointed. He wanted to be exactly like his hero. 'Can you play mandolin?' he asked.

'Can I play mandolin? Can I walk and talk? That's how I learned. I am the best mandolinist I ever heard, except for one or two Italians. In fact the mandolin is the instrument of my heart.'

'Will you teach me?'

'You might need a mandolin. Otherwise we might have to stick to theory.'

Petulantly Iannis pestered his mother and father and his grandmother for a mandolin. Antonia removed her thumb from her mouth and said, 'I'll get you one in Athens, next time I'm there,' and needless to say, she forgot. 'I'll get you one when I go to Naples,' said Alexi, who had no idea when he would be going, or indeed why. Eventually Pelagia told him, 'In fact we have one already, but it's buried under the old house. I am sure Antonio wouldn't mind you digging it up.'

'Who's Antonio?'

'My Italian fiancé who was killed in the war. It belonged to him. You must have heard about him a lot.'

'Oh, him. If it's buried it's going to be all rotten and broken, isn't it?'

'I don't think so. There was a big trapdoor in the middle of the floor, and it was in a hole underneath. But you'll never be able to sift all that rubbish on your own, and I wouldn't let you. It's much too dangerous.'

Iannis pleaded with his father to divert some of his construction workers from one of his sites, was promised, and was then let down because of pressing schedules which were something to do with having a plane-load of tourists arriving shortly at a newly built complex whose plumbing was not even complete yet. Alexi was apoplectic with anxiety about it, and he snapped at his son for the first time in his life, only to hug him and apologise immediately afterwards.

So Spiridon was dragged up the hill by the hand, and shown a ghostly and forlorn ruin overgrown with long clumps of desiccated grass and thorn, its broken stones just visible above the growth. All around it rested the silent and deserted remains of little houses that had all the appearance of regret and loneliness. Tilted steps led nowhere. A communal oven sat at a drunken angle, its cast-iron door seized up and rusted at the hinges, with laminating plates of scale ready to split away either in heat or frost. Inside was a colony of woodlice and the charred scarring of countless forgotten meals eaten by people long dispersed or dead. 'Jesus,' said Spiro, gazing about him at the scene of tranquil desolation, 'it wasn't nearly this bad in Corfu. Doesn't it make you feel sad?'

'It's the saddest place,' said Iannis. 'I come here to explore, and when I'm angry, and when I'm unhappy.' He pointed, 'My great-grandfather died in there. I'm named after him. Grandma says he was the best doctor in Greece, and he could have been a great writer. He could cure people just by touching them.'

Spiro crossed himself, saying, 'Mary preserve us.'

'I've found lots of things,' said Iannis, 'but most of them are broken.' A young brindled cat trotted away, its belly distended with unborn kittens. 'She comes here to hunt for lizards,' said Iannis, pointing. 'She's very good at it. She always leaves the tail, and it sort of writhes around on its own for ages. It's brilliant.'

'Look at this,' said Spiro, pointing to a huge old olive tree that had split down the middle, begun to rot at the bole, but was still exuberant with contorted black branches and small green fruit. 'I climb in this one,' said Iannis, 'there's a branch that's really good for swinging on. That one there.'

'Let's have a swing then,' said Spiro, and Iannis climbed the tree to get there whilst the former sprang upwards and hung. Side by side the two of them swung backwards and forwards for a few moments, aided by the elasticity of the branch, and then dropped to the ground, full of businesslike and manly satisfaction. Spiro rubbed his hands together and said, 'Right, let's get working before it becomes too hot. Do you realise that this will be very bad for my hands? I probably won't be able to play tonight. Did you know that guitarists won't do the washing-up because it softens their fingernails? What a perfect excuse, eh?'

'I like washing up,' said Iannis. 'It gets all the dirt from under your nails, and anyway, Grandma pays me.'

The two of them went through what had once been the door, and scratched their heads in dismay. There was an awful lot of rubbish. 'It's not as bad as it was,' said Iannis apologetically, 'my Dad came and took away all the tiles that weren't broken, and he took most of the beams for new houses. And Grandma came and dug out anything useful.'

Spiro took a stick and lifted out a pale and congealed prophylactic. 'For God's sake!' he exclaimed. 'Shitty tourists.' He flicked it away over the scrub, and Iannis asked, 'What is it?'

'Well, young man, it's what you roll over your pride and joy when you don't want children.'

'How do you go for a pee then? Do you have to take it off?'

'Yes,' said Spiro, sensing that if he was not careful he was letting himself in for some lengthy explanations, 'you take it off. In fact you only put it on when you're at it, see?'

'Oh,' said Iannis, 'it's a condom, is it? I've heard about them. Dmitri told me.'

Spiro raised his eyebrows, blew out his cheeks, and sighed. These kids. He began to throw out the rubble, the pieces of broken tiles, the flattened tin cans, the long and distasteful strips of smeared lavatory paper (also the legacy of tourists), and the innumerable green bottles. 'We've got two days' work here,' he said. 'I suppose we'll just have to get on with it.'

By the next evening there was a clear space in the middle of the old floor, and a dusty stack of broken stones and tiles one metre high outside the walls, along with snapped and rotting lengths of wood. There was also a pile of treasures which Iannis wanted to save; an ancient and smashed wireless with its red tuning needle permanently stuck on 'Napoli', a distorted pan with a jagged hole rusted through the bottom, a broken walking-stick with a silver top, an intact glass jar full of snail shells, a mouldy set of fat books entitled *The Complete and Concise Home Doctor* in English, a stethoscope whose rubber tubes had perished and whose bell was distorted, a photograph in a silver frame with a cracked glass, and inside it a picture of two funny drunks in strange hats with their arms about each other, and, in the distance, the tiny but marvellously naked figure of a lithe girl kicking up the water of the sea, also in a silly hat. He even found a complete photograph album, a little brown, its pages eaten away by insects at the edges, and brown water stains elegantly and delicately spread in undulating patterns across its pages. The first picture was inscribed 'Mama and Papas On Their Wedding Day' and it showed in sepia a young couple standing very formally in clothes so old-fashioned that Iannis could not believe that anyone had really dressed like that. He went through them, sitting on the wall: 'Pelagia's First Steps' – a picture of a baby in a frilly bonnet, flat on its face, looking up in astonishment. He would show them to Grandma later to find out what they all meant. Meanwhile it was fascinating enough to have found a clasp knife with its blade locked by rust, a small glass jar containing a dried pea encrusted with something black and flaky, and a mouldy book of poems by someone called Andreas Laskaratos.

Spiro tried to get his fingers under the iron ring of the long trapdoor, but it had seized in its place and would not budge. Under the wood he slipped the blade of an old screwdriver he had found, but it bent like a piece of cheese and broke. He would have to go and borrow a crowbar, because no doubt the hinges were also rigid with rust. 'Why don't we just smash it?' enquired Iannis.

'Because we don't want to smash the mandolin, that's why. Nothing's to be gained from impatience.' They stood looking at the door, scratching their heads, frustrated at being baulked after having come so far, and then became aware of a very big old man in a black suit and collarless shirt, a heavy silver stubble on his face, standing a little bent in the doorway. 'What are you doing?' he asked. 'O, it's you, young Iannis. I thought you were looters. I was going to give you the back of my hand.'

'We're trying to open this, Kyrie Velisario',' said the boy. 'It's stuck, and it's got something inside that we want.'

The old man shuffled inside and looked down at the trapdoor with his watery eyes. Iannis noticed that he was carrying a red rose. 'I'll lift it in a minute,' he said, 'but first let me put down this flower.' He went back into the yard and placed his flower very carefully on the parched earth. 'I normally do it in October,' he told them, 'but I'll probably be dead myself by then, so I'm putting it there early.'

'What for?' asked Iannis.

'Young man, there's an Italian soldier down there. I buried him myself. A very brave man, as big as me. I liked him, he was very kind. I come every year and put the flower there to show that I have not forgotten. No one has ever seen me do it before, but who cares these days? We have different enemies now, and there's no shame anymore.'

'You mean there's a real skeleton down there?' asked Iannis, wide-eyed with horrified delight, and secretly thinking that it would be ghoulishly exhilarating to try and dig it up. He had always wanted a real skull.

'Not just a skeleton. A man. He deserves his rest. We gave him a bottle of wine and a cigarette, and there's no scolding woman down there to annoy his bones and start tidying up when he only wants his peace. He's got all a man could want.'

Spiro coughed politely but sceptically. 'Don't trouble yourself with trying to lift this door, sir, I've tried it and I can't.'

'I'll have you know,' said Velisarios proudly, 'that I was the strongest man in Greece, if not the world. For all I know, I still am. Do you see that old stone water-trough? In 1939 I lifted it above my head, and no one else has done that before or since. I have lifted mules to my chest with two riders still mounted.'

'It's true, it's true,' said Iannis. 'I've heard about it. And it was Kyrios Velisarios who saved the village.'

'Give me your hand,' said Velisarios to Spiro, 'and see what kind of men there used to be in Cephallonia. Remember that I am seventy-eight years old, and think about what I must have been.'

Smiling a little patronisingly, Spiro held out his hand. Velisarios enfolded it with his own and squeezed. Spiro's expression changed from consternation to alarm to horror as he felt the bones of his hand crushing and creaking as though trapped between the stones of an olive press. 'Ah, ah, ah,' he cried, sinking to his knees and raising his other hand in a gesture of desperate appeasement. Velisarios released him, and Spiro stared at his hand, waggling the

506

fingers and panicking at the thought that he might never play an instrument again.

Velisarios bent down slowly and inserted the tips of the fingers of one hand under the iron ring. He leaned sideways against the strain to put all his weight and strength into the feat, and with a sudden and gratifying rending and splintering of wood and old iron, the door flew upwards in a cloud of dust, torn from its hinges and split down four planks. Velisarios rubbed his hands together, blew on the tips of his fingers, and seemed abruptly to revert to being a tired old man. 'Farewell, my friends,' he said, and shuffled his way slowly down the path to the new village.

'Unbelievable,' said Spiro, still wringing his paralysed hand. 'I just can't believe it. An old man like that. Are his sons giants too?'

'He didn't get married, he was too busy being strong. Did you know that Cephallonia was the original place where the giants lived? It says so in Homer. That's what Grandma says. I'd like to be a giant, but I think I'm going to be average.'

'Unbelievable,' repeated Spiro.

Everything inside that cachette that had been sealed up for nearly thirty-six years was in perfect condition. They found an antique handwound German record-player complete with a set of records and winding handle, a large and intricately crocheted blanket, a little yellowed but still wrapped and interleaved in soft tissue paper, a soldier's knapsack full of wartime curiosities, two bandoliers of bullets, a wad of papers written in Italian, and another wad of papers written in a beautiful Cyrillic script, inside a black tin box, and entitled 'A Personal History of Cephallonia'. There was also a cloth bundle, containing a case, itself containing the most beautiful mandolin that Spiro had ever seen. He turned it over and over in the sunlight, amazed at the exquisite purfling and binding, the gorgeous inlay and the perfect craftsmanship of the tapered sections of the belly. He sighted along the diapason and discovered that the neck was unwarped. Four strings were missing, and the remaining four were black with tarnish, lying loosely upon the frets where Corelli had relaxed their tension for storage in 1943. 'This,' he said, 'is worth more than a whore's memoirs. Iannis, you're a very lucky boy. You've got to look after this better than you love your mother, do you understand?'

But Iannis was at that moment more interested in the Lee-Enfield rifle with a barrel so long that it was almost as tall as himself. Excited and gleeful, he waved it about from the hip, striking Spiro on the backside, and going, 'Bang. Bang. Bang.' He pointed it up towards the tree and squeezed the trigger. The gun leapt in his hands with a terrible and heart-stopping crash, the barrel cracked him in the forehead, and a shower of chips of wood sprayed from the branch above him. He dropped the cumbersome weapon as though it had given him a violent electric shock and he sat down abruptly and burst into tears of shock and terror.

o Carlo.' Then she picked up the wad of Greek papers, and went, 'O Papas, o Papakis,' and she would hug the crocheted blanket to her breasts, and more tears would flood down her face as she clapped her hand to the side of her head and wailed, 'O my poor life that never was, o God in Heaven, o my life, alone and waiting, o . . .' and she would start all over again with the mandolin, kissing it and hugging it as though it were a baby or a cat. She played the scratchy old records over and over, winding the handle furiously and using up all the spare needles in the little compartment at the side, since each one could only be used once, and all the records were of a woman singing German in a smoky voice from a great distance. He liked one of them, called 'Lili Marlene', which was very good for whistling when you walked along the street. The records were very thick, and wouldn't bend, and they had small red labels in the middle. 'Why didn't you have cassettes?' he asked. She would not reply, because she was turning over in her hand the clasp knife that she had once given to her father, or reading the poems of Laskaratos that he had given in return, the voice of the poetry filling her soul as it once had done in the days of a dead and unrecorded world.

Iannis comforted his grandmother as best he could. He sat on her lap, which he was really a little too old for, and he dabbed at her tears with a sodden handkerchief. He submitted without too much dismay to numerous rib-cracking hugs, and he wondered how it was possible to love so much an old woman with dangly jowls, varicose veins, and grey hair so thin that you could see the pink scalp underneath. He stood patiently whilst she went through the photograph album again and again, repeating the same information in the same words, and pointing with her mottled fingers. 'That's your great-grandfather, he was a doctor you know, he died saving us in the earthquake, and that's Drosoula who was a sort of auntie that you never knew, and she was so big and ugly but the nicest person in the world, and that's the old house before it fell down, and look, that's me when I was young – can you believe I was ever so beautiful? – and I'm holding a pine marten we had for a pet, Psipsina, and she was a very funny little thing, and this is Drosoula's son, Mandras – wasn't he handsome? – and he was a fisherman, and I was engaged to him once, but he came to a bad end, God rest his soul, and that's your great-grandmother who died when I was so young I can hardly remember, it was tuberculosis and my father couldn't save her, and that's my father when he was a sailor, so young, good God, so young, and doesn't he look happy and full of life? He saved us in the earthquake, you know. And this is Günter Weber, a German boy, and I don't know what happened to him, and this is Carlo who was as big as Kyrios Velisarios, and it's him who's buried at the old house, he was so kind and he had his own sadness that he didn't mention, and these are the boys of La Scala, singing, all drunk, and that's the olive tree before it split, and that's Kokolios and Stamatis, the funny stories I could tell you about them, old enemies, always fighting about the King and Communism, but the best of friends, and this is Alekos, he's still alive you know, older than Methuselah, still looking after his goats, and that's the Peloponnisos from the top of Mt Aenos, and that's Ithaca if you just turn round in the same place, and that's Antonio, he was the best mandolin player in the world, and I was going to marry him but he was killed, and between you and me I've never got over it, and it's his ghost that comes round the bend at the old village and then disappears . . .' Grandma would pause for tears '. . . and this is Antonio with Günter Weber being silly on the beach, and as for that naked woman, I don't know who she was, but I've got my suspicions, and that's Velisarios lifting a mule – isn't it incredible? – and look at those muscles, and that's Father Arsenios when he was very fat. He got thinner and thinner during the war, and then disappeared completely without anyone knowing why – isn't that strange? – and that's the old kapheneion where Papas, your great-grandfather, used to hide whenever I wanted him for something, and did you know? I was the first woman who ever went into it . . .'

Iannis gazed at those unlined faces from the ancient past, and an eerie feeling came over him. Obviously there weren't any colours in the old days, and everything was in different shades of grey, but it wasn't that. What troubled him was that all these pictures were taken in a present, a present that had gone. How can a present not be present? How did it come about that all that remained of so much life was little squares of stained paper with pictures on? 'Yia, am I going to die?'

Pelagia looked down at him, 'Everybody dies, Ianni'. Some die young, some die old. I'm going to die soon, but I've had my chance. You die, and then someone comes to take your place. "The Deathless Ones have appointed its due time to each thing for man upon this fertile earth." That's what Homer says. Apart from being born, it's the only thing in which we have no choice. One day, I hope when you are very old, you'll die too, so don't be like me. Make the most of everything while you can. When I'm dead, all I want is for you to remember me. Do you think you will? O, I'm sorry, Ianni', I didn't mean to upset you. No, don't cry. O dear. I forgot how young you were . . .'

Iannis begged Antonia to get him some strings for the mandolin from which she had derived her name, and she promised to find him some when she went to Athens. Alexi promised to buy him some when he went to Naples, which he still had found no reason to visit. Pelagia took Iannis on the bus to Argostoli, and bought him some strings in a music shop on one of the sidestreets that goes up the hill at right-angles to the main thoroughfares. 'I love your parents very much,' she told Iannis, 'but they never notice anything that's right under their nose. Athens and Naples! What rubbish!'

Back at the Taverna Drosoula, Spiro carefully cleaned the mandolin and polished it. He rubbed graphite from a pencil tip into the machine-heads, and turned them over and over until everything rotated smoothly, without squeaks, creaks, hesitations or resistance of any kind. He showed the young boy how to pass the upper end of the string through the silver tailpiece, hooking the loop with the polychrome balls of fluff onto the correct hook. He showed him how to wind it through the hole of the machine-heads in such a way that it was less likely to break, and how to settle it in the grooves of the bridge and nut, having first scribbled some graphite into them too, for easy tuning.

He showed him how to tune up each string slowly, going from one to another in turn and then back to the beginning. He demonstrated the use of harmonics to find the correct position of the bridge, he explained the principles of tuning each string to the seventh fret of the pair of strings above it, and then he began to play. He produced three simple chords to accustom his fingers to the reduced space of a mandolin's fretboard, and then he cascaded down a scale at a rapid tremolo.

Iannis was hooked as certainly as the strings with their odd little balls of fluff were hooked to the tailpiece. He digested religiously all of Spiro's information about not letting it sit in the sunshine, not letting it get damp or too cold in the winter, not letting it drop, keeping it polished with special polish such as is used on a bozouki, detuning it for storage, tuning the strings a semitone high in order to get them settled more quickly . . . Spiro told him seriously that he was holding in his hands the most precious thing he would ever own, and it awoke in him a sense of awe and reverence that had never struck him in church when dragged there by Pelagia. He only permitted Spiro and his grandmother to touch it, and was furious if ever anyone knocked it.

Most curiously, even though he had wanted it in order to be able to impress girls when he was older, by the time he was thirteen, and already quite a good player, he had discovered that girls were a complete dead loss. Their intractable mission in life was to frustrate, annoy, and have things that you wanted but that they would not bestow. In fact they were spiteful and capricious little aliens. It was not until he was seventeen and Grandma had begun her wild and frivolous second youth that he met one who made him burst with longing, and who had stopped nearby to listen when he was making Antonia sing.

72

AN UNEXPECTED LESSON

IN OCTOBER 1993 Iannis was impatiently fourteen, and he had just had a whole summer in which to play duets in public with Spiridon and be bombarded with red roses. In order not to annoy his grandmother by his continuous practising – in fact not to make her cry again – he had gone up to the ruins of the old house to play in private, and was concentrating very hard upon creating a decent tremolo by rotating his wrist rather than jerking it up and down, which was exhausting and very soon went out of control. He was biting his lip with the effort, and did not notice the old man who approached him and watched him with a critical but delighted interest. He nearly jumped out of his skin when a voice said, in a very curious accent, 'Excuse me, young man.'

'Ah!' he exclaimed. 'O, you startled me.'

'Too young for a heart attack,' said the man. 'The thing is, I couldn't help noticing that you are doing something wrong.'

'I've had trouble with this tremolo. It keeps breaking up.' It was good to talk to an old man on equal terms; the old were so often remote or incomprehensible, but this one was bright-eyed and had about him an atmosphere of energy and merriment. It seemed flattering to have his attention, and Iannis puffed out his chest a little to feel more like a man. His voice was breaking, sometimes producing disconcerting yodels and squeaks, and so he lowered his voice as far as possible and spoke in that self-consciously adult way that makes an adult smile.

'No, no, no, that'll come very well. It's your left hand. You are trying to use your first and second finger for everything, and that won't do.' He leaned down and started to pull the boy's fingers into place, saying, 'Look, the first finger stops the strings across the first fret, the second finger stops those on the second, the third does the third, and the fourth does the fourth. It's a strain at first because the little finger is not very strong, but it stops you having to twist your hand about, which damps the treble strings by accident.'

'I noticed that. It's very annoying.'

'Just keep that same relationship between the fingers and the frets, wherever you are on the diapason, and it'll make everything much easier.' He stood upright and added, 'You can always tell a really good musician, because a good musician doesn't seem to be moving his hands at all, and the music looks as though it's coming out by magic. If you do as I say, you'll hardly have to move your hand. Just your fingers. And that helps stop the instrument from slipping about. It's always a problem with a roundbacked mandolin, that, and I've often thought of getting a Portuguese one with a flat back. But I've never got round to it.'

'You seem to know a lot about it.'

'Well, I ought to. I've been a professional mandolinist for nearly all my life. I can tell that you're going to be good.'

'Play me something?' asked the boy, offering him the mandolin and the plectrum.

The old man dug in the pocket of his coat and produced his own pick, saying, 'I always use my own. No offence.' He took the mandolin, settled it into his body beneath the diaphragm, stroked a chord experimentally, and began to play the Siziliano from Hummel's Grand Sonata in G. Iannis was gawping with amazement when suddenly the old man stopped, swivelled the mandolin upwards, scrutinised it with an expression of extreme disbelief, and exclaimed, 'Madonna Maria, it's Antonia.'

'How did you know that?' asked Iannis, at once surprised and suspicious, 'I mean, you can't know it's Antonia, can you? Have you seen it before?'

'Where did you find it? Who gave it to you? How do you know it's called Antonia?'

'I dug it out of that hole,' said Iannis, pointing to the open cachette in the middle of the ruin. 'Grandma told me it was there, and that's what she called it, so I called it the same. In fact Grandma named my mother Antonia too, because she sounded like a mandolin when she was a baby.'

'And would your grandma be Kyria Pelagia, daughter of Dr Iannis?'

'That's me. I'm called Iannis, after him.'

The old man sat next to the boy on the wall, still holding the mandolin, and mopped his brow with a handkerchief. He seemed to be very anxious. Iannis noticed a scar across the cheek that was only just hidden by the wisps of white beard. Suddenly the old man said, 'When you found the mandolin, did it have four strings missing?'

'Yes.'

'Do you know where they are?'

'No.'

The old man's eyes twinkled, and he tapped his chest. 'They're in here. Dr Iannis mended my ribs with them, and I've never had them taken out. I was full of bullets, too, and the doctor got them out. What do you think of that?'

The boy was deeply impressed. His eyes widened. Not willing to be outdone, he declared, 'We've got a real skeleton over there.'

'O, I know. That's one of the reasons I came. That's Carlo Guercio. He was the biggest man in the world. And he saved my life. He pulled me behind him at a firing squad.'

The boy was so impressed by now as to be completely dumbfounded; a man with mandolin strings in his ribs who had been in a firing squad and really known the owner of the skeleton? It was better than knowing Spiro.

'Tell me, young man, is your grandmother alive? Is she happy?'

'She cries sometimes, ever since we dug Antonia and all the other things out of the hole. And she's got stiff knees, and her hands tremble.'

'And what about your grandfather? Is he well?'

516

The boy seemed bewildered. He screwed up his face and said, 'What grandfather?'

'Not your father's father. I mean Kyria Pelagia's husband.' The old man mopped his forehead again, and seemed more agitated.

The boy shrugged, 'There isn't one. I didn't even know she had one. I've got a great-grandfather.'

'Yes, I know, it was Dr Iannis. Are you saying that Kyria Pelagia hasn't got a husband? You haven't got a grandfather?'

'I suppose I must have, but I've never heard of him. I've only got my father's father, and he's half-dead. So's my father half the time.'

The old man stood up. He looked about him and said, 'This was a beautiful place. I had the best years of my life here. And do you know what? I was going to marry your grandmother once. I think it's about time I saw her again. By the way, that mandolin used to be mine, but I've heard you play, and I'd like you to keep it. I shall waive my rights.'

As the two of them walked down the hill, Iannis said, 'The biggest man in the world is Velisarios.'

'Porco dio, is he still alive as well?'

Iannis faltered in his steps, 'If you're the one who played the mandolin and was going to marry Grandma . . . does that mean you're the ghost?' A prodigal and autumnal sun broke briefly through the cloud over Lixouri, and the old man paused for thought.

73

RESTITUTION

ANTONIO CORELLI, ALTHOUGH in his seventies, rediscovered a certain amount of youthful agility in his old
limbs. He dodged a cast-iron frying pan, and winced as it
smashed the window behind him. 'Sporcaccione! Figlio
d'un culo!' Pelagia shrieked. 'Pezzo di merda! All my life
waiting, all my life mourning, all my life thinking you were
dead. Cazzo d'un cane! And you alive, and me a fool. How
dare you break such promises? Betrayer!'

Corelli backed against the wall, retreating before the
sharp prods of the broomstick in his ribs, his hands raised
in surrender. 'I told you,' he cried. 'I thought that you were
married.'

'Married!' she exclaimed bitterly. 'Married? No such
luck! Thanks to you, bastardo.' She prodded him again and
moved to swipe him across the head with the broom handle.

'Your father was right. He said you had a savage side.'

'Savage? Don't I have the right, porco? Don't I have the
right?'

'I came back for you. 1946. I came round the bend, and
there you were with your little baby and your finger in its
mouth, looking so happy.'

'Was I married? Who told you that? What's it to you if I
adopt a baby that someone leaves on my doorstep?
Couldn't you have asked? Couldn't you have said, "Excuse
me, koritsimou, but is this your baby?"'

'Please, stop hitting me. I came back every year, you
know I did. You saw me. I always saw you with the child. I

was so bitter I couldn't speak. But I had to see you.'

'Bitter? I don't believe my ears. You? Bitter?'

'For ten years,' said Corelli, 'for ten years I was so bitter that I even wanted to kill you. And then I thought, well, OK, I was away for three years, perhaps she thought I wasn't coming back, perhaps she thought I was dead, perhaps she thought I'd forgotten, perhaps she met someone else and fell in love. As long as she's happy. But I still came back, every year, just to see you were all right. Is that betrayal?'

'And did you ever see a husband? And did you think what it did to me when I ran to you and you disappeared? Did you think about my heart?'

'OK, so I jumped the wall and hid. I had to. I thought you were married, I've told you. I was being considerate. I didn't even ask for Antonia.'

'Ha,' cried Pelagia with a burst of intuition, 'you left it to make me feel guilty, eh? Bestia.'

'Pelagia, please, this is a terrible embarrassment for the customers. Can't we go for a walk and talk about it on the beach?'

She looked around at all the faces, some of them grinning, some of them pretending to be looking the other way. Everywhere there were overturned chairs and tables that Pelagia had flung from her wake in the extremity of her wrath. 'You should have died,' she yelled, 'and left me with my fantasies. You never loved me.' She flounced out of the door, leaving Corelli to tip his hat to the customers, bowing repeatedly and saying, 'Please excuse us.'

Two hours later they were sitting together on a familiar rock, gazing out over the sea as the yellow lights of the harbour reflected in the blackened waters. 'I see you got my postcards, then,' he said.

'In Greek. Why did you learn Greek?'

'After the war all the facts came out. Abyssinia, Libya, persecution of Jews, atrocities, untried political prisoners by the thousand, everything. I was ashamed of being an invader. I was so ashamed that I didn't want to be Italian any more. I've been living in Athens for about twenty-five years. I'm a Greek citizen. But I go home to Italy quite a lot.

I go to Tuscany in the summer.'

'And there's me, so ashamed that I wanted to be Italian. Did you ever write your concertos?'

'Three. I've played them all over the world, too. The first one's dedicated to you, and the main theme is "Pelagia's March". Do you remember it?' He hummed a few bars, until he noticed that she was trying not to cry. She seemed to have become very volatile in her old age, veering between passionate tears and assault. She had actually knocked out his false teeth, so that they had fallen in the sand and had to be washed in the sea. Even now he had a brackish but not unpleasant taste in his mouth.

'Of course I remember it.' She let her head sink, and she wiped her eyes wearily. Suddenly, apropos of nothing in particular, she said, 'I feel like an unfinished poem.'

Corelli felt a sting of shame, and avoided a reply, 'Everything's changed. Everything here used to be so pretty, and now everything is concrete.'

'And we have electricity and telephones and buses and running water and sewers and refrigerators. And the houses are earthquake-proof. Is that so bad?'

'It was a terrible earthquake. I was here. It took me a long time to locate you and find that you were all right.' He caught her look of astonishment, and said, 'I did what you told me to. I joined the fire brigade. In Milan. You said, "Don't fight. Why don't you do something useful, like join the fire brigade?" so I did. It was just like the Army. Plenty of time for practice in between emergencies. When they asked for volunteers, I came straight away. It broke my heart to see it. I worked so hard. And I had a terrible experience. I saw Carlo's grave open and close, and his body down there. Little scraps of uniform, and the bones smashed, and the two coins in his eyes.'

She shuddered, and wondered whether or not to tell him about the secret that Carlo had so perfectly concealed. Instead she asked, 'Did you know that it was Carlo and my father who wrote that pamphlet about Mussolini? Kokolios printed it.'

'I had my suspicions. I decided to let it pass. We all

needed some amusement in those days, didn't we? I see you still have my ring.'

'Only because I got some arthritis in my fingers and I couldn't get it off. I had it altered to fit, and now I regret it.' She looked down at the demi-falcon rising, with the olive branch in its mouth, and 'Semper fidelis' inscribed underneath. She hesitated; 'So did you ever get married? I suppose you did.'

'Me? No. As I said, I was very bitter for years and years. I was horrible to everyone, especially women, and then the music took off, and I was all over the world, flying from one place to another. I had to leave the fire brigade. And anyway, you were always my Beatrice. My Laura. I thought, who wants second best? Who wants to be with someone, dreaming of someone else?'

'Antonio Corelli, I can see that you still tell lies with your silver tongue. And how can you bear to look at me now? I'm an old woman. When you look at me I don't like it, because I remember what I was. I feel ashamed to be so old and ugly. It's all right for you. Men don't degenerate as we do. You look the same, but old and thin. I look like someone else, I know it. I wanted you to remember me properly. Now I'm just a lump.'

'You're forgetting that I came to spy on you. If you see things happen gradually, there's no shock. No disappointment. You are just the same.' He placed his hand on hers, squeezed it gently, and said, 'Don't worry. I'm with you for only a little while, and it's still Pelagia. Pelagia with a bad temper, but still Pelagia.'

'Did it occur to you that my baby might have been a bastard? I could have been raped. I nearly was.'

'It occurred to me. With the Germans and the civil war . . .'

'And?'

'It made a difference. We had some notions about dishonour and tainted goods, didn't we? I admit it made a difference. Thank God we are not so stupid now. Some things change for the better.'

'The man who tried to rape me . . . I shot him.'

He looked at her incredulously, 'Vacca cane! You shot him?'

'I was never dishonoured. He was the fiancé I had before you.'

'You never said anything about a fiancé.'

'You're jealous.'

'Of course I'm jealous. I thought I was the first.'

'Well, you weren't. And don't try to tell me that I was the first, either.'

'The best.' The emotion was beginning to stir him a little too much, and he tried to check himself. 'We're getting sentimental. Two sentimental old fools. Look . . .' He reached into his pocket and brought out something white, wrapped in a plastic bag. He unfolded it and drew out an old handkerchief, which he shook in order to spread it. It had dark, yellow-edged brown streaks upon its fabric. '. . . your blood, Pelagia, do you remember? Looking for snails, and your face was cut by thorns? I kept it. A sentimental old fool. But who cares? There's no one to impress. After all this time, we have the right. It's a beautiful evening. Let's be sentimental. No one's watching.'

'Iannis has been watching. He's behind that coil of rope on the other quay.'

'The little devil. Perhaps he thinks you need protecting. There never was any such thing as a secret on this island, was there?'

'I want to show you something. You never read Carlo's papers, did you? There was a secret. Come back to the taverna and eat, and I'll give you his writing. We do an excellent snails pilaf.'

'Snails!' he exclaimed. 'Snails. Now that's something. I remember all about snails.'

'Don't get any ideas. I'm too old for all that.'

Corelli sat at the table with its chequered plastic cloth, and read through the stiff old sheets that had curled up at the corners. The handwriting was familiar, and the tone of voice and turn of phrase, but it was a Carlo he had never known: 'Antonio, my Captain, we find ourselves in bad times, and I have the strongest feelings that I shall not survive them. You know how it is . . .'

As he read, his brow furrowed, exaggerating its wrinkles and lines, and once or twice he blinked as though in disbelief. When he had finished, he shuffled the papers into order, set them before him on the table, and realised that his snails had gone cold. He began to eat them anyway, but did not taste them. Pelagia came to sit opposite him, 'Well?'

'You know you said that you wished I was dead? So that you could keep your fantasies?' He tapped the sheaf of papers. 'I wish that you hadn't shown me these. I've just realised that I'm more old-fashioned than I thought. I had no idea.'

'He loved you. Are you disgusted?'

'Sad. A man like that should have had children. It's going to take me a while . . . It's a shock. I can't help it.'

'He wasn't just another hero, was he? He was more complicated. Poor Carlo.'

'He wanted to do something to compensate. Poor man, I feel so sorry. I feel guilty. The boys used to make him go to the brothel. What torture. It's terrible.' He paused for reflection, and a thought struck him. 'I traced Günter Weber. It wasn't difficult – he used to talk about his village all the time – he actually thought I was tracing him for revenge, for the War Crimes Commission or something. He was pleading with me. Down on his knees. It was so pathetic that I didn't know whether to laugh or cry. And guess what? He'd followed his father into the Church. There he was, all dressed up as a pastor, grovelling and whining. I couldn't stand it. I wanted to thank him and hit him at the same time. I just walked out and never went back. He's probably in the madhouse by now. Or perhaps he's a bishop.'

Pelagia sighed, 'I still have trouble being pleasant to Germans. I keep wanting to blame them for what their grandfathers did. They're so polite, and the girls are so pretty. Such good mothers. I feel guilty for wanting to kick them.'

'The poor bastards will be doing penance for ever. That's why they're so courteous. Every single one of them has a complex. But I hear that the Nazis are coming back.'

'Everyone's doing penance. We've got the civil war, you've got Mussolini and the Mafia and all these corruption scandals, the British come in and apologise for the Empire and Cyprus, the Americans for Vietnam and Hiroshima. Everyone's apologising.'

'And I apologise.'

She ignored him. She intended to hold out – a little – as long as possible, to get her money's worth. She changed the subject artfully, 'Iannis wants you to teach him to read music properly, and he says why don't you come back next summer and play with him and Spiro. Spiro's gone home to Corfu, but he's very good.'

'Spiro Trikoupis?'

'Yes. How did you know? You've been spying that much?'

'He's the best mandolinist in Greece. I met him years ago. He only plays popular bozouki for tourists. In the winter he comes to Athens sometimes. I went to one of his classes in classical bozouki, because, after all, it's only a big mandolin, and I thought, why not? And we got talking, and he knows some of my pieces. In fact he plays them better than I do. It's old age. It slows the fingers. I have played with him many times. Iannis is going to be good, too, I can tell.'

'He wants to join the Patras Mandolinates Band.'

'Nice happy stuff. Why not? It's a good place to start. We used to have lots of bands like that in Italy, except that we had all the instruments in the shape of mandolins. Can you imagine it? Mandolin basses and cellos? It was funny to see.'

'Are you very famous then?'

'Only in the sense that other musicians have heard of me. I get lots of silly reviews comparing me to the other Corelli. I play up to it. I'm quite cynical. I tried to write all sorts of modern stuff. You know, chromatic scales and microtones, and all sorts of crashes and bangs and squeaks and noises from lawnmowers, but it's only the experts and critics who don't realise what dreadful rubbish it is. My idea of hell; Schoenberg and Stockhausen.' He pulled a grimace. 'To tell the truth I don't even like Bartok, but don't tell anyone, and I even disapprove of Brahms jumping from one key to another without crossing by respectable stages. I realised that I was completely old-fashioned, so I had to find another way to be innovative. Do you know what I did? I took old folk tunes, like some Greek ones, and I set them for unusual instruments. My second concerto has Irish pipes and a banjo in it, and guess what? The critics loved it. Actually it's in exactly the same form, with the same kind of development, as you'd find in Mozart or Haydn or whatever. It sounds good too. I'm just a trickster waiting to be found out. I specialise in finding new ways to be an anachronism. What do you think of that?'

Pelagia regarded him a little wearily, 'Antonio, you haven't changed. You just babble away, assuming that I know what you're talking about. Your eyes light up, and you're off. You might as well be talking Turkish for all the sense I can make of it.'

'I'm sorry, it's enthusiasm that keeps me alive. I forget. I even wrote lots of fake Greek music, for films. When they couldn't get Markopoulos or Theodorakis or Eleni Karaindrou, they asked me instead. Fraud is such a great pleasure, don't you think? Anyway, I've retired now . . . In fact, I was thinking . . . I don't know what you'll think of this, but . . .'

She narrowed her eyes suspiciously, 'Yes? What? You want to defraud me? Again?'

He held her gaze, 'No. I want to rebuild the old house. I've retired, and I want to live in a nice place. A place with memories.'

'Without water and electricity?'

'A pump from the old well, a little filtration plant. I'm sure I can get a power line if I slip a few coins to someone appropriate. Would you sell me the site?'

'You're completely mad. I don't even know if we own it. There aren't any deeds. You'll probably have to bribe everyone.'

'Then you don't mind? Isn't your son-in-law a builder? You know, keep it in the family.'

'You know that if you put a proper roof on you have to pay tax?'

'Merda, is that why all the houses have rusty reinforcing rods sticking out of the top? To look unfinished?'

'Yes. And what makes you think that I'd want an old goat like you living in my old house?'

'I'd pay you to come and clean it,' he said mischievously.

She took the bait by taking him at his word, 'What? Do I need money? With this taverna? And the richest son-in-law anyone ever had? Do you think I'm as mad as you are? Go home to Athens. Anyway, Lemoni would do it.'

'Little Lemoni? She's still here?'

'She's as big as a ship and she's a grandmother. She remembers you, though. Barba C'relli. She never forgot the explosion of the mine, either. She still talks about it.'

'Barba C'relli,' he repeated nostalgically. Time was a complete bastard, no doubt of that. Weak old arms cannot throw grandmother ships up and down in the air. 'I still have tinnitus from that explosion,' he said, and then fell silent for a moment. 'So do I have your permission to rebuild the house?'

'No,' she said, still holding out.

'Oh.' He looked at her doubtfully. He would return to the topic at a later date, he decided. 'I'm going to come and see you tomorrow evening,' he said, 'with a present.'

'I don't want any presents. I'm too old for presents. Go to hell with your presents.'

'Not exactly a present. A debt.'

'You owe me a life.'

'Ah. I'll bring you a life then.'

'Stupid old man.'

He fumbled in his pockets and produced a personal stereo. More fumbling produced a cassette in a very distinguished kind of packaging, which he opened out. He placed the cassette in the stereo and offered her the headphones. She made a dismissive gesture with her hand, waving it in his face as though fending off a mosquito, 'Go away, I wouldn't be seen dead in one of those. I'm an old woman, not some silly girl. Do you think I'm a teenager, to be nodding around with one of those on my head?'

'You don't know what you're missing. They're wonderful. I'm going now. Get Iannis to show you how it works, and listen. I'll see you tomorrow evening.'

After he had gone Pelagia picked up the cassette's container, and extracted the information sheet. It was in Italian, English, French, and German. She was impressed. The picture on the front showed Antonio Corelli, a decade younger, in tails and bow-tie, perhaps at the age of sixty, grinning smugly, with a mandolin clutched at an unrealistic angle in his right hand. She fetched herself a glass of wine for the purposes of general fortification, and began to read the notes. They were by someone called Richard Usborne, an Englishman who, according to yet another note, was a famous critic and expert on Rossini. She began to read: 'This, the long-awaited reissue of Antonio Corelli's first concerto for mandolin and small orchestra, was first published in 1954, and premièred in Milan, with the composer playing the soloist's part. It was inspired by, and dedicated to, a woman named in the score only as "Pelagia". The main theme, scored in 2/2 time, is stated very clearly and emphatically on the solo instrument after a brief flourish on woodwind. It is a simple and martial melody that was described by one of its earliest reviewers as "artfully naïve". In the first movement it is developed in sonata form and . . .'

Pelagia skimmed through the rest. It was all nonsense about fugal elaboration and such stuff. She scrutinised the small row of buttons embellished with arrows going in different directions, gingerly plugged the phones into her ears, and pressed the little button that said 'play'. There was a hissing noise, and then, to her astonishment, music began to play right in the centre of her head instead of in her ears.

As the music flooded her mind, a maelstrom of memories was awakened. She heard 'Pelagia's March', not once, but many times. Snatches appeared out of the blue in curiously distorted and whimsical forms on different instruments. It became so complicated that it was hardly discernible inside such a torrent of notes in different rhythms. At one point it came out as a waltz ('How did he do that?' she thought), and just towards the end there was a thunderous rolling of kettledrums that made her pluck off the phones in panic, believing that there had been another earthquake. Hastily she replaced them, and realised that indeed it was the earthquake, a musical portrait, and it was followed by a long lament on a plaintive instrument that was, although she did not know it, a cor anglais. It was interrupted by single blows on the kettledrum that must be aftershocks. Each one came so suddenly and unpredictably that she jumped in her seat, her heart leaping to her mouth. And then the mandolin broke in and marched confidently through a recapitulation of the theme, eventually becoming quieter and quieter. So quiet that it faded out to nothing. She shook the machine, wondering whether the batteries had run out. This kind of music was supposed to end with barrages of crashing chords, surely? She pressed one of the winding buttons, and the machine clicked. It was the wrong one, so she pressed the other and waited for it to get back to the beginning. This time she heard more than she had before, even some rattles that were just like the machine-pistols on the days of the massacres. There was a slightly frivolous part that might have been crawling about, looking for snails. But there was still the same unsatisfying conclusion that just faded away to silence. She sat, puzzling over it, even a little angry, until she became aware that her adolescent grandson was standing before her, his mouth open in surprise. 'Grandma,' he said, 'you've got a Walkman.'

She eyed him ironically, 'It's Antonio's. He lent it to me. And if you think that I look stupid wearing one, what makes you think that you don't? Nodding about with your mouth open, singing out of tune. If it's all right for you, it's all right for me.'

He did not dare to say, 'It looks silly on an old woman,' and so he smiled instead and shrugged his shoulders. His grandmother knew exactly what he was thinking, and slapped him softly across the cheek, a blow that was almost a caress. 'Guess what?' she said. 'Antonio's going to rebuild the old house. And, by the way, Lemoni told me that your mother told her that you told your mother that I've got a new boyfriend. Well, I haven't. And in future, mind your own business.'

Corelli had the greatest difficulty in proceeding along the quay to the Taverna Drosoula the next night. He was hardly as strong as he used to be, and besides, he had no experience with this kind of thing. It really was no use tugging and pulling, and barking out commands in the best artillery manner did not seem to work either. He had had an exhausting day.

When finally he lurched and strained into the taverna and collapsed in a seat, Pelagia detached herself from the Walkman, switched it expertly to rewind, and demanded, 'And what are you doing here with that?'

'It's a goat. As you see, I've brought you a life.'

'I can see it's a goat. Do you think I don't know a goat when I see one? What's it doing here?'

He glared at her a little balefully, 'You said I don't keep my promises. I promised you a goat, remember? So here's a goat. And I'm sorry the old one was stolen. As you see, this one looks exactly the same.'

Pelagia resisted; she had almost forgotten how enjoyable it was. 'Who says I needed a goat? At my age? In a taverna?'

'I don't care if you don't want it. I promised it, and here it is. One goat the same as the other. Sell it if you want. But if you saw how difficult it was to get it in the taxi, you wouldn't be so hard.'

'In a taxi? Where did you get it?'

'On Mt Aenos. I asked a driver, "Where can I get a good old-fashioned goat?" and he said, "Get in," and we drove up past the Nato base on the mountain. It took hours. And there was this old man called Alekos, and he sold me this goat. I was swindled, I can tell you, and then I had to pay the driver two fares to bring it back. And how it stank. That's how I've suffered, and now you just shout at me and squawk like an old crow.'

'An old crow? Silly old man.' She bent down and clamped the goat's nose firmly in one hand. With the other she lifted its lips and peered at the yellow teeth. Then she burrowed through the hair of its haunches with her fingers, and straightened up. 'It's a very good goat. It's got ticks, but otherwise it's good. Thank you.'

'What are we going to call it?' asked Iannis.

'We'll call it Apodosis,' said Pelagia, already warming to the idea of having a goat again, 'and we can tie it to a tree and feed it on the leftovers.'

'Apodosis,' repeated Corelli, nodding his head. 'A very appropriate name. "Restitution". Couldn't be better. Do you think you'll get much milk from it? You could make yoghurt.'

Pelagia smiled, her face shining with condescension, 'You milk it if you like, Corelli. Personally I only try to milk the females.' She pointed down towards the capacious pink scrotum with its twin tapered oblongs within. 'Udders are they?'

'O coglione,' he said appropriately, burying his face in his hands. Iannis admired people who could swear, especially in foreign tongues, but it seemed strange in an old man. Old people were always trying to reprove you for it. This Corelli was obviously as strange as his grandmother was becoming, skipping about with a personal stereo lodged in her thin grey locks, and smiling coyly when unaware of being observed. This very morning he had caught her before the mirror, posing with different sets of earrings from Antonia's Emporium, and tossing her head into attitudes that could only be described as coquettish.

'Tomorrow, another surprise,' said Corelli, and he raised his battered hat and left.

'O dear,' said Pelagia, her heart full of premonitory misgivings. It occurred to her that she ought to show him her updated 'Personal History of Cephallonia'; he would probably be interested to know that the real reason for the massacres was that Eisenhower had perversely overruled all of Churchill's plans to liberate the islands, and sent the Italian Air Force uselessly to Tunisia instead of Cephallonia. She supposed that he knew that the orders for the atrocities came directly from Hitler himself, but perhaps he did not.

'Is he your boyfriend?' enquired Iannis pertinaciously, having had this same proposition denied repeatedly at every asking.

'Go and do the washing-up, or you don't get paid,'

riposted his grandmother, and she went to fetch a comb so that she could groom the goat, as in the old days. She wondered where she might find a pine marten's kitten these days.

But, she thought, the captain had really surpassed himself when he turned up outside the door with a squeak of brakes, a roaring and revving of pistons, and a cloud of aromatic blue smoke. Pelagia stood with her hands on her hips and shook her head slowly as he clambered carefully off the motorcycle. It was bright red, very high, had thick and knobbly tyres, and looked as though it had been designed for racing. The captain turned the key and shut off the clamour. He kicked out the stand, and propped it. 'Do you know where we're going? We're going to see if Casa Nostra is still there. Just like in the old days . . .' he tapped the handlebars '. . . on a motorbike.'

Pelagia shook her head, 'Do you really think it survived the earthquake? And do you really think I'm going on a thing like that? At my age? Just go away and leave me in peace. Don't give me any more of your harebrained schemes.'

'I hired it specially. It's not as nice as the old one and it makes a horrible noise, like a can of nails, but it goes very well.'

She looked into the old man's face, and fought to suppress a smile. He was wearing a ridiculous blue crash-helmet with a little peak, and a pair of reflective sunglasses that were so new that he had forgotten to remove the label, which dangled down upon one cheek like a small autumnal leaf caught on a filament of cobweb. She saw her own reproving face reflected stereoscopically in the lenses of the sunglasses, and watched herself as she held up her hands, palms outspread, 'Not a chance. I'm too old, and you couldn't even drive straight when you were young. Don't you remember all the crashes? You were mad then, and now you're even madder.'

He defended himself, 'On the old machine we wobbled about because I had to keep fiddling with the advance-retard lever. On this it's all automatic.' He raised his hands

531

and let them drop, as though to signify 'No problem', and then beckoned to her.

'No,' she said. 'My knees are stiff and I can't even raise my legs high enough.' She noticed suddenly that over his shirt he was wearing a bright garment that made him look exactly like the hippies who had appeared on the island in the late sixties. She squinted a little for better focus, and realised that he was wearing the red velvet waistcoat embroidered with flowers, eagles, and fish that she had given him fifty years before. She pretended not to have seen it, and made no comment, but it astounded her that he should have kept it so carefully all this time. She was touched.

'Koritsimou,' he said, aware that she had noticed, and calculating that her opposition might have softened.

'Absolutely not.'

'Don't you want to see Casa Nostra?'

'Not with a madman.'

'You don't want me to have hired it for nothing?'

'Yes.'

'I've got it for two days. We can go to Kastro, and Assos, and Fiskardo. We can sit on a rock and watch for dolphins.'

'Go back to Athens. Old lunatic.'

'I've brought you a crash-helmet too.'

'I don't wear red. Have you ever seen me in red?'

'I'll go on my own.'

'Go then.'

It took an eternity of time to persuade her. As they veered perilously along the stony roads, she clung to his waist, white-knuckled with terror, her face buried between his shoulder-blades, the machine thundering in her groin with a sensation that was at once deeply pleasant and thoroughly disturbing. Corelli noticed that she clutched him even more desperately than in the old days, and cynically he inserted some deliberate swerves into the series of those which were alarmingly accidental.

Pelagia clasped his waist tenaciously. She realised that over the years he had shrunk as much as she had expanded. He swerved suddenly towards the verge of the road, skidding a little and sending up a spray of chippings. 'Gerasimos save me,' she thought, and in search of safety slid her arms right about his waist and linked her fingers together.

A venerable grey moped chugged and popped its way past them. It was adorned not with one but with three girls, all dressed identically in the briefest of white dresses. Corelli caught a glimpse of slender golden thighs, new-grown breasts, arching eyebrows over black eyes, and long loose hair so dark that it was almost blue. He heard a melody begin to rise up in his heart, something joyful that captured the eternal spirit of Greece, a Greek concerto. In composing it he would only have to think of driving along with Pelagia in search of Casa Nostra, and passing three young girls in the most exquisite first flowering of their liberty and beauty. The one driving the moped had her feet up on the fuel tank, the second one was touching up her make-up with painterly gestures and the aid of a small pink mirror, and the third one was facing backwards, her sandalled feet barely skimming above the surface of the road. She had a deeply serious expression on her face as she immersed herself in the newspaper and with elegant fingers tried to prevent the pages from flapping in the breeze.

ACKNOWLEDGEMENTS

PARTICULAR THANKS TO Anne and Arturo Grant, Iannis Stamiris (the novelist), Alexandros Rallis of the Greek Embassy in London, Helen Cosmetatos of the Corgialenios Historical And Cultural Museum in Argostoli, Cephallonia, Giovanni Camisa, and the staff of Earlsfield Public Library in London. None of them, of course, are responsible in any way for my interpretation of the information that they gave.

I am very indebted to innumerable books, but in particular to the following:

RICHARD CAPELL: *Simiomata*, Macdonald and Co, date unknown.

MARIO CERVI: *Storia della Guerra di Grecia*, Sugar Editore, 1965.

KAY CICELLIS: *The Easy Way*, Harvill Press, 1950.

JOHN EVANS: *Time After Earthquake*, Heinemann, 1954.

NICHOLAS GAGE: *Hellas*, Collins Harvill, 1987.

RICHARD LAMB: *War in Italy 1943–1945*, John Murray, 1993.

DENNIS MACK SMITH: *Mussolini*, Weidenfeld and Nicolson, 1981.

E.C.W. MYERS: *Greek Entanglement*, Rupert Hart-Davis, 1955.

MARCELLO VENTURI: *The White Flag*, Blond, 1966.

My apologies to Caroline for so many late meals and neglected duties.

THE HISTORY OF VINTAGE

The famous American publisher Alfred A. Knopf (1892–1984) founded Vintage Books in the United States in 1954 as a paperback home for the authors published by his company. Vintage was launched in the United Kingdom in 1990 and works independently from the American imprint although both are part of the international publishing group, Random House.

Vintage in the United Kingdom was initially created to publish paperback editions of books acquired by the prestigious hardback imprints in the Random House Group such as Jonathan Cape, Chatto & Windus, Hutchinson and later William Heinemann, Secker & Warburg and The Harvill Press. There are many Booker and Nobel Prize-winning authors on the Vintage list and the imprint publishes a huge variety of fiction and non-fiction. Over the years Vintage has expanded and the list now includes great authors of the past – who are published under the Vintage Classics imprint – as well as many of the most influential authors of the present.

For a full list of the books Vintage publishes, please visit our website
www.vintage-books.co.uk

For book details and other information about the classic authors we publish, please visit the Vintage Classics website
www.vintage-classics.info